"Lauren?" Prince Ander Elesseuil spoke the Elf's name softly.

No answer came. He stepped through the entry into the darker shadows beyond. A flicker of movement registered at the edge of his vision, movement that came from somewhere within the surrounding evergreens. A sudden apprehension swept through him, leaving him cold all over.

He stood motionless for a time, waiting for something more. But there was no further movement, no sounds betraying the presence of another living being. Resolutely he went forward.

"Lauren . . . ?"

Then his sight adjusted to the dimmer interior, and the young Elf's name caught in his throat.

Bodies lay strewn about the main room like discarded sacks, torn and broken and lifeless. Lauren, Jase—all of the Chosen were dead, ripped apart as if by maddened animals. Despair filled him. Now no Chosen remained to carry the seed of the Ellcrys in search of the Bloodfire. Now there could be no rebirth of the tree, no salvation for the Elves. Sickened by the carnage, he stood there, horror and revulsion sweeping through him, a single word shrieking in his mind.

Demons!

By Terry Brooks

THE SHANNARA CHRONICLES
The Elfstones of Shannara
The Wishsong of Shannara

BEFORE THE CHRONICLES
THERE WAS . . .
The Sword of Shannara
The First King of Shannara

TO FULLY EXPLORE
THE WORLD OF SHANNARA VISIT
terrybrooks.net/novels/

THE SHANNARA CHRONICLES

Book One:

The Elfstones
of Shannara

Terry Brooks

DEL REY • NEW YORK

2015 Del Rey Mass Market Edition

Copyright © 1982 by Terry Brooks
Map on page vii by the Brothers Hildebrandt copyright © 1977 by Random House, Inc.
All other interior art by Darrell K. Sweet copyright © 1982 by Random House, Inc.

All rights reserved.

Published in the United States by Del Rey, an imprint of Random House, a division of Penguin Random House LLC, New York.

DEL REY and the HOUSE colophon are registered trademarks of Penguin Random House LLC.

Originally published in hardcover in the United States as *The Elfstones of Shannara* by Del Rey, an imprint of Random House, a division of Penguin Random House LLC, in 1982.

ISBN 978-1-101-88605-2
eBook ISBN 978-0-345-44461-5

Printed in the United States of America

randomhousebooks.com

9 8 7 6 5 4 3 2 1

Del Rey mass market edition: December 2015

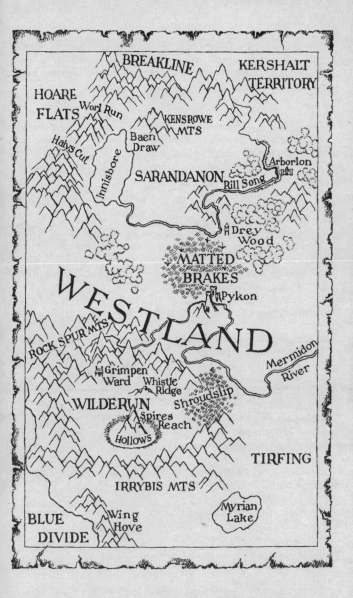

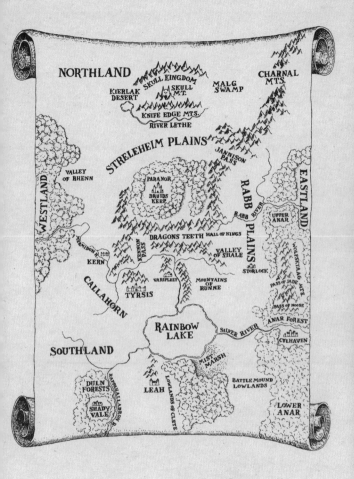

The Elfstones
of Shannara

I

The night sky brightened faintly in the east with the approach of dawn as the Chosen entered the Gardens of Life. Without, the Elven city of Arborlon lay sleeping, its people still wrapped in the warmth and solitude of their beds. But for the Chosen, the day had already begun. Their trailing white robes billowing slightly with a rush of summer wind, they passed between the sentries of the Black Watch, who stood rigid and aloof as such sentries had stood for centuries gone before the arched, wrought-iron gateway inlaid with silver scroll and ivory chips. They passed quickly, and only their soft voices and the crunch of their sandaled feet on the gravel pathway disturbed the silence of the new day as they slipped into the pine-shadowed dark beyond.

The Chosen were the caretakers of the Ellcrys, the strange and wondrous tree that stood at the center of the Gardens—the tree, as the legends told, that served as protector against a primordial evil that had very nearly destroyed the Elves centuries ago, an evil that had been shut away from the earth since before the dawn of the old race of Men. In all the time that had followed, there had been Chosen to care for the Ellcrys. Theirs was a tradition handed down through generations of Elves, a tradition of service that the Elves regarded as both a coveted honor and a solemn duty.

Yet there was little evidence of solemnity in the procession that passed through the Gardens this morning. Two hundred and thirty days of the year of their service had gone by, and youthful spirits could no longer be easily subdued. The first sense of awe at the responsibility given them had long since passed, and the Chosen of the Elves were now just six young men on their way to perform a task they had performed each day since the time of their choosing, a task grown old and familiar—the greeting of the tree at the first touch of sunrise.

Only Lauren, youngest of this year's Chosen, was silent. He lagged a bit behind the others as they walked, taking no part in their idle chatter. His red head was bent in concentration, and there was a deep frown on his face. So wrapped up in his thoughts was he that he was not aware when the noise ahead ceased, nor of the steps that fell back beside him, until a hand touched his arm. Then his troubled face jerked up abruptly to find Jase regarding him.

"What's the matter, Lauren? Are you sick?" Jase asked. Because he was a few months older than the rest, Jase was the accepted leader of the Chosen.

Lauren shook his head, but the frown did not leave his face entirely. "I'm all right."

"*Something* is bothering you. You've been brooding all morning. Come to think of it, you were rather quiet last night, too." Jase's hand on his shoulder brought the younger Elf about to face him. "Come on, out with it. Nobody expects you to serve if you're not feeling well."

Lauren hesitated, then sighed and nodded. "All right. It's the Ellcrys. Yesterday, at sunset, just before we left her, I thought I saw some spotting on her leaves. It looked like wilt."

"Wilt? Are you sure? Nothing like that ever happens to the Ellcrys—at least that's what we've always been told," Jase said doubtfully.

"I could have been mistaken," Lauren admitted. "It was getting dark. I told myself then that it was probably just the way the shadows lay on the leaves. But the more I try to remember how it looked, the more I think it really was wilt."

"There was a disconcerted muttering from the others, and one of them spoke. "This is Amberle's fault. I said before that something bad would come from having a girl picked as a Chosen."

"There were other girls among the Chosen, and nothing happened because of it," Lauren protested. He had always liked Amberle. She had been easy to talk to, even if she was King Eventine Elessedil's granddaughter.

"Not for five hundred years, Lauren," the other said.

"All right, that's enough," Jase interrupted. "We agreed not to talk about Amberle. You know that." He stood silently for a moment, pondering what Lauren had said. Then he shrugged. "It would be unfortunate if anything happened to the tree, especially while she was under our care. But after all, nothing lasts forever."

Lauren was shocked. "But Jase, when the tree weakens, the Forbidding will end and the Demons within will be freed . . ."

"Do you really believe those old stories, Lauren?" Jase laughed.

Lauren stared at the older Elf. "How can you be a Chosen and *not* believe?"

"I don't remember being asked what I believed when I was chosen, Lauren. Were you asked?"

Lauren shook his head. Candidates for the honor of being Chosen were never asked anything. They were simply brought before the tree—young Elves who had crossed over into manhood and womanhood in the prior year. At the dawn of the new year, they gathered to pass beneath her limbs, each pausing momentarily for acceptance. Those the tree touched upon the shoulders became the new Chosen, to serve until the year was done. Lauren could still remember the mix of ecstasy and pride he had felt at the moment a slender branch had bent to touch him and he'd heard her speak his name.

And he remembered, too, the astonishment of all when Amberle had been called . . .

"It's just a tale to frighten children," Jase was saying. "The real function of the Ellcrys is to serve as a reminder to the Elven people that they, like her, survive despite all the changes that have taken place in the history of the Four Lands. She is a symbol of our people's strength, Lauren— nothing more."

He motioned for them all to resume their walk into the Gardens and turned away. Lauren lapsed back into thought. The older Elf's casual disregard for the legend of the tree disturbed him. Of course Jase was from the city, and Lauren had observed that the people of Arborlon seemed to take the old beliefs less seriously than did those of the little northern village from which he came. But the

story of the Ellcrys and the Forbidding wasn't just a story—
it was the foundation of everything that was truly Elven,
the most important event in the history of his people.

It had all taken place long ago, before the birth of the
new world. There had been a great war between good and
evil—a war that the Elves had finally won by creating the
Ellcrys and a Forbidding that had banished the evil
Demons into a timeless dark. And so long as the Ellcrys
was kept well, so long would the evil be locked from the
land.

So long as the Ellcrys was kept well . . .

He shook his head doubtfully. Maybe the wilt was but a
trick of his imagination. Or a trick of the light. And if not,
they would simply have to find a cure. There was always a
cure.

Moments later, he stood with the others before the tree.
Hesitantly, he looked up, then sighed in relief. It appeared
as if the Ellcrys was unchanged. Perfectly formed, her
silver-white trunk arched skyward in a symmetrically
balanced network of tapered limbs clustered with broad,
five-cornered leaves that were blood-red in color. At her
base, strips of green moss grew in patchwork runners
through the cracks and crevices of the smooth-skinned
bark, like emerald streams flowing down a mountain
hillside. There were no splits to mar the trunk's even lines,
no branches cracked or broken. So beautiful, he thought.
He looked again, but could see no signs of the sickness he
had feared.

The others went to gather the tools they would use in the
feeding and grooming of the tree and in the general
upkeep of the Gardens. But Jase held Lauren back. "Would
you like to greet her today, Lauren?" he asked.

Lauren stammered his surprised thanks. Jase was giving
up his turn for the most special of tasks, obviously in an
effort to cheer him.

He stepped forward under the spreading branches to lay
his hands upon the smooth-skinned trunk, the others
gathering about a few paces back to recite the morning
greeting. He glanced upward expectantly, searching for the
first beam of sunlight that would fall upon her form.

Then abruptly he drew back. The leaves directly above
him were dark with patches of wilt. His heart fell. There

was spotting elsewhere as well, scattered throughout the tree. It was not a trick of light and shadow. It was real.

He motioned frantically for Jase, then pointed as the other came forward. As was their custom at this time, they did not speak, but Jase gasped as he saw the extent of the damage already done. Slowly the two walked around the tree, discovering spots everywhere, some barely visible, others already darkening the leaves so badly that their blood-red color seemed drained away.

Whatever his professed beliefs concerning the tree, Jase was badly shaken, and his face reflected his dismay as he went back to confer in whispers with the others. Lauren moved to join them, but Jase quickly shook his head, motioning to the top of the tree, where the dawn's light had almost reached the uppermost branches.

Lauren knew his duty and he turned back again to the tree. Whatever else was to happen, the Chosen must greet the Ellcrys this day as they had greeted her each day since the beginning of their Order.

He placed his hands gently on the silver bark and the words of greeting were forming on his lips when a slender branch from the ancient tree dipped slightly to brush his shoulder.

—Lauren—

The young Elf jumped at the sound of his name. But no one had spoken. The sound had been in his mind, the voice little more than an image of his own face.

It was the Ellcrys!

He caught his breath, twisting his head to glimpse briefly the branch that rested on his shoulder before turning quickly back again. Confusion swept through him. Only once before had she spoken to him—on the day of his choosing. She had spoken his name then; she had spoken all their names. It had been the last time. She had never spoken to any of them after that. Never—except to Amberle, of course, and Amberle was no longer one of them.

He looked hurriedly at the others. They were staring at him, curious as to why he had stopped. Then the branch that rested upon his shoulder slipped down to wrap about him loosely, and he flinched involuntarily with its touch.

—Lauren. Call the Chosen to me—

The images appeared quickly and were gone. Hesitantly, Lauren beckoned to his comrades. They came forward, questions forming on their lips as they stared upward at the silver-limbed tree. Branches lowered to clasp each, and the voice of the Ellcrys whispered softly.

—Hear me. Remember what I tell you. Do not fail me—

A chill swept over them, and the Gardens of Life were shrouded in deep, hollow silence, as if in all the world only they were alive. Images filled their minds, flowing one after the other in rapid succession. There was horror contained in those images. Had they been able, the Chosen would have turned away, to flee and hide until the nightmare that possessed them had passed and been forgotten. But the tree held them fast, and the images continued to flow and the horror to mount, until they felt they could stand no more.

Then at last it was finished, and the Ellcrys was silent once more, her limbs lifting from their shoulders and stretching wide to catch the warmth of the morning sun.

Lauren stood frozen, tears streaming down his cheeks. Shattered, the six Chosen faced one another, and in each mind the truth whispered soundlessly.

The legend was not legend. The legend was life. Evil did indeed lie beyond a Forbidding that the Ellcrys maintained. Only she kept the Elven people safe.

And now she was dying.

II

Far to the west of Arborlon, beyond the Breakline, there was a stirring in the air. Something blacker than the darkness of the early dawn appeared, writhing and shuddering with the force of some blow that appeared to strike it. Momentarily, the veil of blackness held firm. Then it split wide, rent by the force from within it. Howls and shrieks of glee spilled forth from the impenetrable blackness beyond, as dozens of clawed limbs ripped and tore at the sudden breach, straining toward the light. Then red fire exploded all about and the hands fell away, twisted and burned.

The Dagda Mor appeared out of the dark, hissing with rage. His Staff of Power steamed hotly as he brushed aside the impatient ones and stepped boldly through the opening. An instant later, the dark forms of the Reaper and the Changeling followed him. Other bodies pushed forward in desperation, but the edges of the rent came together quickly, closing off the blackness and the things that lived within it. In moments, the opening had disappeared entirely and the strange trio stood alone.

The Dagda Mor looked about warily. They stood in the shadow of the Breakline, the dawn which had already shattered the peace of the Chosen little more than a faint light in the eastern sky beyond the monstrous wall of mountains. The great, towering peaks knifed into the sky, casting pillars of darkness far out into the desolation of the Hoare Flats. The Flats themselves stretched westward from the line of the mountains into emptiness—a hard, barren wasteland in which life spans were measured in minutes and hours. Nothing moved on its surface. No sound broke the stillness of the morning air.

The Dagda Mor smiled, his hooked teeth gleaming. His coming had gone unnoticed. After all these years, he was free. He was loose once more among those who had imprisoned him.

At a distance, he might have passed for one of them. He was basically manlike in appearance. He walked upright on two legs, and his arms were only slightly longer than those of a man. He carried himself stooped over, his movements hampered by a peculiar hunching motion—but the dark robes that cloaked him made it difficult to tell the cause. It was only when close that one could see clearly the massive hump that crooked his spine almost double at the shoulders. Or the great tufts of greenish hair that protruded from all parts of his body like patches of saw grass. Or the scales that coated his forearms and lower legs. Or the hands and feet that ended in claws. Or the vaguely catlike muzzle that was his face. Or the eyes, black and shining, deceptively placid on their surface, like twin pools of water that hid something evil and destructive.

Once these were seen, there was no longer any question as to the Dagda Mor's identity. What was revealed then was not man, but Demon.

And the Demon hated. He hated with an intensity that bordered on madness. Hundreds of years of imprisonment within the black hold that lay beyond the wall of the Forbidding had given his hatred more than sufficient time to fester and grow. Now it consumed him. It was everything to him. It gave him his power, and he would use that power to crush the creatures who had caused him so much misery. The Elves! All of the Elves. And even that would not be enough to satisfy him now—not now, not after centuries of being shut from this world that had once been his—shut into that formless, insentient limbo of endless dark and slow, wretched stagnation. No, the destruction of the Elves would not be enough to salve the indignity that he had suffered. The others must be destroyed as well. Men, Dwarves, Trolls, Gnomes—all those who were a part of the humanity that he so detested, the races of humanity that lived upon his world and claimed it for their own.

His vengeance would come, he thought. Just as his freedom had come. He could feel it. He had waited centuries, posted at the wall of the Forbidding, testing its strength, probing for weakness—all the time knowing that it must, one day, begin to fail. And now that day was here. The Ellcrys was dying. Ah, sweet words! He wanted to shout them aloud! She was dying! She was dying and she could no longer maintain the Forbidding!

The Staff of Power glowed redly in his hands as the hatred flowed through him. The earth beneath its tip charred to ash. With an effort he calmed himself and the Staff grew cool again.

For a time, of course, the Forbidding would still hold firm. Complete erosion would not take place overnight nor, quite possibly, for several weeks. Even the small breach that he had managed had required enormous power. But the Dagda Mor possessed enormous power, more power than any of those still trapped behind the Forbidding. He was chief among them; his word ruled them. A few had defied that word during the long years of banishment—only a few. He had broken them. He had made unpleasant examples of them. Now all obeyed him. They feared him. But they shared his hatred of what had been done to them. They, too, fed on that hatred. It had driven them into a frenzied need for revenge, and when at last they were set free again, that need would take a long, long time to be satisfied.

But for now, they must wait. For now, they must be patient. It would not be long. The Forbidding would weaken a little more each day, decaying as the Ellcrys slowly failed. Only one thing could prevent this—a rebirth.

The Dagda Mor nodded to himself. He knew well the history of the Ellcrys. Had he not been present when she had first seen life, when she had shut his brethren and himself from their world of light into their prison of dark? Had he not seen the nature of the sorcery that had defeated them—a sorcery so powerful that it could transcend even death? And he knew that this freedom could still be taken from him. If one of the Chosen were permitted to carry a seed of the tree to the source of her power, the Ellcrys might be reborn and the Forbidding invoked again. He knew this, and it was because of this knowledge that he was here now. He had by no means been certain that he could breach the wall of the Forbidding. It had been a dangerous gamble to expend so much power in the attempt, for, had he failed, he might have been left badly weakened. There were some behind the wall almost as powerful as he; they would have seized the opportunity to destroy him. But the gamble had been necessary. The Elves did not realize the extent of their danger yet. For the moment, they believed themselves safe. They did not think that any within the confines of the Forbidding possessed sufficient power to break through. They would discover their error too late. By then, he would have made certain that the Ellcrys could never be reborn nor the Forbidding restored.

It was for that reason that he had brought the other two.

He glanced about for them now. He found the Changeling immediately, his body undergoing a steady transition of colors and shapes as he practiced duplicating the life he found here—in the sky, a searching hawk and a small raven; on the earth, a groundhog, then a snake, a multi-legged insect with pincers, then on to something new, almost as quickly as the eye could follow. For the Changeling could be anything. Shut away in the darkness with only his brethren to model after, he had been denied the full use of his powers. There, they had been virtually wasted. But here, in this world, the possibilities were endless. All things, whether human or animal, fish or fowl, no matter their size, shape, color or abilities—he could be any of them. He could assimilate their characteristics perfectly. Even the Dagda Mor was not certain of the Changeling's true appearance; the creature was so prone to adapt to other life forms that he spent virtually all of his time being something or someone other than what he really was.

It was an extraordinary gift, but it was possessed by a creature whose capacity for evil was very nearly as great as that of the Dagda Mor. The Changeling, too, was of Demon spawn. He was selfish and hateful. He enjoyed duplicity; he enjoyed hurting others. He had always been the enemy of the Elven people and their allies, detesting them for their pious concern for the welfare of the lesser life forms that inhabited their world. Lesser creatures meant nothing to the Changeling. They were weak, vulnerable; they were meant to be used by more powerful beings—beings such as himself. The Elves were no better than the creatures they sought to protect. They either could not or would not deceive as he did. All of them were trapped by what they were; they could be nothing else. He could be whatever he wished. He despised them all. The Changeling had no friends. He wanted none. None but the Dagda Mor, that was, for the Dagda Mor possessed the one thing he respected—power greater than his own. It was for that reason and for that reason alone that the Changeling had come to serve him.

It took the Dagda Mor several moments longer to locate the Reaper. He found it finally, not more than ten feet away, perfectly motionless, little more than a shadow in the pale light of early dawn, another bit of fading night hunched down against the gray of the Flats. Cloaked head to foot in robes the color of damp ashes, the Reaper was almost invisible, its face carefully concealed within the shadow of a broad hood. No one ever looked upon that face more than once. The Reaper permitted only its victims to see that much of it, and its victims were all dead.

If the Changeling were to be judged dangerous, then the Reaper was ten times more so. The Reaper was a killer. Killing was the sole function of its existence. It was a massive creature, heavily muscled, almost seven feet tall when it rose to its full height. Yet its size was misleading, for it was by no means ponderous. It moved with the ease and grace of the best Elven Hunter—smooth, fluid, quick, and noiseless. Once it had begun a hunt, it never gave up. Nothing it went after ever escaped. Even the Dagda Mor was wary of the Reaper, though the Reaper did not possess his power. He was wary because the Reaper served him out of whim and not out of fear or respect as did all the others. The Reaper feared nothing. It was a monster who cared nothing for life, even its own. It did not even kill because it enjoyed killing, though in truth it did enjoy killing. It killed because killing was instinctive. It killed because it found killing necessary. At times, within the darkness of the Forbidding, shut away from every form of life but its own brethren, it had been almost unmanageable. The Dagda Mor had been forced to give it lesser Demons to kill, keeping it under his control with a promise. Once they were free of the Forbidding—and they would, one day, be free—the Reaper would be given an entire world of creatures that it might prey upon. For as long as it wished, it might hunt them. In the end, it might kill them all.

The Changeling and the Reaper. The Dagda Mor had chosen well. One would be his eyes, the other his hands, eyes and hands that would go deep into the heart of the Elven people and end forever the chance that the Ellcrys might be reborn.

He glanced sharply to the east where the rim of the morning sun was rising rapidly above the crest of the Breakline. It was time to go. By tonight, they must be in Arborlon. This, too, he had planned with care. Time was precious to him; he had little to waste if he expected to catch the Elves napping. They must not know of his presence until it was too late to do anything about it.

With a quick motion to his companions, the Dagda Mor turned and slouched heavily toward the shelter of the Breakline. His black eyes lidded with pleasure as he tasted in his mind the success tonight would bring him. After tonight, the Elves would be doomed. After tonight, they would be forced to watch their beloved Ellcrys decay without even the faintest hope for any rebirth.

Indeed. Because after tonight, the Chosen would all be dead.

Several hundred yards from the mountains, deep within their concealing shadow, the Dagda Mor stopped. With both hands gripping the Staff of Power, he placed it upright, one end planted firmly in the dry, cracked earth. His head lowered slightly, and his hands tightened about the Staff. For long moments, he stood without moving. Behind him, the other two watched curiously, their dark forms huddled down, their eyes bits of yellow light.

Then abruptly, the Staff of Power began to glow faintly, a pale reddish color that silhouetted the hulking form of the Demon against the darkness. A moment later, the glow intensified sharply and began to pulsate. It ran from the Staff into the arms of the Dagda Mor, turning the greenish skin to blood. The Demon's head came up and fire shot skyward from the Staff in a thin, brilliant arc that flew into the dawn like some frightened, living thing. It was gone in seconds. The glow that lit the Staff of Power flared once and died.

The Dagda Mor stepped back a pace, the Staff lowering. The earth about him was charred and black, and the damp air smelled of burning ash. The whole of the surrounding Flats had gone deathly still. The Demon seated himself, opaque eyes lidding contentedly. He did not move again, nor did the creatures with him. Together, they waited—half an hour, one hour, two. Still they waited.

And finally, down from the vast emptiness of the Northland, swept the monstrous, winged nightmare the Demon had summoned to carry them east to Arborlon.

"Now shall we see," the Dagda Mor whispered.

III

The sun was barely above the horizon when Ander Elessedil stepped through the front door of his small house and moved up the walkway toward the iron gates that fronted the palace grounds. As second son of Eventine, King of the Elves, he could have had his rooms in the royal quarters; but years before, he had moved himself and his books to his present residence and thereby gained a privacy that he would have lacked within the palace. Or so he had thought at the time. Now he was less certain; with his older brother Arion receiving most of their father's attention, Ander would probably have found himself largely undisturbed wherever he chose to live.

He sniffed the cleanness and early warmth of the morning air and smiled briefly. A good day for a ride. Both he and his favorite horse could use the exercise.

At forty, he was no longer a young man. His lean Elven face was lined at the corners of the narrow eyes and the furrow of his sharply angled brow; but his step was quick and easy, and his face was almost boyish when he smiled—though that was seldom these days.

As he neared the gates, he saw that Went, the old groundskeeper, was already at work, tending the flower beds with a hand hoe, his thin frame bent over his work. As he heard Ander approach, Went straightened slowly, one hand going to his back.

"Good morning, Prince. Nice day, eh?"

Ander nodded. "Splendid, Went. Back still bothering you?"

"Now and then." The old man rubbed himself gingerly. "Age catching up to me, I guess. But I can still outwork the young ones they give me for help."

Ander nodded once more, knowing the old man's boast was simple truth. Went should have retired years ago, but he'd stubbornly refused to give up his duties.

As Ander made his way through the front gate, the sentries on watch nodded in greeting, and he nodded back. The guards and he had long since dispensed with formalities. Arion, as Crown Prince, might insist on being treated deferentially, but Ander's position and expectations were somewhat less.

He followed the line of the roadway as it curved left around some decorative bushes toward the stables. Then a thunder of hooves and a shout broke the morning quiet. Ander leaped aside as Arion's gray stallion plunged toward him, scattering gravel and rearing to a sudden halt.

Before the horse was fully at rest, Arion was off and facing his brother. Where Ander was short and dark, Arion was tall and fair, and his resemblance to their father at the same age was striking. That, together with the fact that he was a superb athlete and an accomplished weapons master, hunter and horseman made it inevitable that he should be Eventine's pride and joy. There was also a compelling charisma about Arion—a charisma that Ander had always felt lacking within himself.

"Where bound, little brother?" Arion asked. As usual, when speaking to the younger Prince, his tone held a slight hint of mockery and contempt. "I wouldn't bother our father, if I were you. He and I were up late working on some rather pressing matters of state. He was still sleeping. when I looked in."

"I was heading for the stables," Ander replied quietly. "I had no intention of *bothering* anyone."

Arion grinned, then turned back to his horse. With a hand on the pommel, he leapt lightly into the saddle, disregarding the stirrup. Then he turned to look down at his brother. "Well, I'm off to the Sarandanon for a few days. The people in the farming communities are all stirred up— some old fairy tale of doom overtaking us all. A lot of nonsense, but I've got to settle them down. Don't get your hopes up, though. I'll be back before father leaves for the Kershalt." He grinned. "In the meantime, little brother, look after things, will you?"

He flipped the reins and was off in a rush that carried

him through the gates and away. Ander swore softly to himself and turned back. He was no longer in a mood to go riding.

He should have been the one to accompany the King on the mission of state to the Kershalt. Strengthening the ties between the Trolls and the Elves was important. And while the groundwork had already been laid, it would still require diplomacy and careful negotiating. Arion was too impatient and reckless, with too little feeling for the needs and ideas of others. Ander might lack his brother's physical skills—though he was capable enough—and he might lack as well Arion's natural flair for leadership. But he possessed a gift for thorough, deliberate reasoning and the patience needed in diplomatic councils. On the few occasions when he had been called on, he'd demonstrated such abilities.

He shrugged. There was no sense in dwelling on it now, however. He had already appealed to Eventine to go on the journey and been turned down in favor of Arion. Arion would be King someday; he must have the practice at statescraft he needed while Eventine still lived to guide him. And maybe that made sense, Ander conceded.

Once, Arion and he had been close. That was when Aine was alive—Aine, the youngest of the Elessedil sons. But Aine had been killed in a hunting accident eleven years ago, and after that the bond of kinship had no longer been enough. Amberle, Aine's young daughter, had turned to Ander for support, not to Arion, and the older brother's jealousy had soon manifested itself in open contempt. Then when Amberle had forsaken her position as one of the Chosen, Arion had blamed his brother's influence, and his contempt had degenerated into thinly masked hostility. Now Ander suspected their father's mind was being poisoned against him. But there was nothing he could do about it.

Still deep in thought, he was passing through the gates down the pathway to his house when a shout brought him around.

"My Lord Prince, wait!"

Ander stared in surprise at the sight of a white-robed figure running toward him, one arm waving frantically. It was one of the Chosen, the redheaded one—Lauren, wasn't that his name? It was unusual to see any of them outside the Gardens at this hour. He waited until the young Elf reached him, stumbling to a weary halt, face and arms streaked with sweat.

"My Lord Prince, I must see the King," the Chosen gasped. "And they won't let me through, not until later. Can you take me to him now?"

Ander hesitated. "The King is still asleep . . ."

"I must see him at once!" the other insisted. "Please! This cannot wait!"

There was desperation in his eyes and on his strained, white face. His voice was cracking with his attempt to emphasize the urgency that was driving him. Ander deliberated, wondering what could be that important. "If you're in some kind of trouble, Lauren, maybe I . . ."

"It's not me, my Lord Prince. It's the Ellcrys!"

Ander's indecision vanished. He nodded and took Lauren's arm. "Come with me."

Together they hurried back through the gates toward the manor house, the sentries staring after them in surprise.

Gael, the young Elf who served as personal aide to Eventine Elessedil, shook his head firmly—yet within his dark morning robe his slim form shifted uneasily and his eyes refused to meet those of Ander. "I cannot waken the King, Prince Ander. He told me—very strongly—not to bother him for anything."

"Or anyone, Gael?" Ander asked softly. "Not even for Arion?"

"Arion has left . . ." Gael began. Then he halted and looked even more unhappy.

"Precisely. But I am here. Are you really going to tell me that I cannot see my father?"

Gael did not answer. Then, as Ander started toward the King's bedroom, the young Elf hurried past him. "I'll wake him. Please wait here."

It was several minutes before he came out again, his face still troubled, but he nodded toward Ander. "He will see you, Prince Ander. But for now, just you."

The King was still in his bed as Ander entered, finishing the small glass of wine that Gael must have poured for him. He nodded at his son, then slipped gingerly from beneath the warmth of the bedcovers, his aging body shivering for an instant in the early morning coolness of the room. Gael, who had come in with Ander, was holding out a robe, and Eventine drew it about him, belting it snugly at the waist.

Despite his eighty-two years, Eventine Elessedil was in excellent health. His body was trim and hard. He was still able to ride, still quick and sure enough to be dangerous with a sword. His mind was sharp and alert; when the situation demanded it, as the situation frequently did, he was decisive. He still possessed that uncanny sense of balance, of proportion—the capability of seeing all sides of an issue, of judging each on its merits, and of choosing almost without exception that which would work the greatest benefit to himself and to those he ruled. It was a gift without which he could not have stayed King—would not even have stayed alive. It was a gift Ander had some reason to believe he had inherited, though it seemed worthless enough, in his present circumstances.

The King crossed to the handwoven curtains that draped the far wall, drew them aside, and pushed outward several of the floor-length windows that opened into the forest beyond. Light flooded the chamber, soft and sweet, and the smell of morning dew. Behind him, Gael was moving silently about, lighting the oil lamps to chase the last of the gloom from the corners of the chamber. Eventine hesitated before a window, staring fixedly for an instant at the reflection of his face in the misted glass. The eyes mirrored there were startlingly blue, hard and penetrating, the eyes of a man who has seen too many years and too much unpleasantness. He sighed and turned to face Ander.

"All right, Ander, what's this all about? Gael said something about your bringing one of the Chosen with a message?"

"Yes, sir. He claims he has an urgent message from the Ellcrys."

"A message from the tree?" Eventine frowned. "How long has it been since she gave a message to anyone—over seven hundred years? What was the message?"

"He wouldn't tell it to me," Ander replied. "He insists on delivering the message to you."

Eventine nodded. "Then deliver it he shall. Show him in, Gael."

Gael bowed slightly and hurried out through the chamber doors, leaving them slightly ajar. A moment later a huge, shaggy dog pushed his way through and padded noiselessly to the King. It was Manx, his wolfhound, and he greeted the animal fondly, rubbing the grizzled head, stroking softly the rough coat along the back and flanks. Manx had been with him almost ten years, closer and more faithful than any man could have been.

"Getting a bit gray—like me," Eventine muttered ruefully.

The doors opened wide to admit Gael, followed by Lauren. The Chosen paused in the doorway for a moment, glancing uncertainly at Gael. The King nodded to his aide, dismissing him. Ander was about to leave as well when a slight motion from his father indicated he was to remain. Gael bowed again and left, this time closing the doors tightly behind him. When he was gone, the Chosen came forward a pace.

"My Lord, please forgive . . . they thought that I . . . I should be the one . . ." He was almost choking on the words.

"There is nothing to forgive," Eventine assured him. With a charm that Ander had always known his father could display, the King came forward quickly and put his arm about the young Elf's shoulders. "I know this must be very important to you or you would not have left your work in the Gardens. Here, sit down and tell me about it."

He glanced questioningly at Ander, then guided the Chosen to a small writing table at one side of the room, seating him in one of two chairs while he took the other. Ander followed them over, but remained standing.

"Your name is Lauren, isn't it?" Eventine asked the Chosen.

"Yes, my Lord."

"Very well, Lauren. Now tell me why you've come."

Lauren drew himself up and placed his hands on the table, folding the fingers together tightly.

"My Lord, the Ellcrys spoke to the Chosen this morning." His words were almost a whisper. "She told us . . . she told us that she is dying!"

Ander felt his blood turn cold. For an instant, the King did not respond, but sat rigidly in place, his eyes fixed on the speaker.

"There must be a mistake," he said at last.

Lauren shook his head emphatically. "There is no mistake, my Lord. She spoke to all of us. We . . . we all heard. She is dying. The Forbidding has already begun to crumble."

The King rose slowly and walked to the open window, staring wordlessly out into the forest. Manx, who had curled up at the foot of the bed, rose and followed him. Ander saw the King's hand stray down to scratch the dog's ears mechanically.

"You are certain of this, Lauren?" Eventine asked. "Very certain?"

"Yes . . . yes."

He was crying softly, almost soundlessly, at the table, his face buried in his hands. Eventine did not turn, but continued to stare fixedly into the woodlands that were his home and the home of his people.

Ander was frozen, his eyes on his father, his mind still dazed with shock. The enormity of what he had heard slowly took hold. The Ellcrys dying! The Forbidding ending. The evil that had been shut away free once more. Chaos, madness, war! In the end, the destruction of everything.

He had studied history under his tutors and again in the books of his own library. It was a history that bore the trappings of legend.

Once, long ago, in a time before the Great Wars, before the dawn of civilization in the old world, even before the emergence of the old race of Man, there had been a war between creatures of good and evil magics. The Elves had fought in that war on the side of good. It had been a long, terrible, devastating struggle. But in the end, the forces of good were victorious and the forces of evil were cast down. Yet the nature of the evil was such that it could not be totally destroyed; it could only be banished. Therefore, the Elven people and their allies pooled their magics with the life-force of the earth itself to create the Ellcrys, so that by her presence a Forbidding would be placed upon the creatures of evil. So long as the Ellcrys survived and flourished, the evil could not return upon the earth. Locked in a void of darkness, it might wail in anguish behind the wall of the Forbidding, but the earth was lost to it.

Until now! But if the Ellcrys were to die, the Forbidding must end. It had been written that this must come to pass, for no power could be so strong that it could endure forever. Yet it had seemed that the Ellcrys would, so many generations had it been there, changeless, a fixed point in a shifting maze of life. The Elven people had come to believe it would always be so. Wrongly, it seemed. Foolishly.

The King turned sharply, glanced briefly at Ander, and moved back to the table, reseating himself and taking Lauren's hands in his own to steady him. "You must tell me everything that she said to you, Lauren. Every detail. Leave nothing out."

The Chosen nodded wordlessly. His eyes were dry once more, his face calm. Eventine released his hands and sat back expectantly. Ander pulled over a high-backed chair from across the room and seated himself next to them.

"My Lord, you have heard of the form of her communication with us?" he asked cautiously.

"I was a Chosen once, Lauren," Eventine answered. Ander stared at his father in surprise. This was something he had never known. But Lauren seemed to gain a measure of confidence from the answer. He nodded, turning to Ander to explain.

"Her voice is actually not a voice of sound, but one of images that appear in our minds. There are seldom words as such; the words are our own translation of the thoughts she projects. That is how I translate when she uses my name. The images are brief and not fully drawn, and we have to interpret them as best we can."

He paused and turned back to Eventine. "I . . . the Ellcrys has never spoken to me more than once before this morning, my Lord. She had spoken to the six of us only at the time of our choosing. Until this morning, most of what we knew of her communication was based upon the writings of our Order and the teachings of the Chosen who have served before. Even now, it is very confusing."

Eventine nodded encouragingly. Lauren continued.

"My Lord, the Ellcrys spoke to us at great length this

morning, something she has never done before. She called us to her and told us what was to be and what we, the Chosen, must do. The images were not entirely clear, but there can be no mistake that she is dying. Her time is short; how much time remains isn't certain. Already the erosion has begun. And as she fails, the Forbidding will fail with her. There is only one chance for her—a rebirth."

Eventine's hand shot forth, gripping Lauren's. Ander too had forgotten—shocked and confused by the Ellcrys' forecast of her death. A rebirth! It was written in the oldest histories that the Ellcrys could be reborn and the Forbidding preserved.

"Then there is still hope," he whispered.

Eventine's eyes were fixed on Lauren. "What must be done to give her this rebirth?"

Lauren shook his head. "My Lord, she has entrusted her fate to the Chosen. Only through us will she permit herself to be reborn. I do not pretend to understand her reasons, but the images were clear. She will deliver her seed to one of us—which, she did not say. No face was shown. But it was made known that only one of the Chosen who were selected by her this last time can receive that seed. No other will be considered. Whoever is selected must carry the seed to the life source of the earth—to the fountain of the Bloodfire. There the seed must be immersed within the fire by the bearer. Once returned to the site of the old tree, the seed will take root and a new tree will spring forth to replace the old."

The details of the legend were coming back to Ander now—the bearing of the Ellcrys seed, the ritual of the Bloodfire, the rebirth. It was told in the strange, formal language of the oldest histories—histories that most of the people had forgotten or never known.

"The fountain of the Bloodfire—where is it to be found?" he asked abruptly.

Lauren looked miserable. "A place was shown us, my Lord Prince, but . . . but we could not recognize it. The images were vague, almost as if she lacked the ability to describe it properly."

Eventine's voice remained calm. "Tell me what you were shown. Everything."

Lauren nodded. "There was a wilderness with mountains and swamp all around. There was a deep mist that came and went. Within the wilderness was a lone peak and beneath the peak a maze of tunnels that burrowed deep within the earth. Somewhere within the maze there was a door made of glass—glass that could not break. Behind the door was the Bloodfire."

"No names for any of the parts of this puzzle?" the King asked patiently.

"Only one, my lord. But it was a name we did not recognize. The maze in which the Bloodfire lies hidden appears to be called Safehold."

Safehold? Ander searched his memory, but the name meant nothing to him.

Eventine glanced at Ander and shook his head. He rose to his feet, walked several paces from the table, then stopped abruptly. He turned back to Lauren. "Is there nothing more that you were told? No hints—bits that might not seem to have any meaning?"

"Nothing. That was all."

The King nodded slowly to the young Elf. "Very well, Lauren. You were right in insisting I be told at once. Now, will you wait outside for a little while?"

When the door had closed behind the Chosen, Eventine walked back to his chair and lowered himself slowly. His face seemed to have aged terribly and his movements were those of an old, old man. Manx moved over in front of him, and the grizzled face stared upward sympathetically. Eventine sighed and moved his hand tiredly to the dog's head.

"Have I lived too long?" he muttered. "If the Ellcrys dies, how can I protect my people from what will happen then? I am their King; the responsibility for their protection is mine. I have always accepted that. Yet for the first time in my life, I wish it were otherwise . . ."

He trailed off reluctantly, then turned to look at Ander. "Well, we must do what we can. With Arion gone to the Sarandanon, I will need your help." Ander flushed at the unintended rebuke. "Go with Lauren and question the Chosen carefully. See if there is anything more that may be learned. Anything. I will have the old histories moved up from the vaults and examine them."

"Do you think there might be something there—or in the old world maps?" Ander asked doubtfully.

"No. You have read them more recently than I, but I can remember nothing. Still, what else can we do? If we are to have any chance at all of finding the Bloodfire, we must have more than what Lauren has been able to tell us."

He nodded in dismissal. Ander went out to join Lauren, to return with him to the tree where the other Chosen would be waiting. There he would attempt to discover something more of the mysterious Safehold. It seemed a hopeless effort. But, as his father had said, what else could they do?

IV

The summer day ended with a brilliant burst of red and lavender that flooded the whole of the western skyline. For long, beautiful minutes, the sun seemed to hang at the crest of the Breakline, lighting the roof of the Westland forest and weaving shadows that draped the wooded earth with still, soft bands of darkness. The air cooled slowly, the midday heat fading now as an evening breeze rippled and sighed through the great, silent trees. Then daylight slipped into dusk, and night washed the color from the sky.

The people of the Elven city of Arborlon drifted wearily toward their homes.

Within the Gardens of Life, Ander Elessedil stared upward at the Ellcrys. Seen now against the evening light, the great tree seemed normal, deceptively unchanged. Yet before the sun had set, traces of the sickness that was destroying her had been plainly evident.

The disease was spreading rapidly. On a scattering of smaller limbs, rot had begun to eat away at the silver-white bark. Broad clusters of leaves hung limp with wilt, curling at the tips, the deep red color turned black. The Chosen had scrubbed the bark carefully with herbal salves and plucked the damaged leaves, hoping against reason that the disease could be contained, knowing all the while that it could not. Ander had seen the truth reflected in their eyes. They could not heal the Ellcrys. No one could. She was dying, and there was nothing that anyone could do to prevent it.

He sighed and turned away, not sure why he had made this last visit of the day to the Gardens. The Chosen had returned to their compound an hour earlier, tired and

25

discouraged, silent in their sense of futility. But he had come anyway, drawn by an unreasoning hope that somehow the answers they so desperately needed could be found here. He had not found those answers, of course, and with the coming of nightfall there was little sense in staying longer.

As he passed out of the Gardens, he could feel the sentries of the Black Watch staring after him. They remained unaware of the damage to the tree, but they could sense that something was wrong. The activities of the Chosen had told them that much. Word would soon be spreading, he thought—rumors growing. Soon the people would have to be told.

But for the moment, at least, all was quiet. Lights were already going out and many windows were darkened as the people prepared for sleep. He envied them. There was little chance that he would sleep that night—he or the King.

He sighed again, wishing that there was something he could do for his father. Eventine had always been so sure of himself, had always been so supremely confident that a solution could be found to any problem. But now, in the two visits Ander had made to report his lack of progress, the old King had seemed lost somewhere within himself. He had tried halfheartedly to mask it from his son, but it was obvious that he was looking with despair on the ending of everything he had worked all his life to accomplish. Here, at last, was a challenge that was beyond all his powers. With barely a word to his son, he had sent him back to continue aiding the Chosen in any way he could.

It had proved a futile task. Ander had questioned each of them carefully, then assembled them and probed their collective memory, searching for any small piece of information that might lead to Safehold. But he had learned nothing more than what he already knew.

A search of the carefully preserved records of their Order had yielded nothing, either. He had studied histories that dated back centuries, checking and rechecking. There were repeated references to the sacred Bloodfire, the life source of their world and all its living things. But nowhere was there even the briefest mention of the mysterious place called Safehold.

Nor had the Ellcrys given them any further assistance in their search. At Ander's suggestion, the Chosen had gone back to her again. They had gone to her over and over, one by one and all together, begging her to give them something more to further their understanding of her images. But she would not speak to them. She remained silent.

As he came near the compound of the Chosen, he saw that all the lights were out. Routine had apparently taken over and they must have returned to their sleeping quarters at their usual time, shortly after finishing their evening meal. He hoped they would find some relief in sleep. Maybe they would. Sometimes hopelessness and despair were even more fatiguing than physical labor, and they had experienced little else during the long day.

He was moving quietly past their compound, following a pathway that led toward the manor house to make one final report to his father, when a dark shadow moved from under a low tree beside the path.

"My Lord Prince?"

"Lauren?" he asked. Then, as the figure moved closer, he saw that it was indeed the young Elf. "Why aren't you asleep?"

"I tried to sleep, but I couldn't. I . . . I saw you go up to the Gardens and I hoped that you'd come back this way. Prince Ander, can I speak to you?"

"You are speaking to me, Lauren," Ander reminded him. But his brief attempt at amusement did nothing to lighten the seriousness of the other's expression. "Have you remembered something?"

"Perhaps. Not about what the Ellcrys told us, but something I think you should know. Can I walk with you a ways?"

Ander nodded. They turned back along Ander's chosen path, moving slowly away from the compound.

"I feel as if I ought to be the one to solve this problem," Lauren began after a moment. "Maybe it's because the Ellcrys spoke first to me; that makes finding Safehold seem almost my personal obligation. I know that's probably giving too much importance to myself, but it's the way I feel, nevertheless. In any case, I don't want to overlook anything." He glanced at the Prince. "Do you understand what I am trying to say?"

"I think so. Have we overlooked something, then?"

"Well, something has occurred to me. I thought I should mention it to somebody."

Ander stopped and looked at the young Elf.

"I didn't want to say anything to the King." Lauren's uneasiness increased. "Or to any of the others. I'm not really sure how much of this they know . . . and we don't talk about her . . ."

He trailed off. Ander waited patiently.

"It's about Amberle. My Lord, after her choosing, she spoke with the Ellcrys many times—long conversations." The words came slowly. "It was different with her than with the rest of us. I don't know whether she ever realized that. We never really talked about it . . ."

Ander had stiffened sharply. Lauren saw his reaction and hurried on. "But maybe the Ellcrys would talk to her again. Or she might understand better. Perhaps she might learn something we could not."

There was a long moment of silence as the two faced each other. Then Ander shook his head slowly. "Amberle can't help us now, Lauren. She's gone. Even her mother doesn't know where she went. There's no possible way we could find her in time to make any difference."

The red-haired Elf nodded slowly, the last trace of hope leaving his face. "It was just an idea," he said finally, then turned back toward the compound. "Good-night, Prince Ander."

"Good-night, Lauren. Thank you for telling me, anyhow."

The Chosen nodded again before moving back up the pathway, his white robes rustling softly as he disappeared into the night. Ander stared after him for a moment, his dark face troubled. His father had asked for any hint—anything—that might offer a clue to the location of Safehold. Yet there was really no hope of finding Amberle. She might be anywhere within the Four Lands. And now was hardly the time to bring her name up to Eventine. She had been his favorite, the granddaughter whose choosing had filled him with deep pride and joy. But her betrayal of her trust had been harder for him to bear than even the death of her father Aine.

He shook his head slowly and continued on toward the manor house.

Gael was still on duty, his face drawn with fatigue and his eyes troubled. It was inevitable that he should come to know of the problem they faced, but he could be trusted to maintain secrecy. Now he started to rise, then sank back again at Ander's motion. "The King is expecting you," he said. "He's in his study, refusing to retire. If you could persuade him to sleep, even for a few hours . . ."

"I'll see what I can do," Ander promised.

Within his private study, Eventine Elessedil looked up as his son entered. His eyes studied Ander's face momentarily, reading the failure written there. Then he pushed himself back from the reading table at which he had been seated and rubbed his eyes wearily. He rose, stretched, and walked slowly to the curtained windows, peering through the folds into the darkness beyond. On the book-littered table, a tray of food had been pushed aside, hardly touched. Candles burned low, their wax dripping and puddling on the metal holders. The small study was still and somber, its oak bookcases and tapestry-covered walls a dim mix of faded colors and shadow. Scattered about in piles lay the books that Gael must have spent the day bringing up from the vaults.

The King looked back momentarily at his son. "Nothing?" Ander shook his head silently. Eventine grimaced. "Nor I—" He shrugged, pointing to the book that lay open on the table. "The last hope. It contains a single reference to the Ellcrys seed and the Bloodfire. Read it for yourself."

The book was one of more than a hundred volumes of the histories kept by the Elven Kings and their scribes from days that were lost in myth. They were worn and old, carefully bound in leather and brass, sealed in coverings that served to protect them against the ravages of time. They had survived the Great Wars and the destruction of the old race of Man. They had survived the First and Second Wars of the Races. They had survived the ages and ages of life and death that they chronicled. They contained the entirety of the known history of the Elven people. Thousands and thousands of pages, all carefully recorded through the years.

Ander bent to the open pages; the ink had turned brown

with age and the script was of an ancient style. But the
words were clear enough to read.

"Then shall the One Seed be delivered unto the Bearer
that is Chosen. And the Seed shall be borne by the Bearer
to the Chambers of the Bloodfire, there to be immersed
within the Fire that it might be returned to the earth.
Thereupon shall the Tree be Reborn and the Great Forbidding endure forever. Thus spake the High Wizard to his
Elves, even as he did perish, that Knowledge be not lost
unto his People."

Eventine nodded as Ander looked up again. "I have read
through every one of those books, studying every passage
that might apply. There are others—but none tells more
than the one you read."

He walked back to the reading table and stood fingering
the gilt-edged pages of the volume idly. "This is the oldest
volume. It contains much that may be only myth. The tale
of the ancient war between good and evil magics, names of
heroes, everything that led up to the Forbidding. But no
mention of Safehold or of the location of the Bloodfire. And
nothing on the nature of the sorcery that gave life to the
Ellcrys and to the power of the Forbidding."

The last omission was hardly unusual, Ander thought.
His ancestors had seldom placed the secrets of their magics
in writing. Such things were handed down by word of
mouth so that they could not be stolen by their enemies.
And some sorceries were said to be so powerful that their
use was limited to but a single time and place. It might
have been so with the sorcery that had created the Ellcrys.

The King lowered himself back into his chair, studied the
book a moment longer, then wordlessly closed it.

"We will have to rely on the little we have learned from
the Ellcrys," he said quietly. "We will have to use that to
determine the possible locations of the Bloodfire and then
search each of them out."

Ander nodded wordlessly. It seemed hopeless. There
was only the smallest chance that they could find Safehold
with nothing more than that vague description to aid them.

"I wish Arion were here," his father murmured suddenly.

Ander said nothing. There was good cause for the King
to have need of Arion this time, he admitted to himself. For

the leadership that would be required in directing and furthering the search, Arion was the proper choice. And his presence might give some comfort to their father. Now was no time to begrudge him that.

"I think you should sleep, father," Ander suggested after a moment of silence. "You'll need rest for what lies ahead."

The King rose once more and reached out to extinguish the candles on the table. "Very well, Ander," he said, making an effort to smile at his son. "Send Gael in to me. But your day, too, has been a long one. You go on to bed as well and get whatever sleep you can."

Ander returned to his cottage. To his surprise, he did sleep. While his mind spun dully in useless circles, sheer physical fatigue took over. He awoke only once during the night, his rest broken by a nightmare of indescribable horror that left him damp with sweat. Yet within seconds of waking, he drifted back asleep, the dream forgotten. This time, he slumbered undisturbed.

It was already dawn when he came awake again, slipping hurriedly from the bedcovers to dress. A sense of renewed determination strengthened him as he breakfasted hastily and prepared to leave his house. Somewhere there was an answer to this dilemma, a means by which Safehold could be found. Perhaps it lay with the dying Ellcrys. Perhaps it lay with the Chosen. But there was an answer—there had to be an answer.

As he went down the gravel walkway, he could see the early morning sunlight seeping through the screen of the surrounding forests as the new day began. He would go first to the Chosen—they would be in the Gardens of Life by now, their day already begun—in the hope that by talking once again with them something new would be discovered. They would have been thinking about the matter, turning it over and over in their minds, and possibly one of them might have recalled something more. Or perhaps the Ellcrys would have spoken to them again this morning.

He stopped first at the manor house, where Gael was already at his post. But the young Elf raised a finger to his lips, indicating silently that the King still slept and should not be disturbed. Ander nodded and left, grateful for any rest his father might find.

Dew still glimmered on the palace lawn as he moved toward the gates. He glanced expectantly at the gardens as he passed and was surprised to see that Went was not at work. He was more surprised still to see a scattering of the old fellow's tools at the edge of the rose beds, dirt still fresh upon their metal. It was not like Went to leave a job half done. If he was having that much trouble with his back, he should be checked on. But that would have to wait. There were more pressing concerns at the moment. He glanced through the shrubbery at the flower beds a final time, then hurried on.

Minutes later he was striding past the ivy-grown walls of the Gardens of Life, following the worn pathway that led to their gates. From atop the Carolan—the towering wall of rock that rose abruptly from the eastern shore of the Rill Song, lifting Arborlon above the lands about it—he could see the vast sweep of the Westland stretched forth below: to the east and north, the towers and tree lanes of the Elven home city, wrapped close within the dense tangle of the forestland; to the south, the distant mist-gray crags of the Rock Spur and Pykon, laced with bits and pieces of blue ribbon where the Mermidon River cut apart the aged rock on its long passage eastward into Callahorn; to the west, below the Carolan and beyond the swift flow of the Rill Song, the valley of the Sarandanon, the breadbasket of the Elven nation. The homeland of the Elves, Ander thought with pride. He must find a way, he and the Chosen and his father, to save it.

Moments later he stood before the Ellcrys. There was no sign of the Chosen. The tree stood alone.

Ander stared about in disbelief. It seemed impossible that the Chosen could have all overslept, even though their routine had been so upset by the revelation of the Ellcrys. In hundreds of years, the Chosen had never failed to greet the tree at the first touch of morning light.

Ander left the Gardens hurriedly and was almost running as he came within sight of the walled compound of the Chosen. Evergreens surrounded it, flower gardens banked its stone and brick walkways, and vegetable patches ran in even rows along its backside, the black earth dotted with green stalks and sprouts. A low wall of worn rock enclosed the yard, breached on each side by white picket gates.

The house itself was shadowed and still.

Ander slowed. By now, the Chosen must surely be awake. Yet there was no sign of life. Something cold seemed to settle into the Elven Prince. He moved ahead, eyes peering into the shadowy dimness beyond the open door of the house, until at last he stood at the entrance.

"Lauren?" He spoke the young Elf's name quietly.

No answer came. He stepped through the entry into the darker shadows beyond. A flicker of movement registered at the edge of his vision, movement that came from somewhere within the surrounding evergreens. A sudden apprehension swept through him, leaving him cold all over. What was back there?

Belatedly he thought of the weapons he had left within his lodgings. He stood motionless for a time, waiting for something more. But there was no further movement, no sounds betraying the presence of another living being. Resolutely he went forward.

"Lauren . . . ?"

Then his sight adjusted to the dimmer interior, and the young Elf's name caught in his throat.

Bodies lay strewn about the main room like discarded sacks, torn and broken and lifeless. Lauren, Jase—all of the Chosen dead, ripped apart as if by maddened animals. Despair filled him. Now no Chosen remained to carry the seed of the Ellcrys in search of Safehold and the Bloodfire. Now there could be no rebirth of the tree, no salvation for the Elves. Sickened by the carnage, he nevertheless could not bring himself to move. He stood there, horror and revulsion sweeping through him, a single word shrieking in his mind:

Demons!

A moment later, he staggered outside, retching uncontrollably as he leaned up against the cottage wall and fought to still his shaking. When at last he had recovered, he went at once to give the alarm to the Black Watch, then hurried on to the city. His father would have to be told, and it was best that the news come from his son.

What had befallen the Chosen was all too clear. With the failing of the Ellcrys, the Forbidding had begun to erode. The stronger Demons were breaking loose. Nothing but a Demon could or would have done such a thing to the Chosen. In a single strike, the Demons had made certain that they would never again be imprisoned. They had destroyed all those who might aid in the rebirth of the Ellcrys and the restoration of the Forbidding that had confined them.

Back through the gates that fronted the manor house grounds he ran, down the gravel walkway that led past the gardens that old Went tended. Went was there now, digging and weeding, his leathered face lifting momentarily as the Prince went past. Ander barely saw him, said nothing to him, as he hurried on.

Went's eyes lowered in satisfaction. Hands sifting idly through the black earth, the Changeling went on with his work.

V

It was evening again when Ander Elessedil closed the door to the cottage that had housed the Order of the Chosen, latching it firmly for the final time. Silence fell about him as he paused to stare out into the growing dark. The cottage stood empty now; the bodies of the six murdered youths had long since been taken from it, and Ander had removed the last small personal possessions to return to their relatives. For these few brief moments, he was alone with his thoughts.

But his thoughts were not ones he cared to dwell on. He had supervised the removal of the mutilated bodies and then the gathering of the histories of their Order, taken now for safekeeping to the vaults beneath the Elessedil manor house. At his father's suggestion, he had gone through those records, page by page, searching for that small bit of revelation on Safehold's puzzle that they had somehow overlooked. He had found nothing. He shook his head. What difference anyway, he thought bleakly. What difference now what was learned of Safehold? Without a Chosen to carry the seed, what was the need to locate the Bloodfire? Still, he had been glad to have something to do—anything to do—that would help take his mind from what he had seen when he found Lauren and the others.

He stepped away from the empty cottage, crossed the yard of the compound, and turned down the path leading to the Gardens of Life. All across the Carolan, the flicker of torches burned through the gathering darkness. There were soldiers everywhere; Black Watch ringed the Gardens and Home Guard—the King's personal corps of Elven Hunters—patrolled the streets and tree lanes of the city. The Elves were understandably frightened by what had happened. When word of the slain Chosen had spread, Eventine had acted quickly to reassure his people that they would be protected against a similar fate—though in truth, he believed them to be in no immediate danger. The thing that had killed the Chosen had not been after anyone else. The Chosen had been its sole target. Nothing else made sense. Still, it did no harm to take precautions. Such measures would do as much to stem the panic the King could sense building in his people as to safeguard the city.

The real damage, of course, had already been done. The tree was dying, and now there would be no rebirth. Once she was dead, the Forbidding would fail entirely and the evil locked within would break free. Once free, it would seek out and destroy every last Elf. And with the Ellcrys gone, what miracle of Elven magic could be found to prevent it?

Ander paused outside the wall of the Gardens. He drew a slow breath to steady himself, forcing down the feeling of helplessness that had been building inside all day, little by little, like some insidious sickness. What in the name of sanity were they to do? Even with the Chosen alive, they had not known where the Bloodfire was to be found. With the Forbidding already beginning to crumble, there had never been enough time to search it out. And now, with the Chosen dead . . .

Amberle.

Her name whispered in his mind. Amberle. Lauren's last words to him had been of her. Perhaps she could help, the red-haired Chosen had suggested. Then the idea had seemed impossible. Now anything at all seemed better than what they had. Ander's mind raced. How could he convince his father that he must consider the possibility that Amberle might help? How could he convince his father even to talk to him about the girl? He remembered the old King's bitterness and disappointment the day he had learned of Amberle's betrayal of her trust as a Chosen. Ander balanced that against the despair he had seen in his father's face this morning when he had brought him the news of the slaughtered Chosen. His decision was easily made. The King was desperate for help from some quarter. With Arion gone into the Sarandanon, Ander knew that that help must come from him. And what other help could he give but to suggest to his father that Amberle must be sought?

"Elven Prince?"

The voice came from out of nowhere, startling Ander so that he jumped away from it with a gasp. A shadow slipped from the shelter of the pines that grew close against the walls of the Gardens of Life, darker than the night about it. For an instant Ander stopped breathing altogether, freezing with indecision. Then, as he reached hurriedly for the short sword he wore belted at his waist, the shadow was upon him and a hand lay over his own, an iron grip holding back his arm.

"Peace, Ander Elessedil." The voice was soft but commanding. "I am no enemy of yours."

The shadowy form was that of a man, Ander saw now, a tall man, standing well over seven feet. Black robes were wrapped tightly about his spare, lean frame, and the hood of his traveling cloak was pulled close about his head so that nothing of his face could be seen save for narrow eyes that shone like a cat's.

"Who are you?" the Elven Prince managed finally.

The other's hands lifted and drew back the folds of the hood to reveal the face within. It was craggy and lined, shadowed by a short, black beard that framed a wide, unsmiling mouth and by hair cut shoulder-length. The cat's eyes, piercing and dark, stared out from beneath heavy brows knit fiercely above a long, flat nose. Those eyes stared into Ander's, and the Elven Prince found that he could not look away.

"Your father would know me," the big man whispered. "I am Allanon."

Ander stiffened, his face incredulous. "Allanon?" His head shook slowly. "But . . . but Allanon is dead!"

There was sarcasm in the deep voice, and the eyes glinted once more. "Do I appear to you to be dead, Elven Prince?"

"No . . . no, I can see . . ." Ander's faltered. "But it has been more than fifty years . . ."

He trailed off as the memories of his father's stories came back to him: the search for the Sword of Shannara; the rescue of Eventine from the camp of the enemy armies; the battle at Tyrsis; the defeat of the Warlock Lord at the hands of the little Valeman, Shea Ohmsford. Through it all, Allanon had been there, lending to the beleaguered peoples of the Four Lands his strength and wisdom. When it was finished and the Warlock Lord destroyed, Allanon had disappeared entirely. Shea Ohmsford, it was said, had been the last to see him. There had been rumors afterward that Allanon had come to the Four Lands at other times, in other places. But he had not come to the Westland and the Elves. None of them had ever expected to see him again. Still, where the Druid was concerned, his father had often told him, one soon learned to expect the unexpected. Wanderer, historian, philosopher and mystic, guardian of the races, the last of the ancient Druids, the wise men of the new world—Allanon was said to have been all of these.

But was this truly Allanon? The question whispered in Ander's mind.

The big man stepped close once more. "Look closely at me, Elven Prince," he commanded. "You will see that I speak the truth."

Ander stared at the dark face, stared deep into the glittering black eyes, and suddenly the doubts were gone. There was no longer any question in his mind. The man who stood before him was Allanon.

"I want you to take me to see your father." Allanon was speaking again, his voice low and guarded. "Choose a path little traveled. I wish to keep my coming a secret. Quickly now, before the sentries come."

Ander did not stop to argue. With the Druid following as closely as his own shadow, he slipped past the Gardens of Life and hurried on toward the city.

Minutes later, they crouched within a gathering of evergreens at one end of the palace grounds where a small side gate stood chained and locked. Ander drew a ring of keys from his pocket and fitted one into the lock. It turned with a sharp snick and the lock opened. In seconds, they were inside.

Ordinarily the grounds would have been guarded only by the gate watch. But earlier in the day, following the discovery of the murdered Chosen, the body of Went had been found under a bush at the edge of the south gardens, his neck broken. The manner of his death was wholly different from that of the Chosen, so as yet there was no reason to believe there was any connection. Still, this latest killing was too close to the King to suit the Home Guard. Additional security had been moved onto the grounds. Dardan and Rhoe, the King's personal guards, had taken up watch at the King's door.

Ander would not have believed it possible for anyone to reach the manor house from the exterior walls without being seen by the sentries. But somehow, with the Druid in the lead, they managed to pass without challenge. Allanon seemed little more than another of the night's shadows, moving soundlessly, always keeping Ander close beside him, until at last they reached the floor-length windows that looked in upon the King's study. There they paused momentarily while the Druid listened at the curtained window. Then Allanon gripped the iron entry latch and turned it. The window-doors swung silently open and the Druid and Elven Prince stepped inside.

From a reading table still littered with histories, Eventine Elessedil rose, staring in disbelief, first at his son and then at the man who followed him in.

"Allanon!" he whispered.

The Druid secured the window-doors, drew the curtains carefully back in place, then turned into the candlelight.

"After all these years." Eventine shook his head wonderingly and stepped out from behind the table. Then he saw clearly the big man's face and disbelief turned to astonishment. "Allanon! You haven't aged! You . . . haven't changed since . . ." He choked on the words. "How . . . ?"

"I am who I always was," the Druid cut him short. "That is enough to know, King of the Elves."

Eventine nodded wordlessly, still dazed by the other's unexpected appearance. Slowly he moved back to the reading table, and the two men took up seats across from one another. Ander stood where he was for an instant, uncertain whether to stay or go.

"Sit with us, Elven Prince." Allanon indicated a third chair.

Ander sat down quickly, grateful to be included, anxious to hear what would be said.

"You know what has happened?" The King addressed Allanon.

The Druid nodded. "That is why I have come. I sensed a breach in the Forbidding. Something imprisoned there has crossed over into this world, something whose power is very great indeed. It was the appearance of this creature . . ."

There was the faint sound of footsteps in the hallway beyond the study door, and the Druid was on his feet instantly. Then he paused, his face calm, and he looked back at the King.

"No one is to know that I am here."

Eventine did not question this. He simply nodded, rose from the chair, walked quickly to the door, and opened it. Manx sat there on his haunches, his tail wagging slowly, his grizzled muzzle raised toward his master. Eventine walked out into the hallway and found Gael approaching with a tray of tea. The King smiled and took it from him.

"I want you to go home now and get some sleep," he ordered. When Gael tried to object, he quickly shook his head. "No arguments. We have a lot to do in the morning. Go home. I'll be all right. Ask Dardan and Rhoe to keep watch until I retire. I wish to see no one."

He turned abruptly and re-entered the study, closing the door firmly behind him. Manx had wandered in, sniffed questioningly the stranger he found seated at the reading table, then, apparently satisfied, had dropped down next to the stone fireplace beside them, his muzzle resting comfortably on his paws, his brown eyes closing contentedly. Eventine sat down again.

"Was it this creature, then, that killed the Chosen?" he asked, picking up the conversation.

The Druid nodded. "I believe it to be so. I sensed the danger to the Chosen and came as quickly as I could. Not quickly enough, unfortunately, to save them."

Eventine smiled sadly. "The fault lies with me, I'm afraid. I left them unprotected, even after I was told the Forbidding had begun to fail. But perhaps it makes no difference. Even had they lived, I am not certain the Chosen would have been able to save the Ellcrys. Nothing of what she showed them of the location of the Bloodfire is recognizable. Not even the name she gave them—Safehold. Do you recognize it?"

Allanon shook his head no.

"Our records tell us nothing of Safehold—neither those of my predecessors who ruled nor those of the Chosen," the King continued. "I am faced with an impossible situation. The Ellcrys is dying. In order to save her, one of the Chosen in service to her now must carry her seed to the Bloodfire, immerse it in the flames and then return it to the earth so that a rebirth might be possible."

"I am familiar with the history," the Druid interjected.

The King flushed. The anger and frustration he had held inside was working its way to the fore.

"Then consider this. We do not know the location of the Bloodfire. We have no record of the name Safehold. And now the Chosen are all dead. We have no one to bear the Ellcrys seed. The outcome of all this seems quite inevitable. The Ellcrys will die, the Forbidding will crumble, the evil locked within will be free once more upon the land, and the Elves and very likely all of the races inhabiting the Four Lands will be faced with a war that could easily destroy us all!"

He leaned forward sharply. "I am a King; I am that and nothing more. You are a Druid, a sorcerer. If you have any help to offer, then do so. There is nothing more that I know to do."

The Druid cocked his head slightly, as if considering the problem.

"Before coming to see you, Eventine, I went into the Gardens of Life and spoke with the Ellcrys."

The King stared at him incredulously. "You spoke with. . . ?"

"Perhaps it would be more accurate to say that she spoke with me. Had she not chosen to do so, there would have been no communication between us, of course."

"But she speaks only to the Chosen," Ander interjected, then fell quickly silent as he saw his father frown in annoyance.

"My son is correct, Allanon." Eventine turned back to the Druid. "The Ellcrys speaks to no one but the Chosen—and seldom to them."

"She speaks to those who serve her," Allanon replied.

"Of the Elves, only the Chosen do so. But the Druids have also served the Ellcrys, though in a different fashion. In any case, I simply offered myself to her and she chose to speak with me. What she told me suggests that you are mistaken in your view of matters in at least one respect."

Eventine waited a moment for the Druid to continue. He did not. He simply sat there, staring at the Elf questioningly.

"Very well, I will ask it then." The King forced himself to remain calm. "In what respect am I mistaken?"

"Before I tell you that," Allanon said, leaning forward, "I want you to understand something. I have come to give whatever aid I may, for the evil that is imprisoned within the Forbidding threatens all life in the Four Lands. What aid I can offer, I offer freely. But there is one condition. I must be free to act in this matter as I see fit. Even though you disapprove, Eventine Elessedil. Even then. Do you understand?"

The King hesitated, his blue eyes studying the dark face of the other man, searching for answers that clearly were not to be found there. At last, he nodded.

"I understand. You may act as you wish in this."

The Druid sat back, carefully masking any emotion as he faced Ander and the King.

"First, I believe that I can aid in discovering the location of Safehold. What I was shown of Safehold by the Ellcrys when we spoke was not familiar to me, as I have said. It was not familiar because it was drawn from her memory of the world at the time of her creation. The Great Wars altered the geography of the old world so completely that her perception of it now is quite faulty. Still, we have the name Safehold. You have told me that the histories of the Elven Kings and those of the Order of the Chosen do not record the name. But there is another place to look. At Paranor, within the Druid's Keep, there are histories devoted entirely to the sciences and mystic phenomena of the old world. Within those books, there may be some mention of the creation of the Ellcrys and the location of the Bloodfire. This is a distinct possibility because much of the information contained in those histories was gathered at the time of the First Council of the Druids—drawn from each member as it had been handed down since the holocaust. Remember, too, that the guiding light of that council was Galaphile, and Galaphile was an Elf. He would have seen to it that something about the creation of the Ellcrys and the location of the fountain of the Bloodfire was set down."

He paused. "Tonight, when we are finished here, I will go on to Paranor. The histories are well hidden to any but the Druids, so it is necessary that I go myself. But I believe that within their pages is recorded some mention of the name Safehold. From what is written there, we may hope to discover the location of the Bloodfire."

He folded his hands on the table's edge, and his eyes fixed on those of the King.

"Now as to the Chosen, Eventine, you are mistaken entirely. They are not all dead."

For an instant, the room went deathly still. Amberle! Ander thought in astonishment. He means Amberle!

"All six were killed . . . !" Eventine began, then stopped abruptly.

"There were seven Chosen," the Druid said quietly. "Seven."

The King went rigid, his hands gripping the edges of the table until the knuckles were white. His eyes mirrored anger and disbelief.

"Amberle," he breathed the name like a curse.

The Druid nodded. "She is one of the Chosen."

"No!" The King was on his feet, shouting. "No, Druid!"

There was a scurrying of footsteps in the hallway beyond and then a pounding on the study door. Ander realized what his father had done. His shouts had brought Dardan and Rhoe. Hurriedly, he went to the door and opened it. He was surprised to find not only the guards, but Gael as well. All peered curiously into the study, but the Elven Prince carefully blocked their view. Then his father was beside him.

"I told you to go home, Gael," Eventine reprimanded the young Elf sternly. "Do so now."

Gael bowed mechanically, his face showing the hurt he felt at the other man's words, and disappeared back down the hallway without a word. The King nodded to the Elven Hunters, reassuring them that he was all right, and they returned to their watch.

The King stood silently in the open entry a moment, then closed the door. The penetrating blue eyes swept past his son to Allanon.

"How did you find out about Amberle?"

"When the Ellcrys spoke with me, she told me that seven had been chosen to serve. One was a young girl. Her name was Amberle Elessedil."

The Druid paused, studying carefully the face of the Elven King. It was lined with bitterness. All of its color had drained away.

"It is unusual for a young woman to be selected as a Chosen," Allanon continued calmly. "There have been no more than a handful, I think—not another in the last five hundred years."

The King shook his head angrily. "Amberle's selection was an honor that meant nothing to her. She spurned that honor. She shamed her people and her family. She is no longer one of the Chosen. She is no longer a citizen of this land. She is an outcast by her own choice!"

Allanon came to his feet swiftly, his face suddenly hard.

"She is your granddaughter, and you speak as a fool would."

Eventine stiffened at the rebuke, but held his tongue. The Druid came up to him.

"Hear me. Amberle is a Chosen. It is true that she did not serve the Ellcrys as did the others. It is true that she forsook her duty as a Chosen. It is true that for reasons known only to herself she left Arborlon and the Westland, her home, despite the responsibilities that were clearly hers, that she disgraced her family and particularly you, as King, in the eyes of her people. It is true that she has made herself an outcast. It is true that she does not believe herself to be one of the Chosen any longer.

"But know this. It is not for you nor for her people to take from her what the Ellcrys has given. It is not even for her to do that. It is for the Ellcrys alone. Until the Ellcrys says differently, Amberle remains a Chosen in her service—a Chosen who may bear her seed in search of the Bloodfire, a Chosen who may give her new life."

Allanon paused. "A King may not understand all things, Eventine Elessedil, even though he be a King. Some things you must simply accept."

Eventine stared at the Druid without speaking, the anger gone now from his eyes, replaced with hurt and confusion.

"I was close to her once," he said finally. "After her father—my son Aine—died, I became her father. She was still a child, only five. In the evenings, we would play together . . ." He stopped, unable to continue. He took a deep breath to steady himself. "There was a quality about her that I have not since found; a sweetness, an innocence, a loving. I am an old man speaking these words about his grandchild, but I do not speak blindly. I knew her."

Allanon said nothing. The King moved back to his chair and slowly seated himself once more.

"The histories record no other woman selected to serve as a Chosen since the time of Jerle Shannara. Amberle was the first—the first in more than five hundred years. It was an honor others would have given anything for." He shook his head wonderingly. "Yet Amberle walked away from it. She gave no explanation—not to me, not to her mother, not to anyone. Not one word. She just left."

He trailed off helplessly. Allanon sat down across from him again, his dark eyes intense.

"She must be brought back. She is the only hope that the Elven people have."

"Father." Ander spoke before he had time to think better of it. Impulsively he knelt next to the old man. "Father, on the night before he was killed, Lauren told me something. He told me that the Ellcrys had spoken with Amberle many times after her choosing. That had never happened before. Perhaps Amberle is our best hope."

The King looked at him blankly, as if the words he had spoken meant nothing. Then he placed his hands flat against the worn surface of the reading table and nodded once.

"I find that hope a slim one, Ander. Our people may accept her back again, if only because they have need of her. I am not altogether certain of this; what she has done by her rejection is unpardonable in their eyes. And perhaps the Ellcrys, too, may accept her—accept her both as a Chosen and as the bearer of her seed. I don't pretend to have answers to those questions. Nor do my own feelings matter in this." He turned again to Allanon. "It is

Amberle herself who will stand against us, Druid. When she left this land, she left it forever. She believed strongly that it must be so; something made her believe. You do not know her, as I do. She will never return."

Allanon's expression did not change. "That remains to be seen. We must at least ask her."

"I do not know where she is." The King's voice turned suddenly bitter. "I doubt that anyone does."

The Druid carefully poured a measure of the herb tea and handed it to the King.

"I do."

Eventine stared at him wordlessly for a moment. His face clouded with conflicting emotions, and there were sudden tears in his eyes, tears that were gone as fast as they had come.

"I should have guessed," he said finally. He rose, then stepped away from the table several paces, his face partially turned into the shadows. "You are free to act in this as you will, Allanon. You already know that."

Allanon rose with him. Then, to Ander's surprise, he said, "I will require the services of your son for a brief time before I leave."

Eventine did not turn. "As you wish."

"Remember—no one is to know that I have been here."

The King nodded. "No one shall."

A moment later the Druid was through the curtained windows and gone. Ander stood looking at his father hesitantly, then moved to follow.

He knew the old man's thoughts now were of Amberle.

In the blackness of the Westland forests north of the Carolan, the Dagda Mor sat quietly, his eyes closed. When they opened again, they were bright with satisfaction. The Changeling had served him well. He rose slowly, the Staff of Power flaring sharply as his hands closed about its polished wood.

"Druid," he hissed softly. "I know of you."

He motioned to the formless shadow that was the Reaper, and the monster rose up out of the night. The Dagda Mor looked eastward. He would wait for the Druid at Paranor. But not alone. He could sense the Druid's power, and he was wary of it. The Reaper might be strong enough to stand against such power, but he had better use for the Reaper. No, other help would be necessary. He would bring a handful of the brethren through the eroding wall of the Forbidding.

Enough to snare the Druid. Enough to kill him.

VI

Allanon was waiting for Ander when he stepped from the lighted study, and together they retraced their steps across the palace grounds and through the small side gate to the roadway beyond. Then Allanon asked to be taken to the stables. Wordlessly the two followed a back trail that took them through a small stretch of forest to the stable paddocks and from there to the stable entry. Ander dismissed the old stableman with a word of assurance, and Allanon and he stepped inside.

Oil lamps lit a double row of stalls, and the soft whicker of horses sounded in the stillness. Slowly Allanon passed down the line of stalls, eyes shifting from horse to horse as he walked to the end of the first row and started back up the second. Ander trailed after him and watched.

Finally the Druid stopped and turned back to Ander. "That one," he pointed. "I'll need the use of him."

Ander glanced uneasily at the horse Allanon had chosen. The horse was called Artaq, a huge coal-black stallion standing fully eighteen hands high. Artaq was big enough and strong enough to carry someone of Allanon's size, and he could withstand a great deal of punishment. He was a hunting horse, built for stamina rather than for speed. Yet Ander knew him to be capable of great speed over short distances. His head was narrow and rather small, particularly when viewed in comparison to his great, barrel-chested body. He had eyes that were set rather wide and colored a startling azure. There was intelligence in those eyes; Artaq was not a horse that could be mastered by just any man.

Indeed, that was exactly the problem. Artaq was strong-willed and thoroughly unpredictable. He enjoyed playing games with his riders, games that usually ended with the riders being thrown. More than a few had been injured in those falls. If the man riding Artaq was not strong enough and quick enough to prevent it, Artaq would find a way to shake him off within seconds after he was mounted. Few men bothered to chance this. Even the King seldom rode him anymore, though once he had been a favorite.

"There are others . . ." Ander suggested hesitantly, but Allanon was already shaking his head no.

"This horse will do. What is his name?"

"Artaq," the Elven Prince replied.

Allanon studied the horse carefully for a time, then lifted the stall latch and stepped inside. Ander moved over to watch. The Druid stood quietly before the big black, then lifted his hand in invitation. To Ander's surprise, Artaq came over. Allanon stroked the satin neck slowly, gently, and he bent forward to whisper in the horse's ear. Then he fitted a halter to the black and led him from his stall down the walkway to where the tack was stored. Ander shook his head and followed after. The Druid selected a saddle and bridle and strapped them snugly in place after removing the halter. With a final word of encouragement, he swung up upon the horse's back.

Ander held his breath. Slowly Allanon walked the black down one row of stalls and back along the other. Artaq was obedient and responsive; there would be no games played with this man. Allanon brought him back to where Ander stood waiting and stepped down.

"While I am gone, Elven Prince," he said, his black eyes fixed on Ander, "I entrust to you the care of your father. Be certain that no harm comes to him." He paused. "I depend on you in this."

Ander nodded, pleased that Allanon would show this kind of confidence in him. The Druid studied him a moment longer, then turned away. With the Elven Prince following once more, he walked Artaq to the rear of the stable and pushed ajar the wide double doors.

"Goodbye then, Ander Elessedil," he offered and remounted. Easing Artaq through the open doors, he rode swiftly away into the darkness.

Ander watched after him until he was out of sight.

* * *

For the remainder of that night and for the better part of the three days that followed, Allanon rode Artaq eastward toward Paranor. His journey took him through the deep forests of the Westland to the mouth of the historic Valley of Rhenn and from there onto the sprawling emptiness of the Streleheim Plains. He traveled steadily, pausing only to rest, feed, and water Artaq, carefully keeping within covered areas of the land where possible, steering wide of caravan routes and well-traveled roadways. As yet, no one but the Elven King and his son knew that he had returned to the Four Lands. No one but they knew of the Druid histories at Paranor or of the seventh Chosen. If the evil that had broken through the Forbidding were to discover any of this, his quest would be seriously threatened. Secrecy was his greatest ally, and he intended that it might remain so.

At sunset on the second day of travel, he arrived at Paranor. He was certain that he had not been followed.

While still some distance from the ancient fortress, he left Artaq in a small grove of spruce where there was good grass and water and proceeded the rest of the way on foot. It was not as it had been in the time of the Warlock Lord. The packs of wolves that had prowled the surrounding forests were no more. The barrier of poison thorns that had walled away the Keep was gone. The woodlands were quiet and peaceful in the early evening dusk, filled with the pleasant sounds of nightfall.

Within minutes, he stood at the foot of the Druid's Keep. The aged castle sat atop a great mass of rock, rising above the forest trees as if it had been thrust from out of the bowels of the earth by some giant's hand. It was a breathtaking vision from a child's fairy tale, a dazzling maze of towers and walls, spires and parapets, their weathered white stones etched starkly against the deep blue of the night sky.

Allanon paused. The history of Paranor was the history of the Druids, the history of his forebears. It began a thousand years after the Great Wars all but annihilated the race of Man and changed forever the face of the old world. It began after years of desolation and savagery as the survivors of the holocaust struggled to subsist in a lethal new world where man was no longer the dominant species. It began after the one race of Man became reborn into the new races of Men, Dwarves, Gnomes and Trolls—after the Elves reappeared. It began at Paranor, where the First Council of the Druids came together in a desperate effort to save the new world from total anarchy. Galaphile called them here—Galaphile, who was the greatest of the Druids. Here the histories of the old world, written and spoken, were set down in the Druid records, to be preserved for all the generations of man yet to come. Here the mysteries of the old sciences were explored, the fragments patched together, the secrets of a few restored to knowledge. For hundreds of years, the Druids lived and worked at Paranor, the wise men of the new world seeking to rebuild what had been lost.

But their efforts failed. One among them fell victim to ambition and ill-advised impatience, tampering with power so great and so evil that in the end it consumed him entirely. His name was Brona. In the First War of the Races, he led an army of Men against the other races, seeking to gain mastery over the Four Lands. The Druids crushed this insurrection and drove him into hiding. They believed him dead. But five hundred years later, he returned—Brona no longer, but the Warlock Lord. He trapped the unsuspecting Druids within their Keep and slaughtered them to a man—all save one. That one was Bremen, Allanon's father. Bremen forged an enchanted Sword and gave it to the Elven King, Jerle Shannara, a talisman that the Warlock Lord could not stand against. It won for the Elves and their allies the Second War of the Races and drove the Warlock Lord again from the world of men.

When Bremen died, Allanon became the last of the Druids. He sealed the Keep forever. Paranor became history to the races, a monument of another time, a time of great men and still greater deeds.

The Druid shook his head. All that was past now; his concern must be only with the present.

He began to skirt the stone base of the castle, his eyes studying the deep crevices and jagged outcroppings. Finally he stopped, his hands reaching to the rock and touching. A portion of the stone swung inward, revealing a cleverly concealed passageway. The Druid slipped quickly through the narrow opening, and the stone sealed itself behind him.

There was total blackness within. Allanon's hands searched until they found a cluster of wall torches set in iron brackets hammered into the rock. Lifting one free, he worked with the flint and stone he carried in a pouch at his waist until a spark ignited the pitch that coated the torch head. Holding the burning brand before him, he allowed his eyes a moment to adjust. A passage stretched away before him, the faint outline of rough-hewn steps cut into the rock floor disappearing upward into darkness. He began to climb. The smell of dust and stale air filled his nostrils, and he wrinkled his nose in distaste. The caverns were cold, their chill sealed in permanently by tons of rock. The Druid pulled his heavy cloak about him. Hundreds of steps passed beneath his feet, and still the tunnel twisted through the black.

It ended finally at a massive wooden door. Allanon paused and bent close, his eyes studying the heavy iron bindings. After a moment, his fingers touched a combination of metal studs, and the door swung open. He stepped through.

He stood in the furnace of the Keep. It was a round, cavernous chamber that consisted wholly of a narrow walkway encircling a great dark pit. A low iron railing rimmed the pit at its edge. About the walkway, a succession of wooden and ironbound doors were set into the chamber wall, all closed and barred.

The Druid moved to the railing and, holding the torch before him, peered downward into the pit. The faint illumination of the fire danced off blackened walls crusted over with ash and rust. The furnace was cold now, the machinery that once pumped heat to the towers and halls of the castle locked and silent. But far below, beyond the pale glimmer of the torchlight, beneath massive iron dampers, the natural fires of the earth still burned. Even now, their stirrings could be felt.

He remembered another time. More than fifty years ago, he had come to Paranor and the Druid's Keep with the little company of friends from the Dwarf village of Culhaven: the Ohmsfords, Shea and Flick; Balinor Buckhannah, Prince of Callahorn; Menion, Prince of Leah; Durin and

Dayel Elessedil; and the valiant Dwarf Hendel. He had come in search of the legendary Sword of Shannara, for the Warlock Lord had returned to the Four Lands, and only the power of the Sword could vanquish him. Allanon had come with his little band into the Keep and very nearly had not come out again. In this very room, he had battled to the death with one of the Skull Bearers. The Warlock Lord had known he was coming. It had been a trap.

His eyes lifted sharply, and he listened to the deep silence. A trap. The word disturbed him; it triggered some instinct, a sixth sense of warning. There was something wrong. Something . . .

He stood there for a moment, indecisive. Then he shook his head. He was being foolish. It was the memory, nothing more.

Carrying the torch before him, he moved along the walkway until he reached a tight spiral stairway that led upward. Without a backward glance to the pit or the furnace chamber, he climbed the stairs quickly and entered the upper halls of the Druid's Keep.

All was as it had been fifty years earlier. Starlight filtered through high windows in thin ribbons of silver, touching softly the heavy wooden panels and polished timbers that framed up the towering corridor. Paintings and tapestries hung the length of the hall, their rich colors muted into grays and deep blues by the nightfall. Statues of stone and iron stood silent watch before massive wooden doors with handles of brass. Dust lay over everything, a thick soft carpet, and long streamers of cobweb fell from ceiling to marble floor.

Allanon moved down the hallway slowly, the torchlight burning through the haze of musty air that hung motionless through the Keep. All was silence, deep and penetrating. His footfalls echoed eerily as he walked, and small puffs of dust rose in the air behind him, stirred by the passing of his feet. Doors came and went to either side, all closed, their metal fittings glinting fire as the torchlight struck the mirrored surface. The hall he traveled intersected another, and he turned right. He walked almost to its end, stopping finally before a smallish door of white oak and iron. A huge lock secured this door. The Druid fumbled for a moment at the pouch about his waist, finally producing a large metal key. He placed the key in the lock and turned it twice. The mechanism creaked in protest, its workings rusty with disuse, but the heavy bolt drew back. The iron handle slipped free of its catch. Allanon stepped inside and closed the door behind him.

The room he had entered was small and windowless. It had once been a study. Shelves of fraying, cloth-bound books lined its four walls, the colors of the bindings long since faded, the pages dried almost to dust. Against the far wall were placed two small reading tables with chairs constructed of reed and cane, stiff and solitary, like sentries at attention. Closer to the doorway were two more comfortable-looking armchairs formed of thickly padded leather. An aged, handwoven rug lay loosely across wooden plank flooring hammered down with iron nails. The fabric of the rug was laced with heraldic designs and bits of gold leaf.

The Druid glanced about the room perfunctorily and moved to the wall on his left. Reaching behind the books at the end of the third shelf down, he located two large iron studs. When he touched these, a section of the bookcase swung silently ajar. He pushed the shelving out a bit to allow himself room to pass through, then pulled the casing closed behind him.

He stood within a vault constructed entirely of massive granite blocks cut to interlock with one another and then tightly sealed with mortar. Except for a single long wooden table and half a dozen high-backed chairs, the chamber was bare. There were no windows and no door save the one through which he had entered. The air here was stale with age, but breathable. Not surprisingly, given the chamber's tight construction, there was an almost total absence of dust.

Using the torch he carried, Allanon lit torches bracketed in the wall to either side of the entry and two squat candles that rested on the table. Once that was done, he moved to the wall to the right of the door and began running his hands lightly over the smooth stone. After a moment, he placed the tips of his fingers and thumbs firmly in place against the granite, bridging both palms out, and lowered his head in concentration. At first nothing happened, but then suddenly a deep blue glow began to spread outward from his fingers and ran through the stone like veins through flesh. An instant later the wall erupted in soundless blue fire; then both wall and fire were gone.

Allanon stepped back. Where the granite wall had been stood row upon row of massive, leather-bound books elaborately engraved with gold. It was for this that the Druid had come to Paranor—for these were the histories of the Druids, the whole of the knowledge of the old and new world salvaged from the holocaust of the Great Wars, recorded from the time of the First Council of the Druids to the present.

Allanon reached up and carefully removed one of the heavy tomes. It was in good condition, the leather soft and pliable, the edges of the pages sharp, the binding solid. They had weathered the ages well. Five centuries earlier, after the death of Bremen, after he had come to the realization that he was the last of the Druids, he had constructed this vault to protect these histories so that they might be preserved for the generations of men and women who would one day live upon this earth and would have need of the knowledge the books contained. From time to time he returned to the Keep, dutifully recording what he had learned in his travels about the Four Lands, setting down the secrets of the ages that might otherwise be lost. Much of what was recorded here dealt with the secrets of sorcery, with power that no one, be he Druid or ordinary man, could hope to comprehend fully—much less put to practical use. The Druids had thought to keep those secrets safe from men who might use them foolishly. Yet the Druids were gone now, save for Allanon, and one day he, too, would be gone. Who then would inherit the secrets of power? It was a matter of no small concern to Allanon—a dilemma for which, as yet, he had found no agreeable solution.

He leafed quickly through the book he held and placed it back again, selecting another. He glanced at this second book, then moved to the long table and seated himself. Slowly, he began to read.

For nearly three hours, he did not stir, other than to turn the pages of the history, his face bent close to the carefully inscribed writing.

At the end of the first hour, he discovered the location of

Safehold. But he continued to read. He was looking for something more.

At last his eyes lifted and he leaned back wearily. For a time he just sat there in the high-backed chair, staring fixedly at the rows of books that comprised the Druid histories. He had found all that he had been looking for and wished that he had not.

He thought back to his meeting with Eventine Elessedil two days earlier. He had told the Elven King that he had gone first to the Gardens of Life and that the Ellcrys had spoken with him. But he had not told the King all that she had revealed. In part, he had not done so because much of what she had shown had been confusing and unclear, her memories of a time and a life long gone altered beyond anyone's recognition. But there had been one thing that she had shown him that he had understood all too well. Yet it had been so incredible that he felt he could not accept it without first checking the Druid histories. This he had done. Now he knew it to be true and knew it must be kept hidden—from Eventine, from everyone. He experienced a sense of despair. It was as it had been fifty years ago with young Shea Ohmsford; the truth must be left to reveal itself through an inexorable passage of events. It was not for him to decide the time and the place of its revelation. It was not for him to tamper with the natural order of things.

Yet he questioned this decision. Alone with the ghosts of his ancestors, the last of his kind, he questioned this decision. He had chosen to conceal the truth from Shea Ohmsford—indeed, from all who had comprised the little company of adventurers from Culhaven, all who had risked their lives in search of the Sword of Shannara because he had convinced them that they must—but most especially from Shea. In the end, he had come to believe that he had been wrong to do so. Was he wrong now, as well? This time, should he not be candid from the beginning?

Still lost in thought, he closed the book in front of him, rose from the table, and carried the heavy volume back to the niche from which he had taken it. He made a quick circular motion of one hand before the bank of histories, and the granite wall was restored. He stared absently at it for a moment, then turned away. Retrieving the torch he had brought with him into the Keep, he extinguished the vault's remaining lights and triggered the release on the concealed door.

Within the Druid study once more, he paused long enough to close the open section of shelving so that all was as it had been. He looked about the little room almost sadly. The castle of the Druids had become a tomb. It had the smell and taste of death in it. Once it had been a place of learning, of vision. But no more. There was no longer a place for the living within these walls.

He frowned his displeasure. His attitude had soured considerably since reading the pages of the Druid history. He was anxious to be gone from Paranor. It was a place of ill-fortune—and he, in chief, must bear that ill-fortune to others.

Silently he walked to the study door, pulled it open, and stepped through into the main hallway.

Not twenty feet beyond stood the humped form of the Dagda Mor.

Allanon froze. The Demon waited alone, his hard gaze fixed upon the Druid, the Staff of Power cradled loosely in his arms. The harsh sound of his breathing cut sharply through the deep silence, but he did not speak a word. He simply stood there, studying carefully the man he had come to destroy.

The Druid stepped away from the study door, moving cautiously to the center of the corridor, his eyes sweeping the hazy blackness about him. Almost immediately he saw that there were others—vague, wraithlike forms that crept from out of the shadows on four limbs, their eyes slits of green fire. There were many, and they were all around him. They edged steadily closer, circling slightly from side to side in the manner of wolves gathered about some cornered prey. A low mewling sound came from their faceless heads, a horrible catlike whining that seemed to find pleasure in the anticipation of what was to come. A few slipped into the pale fringes of his torchlight. They were grotesque creatures, their bodies a sinuous mass of gray hair, their limbs bent and vaguely human, their multiple fingers grown to claws. Faces lifted toward the Druid, faces that turned him cold. They were the faces of women, their features twisted with savagery, their mouths had become the jaws of monstrous cats.

He knew them now, though they had not walked the earth for thousands of years. They had been shut behind the wall of the Forbidding since the dawn of Man, but their legend was written in the history of the old world. They were creatures who lived on human flesh. Born of madness, their bloodlust drove them beyond reason, beyond sanity.

They were Furies.

Allanon watched them circle, creeping about the edges of his torchlight, savoring the prospect of his death. It was a death that seemed assured. There were too many for the Druid; he knew that already. His power was not great enough to stop them all. They would attack as one, lunging at him from all sides, tearing and ripping him until nothing remained.

He glanced quickly to the Dagda Mor. The Demon remained where he was, beyond the circle of his minions, his dark gaze fixed on the Druid. It was obvious he felt no need to bring his own power to bear; the Furies would be enough. The Druid was trapped and hopelessly outnumbered. He would struggle, of course; but in the end, he would die.

The mewling of the Furies rose sharply, a dry wailing that reverberated the length of the Keep, echoing hollow and shrill through the castle of stone. Clawed fingers raked the marble floor like the scraping of shattered bone, and the whole of Paranor seemed to freeze in horror.

Then, without warning, Allanon simply disappeared.

It happened so abruptly that for an instant the bewildered Furies ceased all movement and stared in disbelief at the spot where the Druid had stood just one moment earlier, their cries dying into stillness. The torch still hung suspended in the haze of darkness, a beacon of fire that held them spellbound. Then it dropped to the floor of the hall in a shower of sparks. The flame disintegrated and the corridor was plunged into blackness.

The illusion lasted only seconds, but it was long enough to permit Allanon to escape the circle of death that had ensnared him. Instantly, he was through the Furies and racing toward a pair of massive oaken doors that stood closed and barred at the near end of the hall. The Dagda Mor shrieked in anger, and the Staff of Power came up. Red fire blazed the length of the corridor, scattering the maddened Furies as it arced toward the fleeing Druid. But Allanon was too quick. With a sweep, his cloak came up, deflecting the attack. The Staff's fire shot past him and burst apart the double doors, tearing them from their iron bindings and leaving them shattered. The Druid leaped through the entryway into the room beyond and was lost in the darkness.

Already the Furies were after him, bounding down the hallway like animals, their cries thick with hunger. The fleetest among them surged through the gaping doorway and caught the Druid as he struggled to free the clasp that secured a floor-length window leading to the battlements. Allanon turned to face them, his tall form crouching. He seized the two closest to him as they leaped for his throat and threw them into the rest. His hands came up and blue fire scattered from his fingers, turning the floor between them into a wall of flame. Still the Furies came after him. The nearest hurtled recklessly into the flames and perished. When the fire vanished a moment later, the windows stood open, and the Druid was gone.

A thousand feet above the canopy of the surrounding forestland, his back pressed against the towering wall of the Druid's Keep, Allanon edged his way along a narrow stone ledge that dropped away into blackness. With each step he took, the wind threatened to tear him loose. He worked his way quickly to a slender stone catwalk that bridged to an adjoining tower. The catwalk was less than three feet wide; below there was only emptiness. The Druid did not hesitate. This was his only chance to escape. He started across.

Behind him he heard the screams of rage and frustration that burst from the throats of the Furies as they followed him through the open windows. They came after him in a rush, more sure than he on the smooth castle stone, their clawed limbs gripping tightly as they raced to catch him. At the windows, the Dagda Mor raised the Staff of Power once more, and the killing fire streaked toward the fleeing Druid. But Allanon had seen that he would not cross before the Furies reached him. Dropping to one knee, he brought both arms up in a wide circle, and a shield of blue fire materialized in front of him. The flame from the Demon's staff shattered harmlessly against it. Yet the force of the attack threw the Druid backward, and he tumbled down upon the narrow bridge. In the next instant, the foremost of his pursuers were upon him.

This time Allanon was not quick enough. Clawed fingers ripped through the fabric of his cloak and tore into his flesh. Searing pain wracked his shoulders and chest. With a tremendous heave, he threw back the Furies that held him, and they fell from the narrow arch, screaming. Staggering to his feet, he lurched toward the waiting tower. Again the Furies came at him, stumbling over one another in their eagerness to reach their prey, howling their frustration; their strange, half-woman faces twisted with hate. Again the Druid threw them back, his body shredded further, his clothing soaked with blood.

Then at last he reached the far end of the bridge, his body sagging against the wall of the tower. He turned, hands raising. Blue fire erupted downward into the stone walk, shattering it apart. With a shudder, the whole of the arch collapsed. Shrieking with horror, the Furies tumbled down into the night and disappeared.

Fire from the Staff of Power flared all about him, yet the Druid managed to evade it, dodging quickly around the circle of the tower wall until he was beyond the Demon's sight. There he found a small iron door, closed and locked. With a single powerful shove of one shoulder, he burst through the door and was gone.

VII

I t was midmorning. In the Village of the Healers, the tiny Gnome community of Storlock, the thunderstorm was finally ending. It had been spectacular while it had lasted—masses of rolling black clouds streaked with wicked flashes of lightning and punctuated by long, booming claps of thunder—torrential rains that hammered the forestland with the force of winter sleet—winds that uprooted whole trees and stripped roofs from the low stone and plaster buildings that comprised the village. The storm had blown out of the Rabb Plains at dawn, and now it was drifting eastward toward the dark ridge of the Wolfsktaag, leaving the woodlands of the central Anar sodden and muddied with its passing.

Wil Ohmsford stood alone on the porch of the Stor rest center, the major treatment facility for the community, and watched absently as the rain slowed to a thin trickle. The clouds still screened away the sunlight, leaving the day wrapped in somber tones of gray, and a fine mist had formed in the mix of cool storm air and warm earth. The eaves and walls of the center were wet and shiny, and droplets of moisture clung to the leaves of the vines that grew about them, glistening with green freshness. Bits of wood littered the ground, forming small dams against the rivers of surface water that flowed everywhere.

The Valeman yawned and stretched wearily. He had been up all night, working with children afflicted by a particularly nasty fever that dried away the fluids of the body and sent temperatures soaring. He could have asked to have been relieved earlier, of course, but he would not have felt comfortable doing that. He was still a student among the Stors, and he was very conscious of the fact that he must continue to prove himself if he were to one day become a Healer. So he had stayed with the children, all yesterday, all night, until at last the fever had broken.

Now he was too tired to sleep, too keyed up from his night's work. Besides, he knew he should spend some time with Flick. He grinned in spite of his exhaustion. Old Uncle Flick would very likely drag him bodily from his bed if he failed to visit for at least a few minutes before trundling off to sleep.

He swung down off the porch, the muddied earth sucking at his boots as he plodded through the damp, head lowered. He was not very big, an inch or two taller than Flick perhaps, and his build was slight. He had his grandfather's halfling Elven features—the slim nose and jaw, the slightly pointed ears hidden beneath locks of blondish hair, the narrow eyebrows that angled up sharply from the bridge of his nose. Distinctive features, they had marked Shea Ohmsford and now they marked his grandson as well.

The sound of running footsteps brought him about. It was one of the Servers, Gnome aides to the Stors. He came up to Wil, wizened yellow face streaked with rain, forest cloak wrapped close to ward off the weather.

"Sir, your uncle has been asking for you all night," he panted, slowing. "He insisted I ask after you . . ."

Wil nodded understandingly and reached out to clasp the Gnome's shoulder. "I am on my way to see him now. Thank you."

The Server turned and darted back through the mist to whatever shelter he had been forced from. Wil watched him disappear from view, then started back up the roadway.

A smile creased his face. Poor Uncle Flick. He would not be here at all if Shea had not taken ill. Flick cared little for the Eastland, a country he could live without quite nicely, as he was fond of reminding Wil. He particularly disliked Gnomes, though the Stors were decent enough folk. Too many Gnomes had tried to do away with him in the past, particularly during the search for the Sword of Shannara. That was not something he could forget easily; such memories lingered on and could not be put aside simply for the sake of being fair-minded about Gnomes.

In any case, Flick really didn't care to be here at all and wouldn't have been, except that Shea had not been able to come as he had promised Wil he would and Flick had felt duty-bound to come in his place. Viewed in that perspective, the whole thing was Shea's fault—as Flick had announced to Wil ten seconds after his arrival. After all, if Shea hadn't made his ill-advised promise to visit Wil, then Flick would be back in the Vale instead of sitting around in Storlock where he did not want to be in the first place. But Flick was Shea's brother and therefore Wil's uncle—Flick refused to think of himself as anyone's granduncle—and since Shea could not come, someone had to make the trip in his stead. The only other someone was Flick.

The little guest cottage where Flick was staying came into view, and Wil turned reluctantly toward it. He was tired and he did not feel like an argument, but there would probably be one, because he had spent very little time with Flick during the few days his uncle had been in Storlock and none at all in the past thirty-six hours. His work was demanding, but he knew that his uncle viewed that as a lame excuse.

He was still mulling the matter over when Flick appeared abruptly on the porch of the cottage, gray-bearded face lapsing into stony disapproval. Resigned to the inevitable, Wil mounted the steps and brushed the water from his cloak.

Flick studied him wordlessly for a moment, then shook his head.

"You look exhausted," he declared bluntly. "Why aren't you in bed?"

Wil stared at him. "I'm not in bed because you sent word that you wanted to see me."

"Not right away, I didn't!"

"Well," Wil shrugged helplessly. "I guess I thought I should come to see you now. After all, I haven't been able to give you much time so far."

"True enough," his uncle grunted, a hint of satisfaction in his voice at eliciting this admission. "Still, you pick an odd time to mend the error of your ways. I know you were up all night. I checked. I just wanted to see if you were all right."

"I'm fine." Wil managed a brief smile.

"You don't look fine. And it's this weather as much as anything." Flick rubbed his elbows gingerly. "Confounded rain hasn't stopped since I got here. It doesn't bother just old people like me, you know. Bothers everyone—even would-be Healers." He shook his head. "You would be better off back in the Vale."

Wil nodded absently.

It had been a long time since Shady Vale. For almost two years now he had been living and working in the village of the Stors, learning the art of Healing from the recognized masters of the craft, preparing himself for the time when he might return to the Southland as a Healer, to lend the benefit of his skills to his own people. Unfortunately the whole business of becoming a Healer had proven a source of constant irritation to Flick, though Wil's grandfather had come to accept it well enough. When the fever had taken Wil's parents, a very young Wil Ohmsford had bravely resolved that, when he grew older, he would become a Healer. He had told his grandfather and Flick, in a child's way and with a child's determination, that he wished to save others from sickness and pain. That was fine, they agreed, thinking it a child's whim. But his ambition had stayed with him. And when, on reaching manhood, he announced that it was his intention to study, not with the Healers of the Southland, whom he knew to be only adequate in their skills, but with the very best Healers in the Four Lands—with the Stors—their attitude had undergone an abrupt change. Good old Uncle Flick had long ago made up his mind about Gnomes and the Eastland. Even his grandfather had balked. No Southlander had ever studied with the Stors. How could Wil, who did not even speak the language, expect to be taken into their community?

But Wil had gone despite their reservations—only to be taken before the Stor council upon his arrival and told politely but firmly that no one who was not of the village of Storlock had ever been permitted to study with them. He might stay as long as he wished, but he could not become one of them. Wil did not give up. He decided that he must first learn their language, and he spent almost two months doing so. Then he appeared again before the council and again attempted to persuade them, this time speaking to them in their own tongue. He was not successful this time either. Every week for nearly a month after that, he went before the council to plead his cause. He told them everything about himself and his family, everything that had led to his decision to become a Healer—everything that he thought might convince them that he should be allowed to study with them. Something must have worked, because finally, without a word of explanation, he was told that he would be permitted to remain and that they would teach him what they knew. In time, if he proved diligent and capable, he would become a Healer.

He smiled fondly at the memories. How pleased he had been—and his grandfather and Flick, when they had learned of his acceptance, though the latter would never admit it any more than he would admit to the real reason for his disapproval of the whole venture. What really distressed Flick was the distance separating him from Wil. He missed the hunting, fishing, and exploring that they had shared while Wil was growing up. He missed having Wil there in the Vale with him. Flick's wife had died a long time ago, and they had never had any children of their own. Wil had been his son. Flick had always believed that Wil would stay on in the Vale and manage the inn with Shea and him. Now Wil was gone, settled in Storlock, far from the Vale and his old life, and Wil knew that his uncle simply could not accept the way things had worked out.

"Are you listening to me?" Flick asked suddenly, a frown creasing his bearded face.

"I'm listening," Wil assured him. He placed a hand gently on his uncle's shoulder. "Be patient, Uncle Flick. I'll be back some day. But there is so much to learn yet."

"Well, it's you I'm concerned about, not me," Flick pointed out quickly, his stocky form straightening. "Your grandfather and I can manage just fine without you, but I'm not so sure you can manage without us. Look at you. You push yourself too hard, Wil. You have this stubborn streak in you that seems to have blinded you to the fact that you cannot do everything that you might like to do. You are a normal human being like the rest of us. What do I have to do to get you to see that?"

It appeared that he wanted to say more, but with an effort he stopped himself. "This isn't the time for it." He

sighed. His hand came to rest on Wil's. "Why don't you go
to bed? We can talk when you . . ."

His gray eyes shifted suddenly, and his voice trailed off.
Wil turned to follow his gaze. There was movement in the
mist—a shadow, dark and solitary. They stared at it
curiously, watching it slowly materialize. It became a horse
and rider, each blacker than the other. The rider sat bent
forward in the saddle, as if quite weary from the ride, dark
clothing soaked by the rain and plastered against his tall
frame.

A sudden apprehension stole through Wil. This was no
Stor that came; indeed, this looked to be no man the like of
which he had ever seen.

"It cannot be . . ." he heard Flick mutter.

His uncle did not finish the thought. He brushed past
Wil and stepped to the edge of the porch, bracing himself
with an outstretched arm against the rain-slicked railing.
Wil moved to stand with him. The horseman was coming
directly toward them. So strong was the sense of foreboding that the rider's approach engendered within him that
the Valeman gave momentary consideration to fleeing. Yet
he could not flee. He could only wait, eyes fixed on the
spectral form.

The rider drew to a halt before the Valemen. His head
was lowered, his face hidden within the folds of a dark
cowl.

"Hello, Flick."

The rider's voice was a deep, low whisper. Wil saw his
uncle start.

"Allanon!"

The big man slipped from the back of his horse, but one
arm remained hooked about the animal's neck, as if he
could not stand alone. Wil came forward a pace and
stopped. Something was clearly wrong.

Allanon's gaze shifted slowly to meet his own. "Wil
Ohmsford?" The Valeman nodded, surprised. "Go quickly
and ask the Stors to come . . ." he began, then sagged
downward, barely catching himself in time to keep from
collapsing.

Wil came down the porch steps instantly, moving to the
Druid's aid, but stopped as the big man's hand came up in
warning.

"Do as I say, Valeman—go!"

Then Wil saw clearly what the rain had hidden from him before. Allanon's clothes were deeply stained with blood. Without another word the Valeman bounded back up the roadway toward the center, the weariness and discomfort slipping from him like a dream lost in waking.

VIII

The Stors took Allanon to the rest center, and although both Wil and Flick sought to accompany the injured Druid, they were told gently but firmly that their assistance was not needed. Enigmatic and silent, Stors and Druid disappeared into the corridors of the center, and the Valemen were left standing in the rain. Since it was apparent that for the moment nothing further would be learned of the Druid's coming, Wil Ohmsford bade his uncle goodnight and went off to bed.

Later that same day, during the early evening hours, Allanon sent word that he wanted to see both Valemen. Wil received the news with mixed emotions. On the one hand, he was curious to discover what had befallen the Druid. Stories of Allanon were familiar territory; his grandfather and Flick had told them all a dozen times over. Yet never in those tales had there been mention of injuries like those the big man had suffered in coming to Storlock. Not even the Skull Bearer that had attacked him in the furnace room at Paranor during the search for the Sword of Shannara had done this kind of damage, and Wil wanted to know what manner of creature walked the Four Lands that was more dangerous than the winged servants of the Warlock Lord. On the other hand, he was disturbed by the Druid's presence in Storlock. It might have been coincidence that Allanon came at a time when he found both Flick and Wil in the village. It might have been by chance that he stumbled upon them rather than the Stors. But Wil did not believe it for a moment. Allanon had come to them deliberately. Why had he done that? And why had he summoned them to this meeting? Wil could understand Allanon's wish to confer with Flick; after all, they had met before and shared common adventures. By why Wil? The Druid didn't even know the youngest Ohmsford. Why would Allanon be interested in meeting with him?

Nevertheless, he left his quarters and dutifully trooped off through the growing darkness across the village square toward the guest house where he knew Flick would be waiting. Much as he mistrusted the purpose behind this meeting, he was determined to go anyway. He was not one to back away from trouble—and besides, he could be wrong in his suspicions. Perhaps the Druid merely wanted to thank him for his help.

He found Flick waiting on the porch of the guest cottage, wrapped tightly in his heavy travel cloak, mumbling irritably about the weather. The elder Ohmsford came down the porch steps to join him, and they struck off together down the roadway toward the Stor rest center.

"What do you think he wants, Uncle Flick?" Wil asked after a moment, pulling his own cloak closer about him to ward off the evening chill.

"Hard to say," Flick grunted. "I'll tell you one thing. Every time he appears, it means trouble."

"His coming to Storlock has something to do with us, doesn't it?" Wil ventured, watching his uncle's face.

Flick shook his head uncertainly. "He's come here for a purpose sure enough. And he's called us over to say something more than hello and how are you. Whatever it is he has to say, it won't be anything we want to hear. I know that much. It never has been before and I see no reason to expect anything different this time around." He stopped abruptly and faced his nephew. "You watch yourself in there with him, Wil. He is not to be trusted."

"I'll be careful, Uncle Flick, but I don't think there is much to worry about," Wil replied. "We both know something of Allanon, don't we? Besides, you'll be there to keep an eye on things."

"I fully intend to." Flick turned and they continued walking. "Just remember what I said."

Moments later they mounted the porch steps of the rest center and stepped inside. The center was a long, low building constructed of stone and mortar walls and a clay-tiled roof. A large, comfortably furnished lobby opened on either side into hallways that disappeared into the wings of the center, where numerous small rooms provided for the care of the sick and injured. As they entered, one of the white-robed Stors in attendance came up to greet them. He beckoned wordlessly, then led them down a long, empty hallway. At its end was a single closed door. The Stor knocked once, turned, and left. Wil glanced uneasily at Flick, but the elder Ohmsford was staring fixedly at the closed door. Together they waited.

Then the door swung open and Allanon stood before them. He looked for all the world as if he had not been injured at all. No wounds were visible. The black robes that cloaked his tall frame were clean of blood. His face was somewhat drawn, but showed no sign of any pain. His penetrating gaze settled on the Valemen for a moment, then one hand motioned toward a small table with four chairs set about it.

"Why don't we sit there while we talk?" He made the suggestion seem almost an order.

They entered and seated themselves on the chairs. The room was windowless and bare of furnishings, except for the table and chairs and a large bed. Wil glanced about briefly, then turned his attention to the Druid. Allanon had been described to him by both Flick and Shea on dozens of occasions, and he looked now exactly as he had been described. But how could that be, Wil wondered, when the descriptions were of a man they had not seen since before the time of his birth?

"Well, here we are," Flick said finally, when it appeared that no one was ever going to say anything.

Allanon smiled faintly. "It seems so."

"You look well enough for a man who was half-dead just a few hours earlier."

"The Stors are very adept at their art, as you of all people should know," the Druid replied rather too pleasantly. "But I'm afraid I do not feel half so well as I should. How are you, Flick?"

"Older and wiser, I hope," the Valeman declared meaningfully.

Allanon did not respond. His gaze shifted abruptly to Wil. For a moment he said nothing further, his dark face inscrutable as he studied the younger Ohmsford. Wil sat quietly and did not turn away, though the Druid's eyes made him uneasy. Then slowly Allanon leaned forward in his chair, his great hands settling on the table top and folding together.

"I need your help, Wil Ohmsford," he stated quietly. Both Valemen stared at him. "I need you to come with me into the Westland."

"I knew it," muttered Flick, shaking his head.

Allanon smiled ruefully. "It is comforting to know, Flick, that some things in this life never change. You are certainly proof of that. Would it matter at all if I were to tell you that Wil's help is needed not for me, but for the Elven people and in particular, a young Elven girl?"

"No, it would not," the Valeman replied without a moment's hesitation. "He's not going and that's the end of it."

"Wait a minute, Uncle Flick," Wil interjected quickly. "It may well be that I'm not going, but I would like to be the one who makes that decision. At least, we can hear something more about what it is that I'm needed to do."

Flick ignored the reprimand. "Believe me, you do not want to hear another word. This is exactly how the trouble begins. This is exactly how it began for your grandfather fifty years ago." He looked quickly at Allanon. "Isn't that true? Isn't this exactly how things started when you came to Shady Vale and told us all about the Sword?"

Allanon nodded. "It is."

"There—you see!" Flick declared triumphantly. "Exactly the same. I'll wager this journey you've got planned for him is dangerous, too, isn't it?"

Again the Druid nodded.

"Well, then," the Valeman sat back, satisfaction etched into his bearded face. "I should think that settles the matter. You're asking too much. He's not going."

Allanon's dark eyes glittered. "He must go."

Flick looked startled. "He must?"

The Druid nodded. "You will see why, Flick, once I have explained what has happened in the Four Lands these past few days. Listen closely to me, Valemen."

He edged his chair closer to the table and leaned forward. "A long time ago, a very long time ago, before the Great Wars and the evolution of the new races, even before the development of Man as a civilized species, there was a terrible war fought between creatures that, for the most part, no longer exist. Some of these creatures were good and caring; they revered the land and sought to protect and preserve it against misuse and waste. For them, all life was sacred. But there were others who were evil and selfish; their ways were destructive and harmful. They took from the land and from its life without need or purpose. All were creatures whose physical characteristics and capabilities differed in the main from your own—that is to say, their appearance was different from yours, and they were capable of behavior no longer innate to the men of this world. In particular, they possessed to varying degrees powers of magic—at least, we would call it magic or sorcery or the mystic. Such power was common at that time, though some among these creatures possessed the power to a greater extent than others; thus their capacity for good or evil was enhanced proportionately. All of these creatures, both good and evil, existed together in the world and, because Man had not yet developed beyond a primitive life form existing within a narrow geographical space, the world was theirs alone. It had been so for centuries. But their existence together had never been harmonious. They lived in continuing conflict, for they worked at cross-purposes—the good to preserve, the evil to destroy. From time to time the balance of power between the conflicting sides would shift, as first the good and then the evil would dominate the drift of things.

"The struggle between them intensified through the years until finally, after centuries had passed without resolution of the conflict, the leaders in each camp banded together all who supported them, and the war began. This was not a war the like of which we have seen since. This was not a war on the order of the Great Wars, for the Great Wars employed power of such awesome proportion that the men who wielded it lost control entirely and were engulfed in the resulting cataclysm. Rather it was a war in which power and strength were skillfully employed at each turn—in which the creatures involved stood toe to toe in battle and lived and died on the skill they wielded. This was like the Wars of the Races, which have dominated the history of the new world; in the Race Wars, the Warlock Lord perverted the thinking of those who served him,

turning them against one another so that in the end he might enslave and rule them all. But in this war, there was never any deceit or illusion that swayed those who fought it. Good and evil were polarized from the beginning; no one stood aside in neutrality, for there were no neutral corners to be found. This was a war fought to determine forever the character and mode of evolution of life on the earth across which it was waged. It was a war that would decide whether the land would be forever preserved or forever desecrated. Each camp had resolved once and for all to achieve total victory over the other. For the creatures of evil, if they were defeated, it meant banishment; for the creatures of good, if they lost, it meant annihilation.

"So the war was fought—a terrible, monstrous war that I will not even attempt to describe, for there would be no point in doing so. For our purposes here it is only important that you know that the evil ones were defeated. Their power was broken and they were driven back and finally trapped. Those who had defeated them used their powers to create a Forbidding, a wall of imprisonment behind which the evil was to be placed. Their prison was not of this world nor any world, but a black hole of emptiness and isolation where nothing but the evil would be permitted to exist. Into this hole the evil was banished, sealed away behind the wall of the Forbidding for all time.

"The strength behind the Forbidding was a marvelous tree called an Ellcrys. The creatures of good created the Ellcrys out of the earth's life source, which they called the Bloodfire, and out of their own power. They gave her life so that, by her presence in the world, the Forbidding might endure long after they themselves were gone, long after the world they had struggled so long and desperately to preserve had altered and evolved beyond any recognition. Her life span was not to be measured by any standard that they possessed. But so long as she lived, the Forbidding continued, and so long as the Forbidding continued, the evil would remain shut within its prison."

He settled back in his chair, easing his tall frame gingerly away from the table to relieve cramped muscles, his arms slipping down into his lap. His dark eyes stayed locked on those of the Valemen.

"It was believed that the Ellcrys would live forever—not

by those who gave her life, for they knew that all things must eventually pass away—but by those who followed them, by all who nurtured and loved and honored this wondrous tree that was their protector for countless centuries. For them, the Ellcrys became a symbol of permanency; she survived the destruction of the old world in the holocaust of the Great Wars, she survived the Race Wars and the power of the Warlock Lord, and she survived after every other living thing that had existed with her had passed away—everything but the earth herself, and even the earth had changed while the Ellcrys had remained constant."

He paused. "So the legend grew. The Ellcrys would live forever. It was eternal. That belief never faltered." His face lifted slightly. "Until now. Now the belief is shattered. The Ellcrys is dying. The Forbidding begins to erode. The evil ones imprisoned within begin to break free once more and come back into this world that was once theirs."

"And these creatures caused your injuries?" Wil surmised.

Allanon nodded. "Some already walk the Four Lands. Though I thought to keep my presence secret, they have discovered me. They found me at Paranor within the Druid's Keep and very nearly finished me."

Flick looked alarmed. "Are they still searching for you?"

"They are—but I have reason to believe that they won't be so quick to find me this time."

"That doesn't reassure me much," the Valeman grumbled, glancing toward the doorway of the little room a bit apprehensively.

Allanon let the remark pass. "You may remember, Flick, that I once told to Shea and to you the history of the races. I told you how all of the races evolved from the old race of Man following the destruction wrought by the Great Wars—all of the races but one. The Elves. I told you that the Elves were always there. Do you remember?"

Flick grunted. "I remember. That was something else you never explained."

"I said that theirs was another story for another time. That time is now—in part, at least, though I don't propose to digress on the history of the Elven people at any great length. But some things you should know. We have spoken only in the abstract of the creatures that fought this war of good and evil that culminated in the creation of the Ellcrys. We must give them identity. All were creatures that became part of the old legends of faerie when men emerged from the darkness of barbarism and began to populate and build upon the world. They were creatures of magics, as I have said, both great and small. There were diverse species— some all good, some all bad, some whose individual peoples divided and went in opposite ways. They had names that you will recognize—Faeries, Sprites, Goblins, Wraiths, and the like. The new races, though human in ancestry, were named from four of the more numerous and best recorded of these creatures of supposed legend— Dwarves, Gnomes, Trolls, and Elves. Except, of course, that the Elves are different. They are different because they are not simply a legend reborn—they are the legend survived. The Elven people are the descendants of the faerie creatures that existed in the old world."

"Now wait a minute," Flick cut in quickly. "You mean to say that the Elven people are the same Elven people that all the old legends tell about—that there really were Elves in the old world?"

"Certainly there were Elves in the old world—just as there were Trolls and Dwarves and all the other creatures that gave birth to the legends. The only difference is that all of the others have been gone from the world for centuries, while the Elves have remained. They have altered, of course; they have evolved considerably. They were forced to adapt."

Flick looked as if he didn't understand one word of what he was hearing.

"There were Elves in the old world?" he repeated incredulously. "That is just not possible."

"Of course it's possible," the Druid replied calmly.

"Well, how did they survive the Great Wars?"

"How did Man survive the Great Wars?"

"But the old histories tell us of Man—they do not mention a single word about Elves!" the Valeman snapped. "Elves were a fairy tale people. If there really were Elves in the old world, where were they?"

"Right where they had always been—Man just couldn't see them."

"Now you're telling me Elves were invisible?" Flick threw up his hands. "I don't believe any of this!"

"You didn't believe any of what I told you about Shea and the Sword of Shannara either, if I remember correctly," Allanon pointed out, the faintest hint of laughter on his lips.

"I don't see what any of this has to do with why the Elves need my help," Wil interjected, heading off another outburst from Flick.

The Druid nodded. "I'll try to explain if Flick will just be patient with me for a moment longer. The history of the Elves is important to this discussion for one reason only. The Elves were the ones who conceived the idea of the Ellcrys and who brought her into being. It was the Elves who gave her life and afterwards cared for her down through the ages. Her protection and well-being are entrusted to an order of Elven youth called Chosen. For a single year, the Chosen stand in service to the tree, their task to see to it that she is properly looked after. At the end of that year, they are replaced. It has been so since the tree's creation. One year of service only. The Chosen are revered and honored among the Elven people; only a few are ever selected to serve and those who do so are guaranteed a position of high esteem in the Elven culture.

"All of which brings us to the present. As I have told you, the Ellcrys is dying. A few days earlier, she made this known to the Chosen. She was able to do this because she is a sentient being and possesses the ability to communicate. She revealed to them that her death was inevitable and close. She revealed as well what the Elven legends had foretold, what the first Elves had known, but what generations of Elves thereafter had virtually forgotten—that although the Ellcrys must die in the manner of other living creatures, unlike them she could be reborn. Yet her rebirth must depend heavily on the efforts of the Chosen. One among them would be required to bear her seed in search of the earth's life source—the Bloodfire. Only one of the Chosen presently in her service could do this. She told them where the Bloodfire might be found and bade them make preparations to seek it out."

He paused. "But before this could be done, some of the evil ones locked within the Forbidding broke free, finding the wall sufficiently weakened as the strength of the Ellcrys began to fail. One slipped into the Elven city of Arborlon, where the Ellcrys stands, and killed the Chosen it found there, believing that with their deaths any chance for a rebirth would be ended. I arrived too late to prevent this from happening. But I spoke with the Ellcrys and discovered through her that one of the Chosen still remains alive—a young girl who was not within the city when the others were killed. Her name is Amberle. I left Arborlon in search of her."

He leaned forward once more. "But the evil ones have learned of her also. They sought once already to prevent me from reaching her and very nearly succeeded. They will certainly try again if they have the chance to do so. But they do not know where she can be found nor, for the moment at least, do they know where I am. If I am quick enough, I should be able to reach her and return her safely to Arborlon before they discover me again."

"Then I should think that you are wasting valuable time conversing with us," Flick declared firmly. "You should be on your way to the girl."

The Druid ignored him, though his face darkened slightly. "Even though I return Amberle to Arborlon, there are problems still that must be dealt with. As the last of the Chosen, it will fall to her to bear the Ellcrys' seed in quest of the Bloodfire. No one, myself included, knows exactly where the Fire can be found. Once, the Ellcrys knew. But the world she remembers is gone now. She gave the Elves a name—Safehold. It is a name that means nothing to them, a name from the old world. When I left Arborlon, I traveled first to Paranor to search the Druid histories compiled by the Council after the Great Wars—histories which record the mysteries of the old world. Reading through those histories, I was able to discover the country within which Safehold lies. Still, the exact location of the Bloodfire must be discovered by those who seek it."

And suddenly Wil Ohmsford realized why it was that Allanon wanted him to go into the Westland.

He realized it and still he could not believe it.

"Amberle cannot undertake this search alone," Allanon continued. "The country into which she must go is dangerous—much too dangerous for a young Elven girl to travel by herself. It will be a difficult journey at best. Those who have crossed through the Forbidding will continue to seek her out; if they find her, she will have no protection against them. She must not be harmed in any way. She is the last hope of her people. If the Ellcrys is not reborn, the Forbidding will eventually fail altogether and the evil locked within it will be loose once more upon the earth. There will be war with the Elves that they cannot, in all probability, win. If they are destroyed, the evil will move into the other Lands as well. It will grow stronger as it comes, as is the nature of beings such as these. In the end, the races will be devoured."

"But you will be there to help her . . ." Wil began, searching for a way out of the trap he felt closing about him.

"I cannot be there to help her," Allanon cut in quickly.

There was a long silence. Allanon spread his hands on the table.

"There is good reason for this, Wil Ohmsford. I have told you that the evil already begins to break through the wall of the Forbidding. The Ellcrys will grow steadily weaker; as she does so, the creatures she imprisons will grow bolder. They will continue to push against the wall of the Forbidding. They will continue to break through. Eventually, they will tear down the wall entirely. When this happens, they will converge upon the Elven nation and attempt to destroy it. This may very well happen long before the Bloodfire is found. There is also a possibility that the Bloodfire may never be found or that it may be found too late. In either case, the Elven people must be prepared to stand and fight. But some of the creatures within the Forbidding are very powerful; at least one possesses sorcery very nearly as great as my own. The Elves will have no defense against such power. Their own magic is lost. The Druids who once aided them are gone. There is only me. If I leave them and go with Amberle, they will be defenseless. I cannot do that. I must give them whatever aid I can.

"Yet someone must go with Amberle—someone who possesses power enough to resist the evil that will pursue her, someone who can be trusted to do everything humanly possible to protect her. That someone is you."

"What are you talking about?" Flick exclaimed in exasperation. "What possible help can Wil be against creatures such as these—creatures that very nearly succeeded in doing you in? You don't mean for him to use the Sword of Shannara?"

Allanon shook his head. "The power of the Sword works only against illusion. The evil we face is very real, very tangible. The Sword would have no power against it."

Flick almost came to his feet. "What then?"

The Druid's eyes were dark and filled with insight and Wil Ohmsford felt his heart sink.

"The Elfstones."

Flick was aghast. "The Elfstones! But Shea has the Elfstones!"

Wil put his hand quickly on the other's arm. "No, Uncle Flick, I have them." He groped within his tunic and then withdrew a small leather pouch. "Grandfather gave them to me when I left Shady Vale to come to Storlock. He told me that he no longer had need of them and that he thought they should belong to me." His voice was shaking. "It's strange; I only took them to please him—not because I ever thought that I would use them. I've never even tried."

"It would do you no good, Wil." Flick turned back hurriedly to Allanon. "He knows. No one but Shea could ever use the Elfstones. They are useless to anyone else."

Allanon's expression did not change. "That is not entirely true, Flick. They can only be used by one to whom they are freely given. I gave them to Shea to use when I warned him to flee the Vale to Culhaven. They remained his until he gave them to Wil. Now they belong to Wil. Their power is his to invoke, just as it was once Shea's."

Flick looked desperate. "You can give them back," he insisted, turning once more to Wil, seeing the confusion in his eyes. "Or you can give them to someone else—anyone else. You don't have to keep them. You don't have to become involved in any of this madness!"

Allanon shook his head. "Flick, he is already involved."

"But what of my plans to become a Healer?" Wil interjected suddenly. "What of the time and work I have put into that? Becoming a Healer is all that I have ever wanted to do, and I am finally on my way to doing it. Am I expected just to give it all up?"

"If you refuse your aid in this matter, how can you then become a Healer?" The Druid's voice turned hard. "A Healer must give whatever help he can, whenever he can, in any way that he can. It is not something he can pick and choose. If you refuse to go and all that I have foreseen comes to pass—as I am certain that it then will—how will you live with yourself, knowing that you never even tried to prevent it?"

Wil flushed. "But when will I be able to return again?"

"I don't know. It may be a long time."

"And even if I come with you, can you be certain that the power of the Elfstones will be strong enough to protect this girl?"

Allanon's face closed in about itself, dark, secretive.

"I cannot. Such power as the Elfstones possess draws its strength from the holder. Shea never tested their limits; you may have to."

"Can you give me no assurances, then?" The Valeman's voice had dropped to a whisper.

"None." The Druid's gaze never left him. "Still, you must come."

Wil slumped back in his chair, stunned. "It seems I have no choice."

"Of course you have a choice!" Flick snapped angrily. "Will you give up everything for no other reason than this—that Allanon says you must? Will you go with him for that alone?"

Wil's eyes lifted. "Didn't you, Uncle Flick—grandfather and you—to search out the Sword of Shannara?"

Flick hesitated uncertainly; then he reached over and took his nephew's hands in his own, clasping them tightly.

"You are too quick in this, Wil. I warned you of Allanon. Now you listen to me. I see more in this than you. There is something hidden behind the Druid's words. I can feel it." His voice tightened, and the lines in his gray-bearded face creased even more deeply. "I am afraid for you. It is because I am afraid that I speak to you as I do. You are like my own son; I don't want to lose you."

"I know," Wil whispered. "I know."

Flick straightened. "Then don't go. Let Allanon find another."

The Druid shook his head. "I cannot, Flick. There is no

other. There is only Wil." His eyes again sought those of the young Valeman. "You must come."

"Let me go instead," Flick offered suddenly, a hint of desperation in his voice. "Wil can give the Elfstones to me, and I can watch over the Elven girl. Allanon, we have traveled together before . . ."

But the Druid was already shaking his head no. "Flick, you cannot come," he said gently. "Your heart is greater than your strength, Valeman. The journey that lies ahead will be long and hard and must be made by a younger man." He paused. "Our travels together are over, Flick."

There was a long silence, and then the Druid turned again to Wil Ohmsford, waiting. The Valeman looked at his uncle. They stared at each other wordlessly for a moment, Flick's gray eyes uncertain, Wil's now steady. Flick saw that the decision had been made. Almost imperceptibly, he nodded.

"You must do what you feel is right," he mumbled, reluctance sounding in his every word.

Wil turned to Allanon. "I will come with you."

IX

Early the next morning, Allanon came to Wil Ohmsford and told him that they were leaving Storlock at once. Dark and grim-visaged, the Druid appeared at the door of the Valeman's cottage without a word of forewarning and while Wil gave thought to arguing against such an abrupt departure, something in the big man's face and voice convinced him that he should not. Last evening, when they had parted company, there had been no urgency in the Druid's behavior; now there clearly was. Whatever it was that had persuaded Allanon to make this decision, it was compelling. Wordlessly the Valeman packed his few belongings and latched the door of the cottage behind him as he followed the Druid out.

It was raining once more as a new storm approached from out of the northwest, and the dawn skies were heavy and leaden. Allanon led the Valeman up the muddied roadway, his tall form wrapped in the black robe, his cowled head bent slightly against a steadily rising wind. A handful of white-robed Stors waited to receive them on the steps of the rest center with a small kit for Wil and provisions for the journey. Artaq was saddled and shaking his head with impatience, and Allanon mounted the black at once, a gingerliness in his movements suggesting that his wounds were not yet fully healed. A wiry gray gelding named Spitter was given to Wil, and he had one foot in the stirrup when Flick came dashing up, bearded face dripping and flushed. Hastily his uncle pulled him back into the shelter of the rest center's covered porch.

"They just told me," he panted, wiping the rain from his eyes. "I'm surprised they bothered!" He glanced angrily toward Allanon. "Is it necessary that you leave so quickly?"

Wil nodded slowly. "I think something may have made it necessary."

Frustration and concern showed in Flick's eyes. "It is not too late to rethink your decision in all this," he whispered harshly and would have said more, but Wil was already shaking his head. "Very well. I'll tell your grandfather what has happened, though I am certain he won't like it any better than I do. Be careful, Wil. Remember what I said about all of us having our limitations."

Wil nodded. They said their goodbyes quickly and gruffly, almost as if they were afraid to express what they were really feeling, their faces fixed and drawn as they exchanged uneasy glances and hurriedly embraced. Then Allanon and he were riding away. Flick, the Stors, and the village became dark shadows that faded into the mist and gray of the Eastland forests and disappeared from view.

The Druid and the Valeman rode west out of Storlock to the edge of the Rabb Plains, then turned south. Allanon paused long enough to tell Wil that the first leg of their journey would take them below the Silver River to a small village on the western edge of the lower Anar called Havenstead. It was at Havenstead that they would find Amberle. The Druid did not volunteer anything further on the matter, and Wil did not ask. Rain washed over them in sheets as the storm worsened; keeping within the fringe of the forestland, they bent their heads over their horses' necks and rode without speaking.

As they traveled, Wil's thoughts drifted back to the events of the previous evening. Even now, he was not sure exactly why he had decided to go with the Druid. And that disturbed him. Surely he should be able to explain why he had agreed to such an improbable journey—to himself, at least, if to no one else. Yet he could not. There had been sufficient time to think about his reasons for making the decision, and indeed he had thought about little else. Hindsight should have lent clarity to his actions; it did not. Rather, he felt a lingering sense of confusion. Everything seemed to jumble together in his mind—all the disparate, incomplete reasoning, all the emotions that intertwined and colored. They would not sort themselves out for him; they would not arrange themselves in a neat, orderly fashion. They merely shuffled about like stray sheep and he chased after them hopelessly.

He wanted to believe that he had chosen to go because he was needed. If all that Allanon had told him were true—and he felt it was, despite Flick's obvious doubts—then he could be of great service to the Elven people and particularly to the girl Amberle. But who was he fooling? He had no idea at all whether he could use the Elfstones that his grandfather had entrusted to him. Suppose their power was beyond him. Suppose Allanon was wrong in thinking that the Elfstones could be passed down to him. Suppose anything at all. The fact was that he had made a rather impulsive decision, and now he must live with it. On the other hand, the impulsiveness of the decision did not necessarily detract from its merit. If he possessed aid to offer the Elves, he must extend that aid. He must at least try to help them. Besides, his grandfather would have gone; he knew that as surely as he knew anything. Shea Ohmsford would have gone, had Allanon asked him, just as he had gone on his quest for the Sword of Shannara. Wil could do no less.

He took a deep breath. Yes, he had made the right decision in going, and he believed that he had made that decision for the right reasons, though they seemed jumbled and out of order to him now. What bothered him most, he realized suddenly, had nothing to do with the decision itself or the reasons for that decision. It had to do with Allanon. Wil would have liked to believe that the decision to go with the Druid had been his own. Yet the more he considered the matter, the more certain he became that the decision had not really been his at all. It had been Allanon's. Oh, he had spoken the words as if they were his own, spoken them bravely and despite his uncle's warnings. Yet he knew that the Druid had been able to foresee exactly what it would take to persuade Wil to speak those words, and he had directed the conversation accordingly. Somehow he had known what the younger Valeman's reactions would be, what Flick's would be, how the two would interact, and how his own comments would influence them. He had known all this and used that knowledge accordingly. Shea Ohmsford had once told Wil that Allanon possessed the ability to see into the minds of other men, to know their thoughts. Wil understood now exactly what his grandfather had been talking about.

Thus he had committed himself. It was not something that could be undone, even if he should choose to do so, and he did not. But from here forward, he would be on his guard against such clever manipulation by the Druid. In so far as it was possible for him to do so, he would look beyond the words and actions of the big man to the reasons that lay behind them, the better to see where it was that he was being led. Wil Ohmsford was nobody's fool. He had been looking after himself for several years, and he was not about to quit doing so now. He must be wary of the Druid. He would trust him, but not blindly and not without proper consideration. Perhaps he could be of service to the Elves and to the girl Amberle; he did not reject that possibility simply because of what he felt about the manner in which his cooperation in all this had been secured. But he would be careful to choose his own manner of giving aid. He would be careful to decide for himself whose interests he might best look after. He would accept nothing as he found it.

His face lifted guardedly, and he peered through the rain at the dark form riding ahead of him—Allanon, last of the Druids, a being who came from another age, whose powers dwarfed anything known to this current world. And Wil must both trust him and yet not trust him. He felt a moment of deep consternation. What had he gotten himself into? Perhaps Flick had been right after all. Perhaps he would have done well to have given a little more thought to his decision. But it was too late for that now. Too late, as well, for thoughts such as these. He shook his head. There was little point in dwelling on it further. He would be well advised to turn his thoughts in another direction.

He spent the remainder of the day trying unsuccessfully to do so.

The rain turned to drizzle as the day lengthened, then at last died away entirely in the cold gray of early evening.

Thunderclouds continued to blanket the skies as nightfall turned from gray to black, and the air filled with mist that wandered at the forest's edge like a child lost. Allanon turned into the shelter of the great trees, and they made camp in a small clearing several hundred yards from the borders of the Rabb. Behind them, rising above the roof of the forest, was the dark wall of the Wolfsktaag, little more than a deeper shade of black against the night. Despite the damp, they managed to salvage enough dry wood and kindling to make a small fire, and the flames lent some warmth to the evening chill. Travel cloaks were hung on lines stretched overhead, and the horses were tethered close by.

They consumed a sparse meal of cold beef, fruit, and nuts that they had packed before leaving Storlock, exchanging only a few perfunctory words as they ate. The Druid sat in brooding silence, preoccupied with his own thoughts, as he had been ever since they had left the village, and seemingly uninterested in carrying on any sort of conversation. But Wil had determined to learn something more of what lay ahead and he had no intention of waiting any longer to begin talking about it. When they had finished their meal, he eased himself a bit closer to the fire, making sure the movement caught Allanon's attention.

"Can we talk a bit?" he asked carefully, bearing in mind his grandfather's many tales of the big man's uncertain temperament.

The Druid stared at him expressionlessly for a moment, then nodded.

"Can you tell me something more about the history of the Elven people?" Wil decided the conversation should begin there.

Allanon smiled faintly. "Very well. What would you like to know, Wil Ohmsford?"

The Valeman hesitated. "Last night you told us that even though the histories of the old world make no mention of the Elven people other than in fairy tales and in folklore, they were a real people nevertheless, just as men were. You said they were there, but humans couldn't see them. I didn't understand that."

"You didn't?" The big man seemed amused. "Well, then you shall have an explanation. Simply put, the Elves have always been creatures of the forest—but more so in the times before the Great Wars. In those days, as I've told you before, they were creatures of magic. They possessed the ability to blend in quite naturally with their surroundings, much as if they were a bush or plant that you might pass by a thousand times and never notice. Humans couldn't see them because they did not know how to look for them."

"But they weren't invisible?"

"Hardly."

"Just difficult to see?"

"Yes, yes." There was a touch of annoyance in the Druid's answer.

"But why don't we have trouble seeing them now?"

Allanon straightened himself. "You're not listening. In the old world, the Elves were creatures of magic, as were all the creatures of faerie. They are creatures of magic no longer. They are men, just as you are a man. Their magic is lost to them."

"How did this happen?" Wil settled his elbows against his knees and propped his chin in his hands, somewhat in the manner of a curious child.

"That is not so easy to explain," the Druid advised him. "But I can see that you will not be satisfied until I've tried, so I will attempt to do so."

He leaned forward slightly. "After the creation of the Ellcrys, after the banishment of the creatures of evil magic from the earth, the Elves and their faerie brethren drifted apart once more. It was natural enough that this should happen, since they had united in the first place only for the purpose of defeating their common enemy and, once that was accomplished, there was little left to keep them together. Beyond their general concern in preserving the earth as a homeland, they had almost nothing in common. Each species of creature had its own way of life, its own habits, its own interests. Elves, Dwarves, Sprites, Gnomes, Trolls, Witches, and all the rest, were as different from each other as the beasts of the forest from the fish in the sea.

"Humankind had not yet begun to emerge from its early, primitive existence, and would not do so for hundreds of years to come. The faerie creatures paid the humans little attention, and indeed there seemed little reason to do so. After all, at this stage in time humans were simply a higher form of animal life, possessing greater innate intelligence than other animals, but lesser instincts. The Elves and their brethren did not foresee the influence that humans would eventually have upon the development on the earth."

The Druid paused. "It was something they could have foreseen, had they paid closer attention to the differences between themselves and humankind. Two differences were of particular importance. The Elves and their brethren did not procreate rapidly; humans did. The Elves, for example, were one of the more populous faerie people, yet their longer life spans resulted in fewer births. Many of the other faerie creatures gave birth only once every several hundred years. But humans had frequent multiple births within the family unit, and their population grew quickly. In the beginning, the creatures of magic far outnumbered the humans. Within a thousand years time, that situation reversed itself dramatically. Thereafter the human population expanded steadily, while the faerie population began to diminish—but I'll get to that in a moment.

"The second difference between the Elves and their brethren and humankind had to do with the ability to adapt, or lack thereof. The Elves were creatures of the forestland; they seldom left the shelter of their woods. It was the same with most of the others. Each resided within a particular geographic area, a carefully bounded terrain. It had always been so. Some lived within the forests, some within the rivers and seas, some within the mountains, some within the plainlands. They had adapted their way of life to the terrain that served as their homeland; they could not and would not live anywhere else. But humans were more adaptable; they lived everywhere. The forests, the rivers, the mountains, the plains—they claimed it all. Thus their expansion as their population grew came naturally, easily. They adapted to any change in environment. The Elves and their brethren resisted all change."

Allanon paused, then smiled faintly. "There was a time, Wil Ohmsford, when life in the old world was much as life is now—when humans lived and worked and played much as the races do in this world. Does that surprise you?"

Wil nodded. "A little, I guess."

The Druid shook his head. "There was such a time. It was then that the Elves should have come forward and joined with humans to shape their world. But they did not—neither they nor their brethren. They chose instead to remain hidden within their forestland, observers only, still believing that their own existence would not be affected by the development of humankind. They saw no threat to themselves; the humans possessed no magic and their ways were not destructive—not then. So the Elves kept to their policy of isolation, foolishly thinking it could always be so. It was their undoing. The human population continued to expand and to develop. As time wore on, they learned of the Elves and their brethren. But because the faerie creatures chose concealment as their way of life, they earned the distrust of humans. They were deemed creatures of ill-fortune, creatures who spied and connived against others, creatures who performed acts of mischief and whose favorite pastime was to discover new ways of making the lives of hardworking humans more difficult. There was some truth to the charges, since a few of the faerie creatures did indeed delight in tormenting humans with small acts of enchantment, but by and large the reputation was undeserved. In any case, the Elves and their brethren chose to ignore it all. The attitude of humankind toward them did not concern them. Their sole concern was with the preservation and protection of the land and the living things within it, and this they could accomplish very well, despite the ill feelings humans bore them.

"Then even this state of affairs began to change. Humans continued to populate the earth with increasing rapidity, growing, expanding, now building cities and fortresses, now sailing the seas in search of new lands, now pushing back the wilderness about them. They began, for the first time, seriously to affect the character of the land, changing whole regions for habitation and consumption needs. The Elves were forced to move deeper and deeper into the forestlands that were their homes, as the human population cut away the trees and brush. All of the faerie creatures found their homelands being encroached upon by this expansion until finally, for some, there were no homes at all."

"But didn't they resist this intrusion?" Wil interrupted suddenly.

"It was far too late for that," Allanon replied, his smile bitter. "By this time, many of the faerie creatures had become extinct, some by failure to reproduce sufficient young, some by their failure to adapt to a changing environment. Those who remained were no longer able to unite as they once had done; it had been hundreds of years since their war with the faerie creatures of evil magic, and they had scattered far and wide about the earth and long since lost contact with one another. Worst of all, they no longer had their own magic. When the evil magic had flourished upon the earth, there had been need for good magic to withstand it. But once that evil had been banished, the need for the good magic was past. The faerie creatures ceased using most of it. As time passed, much of it was forgotten altogether. Human beings used no magic of any consequence, so the Elves and their brethren saw no need for the very powerful magics that had once been employed to defeat their evil counterparts. By the time they recognized the need for it again, it was lost to them— all but a small part of it. Thus their resistance to the expansion of the human population into their homelands was weakened badly. At first they fought very hard, using all the power they still possessed to stop what was happening. It availed them nothing. There were too many humans and too few of them. Their magic was ineffective. It won them small victories, brief respites, nothing more. They were simply overwhelmed in the end, driven from their homes to find new ones or to perish—driven out, in the final analysis, by sciences and technologies against which they had no real defense."

"And the Elves—what of them?" Wil asked quietly.

"They learned to survive. Their population dwindled, but they did not become extinct as did so many of the others. They remained within their forestland, moving steadily deeper, hidden now completely from the humans who had come to occupy almost the whole of the earth. They watched in horror the destruction that was being

performed on their world. They watched it being stripped
of its resources and its animal life. They watched as its
ecological balance was utterly and irreversibly disrupted.
They watched the humans war between themselves inces-
santly as the separate governments struggled to achieve
domination over one another. They watched and they
waited and they prepared—for they saw how it all must
end."

"The Great Wars." The Valeman anticipated the Druid.

"The Great Wars." Allanon nodded. "The Elves foresaw
that such horrors would come. They used what magic they
still possessed in an effort to preserve themselves and a few
carefully chosen treasures of their past—among these, the
Ellcrys—from the holocaust that followed. It was a remark-
able effort, and it allowed them to survive. Most of the
other faerie creatures were destroyed. A small number of
humans survived, though it was not through their foresight that they did so. They survived because there were so
many of them in so many different parts of the earth that
the holocaust simply missed a few of them. But everything
that the humans had built was destroyed. All of their vast,
sprawling civilization was erased. The old world was
reduced to a barren, desolate wilderness.

"For hundreds of years after, all life was caught up in a
savage struggle to stay alive. The few creatures that
remained alive in this new world were forced to adapt to
the primitive environment about them, an environment in
which nature had been altered beyond recognition.
Humankind was changed forever. From out of the old race
of humans emerged four new and distinct races: Men,
Dwarves, Gnomes, and Trolls. It was believed, and is still
believed by most, that the Elves were a fifth race born of
the holocaust. For the new races, it was the beginning of
life. Most of the history of the old world was quickly
forgotten; most of the old ways vanished. The Elves kept
much of their history and their tradition. Only their magic
was lost to them—but this time it was lost for good. Their
need to adapt resulted in changes that would not otherwise
have occurred, changes that brought them closer culturally
and physiologically to the new races. Reborn humans and
surviving Elves assimilated together in their new world
until finally, inexorably, they became much the same.

"And when at last, almost a thousand years after the Great Wars had ended, the new races began to emerge from the primitive lives they had endured while struggling to survive the aftereffects of the holocaust, the Elves stood with them. No longer would they hide in their forestland as impartial observers to the development of a world. This time they would be a part of that development, working openly with the new races to be certain that men did not travel a second time that roadway which had almost ended with the destruction of all life. Thus did the Elves, through the Druid Galaphile, convene the First Council at Paranor. Thus did the Elves seek to turn the races from an ill-advised search for the old sciences of energy and power, counseling instead a more cautious approach to life's mysteries. Thus did they seek to regain the small magics they had lost, believing these arts would help them best in their efforts to preserve their new world and its life."

"Yet the Elves have no magic," Wil reminded the big man. "Only the Druids did."

"The Druids and a handful of others scattered through the land," Allanon corrected. He seemed to lose himself momentarily. When he spoke again, his voice was distant. "The Druids learned early of the dangers inherent in the search for the lost magic. A Druid named Brona taught them well. His need to explore the limits of the magic destroyed him, created in his physical shell the creature we know as the Warlock Lord. When the Druids realized what hunger for the magic had done to him, they forbade further exploration. The magic they had found was not altogether good, nor altogether bad; it was simply powerful—too powerful for mortal men to master. For a time, it was left alone. Then Brona caught and killed all of the Druids at Paranor, signaling the start of the Second War of the Races, and suddenly there was only Bremen left to teach the magic. Then, when he was gone, there was only me . . ."

He trailed off momentarily, dark eyes narrowing as he stared down into the little fire at their feet. Then he looked back suddenly at Wil.

"What else would you know, Valeman?"

The tone of his voice was sharp, almost angry. Its abruptness caught Wil by surprise, but he kept his gaze steady, forcing his eyes to meet the Druid's.

"What else would you have me know?" he replied quietly.

Allanon said nothing, waiting. There was a long, uncomfortable silence as the two men faced each other. At last the Valeman looked away again, poking idly at the embers of their fire with the toe of one boot.

"These creatures that were shut within the place beyond the Forbidding—what of them?" he asked finally. "How have they survived for so many years? Why have they not perished?"

Allanon's dark expression did not change. "Call them Demons, for that is what they have become. They were sent to a non-place, a dark emptiness beyond any living world. Within that darkness, there was no passing of time to bring age and death. The Elves failed to realize this, I suppose, or perhaps thought it of little importance, since their only concern was to remove the evil from their own world. In any case, the Demons did not die; rather, they multiplied. The evil that lived within them fed upon itself and grew stronger. It bred new life. For evil left to itself, Valeman, does not simply perish; it thrives. Evil contained is not evil destroyed. It nourishes itself, grows within its confinement, swells and rages until it works loose, and then . . . then it runs free."

"And its magic?" Wil followed quickly. "Has its magic grown also?"

Some of the harshness faded from the other's visage, and he nodded. "Fed in the same way, and practiced, for the evil ones warred with each other in their prison, driven nearly mad with need to release their hatred of what had been done to them."

Now it was the Valeman's turn to be silent. His face lowered into shadow; his arms wrapped protectively about his knees as he drew his legs up tightly to his chest. In the east, there sounded the faint, distant thunder of the departing storm as it faded into the broken wall of the Wolfsktaag.

A touch of impatience revealed itself in Allanon's dark face as he watched the young man. He leaned forward once more.

"Are all of your questions answered now, Wil Ohmsford?"

The Valeman blinked. "No." His head lifted sharply. "No, I have one more."

Allanon frowned. "Indeed. Let's have it, then."

He was clearly displeased. Wil hesitated, weighing inwardly the advisability of proceeding any further with this. He decided that he must. He chose his words carefully.

"Everything that I've heard suggests that these Demons are more than a match for the Elves. It seems from your own encounter with them that they are a match even for you." There was anger now in the big man's face, but Wil pushed ahead quickly. "If I accompany the Elven girl Amberle in search of the Bloodfire, as you have asked me, they will surely come after us. Suppose we are found. What chance do I stand against them, Allanon? Even with the Elfstones, what chance do I have? You would not answer me before. Answer me now."

"Well." The Druid rocked back slightly, the lean, dark visage suddenly expressionless in the firelight, creased in shadow. "I thought this was all leading up to something."

"Please give me an answer to my question," Wil persisted quietly.

Allanon cocked his head reflectively. "I don't know the answer."

"You don't know?" the Valeman repeated the words incredulously.

The Druid blinked. "In the first place, I hope to keep them from finding you. If they cannot find you, they cannot harm you. At the moment, they know nothing of you at all. I intend that it should stay that way."

"But if they do find me—then what?"

"Then you have the Elfstones." He hesitated. "Understand this, Wil. The Elfstones are a magic from the old world—a magic that existed when the Elves first defeated these creatures. The power of the Stones is measured by the strength of the man or woman who wields them. There are three Elfstones—one each for the heart, mind, and body of the user. All three must unite as one; when this is done properly, the power released can be very great."

He looked at the Valeman sharply. "Do you understand, then, why I cannot answer your question? You will determine the strength of your defense against your

enemies; it must come from within you, not from the
Stones themselves. I cannot measure that in you. Only you
can do that. I can only tell you that I judge you to be as
good a man as your grandfather—and I've met no better
man, Wil Ohmsford."

The Valeman stared wordlessly at the Druid for a
moment, then looked down at the fire.

"Nor have I," he whispered.

Allanon smiled faintly. "Your grandfather's chances
seemed very poor when he went in quest of the Sword of
Shannara. He would admit to that. The Warlock Lord knew
of him from the beginning; the Skull Bearers actually came
into the Vale in search of him. He was hunted every step of
the way. Yet he survived—and he did so despite his own
considerable doubts."

He reached over and put his hand on Wil's shoulder, the
cavernous eyes glinting in the firelight. "I like your chances
in this. I believe in you. Now you must start believing in
yourself."

He took his hand away and rose. "We've talked enough
this night. You need to sleep. We've a long ride ahead of us
tomorrow." He wrapped his black robes tightly about him.
"I'll keep watch."

He started to move away from the Valeman.

"I can keep watch," Wil offered quickly, remembering
the Druid's injuries.

"You can sleep," Allanon grunted, and the night shadows swallowed him up.

Wil stared after him for a second, then shook his head.
Spreading his blankets next to the fire, he rolled himself
into them and stretched wearily. He would not sleep, the
Valeman told himself. Not yet. Not until he had taken time
to consider carefully all that had been said this evening,
until he had decided how much of it he should believe,
until he was convinced that he knew what he was doing in
all this. Not until then.

He let his eyes close for just a moment. Immediately he
was asleep.

X

They resumed their journey at daybreak. Although the forestland still glistened damply with yesterday's rain, the skies were clear and blue and filled with sunlight as the pair rode southward along the fringes of the Anar. The drab emptiness of the Rabb brightened into rolling grasslands, and the enticing smell of fruit-bearing trees was carried past them on a gentle morning breeze.

Late that afternoon they arrived at the legendary Silver River and came upon a company of Dwarf Sappers engaged in the construction of a footbridge at a heavily forested narrows. Leaving Wil concealed in a copse of fir with the horses, the Druid went down to the river's edge to confer with the Dwarves. He was gone for a time and, when he returned, seemed preoccupied with something. It was not until they had remounted and were riding downriver away from the Dwarves that he volunteered to Wil that he had given warning of the danger to the Elves and requested that the Dwarves send aid as quickly as possible. One among the Sappers had recognized the Druid and had promised that help would be sent. Still, marshaling any sizable force would take time . . .

Allanon left the matter there. Minutes later they forded the Silver River at a shallows where a broad sandbar split the clear waters apart and rock shallows slowed the current enough to permit horse and rider safe passage. From there they rode south at a leisurely pace, watching the shadows they cast lengthen as the day wore on. It was nearly sunset when Allanon reined in Artaq at the crest of a tree-lined rise and dismounted. Wil followed him down, leading Spitter forward several paces to where the Druid waited.

They tethered the horses in a small grove of hickory and together walked ahead to where an outcropping of rock split apart the wall of trees. With Allanon in the lead, they moved up into the rocks and peered out.

Below them lay a broad, horseshoe-shaped valley, its slopes and floor heavily forested, but open at its western end to grasslands that had been tilled and planted with farm crops. A village sat at the juncture between forest and field, and a narrow stream ran from the woodlands through the cluster of homes north across the top of the farmland, its waters irrigating the soil in dozens of neatly inscribed ditches. Men and women moved busily about the little community, tiny figures to the two who looked down on them from the valley rim. Far to the south, the grasslands ended in a rock-strewn lowland that stretched unbroken to the horizon and disappeared.

"Havenstead," Allanon announced, indicating the village and the farmlands. His finger lifted slightly and pointed into the lowland. "Out there is the Battlemound."

Wil nodded. "What do we do now?"

The Druid seated himself comfortably. "We wait until it gets dark. The fewer people who see us, the better. The Stors would say nothing in any case, but these villagers are free with their talk. Secrecy is still our greatest ally, and I don't intend to lose it unnecessarily. We'll go in quickly and quietly and leave the same way." He glanced up at the sun, already beginning to drop rapidly into the western horizon. "We only have about an hour."

They sat together without talking until the rim of the sun was barely visible above the tree line, and the dusk had begun to slip her gray shadow over the length of the valley. Finally, Allanon rose. They walked back to where they had tied the horses, remounted and started out once more. The Druid led them eastward for a time, skirting the valley rim until they had reached a heavily forested section of the slope that concealed a narrow draw. There they started down. They wound their way slowly through the trees, watching the woodlands darken steadily into night, allowing the horses to pick their way through the brush. Wil quickly lost all sense of direction, but Allanon seemed to know exactly where he was going and did not slow as he guided them forward.

After a time, they reached the valley floor, and travel grew easier. A clear, moonlit sky peeked down on them through breaks in the forest roof, and night birds called out sharply at their passing. The air was sweet and heavy with the smell of the woods, and Wil grew drowsy.

Finally, scattered bits of yellow light began to flicker into view ahead of them, slipping through the screen of the forest, and the faint sounds of voices reached out through the stillness. Allanon dismounted, motioning for Wil to do likewise, and they walked the horses forward afoot. The forest thinned out noticeably, clear of heavy brush and deadwood, and ahead of them they could see a low stone wall with a wooden gate. A line of tall evergreens bordered the wall and screened away most of what lay beyond, though it was clear to Wil that they were at the eastern edge of the farming village and the yellow lights were the flames of oil lamps.

Upon reaching the wall, they tied the horses to an iron post. Allanon put a single finger across his lips. Silently, they passed through the little wooden gate.

What they found on the other side brought Wil up short. A sweeping, terraced garden spread out before them, its tiers of multicolored flowers dazzling even in the pale moonlight. A stone walkway, glistening with flecks of silver, wound downward out of the gardens to a gathering of wooden benches and from there to a small cottage constructed of timber and stone. The cottage was a single story with a loft and was fronted by the familiar open-air porch. Flower boxes hung below latticed windows, and thick, low bushes bordered the roughened walls. Crimson yews and blue spruce grew at the immediate front of the home. A second walkway ran from the porch beneath the arch of a magnificent white birch and disappeared through a hedgerow to a roadway beyond. In the distance, glimmerings of light from other cottages broke the night.

Wil stared at it all in wonderment. Everywhere there were touches of color and life—all with the look of something drawn from a child's storybook. Everything was perfectly ordered.

He glanced questioningly at Allanon. The mocking smile flashed briefly, and the Druid motioned for him to come. They followed the pathway through the gardens to the benches, then moved on toward the cottage. Light shone brightly through the curtained windows of the little house, and from within came the low, gentle sound of voices—no, Wil corrected himself, children's voices! He was mildly surprised at his discovery and very nearly missed seeing the fat, striped house cat that lay sprawled across the first step of the porch. He caught himself just in time to keep from stepping on the sleeping animal. The cat raised its bewhiskered face and stared up at him insolently. Another cat, this one coal black, scooted off the porch hurriedly and slipped down into the bushes without a sound. Druid and Valeman climbed the porch steps and moved to the front door. From within, the children's voices rose sharply in laughter.

Allanon knocked firmly and the voices went still. Footsteps came to the other side of the door and stopped.

"Who is it?" a voice asked softly, and the patterned curtains that screened a glass port parted slightly.

The Druid leaned forward, allowing the light from within to fall across his dark countenance.

"I am Allanon," he answered.

There was a long silence, then the sound of a latch drawn back. The door opened and an Elven girl stepped through. She was small, even for an Elf, her body slender and brown with sun. Chestnut hair fell all the way to her waist, shadowing a child's face at once both innocent and knowing. Her eyes flashed briefly to Wil—eyes that were green and deep with life—then settled once more on the Druid.

"Allanon has been gone from the Four Lands for more than fifty years." Her voice was steady, but there was fear in her eyes. "Who are you?"

"I am Allanon," he repeated. He let a moment of silence pass. "Who else could have found you here, Amberle? Who else would know that you are one of the Chosen?"

The Elven girl stared up at him speechlessly. When she tried to speak, the words would not come. Her hands came together tightly; with a visible effort, she composed herself.

"The children will be frightened if they are left alone. They must be put to bed. Wait here, please."

Already there was a scurrying of small feet at the other side of the door and the faint whisper of excited voices.

Amberle turned and disappeared back into the cottage. They could hear her voice, low and soothing, as she ushered the children up wooden stairs to the loft overhead. Allanon moved to a wide-backed bench at the other end of the porch and seated himself. Wil remained where he was, standing just to one side of the door, listening to the sounds of the Elven girl and the children from within, thinking as he did so: she is only a child herself, for goodness' sake!

A moment later she was back, stepping lightly onto the porch, closing the cottage door carefully behind her. She glanced at Wil, who smiled at her awkwardly.

"This young man is Wil Ohmsford." Allanon's voice floated out of the dark. "He studies at Storlock to become a Healer."

"Hello . . ." Wil began, but she was already walking past him to the big man.

"Why have you come here, Druid—if Druid you are?" she demanded, a mixture of anger and uncertainty in her voice. "Has my grandfather sent you?"

Allanon rose. "Can we sit in the gardens while we talk?"

The girl hesitated, then nodded. She led them from the porch back along the stone walkway to the benches. There she seated herself. The Druid sat across from her, Wil a little off to one side. The Valeman recognized that his role in this confrontation was that of a spectator and nothing more.

"Why are you here?" Amberle repeated, her voice a bit less unsettled than a moment earlier.

Allanon folded his robes about him. "To begin with, no one has sent me. I am here of my own choice. I am here to ask you to return with me to Arborlon." He paused. "I will be brief. The Ellcrys is dying, Amberle. The Forbidding begins to crumble; the evil within breaks free—Demons all. Soon they will flood the Westland. Only you can prevent this. You are the last of the Chosen."

"The last . . ." she whispered, but the words caught in her throat.

"They are all dead. The Demons have found and killed them. The Demons search now for you."

Her face froze in horror. "No! What trick is this, Druid? What trick . . ." She did not finish this either, but stopped

as tears formed in her eyes and streaked her child's face.
She brushed them away swiftly. "Are they really all dead?
All of them?"

The Druid nodded. "You must come with me to Arborlon."

She shook her head quickly. "No. I am no longer one of
the Chosen. You know that."

"I know that you would wish it so."

The green eyes flared angrily. "What I would wish is of
no matter in this. I no longer serve; that is all behind me. I
am no longer one of the Chosen."

"The Ellcrys selected you as one of the Chosen," Allanon
replied calmly. "She must decide whether you remain one.
She must decide whether you shall carry her seed in search
of the Bloodfire, so that she may be reborn and the
Forbidding restored. She must decide—not you, not I."

"I will not go back with you," Amberle stated quietly.

"You must."

"I will not. I will never go back. This is my home now;
these are my people. I have made this choice."

The Druid shook his head slowly. "Your home is wherever you make it. Your people are whomever you wish them
to be. But your responsibilities are sometimes given you
without choice, without consent. It is so in this, Elven girl.
You are the last of the Chosen; you are the last real hope of
the Elves. You cannot run away from it; you cannot hide
from it. You most certainly cannot change it."

Amberle rose, paced away a step, and turned. "You do
not understand."

Allanon watched her. "I understand better than you
think."

"If you did, you would not ask me to return. When I left
Arborlon, I knew that I would never go back again. In the
eyes of my mother, my grandfather, and my people, I had
disgraced myself. I did something that could not be
forgiven—I rejected the gift of being a Chosen. Even
should I wish it, and I do not, this cannot be undone. The
Elves are a people whose sense of tradition and honor runs
deep. They can never accept what has happened. If it were
made known to them that they would all perish from the
earth unless I alone chose to save them, still they would

not have me back. I am outcast from them, and that will not change."

The Druid rose and faced her, tall and black as he towered over her small form. His eyes were frightening as they fixed on hers.

"Your words are foolish ones, Elven girl. Your arguments are hollow and you speak them without conviction. They do not become you. I know you to be stronger than what you have shown."

Stung by the reprimand, Amberle went taut.

"What do you know of me, Druid? You know nothing!" She stepped close to him, green eyes filled with anger. "I am a teacher of children. Some of them you saw this night. They come in groups of half a dozen or eight and stay with me one season. They are given into my care by their parents. They are entrusted to me. While they are with me, I give to them my knowledge of living things. I teach them to love and to respect the world into which they were born—the land and sea and sky and all that lives upon and within it. I teach them to understand that world. I teach them to give life back in exchange for the life they were given; I teach them to grow and nurture that life. We begin simply, as with this garden. We finish with the complexity that surrounds human life. There is love in what I do. I am a simple person with a simple gift—a gift I can share with others. A Chosen shares nothing with others. I was never a Chosen—never! That was something I was called upon to be that I did not wish to be nor was suited to be. All that, I have left behind me. I have made this village and its people my life. This is who I am. This is where I belong."

"Perhaps." The Druid's voice was calm and steady and it brushed aside her anger. "Yet will you turn your back on the Elves for no better reason than this? Without you, they will surely perish. They will stand and fight as they did in the old world when the evil first threatened. But this time they lack the magic to make them strong. They will be destroyed."

"These children have been given into my keeping . . ." the girl began hurriedly, but Allanon's hand rose abruptly.

"What do you think will happen once the Elves are destroyed? Do you think the evil ones will be content to stay within the borders of the Westland? What of your children then, Elven girl?"

Amberle stared at him wordlessly for a moment, then dropped slowly back down onto the bench. Tears ran again from her eyes, and she closed them tightly.

"Why was I chosen?" she asked softly, her words barely more than a whisper. "There was no reason for it. I did not seek it—and there were so many others who did." Her hands clenched in her lap. "It was a mockery, Druid—a joke. Do you see that? No woman had been chosen in over five hundred years. Only men. But then I was chosen—an impossible, cruel mistake. A mistake."

The Druid stared at the gardens, his face expressionless once more.

"There was no mistake," he responded, though Wil believed he was speaking almost to himself. The Druid looked back at her, turning quietly. "What frightens you, Amberle? You are afraid, aren't you?"

She did not look up, did not open her eyes. Her head nodded once.

Allanon reseated himself. His voice was gentle now. "Fear is part of life, but it should be faced openly, never hidden. What is it that frightens you?"

There was a long silence. Wil leaned forward quietly on his seat several benches away.

Finally Amberle spoke, her words whispered. "She does."

The Druid frowned. "The Ellcrys?"

But this time Amberle did not answer him. Her hands lifted to her stricken face and wiped away the tears. Her green eyes opened, and she came to her feet once more.

"If I were to agree to travel with you to Arborlon, if I were to agree to face my grandfather and my people, if I were to go before the Ellcrys one final time—if I were to do all this, all that you have asked, what then if she will not give to me her seed?"

Allanon straightened. "Then you may return to Havenstead, and I will trouble you no more."

She paused. "I will think about it."

"There is no time to think about it," Allanon insisted. "You must decide now, tonight. The Demons search for you."

"I will think about it," she repeated. Her eyes settled on Wil. "What is your part in all of this, Healer?" Wil started to reply, but her quick smile stopped him. "Never mind. Somehow I sense that we are alike in this. You know no more than I."

Less, Wil wanted to tell her, but she had already turned away.

"I have no place for you in my home." She spoke to Allanon again. "You may sleep here, if you like. Tomorrow we'll talk about this further."

She started toward the cottage, chestnut hair trailing sail-like down her back.

"Amberle!" the big man called after her.

"Tomorrow," she replied and did not slow.

Then she was gone, disappearing silently through the cottage door, leaving Druid and Valeman staring after her in the dark.

XI

The creature came for Wil through the sluggish haze of his sleep, a formless creation of his dreams that rose up hauntingly out of the depths of his subconscious. It was a thing of terror, a thing that lurked in the dark recesses of his mind where he hid his deepest fears. It came for him with stealth and cunning, slipping easily past the obstacles with which he sought to block it, its motion fluid and quick as it pressed in about him. He could not see it as it came; he never would. It lacked substance or identity; it lacked reason. There was only the overwhelming sense of terror it created by its being. He ran from it, of course—ran swiftly through the landscapes of his imagination, ran and ran until it seemed he must surely have left it behind. But he had not. It was there at once, closing swiftly, surely. He lunged from it in desperation, screaming soundlessly for help, anyone's help. But there was no one. He was alone with this thing and he could not escape it. Yet he must, for if it were to reach him, if it were to touch him, he knew with certainty that he would die. So he ran in fear, blindly, feeling the breath of the thing hot upon his neck . . .

He came awake with a start, lurching upward from beneath the blankets to a sitting position. The night air was cold on his face and body. Sweat ran from beneath his arms, and from within his head he could hear the sound of his heart pounding wildly.

Allanon's dark form crouched next to him, strong hands holding fast to Wil's shoulders. The Druid's voice was a harsh whisper.

"Quick, Valeman. They have found us."

Wil Ohmsford did not need to ask who it was that had found them. It was his dream become reality. He came to his feet with a bound, grabbing up his blanket and hurrying after the Druid, who was already moving toward the little cottage. As if by intuition, Amberle appeared at the edge of the porch, white night dress blowing eerily about her slender form, giving her a ghostly appearance. Allanon went to her at once.

"I told you to dress," he whispered angrily.

She looked unconvinced. "You would not seek to trick me, Druid? This would not be some game you are playing to help me make up my mind to come back with you to Arborlon?"

Allanon's face went black. "Another few minutes of standing around and you will have your answer! Now dress!"

She stood her ground. "Very well. But I cannot leave the children. They must be taken to a place of safety."

"There is not time enough for that," the Druid urged. "Besides, they will be safer here than stumbling about in the dark."

"They will not understand being left like this."

"Remain and they will share your fate!" Allanon's patience was gone. "Wake the oldest. Tell him that you must go away for a time, that you have no choice. Tell him that when it is light out, to take the others to a neighbor's home. Now do as I say—hurry!"

This time she did not argue, but turned and disappeared back inside the cottage. Wil straightened his clothing and rolled his blanket tight. Together, Druid and Valeman saddled the horses and brought them around to the front of the darkened home to wait for the Elven girl. She was with them almost immediately, dressed in boots, slacks, belted tunic and a long blue riding cloak.

Allanon brought the girl and the Valeman close before Artaq, whispering softly to the animal, stroking the satin neck. Then he handed the reins to Wil. "Get on."

Wil did as he was told, scrambling aboard the big black. Artaq shook his head and whickered. Allanon continued to whisper gently, then took Amberle by the waist and swung her up behind the Valeman as if she were no more than a feather's weight. Then he mounted Spitter.

"Quiet, now," he cautioned. "Not a word."

They turned onto the roadway that ran in front of the little cottage and followed it eastward through the sleeping village. Only the sound of their horses' hooves thudding softly on the earthen trail broke the deep stillness. In minutes, the buildings of the village were behind them, and they were at the forest's edge. Before them stretched the tilled fields, the waters of the irrigation ditches sparkling with moonlight as they crisscrossed through neatly planted rows of grain and corn already grown and ripening. In the distance, on either side, the wooded slopes of the valley fell away into the grasslands.

Allanon dismounted wordlessly. He stood motionless for a time, listening to the silence of the night, his dark face anxious. Finally he stepped close to Artaq, motioning for Wil and Amberle to bend close.

"They are all around us." He breathed the words. Wil went cold. The Druid looked at him as if to measure his worth. "Have you ridden in hunt before?" Wil nodded. "Good. You and Amberle will stay with Artaq. If you are pressed, give him his head. He will see you safely through this. We will ride north along the edge of the village to where the valley drops into the grasslands. Once there, we will break through their circle. Do not stop for anything, do you understand? If we become separated, do not turn back. Ride north until you reach the Silver River. If I do not come at once, cross and ride west to Arborlon."

"What will you . . . ?" Wil asked hurriedly.

"Do not concern yourself with what I might be doing," the Druid cut him short. "Just do as you are told."

Wil nodded reluctantly. He did not like the sound of this at all. When Allanon turned away, he glanced back at Amberle.

"Hold tight," he whispered and tried a quick smile. She did not smile back. There was undisguised fear in her eyes.

Allanon remounted. Slowly, cautiously they made their way along the forest's edge, skirting the western borders of the village of Havenstead. Silence hung deep and penetrating across the whole of the valley. Like shadows, they slipped through the darkness of the trees, their eyes searching the night for movement. Ahead of them, the north slope of the valley began to loom up darkly through breaks in the forest.

Then Allanon reined in sharply, motioning for them to be still. He pointed wordlessly toward the fields on their left. Wil and Amberle followed the line of his arm. At first, there was nothing to be seen, only row upon row of stalks shaded dark gray in the moonlight. But a moment later their eyes picked out the quick movement of something vaguely like an animal as it crept from one of the irrigation ditches and disappeared into the stalks of the field.

They waited for a time, frozen against the trees, then started forward once more. They had only gone a short distance when, from out of the woodlands behind them, a deep, searing howl rose. Amberle tightened her grip about Wil's waist and put her head against his back.

"Demon-wolves." Allanon spoke the name quietly. "They've found our trail."

He kicked Spitter's flanks firmly and urged the horse into a slow trot. Artaq snorted anxiously and followed. The howl was picked up by others, and there was the sudden sound of bodies plunging through the trees.

"Ride!" Allanon shouted.

The horses lunged forward, veering sharply left from the cover of the woodlands. At a gallop, they raced along the edge of the fields, following the line of the irrigation ditch toward the break that led to the grasslands. The howling rose all about them, fierce and hungry. Huge, leaping shadows sprang above the stalks of grain and corn in the darkness on their left, crashing wildly toward them. Wil bent low over Artaq's neck and urged the big horse on. Before them, the pass leading from the valley came into view.

Half a dozen bristling, dark forms broke from the woods ahead of them, things that were wolflike, but much larger, and with faces that appeared grotesquely human as they lifted in the moonlight, long teeth snapping. Allanon turned Spitter directly toward them, blue fire sparking on the fingers of one hand as it raised menacingly. An instant later the fire lanced out, burning into the pack, scattering it wildly. Spitter surged through its midst, his call shrill with terror.

Artaq was already past both Druid and Demon-wolves, his sleek body leveled out as he raced for the open plains. Several dark bodies lunged from out of the fields before them, jaws snapping at the horse's legs. Artaq did not slow. He caught one beast with his shoulder and knocked him spinning. The others were quickly left behind. Wil bent lower, pulling Amberle down with him against Artaq's back, loosening slightly his grip on the reins. To their right, more Demon-wolves bolted from the trees, their howls filling the night air. Streaks of blue fire cut through them, and the howls turned to shrieks of pain. Artaq ran on.

Then a single huge Demon-wolf appeared at the forest's edge ahead of them, running parallel to the woodland stream that fed the irrigation ditches. It lunged forward to intercept them, moving with astonishing speed, bounding through the long grass, its movements fluid and soundless. Wil felt something cold and hard tighten in his chest. The beast was narrowing the gap between them too quickly; they would not escape it. He did the only thing he could think to do. He shouted wildly to Artaq and gave him his head. The big black responded. From somewhere deep within, he found new strength. His stride lengthened. The beast was almost upon them, a massive, dark terror that seemed to rise up suddenly out of the night beside them. Wil closed his eyes and yelled one final time. Artaq screamed in response. Gathering himself, the stallion hurdled the woodland stream that lay across his path. Gaining the far bank, he raced from the woodlands and fields of Havenstead into the open plains beyond.

For an instant after, Wil's eyes remained closed, locked tight with fear. He simply clung to Artaq's neck, feeling the comforting movement of the great horse beneath him as they fled into the night. When he finally lifted his head once more and risked a quick look behind him, past Amberle's huddled form, he found that they were alone. Fire and smoke rose out of the darkness from within the valley, and the air was filled with frenzied yowling. There was no sign of the Demon-wolves. There was no sign of Allanon.

Almost without thinking, Wil reined in Artaq sharply and wheeled him about. Allanon had been firm in his instructions. Under no circumstances was he to turn back. Amberle was his first consideration. She had been given into his safekeeping; she was to be protected at all costs. He glanced quickly at her child's face as it rose out of the shadow of his back, green eyes questioning. He knew what he should do. Yet he knew that the Druid was still back there, probably in trouble. How could he simply leave him and go on?

His indecision lasted only a moment. From out of the valley behind them galloped a terrified Spitter, wiry gray body extended in full stride. Bent low over his back, black robes billowing out wildly, his dark figure silhouetted against a horizon colored red with fire, was the Druid. Close behind ran the Demon-wolves, their shaggy forms leaping madly through the tall grass, howling their hatred of the humans who had escaped them.

Wil turned Artaq north instantly and put his heels to him. The big black snorted and leaped ahead. The Valeman did not give him his head this time, but held him carefully in check. Their chase might be a long one, and the black's great strength was not without its limits. Artaq did not fight him, but followed his lead, running easily. Wil bent forward, feeling Amberle's grip about his waist tighten, her face burying itself against his back once more.

A mile further on, Spitter drew abreast, his heaving body streaked with sweat and dirt, his nostrils flaring. Already, he was growing tired. Wil glanced anxiously at Allanon, but the Druid did not look over; his dark gaze was fixed on the land ahead as he urged his horse on with small movements of his hands.

The chase through the grasslands of the Silver River country wore on with grim determination. The maddened howling of the Demon-wolves died quickly, changing to the sound of ragged breathing punctuated by snarls of frustration. For the fleeing horsemen, there was only the muffled whistle of the wind and the steady pounding of their horses' hooves. Through vales that cut between gently sloping hills and over broad, empty rises they ran, hunter and hunted—past groves of fruit trees, past solitary oaks and willows, past small winding streams of water, all through the silence and dark of the plains. Time slipped away without meaning. They had run nearly a dozen miles. Still the distance between them and their pursuers remained unchanged.

At last the Silver River slipped into view, a broad ribbon of moonlit water shining out of the dark through breaks in the low hills that bounded her near bank. Wil saw the river first and shouted. Artaq jumped ahead instantly at the sound of his voice, moving in front of Spitter once more. Belatedly, Wil sought to hold him back, but the big black would not be curbed this time. He was still running easily, smoothly, and he quickly left the tiring Spitter behind.

The gap between Artaq and those who came after widened further. Wil was still trying to rein in the black when he caught sight of the crouching, dark forms that appeared abruptly from out of the night ahead of him— forms that were bent and twisted and covered with bristling gray hair. Demons! Wil felt his stomach tighten. It was a trap. They had been waiting here, waiting in case any managed to escape from the Demon-wolves at Havenstead. Now they were spread out all along the banks of the Silver River, closing as the horsemen approached.

Artaq saw them and veered sharply left toward a small rise. Fifty yards further back, Spitter followed his lead. Further back still, but closing now on the tiring animal, ran the Demon-wolves, howling once more. Artaq gained the summit of the rise at full gallop and broke downward for the Silver River. The Demons in front of him moved quickly to bar his passage. Wil could see them clearly now, catlike beasts with the faces of women, twisted and grotesque. They bounded toward the big black, mewling hideously, muzzles lifting to reveal their long, sharp teeth.

At the last second, Artaq wheeled sharply and circled back toward the rise, leaving the cat things screeching with frustration. In that moment, Spitter topped the rise, stumbled wearily and went down. Allanon tumbled to the ground in a tangle of robes, rolled over several times, and sprang back to his feet. Demon-wolves came at him from all sides, but the blue fire spread from his fingers in a broad, cutting sweep that scattered them like leaves in a strong wind. Artaq wheeled left again, Wil and Amberle clinging desperately to his back to keep from being thrown.

Screaming his hatred of the cat-things that sought to trap him, he ran at them once more, parallel now to the riverbank, moving so swiftly that he was on top of them before they had time to realize what he was about. Several of the beasts reached for him, clawed limbs ripping, but he was past them almost at once, clearing their grasping talons with a mighty leap and racing away into the night. Behind him, an arc of blue fire lanced into the nearest pursuers, burning them to ash. Wil glanced back once and saw Allanon still standing atop the rise, Demon-wolves and cat things alike closing about him from every direction. Too many! Wil heard the words scream through his brain. Fire sprang from the Druid's hands, and he disappeared in a haze of smoke and dark, leaping forms.

Then some sixth sense triggered within the Valeman, warning of new danger. His gaze shifted hurriedly from the battle atop the rise. From out of nowhere appeared half-a-dozen more of the Demon-wolves, racing toward Artaq in great, silent bounds. Wil felt a quick moment of panic. He and Amberle were trapped between the beasts and the river. Ahead of them a dense stretch of wood blocked their passage. Behind them were the Demons they had just fled. There was nowhere for them to go.

Artaq did not hesitate. He veered toward the Silver River. The wolves came after, soundless, fluid, black terror. Wil was sure that this time they would not escape. Allanon was no longer there to help them; they were all alone.

The Silver River drew closer. There were no shallows in view—only an open expanse of water too broad, too deep and too swift for them to cross; if they were to try, Wil realized, they would most certainly be swept away. Yet Artaq did not slow. Whatever the danger might be to them, the big black had made his choice. He was going into the river.

The Demon-wolves sensed it as well. Less than a dozen yards back, they threw themselves forward in a determined effort to catch Wil and the Elven girl. Amberle screamed in warning. Frantically Wil fumbled in his tunic for the leather pouch that contained the Elfstones, not knowing if he could even use them, only knowing that he must do something. He was too late. As his hand closed

about the stones, they reached the edge of the Silver River.
Artaq gathered himself and sprang clear of the riverbank,
Wil and Amberle clinging to his back. In that same instant,
white light burst all about them, freezing their motion as if
they had been captured in a painting. The wolves disappeared. The Silver River vanished. Everything was gone.
They were alone, rising upward in a slow, steady climb into
the light.

XII

Before time became time recorded, he was there. Before men and women, before nations and governments, before all the history of humankind, he was there. Even before the world of faerie split in war between good and evil, fixing unalterably the character of life thereafter, he was there. He was there in that time when the world was a sacred Eden and all living things existed together in peace and harmony. He was young then, a faerie creature himself while the faerie creatures of the earth were just being born. He lived within gardens that had been given over into his keeping, entrusted with the responsibility of seeing that they and all the living things that dwelt within were cared for and preserved, sheltered and renewed. He had no name, for names were not needed. He was who he was, and his life was just beginning.

He had not understood what he was to become. His future was a vague and distant promise whispered in the corridors of his dreams, and he could not have foreseen its reality. He could not have foreseen that his life was not to be finite in the manner of other living things, but was to extend down through centuries of lives celebrated in birth and forgotten in death until his own became cloaked in the trappings of immortality. He could not have foreseen that all who had been born into the world with him and all who were thereafter to be born, whether faerie or human, would fade and be lost while he alone would continue on. Nor would he have wanted to, for he was still young enough to be filled with the conviction that his world would always be as it was then. Had he known that he would live to see it all changed beyond any possible recognition, he would not have wished to survive. He would have wished to die and become one again with the earth that had bred him.

It would have been an irreparable loss, for he was to become the last remnant of that fabled time that was the world in its inception, the last remnant of peace and harmony, of beauty and light that was the Eden of life. It had been decreed in the twilight of the beginning, changing forever the course of his existence, changing forever the purpose of his life. He was to become for a world fallen from grace a small reminder of what had been lost. He was to become as well the promise that all that had once been might one day come again.

In the beginning, he had not comprehended this. There was only shock and dismay at discovering that the world was changing, its beauty fading, its light dying—that all that had been so filled with peace and harmony was to be lost. Soon his gardens were all that remained. Of all who had come into the world with him, not one was left behind. He was alone. He despaired for a time, consumed with grief and self-pity. Then the changes that had altered the land about him began to encroach upon his own small world, threatening to change it as well. He remembered then his responsibilities, and he began the long and difficult struggle to preserve the gardens that were his home, determined that this last bit of the first world would survive, though all else had been lost. The years slipped away, and his struggle wore on. He found himself aging only slightly. He found within himself power that he had not known he possessed. After a time, he began to realize the purpose for his solitary existence—that a new trust had been given him, a trust he must not abandon. With realization came acceptance, and with acceptance came understanding.

For centuries he labored in anonymity, his existence little more than a myth that became part of the folklore of the nations building about him, a fantasy told with wry smiles and smug indulgence. It was not until after the cataclysm men called the Great Wars, the final destruction of the old world and the emergence of the new races, that the myth began to gain acceptance as truth. For it was then that he chose for the first time ever to go out from the gardens into the land beyond. His reasons were carefully drawn. There was magic in the world again, and his was the highest and best magic—the magic of life. The land without was new and fresh once more, and he saw in that rebirth an opportunity to recapture all that he had known when he was young. Through him, the past and future might at last be joined. It would not come easily or quickly; still, it would come. But he could no longer remain secluded and hidden within his gardens. He must go out from them. Contained within his small sanctuary was the seed of all that the world so desperately needed to regain; it was the trust he had first been given. He saw that it was not enough that it be preserved. He saw that it must be built upon—more, that it must be made visible and accessible. He must see that this was done.

Thus he went out from the gardens that had been his home for so many centuries, traveling into the country that lay about it—a country of sweet grasslands and gently rolling hills, of shaded woodland glens and quiet ponds, all bound together by a river that was the lifestream of the land. He would not travel far from the gardens, however, for they were his first concern and their need for his protection demanded that he stay close. Still, it did not prove necessary to journey farther than he did. The country he found pleased him. He planted the seed of the first world within its heart, marking it as his own, giving to it a special radiance that made it easily recognizable, giving to its inhabitants and to its travelers, whomsoever should require it, his blessing and protection from harm. In time, the new races came to understand what he had done; they spoke of him and of his land with awe and with respect. They began to tell his story throughout the Four Lands. The story grew with each new telling until at last they had made of him a legend.

They named him after the country he had made his own. They called him the King of the Silver River.

He came to Wil and Amberle in the guise of an old man, appearing from out of the light, wizened and bent with

age, his robes hanging about his thin frame as if he were
made of brittle sticks. His hair fell about his shoulders in
thick, white locks. His ancient face was wrinkled and
brown with sun; his deep blue eyes were the color of sea-
water. He smiled in greeting, and Wil and Amberle smiled
in response, sensing that there was no harm in this man.
They still clung tightly to Artaq's broad back, the black
extended in full stride, unmoving in the light that held
them all frozen. Neither Valeman nor Elven girl understood what had happened, yet there was no fear in them,
only a deep, comforting drowsiness that immobilized
them with the strength of iron chains.

The old man stopped before them, blurred and indis-
tinct in the haze of the light. His hand touched Artaq's
sleek face and the black nickered softly. The old man
looked at Amberle then, and there were tears in his
eyes.

"Child, that you were mine," he whispered. He stepped
closer, reaching up to take her hand in his own. "No harm
shall come to you in this land. Be at peace. We are joined
in purpose and shall be one with the earth."

Wil struggled to speak and could not. The old man
stepped back again, and one hand raised in farewell.

"Rest, now. Sleep." He began to fade, slipping back into
the light. "Sleep, children of life."

Wil's eyes grew heavy. It was a pleasant, welcome sensation and he did not fight it. He was conscious of Amberle's small form slumped heavily against his own, her
hands locked loosely about his waist. The light seemed to
draw back from them, fading into darkness. His eyes
closed, and he drifted into slumber.

He began to dream. He was standing in the midst of a
garden filled with incredible beauty and serenity, dazzling
in its color and fragrance, so wondrous that all else that he
had known in life or had imagined possible paled in
comparison. There were streams shimmering silver as
they flowed from out of springs hidden within the earth
and spilled into quiet ponds. There were trees canopied
overhead, filtering sunlight that speckled with touches of
golden warmth. There were soft, sweet grasses that
carpeted the lanes and walkways in emerald silk. All
manner of birds flew, fish swam, and animals walked

through these gardens—passed in harmony and contentment and in peace. The Valeman was filled with a sense of deep, abiding tranquillity, fulfillment, and a happiness so intense that he cried.

Yet when he turned to share what he was feeling with Amberle, he found her gone.

XIII

When Wil Ohmsford awoke once more, it was dawn. He lay in a grassy vale beneath the sheltering limbs of twin maples, the morning sun filtering down through masses of broad green leaves in long streamers of brightness that made him blink. Close by, there was the faint sound of water lapping against a shore. For an instant, he believed himself still within the wondrous gardens of his dream. So real had they seemed to him that, almost without thinking about it he pushed himself up on one elbow and looked about hurriedly for them. But the gardens were gone.

Amberle lay next to him, still sleeping. He hesitated, then reached over and shook her shoulder gently. She stirred restlessly and her eyes opened. She looked at him in surprise.

"How are you?" he asked.

"I'm fine." She brushed the sleep from her eyes. "Where are we?"

Wil shook his head. "I don't know."

The Elven girl sat up slowly and looked about the small vale.

"Where is Allanon?"

"I don't know that either." Wil stretched his legs tentatively, surprised to find them loose and uncramped. "He's gone. They're all gone—Allanon, those creatures . . ." He paused, hearing movement in the brush at the far end of the hollow. A familiar black face poked through the leaves, nickering softly. Wil smiled. "Well, at least we still have Artaq with us."

The black cropped lazily at the grass, shook himself clear of the brush, and trotted over to nuzzle Wil. Wil stroked

120

the sleek head for a moment, rubbing at the horse's ears. Amberle watched quietly.

"Did you see the old man?" Wil asked her.

She nodded solemnly. "That old man was the King of the Silver River."

Wil looked at her. "I thought as much. My grandfather saw him once, years ago. I don't think I was ever really sure whether he was real or not until now, though. Funny." Artaq moved off several paces and began feeding. Wil shook his head. "He saved our lives back there. The Demon-wolves almost had us . . ." He caught the look that crept into the Elven girl's eyes and stopped. "Anyway, I guess we're safe now."

"It was like a dream, wasn't it?" she said softly. "We were floating in the light, riding Artaq with nothing beneath us but the light. Then he came up to us, walking, came out of nowhere and said something . . ." She trailed off, as if the memory of it confused her. "Did you see it?"

The Valeman nodded.

"And then he disappeared," she continued, speaking more to herself than to him, as if trying to recall all that had happened. "He disappeared and the light disappeared and . . . and then . . ." She looked at him curiously.

"The gardens?" he suggested. "Did you see the gardens?"

"No." She hesitated. "No, there were no gardens, just a darkness and a . . . a sensation I can't describe. I . . . a sort of reaching, I think." She looked at him for help, but he just stared back at her in confusion. "You were standing there with me," she went on. "You were standing there, but you couldn't see me. I called to you, but you didn't seem to hear me. It was so strange."

Wil hunched forward. "I remember the old man and the light, just as you've described them. I remember that. When they disappeared, I remember falling asleep . . . or at least, I think I fell asleep. Anyway, you were there with me on Artaq. I could feel your arms about my waist. The next thing I knew, I was standing in these gardens—I'd never seen anything like them; they were so peaceful and beautiful and quiet. But when I looked around for you, you weren't there. You were gone."

They looked at each other wordlessly for a moment.

"I suppose we had better worry about where we are now," Wil said finally.

He climbed to his feet and looked about again. Belatedly, he thought about helping Amberle up, but by then she was already standing next to him, brushing leaves and grass from her hair. He hesitated a moment, then led the way through the brush surrounding them toward the sound of the water.

Moments later, they stood at the edge of a lake so vast that its shoreline circled in either direction to the horizon and disappeared. Waves crested in sudden flashes of silver foam, the waters deep and clear blue in the morning sun. Groves of trees bordered its grass-covered banks, willow and elm and ash, leaves rippling softly in a light southerly wind that carried with it the scent of honeysuckle and azaleas. In the cloudless blue sky that canopied above the lake arced a brilliant, shimmering band of colors that seemed to rise from one end of the horizon and disappear into the other.

Wil glanced upward to fix the sun's location, then turned to Amberle, shaking his head in disbelief.

"Do you know where we are? We're somewhere on the north shore of the Rainbow Lake. The old man carried us all the way down the Silver River and across the lake to wherever it is we are now. We're miles from where we started."

The Elven girl nodded almost absently. "I think you're right."

"I know I'm right." Wil paced away excitedly and stopped at the water's edge. "I just don't know how he managed it."

Amberle sat down on the grass, gazing out over the lake.

"The legend says he helps those who need it when they travel in his land—that he keeps them safe from harm." She paused, her mind clearly elsewhere. "He said something to me . . . I wish I could remember . . ."

Wil was not listening. "We should get moving. Arborlon's a long way off. But if we travel in a northwest direction, we should be able to find the Mermidon, then follow it all the way to the Westland. That's a lot of open country, but we won't be so easy to find now. There's no trail to follow this time."

He missed entirely the look of annoyance that crossed Amberle's face, his mind preoccupied with the journey ahead.

"It should only take us about four days—maybe five, since we only have one horse between us. If we get lucky, we might find another one somewhere along the way, but I suppose that's asking a bit much. It would help if we had some weapons, too; we don't even have a hunting bow. That means eating fruit and wild vegetables, I guess. Of course we might . . ."

He trailed off, suddenly aware that Amberle was shaking her head in disapproval. The Elven girl crossed her legs before her and sat back.

"What's the matter?" he asked, dropping down next to her.

"You are, for one thing."

"What do you mean, I am?"

"You seem to have fixed in your mind everything that happens from here on. Don't you think you ought to hear my thoughts on the matter?"

Wil stared at her, somewhat taken aback. "Well, sure, I . . ."

"I haven't noticed you asking for them," she continued, ignoring him. "Do you not think it necessary to ask?"

The Valeman reddened. "I'm sorry. I was just . . ."

"You were just making decisions that you have no right to make." She paused and regarded him coolly. "I don't even know what you're doing here. The only reason I've come this far with you is that I really didn't have any choice in the matter. It's time to find out a few things. Why did Allanon bring you along in the first place, Wil Ohmsford? Who are you?"

Wil told her, starting with the story of Shea Ohmsford and the quest for the Sword of Shannara and ending with Allanon's visit to Storlock to seek his aid in tracking the Bloodfire. He told her everything, deciding that it was pointless to hold anything back, sensing that if he were not completely honest with this girl, she would have nothing further to do with him.

When he finished, Amberle stared at him wordlessly for a moment, then shook her head slowly.

"I don't know whether to believe you or not. I should, I

suppose. I really don't have any reason not to. It's just that so much has happened that I'm not really very certain of anything right now." She hesitated. "I've heard stories of the Elfstones. They were an old magic, said to have all been lost long before the Great Wars. Yet you claim Allanon gave three to your grandfather and he in turn gave them to you. If that much of what you've told me were true . . ." She trailed off, her eyes fixed on his. "Would you show them to me?" she asked.

The Valeman hesitated, then reached into his tunic. He realized that she was testing him, but then he guessed that she had a right to do that. After all, she had only his word for everything he had told her, and she was being asked to place her safety in his hands. He pulled out the worn leather pouch, loosened the drawstrings and dropped the stones in his hand. Perfectly formed, their color a deep, brilliant blue, they flashed sharply in the morning sunlight.

Amberle bent close, regarding them solemnly. Then she looked back at Wil again.

"How do you know these are Elfstones?"

"I have my grandfather's word on it. And Allanon's."

She did not look impressed. "Do you know how to use them?"

He shook his head. "I've never tried."

"Then you don't really know whether they're any good to you or not, do you?" She laughed softly. "You won't know until you need them. That's not very comforting, is it?"

"No, not very," he agreed.

"Yet here you are anyway."

He shrugged. "It seemed like the right thing to do." He dropped the Elfstones back in the pouch and tucked the pouch into his tunic. "I guess I'll have to wait and see how it works out to know whether or not I was mistaken."

She studied him carefully for a moment, saying nothing. He waited.

"We have much in common, Wil Ohmsford," she said finally. She crossed her arms about her knees, drawing them up. "Well, you've told me who you are—I think you're entitled to the same courtesy. My family name is Elessedil. Eventine Elessedil is my grandfather. In a sense, we're both involved in this because of who our grand-fathers are."

Wil nodded. "That's true, I suppose."

The wind caught her chestnut hair and blew it across her face like a veil. She brushed the strands away and looked out across the lake again.

"You know that I do not want to go back to Arborlon," she said.

"I know."

"But that's where you think I ought to go, isn't it?"

He eased back on his elbows, watching the rainbow's arc above him.

"That's where I think you have to go," he replied. "Obviously you cannot go back to Havenstead; the De-mons will be looking for you there. Pretty soon, they'll be looking for you here as well. You have to keep moving. If Allanon escaped . . ." He paused, distracted by the impli-cations of that statement. "If Allanon escaped, he will expect us to go on to Arborlon, and that's where we'll find him." He looked over at her. "If you've got any better ideas, I'm ready to listen."

For a long time, she didn't say anything. She just kept staring out over the Rainbow Lake, watching the graceful movement of the water, letting the wind blow freely across her face. When she finally spoke again, it was just a whisper.

"I'm afraid."

Then she looked at him, seemed about to say something more, and thought better of it. She smiled—the first genuine smile he had seen from her.

"Well, we're a pair of fools, aren't we? You with your Elfstones that may or may not be what you think and me about to do the one thing I swore I'd never do." She rose, walked away a few paces, then turned as he came to his feet behind her. "I want you to know this. I think that going to Arborlon is pointless. I think that Allanon is wrong about me. Neither the Ellcrys nor the Elven people will accept me back again because, despite what the Druid may think, I am no longer one of the Chosen."

She paused. "Still, doing anything else wouldn't make much sense, would it?"

"Not to me, it wouldn't," he agreed.

She nodded. "Then I guess it's settled." Her child's face regarded him soberly. "I just hope this isn't a mistake."

Wil sighed. "If it is, we'll probably know soon enough." He forced a thin smile. "Let's collect Artaq and find out."

They spent the remainder of that day and all of the next traveling north and west through the grasslands of Callahorn. The weather was warm, dry, and pleasant, and the time passed quickly. Dark thunderclouds appeared to the north around noon of the first day, hanging ominously over the craggy expanse of the Dragon's Teeth, but by sunset they had blown east into the Rabb and were gone. The Valeman and the Elven girl alternated between riding Artaq and walking, doubling up when they rode, then both traveling afoot for a time in order to rest the big black. Artaq looked fresh even after several hours of being ridden, but Wil was not about to risk tiring the horse. They saw nothing of the Demons that they had lost at the Silver River, but the creatures were certainly still out there and looking for them. If they were unlucky enough to be found again, Wil wanted Artaq ready to run.

Bereft of any weapons at all, save for a small hunting knife Wil carried tucked in his belt, they were forced to eat fruits and vegetables that grew wild on the grasslands. Wil found the fare ample, if somewhat less than satisfying, but Amberle seemed not to mind at all. If anything, she seemed quite pleased with their meals. She showed the Valeman a talent for discovering food where he would not have guessed food existed, pulling from the most unlikely places edible plants and roots that she readily identified and described in quite thorough detail. Wil listened attentively and asked questions from time to time, finding this the one topic of conversation she seemed willing to pursue. Initially, he had tried to draw her out on other subjects, but had met with little success. So they talked of plants and roots and the rest of the time traveled in silence.

They slept that first night in a grove of cottonwood near a small spring that provided them with clean drinking water. By midafternoon of the second day, they reached the Mermidon and began following it north. Up until that point, they had seen no one, but thereafter passed half a dozen travelers, some afoot, some on horseback, one

riding in a small wooden cart drawn by oxen. All exchanged with them a word of friendship and a wave before
continuing on their way.

At sunset they made camp along the Mermidon, west
and south of the city of Tyrsis, finding shelter in a grove of
white pine and willow. Using a willow branch, a length of
twine, and a hook from his clothing, Wil fashioned a crude
fishing pole. Within half-an-hour he had landed a pair of
striped bass. He was cleaning the fish by the river's edge
when a caravan of wagons swung into view from the south
and wound its way down toward the far bank. Gaily
painted houses on wheels, with peaked roofs of cedar
shingles, hand-carved wooden doors, and windows
studded with brass, the wagons flashed brightly in the
setting sun. Teams of finely groomed horses pulled the
wagons, their traces laced with bits of silver. Several riders
kept pace, their graceful forms cloaked in silk and trailing
streamers of color from their throats and from the bridles of
their mounts. In spite of himself, Wil stopped what he was
doing and watched the strange procession approach the
river, wagon axles groaning, leather harness creaking,
voices calling and whistling encouragement. Almost directly across from where the Valeman sat, the caravan swung
into a loose circle and lurched to a halt. Men, women, and
children climbed from the wagons and began unhitching
the teams and setting up camp.

Amberle appeared from the trees behind Wil and joined
him. The Valeman glanced over at her briefly, then followed her gaze back across the river to the gathering on the
far bank.

"Rovers," he announced thoughtfully.

She nodded. "I've seen them before. The Elves don't
have much use for them."

"No one has." He went back to cleaning the fish.
"They'll steal anything that isn't nailed down—or if it is,
find a way to talk you out of it. They have their own rules
and they don't pay any attention to anyone else's."

Amberle touched his arm, and he looked up to watch a
tall man, dressed all in black save for a cloak and sash of
forest green, accompany two older women in long, multicolored skirts and blouses as they carried water buckets
down to the water's edge. As the women stooped to fill the

buckets, the tall man removed a wide-brimmed hat and, with a flourish, bowed low to Wil and Amberle, his darkly tanned face flashing a broad smile through a shading of black beard. Wil raised one arm and waved back cordially.

"I'm just as glad that they're on that side of the river," he muttered to Amberle as they rose to return to their camp.

They enjoyed a savory meal of fish, fruit, vegetables and spring water, then settled back next to the campfire and gazed out through breaks in the forest to the glimmer of the Rover fires as they blazed up from out of the darkness across the river. They were quiet for a time, lost in their own thoughts. Then Wil looked over at the Elven girl.

"How is it that you know so much about growing things—the gardens at your cottage in Havenstead, the roots and plants you found for us during our journey? Did someone teach you all that?"

A look of surprise crossed her face. "For being part Elf, you certainly don't know very much about us, do you?"

Wil shrugged. "Not really. The Elven blood is all on my father's side, and he died when I was very young. I don't think that my grandfather has ever gone into the Westland—at least he never speaks about it. In any case, I guess I've just never thought that much about being part Elf."

"It is something that you should have thought about," she said quietly. Her green eyes found his. "We first need to understand who we were before we can understand who we are."

The words were spoken not as a criticism of the Valeman, but almost in self-reproach. Wil found himself suddenly wishing that he knew more about this girl, that he could find a way to persuade her to confide even a small piece of herself in him, rather than keeping it all so tightly locked away.

"Maybe you could help me gain at least a part of that understanding," he offered after a moment's thought.

There was instant doubt in her eyes, almost as if she believed that he was playing some game with her. She hesitated a long time before answering him.

"Very well, maybe I can." She squared herself around so that she was seated facing him. "You must first understand that the Elven people believe that preservation of the land and all that lives and grows upon it, plant and animal alike, is a moral responsibility. They have always held this belief foremost in their conduct as creatures of the earth. In the old world, they devoted the whole of their lives to caring for the woodlands and forests in which they lived, cultivating its various forms of vegetation, sheltering the animals that it harbored. Of course, they had little else to concern them in those days, for they were an isolated and reclusive people. All that has changed now, but they still maintain a belief in their moral responsibility for their world. Every Elf is expected to spend a portion of his life giving back to the land something of what he has taken out of it. By that I mean that every Elf is expected to devote a part of his life to working with the land—to repairing damage it may have suffered through misuse or neglect, to caring for its animals and other wildlife, to caring for its trees and smaller plants where the need to do so is found."

"Is that a part of what you were doing in Havenstead?"

She nodded. "In a way. The Chosen are exempt from this service. When I ceased to be one of the Chosen and no longer felt welcome in my homeland, I decided that I should do service to the land. Most of the work done by the Elves is carried out in the Westland because that is the Elven homeland. But we believe that the care of the land is not simply an Elven responsibility, but the responsibility of all men. To some extent the Dwarves share our concern, but the other races have never been much persuaded. So some of the Elves go out from the Westland to other communities, trying to teach the people living there something of their responsibility for the care and preservation of their land. This is what I was trying to do at Havenstead."

"And you were working with the children of the village," Wil surmised.

"Primarily the children, for the children are more receptive to what I teach and have the time to learn. I was taught of the earth when I was a child; it is the Elven way. I was more adept than most at translating the lesson into use—one of the reasons, I guess, that I was selected to be a Chosen. The skills of the Chosen in the preservation and care of the earth and its life forms are of the highest order; the Ellcrys has some sense of this. She has this ability . . ."

Amberle seemed to catch herself in the middle of a thought she did not wish to express. She stopped abruptly, shrugging.

"Anyway, I was very good at teaching the children of Havenstead, and the people of the village were very kind to me. Havenstead was my home, and I did not want to leave."

She shifted her gaze abruptly to the fire between them. Wil said nothing, leaning forward to add several pieces of stray wood to the flames. After a moment's silence, Amberle looked up at him again.

"Well, now you know something of the Elven feeling for the land. It's a part of your heritage, so you should try to understand it."

"I think I do understand it," the Valeman replied, reflecting. "At least in part. I have not been trained in the Elven manner, but I have been trained by the Stors as a Healer. Their concern for human life is much the same as the Elven concern for the land. A Healer must do whatever is in his power to do to preserve the lives and health of the men, women, and children whom he treats. This is the commitment I made when I chose to become a Healer."

The Elven girl looked at him curiously. "Somehow that makes it seem even stranger that you were persuaded by Allanon to look after me. You are a Healer, dedicated to preserving life. What will you do if you are placed in a situation where, in order to protect me, you must harm others, perhaps even cause them to die?"

Wil stared at her wordlessly. He had never even considered the possibility that such a thing might happen. Thinking on it now, he experienced an unpleasant feeling of doubt.

"I don't know what I'll do," he admitted uncomfortably.

They were silent for a moment, staring across the fire at each other, unable to break through the awkwardness of the moment. Then Amberle rose abruptly, came over to the Valeman, and sat next to him, impulsively clasping his hand in her own. Her winsome face looked out at him through the shadow of her hair.

"That wasn't a fair question to put to you, Wil Ohmsford. I'm sorry I asked it. You came on this journey because you believed that you might help me. It is wrong of me to doubt that you would do so."

"It was a fair question," Wil replied firmly. "I just don't have an answer to it."

"Nor should you," she insisted. "I, of all people, should know that some decisions cannot be made in advance of the time that will demand them. We cannot always anticipate the way in which things will happen and therefore cannot anticipate what we will do. We must accept that. Again, I am sorry. You might as well ask me what decision I will make if the Ellcrys tells me that I am still one of the Chosen."

Wil smiled faintly. "Be careful. I am tempted to ask exactly that."

She released his hand instantly and rose. "Do not. You would not like the answer I would give you." She shook her head sadly. "You think my choice in this is a simple one, one that you could make easily. You are wrong."

She walked back to the other side of the fire and reached down for her travel cloak, shaking it out upon the ground. As she prepared to roll herself in it to sleep, she turned back to him one final time.

"Believe me, Valeman, should our decisions become necessary, yours will be the easier of the two."

She lowered her head to the folds of the cloak and was asleep in moments. Wil Ohmsford stared thoughtfully into the fire. Although he could not begin to explain why, he found that he believed her.

XIV

When they awoke the following morning, Artaq was missing. At first they thought that he might have wandered off during the night, but a quick check of the woods in which they were camped and the open grasslands beyond failed to turn up any sign of the big black. It was at this point that an unpleasant suspicion began to form in the back of Wil's mind. Hurriedly, he examined the area in which Artaq had been left to graze, moving from there along the perimeter of their campsite, dropping to his knees from time to time as he went to smell the earth or touch it with his fingers. Amberle watched him curiously. After a few minutes of this, the Valeman seemed to find something. Eyes still fixed on the ground before him, he began walking southward through the small stand of timber and into the grasslands—one hundred feet, two. He began to angle toward the river. Wordlessly, the Elven girl trailed after. Moments later, they both stood at the edge of the Mermidon, staring out across a series of shallows several hundred yards downstream from their camp.

"Rovers." Wil spat the word out like a bitter pill. "They crossed here during the night and stole him."

Amberle looked surprised. "Are you sure?"

"I'm sure." Wil nodded. "I found their tracks. Besides, no one else could have managed it. Artaq would have called out if it were anyone but an expert horse handler, and the Rovers are the best. Look, they're already gone."

He pointed across the river to the spot on the empty grasslands the caravan had occupied the previous night. They stared at it silently for a moment.

"What do we do now?" Amberle asked finally.

Wil was so mad he could barely speak. "First we go back

and pack our things. Then we cross the river and have a look at their campsite."

They returned to their own camp, hastily put together the few items they had carried with them, and returned to the river. They crossed at the shallows without difficulty. Minutes later they stood at the now-deserted Rover camp. Once more Wil began studying the ground, moving more quickly this time as he paced the area from end to end. Finally he walked back to where Amberle stood waiting.

"My Uncle Flick taught me to read signs when I hunted the woods about my home in Shady Vale," he informed her conversationally, his mood considerably improved. "We used to fish and trap the Duln Forests for weeks at a time when I was little. Always thought I might again have need of what I learned someday."

She nodded impatiently. "What did you find?"

"They've gone west, probably just before daybreak."

"Is that all? Isn't there some indication of whether or not Artaq is with them?"

"Oh, he's with them, all right. Back at the shallows, there are signs of a horse going into the river from the other side and coming out again over here. One horse, several men. No mistake, they've got him. But we're going to get him back again."

She looked at him doubtfully. "You mean you're going after them?"

"Of course I'm going after them!" He was getting angry all over again. "We're both going after them."

"Just you and me, Valeman?" She shook her head. "On foot?"

"We can catch up to them by nightfall. Those wagons are slow."

"That assumes that we can find them, doesn't it?"

"There's no trick to that. At one time, I could track a deer through wilderness timber where there hadn't been rain for weeks. I think I can manage to track an entire caravan of wagons across open grasslands."

"I don't like the sound of this at all," she announced quietly. "Even if we do find them and they do have Artaq, what are we supposed to do about it?"

"We'll worry about that when we catch up to them," he replied evenly.

The Elven girl did not back away. "I think that we should worry about it right now. That's an entire camp of armed men you're talking about chasing after. I don't like what's happened any better than you do, but that's hardly sufficient excuse for failing to exercise sound judgment."

With an effort, Wil held his temper. "I am not about to lose that horse. In the first place, if it weren't for Artaq, the Demons would have had us, back at Havenstead. He deserves a better fate than spending the rest of his years in the service of those thieves. In the second place, he is the only horse we had and the only horse we are likely to get. Without him, we will be forced to walk the rest of the way to Arborlon. That will take more than a week, and most of that week will be spent crossing these open grasslands. That increases rather substantially the chances of our being discovered by those things still searching for us. And I don't like the sound of that. We need Artaq."

"You seem to have made up your mind on this," she said expressionlessly.

He nodded. "I have. Besides, the Rovers are traveling toward the Westland anyway; at least we'll be headed in the right direction."

For a moment she didn't say anything; she merely looked at him. Then finally she nodded.

"All right, we'll go after them. I want Artaq back too. But let's think this through a bit further before we catch up to them. We had better have some sort of plan worked out by then, Valeman."

He grinned disarmingly. "We will."

They walked all day through the open grasslands, following the trail of the Rover caravan. It was hot and dry, and the sun beat down on them from out of a cloudless blue sky. They found little shade along the way to relieve them from the heat. What water they carried was soon gone, and they did not run across even a small stream to replenish their supply. By late afternoon, all they could taste in their mouths was the dust of the plains and their thirst. Leg muscles ached and their feet blistered. They spoke to each other only infrequently, conserving their strength, concentrating on putting one foot in front of the other, watching the sun sink slowly into the horizon ahead of them until all that remained of the day was a dull orange glow above the sweep of the land.

A short time later, it began to darken, the day to disappear into dusk, the dusk into night. Still they walked on, no longer able to find the marks of the wagon wheels in the plains grass, relying now on their sense of direction to keep them moving in a straight line westward. Moon and stars brightened in the night sky, casting down upon the open grasslands their faint light to guide the Valeman and the Elven girl as they moved steadily forward. Dirt and sweat cooled and dried on their bodies, and they felt their clothing stiffen uncomfortably. Neither suggested stopping to the other. Stopping meant admitting they would not catch up to the caravan that night, that they would be forced to go on like this for another day. They kept walking, silent, determined, the girl as much so as the man now, a fact that surprised him and caused him to feel genuine admiration for her spirit.

Then they saw light in the distance ahead, a fire burning through the dark like a beacon, and they realized that they had found the Rovers. Wordlessly, they trudged to within shouting distance of the firelight, watching the peaked roofs of the wagon homes gradually take shape in the night until finally the entire caravan stood revealed, wound into a loose circle as it had been on the banks of the Mermidon.

Wil took hold of Amberle's arm and gently pulled her down into a crouch.

"We're going in," he whispered, his eyes never leaving the Rover camp.

She looked at him in disbelief. "That's your plan?"

"I know something of these people. Just go along with whatever I say, and we'll be fine."

Without waiting for her response, he stood up and began walking toward the caravan. The Elven girl stared after him for a moment, then rose to her feet and followed after. As they drew closer to the circled wagons, the faces of the men, women, and children passing within the firelight grew visible. Laughter and bits of conversation became audible and distinct. The Rovers had just finished their evening meal and were visiting casually with one another. From somewhere within the camp came the soft thrum of a stringed instrument.

Twenty yards from the perimeter of the circle, Wil called out. It surprised Amberle so that she jumped. Within the camp, everyone instantly stopped what was being done, and all heads turned in their direction. There was a sudden scrambling of feet as a handful of men appeared at the gap between the wagons nearest the approaching pair. Wordlessly, the men peered out into the night, the firelight behind them now, leaving them shadowed and faceless. Wil did not slow. He kept walking directly toward them, Amberle a step or two behind. The entire caravan had gone suddenly still.

"Good evening," Wil said cheerfully as he reached the gathering of Rovers who blocked their passage into the camp.

The men said nothing. In the glimmer of the firelight, the Valeman caught a glimpse of metal blades.

"We saw your fire and we thought you might give us something to drink," he continued, still smiling. "We've been walking since daybreak without water and we're about worn out."

Someone pushed his way through the knot of silent men, a tall man in a cloak of forest green and a broad-brimmed hat—the man they had seen at the river.

"Ah, our young travelers from last evening," he announced quietly and not in greeting.

"Hello again," Wil responded pleasantly. "I'm afraid we've had some very bad luck. We lost our horse during the night—he must have wandered off while we were sleeping. We've been walking all day without water and we could use something cool to drink."

"Indeed." The big man smiled without warmth. He was tall, well over six feet, lean and rawboned, his dark face shaded with a black beard and mustache that gave his smile an almost menacing appearance. Eyes that looked blacker than the night about them peered out from beneath a lined and weathered brow that sloped into a nose hooked slightly at the bridge. The hand that came up to beckon to the men behind him was ringed on each finger.

"Have water brought," he ordered, his eyes still on the Valeman. His expression did not change. "Who are you, young friend, and what is your destination?"

"My name is Wil Ohmsford," the Valeman replied. "This is my sister, Amberle. We're on our way to Arborlon."

"Arborlon." The tall man repeated the name thoughtfully. "Well, you're Elves, of course—in part, at least. Any fool can see that. But now, you say that you lost your horse. Would you not have been wiser to stay along the Mermidon in your travels, rather than coming straight west as you did?"

Wil smiled some more. "Oh, yes, we thought about that; but you see, it's important that we reach Arborlon as soon as possible, and walking would take much too long. Of course, we saw you camped across the river from us last night and we saw, too, that you seemed to have a number of very fine horses. We thought that if we could manage to catch up with you by nightfall, we might trade something of value for one of your horses."

"Something of value?" The big man shrugged. "Possibly. We would have to see what it is that you propose to trade, of course."

Wil nodded. "Of course."

An old woman appeared, carrying a pitcher of water and a single wooden cup. She handed these to Wil, who accepted them wordlessly. With the Rovers looking on, he poured some of the water into the cup. He did not offer it to Amberle, who looked at him in surprise as he ignored her completely and drank the water down. Then he poured a second cup and drank it as well. When he was finished, he handed her the empty cup and pitcher without comment.

"You know something of the Way," the tall man remarked, interest showing in his dark eyes. "You know also that we're Rovers, then."

"I have treated Rovers before," Wil said. "I'm a Healer."

A quick murmur went through the assemblage, which had grown considerably since the conversation had begun and now consisted of almost the entire camp, some thirty men, women, and children, all dressed colorfully in bright silks with woven ribbons and scarves.

"A Healer? This is unexpected." The tall man stepped forward, removed his hat with a flourish, and bowed low. Straightening once more, he extended his hand in greeting. "My name is Cephelo. I am Leader of this Family."

Wil accepted the hand and shook it firmly. Cephelo smiled.

"Well, you mustn't stand out here while the night grows cold about you. Come with me. Your sister is welcome, too. You both look as if you could do with a bath and something to eat."

He led the way through the crowd of Rovers into the circle of the wagons. An immense fire burned at the center of the camp, a tripod and iron kettle suspended above it. The glow of the fire reflected off the gaily painted wagons, mixing the rainbow of colors with shadows of the night. Wooden benches sat beneath the wagons, intricately carved and polished, their broad seats cushioned by feather pillows. Brass-handled windows stood open to the light, laced with curtains and strings of beads. On a long table to one side lay an assortment of wicked-looking pikes, swords, and knives, all carefully arranged. Two small boys were diligently oiling the metal blades.

They reached the cooking fire and Cephelo turned abruptly.

"Well now, which shall it be first—a meal or a bath?"

Wil did not even glance at Amberle. "A bath, I think— my sister, as well, if you can spare the water."

"We can spare it." Cephelo nodded, then turned. "Eretria!"

There was a whisper of silk, and Wil found himself face to face with the most stunning girl he had ever seen. She was small and delicate, in the manner of Amberle, but without the childlike innocence that marked the Elven girl. Thick, black hair tumbled in ringlets to her shoulders, framing eyes that were dark and secretive. Her face was beautiful, her features perfectly formed and immediately unforgettable. She was wearing high leather boots, dressed in pants and tunic of scarlet silk that failed to hide anything of the woman beneath. Bands of silver flashed on her wrists and neck.

Wil looked at her in astonishment and could not look away.

"My daughter." Cephelo sounded bored. He motioned toward Amberle. "Take the Elven girl and let her bathe herself."

Eretria smiled wickedly. "It would be much more interesting to bathe him," she offered, nodding toward Wil.

"Just do as you're told," her father ordered sharply.

Eretria kept her eyes on the Valeman. "Come along, girl," she invited. She turned and was gone. Amberle followed after, looking none too happy.

Cephelo led Wil to the far side of the encampment where a series of blankets hung across a small area between two of the wagons. Within stood a tub of water. Stepping behind the blankets, Wil stripped off his clothing and laid it neatly on the ground beside him. He was well aware that the Rover was watching everything he removed, looking to see if he possessed anything of value, and he was careful to see to it that the pouch containing the Elfstones did not fall loose from its pocket within his tunic. He began to pour water over himself with a ladle, washing away the dirt and sweat of the day's travel.

"It is not often that we encounter a Healer who will treat Rovers," Cephelo said after a moment. "We usually must care for our own."

"I was trained by the Stors," Wil answered him. "Their help is given freely."

"The Stors?" Cephelo was surprised all over again. "But the Stors are all Gnomes."

The Valeman nodded. "I was an exception."

"You appear an exception in many ways," the tall man declared. He seated himself on a nearby bench and watched the Valeman towel dry and begin rinsing his clothes. "We have work for you that will enable you to pay for your food and rest, Healer. There are some among us who have need of your skills."

"I will be happy to do what I can," Wil replied.

"Good." The other man nodded in satisfaction. "I'll find you some dry clothing to use."

He rose and walked away. Instantly Wil slipped the Elfstones from his tunic pocket into his boot, then quickly resumed washing out his clothing. Cephelo was back almost at once, carrying Rover silks for Wil to wear. The Valeman accepted the clothes and dressed himself. Despite the uncomfortable knot at the toe of his right boot, he pulled it on firmly, then the left boot. Cephelo summoned the old woman who had brought the water earlier to take

Wil's damp clothing. The Valeman handed the clothes over
without comment, knowing they would be thoroughly
searched and nothing found for the effort.

Then they returned to the fire at the center of the
encampment, where Amberle joined them, washed clean
and dressed in clothing similar to Wil's. Each was given a
plate of steaming food and a cup of wine. They sat next to
the fire and ate silently while the Rovers settled about
them, watching curiously. Cephelo took up a position
across from them, sitting cross-legged on a wide, gold-
tasseled cushion, his dark face expressionless. There was
no sign of Eretria.

When the meal was finished, the Rover Leader assembled the members of his Family who needed Wil's attention. Without comment, the Valeman examined them one
by one, treating a series of infections, internal disorders,
skin irritations, and minor fevers. Although she was not
asked to do so, Amberle worked next to him, providing
bandages and hot water, aiding in the application of simple
herb medicines and salves. It took the better part of an
hour for Wil to complete his work. When he was finished,
Cephelo stepped up to him.

"You have done your work well, Healer." He smiled a bit
too pleasantly. "Now we must see what we can do for you
in return. Walk with me a bit—this way."

He put one long arm about the Valeman's shoulders and
steered him away from the fire, leaving Amberle by herself
to clean up after their work. They walked toward the far
side of the Rover camp.

"You say that you lost your horse last night near where
we camped on the Mermidon." Cephelo's voice was
thoughtful. "What did this animal look like?"

Wil's face remained expressionless. He knew the game
that was being played.

"A stallion, all black."

"Well, now." Cephelo appeared even more thoughtful.
"We found a horse such as you have described, a very fine
animal, just this morning, quite early. It wandered into our
camp from out of the grasslands as we were getting our
teams hitched for the day's travel. Perhaps this was your
horse, Healer."

"Perhaps," Wil agreed.

"Of course, we didn't know whose animal he was." Cephelo smiled. "So we brought him along with our own. Why don't we take a look at him?"

They passed through the ring of wagons into the plains beyond. Fifty feet from the camp, the Rover horses were tethered in a line. Two dark forms materialized from out of the night, Rovers armed with pikes and bows. A word from Cephelo sent them back into hiding. The tall man led Wil down the tether line to its furthest end. There stood Artaq.

Wil nodded. "That's the horse."

"Does he bear your mark, Healer?" the other man asked, almost as if the question embarrassed him. Wil shook his head. "Ah, that is most unfortunate, for now we can't be certain that he really is your horse, can we? After all, there are a fair number of black stallions in the Four Lands, and how are we to tell them apart if their owners do not mark them? This presents quite a problem, Healer. I wish to give this horse to you, but there is a great risk to me in doing so. I mean, suppose I give him to you, as I wish to do, but then another man comes to me and tells me that he has lost a black stallion as well, and we then discover that I have mistakenly given his horse to you. Why then, I would be responsible for that man's loss."

"Yes, that's true, I guess." Wil nodded with just the right touch of doubt, carefully avoiding any argument with the big man's ridiculous supposition. It was, after all, just a part of the game.

"I believe you, of course." Cephelo's bearded face turned solemn. "Certainly a Healer is to be trusted, if anyone is to be trusted in this world." He grinned at his own humor. "However, there is still some risk to me if I choose to hand this animal over to you—I must accept that fact, being a practical man in an often hard business. And then there is the matter of feed and care given to this animal. We groomed him and tended him as we do our own; we fed him with meal we carry for our own. You will understand if I tell you that I feel we are owed something for all this."

"Indeed." Wil nodded.

"Well, then." Cephelo rubbed his hands in satisfaction. "We are in agreement. All that requires settling is the price. You spoke earlier of trading something of value for a horse.

Perhaps now we can make a fair exchange—whatever you carry with you in satisfaction of your debt to us. And in the bargain, I would say nothing of finding this horse to any other who might claim the loss of a black stallion."

He winked knowingly. Wil walked up to Artaq and stroked his sleek forehead, letting the horse nuzzle up against his chest.

"I'm afraid I don't have anything of value, after all," he said finally. "I brought nothing with me in my journey that could possibly repay you for what you've done."

Cephelo's jaw dropped. "Nothing?"

"Nothing at all."

"But you said you brought something of value . . ."

"Oh, yes." Wil nodded quickly. "I meant that I could offer you my services as a Healer—I thought that might have some value."

"But you've given those services in payment of food and shelter and clothes for yourself and your sister."

"Yes, true." The Valeman looked less than happy with the thought. He took a deep breath. "Perhaps I could suggest something?" A look of renewed interest appeared in the other's face. "Well, it seems that we are both traveling to the Westland. If you would allow us to accompany you, we might find some opportunity to repay you yet—possibly you might have need of my skill another time."

"That seems unlikely." Cephelo pondered the thought. He shook his head. "You've nothing of value to give for the horse—nothing at all?"

"No, nothing."

"That seems a poor way to travel," the Rover muttered, rubbing his bearded chin. The Valeman said nothing, waiting. "Well, I suppose it will do no harm to have you travel with us as far as the forestland. That's only a few days travel, though, and if you've done nothing for us by then, we may have to keep the horse for our trouble. You understand that."

Wil nodded wordlessly.

"One thing more." Cephelo stepped close, his face no longer pleasant. "I trust that you would not be so foolish as to try to steal that horse from us, Healer. You know us well enough to realize what would happen to you if you were to try such a thing."

The Valeman took a deep breath and nodded once more. He knew.

"Good." The big man stepped back. "See to it that it doesn't slip your mind." He was clearly unhappy at the way in which matters had worked out, but he shrugged his indifference. "Enough of business. Come to my home and drink with me."

He led the way back through the caravan circle, clapping his hands sharply as he entered, calling to those within to gather and to join with wine and music in celebrating the good fortune of the day and in welcoming the young Healer who had shown them such kindness. Wil was seated next to the Leader on a cushioned bench set before the big man's wagon home as the men and women and children of the Rover camp crowded about eagerly. Wine was drawn from a great vat and cups were passed about to everyone. Cephelo came to his feet and offered a flowery toast to the good health of his Family. Cups were raised high in answer and quickly drained. Wil drank his with the rest. He looked about hurriedly for Amberle and found her seated near the perimeter of the circle of faces surrounding him. She did not look at all pleased. He wished he could take time to explain all that had happened, but that would have to wait until they had a moment alone. For now, she would simply have to bear with him.

Cups were refilled now, another toast was proposed, and they all drank again. Cephelo called loudly for the music. Stringed instruments and cymbals were brought forth, and their owners began to play. The music was at once wild, haunting, and free as it rose into the night. The laughter of the Rovers rose with it, careless and gay. More wine was poured and quickly consumed, followed by shouts of encouragement for the musicians. Wil felt himself growing light-headed. The wine was strong, too strong for one not used to drinking it as the Rovers did. He must be careful, he thought to himself, raising his cup once more as a new toast was proposed, yet sipping this time rather than draining the amber liquid. In the toe of his right boot, he felt the reassuring bulk of the Elfstones pressed against his foot.

The musicians played faster, and now the Rovers were on their feet and dancing, half a dozen or eight, forming a circle with arms interlocked as they wheeled about the fire. More rose quickly to join the procession, and those still seated began to clap wildly. Wil joined them, setting his cup on the bench beside him. When he reached down for it a moment later, it was full again. Caught up in the spirit of the music, he drank it down without thinking. The dancers broke apart, pairing off now, spinning and leaping before the flames. Someone was singing, a wistful cry that blended eerily with the music and the dance.

Then suddenly Eretria was there before him, dark and beautiful, her slender form clad all in scarlet silk. Her smile was dazzling as she reached down for his hands and brought him to his feet. She pulled him into the midst of the dancers, broke from him for an instant, and twirled away in a flash of ribbons and trailing black hair. Then she was before him once more, slim arms holding him as they danced. The fragrance of her hair and body mingled with the warmth of the wine coursing through his blood. He felt her press close against him, feather light and soft, speaking words that he could not seem to hear clearly. The movement of the dance dizzied him; everything about him began to blend in a maze of colors that whirled against the backdrop of the night. The music and the clapping roared louder, and the shouts and whistles of the Rovers. He felt himself begin to leave the ground, still holding Eretria close.

And then she was gone as well, and he began to fall.

XV

he came awake with the worst headache of his life. It was the sensation of being shaken like a slender branch in a high wind that brought him around, and it took him several long minutes to realize that he was stretched out in the back of one of the Rover wagons. He lay on a straw-filled pallet in a wooden frame bed against the rear wall of the mobile house, staring upward at a strange assortment of tapestries, silks and laces, and metal and wooden implements, all swaying with the motion of the wagon as it bounced and rolled across the grasslands. A shaft of bright sunlight slipped through a partly cracked window, and he knew he had slept the night.

Amberle appeared next to him, a look of reproof in her sea-green eyes.

"I don't need to ask how you're feeling this morning, do I?" she declared, her words barely audible above the rumble of the wheels. "I hope it was worth it, Valeman."

"It wasn't." He sat up slowly, feeling his head throb violently with the movement. "Where are we?"

"In Cephelo's wagon. Since last night, if you can remember that far back. I told them that you were still recovering from a fever and that you might be sick from more than the wine. So they put me in here with you to look after you until I was sure you were feeling better. Drink this."

She handed him a cup with some dark liquid in it. Wil eyed the unpleasant-looking concoction suspiciously.

"Drink it," she repeated firmly. "It's an herbal remedy for excessive use of wine. There are some things you don't need to be a Healer to know."

He drank it down without arguing. It was then that he noticed that his boots were gone.

"My boots! What happened to . . . ?"

"Be quiet!" she warned, motioning quickly toward the front of the wagon where a small wooden door stood closed. Wordlessly, she reached beneath the bed and produced the items in question, then pulled from the sash about her waist the small leather pouch containing the Elfstones.

The Valeman sat back with a look of relief.

"The party proved to be a bit too much for you," she continued, a trace of sarcasm in her voice. "After you passed out, Cephelo had you carried to his wagon to sleep. He was about to have that old woman strip you when I convinced him that if the fever had come back, it would be contagious and that, any case, you would be offended if your clothes were taken without your permission. Apparently he didn't consider the matter all that important because he ordered the old woman out. After he was gone, as well, I searched you and found the Elfstones."

He nodded approvingly. "You've kept your wits about you."

"Good thing one of us did." She brushed aside his compliment with an arch of her eyebrows. She glanced again toward the closed door. "Cephelo left the old woman in the next compartment to keep an eye on us. I don't think he was entirely persuaded that he knows everything he should about you."

Wil leaned forward, resting his chin on his hands. "That wouldn't surprise me."

"Then why are we still here—other than the fact that you drank too much wine last night?" she wanted to know. "For that matter, why are we here in the first place?"

He reached for the Elfstones and she gave them to him. He put the leather pouch back into his right boot and pulled both boots on firmly. Then he motioned for her to lean close.

"Because we have to find a way to get Artaq back from these people and we can't do that if we don't stay with them," he whispered loud enough for her to hear him over the creaking of the wagon. "And there's another reason. The Demons that chased us from Havenstead will be looking for just two people—not an entire caravan. Perhaps traveling with the Rovers will throw them off. Besides, we're still traveling west, which is where we want to go, and we're traveling faster than we could on foot."

"Fine. But this is dangerous as well, Valeman," she pointed out. "What do you plan to do when we reach the Westland forests and Cephelo still refuses to give you Artaq?"

He shrugged. "I'll worry about that when it's time."

"We've been over this ground before." She shook her head in disgust. "At least you might try confiding in me a bit more than you have so far. It is not very reassuring to have to rely on you and not have the faintest idea what you're about."

"You're right," he agreed. "I'm sorry about last night. I should have told you more before we entered the camp, but, to tell you the truth, I hadn't made up my mind what we were going to do until just after we found it."

"I believe that." She frowned.

"Look, I'll try to explain some of it now," he offered. "Rovers travel in Families—you already know that much. The term 'Family' is somewhat misleading though, because its members are not always blood-related. Rovers frequently trade or even sell wives and children to other camps. It is a kind of communal property situation. Each Family has one Leader—a father figure who makes all the decisions. Women are considered subservient to men; that is what is called the Way. For the Rovers, that is the natural order of things. They believe quite firmly that women are to serve and obey the men who protect and provide for them. It is a tradition among them that those entering their camp should observe this custom in order to be made welcome. That's why I took the water first. That's why I left you to clean up after we treated the sick. I wanted to convince them that I understood and honored their beliefs. If they believed that, there was a chance they would give Artaq back to us."

"It doesn't seem to have worked out that way," Amberle remarked.

"No, not yet," he admitted. "But they have let us come along with them; ordinarily they would not even consider such a thing. Rovers have little use for outsiders."

"They have let us come along because Cephelo is curious about you and wants to find out more than he has been told." She paused. "Eretria has more than a passing interest in you as well. She made that quite apparent."

He grinned in spite of himself. "And I suppose you think I enjoyed all that dancing and drinking last night?"

"If you really want to know—yes, that is exactly what I think."

She said it without the faintest trace of a smile. Wil sat back, his head throbbing with the movement.

"All right, I admit that I overdid it. But there was a good reason for what I did, despite what you may think. It was necessary for them to believe that I wasn't smarter than they were. If they believed that I was, we would both be dead. So I let myself drink and dance and behave as any other outsider would under the same circumstances—just to keep them from becoming suspicious." He shrugged. "I cannot help what Eretria thinks about me."

"I am not asking you to." She grew suddenly angry. "I don't care what Eretria thinks about you. I only care that you don't give us both away by being foolish!"

She saw the look of surprise that crept into his eyes and she flushed darkly.

"Just be careful, will you?" she added quickly, took the empty cup from his hands, and turned away, moving to the far end of the wagon. Wil stared after her curiously.

A moment later she was back, calm and collected once more.

"There is something else you should know about. Early this morning the caravan met with an old line trapper traveling east. He had just passed through the Tirfing—the lake country fronting the Westland forests below the Mermidon. He warned Cephelo not to go in. He said there was a Devil there."

Wil frowned. "A Devil?"

"He called it a Devil—it is a name the Rovers use for something not human, something evil." She paused meaningfully. "It may be that this Devil is one of the Demons that has broken through the Forbidding."

"What did Cephelo say about this Devil?"

Amberle smiled faintly. "He is not afraid of Devils. He intends to go into the Tirfing anyway—his mind is made up on that. I think he has business that requires that he pass that way. The rest of the Family is not too happy about his decision."

Wil nodded. "I would be inclined to go along with them."

The Elven girl gave him a long, careful look. "I would not be inclined to go along with anyone in this camp, if I were you. Keep that in mind if you are offered any more wine."

She wheeled without a word and moved back once again to the far end of the wagon, hiding her movements from the Valeman. Wil started up after her irritably, but the pain in his head made him reconsider quickly. He sat back carefully, resting his throbbing head against a piece of woven reed backing lining the wagon wall. One thing was certain, he thought glumly. She need not worry about him drinking any more of that wine.

The caravan traveled steadily westward until midday, then halted long enough for the Rovers to partake of a quick lunch. By this time, Wil was feeling much improved and was able to eat some of the dried meat and vegetables that comprised the meal. Cephelo spoke to him briefly, inquiring politely as to his health, then moved away, his mind clearly on other matters. There were vague mutterings among the Rovers of the rumored Devil, and it was apparent to the Valeman that the Family was more than a little concerned with the old trapper's report. Rovers were a superstitious lot anyway, and Cephelo's decision to ignore a warning such as this one was not popular.

The remainder of the afternoon passed quickly. Wil took a turn at driving Cephelo's wagon while the old woman napped in the back. Amberle rode beside him as he guided the four-horse team forward in the caravan line through the broad expanse of the grasslands, humming and singing softly to herself but saying very little to him. The Valeman left her alone, concentrating on the task at hand, staring out thoughtfully into the emptiness of the plains. Several times Cephelo rode a big sorrel past them, his forest green cloak billowing out behind him, his dark face covered with a sheen of sweat from the heat of the day. Once Wil caught a quick glimpse of Artaq as the Rover relief horses were driven past the wagons toward a watering hole somewhere ahead of the caravan. He was not being ridden, and it appeared that as yet Cephelo had not decided how he would use the big black—which meant, hopefully, that he had not decided if he intended to keep him.

A little more than an hour before sunset, they entered the Tirfing, a land of small lakes and surrounding woodlands spread out beneath the rim of the grasslands. Far to the west, beneath the red ball of the setting sun, lay the dark mass of the Westland forests. The Rover wagons wound their way down out of the plains into the wooded stretches of the Tirfing along a rutted earthen trail worn by the passing of countless other travelers before them. The heat of the open grasslands dissipated quickly as they entered the sheltering trees, shadows lengthening across the trail before them with the onset of dusk. Through breaks in the woodlands, they began to glimpse bits and pieces of the lakes that dotted the country about them.

It was dark when Cephelo finally brought them to a halt in a large clearing, ringed by oaks and overlooking a small lake several hundred feet to the north. The wagons swung into the familiar circle, rumbling and creaking to a weary halt. Wil was so stiff that he could barely move. While the Rover men worked to unhitch the teams and the women began preparations for the evening meal, the Valeman climbed down gingerly from the hard board seat and tried walking off the stiffness. Amberle chose to walk another way, and he did not bother to follow her. He limped through the caravan circle to the fringes of the surrounding trees, pausing there to stretch himself painfully and allow the blood to circulate through cramped limbs.

Moments later he heard footsteps and turned to find Eretria approaching, her slim form another shadow in the evening dusk. She was dressed in high boots and leather riding clothes, a red silk scarf about her waist and another at her throat. Black hair tumbled down about her shoulders, loose and windblown. She smiled as she came up to him, her dark eyes twinkling mischievously.

"Do not stray too far, Wil Ohmsford," she advised. "A Devil might find you and then what would you do?"

"Let him have me." Wil grimaced, rubbing his backside. "Anyway, I do not plan on doing much straying until after I've been fed."

He eased himself down into the tall grass, placing his

back against one of the oaks. Eretria watched him word-lessly for a moment, then sat down beside him.

"Where have you been all day?" the Valeman asked conversationally.

"Watching you," she replied, then smiled wickedly as she saw the look that appeared on his face. "You didn't see me, of course. You weren't supposed to."

He hesitated uncomfortably. "Why were you watching me?"

"Cephelo wanted you watched." She arched her eye-brows. "He doesn't trust you—or the Elven girl you claim is your sister."

She was staring at him boldly now, as if daring him to contradict her. Wil felt a quick moment of panic.

"Amberle is my sister," he stated as assertively as he could.

Eretria shook her head. "She is no more your sister than I am Cephelo's daughter. She does not look at you as a sister would; her eyes say that she is something else. Still, it makes little difference to me. If you wish that she be your sister, then so shall she be. Just don't let Cephelo catch you playing this little game."

Now it was Wil's turn to stare. "Wait a minute," he said after a moment's pause. "What do you mean she is no more my sister than you are Cephelo's daughter? He said you were his daughter, didn't he?"

"What Cephelo says and what is true are not necessarily the same—in fact, very seldom the same." She leaned forward. "Cephelo has no children. He bought me when I was five from my father. My father was poor and could offer me nothing. He had other daughters, so one would not be missed. Now I belong to Cephelo. But I am not his daughter."

She said it so matter-of-factly that for a moment Wil could think of nothing to say in response. She saw his confusion and laughed merrily.

"We are Rovers, Wil—you know our ways. Besides, it could have been much worse for me. I could have been given to a much lesser man. Cephelo is a Leader; he has respect and position. As his daughter, I benefit from this. I have more freedom in my life than most women. And I have learned much, Healer. It has made me more than a match for most."

"I would not want to be the one to test that," he admitted. "But why are you telling me this?"

She pursed her lips teasingly. "Because I like you—why else?"

"That is what I am wondering." He ignored the look. She straightened abruptly, her face petulant.

"Are you married to this Elven girl? Is she promised to you?"

His surprise was evident. "No."

"Good. I thought not." The petulance disappeared. She paused, her smile wicked once more. "Cephelo does not plan to return your horse to you."

Wil considered the statement carefully. "You know this?"

"I know how he is. He will not return your horse. He will let you go on your way if you do not cause him any trouble or try to take back the horse, but he will never give it back to you willingly."

The Valeman's face was expressionless. "I'll ask again— why are you telling me this?"

"Because I can help you."

"And why should you do that?"

"Because you, in turn, can help me."

Wil frowned. "How?"

Eretria crossed her legs before her and placed her hands on her knees, rocking back. Her dark eyes danced with amusement.

"I would guess, Wil Ohmsford, that you are much more than what you have told us—that you are most certainly more than a simple Healer traveling the grasslands of Callahorn with your sister. I would guess that this Elven girl has been given into your care and that you accompany her as an escort, perhaps a protector." One brown hand came up hurriedly. "Do not bother to deny this, Healer—a lie from your lips would be wasted on me, for I am the daughter of the world's foremost liar and know the art far better than you."

She smiled and put one hand on his arm. "I like you, Wil—there is no lie in that. I want you to have your horse back again. Obviously it is important that you get him back or you would not have come after us. Alone, you will not be successful. But I could help you."

Wil looked doubtful. "Why would you do that?" he asked finally.

"If I help you regain your horse, then I want you to take me with you when you go."

"What!" The exclamation was spoken before he could think better of it.

"Take me with you," she repeated firmly.

"I cannot do that!"

"You can if you wish your horse back."

He shook his head helplessly. "Why would you want to leave? You just finished telling me that . . ."

She cut him short. "All that is in the past. Cephelo has decided that it is time that I married. In Rover tradition, he will select my husband and for a price, turn me over to him. My life has been good, but I have no intention of being sold a second time."

"Couldn't you just leave on your own? You seem capable of that."

"I am capable of a great deal more, should it come to that, Healer. That is why you have need of me. If you take back your horse—something I doubt you can do without my help—the Rovers will come after you. Since you will be pursued in any event, it will cause you no further burden to take me as well as the horse—especially since I know enough of Rovers to give you the guidance you will need to elude them."

She shrugged. "As for leaving on my own, I have given thought to that. If there were no other choice, I would do so rather than be sold again. But where would I go? A Rover is welcome nowhere and, like it or not, a Rover is what I am. Alone, I would be little better than an outcast among the races, and my life would not be a pleasant one. But with you I could find acceptance; you are a Healer and you have respect. I could even travel with you. I could aid you in the mending of the ill. You would find that I . . ."

"Eretria," Wil cut in gently. "There is no point in discussing it. I cannot take you with me. I can take no one with me but Amberle."

Her face darkened. "Do not be so quick to spurn me, Healer."

"This has nothing to do with spurning you," he responded, at the same time trying to decide how much he could tell her. Not very much, he quickly realized. "Listen. It would not be safe for you to travel anywhere with me right now. When I leave, Cephelo will not be the only one looking for me. There will be others, much more dangerous than he. They search for me now. If I took you along, you would be in great danger. I cannot allow that."

"The Elven girl travels with you," she insisted.

"Amberle travels with me because she must."

"Words. I do not believe them. You will take me with you, Wil Ohmsford. You will take me with you because you must."

He shook his head. "I cannot."

She rose abruptly, her beautiful dark face angry and set. "You will change your mind, Healer. The time will come when you will have no other choice."

She turned and stalked away. A dozen yards from him, she paused and glanced back suddenly, her black eyes fixing on his. From out of the shadow of her face flashed that wondrous, dazzling smile.

"I am for you, Wil Ohmsford," she called.

She held his gaze a moment longer, then turned and continued walking back toward the Rover caravan. The Valeman stared after her in mild amazement.

XVI

Dinner was set out and eaten, and it was shortly thereafter that the deep, booming cough broke through the peaceful sounds of the night and froze them into stillness. It came from the south end of the lake on which the Rovers were encamped—once, twice and then was gone. All heads turned as one, faces startled and expectant. Moments later the cough sounded again, rumbling out of the darkness like the huffing roar of some monstrous bull calling in challenge. The Rovers scrambled hurriedly for their weapons, then rushed to the perimeter of the circle of wagons and peered out into the night. But the sound died, and this time it did not repeat. Cephelo and more than a dozen of his men stood waiting for a time, anticipating something further. When nothing happened, he gruffly ordered everyone back to the fire and the evening wine. Joking loudly about Devils and things that prowled the night, he boasted that none of these would dare to come into a Rover camp without first seeking permission. Cups of wine were refilled and distributed, and everyone drank heartily. Yet glances continued to stray in the direction of the sound.

Half an hour later it came again, closer than before, sudden and heavy in the night. Startled Rovers sprang to their feet, snatching up their weapons a second time and racing for the edge of the camp. Wil went with them this time, Amberle only a step behind as he reached a gap between two of the Rover wagons and stared out guardedly. There was nothing to be seen. Nothing moved. Hesitantly, Cephelo stalked to the very edge of the woods surrounding the small clearing, both hands securely grasping the handle of a heavy broadsword. He stood for a time, his tall form black against the trees, poised to defend himself. There was only silence. Finally he turned and walked back again, his face set. There was no further joking. The horses, which were tethered on a line along a small inlet from the lake, were brought close in to the caravan in order that they could be better watched. Guards were placed all about the perimeter of the clearing and warned to keep their eyes open. Everyone else was taken back inside the circle of the wagons where they settled themselves within the comforting light of the fire. The wine was passed about, though fewer drank this time. Conversation resumed, but it was low and guarded and the word "Devil" was mentioned frequently. The men kept the women and children close, and everyone looked thoroughly disquieted.

Wil walked Amberle several paces back from the anxious group, his head lowered.

"I want you to stay close," he said quietly. "Do not leave me for any reason."

"I won't," she promised. Her eyes were intense as they found his and then glanced away quickly. "Do you think . . . ?"

Cephelo cut short her thought, calling suddenly for music, clapping his hands and encouraging those about him to do likewise. The Valeman and the Elven girl joined in obediently. A few weak cheers greeted Cephelo as he moved about the fire.

Wil glanced about uneasily. "If there is anything out there, and if whatever it is attacks this camp, then you and I are getting out. We will try to reach Artaq, then make a run for it. Are you willing to risk it?"

She nodded. "Very."

Cymbals shivered their silver cry, and the stringed instruments hummed softly. Hands began to clap, steady and confident.

Then the cough broke almost on top of them, booming out of the darkness with frightening suddenness, heavy and terrible. Shouts sounded from the guards—shouts filled with terror, shouts that cried, "Devil, Devil!" Those gathered about the fire scattered, the men rushing for their weapons, the women and children fleeing in confusion. A scream rose above the clamor, high and quick, dying

almost immediately into stillness. Beyond the circle of the
wagons, something huge and dark moved in the night.
"Demon!" Wil whispered the name almost without
thinking.

An instant later the creature appeared through a gap
between two of the wagons, pushing aside the wooden
homes as if they were made of paper. It was unquestionably a Demon—but much bigger than anything the Valeman and the Elven girl had encountered fleeing Havenstead. It stood on two legs, more than fifteen feet tall, its
massive body bent and heavy and covered with mottled
brown and gray hide that hung from it in thick folds. A
crest of scales ran from its neck the length of its back and
down either leg. Its face was blasted and empty, a mass of
teeth curving out from jaws that opened wide to emit its
deep, booming cough. From two great, clawed hands
dangled the broken body of a Rover guard.

It flung the dead man aside and came forward. Cephelo
and a dozen more Rovers met it with pikes and swords. A
few thrusts penetrated the thick hide, but most were
turned aside. The creature was slow and ponderous, but
incredibly strong. It shambled forward through the wall of
defenders, swatting them aside effortlessly. Cephelo threw
himself directly into the Demon's path, leaping up to thrust
his broadsword deep into the creature's gaping mouth. The
monstrous thing barely slowed, jaws snapping the sword
into splinters, clawed hands reaching for the Rover Leader.
Cephelo was too quick, but another Rover went down,
tripping over his own feet in his haste to escape. The
Demon's foot dropped on the struggling man like a rock.

Wil was already moving Amberle toward the far side of
the encampment, intent on reaching the tethered horses,
when he saw Cephelo go down as well. The defenders
were attempting to entangle the Demon's legs when one
massive arm caught the big man a glancing blow and sent
him tumbling head over heels. Hesitating in a gap between
the wagons, Wil watched the other Rovers spring to
Cephelo's defense, two grabbing the inert form and pulling
it to safety while the others feinted and jabbed at the
monster to draw its attention. The Demon swung about,
pikes and swords hacking at its armored body, and reached
for the nearest Rover wagon. It seized the heavy carrier

and, with a single lunge, threw it over. The wagon fell with a crash, splitting apart, metal ornaments and silk rolls spilling into the firelight. The defenders cried out in fury and resumed their hopeless attack.

Amberle was pulling urgently on Wil Ohmsford's arm, but still the Valeman hesitated. He could not bring himself to believe that something so huge and so slow had managed to track them all the way from Havenstead. No, this creature had escaped through the wall of the Forbidding on its own, wandered down into the Tirfing, and simply stumbled on their caravan. It had come alone, blindly, stupidly—but a thing of such destruction that it was clear already that the Rovers were no match for it. Despite their efforts to turn or stop it, the Demon would surely destroy the entire caravan.

But the Rovers would not run. The garish wagons, the cumbersome wheeled houses—these were their homes. Everything they owned was in them. No, the Rovers would not run. They would stand and fight; and if they did so, they would die. The Demon was a thing of another age; its power was greater than that of flesh and blood and bone. It would take power as great as its own to stop it. Only he possessed that power. But this was not his fight. These people had stolen from him; he owed them nothing. His first and only responsibility was for Amberle. He should take her and go quickly. Yet if he did, what would become of the Rovers—not only the men, but the women and children as well? Had they harmed him? Without his help, they stood no chance at all against the Demon.

His indecision was complete when he remembered that his grandfather had once told him that when he had used the Elfstones in his flight from the Warlock Lord, he had inadvertently told his enemy exactly where he could be found. It might well be the same now. Some of these Demons were creatures capable of using magic; Allanon had told him this was so. If he were to use the Elfstones, he might lead them right to him.

He looked quickly at Amberle. What she saw in his eyes told her at once what he intended to do. Wordlessly she released his arm. He pulled off his right boot and reached into it for the Elfstones. At least he must try, he told himself. At least he must do that much. He could not let these people die. He opened the pouch and poured the three blue Stones into his open palm. Closing his fists over them tightly, he stared back into the camp.

"Stay here," he told the Elven girl.

"No, wait . . ." she called after him, but he was already running.

The Demon had turned away from the wagons and was driving the Rovers before it as it advanced toward the center of the encampment. Cephelo was back on his feet, swaying unsteadily as he leaned against a wagon at one side and yelled encouragement to the defenders. Wil closed the distance between himself and the combatants until no more than twenty yards separated them. Raising his fist above his head, he willed forth the power of the Elfstones.

Nothing happened.

He experienced a sinking sensation in the pit of his stomach. The one thing he had feared most had come to pass—he could not control the power of the Elfstones. Allanon had been wrong. Only his grandfather could invoke their power, not he. They were not his to command. They would not obey him.

Yet they must! He tried again, concentrating on the feel of the Stones in his hand, calling down to the magic that lay buried somewhere within them. Still nothing. Yet this time he sensed something he had missed before—a barrier of some sort that blocked his efforts, a barrier somewhere within himself.

The shouts of the Rovers broke sharply through his thoughts, and he saw that the Demon was coming directly toward him. The defenders were behind the creature now, stabbing and thrusting with their weapons at its legs and flanks, trying to turn it from the Valeman. One massive arm swung out, knocking two men sprawling, and scattering the rest. The booming cough rolled out of its throat. Cephelo began hobbling frantically toward the battle, supporting himself with a broken pike, his dark clothing torn and covered with dust and blood. Wil saw them all as if they had been frozen in a single instant of still life, struggling as he did so to free the power that lay locked within the Elfstones. It did not occur to him to run; he simply stood there in the center of the Rover camp, a solitary figure with one arm raised to the night sky.

Then Eretria appeared from out of nowhere, darting forward, her slender form a shadow of sudden movement that flashed between the Demon and the Valeman, one brown hand hurtling a fiery torch into the monster's face. The creature caught the burning stick of wood in its jaws, snapping at it reflexively—yet slowing as it did, as if somehow bothered by the fire and smoke. Taking advantage of its momentary hesitation, Eretria caught hold of Wil and began pulling him backward until both lost their footing, stumbled and went down. The Rover defenders rallied at once, snatching up brands from the fire and throwing them at the Demon in an effort to confuse it. But the monster had already started forward again. Wil scrambled back to his feet hurriedly, pulling Eretria up with him. At that same moment Amberle reached his side, a long pike held firmly in both small hands as she prepared to defend them all. Wordlessly the Valeman grabbed her arm, pushed both women behind him, and turned to face the advancing Demon.

The creature was almost on top of them. Wil Ohmsford held forth the hand that gripped the Elfstones. There was no hesitation, no confusion within him now. Driving inward, he smashed aside the barrier that stood between himself and the power of the Stones, smashed it aside through strength of will born of desperation and need, without yet understanding what it was. As he did so, he sensed something change within himself that he could not explain and did not feel was altogether good. There was no time to give it thought. Reaching down within the heart of the Elfstones, he brought them to life at last. Brilliant blue light flared up from his clenched hand, gathered itself, then burst forward to strike the Demon. The monstrous thing roared as the power of the Stones burned through it. Still it came on, its clawed hands grasping. Wil did not give ground. He took himself further into the Stones, feeling their power intensify. Everything about him grew hazy with their glow, and again the Elfstones lashed out at the Demon. This time the creature could not withstand the Elven magic. Its massive form erupted in flames and became a pillar of blinding light. For an instant it burned deep blue in the night, then exploded into ash and was gone.

Wil Ohmsford brought his arm down slowly. Where the Demon had stood, there was only charred earth and a wisp of black smoke rising into the night. The whole of the surrounding woodlands had gone deathly still, and only the crackling of the Rover fire disturbed the silence. The Valeman looked about uncertainly. Not a single Rover moved; they just stood there, the men with their weapons still poised to do battle, the women and children huddled close to one another, all with disbelief and fear reflected in their faces. Wil felt a moment of panic. Would they turn on him, knowing now that he had deceived them? He looked back quickly at Amberle, but she, too, stood frozen, her deep green eyes filled with wonder.

Then Cephelo hobbled forward, casting aside the broken spike as he came up to the Valeman, his dark bearded face streaked with blood and soot.

"Who are you?" he asked softly. "Tell me who you are."

The Valeman hesitated. "I am who I said I was," he said finally.

"No." Cephelo shook his head. "No, you are surely no simple Healer. You are more than that." His voice was hard and insistent. "I was right about you all along, wasn't I?"

Wil did not know how to respond.

"Tell me who you are," Cephelo repeated, his voice low and dangerous.

"I have already told you who I am."

"You have told me nothing!" The Rover Leader's face flushed with anger. "I think you knew of this Devil. I think that he came here because of you. I think that all of this was because of you!"

Wil shook his head. "The creature found you by chance; it was chance that I was with you when he did."

"Healer, you are lying to me!"

Wil felt his temper slip. "Who has lied to whom, Cephelo? This was your game we played—you made all the rules!"

The big man took a quick step forward. "There are rules you might yet be taught."

"I do not think so," the Valeman replied evenly.

He brought the fist that held the Elfstones up slightly.

Cephelo did not miss the gesture. He stepped back slowly. The smile that followed was painfully forced.

"You said you carried nothing of value, Healer. Did you forget these?"

Wil shook his head. "The Stones have no value to anyone but me. They would be worthless to you."

"Indeed." The Rover did not bother to conceal the sneer in his voice. "Are you a sorcerer, then? A Devil yourself? Why not tell me who you are?"

Wil hesitated. He was getting nowhere this way. He had to put an end to this whole conversation. Amberle stepped up beside him, one small hand reaching out to take his arm, touching it lightly. It was reassuring to have her there.

"Cephelo, you must return my horse to me," he said quietly. The Rover's face went black. "Amberle and I must go at once. There are more Devils than this one I destroyed—that much I will tell you. They track both the Elven girl and me. Because I used the Stones, they will know now where we can be found. We must go—and you must leave here, as well."

Cephelo stared wordlessly at him for several long moments, obviously trying to determine if what he was being told was the truth. In the end, caution overruled mistrust. He nodded curtly.

"Take your horse and go. I want no more of either of you."

He wheeled and walked away, calling loudly to his people to strike camp. Clearly he wished to be gone from the Tirfing as well. Wil watched him for a moment, then dropped the Elfstones into their leather pouch and tucked the pouch back within his tunic. Taking Amberle by the arm, he began moving toward the horses. Then he remembered Eretria. He looked for her and found her in the shadow of the wagons, her dark eyes watching him.

"Goodbye, Wil Ohmsford," she said quietly.

He smiled faintly. She knew that she had lost her chance to go with him. For an instant, he hesitated. She had saved his life; he owed her something for that. Would it be so wrong for him to help her now? Yet he knew that he could not. His sole concern now must be for Amberle. He could not distract himself from that, even for this Rover girl he found so enchanting. The debt he owed her must be paid another time.

"Goodbye, Eretria," he replied.

A touch of that dazzling smile broke through the shadow of her face.

"We will meet again," she called, then whirled and was gone.

Five minutes later, Wil and Amberle rode Artaq north out of the Rover camp and disappeared into the night.

XVII

With little more than an hour remaining before dawn, they arrived at the south bank of the Mermidon several miles downstream from where the river emerged from the forests of the Westland into Callahorn. They had ridden Artaq for most of the night, maintaining a steady pace as they journeyed north through the open, more easily traveled grasslands, seeking to put as much distance as possible between themselves and the Tirfing. They had rested only once, a brief stop for water and relief from rapidly cramping muscles, then remounted and gone on. By the time they reached the river's edge, both horse and riders were close to exhaustion. The Valeman could discern no readily accessible point for crossing, the Mermidon being both wide and deep for as far as the eye could see in both directions, and it quickly became apparent that they either would have to swim the river or follow its banks until a shallows was found. Having no wish to attempt either while it was still dark, Wil decided that the best thing for them to do was to rest until daylight. Turning Artaq into a grove of cottonwood, he unsaddled and tethered the big black, then spread blankets for both Amberle and himself. Screened by the trees, all three fell quickly asleep.

It was almost noon when Wil awoke once more, feeling the warmth of the summer day filter through the cottonwoods from out of yet another clear, sunlit sky. The Valeman touched Amberle gently, and she came awake. They rose, washed, ate a brief meal, and resumed their journey toward Arborlon.

They rode Artaq upstream for several miles, almost to the edge of the Westland forests, but found no shallows

that would afford them a safe crossing. Rather than waste
further time retracing their steps downstream, they decided they would chance swimming the river. Strapping
their few possessions about Artaq's neck, they tied themselves to his saddle with a length of rope, led the big black
down to the water's edge, and plunged in. The water was
chill, and the shock of the sudden immersion numbed
them. They thrashed wildly for a few minutes, fighting the
cold and the pull of the current, then settled into a steady
kick, hands gripping the safety rope tightly. Artaq swam
strongly. Even though the river swept them downstream
for nearly half a mile, they reached the far bank unharmed.

From there they rode north at a leisurely pace, walking
Artaq frequently to rest him. Wil believed that they had
traveled far enough from the Tirfing to confuse any
immediate pursuit, and he saw no reason to tire the black
further. The previous night's run had taken a lot out of the
gallant horse, and he needed a chance to regain his
strength. If he were not given that chance now, he would
be useless to them later—and Wil was not about to
discount the possibility that they might have great need for
him before Arborlon was reached. Besides, even at this
slower pace, they would reach the Valley of Rhenn by the
following morning. That was soon enough, he reasoned.
They would be safe until then.

Amberle might have had a different opinion, but she
kept it to herself. Free of the Rovers, her spirits were
noticeably improved. She sang and hummed once more as
they walked, pausing frequently to observe small flowers
and plants, bits and pieces of tiny life that would have gone
unnoticed by the Valeman in the vast carpet of the
grasslands. She had little to say to Wil, although she
answered pleasantly when he spoke to her and smiled
patiently at his questions about the growing things she was
drawn to. But for the most part, she stayed reserved and
distant in her attitude toward him, refusing to engage in
general conversation, walled away in that private world
she had chosen for herself since the time they had begun
this journey north from the banks of the Rainbow Lake.

As the day wore on, Wil found himself thinking of
Eretria, wondering if she would leave Cephelo and the
caravan as she had threatened and if he would indeed see

her again one day. There was an excitement to the Rover girl that he found fascinating. She reminded him of a brief vision created by the Sirens that grew on the Battle-mound—mesmeric and alluring, stirring within the mind wild and beautiful thoughts. He smiled at the comparison. It was foolish, really. She was flesh and blood, no vision. Still, if he were to probe the surface of her, would he find that she, like the Siren, was a thing of deception? There was something to her that suggested this, and it bothered him more than a little. He had not forgotten how she had risked her own life to save his; he would hate to discover that there had been any deception in that.

By nightfall, they were angling west, following the line of the forestland as it wound northward toward the vast expanse of the Streleheim. As darkness closed about them, Wil turned Artaq into the woods, trailing a small stream through the trees for several hundred feet until it pooled below a rapids, providing them with suitable drinking water. There they made camp, bedding down Artaq in a patch of thick grass, feeding and watering him before turning to their own needs. A cooking fire would call attention to their presence, so they settled for fruits and vegetables provided by Amberle. Once again, these were unfamiliar foods to the Valeman, but he enjoyed them nonetheless. He sensed that, given enough time, he might even become used to the strange fare. He was almost finished with the last of the peculiar, elongated, orange fruits when the Elven girl turned to him suddenly, a quizzical look on her face.

"Do you mind if I ask you something?" she wanted to know.

He grinned. "How do I know if I mind, if I don't know what it is you plan to ask?"

"Well, you needn't answer if you don't wish to—but this has been bothering me ever since we left the Rover camp."

"In that case, ask."

The small clearing in which they sat was very dark, the pale light of the moon and stars screened by the tangle of tree limbs that interlocked above them, and she moved close to him so that she could see his face clearly.

"Will you be honest with me?" Her eyes fixed on his.

"I will."

"When you used the Elfstones, did you . . . ?" She hesitated, as if not sure of the word she wanted. "Did you . . . hurt yourself?"

He stared at her, a sudden premonition stirring at the back of his mind, undefined still, but there nevertheless.

"That is a curious question."

"I know." She nodded, and a faint smile escaped before her face grew serious once more. "I cannot explain it, really—it was a feeling I had when I watched you. At first you could not seem to control the Elfstones. You held them up and nothing happened, although it was clear enough that you were trying to use their power to stop the Demon. Then, when they did at last come alive, there was a change in you—a change that showed in your face . . . almost like pain."

The Valeman was nodding slowly. He remembered now, and the memory was not pleasant. After it had happened, he had blocked it from his mind—blocked it without thinking, almost as a reflex action. Even now, he did not know why. It was not until this moment, when she recalled it to him, that he remembered what he had felt.

There was concern mirrored in the Elven girl's eyes as he stared into them now. "If you do not wish . . ." she began quickly.

"No." His voice was quiet, firm. He shook his head slowly. "No. I do not know if I understand it myself, though—but it would help to talk about it, I think."

He took a deep breath, choosing his words carefully. "There was a block somewhere within me. I do not know what it was or what caused it, but it was there and it would not let me use the Stones. I could not seem to pass around it or go through it." He shook his head again. "Then the Demon was almost on top of me, and you and Eretria were both there, and all of us were going to die, and I somehow smashed the block—smashed it apart and reached down into the Stones . . ."

He paused. "There was no pain, but a sense of something unpleasant happening within me, something . . . I don't know how to describe it. A sense of having done something wrong—yet there was nothing wrong in what I did."

"The wrong may have been to yourself," she murmured

after a moment's consideration. "Perhaps the Elven magic is harmful to you in some way."

"Perhaps," he agreed. "Yet my grandfather never spoke of this. Can it be that the magic did not affect him, yet does affect me? Why would it be different with me?"

She shook her head doubtfully. "Elven magic causes different reactions in different people. It has always been so. It is a magic born of the spirit, and the spirit is never a constant."

"But my grandfather and I are so much alike—even more so than my father and I were." Wil pondered. "Kindred spirits, you might say—and not so diverse as to cause this . . . this difference in our use of the Stones. Surely he would have felt this as well—and he would have told me."

Amberle's hand reached for his arm, holding it firmly. "I do not think you should use the Elfstones again."

He smiled. "Even to protect you?"

He said it lightly, but she did not return the smile. There was nothing humorous in this to her.

"I would not be the cause of any injury to you, Healer," she announced quietly. "It was not my choice that brought you on this journey, and I feel badly that you are here at all. But since you are here, I will speak my mind. Elven magic is nothing to be toyed with; it can prove to be more dangerous than the evil it was created to protect against. Our histories have left us with that warning, if little else. The magic may act against not only the body, but the spirit as well. Wounds of the body may be treated. But what of wounds to the spirit? How will you treat them, Healer?"

She bent close. "No one is worth such injury—no one. Especially me."

Wil stared at her silently for a moment, startled to see tears glistening at the corners of her eyes. He reached out his hand to cover hers.

"We shall be careful for each other," he promised. He tried a quick smile. "Maybe we won't have need of the Stones again."

The look she gave him in response suggested that she did not believe a word of it.

It was midnight when the howl of the Demon-wolves rose out of the stillness of the grasslands, shrill, hungry, and filled with hatred. Wil and Amberle came awake at once, the contentment of their sleep twisted with fear. For an instant they did not move, their bodies pushed upright from beneath the blankets, their eyes wide and staring as they sought each other out in the dark. The cry died, echoed in the silence that followed, then rose again, piercing and high. This time neither Valeman nor Elven girl hesitated. Without a word, both were on their feet, pulling on their boots, slipping their riding cloaks about their shoulders. In seconds they had saddled Artaq, mounted, and were riding north once more.

They moved ahead at a steady trot, keeping to the open plains where the way was clear and lit by moon and stars, following the line of the forestland. Cool night air rushed over them as they rode, damp with moisture gathering into morning dew, filled with the smells of the dark. Behind them, the howling continued, far back still, somewhere above the line of the Mermidon. The Demon-wolves were searching. The trail they followed was a day old; they did not realize yet how close they actually were to their prey.

Artaq ran smoothly, his great body working effortlessly as he raced across the grasslands, little more than another shadow slipping through the summer night. He had gotten most of the rest he needed for this run and he would not be winded quickly. Wil rated him carefully, keeping the pace steady, not letting the black overextend himself. It was early still; the chase had just begun. Their pursuers would discover soon enough the truth of matters. The Valeman was angry with himself; he had not believed they could be found again so quickly. The Elfstones must have revealed their presence in the Tirfing. The Demon-wolves had come for the Valeman and the Elven girl immediately, tracked them north, and now flushed them from the Westland forests. Once they found the campsite their quarry had abandoned, the wolves would come after them with a vengeance. The Demons would run them until they were caught.

They rode on for better than an hour without sighting the valley, the howling trailing after them as they fled. It was answered now by cries that rose out of the grasslands below the Dragon's Teeth and the plains to the north. Wil felt his heart sink. The wolves had them ringed. Only the

Westland had been left open to them. He wondered suddenly if that way, too, might be closed. He remembered how it had been at the Silver River. The Valley of Rhenn might be a trap as well. Perhaps they were purposely being driven into the valley and it was there that the Demons planned to finish them. Yet what other choice was left them but to take that chance?

Moments later the howls behind them rose in a frenzy. The Demon-wolves had found their camp.

Wil put Artaq into a full gallop. The Demons would come quickly now, certain that their prey was close ahead, knowing that they could be caught. Cries north and east of them sounded in answer to those behind, shrill and ragged as the hunters began to run. Artaq was sweating, his head extended forward, his ears laid back. The grasslands thinned into barren scrub; they had crossed into the Streleheim. The Valley of Rhenn could not be far. Wil stretched himself low over Artaq's straining neck and urged the gallant horse onward.

It was during the third hour of the chase, when the grasslands of Callahorn had been left far behind and the earth beneath Artaq's pounding hooves had gone hard and cracked, when the howls of the Demon-wolves had drawn so near that it seemed the huge gray forms must spring into view at any moment, when wind and dust had blinded them and sweat from fear had streaked their bodies beneath their tangled clothes, that Valeman and Elven girl at last caught sight of the broken ridges that formed the mouth of the Valley of Rhenn. They rose out of the flatlands below the Elven forests, rock and scrub black against the night sky. The riders turned toward the pass without slowing. Artaq's flanks were heaving, his nostrils flaring; sweat and lather coated his sleek black body. He stretched out further, racing through the darkness, the two hunched forms on his back holding on desperately.

In seconds, the pass was before them, craggy ridges looming up on either side. Down into the narrow slot of the valley thundered the black. Wil peered frantically through tear-filled eyes as the wind ripped across his face, searching for the Demons that he had feared would be waiting to trap them. Astonishingly, he found none. They were alone in the valley. He felt a quick sense of exhilara-

tion. They were going to escape! Their pursuers were too
far back to catch them before they were safely into the
Westland forests, into the country of the Elves. By then
there would be help . . .

The incomplete thought hung suspended in his mind,
repeating itself over and over in cadence with the sound of
Artaq's pounding hooves as the black raced along the floor
of the valley. Wil went cold. What was he thinking? There
would be no help for them. No one even knew they were
coming—no one but Allanon, and the Druid was gone.
Help? What help did he expect? Already the Demons had
gone into the very heart of the city of Arborlon to destroy
the Chosen. What did he think would stop them from
trailing one incredibly foolish Valeman and an unarmed
Elven girl into forestland miles from anything? All he had
succeeded in doing in gaining the Valley of Rhenn was to
take Artaq out of the open grasslands, where he could run,
into the confinement of the woods, where he could not.
There was nothing there that would prevent the wolves
from coming after them—creatures that were quicker and
more agile than they, better able to penetrate the maze of
trees and brush, better able to pursue than they would be
able to flee. He wanted to scream what he was feeling.
Stupid! His shortsightedness had taken away their one
slim chance of escape. He had been so concerned with
what they had been running from that he had forgotten to
consider what they had been running into. They were not
going to escape at all. They would be caught; they would
be killed. It was his fault. He had done this to them.

He must do something.

His mind raced, searching desperately. He had only one
weapon left.

The Elfstones.

Then Amberle screamed. The Valeman jerked about,
following the Elven girl's rigid arm as it pointed skyward.

Through the mouth of the valley flew a monstrous black
creature with leathered wings that spanned the line of the
ridges and a head hooked and bent like some twisted limb.
Shrieking, it swept out of the Streleheim into the crease of
the valley and came for them. Wil had never seen anything
so huge. He yelled frantically to Artaq, but the black had
nothing left to give—he was running now on spirit alone.

A hundred yards away loomed the draw that marked the far pass. Beyond lay woods that would hide them from this nightmare, woods into which a thing of such size could not possibly go. All they needed was a few seconds more.

The creature dove for them. It seemed to fall toward them like some massive rock, plummeting downward out of the night. Wil Ohmsford saw it come and glimpsed momentarily the rider it bore, a thing vaguely manlike, yet humped and misshapen, its eyes red against the black of its face. The eyes seemed to transfix him, and he felt his courage melt.

For an instant he thought they were finished. But then, with a final lunge, Artaq gained the far pass, broke clear of the high ridges, and plunged into the darkness of the trees.

Down a narrow rutted earthen trail the big horse thundered, barely slowing as his sleek body dodged and twisted through the tangle of trunks and heavy brush. Wil and Amberle hung on desperately, limbs and vines whipping across them, threatening to unseat them at every turn. Wil tried to slow the black, but Artaq had taken the bit between his teeth. The Valeman had lost control of him entirely. He was running his own race now.

In seconds the riders lost all sense of direction, confused by the forest dark that had closed about them and by the winding trail. Although he could no longer hear the howl of the Demon-wolves nor the shriek of that flying monster, Wil was terrified that they might inadvertently become turned about and end up traveling back toward the very creatures from whom they sought to escape. He sawed angrily on the reins in an effort to free the bit, but Artaq held on firmly.

The Valeman had just about given up hope of ever stopping the black when the big horse abruptly slowed and then stopped altogether. Standing in the middle of the forest trail, sides heaving, nostrils flaring, he lowered his finely shaped head and nickered softly. A long moment of silence followed. Wil and Amberle glanced at one another questioningly.

Then a tall, black form appeared right in front of them, slipping from the forest night without a sound. It happened so quickly that Wil did not even have time to think to reach for the Elfstones. The dark figure stepped forward, one hand touching gently Artaq's sweating neck, slowly stroking the satin skin. From out of the shadow of a hooded cloak, his face lifted to the light.

It was Allanon.

"Are you all right?" he asked softly, reaching up to take Amberle from the saddle and lower her carefully to the ground.

The Elven girl nodded wordlessly, astonishment filling her sea-green eyes—astonishment, and a touch of anger. The Druid frowned, then turned to aid Wil, but the Valeman was already scrambling down from Artaq's back.

"We thought you dead!" he burst out in disbelief.

"It seems that someone is forever declaring me dead before the fact," the mystic remarked somewhat petulantly. "As you can see, I am quite . . ."

"Allanon, we have got to get out of here." Wil was already glancing anxiously over his shoulder. His words tripped over one another in his haste to get them out. "The Demon-wolves chased us north all the way from the Mermidon, and there's a black, flying thing that . . ."

"Wil, slow down."

". . . almost caught us in the valley, bigger than anything I've ever . . ."

"Wil!"

Wil Ohmsford went silent. Allanon shook his head reprovingly.

"Would you please let me get a word in edgewise?" The Valeman flushed and nodded. "Thank you. First of all, you are quite safe now. The Demons no longer pursue you. The one who leads them can sense my presence. He is wary of me and has turned back."

The Valeman looked doubtful. "Are you sure?"

"Very sure. No one has followed you. Now come over here with me, both of you, and sit down."

He led them to a fallen log that lay next to the trail, and the Valeman and Elven girl seated themselves wearily. Allanon remained standing.

"We must go on to Arborlon tonight," he advised them. "But we can spare a few moments to rest before we leave."

"How did you get here?" Wil asked him.

"I might ask you the same question." The big man hunched down on one knee, drawing the black robes close about him. "Do you understand what happened to you at the river?"

The Valeman nodded. "I think so."

"It was the King of the Silver River," Amberle interjected quietly. "We saw him; he spoke to us."

"It was to Amberle that he spoke," Wil corrected. "But what happened to you? Did he help you as well?"

Allanon shook his head. "I am afraid I did not even see him—only the light which enveloped and took you away. He is a reclusive and mysterious being, and he shows himself to very few. This time, he chose to appear to you. His reasons must remain his own, I suppose. In any case, his appearance caused considerable confusion among the Demons, and I took advantage of that confusion to make my own escape."

He paused. "Amberle, you said that he spoke with you. Do you recall what it was that he said?"

The Elven girl looked uneasy. "No, not exactly. It was like a dream. He said something about . . . joining."

For an instant there was a flicker of understanding in the Druid's dark eyes. But neither Wil nor Amberle saw it, and it disappeared at once.

"No matter." The mystic brushed the incident aside casually. "He helped you when you needed help, and for that we are in his debt."

"His debt, to be sure—but certainly not yours." Amberle did not bother to disguise her anger. "Where have you been, Druid?"

Allanon seemed surprised. "Looking for you. Unfortunately, when he helped you, the King of the Silver River caused us to become separated. I knew you were safe, of course, but I did not know where you had been taken or how to go about finding you again. I might have used magic, but that seemed unnecessarily risky. The one who leads these Demons who have broken through the Forbidding has power as great as my own—perhaps greater. Using magic might have led him to us both. So I chose instead to continue on toward Arborlon, searching for you as I went, believing that you would remember and follow accordingly the instructions I had given you. Because I was forced to go afoot—your gray, Wil, was lost in the battle—I was certain that you were ahead of me the entire time. It was not until you used the Elfstones that I realized I was mistaken."

He shrugged. "By then I was almost to Arborlon. I started back at once, traveling south through the forest-land, thinking that you would seek sanctuary by entering the woods below the Mermidon. Again, I was mistaken. When I heard the howling of the Demon-wolves, I realized that you were trying to reach the Valley of Rhenn. That brought me here."

"It appears that you have been mistaken much of the time," Amberle snapped.

Allanon said nothing, his eyes meeting hers.

"I think you were mistaken in coming to me in the first place," she continued, her voice accusing now.

"It was necessary that I come."

"That remains to be seen. What worries me at the moment is that the Demons have been one step ahead of you from the beginning. How many times now have they almost had me?"

Allanon rose. "Too many times. It will not happen again."

Amberle rose with him, her face flushing darkly. "I no longer feel particularly reassured by your promises. I want this journey finished. I want to go home again—to Haven-stead, not to Arborlon."

The Druid's face was expressionless. "Understand—I do what I am able to do for you."

"Perhaps. Perhaps you only do what suits you."

The Druid stiffened. "That is unfair, Elven girl. You know less about this than you suppose."

"I know one thing. I know that neither you nor your choice for my protector have proven very capable. I would be much happier if I had never seen either one of you."

She was so angry she was almost in tears. She stared at them furiously, daring them to contradict her. When they did not, she turned away and started walking down the darkened trail.

"You said we must go on to Arborlon tonight, Druid," she called out. "I want this finished!"

Wil Ohmsford stared after her, resentment and confusion showing in his face. For a moment he seriously considered just sitting there and letting the Elven girl go her own way. She obviously had little enough use for him. Then he felt Allanon's hand on his shoulder.

"Do not be too quick to judge her," the Druid said softly.

The hand withdrew, and Allanon moved over to gather up Artaq's reins. He looked back at Wil inquiringly. The Valeman shook his head and rose. After all, he had come this far. There was nothing to be gained by not going on.

The Druid had already started after the slender figure of the Elven girl as she disappeared up the pathway into the trees. Grudgingly, Wil followed.

XVIII

It was evening of the following day. Shadows lengthened across the forested city of Arborlon and gray dusk deepened steadily into night. Eventine Elessedil sat alone in the seclusion of his study, poring over Gael's list of matters that would require his attention in the morning. Fatigue lined his face, and his eyes squinted wearily in the light of the oil lamp that sat atop the wooden desk he occupied. The room was still, closing the aged King of the Elves away in the silence of his thoughts.

He glanced over briefly at Manx, who lay sprawled across the room against a bookcase, sleeping soundly. The wolfhound's graying flanks rose and fell rhythmically, his breath exhaling through his nose with a curious nasal whine. Eventine smiled. Old dog, he thought, sleep comes easily to you, deep and dreamless and troublefree. He shook his head. He would give much to enjoy just a single night's undisturbed sleep. There had been little rest for him. Nightmares crowded his slumber—nightmares that were distortions of the unpleasant realities of his waking hours, carried with him into sleep. They teased and tormented him; they stole wickedly through his slumber, disruptive and hateful. Each night they returned, prodding at his subconscious, fragmenting his sleep so that time and again he shook himself awake, until at last dawn brought an end to the struggle.

He rubbed his eyes, then his face, closing off the light with his hands. He would have to sleep soon because sleep in some form was necessary. But he knew that he would find little rest.

When he took his hands away again, he found himself staring at Allanon. For an instant he did not believe that he was seeing the Druid; this was only a trick of his mind, brought on by his weariness. But when he squinted sharply and the image did not disappear, he came to his feet with a start.

"Allanon! I thought I was seeing things!"

The Druid came forward and they locked hands. There was the barest flicker of uncertainty in the Elven King's eyes.

"Did you find her?"

Allanon nodded. "She is here."

Eventine did not know how to respond. The two men stared at each other wordlessly. Against the bookcase, Manx raised his head and yawned.

"I did not think she would ever come back," the King said finally. He hesitated. "Where have you taken her?"

"Where she can be protected," Allanon responded. He released the King's hand. "We do not have much time. I want you to summon your sons and the most trusted of your advisers—those to whom you have confided the truth of the danger that threatens the Elves. Be certain of your choice. Have them gather in one hour in the chambers of the Elven High Council. Tell them that I would speak with them. Tell no one else. See to it that your guard keeps watch without. One hour. I will meet you then."

He turned and started back toward the open windows he had come through.

"Amberle . . . ?" Eventine called after him.

"One hour," the Druid repeated, then slipped through the curtains and was gone.

The allotted hour passed, and those summoned by the Elven King assembled in the High Council. The council room was a cavernous, hexagonal chamber built of oak and stone with its cathedral ceiling peaked starlike overhead at a joinder of massive beams. A set of huge wooden doors opened into the room, lighted by low-hanging oil lamps suspended at the ends of black iron chains. Against a facing wall was settled the dais of the King, a riser of steps leading to a great, hand-carved oaken throne flanked by a line of standards from which hung flags bearing the insignia of the houses of the Elven Kings. Gallery seats bordered the remaining walls, each set a dozen rows deep, all overlooking a broad expanse of polished stone flooring encircled like an arena by a low iron railing. At the exact center of the room stood a wide oval table with twenty-one chairs where sat the members of the Elven High Council.

Only six of these chairs were occupied this night. At one of them sat Ander Elessedil. He spoke little to the five seated with him, his eyes straying restlessly to the closed double doors at the far end of the chamber. Thoughts of Amberle crowded together in his mind. Although the girl had not been mentioned by his father when he had come to him with the news of Allanon's return, he was certain nevertheless that the Druid had succeeded in bringing her back to Arborlon; if not, this Council would not have been convened in such haste. He was equally certain that Allanon intended to bring her before the Council and ask that they entrust to her the search for the Bloodfire. He was not certain what the Council would say in response. If the King chose to speak first on the Druid's request and to lend it his support, then the others would probably acquiesce to his wishes—though this was by no means a foregone conclusion, given the strong feelings the Elves bore about Amberle. In any case, he did not believe that his father would do that. He would listen first to the advice of the men he had gathered about him. Then he would decide.

Ander glanced briefly at his father, then looked away again. What would his own advice be, he wondered suddenly? He would be asked to speak, yet how could he trust himself to be objective where Amberle was concerned? Conflicting emotions colored his reason with their intensity. Love and disappointment intermingled. His hands locked before him on the table in response to what he was feeling. Perhaps it would be best if he said nothing. Perhaps it would be best if he simply deferred to the judgment of the others.

His gaze shifted momentarily to their faces. Other than Dardan and Rhoe, who kept watch outside the chamber doors, no one else had been told of this meeting. There were others his father might have called—good men. But he had chosen these. It was a balanced choice, Ander thought to himself as he considered the character of each. But what sort of judgment would they exercise when they heard what was being asked?

He found that he was not sure.

Arion Elessedil sat on his father's right, the place at the Council table reserved for the Crown Prince of the realm. It was Arion to whom the King would look first, just as he always did whenever an important decision was required. Arion was his father's strength, and the old man loved him fiercely. Just his presence lent Eventine a sense of reassurance that Ander knew he could not provide, however he might try. But Arion lacked compassion and at times exhibited a stubbornness that obscured his good sense. It was difficult to predict what he might do where Amberle was concerned. Once he had been fond of the girl, the only child of his beloved brother Aine. But all that was long since past. His feelings had changed with the death of his brother—changed further with Amberle's betrayal of her trust as a Chosen. There was great bitterness within the Crown Prince, much of it caused by the obvious hurt that this girl had brought to the King. It was impossible to tell how deep that bitterness ran. Deep, Ander thought and was troubled by what that might mean.

The King's First Minister, Emer Chios, occupied the chair next to Arion. As First Minister, it was Chios who presided over the Council in the King's absence. An articulate, persuasive man, he could be depended upon to express his feelings candidly. Although Eventine and his First Minister were not always in agreement on matters that came before the Council, they nevertheless had great respect for each other's opinions. Eventine would listen closely to what his First Minister had to say.

Kael Pindanon, Commander of the Elven Army, was the King's oldest and closest friend. Though ten years younger than the King, Pindanon looked at least that much older, his face seamed like dry wood, his gnarled frame rawhide tough, scarred and knotted from a lifetime of combat. White hair flowed down below his shoulders, and a great, drooping mustache arched about the thin line of his mouth. Iron hard and fixed of purpose, Pindanon was the most predictable of Eventine's advisers. The old soldier was completely devoted to the King; he always advised with the King's best interests foremost in mind. It would be so with Amberle.

The last man at the table was not a member of the High

Council. He was younger even than Ander, a slim, dark-haired Elf with an alert air and anxious brown eyes. He sat next to Pindanon, his chair drawn back slightly from the oval table, not speaking to the others but watching them in silence. Twin daggers were strapped about his waist and a broadsword hung in its scabbard from the back of his chair. He wore no insignia of office save for a small medallion that bore the crest of the Elessedils and dangled from a silver chain about his neck. His name was Crispin. He was Captain of the Home Guard, the elite corps of Elven Hunters whose sole duty was the protection of the King. His presence at this Council was something of a mystery; he was not a man from whom Ander would have expected his father to seek advice. But then, his father did not always do what Ander expected.

He paused in his evaluation. With different backgrounds and different personalities, the men his father had gathered were alike only in their absolute loyalty to the old King. Perhaps because of that loyalty, they were men to whom Eventine felt he might safely entrust the decision, however difficult, that must be made concerning Amberle. Perhaps, too, they were here because they were the ones whose counsel he would seek when it came time to defend the Elven homeland.

And that time was near. The inevitability of a terrible struggle between Elves and Demons confronted them at every turn. Each day the Ellcrys weakened further, decay and wilt spreading inexorably through her branches, stripping her of beauty and life, weakening the power that maintained the Forbidding. Each day new reports were received of strange and frightening creatures, things born of nightmares and dark fantasies, prowling the borders of the Westland. Elven soldiers patrolled from the Valley of Rhenn to the Sarandanon, from the Matted Brakes to the Kershalt, and still the number of these creatures grew. It was certain that more would follow, until at last enough had broken free to unite and attack the Elves in force.

Ander rested his elbows on the table and folded his hands together against his forehead, shading his eyes against the light. The Ellcrys was failing so quickly that he wondered whether enough time remained to reach the

Bloodfire, even if Allanon had succeeded in his quest. Time! It all came down to that.

The massive doors at the far end of the chamber swung open and six heads turned as one. Allanon strode through, tall and forbidding in his black robes. With him came two smaller figures, cloaked and hooded, their faces hidden.

Amberle! Ander thought at once. One of them must be Amberle!

But who was the second?

All three moved wordlessly to the opposite end of the wide oval table. There the Druid seated his companions, then raised his dark face toward the King.

"My Lord Eventine." He bowed slightly.

"Allanon," the King replied. "You are welcome."

"All are assembled?"

"All," Eventine assured him, then named them one by one, "Please say what you have come to say."

Allanon came forward several paces until he stood midway between the Elves and the two cloaked figures.

"Very well. I would say this once only, so I ask that you listen and heed. The Elven nation stands in grave peril. The Ellcrys is dying. She fails quickly now, more quickly with the passing of each day. As she fails, the wall of the Forbidding weakens. Already the Demons your forefathers imprisoned within begin to break loose once more into your world. Soon all will be free and, once free, they will seek your annihilation."

The Druid came forward a pace. "Do not disbelieve this, Elven Lords. You do not yet appreciate, as I do, the extent of the hatred that drives them. I have seen but a handful of these creatures, a handful that have crossed already through the Forbidding, but even those few conveyed to me the whole of the hatred that has consumed them all. That hatred is awesome. It gives them power—more power than they possessed when they were first shut from the earth. I do not think that you will be able to stand against it."

"You do not know the Elven army!" Pindanon's face was dark.

"Commander." Eventine spoke softly. The old soldier turned at once. "Let us hear him out."

Pindanon sat back, frustration lining his jaw.

"The Ellcrys is the key to your preservation," Allanon continued, ignoring Pindanon. "When the Ellcrys dies, the Forbidding will be lost. The magic that created it will be lost. One thing can prevent that, and one thing only. In accordance with the Elven legend and the laws of magic that gave her life, the Ellcrys must undergo a rebirth. That can be accomplished in only one way. You know it well. A Chosen in service to the tree must carry her seed to the source of all life, the earth's Bloodfire. There the seed must be wholly immersed in the Fire, then returned to the earth where the mother tree roots. Then will there be new life for the Ellcrys. Then will the wall of the Forbidding be restored and the Demons shut once more from the earth.

"Men of Arborlon. Two weeks earlier, having discovered that the Ellcrys was dying, I came to Eventine Elessedil to offer what aid I could. I came too slowly. The Forbidding had begun to weaken already, permitting a few of the Demons imprisoned within to escape. Before I could act to prevent it, they had slain the Chosen, killing them as they slept, killing all they found.

"Nevertheless, I told the King that I would seek to aid the Elves in two ways. First, I would travel to Paranor to the castle of the Druids and there search the histories of my predecessors in an effort to learn the secret of the word 'Safehold.' I have done this. I have discovered where the Bloodfire can be found."

He paused, studying the faces of the men who listened. "I told the King as well that I would seek out one who might bear the seed of the Ellcrys in quest of the Bloodfire, for I believed that such a person existed. I have done this also. I have brought that person with me to Arborlon."

Ander tensed expectantly as a murmur of disbelief rose out of the men assembled. Allanon turned and beckoned to the smaller of the two cloaked figures.

"Come forward."

Hesitantly, the dark form rose, then walked to stand beside the Druid.

"Lower your hood."

Again there was hesitation. The Elves leaned forward impatiently—all but Eventine, who sat rigidly in his chair, hands gripping the carved wooden arms.

"Lower your hood," Allanon repeated gently.

This time the cloaked figure obeyed. Slim brown hands reached from beneath the folds of the robe and pulled back the concealing hood. Amberle's sea-green eyes, frozen with uncertainty, met those of her grandfather. There was an instant of stunned silence.

Then Arion sprang to his feet, livid with rage. "No! No, Druid! Take her out of here! Take her back to wherever it was you found her!"

Ander rose halfway out of his chair, shock reflected in his face at his brother's words, but his father caught his arm and brought him back to his seat. Quick, angry comments were exchanged, but the words were lost in a jumbled mix of voices that drowned one another out.

Eventine's hand went up sharply, and the room was still again.

"We will hear Allanon out," he repeated firmly, and Arion slipped back into his chair.

The Druid nodded. "I would ask you all to remember this. Only a Chosen in service may bear the seed of the Ellcrys. When the year began, there were seven. Six are dead. Amberle Elessedil is your last hope."

Arion leaped up. "She is no hope! She is no longer a Chosen!" The Elven Prince's voice was hard and bitter. Kael Pindanon nodded in agreement, distaste showing on his seamed face.

Allanon came forward a step. "You would question whether she is still a Chosen?" The faint, mocking smile passed quickly across his lips. "Know then that she questions this as well. But I have told her, and I have told her grandfather, and now I tell you, that no feelings in this, neither yours nor hers, will determine the truth of what she is. Your feelings are not of any consequence. King's grandchild or outcast from her people—what matter, Elven Prince? Your concern should be with the survival of your people—your people and the peoples of all the Lands, for this danger threatens them as well. If Amberle can be of service to you and to them, then what has gone before must be forgotten."

Arion stood his ground. "I will not forget. I will never forget."

"What is it that you ask of us?" Emer Chios interrupted quickly, and Arion sat down once more.

Allanon turned to face the First Minister. "Just this. Neither you nor I nor Amberle herself has the right to determine whether she is still a Chosen. Only the Ellcrys has that right, for it was the Ellcrys who determined that she should be a Chosen in the first place. Therefore we must know the tree's feelings. Let Amberle go before the Ellcrys; let the Ellcrys decide whether to accept or reject her. If she is accepted as a Chosen, she will be given a seed and she will go in search of the Bloodfire."

"And if she is rejected?"

"Then we had best hope that Commander Pindanon's faith in the Elven army is well placed."

Arion rose once more, ignoring the warning glance his father gave him.

"You ask too much of us, Druid. You ask that we place our trust in one who has already proven untrustworthy."

Allanon's voice was steady. "I ask that you place your trust in the Ellcrys, much as you have done for countless centuries. Let the decision be hers."

Arion shook his head. "No, I sense a game being played here, Druid. The tree speaks to no one; she will not speak to this girl." His angry gaze shifted to Amberle. "If the girl would have us trust her, let her tell us why she left Arborlon in the first place. Let her tell us why she disgraced herself and her family."

Allanon seemed to consider the request for a moment, then finally looked down at the Elven girl beside him. Amberle's face was white.

"I did not mean to bring disgrace to anyone," she replied quietly. "I did what I felt I had to do."

"You disgraced us!" Arion exploded. "You are my brother's child, and I loved my brother very much. I would like to understand what you did, but I do not. What you did brought shame to your family—to all of us. It brought shame to the memory of your father. No Chosen has ever rejected the honor of serving. None! But you, you discarded the honor as if it meant nothing!"

Amberle was rigid. "I was not meant to be a Chosen, Arion. It was a mistake. I tried to serve as did the others, but I could not. I know it was expected of me, but I . . . could not do it."

"Could not do it?" Arion came forward threateningly. "Why? I want to know why. This is your chance to explain—now do so!"

"I cannot!" she answered in a tight whisper. "I cannot. I could not make you understand, not if I wished, not if . . ." She looked imploringly at Allanon. "Why did you bring me back, Druid? This is senseless. They do not wish me here. I do not want to be here. I am frightened, do you understand? Let me return home."

"You are home," the Druid answered gently, a sadness in his voice that had not been there before. He looked over at Arion. "Your questions are pointless, Elven Prince. Give thought to the purpose for those questions. Give thought to their source. Hurt gives way to bitterness, bitterness to anger. Travel too far that road and the way is lost."

He paused, dark eyes fixing those of the Elven Council. "I do not pretend to understand what caused this girl to leave her people. I do not pretend to understand what caused her to choose a life different from that which was offered her in Arborlon. It is not my place to judge her, nor is it yours. What has gone before is done. She has shown courage and resolve in making the journey back to Arborlon. The Demons have learned of her; they have hunted her. They hunt her still. She has endured hardship and risked danger in returning. Should that have been for nothing?"

At the mention of danger to Amberle, alarm flickered briefly in Eventine's eyes. Ander saw it; it was there and then quickly gone.

"You might have taken this girl before the Ellcrys without consulting us," Emer Chios pointed out suddenly. "Why didn't you?"

"Amberle did not wish to return to Arborlon," Allanon responded. "She came because I persuaded her that it was necessary, that she must help her people if she could. Still, she should not be forced to come in secrecy and stealth, but openly. If she is to go before the Ellcrys, it should be with your approval."

His arm slipped about her slender shoulders. She glanced up at him, surprise reflected in her child's face.

"You must make your choice." The Druid's face was impassive. "Which of you will stand beside her, Elven Lords?"

The chamber grew still. Elves and Druid stared wordlessly at one another, eyes locked. All but forgotten by now, the second cloaked form shifted nervously at the far end of the table. The seconds slipped away. No one rose.

Then suddenly Ander Elessedil found Allanon looking directly at him. Something unspoken passed between them, an understanding almost. In that instant Ander knew what he must do.

Slowly he came to his feet.

"Ander!" he heard his brother protest.

He glanced quickly at Arion's dark face, saw the warning mirrored in the other's hard eyes, then looked away again. Wordlessly, he moved around the table until he stood before Amberle. She stared up at him, frightened, like a wild thing poised to flee. Gently he took hold of her shoulders and bent to kiss her forehead. There were tears in her eyes as she hugged him back.

Emer Chios rose. "I do not see that there should be any difficulty in making this decision, my Lords," he addressed them. "Whatever options we may have, we should certainly take advantage of them."

He stepped over to join Ander.

Crispin glanced briefly at Eventine. The King sat rigid, his face expressionless as he met his Captain's eyes. Crispin stood up and crossed to stand beside Ander.

The Council had divided evenly. Three stood with Amberle; three remained seated at the table. Eventine looked at Arion. The Crown Prince of the Elves met his father's gaze squarely, then turned his bitter eyes on Ander.

"I am not the fool that my brother is. I say no."

The King looked at Pindanon. The old soldier's face was hard.

"My trust is in the Elven Army, not this child." Then he seemed to hesitate. "She is your flesh and blood. My vote will be as yours, my King. Cast it well."

All eyes fixed now on Eventine. For an instant he did not seem to have heard. He sat staring at the table before him, a look of sadness and resignation on his face. His hands slid slowly across the polished wooden surface, then locked tightly.

He came to his feet.

"It is decided then. Amberle shall go before the Ellcrys. This Council is adjourned."

Arion Elessedil rose, cast a withering glance at Ander, and stalked from the High Council without a word.

Within the concealing shadow of his cowl, Wil Ohmsford saw the pain and disbelief mirrored in Ander Elessedil's eyes as he stared after his brother. A breach had been opened between these two that would not quickly be closed again. Then the Elven Prince's gaze shifted suddenly to meet his own, and he looked away self-consciously.

Allanon was speaking again, advising those who remained that Amberle would rest a day or two before going to the Ellcrys and that after she had done so they would meet once more. Wil rose, keeping his robes drawn close about him, for Allanon had warned that he was not to reveal himself. The chamber began to empty, and he moved over to stand with Amberle. He saw Ander Elessedil cast a glance back at them, hesitate, then follow the others out. Allanon had drawn Eventine aside and was speaking to him, their words hushed and secretive. There appeared to be some argument between them. Then, with a reluctant nod, the Elven King departed as well. Wil and Amberle were left alone with the Druid.

Allanon beckoned. "Follow me."

Quickly he led them from the council room, ushering them back down the outer hallway until they stood once more in the cool dark of the entry beyond. The Druid paused, listened, and then turned to them.

"Amberle." He waited until her eyes were fixed on his. "I want you to go to the Ellcrys tonight."

Surprise and confusion registered on the Elven girl's face.

"Why?" she asked in disbelief, then quickly shook her head. "No. No, this is too quick! I want time to prepare myself before I do this. Besides, you just finished telling my father and the others that it would be a day or two before I went to her!"

Allanon nodded patiently. "A small but necessary deception. As for preparation, what preparation will you make? This is not a test of skill or endurance; no amount of preparation will help you. Either you are still a Chosen in service to the tree or you are not."

"I am tired, Druid!" She was angry now. "I am tired and I need to sleep! I cannot do this thing now!"

"You must." He paused. "I know that you are tired; I know that you need sleep. But that will have to wait. You must first go to the tree—and you must do so now."

She went rigid at his words, a trapped look springing into her eyes. Then she began to cry, uncontrollably. It was as if everything that had happened—the unexpected appearance of the Druid at her cottage, the news that the Ellcrys was dying and the Chosen slain, the realization that she must return to Arborlon, the harrowing flight north from Havenstead, the confrontation with the Council and her grandfather, and now this—had caught up with her all at once and overwhelmed her completely. All of her defenses seemed to give way. She stood before them, small and vulnerable, sobbing, choking on words that would not come. When Allanon reached for her, she pulled quickly away, stepping apart from them both for several long minutes. Wil Ohmsford stared after her helplessly.

She stopped crying finally, her face still turned away from them. When she spoke, her voice was barely a whisper.

"Is it truly necessary, Allanon—truly necessary—that I go to her tonight?"

The Druid nodded. "Yes, Elven girl."

There was a long silence. "Then I will do so."

Quiet and composed once more, she rejoined them. Without a word, Allanon led them out into the streets of the city.

XIX

Pale silver moonlight spilled down out of the heavens and washed the summer night. Sweet smells and comforting hums rose out of the dark in slow, dizzying waves that floated and danced in the warm breezes and brushed the hedgerows and stands, the flower banks, and the bushes of the Garden of Life. Dappled shadows layered the Gardens' colors in oddly knit patterns of black and white. Tiny life forms that awoke with darkness skittered and flew with sudden, invisible bursts that left no trace of their passing.

In the midst of it all, solitary and ignored atop the small hillock that overlooked the homeland of the Elves, the wondrous tree they called the Ellcrys continued its slow, inevitable march toward death. The long journey had begun to take its toll. The perfect beauty that had marked the Ellcrys in health was gone, the perfect symmetry of her form marred and broken. Silver bark peeled away from trunk and limbs, black and rotting, hanging in strips like tattered skin. Blood-red leaves curled tight with wilt, a scattering of those that had already fallen dotting the earth beneath, dried and withered husks, rustling with the wind. Like some weathered scarecrow set upon a pole above the fields, she stood stark and skeletal against the night horizon.

Allanon, Wil Ohmsford, and Amberle stared up at her wordlessly from the base of the rise, cowled faces lifted against the screen of moonlight. For a long time they were still, motionless save for the ripple of cloth garments in the light breezes, silent. When Amberle finally spoke, her whisper filled the quiet with deep, sudden poignancy.

191

"Oh, Allanon, she looks so sad."

The Druid did not respond, his tall spare frame rigid beneath the robes, his face hidden within the shadow of the cowl. The smell of lilacs wafted past them, lingered momentarily, and was gone. After a moment, Amberle glanced over at the big man, arms folding tightly into her robe.

"Is she in pain?"

The movement of the Druid's head was barely perceptible. "Some."

"She is dying?"

"Her life is ending. Her time is almost gone."

There was a long pause. "Can you do nothing for her?"

"What can be done for her must be done by you." Allanon's deep voice was a gentle murmur.

Amberle's sigh was audible, a shiver of acceptance that passed through her slender body. The seconds slipped away. Wil shuffled his feet wearily, waiting for the Elven girl to come to terms with herself. This was not easy for her. She had not expected even to be here tonight; neither of them had. They had expected that, with the adjournment of the Council, they would be allowed at long last to sleep. There had been no sleep since before their flight into the Valley of Rhenn and their unexpected reunion with Allanon. They were exhausted.

"She is sleeping," Amberle whispered suddenly.

"She will wake for you," the Druid responded.

She does not want this, Wil thought. *She has never wanted this. She is not simply unwilling, she is frightened. She said so that first night in the little garden behind her home. Yet she has never said why.*

Wil looked toward the summit of the rise. What was it about the Ellcrys that frightened her so?

"I am ready."

She said it simply, her voice calm. Allanon was silent for a moment, then nodded, the cowl bending slightly with his response.

"Then go. We will wait for you here."

She did not move at once, but stood quietly for a moment as if seeking something more from the Druid. But there was nothing more offered. Gathering her robes about her, she started forward, moving up the gentle slope, face lifted toward the still, ragged tree that waited at the top.

She did not look back.

She completed the climb in only moments and stood alone before the Ellcrys. She stood, not yet within reach of the tree, but just beyond, her small form withdrawn into the concealing folds of the dark robe, her arms clenched tightly against her sides. From atop the rise, the Westland lay open to the sweep of the horizon, and she felt small and unprotected. The night breeze blew across her face, laced with the scents of the garden, and she breathed it deeply, steadying herself.

I need only a moment, she told herself. Just one moment.

But she was so afraid!

She still did not understand why this was, not even now, after all this time. She should be able to understand it; she should be able to control it. Yet she could not. That made it all the worse. The fear was unreasoning, senseless, blind. It was always there, lurking in the back of her mind like some beast of prey, slipping from its place of hiding whenever she gave thought to the Ellcrys. She fought against it, struggled determinedly, but it swept through her nonetheless, irrepressible, dark. She had been able to suppress it in Havenstead, for in Havenstead the cause was distant and past. But now, returned once more to Arborlon, standing less than a dozen feet away, remembering the touch of the Ellcrys . . .

She shuddered at the memory. It was the touch she really feared. Yet why should that be? No harm came from it, no injury. It served only to allow the Ellcrys to communicate her thoughts through images. But there was this sense of something more that had always come with the touch, ever since that first time the Ellcrys had spoken with her. Something.

Her thoughts scattered at the sound of an owl's soft hoot. She was aware that she had been standing there for several minutes and that the two men waiting below must be watching her. She did not want that.

Quickly, she began to walk around to the far side of the tree.

* * *

Druid and Valeman watched silently as the dark figure of the Elven girl circled the Ellcrys and disappeared from view. They remained standing a moment longer; but when she did not reappear, Allanon seated himself wordlessly on the grass. Wil paused, then sat down next to him.

"What will you do if the Ellcrys decides that she is no longer one of the Chosen?"

The Druid did not turn his head. "That will not happen."

The Valeman hesitated a moment before speaking again.

"You know something about her that you have not told either of us, don't you?"

Allanon's voice was cold. "No. Not in the sense that you mean."

"But in some sense."

"What must concern you, Valeman, is seeing that nothing happens to her after you leave Arborlon."

The way he said it left Wil with the very distinct impression that this particular subject was closed. The Valeman shifted his weight uncomfortably.

"Can you tell me something else, then?" he asked a moment later. "Can you tell me why she is so afraid of the Ellcrys?"

"No."

Wil flushed heatedly within his cowl. "Why not?"

"Because I am not sure that I understand it myself. Nor do I think that she does. In any case, when she is ready for you to know about it, she will tell you herself."

"I doubt it." Wil slouched forward, arms resting loosely on his knees. "She does not seem to think much of me."

Allanon did not respond. They sat in silence for a time, glancing periodically toward the summit of the rise and the solitary tree. There was no sign of Amberle. Wil glanced over at the Druid.

"Is she safe up there alone?"

The mystic nodded. Wil waited for him to explain why she was safe, but he did not offer an explanation. The Valeman shrugged. Being this close to her, he must have some means of seeing to it that she was protected, he decided.

At least he hoped so.

* * *

For a long time Amberle did not move. She could not. Her fear had paralyzed her. She stood rigid and chilled not five feet from the nearest branches, staring hypnotically at the Ellcrys. Within her, the fear ran like liquid ice, numbing even her thoughts. She lost all sense of time, of place, of everything but her inability to take those last few steps forward.

When at last she did take them, it seemed that it was someone else who took them for her. She remembered only the distance between herself and the Ellcrys closing and then disappearing altogether. She was beneath the canopy of the tree, lost in shadow. The night breeze died into stillness, and the cold within her turned to heat.

Wordlessly, she dropped to her knees amid the clutter of dead leaves and broken twigs that blanketed the ground, her hands folding tightly in her lap. She waited.

Moments later, a ragged branch dipped downward and wrapped gently about her shoulders.

—Amberle—

The Elven girl began to cry.

There had been silence between them for quite some time when Wil suddenly recalled something odd that Allanon had said earlier. He had determined that he would ask nothing further of the Druid following their last exchange, but his curiosity got the better of him.

"Allanon?"

The Druid looked at him.

"Something is bothering me." He took a moment to arrange his words. "When you told Amberle that we must come here tonight, she reminded you that you had informed the Elves at the High Council that she would be given a day or two to rest. You answered her by saying that what you told them was a necessary deception. What did you mean by that?"

Moonlight revealed the familiar mocking smile as it slanted across the mystic's lean face.

"I was wondering when you would get around to that question, Wil Ohmsford." He laughed softly. "Your inquisitiveness is all-encompassing."

Wil grinned ruefully. "Do I get an answer to my question?"

Allanon nodded. "An answer that will not please you. The deception was necessary because there is a spy within the Elven camp."

The Valeman went cold. "How do you know that?"

"Logic. When I arrived at Paranor, the Demons were waiting for me. Waiting for me, Valeman—I was not followed. That suggests rather strongly that they knew in advance that I would be coming there. How did they know that? For that matter, how did they know about me in the first place? Only Eventine knew that I had returned to the Four Lands. Only Eventine knew of my plans to travel to Paranor; I told him in confidence that I would go there to study the Druid histories in an effort to discover the location of Safehold. Eventine was cautioned to say nothing and would have done exactly that."

He paused. "That leaves only one possibility. Someone listened in on our conversation—someone who had reason to betray us to the Demons."

Wil looked doubtful. "But how could that have happened? You said yourself that no one even knew that you had returned to the Four Lands before you spoke to Eventine."

"That puzzles me, also," the Druid admitted. "The spy must be someone with easy access to the King, someone who would know everything that he is about. One of his household staff, perhaps."

He shrugged. "In any case, it was fortunate that I did not mention to the King where Amberle could be found or the Demons would almost certainly have reached her before I did." He paused, black eyes fixing on the Valeman. "They would have reached you, as well, I imagine."

Wil felt his skin crawl. The suggestion was a thoroughly disconcerting one, even now. For the first time since he had met Allanon, he was grateful that the Druid was so closemouthed about what he knew.

"If all this is so, then why did you tell the Elves at the High Council so much?" he asked. "If there is a spy, isn't there a rather good possibility that he may discover everything that was said at that meeting?"

The Druid leaned forward. "A very good possibility. In fact, I intend to make certain that he does. That is the reason for the deception. You see, the Demons already know that we are here, and they know why we are here. They know who I am; they know who Amberle is. They do not yet know who you are. All this they have discovered from my conversation with Eventine and from what they have seen in pursuing us from Havenstead. We have told the Elves at the High Council nothing new—except for one small item. We have told them that Amberle will rest for several days before she goes to the Ellcrys. So, for the next several days, at least, the Demons will expect us to do nothing. That deception, I hope, will give us a small but very useful advantage."

"What kind of advantage?" Wil frowned. "What do you have in mind, Allanon?"

The Druid pursed his lips. "As to that, Wil, I am afraid that I will have to ask you to be patient for a bit longer. But I promise that you will have your answer before the night is done. Fair enough?"

There was nothing particularly fair about any of this, Wil thought glumly. Still, there was no point in pressing the matter. When Allanon had made up his mind, Wil knew that that was the end of it.

"One thing more." The Druid put a cautionary hand on his shoulder. "Say nothing of this to Amberle. She is frightened enough as it is, and there is no reason that she should be frightened further. Let this remain a secret between you and me."

The Valeman nodded. That much, at least, they could agree upon.

Only minutes later, Amberle appeared suddenly from beneath the shadow of the tree. She stood for a moment silhouetted against the night sky, hesitated, then started toward them. She walked slowly, carefully, as if uncertain of her movements, hands held clasped together against her breast. Her cowl was lowered, her long, chestnut hair fanning out behind her in the breeze. As she neared them, they could see plainly her stricken face. It was pale and drawn and streaked with tears, and fear reflected brightly in her eyes.

She came up to them and stopped. Her slender form was trembling.

"Allanon . . . ?" she cried softly, choking on his name.

The Druid saw that she was on the verge of collapsing. He reached for her at once, took her in his arms and held her close against him. She allowed herself to be held this time, crying soundlessly. For a long time he held her, all the while saying nothing. Wil watched uncomfortably and felt generally useless.

After a time, the crying stopped. Allanon released the Elven girl and stepped back. Her face remained lowered for a moment, then lifted to his.

"You were right," she whispered.

Clasped hands came away from the folds of her robe and slowly opened. Nestled in her palms, like a perfectly formed silver-white stone, was the seed of the Ellcrys.

XX

Moments later, Allanon led them from the Gardens. Cowls drawn close about their faces and cloaks laced tight, they slipped through the gates and past the sentries of the Black Watch and started back toward the city. The Druid did not offer any explanation as to where he was taking them, and they did not ask. They walked in silence, Allanon a step or two ahead, Wil and Amberle following. Both were exhausted. The Valeman glanced often at the Elven girl, more worried about her than he cared to admit even to himself, but she gave little indication of her emotional state, and he caught only an occasional glimpse of her face within the covering of the hood. Once he asked quietly if she was all right, and she nodded back to him without speaking.

A short time afterward, they found themselves approaching the manor house of the Elessedils. Beckoning wordlessly, Allanon led them onto the grounds surrounding the darkened home, directing them through a screen of pine that bordered the south lawn, then along a series of hedgerows to a small alcove and a pair of floor-length glass windows draped in heavy shadow. Standing before the doors, Allanon tapped softly on the glass. There was a moment's wait, then the curtains covering the window moved slightly. A latch within was released, and the doors swung open. Quickly Allanon motioned them through, glanced furtively about, and followed, closing the doors behind him.

They stood for a few seconds in darkness, listening to the faint sound of footfalls as someone moved slowly about the room. Then a light was struck to a candle's wick. Wil found that they were in a small study, burnished oak from walls and shelving gleaming in the candle's dim flame, soft tracings of color from leather-bound books and tapestries visible through the heavy shadows. At the far side of the little room, an aged wolfhound raised his grizzled head from a small earthen-colored rug on which he lay and thumped his tail in greeting.

Eventine Elessedil placed the candle on a small work-table and turned to face them.

"Is everything arranged?" Allanon's deep voice broke the stillness.

The old King nodded.

"And your household?" The Druid was already moving across the room to the single door that led into the rest of the home. He opened it, looked through briefly, then closed it again.

"Everyone sleeps but Dardan and Rhoe, and they stand watch at my bedroom door, believing me asleep as well. There is no one here but old Manx."

The wolfhound glanced over at the mention of his name, then lowered his head between his paws and closed his eyes.

Allanon walked back across the room. "Then we can begin."

He motioned Wil and Amberle to take chairs about the worktable, drawing a third chair over for himself. The Valeman sat down wearily. Amberle started forward, then stopped, her eyes on her grandfather. Eventine looked back at her, hesitated, then moved quickly to embrace her. The Elven girl went rigid for a moment, then her arms went about him.

"I love you, grandfather," she whispered. "I missed you."

The old King did not speak, but nodded into her shoulder, one hand coming up to stroke her hair. Then he took her head gently in his hands and tilted it back so that she was facing him.

"What has happened is behind us, Amberle. Forgotten. There will be no more harsh words between us. This is your home. I want you here with me, with your family."

The Elven girl shook her head sadly. "I have spoken with

the Ellcrys, grandfather. She has told me that I am her Chosen. She has given to me her seed."

The old man's face went pale, and his eyes dropped. "I am sorry, Amberle. I know that you wish it could be otherwise. Believe me, I wish it could be otherwise, too."

"I know you do," she replied, but there was despair in her eyes.

She separated from him and seated herself at the table with Allanon and Wil. The King remained standing for a moment, his eyes staring over at his granddaughter. There was a lost and frightened look to him that suggested a child strayed. Slowly he recovered himself, then moved to sit with the others.

Allanon leaned forward, hands folding carefully atop the table.

"Eventine and I agreed at the close of the High Council that we would meet in secret later this night. What is said here shall remain between the four of us and no other. Time slips away from us, and we must act quickly if we are to save the Elven people. The Ellcrys is failing. Soon the Demons contained within the Forbidding will break through into the Four Lands. Eventine and I shall be there to meet them when they do. But you, Amberle, and you also, Wil, must go in search of the Bloodfire."

He turned to the Elven girl. "I would go with you if I could. I would go with you if there were any possible way to do so, but there is not. One of the Demons that has already broken through the Forbidding, as well as some still locked within, possess powers that your grandfather and the Elven people cannot stand against without my help. It will be my task to shield the Elves from those powers. Sorcery to withstand sorcery. It must be so.

"But in my place, I send Wil Ohmsford, and I have not chosen lightly to entrust your care and safety to him. It was his grandfather who went with me in search of the Sword of Shannara, who found it, and who then stood alone against the Warlock Lord and saw him destroyed. His great-uncle Flick once saved your grandfather's life. Wil has the strength of character that marked both men; he has their sense of honor. You have seen that he holds the Elfstones that I once gave to his grandfather. He will protect you as I would. He will stand with you, Amberle— he will not fail you."

There was a long moment of silence. The Valeman felt embarrassed by the Druid's words—embarrassed and uneasy. He was not so sure of himself. He glanced quickly at Amberle and found her staring back at him.

"You are a Chosen in service to the Ellcrys," Allanon continued, drawing the Elven girl's eyes back to meet his own. "Though we all might wish it were otherwise, the matter has been settled as we agreed that it should be. You are the last of the Chosen, and therefore the last hope of your people. You alone can restore the Forbidding. A terrible responsibility, Amberle, but it belongs to you. If you fail, Demon and Elf will do battle until one or both have been utterly destroyed. The Ellcrys has given you her seed, and so you must take it in quest of the Bloodfire. That will not be easily done. The Bloodfire lies within a place called Safehold, and Safehold is a part of the old world. That world is gone, forever changed. Down through the ages, the place called Safehold has been all but forgotten. Even the Ellcrys no longer recognizes the path that leads there. If not for the Druid histories, Safehold might have been irretrievably lost to us. Yet the histories are a link between past and present. I have read them and know where Safehold lies."

He paused. "It lies within the Wilderun."

No one said a word. There was no need. Even Wil Ohmsford, a Southlander and a Valeman who until now had never set foot in the Westland, had heard of the Wilderun. Buried within the forests that lay south of the Elven homeland, it was a treacherous and forbidding stretch of wilderness virtually encircled by mountains and swamp. Fewer than half a dozen hamlets could be found there, and those were peopled by thieves, cutthroats, and outlaws of every conceivable sort. Even they seldom strayed far from their villages or the few well-worn trails that crisscrossed the region, for in the timber beyond, the rumors said, were creatures no man would care to encounter.

Wil took a deep breath. "You wouldn't happen to know where within the Wilderun we are to find the Bloodfire?"

Allanon shook his head. "I cannot be sure. Even the Druid histories refer in part to the geography of the old world, and the landmarks that existed then are gone. You will have to rely on the Elfstones."

"I thought as much." The Valeman sagged back in his chair. "Use of the Elfstones will tell the Demons where we can be found."

"Unfortunately true. You will have to exercise great discretion, Wil. I will relate to you what the Ellcrys told the Chosen about Safehold before they were slain—what she later told also to me. This may help you in your search. The Bloodfire lies within a wilderness with mountains and swamp all around—obviously the Wilderun, as the Druid histories record. Now here is the rest of what she said. There is a deep mist that comes and goes. Within the wilderness can be found a lone peak; beneath the peak is a maze of tunnels that burrow deep within the earth. Somewhere within the maze is a door made of glass that will not break. Behind the door you will find the Bloodfire."

He cocked his head reflectively. "As you can see, the general description of the Wilderun remains surprisingly accurate, even after the passage of so many years and the cataclysmic changes wrought in the geography of the earth by the Great Wars. Perhaps the balance of the description remains accurate as well. Perhaps the Bloodfire may still be found beneath a lone peak, within a maze of tunnels." He shrugged. "I would give you more help if I had it to give, but I do not. You must do the best you can with that."

Wil managed a faint, if somewhat forced, smile of encouragement. He did not dare look over at Amberle.

"How do we reach the Wilderun?" he asked.

The Druid glanced questioningly at Eventine, but the Elven King appeared preoccupied. At last, distracted by the silence, he looked over at Allanon and nodded absently.

"Everything has been arranged."

The Druid seemed to hesitate, then turned to Amberle. "Your grandfather has selected Captain Crispin, who commands the Home Guard, to be your guide and protector on this journey. Crispin is a very resourceful and courageous soldier; he will serve you well. He has been instructed to choose half a dozen Elven Hunters as your escort. Six is a small number, but a small number may be best in this case. It will attract far less attention than a large command and it should enable you to travel more swiftly.

"The plan that the King and I have settled on is this. You will be taken from the city in secret; the means have been left to Captain Crispin. Only Crispin will be aware of your mission. He and the Elven Hunters under his command will go with you as far as you need them. All will have been instructed that no harm is to befall you, that they are to do whatever is necessary to protect you."

"Allanon."

It was Eventine who spoke, glancing over suddenly, a worried look on his face. His penetrating blue eyes found those of the Druid.

"There is something I have not yet told you. I did not speak of this before because we had only those few moments at the close of the Council. But I think something should be said now. There is reason for concern in this venture beyond the obvious danger of being tracked by the Demons who have pursued you this far."

He leaned forward, arms crossing loosely on the table to support his weight. His face, caught in the dim light of the candle, seemed very old.

"You know how the Chosen died—perhaps Wil and Amberle do not." His gaze shifted. "They were torn apart, mangled almost beyond recognition."

Horror reflected in the faces of the Elven girl and the Valeman. The King put his hand gently on his grand-daughter's shoulder.

"I do not tell you this to frighten you more, Amberle, nor you, Wil, but because of this." He looked back at Allanon. "Since you have been gone from Arborlon, there have been more deaths like those of the Chosen. A great many deaths. Whatever it was that killed them has been roaming the surrounding country, systematically destroying every-thing and everyone it encounters, man or beast, young or old. Over fifty Elves have died—all in the same manner, all by being ripped apart. Three nights ago, an entire Elven patrol was waylaid and destroyed. Six armed men. A week earlier, an army compound at the north edge of the city was invaded and twenty men were killed while they slept. There has been an increasing number of Demons sighted in the Westland since the Ellcrys began to fail and more than a few unpleasant pitched fights as well—but nothing on this order, nothing as deliberate and premeditated. This creature knows what it is about; it kills with purpose. We have tried without success to track it. We cannot find it. We have not even seen it. No one has. But it is out there—and it hunts us."

He paused. "It was sent once, Allanon, for the purpose of destroying the Chosen. It did so—all but one. It may be that it will be sent again."

Amberle had gone white. Allanon rubbed his bearded chin thoughtfully.

"Yes, there was such a Demon in the old days," he mused. "A Demon that killed out of instinctive need. They called it a Reaper."

"I don't care what they called it," Wil spoke up suddenly. "What I want to know is how to avoid it."

"Secrecy," the Druid offered. "However vicious and cunning this Demon, it will have no more reason than its brethren to suspect that you have left Arborlon. If it believes that you are still here—if they all believe that you are still here—they will not be looking for you elsewhere. Perhaps we can give them that impression."

He turned to Eventine. "The time will come very soon now when the Ellcrys can no longer maintain the wall of the Forbidding with sufficient strength to contain the remainder of the Demons still imprisoned within. When that time comes, the Demons will concentrate their strength at the wall's weakest point and break free. We cannot wait for that to happen. We must find the place where they will attempt their crossover and do what we can to prevent it. Even if we fail, we can fight a delaying action which will slow them in their march on Arborlon. They will try to march here, for they will seek to destroy the Ellcrys. They must. They cannot tolerate her. Remember that while she was strong, she was anathema to them. But as she weakens, she becomes less so. Once they have broken through her wall, they will move quickly to destroy her. We must do what we can to prevent that. We must give

Amberle time to reach the Bloodfire and return again. We must keep the Demons from Arborlon until then.

"So." He let the word hang for a moment in the silence of the little room. "We shall deceive the Demons who are already through the Forbidding by acting as if preparations to seek the Bloodfire are yet to be completed. We shall make it appear as if you have not left. The Demons know that it was I who brought Amberle here; they will expect me to be with her when she leaves. We can make use of that. We can focus their attention on me. By the time they realize that they have been misled, you should be well beyond their reach."

Unless their spy is more resourceful than you anticipate, Wil wanted to say; but he decided not to.

"It all sounds very promising," he said instead. "That seems to settle everything except the matter of when we should leave."

The Druid leaned back in his chair. "You will leave at dawn."

Wil stared at him in disbelief. "At dawn? Tomorrow?"

Amberle sprang to her feet. "That is impossible, Druid! We are exhausted! We have not slept in almost two days— we have to have more than a few hours rest before setting out again!"

Allanon held up his hands. "Peace, Elven girl. I understand this as well as you. But consider. The Demons know that you have come here for the purpose of carrying the seed of the Ellcrys to the Bloodfire. They know that you will attempt to leave the city, and they will be watching closely. But they will not be watching as closely now as they will in a day or two. Do you know why? Because they will expect you to rest first. That is exactly why you must leave at once. Surprise offers you your best chance to slip past them."

Understanding flickered in Wil's eyes. This was the advantage that the Druid had hoped his deception at the High Council might yield them.

"There will be sufficient rest for you after you are gone from the city," Allanon promised. "Two days of travel will enable you to reach the Elven outpost in Drey Wood; you can catch up on your lost sleep there. But delay in Arborlon is dangerous. The quicker you are gone from here, the better your chances."

Wil hated to admit it, but there was logic in the Druid's argument. He glanced quickly at Amberle. She stared down at him silently for a moment, frustrated and angry, then turned back to Allanon.

"I want to see my mother before I leave."

The Druid shook his head. "That is not a good idea, Amberle."

Her jaw tightened. "You seem to think that you have the final say in whatever I wish to do, Druid. You don't. I want to see my mother."

"The Demons know who you are. If they know also of your mother, they will expect you to go to her. They will be waiting for just that. It is dangerous."

"Just being here is dangerous. Surely you can find a way for me to spend five minutes with my mother." Her eyes dropped. "Do not be so foolish as to suggest that I should see her when I return."

There was an unpleasant moment of silence. Allanon's dark face turned suddenly expressionless, as if he were afraid he might reveal something he wished to remain hidden. Wil did not miss the change, and it puzzled him.

"As you wish," the Druid agreed. He rose. "Now you must sleep while you can. We must go."

Eventine stood up with him, turning to face his grand-daughter.

"I am sorry that Arion spoke so harshly at the Council," he apologized, looking as if he had something more to say, but could not. He shook his head. "I think that in time he will come to understand as I did . . ."

He trailed off awkwardly, then put his arms around Amberle and kissed her cheeks.

"If I were not so old . . ." he began emotionally, but the girl put her fingers to his mouth to stop him. She shook her head.

"You are not so old that you do not see that you are needed here more than you are needed to go with me." She smiled, and there were tears in her eyes as she kissed him back.

Feeling a bit self-conscious, Wil stepped away from the

table and moved quietly over to the sleeping Manx. The aged wolfhound heard his approach. One eye stared up at him questioningly. On impulse, Wil reached down to pet the dog, but Manx gave a low, barely audible growl of warning. Wil drew back.

Unfriendly beast, the Valeman thought to himself.

He returned to the others. Eventine shook hands with him and wished him well. Then with Amberle beside him, Wil followed Allanon back through the floor-length windows into the night.

XXI

The Druid took them to a small cottage nestled on a forested slope at the northern edge of the city amid a cluster of similarly structured homes. There was nothing to set this particular cottage apart from any of the others, and this suggested to Wil the principal reason for its selection. Though unoccupied when they entered, it was fully furnished and had been lived in recently. Allanon did not offer to explain what had become of the owners. He entered the cottage as if it were his own, moved through the darkness of a living room to light several oil lamps, then carefully drew closed all the curtains that decorated the cottage windows. Having checked once through the remaining rooms while Wil and Amberle sat waiting at a small table graced with freshly cut flowers and embroidered mats, he returned momentarily with bread, cheese, fruit, and a pitcher of water. They ate in silence, Wil consuming a full meal despite the late hour, Amberle eating almost nothing. When dinner was finished, Allanon led the Elven girl to a small bedroom at the rear of the home. A single shuttered window stood latched and barred behind drawn curtains. The Druid checked the fastenings thoroughly, then nodded. Wordlessly, Amberle moved to the feather bed. She was so tired that she did not even bother to undress, but simply kicked off her boots and fell wearily across the covers. She was asleep almost immediately. Allanon paused long enough to place a light blanket over the exhausted girl, then stepped from the room, closing the door noiselessly behind him.

Alone in the living room, Wil Ohmsford stared through the curtained windows into the darkness beyond, where the lights of the city proper winked back at him like fireflies in the forest shadows. He glanced about restlessly as the Druid reappeared.

"We have to talk, Allanon."

The big man did not look surprised.

"Still more questions, Wil Ohmsford?"

"Not exactly." The Valeman looked uncomfortable.

"I see. Well then, why don't we sit down?"

Wil nodded, and they moved over to take chairs across from one another at the little table where they had eaten their meal. Once seated, the Valeman seemed uncertain as to how to proceed. Allanon regarded him expressionlessly, waiting.

"Something happened to me when I tried to use the Elfstones on that Demon in the Tirfing—something that I do not understand," Wil began finally, avoiding the other's dark eyes. "I had almost decided against saying anything to you about it because I did not want you to think that I was looking for an excuse not to make the journey into the Wilderun."

"That would have been foolish." Allanon spoke quietly. "Tell me what it is that happened."

The Valeman did not seem to hear him. "The only reason I decided to speak about it was that I grew concerned for Amberle's safety if I remained quiet. If I am to be her protector, then I cannot afford to play games with my pride."

"Tell me what happened," the Druid repeated.

Wil looked up uneasily. "I will explain it in the best way I can. As I said, when the Demon came at me and I tried to use the Elfstones, something inside of me resisted. It was like some sort of blockage, like a wall that had imposed itself between me and the Elfstones so that I could not call upon them for aid. I held them out before me and tried to reach down into them, to call forth their power, but nothing happened. In that instant, I was certain that you had been wrong in your belief that I could use the Stones as my grandfather had done. I thought that I was going to die. But then, just before the Demon reached me, the wall within me seemed to break apart, and the power of the Stones flared out and destroyed the creature."

He paused. "Since then, I have thought carefully about what happened. At first I decided that I simply had not understood how to use the Elfstones, that it was my inexperience or confusion that caused the resistance. But I no longer believe that. It was something different. It was something about me."

The Druid stared back at him wordlessly for several minutes. One hand toyed idly with the small black beard, pulling at it, twisting it. Finally the hand moved away.

"You will remember that I told you that the Elfstones were an old magic, a magic from the days before Man, a magic that belonged to the age when the faerie people ruled the earth and magic was commonplace. There were many different Elfstones then, and they served many different purposes. Their colors identified their uses. The blue Elfstones, such as those that you hold, were the seeking Stones. Possession of the blue Elfstones enabled the holder to find that which was hidden from him merely by willing that it be so—for example, the Bloodfire for which you will search. Other Elfstones exhibited other characteristics. All possessed the common characteristic of offering the holder protection against other magics and things created of magic and sorcery. But the extent of that protection—indeed, the extent of the power of the Stones —was dependent entirely on the strength of character of the holder. The Stones were grouped in sets of three; there was a reason for this. Each Stone represented a part of the holder: one Stone for the heart, one Stone for the body, one Stone for the mind. For the magic to be given life, the three would have to act in concert—three individual strengths joining as one. The success of the holder in employing the Elfstones was a measure of his ability to unite those strengths."

He spread his hands upon the table. "The Elfstones have another characteristic, Wil—one basic to their use. The Elfstones are an Elven magic; they were created by Elven wizards for the Elves only. They have been passed from generation to generation, family to family, hand to hand— but always by Elves to Elves, for none other could ever use the Stones."

A look of disbelief crossed the Valeman's face. "Are you trying to tell me that I cannot use the Elfstones because I am not an Elf?" he exclaimed.

Allanon shook his head. "It is not as simple as that." He

leaned forward, choosing his words carefully. "You are partially an Elf, Wil. It is so with your grandfather as well. But he is half Elf, having been born the child of an Elf and a Man. You are something quite different. Neither your mother nor your grandmother was an Elf; both were of the race of Man. All that is Elf in you is that part inherited from your father by way of your grandfather."

"I do not see what difference any of that makes," Wil persisted. "Why should I have difficulty using the Elfstones when my grandfather did not? There is at least some of his Elven blood in me."

"It is not your Elven blood that would cause you difficulty," the Druid replied quickly. "It is your Man blood. You have the physical characteristics of your grandfather— that part of you marks your Elven heritage unmistakably. But that is only a small part of the whole; the greater part of you is Man. Much of the Elf has been bred out of you."

He paused. "Understand, when you attempt to use the Elfstones, only that small part of you that is Elf can link you to their power. The balance of your heart and mind and body resists the intrusion of the magic. It forms a block against it. The three strengths are weakened, for the strength of each is diminished to that which is solely due to your Elf blood. That may be what you have experienced in your use of the Stones—a rejection by that considerable part of you that is Man of the Elven magic."

Wil shook his head in confusion. "But what of my grandfather? He did not experience this rejection."

"No, he did not," Allanon agreed. "But your grandfather was half Elf. The Elf half dominated and gave him command over the power of the Elfstones. The resistance that he experienced was barely measurable. For you, it is a different matter entirely. Your link with the power of the Elfstones is more tenuous."

Wil stared at him. "Allanon, you knew this when you came to me in Storlock. You had to know. Yet you said nothing. Not one word. Not one."

The Druid's expression did not change. "What was I to say, Valeman? I could not determine the extent of the difficulty that you might encounter in using the Elfstones. Any use of the Stones depends greatly on the character of the holder. I believed you strong enough to overcome any resistance within yourself. I still believe that. Telling you then of the problem would have caused you considerable doubt—doubt that might have resulted in your death in the Tirfing."

The Valeman rose wordlessly, a stunned look on his face. He walked away from the table several paces, then turned back again.

"This could happen again, couldn't it?" he asked quietly. "Every time I try to use the Elfstones."

The Druid nodded. Wil studied the dark face silently for a moment, the implications of this admission whirling through his mind like blown leaves.

"Every time," he repeated. The leaves froze sharply. "Then there could come a time when the resistance within me might prove too great. There could come a time when I would call upon the power of the Elfstones and they would not respond."

Allanon took a long time to answer. "Yes, that is possible."

Wil sat down again, the disbelief in his face changing now to horror.

"How can you entrust Amberle's protection to me, knowing that?"

The Druid's hand came down on the table like a hammer. "Because there is no one else!" His dark face flushed with anger, but his voice remained calm. "I suggested to you once before that you should start believing in yourself. I will suggest it one time more. We are not always properly equipped to face the difficulties life places in our path. It is so now. I wish that my power was such that your aid were not necessary in this matter; I wish that I could give you something more with which to protect the Elven girl and yourself. I wish much that cannot be. I brought you to Arborlon because I knew that I alone could not hope to save the Elves from the danger that threatens them. We are both inadequate in this, Wil Ohmsford. But we must do the best we can with what we are. The Druids are gone; the Elven magics of the old world are lost. There is only you and me. There are only the Elfstones that you hold and the magic that I wield. That is all, but that must do."

Wil held his gaze steady. "I am not afraid for me; I am afraid for Amberle. If I should fail her . . ."

"You must not fail her, Valeman." The Druid's voice was hard, insistent. "You must not! You are all that she has."

Wil straightened. "I may not be enough."

"Not enough?" The words were laced with sarcasm. Allanon shook his head. "Your grandfather once believed as you did, not so many years ago. He could not understand how I thought it possible that he might possess the means of destroying a being as awesome as the Warlock Lord. After all, he was only one insignificant little Valeman."

There was a long silence. Valeman and Druid stared wordlessly at one another in the stillness, the flicker of the oil lamp flame dancing across their faces. Then Allanon's black form rose, slowly and deliberately.

"Believe in yourself. You have already used the Elfstones once; you have experienced and overcome the resistance within you and summoned the magic. You can do so again. You *will* do so. You are a son of the house of Shannara; yours is a legacy of strength and courage stronger than the doubt and fear that makes you question your Elven blood."

He leaned down. "Give me your hand."

The Valeman obeyed. Allanon clasped it tightly in his own.

"Here is my hand and thus my bond. Here is my oath to you. You shall succeed in this quest, Wil Ohmsford. You shall find the Bloodfire and bring safely home again the last of the Chosen, she who shall restore the Ellcrys." His voice was low and commanding. "I believe that, and so must you."

The hard, dark eyes penetrated deep into the Valeman's own, and Wil felt himself laid bare. Yet he would not look away. When he spoke, his words were almost a whisper.

"I will try."

The Druid nodded. He was wise enough to leave it at that.

Eventine Elessedil remained in the small study for a long time after the other three had departed. He sat in silence at the fringe of the circle of light cast by the solitary flame of the oil lamp, a rumpled figure formed of shadows and gathered robes. Collapsed in the familiar embrace of his favorite chair, a leather-bound furnishing worn with age and shaped with use, the King of the Elves stared unseeing at the bookcases, paintings, and woven tapestries that lined the wall across from him, thinking of what had been and what was yet to be.

Midnight came and went.

Finally the King rose. Gathering his scattered thoughts and half-drawn plans as he went, he extinguished the oil lamp and moved wearily through the study door into the hallway beyond. There was nothing more to be done this night, nothing more that he could expect to accomplish. By dawn, Amberle would be on her way toward the Wilderun. His concern must no longer be with her; it must be with his people.

Down the length of the darkened hallway the old King passed, anxious now for the rest that sleep would bring him.

All the while, the eyes of the Changeling watched him go.

In the deep blackness of the forest south of the city of Arborlon, the Dagda Mor rose up from the stone on which he had been seated. Cruel red eyes reflected the Demon's sense of exhilaration. This time there would be no mistake, he thought. This time he would make certain that they were all destroyed.

His humped form slouched forward. First he would see to the Elven girl.

One clawed hand beckoned, and from out of the shadows stepped the Reaper.

XXII

Dawn broke misted and iron-gray across Arborlon, and the sky was filled with rolling black clouds. By the time Wil and Amberle had dressed and eaten, the rains had begun, a spattering of drops that turned quickly to a steady downpour, thrumming against the cottage roof and windows. Thunder rolled in the distance, long booming peals that shook the forestland.

"You will not be so easily found in this," Allanon observed with satisfaction and took them out into the storm.

Wrapped in long, hooded traveling cloaks that covered woolen tunics and breeches and high leather boots, they trailed after the Druid as he led them through sheets of driving rain down wooded pathways that skirted the westernmost edge of the city along the broad bluff of the Carolan. Barely able to find their way through the dawn gloom, Valeman and Elven girl followed closely. Fragmented images of cottages, and fence lines, and gardens slipped into view and away again, appearing miragelike through the haze of the storm, then melting back into it once more. A sharp, chill wind blew rain into their faces through the folds of their cowls, and they bent their heads against its force. Boots sloshed wetly through puddles and gullies of surface water that formed before them as they passed along the rutted forest trail.

At the far side of the city, Allanon abruptly departed from the pathway and led them toward a solitary stable that sat back against a hillside to their left. Double wooden doors stood slightly ajar, and they stepped quickly inside out of the weather. Cracks in shuttered windows and ruined walls filled the interior of the structure with gray, hazy light. Rows of stalls and a high loft stood empty, layered in shadows and dust. The air had a stale, pungent smell. They paused momentarily to brush the water from their cloaks, then moved toward a solitary door at the rear of the stable. Almost immediately they were flanked by two heavily armed Elven Hunters, who appeared soundlessly from out of the gloom to either side. Allanon took no notice of them. He walked directly to the door without turning. Tapping softly, he placed one hand on the rusted iron handle and looked back at Amberle.

"Five minutes. That is all the time we can spare."

He pushed the door open. Valeman and Elven girl stared in. A small tack room lay below. Crispin waited there and with him an Elven woman, cloaked and hooded. The woman slipped the hood to her shoulders, and Wil was startled to find that her face, though older, mirrored Amberle's. Allanon had kept his promise; it was the Elven girl's mother. Amberle went to her at once, held her, and kissed her. Crispin stepped from the room and closed the door softly behind him.

"You were not followed." The Druid made it a statement of fact.

The Captain of the Home Guard shook his head. He was dressed as were the other Elven Hunters, clothed in gray and brown colored garments that were loose and comfortable and blended well with the forestland. Beneath a cloak draped across his shoulders, he wore a brace of long knives belted at his waist. Across his back were strapped an ash bow and short sword. Rain had dampened his light brown hair, giving him a decidedly boyish look, and only the hard brown eyes suggested the boy in him was long since gone. He nodded briefly to Wil in greeting, then stepped over to speak with the Elves. One turned and disappeared wordlessly back out into the rain, the other into the loft. They moved on cat's feet, silent, fluid.

The minutes slipped away. Wil stood silently beside Allanon, listening to the drumming of the rain against the stable roof, feeling the dampness of the air work through him. At last the Druid stepped back to the tack room door and tapped softly once more. A moment later it opened, and Amberle and her mother reappeared. Both had been crying. Allanon reached for the Elven girl's hand and held it in his own.

"It is time to go now. Crispin will see you safely out of Arborlon. Your mother will remain here with me until you are gone." He paused. "Keep faith in yourself, Amberle. Be brave."

Amberle nodded silently. Then she turned back to her mother and embraced her. As she did so, Allanon drew Wil aside.

"I wish you good fortune, Wil Ohmsford." His voice was barely audible. "Remember that I depend on you most of all."

He gripped Wil's hand and stepped back. Wil stared at him a moment, then turned as he felt Crispin's hand on his shoulder.

"Stay close," the Elf advised, and started toward the double doors.

Valeman and Elven girl moved after him wordlessly. He stopped them as he reached the doors, whistling sharply to signal the other Elven Hunters. The call was answered almost immediately. Crispin slipped through the doors into the rain. Tightening their cloaks about them, Wil and Amberle followed.

They hastened quickly down the rise to the pathway, backtracked in the direction from which they had come for some fifty feet or so, then turned down a new trail that ran east toward the Carolan. In a matter of seconds, three Elven Hunters had fallen in behind them like shadows slipped from the forest. Wil glanced back once at the solitary barn, but it had faded already into the mist and the rain.

The trail narrowed sharply now, and the woods closed in about them. Slipping through dark, glistening trunks and sagging boughs heavy with rain, the six cloaked figures followed the rutted pathway as it began to slope downward. The path ended at a long, rambling flight of wooden stairs that wound down out of the Carolan through the tangle of the forest. Far below and barely visible through clouds of thinning mist lay the gray ribbon of the Rill Song. To the east, meadowland and forest mixed in patchwork fashion across the sweep of the land.

Crispin motioned them forward. It was a long and

somewhat arduous descent, for the steps were rain-slicked
and narrow, and the footing was uncertain. A guide rope,
frayed and rough, hung loosely from posts fastened to the
stairs, and Wil and Amberle gripped it cautiously as they
went. Hundreds of steps later the stairway ended, and
they started along a new pathway that disappeared into a
short stretch of pine. Somewhere ahead they could hear
the sullen rush of the river, rain-swollen and sluggish, its
roar blending with the deep howl of the wind coming
down off the heights.

When the forest broke in front of them several hundred
yards further on, they found themselves at a heavily
wooded cove that opened through a wall of great, drooping willows and cedar into the main channel of the Rill
Song. Within the shelter of the cove, anchored beside a
creaking, badly rotted dock, rode a solitary barge, its deck
laden with canvas-covered crates and stores.

Crispin signaled for them to halt. The Elven Hunters
behind him faded into the trees like ghosts. Crispin
glanced about, then whistled sharply. A response sounded
almost at once from aboard the barge, then another from
the head of the cove. Nodding to Wil and Amberle to
follow, the Captain of the Home Guard left the cover of the
forest. Bent against the force of the wind, the three moved
quickly onto the dock, boots thudding hollowly, then
aboard the waiting barge. An Elven Hunter appeared
suddenly from beneath the canvas, pulling back a section
hastily, to reveal an opening between the stacked crates.
Crispin motioned for the Valeman and the Elven girl to
enter. They did so, and the canvas dropped silently behind
them.

Inside, it was sheltered and dry. The darkness confused
them at first, and they stood uncertainly, feeling the
rocking of the boat beneath them. But a faint sliver of light
filtered through where the canvas dropped to the deck,
and slowly their eyes adjusted. They discovered that a
space had been cleared to form a small cabin within the
center of the crates. Foodstuffs and blankets lay neatly
stacked against the far wall, and there were weapons
bundled carefully in leather casings in one corner. Stripping their cloaks away, they stretched them out to dry next
to the stores and sat down to wait.

Moments later they felt the barge lurch free of the old dock and begin to move with the current. Their journey to the Wilderun was under way.

They spent all of that day and the next concealed within their little cabin, forbidden by Crispin to make even the briefest appearance on deck. The rain continued to fall in a steady drizzle, and the land and the sky remained gray and shadowed. Occasional glances through the flaps of the canvas covering showed to them the land through which they traveled, a mix of forestland and rolling hills for the most part, although, at one point during their journey, a series of high bluffs and ragged cliff sides hemmed in the Rill Song for several hours as she churned her way sluggishly southward. Through it all, mist and rain masked everything in shimmering gray half-light and gave the impression of some vaguely remembered dream. The river, swollen with the rains, roiling with limbs and debris, rocked and buffeted the barge.

Sleep was impossible. They took what rest they could get, brief naps that left them disoriented when they awoke and always tired still. Muscles and joints ached and stiffened, and the constant rolling motion of the boat took away what little appetite they might have been able to muster.

Time seemed to drag endlessly. They spent it alone with each other, save for the few occasions when Crispin or one of the other Elven Hunters came in out of the weather. When the Elves ate or slept was anybody's guess, for it appeared that most of their time was spent navigating the river and keeping close watch over their passengers. There was always at least one Elf on guard directly outside the entry to their little cabin. They came to know the names after a time, some when one ducked into the cabin momentarily, some by conversations that took place without. A few they could put faces to, such as Dilph, the small, dark Elf with the friendly eyes and the iron grip, and Katsin, the big, rawboned Hunter who never spoke at all. Kian, Rin, Cormac, and Ped remained little more than voices, though they came to recognize Kian's quick, deep oaths of irritation and Ped's cheerful whistling. They saw more of Crispin than any of the others, for the Elven

Captain made regular visits to inquire of their needs and to inform them of their progress. But he never stayed for more than a few minutes, always excusing himself politely but firmly, to return to the Elves under his command.

In the end, it was the talks with each other that made the confinement, the dreariness, and the loneliness of the journey bearable. The talks began out of mutual need, Wil thought, but cautiously and awkwardly, for they still regarded each other with a strong sense of uncertainty. The Valeman was never sure why the Elven girl chose to discard the shell into which she had withdrawn for much of their journey north from Havenstead, but her attitude seemed to undergo a surprising transformation. Before, she had been reluctant to discuss much of anything with Wil. Now she was eager to converse with him, drawing out by her questions stories of his early years in Shady Vale, the years when his parents had been alive, then later when he had lived with his grandfather and Flick. She wanted to know of his life with the Stors and the work that he would be doing when he left their village again and returned to the Southland as a Healer. Her interest in him was genuine and pervasive, and it whispered of need. Nor did they speak only of him. They spoke of her as well, of her childhood as the granddaughter of the King of the Elves, of growing up the only child of Eventine's lost son. She told Wil of the Elven way of life, of their strong belief in giving back to the land that nourished and sheltered them something of themselves, something of their lives. She exchanged with him ideas on the ways in which the races might better serve the needs of one another and of the land. Each argued gently and persuasively for understanding, compassion, and love, discovering as they did so, with some surprise, that their beliefs were very much the same, that their values were values shared.

Carefully, by cautious degrees, they bound themselves, each to the other. Deliberately, they avoided saying anything of the journey on which they had been sent, of the danger that threatened the Elven people and of their own responsibility for putting an end to that danger, or of the ancient and mysterious tree they called the Ellcrys. There would be time enough later for that; this time could be better used. It was an agreement arrived at not by words spoken, but by simple understanding. They would speak openly of the past and the future; they would say nothing of the present.

The talks gave them comfort. Without, the rains fell unceasingly, the gray haze of the storm washed the land, and the Rill Song rumbled in discontent on its passage south. Shut within their dark concealment, buffeted by winds and water, lacking sleep and appetite, they might easily have given way to apprehension and doubt. But the talks gave them comfort, born of feelings shared, of companionship, and of understanding. It gave them a sense of security in each other's presence, muting at least in part the unpleasant sensation that the whole of their world was passing away and that, with that passing, their lives would be forever changed. It gave them hope. Whatever was to befall them in the days to come, they would face together. Neither would be forced to stand alone.

Sometime during those gray, rain-filled hours, a strange thing happened to Wil Ohmsford. For the first time since that night in Storlock when he had agreed to travel to the Westland with Allanon, he found himself caring, deeply and compellingly, about what was to become of Amberle Elessedil.

It was late afternoon on the second day of their journey when they arrived at Drey Wood. The heavy rains had diminished to a slow drizzle, and the air had gone sharply chill with the approach of nightfall. Gray dusk shrouded the forestland. From out of the west, a new bank of threatening black clouds had begun to roll toward them.

Drey Wood was a stretch of dense forest covering a series of low rises which ran eastward from the left bank of the Rill Song to a line of high, craggy bluffs. Elms, black oaks, and shag-bark hickories towered over a choked tangle of scrub and deadwood, and the forest smelled of rot. A dozen yards inland from the riverbank, there was nothing but blackness, deep and impenetrable. Rain falling into the trees in a steady patter was the only sound that broke the stillness.

The Elven Hunters guided the unwieldy barge into a shallow bay where a docking slip jutted outward from the bank, waves breaking against its pilings and washing over its wooden slats. On shore, just within the fringe of the woods, stood a weathered, empty cabin, its single door and windows closed and shuttered. Easing the barge against the pilings, the Elves fastened the mooring lines and stepped off.

Crispin brought Wil and Amberle out from their cabin, carefully admonishing them to keep their hooded cloaks securely in place. Stretching gratefully, they joined him on the docking slip. The Rill Song splashed up at them, and they hastened ashore.

Dilph moved to the cabin, opened its door, peered momentarily about, and withdrew. He shook his head at Crispin. The Elf Captain frowned and glanced about guardedly.

"Is something wrong?" Wil asked.

Crispin looked away. "Just being cautious. The main post is half a mile inland, built into the trees at the top of a rise to permit an overview of the surrounding country. I thought that the Hunters stationed there would have seen us coming, but the weather might have prevented that."

"What about this cabin?" the Valeman wanted to know.

"One of several watches the post keeps. Usually there is someone on duty." He shrugged. "With the weather this bad, though, the commander of the post may have pulled in all one-man sentries. He was not told that we would be coming and had no reason to expect us."

He glanced back at the forest. "Excuse me for a moment, please."

He signaled the other Elves to join him, and they huddled quickly, their voices low and furtive.

Amberle stepped close to Wil. "Do you believe him?" she whispered.

"I'm not sure."

"I am. I think something is wrong."

The Valeman did not reply. Already the conference was ending. Katsin had moved back to the dock to stand close to the moored barge. Cormac and Ped had taken up positions at the edge of the forest. Crispin was talking now to Dilph, and Wil edged closer to hear what was being said.

"Take Rin and Kian and scout to the outpost." The Elf

Captain glanced over his shoulder at the Valeman. "If all is well, come back for us."

Wil made a quick decision and stepped forward. "I'm going, too."

Crispin frowned. "I don't see any reason for that."

Wil stood his ground. "I think I can give you one. Protecting Amberle is my responsibility as well as yours; that is why Allanon sent me with her. Exercising that responsibility is a matter of judgment, Captain, and in this instance I think I should scout ahead with Dilph."

Crispin thought it over for a moment, then nodded. "As long as you do exactly as Dilph tells you."

Wil turned back to Amberle. "Will you be all right?"

She nodded, then watched wordlessly as he followed the Elven Hunters into the darkness of the trees and disappeared from view.

Like ghosts, the four slipped through the sodden curtain of the woods, their steps soundless. Mist trailed about them in streamers thick with dampness, and rain fell softly. Rows of dark trunks and masses of scrub and thicket passed away as the forest wound on over steep rises and ridge lines. The minutes slipped by, and Wil Ohmsford felt himself grow increasingly uneasy.

Then Kian and Rin split off to either side, disappearing into the trees, and Wil found himself alone with Dilph. An empty clearing appeared suddenly from out of the gloom, and Dilph dropped to a crouch, motioning Wil down behind him. The Elf pointed upward into the trees.

"There," he whispered.

High in the interwoven branches of two great oaks sat the Elven outpost. Rain and mist shrouded the buildings and their connecting passageways. Neither oil lamp nor torchlight burned from within. Nothing moved. Nothing sounded. It was as if the post were deserted.

But that should not be.

Dilph eased forward slightly, peering left through the gloom until he caught sight of Rin, then right until he found Kian. Both knelt within the cover of the trees some thirty yards to either side, watching the silent post. Dilph whistled softly to catch their attention. When he had it, he

signaled for Kian to go in for a closer look. Rin he sent left
to scout the perimeter of the clearing.

Wil watched Kian sprint to the base of the oaks which
supported the post, find the concealed footings in one
massive trunk, and begin to climb. Then, with Dilph
leading, Wil started right, staying just within the fringe of
the clearing, eyes searching the forest for some sign of the
missing Elves. The woodland was sodden and murky, and
it was difficult to see much of anything through the tangle
of scrub.

The Valeman glanced back to the post. Kian had almost
reached the lowest building, a small command hut set just
below the main living quarters. Rin was nowhere to be
seen. Wil was still looking for the Elf when he took a step
forward and tripped, sprawling face down across the
broken, lifeless body of an Elven Hunter. He sprang back to
his feet in horror, eyes sweeping the gloom about him. To
his left lay two more bodies, limbs twisted, bones shattered
and crushed.

"Dilph!" he whispered harshly.

At once the Elf was beside him. Pausing only an instant
to survey the grisly scene, Dilph stepped to the edge of the
clearing and whistled sharply. Rin appeared from out of the
forest, a startled look on his face. At the rail of the platform
surrounding the command hut, Kian looked down. Frantically, Dilph motioned them back.

But almost immediately, Kian disappeared. Something
seemed to reach out and snatch him from view, so
suddenly that it appeared to an astonished Wil as if he had
simply evaporated. Then Kian's scream sounded, short
and strangled. His body flew out of the trees, sailing like a
fallen limb into the rain, tumbling lifelessly to the ground
below.

"Run!" Dilph cried to Wil and bolted into the trees.

The Valeman froze for a single, terrible instant. Kian was
dead. Almost certainly, the entire Elven outpost of Drey
Wood was dead as well. All of his thoughts scattered, save
one—if he did not get to Amberle in time, she would be
dead as well. Then he ran, darting like some stricken deer
through the tangle of the forest, leaping and twisting
through scrub and deadwood, desperate to reach the barge
and the unsuspecting Elven girl whose life he guarded.

Somewhere off to his right he could hear Dilph, fleeing as he did, and further back Rin. He knew instinctively that something pursued them. He could not see it, could not hear it, but he could sense it, terrible and black and pitiless. Rain streaked his face and ran into his eyes, clouding his vision as he sought to avoid fallen logs and thorny brush. Once he went down, but he was up again almost immediately, never slowing, his lean form straining to put further distance between himself and his unseen pursuer. His chest heaved with the effort, and his legs ached. There had been few times in his life when he had been afraid, but he was afraid now. He was terrified.

Rin's scream sounded sharply through the stillness. The thing had him. Wil gritted his teeth in fury. Perhaps the Elves at the barge would be warned now. Perhaps they would cast off at once, so that, even if he too were caught, at least Amberle would escape.

Branches and leaves tore at him like clutching hands. He looked for Dilph, but the Elf was no longer in view. Alone, he ran on.

Dusk began to slip rapidly over Drey Wood, turning gray afternoon to night. The drizzle which had fallen at a steady rate for most of the day changed abruptly to a heavy downpour, the wind gusting sharply as a new mass of black stormclouds rolled across the sky. Thunder rumbled in the distance, deep and ominous. On the banks of the Rill Song, the Elven Hunters and their charge pulled rain-soaked cloaks closer about their chilled bodies.

Then the scream sounded from somewhere within the wood, high and short, almost lost in the heavy rush of the wind. For an instant no one moved, staring wordlessly at the dark wall of trees. Then Crispin was barking orders, sending Amberle back to the barge and into hiding once more, calling Ped and Cormac to him. Weapons drawn, the three Elven Hunters backed to the end of the dock, scanning the hazy tangle of the forest. Aboard the barge, Katsin loosened the mooring lines and stood ready to cast off.

Amberle huddled for a few moments within the dark of the cabin, listening to the sound of the wind and the rain without. Then abruptly she rose, pushed aside the canvas flap, and stepped back out into the weather. Whatever the consequences, she could not stay hidden in that cabin without knowing what was going on out here. She edged her way along the stacked crates until she was able to gain the dock. Katsin had looped the lines that moored the barge several turns about a piling; with the loose ends gripped firmly, he stood braced to release them on command. He gave Amberle a sharp look when he saw her, but the girl ignored it. At the edge of the bank, several feet from the dock, the remaining Elven Hunters faced the wood, sword blades glistening dully with rain.

Abruptly a disheveled figure broke from the trees not twenty yards downriver, stumbled, and pitched forward. When he scrambled up again, they saw that it was Dilph.

"Get away!" he cried in warning, his voice ragged. "Quick, get away!"

He started toward them, lost his footing once more and went down.

Crispin was already moving. A sharp command sent Ped and Cormac to the barge as he raced for the fallen Dilph. Barely slowing, he snatched the other man up in his arms, flung him over one shoulder and streaked back toward the waiting boat.

Amberle peered through the mist and rain into the forest. Where was Wil Ohmsford?

"Drop the lines!" Crispin was shouting.

Katsin did as he was told, then hurriedly shoved Amberle aboard the barge where Ped and Cormac already waited. A second later Crispin had Dilph aboard as well, and the heavy craft began to drift.

Then suddenly Wil appeared, thrusting clear of the forest and racing for the dock. Amberle saw him, started to cry out, and then went cold. In the shadow of the trees behind the fleeing Valeman, something huge followed in pursuit.

"Look out!" she screamed in warning.

Spurred by her cry, the Valeman gained the dock in a single bound, sprinted its length without slowing, and sprang to reach the drifting barge, barely catching its deck with an outstretched foot. He would have tumbled into the river but for the Elven Hunters, who reached out and pulled him to safety.

The barge swung into the main channel of the Rill Song and began to pick up speed. Katsin seized the tiller, bringing the cumbersome boat about. As Wil stumbled back against the crates and sank down in exhaustion, Amberle quickly removed her own cloak and wrapped it tightly about him. Close at hand, Crispin bent over Dilph. Wind and the roar of the river scattered Dilph's words.

". . . Dead, all of them—smashed, broken like twigs . . . like the patrol in Arborlon, like . . . the Chosen." His mouth opened and he choked for breath. "Kian, too . . . and Rin, both dead . . . the Demon caught them . . . it was waiting for us. . . ."

Amberle didn't hear the rest. Her eyes were locked on Wil's. With terrible certainty, each had realized the truth.

It was waiting for them. The Demon.

Allanon had given it a name. He had called it the Reaper.

XXIII

It was midnight when Crispin took the barge ashore again. Immediately below Drey Wood, the Rill Song swung westward on its twisting journey to the Innisbore. When the Elves finally guided the barge into a narrow, heavily wooded inlet that broke south from the main channel, they found themselves at the northernmost edge of the Matted Brakes, miles from where they had intended to leave the river. The rains had diminished once more to a soft drizzle that hung in the chill air like fine mist. Heavy clouds obscured moon and stars, and the night was so black that even Elven eyes could see no further than a dozen paces. The wind had died away into stillness, and a deep haze had settled over the whole of the land.

The Elven Hunters grounded the barge on a low sand bar at the head of the inlet, pulled her nearly clear of the river and made her fast. Moving safely and quietly, they scouted the land about them for several hundred yards in all directions, determined that nothing threatened them, then reported back to Crispin. The Elf Captain decided that it would be pointless to attempt further travel until morning. Wil and Amberle were told to remain in their cabin. Wrapped in warm blankets to ward off the cold, free for the first time in two days from the river's discomforting pitch and roll, they fell asleep at once. The Elves ringed the barge and its sleeping passengers, standing watch in shifts. Crispin posted himself beside the cabin entry and settled in for the night.

At dawn, the little company rose, packed what provisions and weapons they could carry, then freed the barge from its moorings and let the river carry it away. It disappeared swiftly, twisting in the pull of the current. As soon as it was gone, they struck out across the Matted Brakes.

The Brakes were lowlands choked with scrub and brush and dotted with stagnant lakes, bramble runs, and sink holes. They split apart the vast Westland forests from the banks of the Rill Song to the wall of the Rock Spur, a maze of wilderness through which few travelers dared to journey. Those who did risked losing themselves hopelessly in a tangle of thicket and clustered bogs shrouded in mist and darkness. Worse, they risked an encounter with any number of unpleasant denizens of the Brakes, creatures that were vicious, cunning, and indiscriminate in their choice of prey. Not much of anything lived within these lowlands, but what did live there understood well that all creatures were either hunter or hunted and that only the former could survive.

"If there were another alternative, we would not come this way," Crispin advised Wil, dropping back momentarily to share his thoughts with the Valeman. "If all had gone as planned, we would have taken horses from the outpost south along the western edge of the Brakes to the Mermidon, then ridden west into the Rock Spur. But Drey Wood has changed all that. Now we have to be concerned as much with what may follow as with what may lie ahead. The one virture to the lowlands is that they will hide any trace of our passing."

Wil shook his head doubtfully. "A thing like the Reaper won't give up easily."

"No, it will keep hunting us," the Elf agreed. "But it won't catch us like that a second time. It was waiting for us at Drey Wood because it knew we were coming. I don't know how it knew, but it did." He glanced at the Valeman, but Wil said nothing. "In any case, it won't know where we are now. If it expects to find us again, it will have to track us. That might have been done easily enough if we had stayed within the forestland, but it will be very difficult here. It will have to determine first where we left the River; that alone could take days. Then it will have to follow us into the Brakes. But the Brakes swallow you up without a trace; this marsh hides tracks ten seconds after you've made them. And we've got Katsin, who was born in this country and has crossed the Brakes before. The Demon, however powerful it may be, is in strange country. It will have to hunt by instinct alone. That gives us a very definite edge."

Wil Ohmsford did not agree. Allanon had thought that the Demons would not track him when he fled Paranor. But they did. The Valeman had thought they would not find him again once Amberle and he were carried to the far shores of the Rainbow Lake by the King of the Silver River. But again they did. Why should it be any different this time? The Demons were creatures of another age; their powers were the powers of another age. Allanon had said that himself. He had said as well that the one who led them was a sorcerer. Would it be so difficult for them to track a handful of Elven Hunters, a young girl, and a Valeman?

Still, there was nothing to be done about it, the Valeman knew. If the Reaper could track them in the Brakes, it would track them anywhere. Crispin had made the right decision. The Elven Hunters possessed considerable skill; perhaps that would be enough to see them safely through.

The Valeman was far more concerned about another unpleasant possibility, and since their encounter with the Reaper at Drey Wood he had been able to think of little else. The Reaper had known that they were coming to that Elven outpost. It had to have known, because it had lain in wait for them. Crispin was right about that. But there was only one way it could have known—it must have been told by the spy concealed within the Elven camp, the spy whom Allanon had worked so carefully to deceive. And if the Demons knew of their plan to travel south to the Elven outpost at Drey Wood, then how much more about this journey did they know? It was altogether possible, the Valeman realized, that they knew everything.

It was a chilling possibility, one that he would have preferred not to consider further, but which seemed more and more plausible as he weighed the facts. Allanon had been certain that there was a spy within the Elven camp. Somehow the spy had managed to overhear their conversation in Eventine's study. He could not conceive of how that could have been accomplished, but he was certain that it had. Drey Wood had been mentioned; that would account for the Reaper. But the Wilderun had also been mentioned. That meant that the Demons knew exactly where they were going after Drey Wood; and if the Demons knew that, then regardless of the route the little company chose to follow or the deceptions they chose to employ to elude would-be pursuers, chances were excellent that when the company arrived at the Wilderun there would be Demons waiting for them.

The thought lingered with Wil Ohmsford all that day as the little company slogged through the marshy tangle of the Brakes. Thorny brush and saw grass cut them at every passing, mist turned their clothing damp and chill, and mud and foul-smelling water seeped through their boots and filled their nostrils with its stench. They walked separate and apart from each other, speaking little, eyes peering guardedly through rain and swirling haze as the land passed away about them in a changeless wash of gray. By nightfall, they were exhausted. They made their camp in a sparse outcropping of brush that grew up against a low rise. There was too much risk in a fire, so they wrapped themselves in blankets that were damp with the lowland's chill and ate their food cold.

The Elven Hunters finished quickly and prepared to stand watch in shifts. Wil had just completed his own small meal of dried meat and fruit, washed down with a little water, when Amberle came over and huddled down beside him, her child's face peering out at him from within the folds of the blanket she had pulled up about her head. Stray locks of chestnut hair fell loosely over her eyes.

"How are you holding up?" he inquired.

"I'm fine." She had the look of a lost waif. "I need to talk."

"I'm listening."

"I have been thinking about something all day."

He nodded wordlessly.

"The Reaper was waiting for us at Drey Wood," she said quietly. She hesitated. "You realize what that means?"

He said nothing. He knew what was coming next. It was as if she had read his mind.

"That means that it knew we were coming." She spoke the words he was thinking. "How could that have happened?"

He shook his head. "It just did."

That was the wrong answer, and he knew it. Her face flushed.

"Just as the Demons found us at Havenstead? Just as they found Allanon at Paranor? Just as they seem to find us everywhere we go?" Her voice stayed low, but there was anger in it now. "What kind of a fool do you think I am, Wil?"

It was the first time that she had ever used his given name, and it startled him so that for a moment he simply stared at her. There was hurt and suspicion in her eyes, and he saw that he must either tell her what Allanon had directed him to keep secret or lie to her. It was an easy decision to make. He told her about the spy. When he had finished, she shook her head reprovingly.

"You should have told me before now."

"Allanon asked me not to," he tried to explain. "He thought that you already had enough to worry about."

"The Druid does not know me as well as he thinks. Anyway, you should have told me."

He no longer felt like arguing the point. He nodded in agreement.

"I know. I just didn't."

They were silent for a moment. One of the Elves on watch appeared, wraithlike, out of the mist, then disappeared into it again. Amberle stared after him, then glanced over at Wil. Her voice floated out of the folds of her hood, her face masked in shadow.

"I'm not angry. Really, I'm not."

He smiled faintly. "Good. This marsh is dismal enough as it is."

"I would have been angry if you had not told me the truth just now."

"That was why I told you."

She let the matter drop. "If this spy overheard what was said in my grandfather's study that night before we left Arborlon, then the Demons know where we are going, don't they?"

"I imagine so," he replied.

"That means they know about Safehold as well; they know everything the Ellcrys told the Chosen, because Allanon repeated it to us. They have as much chance of finding the Bloodfire as we do."

"Maybe not."

"Maybe not?"

"We have the Elfstones," he pointed out, wondering as he did so if it made any difference that they did. After all, he did not really know if he could use the Stones again. The thought depressed him.

"Who could have gotten close enough to hear what we were saying?" She frowned and looked at him.

He shook his head wordlessly. He had been wondering that, too.

"I hope that my grandfather is all right," she murmured after a minute.

"I would guess that he is better off than we are." Wil sighed. "At least he has someplace warm to sleep."

He hunched his knees up to his chest, trying to find an extra bit of warmth. Amberle moved with him, shivering with the cold. He let her settle close against him, bundled in her coverings.

"I wish this were finished," she whispered distantly, almost as if she were saying it to herself.

The Valeman grimaced. "I wish it had never begun."

She turned her head to look at him. "As long as we are wishing, I wish you would be honest with me after this. No more secrets."

"No more secrets," he promised.

They were quiet after that. A few moments later, Amberle's head slipped down against his shoulder and she was asleep. The Valeman did not disturb her. He left her that way and stared out into the dark, thinking of better times.

For the next two days, the little company trudged through the gloom of the Matted Brakes. It rained most of the time, a steady drizzle interspersed with heavy showers that drenched further an already sodden earth and left the travelers cold and miserable. Mist hung overhead and swirled thick across ridge tops and still, marshy lakes. The sun remained screened by banks of stormclouds, and only a faint lightening of the sky for several hours near midday gave any indication of its passing. At night, there was only the impenetrable dark.

Travel was slow and arduous. In single file, they worked their way across the tangle of the Brakes, through bramble thickets that sword blades could barely hack apart, past bogs that bubbled wetly and sucked from sight everything that came within their grasp, and around lakes of green slime and evil smells. Deadwood littered the ground, mingling with pools of surface water and twisting roots. The vegetation had a gray cast to it that muted its green and left the whole of the land looking sick and wintry. What lived within the Brakes stayed hidden, though faint sounds skittered and lurched in the stillness, and shadows slipped like wraiths through the rain and the gloom.

Then, shortly before noon on the third day, they arrived at a massive body of stagnant water, choked with roots and deadwood that protruded like the earth's broken bones from amid a covering of lily pads rippling gently with the rainfall. The shores of the lake were massed thick with bramble runs and scrub as far as the eye could see. Mist rolled across the surface of the water in a deep haze, and there was no sign of the far shore.

It was apparent immediately that any attempt at circling the lake would require several hours of backtracking to escape the heavy brush. There was only one other alternative open to them, and they took it. Katsin led them, as he had for most of their journey through the Brakes, with the other four Elven Hunters split in pairs so that two walked before Wil and Amberle and two followed. Cutting through the scrub that blocked their passage, they stepped onto a narrow bridge of earth and roots that jutted out from the shoreline and disappeared into the mist. If they were lucky, the bridge would span to the far shore.

They proceeded cautiously, picking their way along the uneven course, carefully staying back from the mire that lay to either side. The mist closed about them almost at once, and the land behind faded into it. The minutes slipped away. Rain blew sharply into their faces, caught on a sudden gust of wind. Then the mist cleared unexpectedly, and they saw that their bridge dropped away into the lake not a dozen yards ahead. Beyond lay a huge mound of earth encrusted with rock and vegetation. The far shore of the lake was nowhere to be seen. They had reached a dead end.

Crispin started forward for a closer look at what lay
beyond the mound of earth, but Katsin's hand came up
sharply in warning. He glanced back quickly at the others
of the little company, placing a finger to his lips. Then he
pointed to the mound, his hand moving to a long ridge that
curved downward into the lake. At its tip, steam rose in
small jets from two ragged holes that protruded from just
above the water line.

Breathing holes!

Wordlessly, Crispin motioned them back. Whatever it
was that lay sleeping out there, he had no intention of
disturbing it.

But he was too late. The creature had sensed them. Its
bulk heaved up suddenly out of the lake, showering them
with stagnant water. It huffed loudly as yellow eyes
snapped open from beneath the covering of lily pads and
vines. Writhing feelers flared from its mud-covered body,
and a broad, flat snout swung toward them, jaws gaping
wide in hunger. It hung suspended above the lake for an
instant, then sank quietly beneath the water and was gone.

Wil Ohmsford had only a glimpse of the monstrous
thing. Then he was fleeing through the mist behind Ped
and Cormac, pulling Amberle with him, struggling to keep
his footing on the rutted path. He heard Katsin, Dilph and
Crispin coming up quickly behind him and risked a quick
glance back to see if the creature had followed them. In the
same moment that he looked back, his foot caught and he
went down, dragging Amberle with him.

The fall saved both their lives. Out of the mist rose the
creature, massive jaws sweeping across the narrow bridge
before them like a fisherman's net. Cries of terror sounded
from Ped and Cormac as the thing caught them up and
pulled them into the lake. The huge bulk settled downward into the water and disappeared.

Wil froze in horror, staring fixedly into the mist where
the monstrous thing had gone. Then Crispin leaped
forward, catching Amberle up over his shoulder and
sprinting for the safety of the shore. Katsin snatched up
Wil before the Valeman could think to act on his own and
followed. Dilph raced after them, short sword drawn. In
seconds, they were stumbling back through the wall of

scrub and bramble. Far back from the water's edge, they collapsed in the muddied earth, their breathing heavy in the stillness as they listened for the sounds of any pursuit. There were none. The creature was gone.

But now they were only five.

XXIV

Nightfall drifted down across the Westland in gossamer sheets of gray dusk, and the chill of evening settled into the forestland. The clouds which had masked the summer sky for nearly seven days began to break apart so that thin strips of blue glimmered brightly in the fading sunlight. In the west, the horizon turned scarlet and purple, the glow falling softly across the rain-drenched woodlands.

From beneath the smudge of haze that shrouded the Matted Brakes appeared the five who remained of the little company from Arborlon, surfacing like lost souls out of the netherworld. Haggard and worn, their hands and faces covered with welts and bruises, their clothing soiled and torn and hanging damply from their bodies, they had the look of beggars. Only their weapons suggested that they were something more. Trudging wearily through the last row of thicket, past the last clump of bramble, they scrambled up a small rise of loose rock and scrub and came to a ragged halt before the twin towers of the Pykon.

It was an awesome, spectacular sight. Straddling the broad channel of the Mermidon as the river wound its way eastward toward the grasslands of Callahorn, the Pykon formed a natural gateway into the sprawling, humpbacked mountain range the Elves had named the Rock Spur. The Pykon stood solitary and aloof, twin pinnacles of rock towering into the skyline like massive sentinels set guard over the land below. Ridge lines and crevices scarred the surface in a maze of creases and splits that shadowed the stone cliffs like the lines on an oldster's seamed face. A pine forest grew at the north base of the peaks, thinning as the slope grew steeper, until all that remained was scrub and wildflowers that spotted the dark rock with brilliant dabs of color. Higher up, pockets of snow and ice glistened dazzling white.

Crispin held a hurried conference. In their meanderings through the tangle of the Brakes, they had drifted further eastward than he had intended, coming out here rather than at the edge of the Rock Spur. It might seem logical that they should skirt the Pykon, then travel upriver along the Mermidon until it intersected the Rock Spur. But the entire journey would have to be made on foot, and it would take them at least two days more to get that far. Worse, they would risk leaving a trail that could be followed. The Elf Captain thought that he had a better alternative. Nestled deep within the Pykon, bridging a massive split in the near peak, was an Elven fortress that had stood abandoned since the Second War of the Races. Crispin had been there once years ago, and if he could find it again, there were passages leading from that ancient stronghold downward through the mountain rock to the Mermidon where it split apart the twin peaks. There were docks on the river and a boat as well, perhaps; or if not, there would be wood enough to construct one. From there, the Mermidon flowed eastward for several miles, but then doubled back on itself to where the Rock Spur bordered on the impenetrable mire of the Shroudslip. If they were to utilize the river as their means of travel, the journey could be completed in half the time it would take them if they went on foot—a day, perhaps less than a day. There was another reason for going this way, the Elf Captain added. The river would hide all trace of their passing.

This last argument decided them. None of them had forgotten the encounter with the Reaper at Drey Wood. The Demon would still be searching for them, and anything they might do to thwart that hunt must be tried. It was quickly agreed that it would be best to follow Crispin's advice.

Without wasting any further time, they began the climb onto the Pykon. They passed quickly through the scattered pines that grew at the base of the near peak, reaching the lower slopes as the afternoon sun dipped down behind the forest horizon and night descended. A half-moon began to brighten in the east and clusters of stars winked into view against the deep blue of the sky, lighting the way for the five as they hiked upward onto the rock. It was a still, peaceful night, filled with sweet smells carried from the forest on a gentle south wind. A pathway was found, broad, well-trodden, twisting its way through clumps of boulders and past craggy drops, winding steadily upward into the shadow of the mountain. Behind them, the forestland began to drop away, revealing the dark vista of the Brakes as they spread northward below them toward the thin line of the Rill Song.

It was nearing midnight when the Elven fortress at last came into view. The great stronghold sat back within a deep crevice, a twisting maze of parapets, towers, and bulwarks rising up darkly against the moonlit stone of the cliffs. A long, winding stairway ran up the slope to a gaping entry in the castle's outer wall. Ironbound wooden doors, weathered and split with age, their hinges rusted fast, stood open against the night. Watchtowers perched like squat beasts of prey atop massive stone-block walls, their narrow windows black and vacant. Spikes protruded from the crest of the parapets; high within the cluster of peaked turrets, chains that had once carried the standards of the Elven Kings clanged sharply against iron poles. From somewhere above the fortress, deep within the mountain's crags, sounded the piercing cry of a night bird, its shriek rising until it matched the shrill pitch of the wind, hanging momentarily, then fading into echo.

The five who remained of the little company from Arborlon climbed the steps to the entrance of the abandoned fortress and stepped cautiously through. A high, tightly enclosed walkway ran back to a second wall. Weeds and scrub had grown through the stone block that formed the walk. The five started forward, boots echoing hollowly in the stillness of the passage. Bats flew from chinks and cracks, their leathery wings flapping wildly. Small rodents scurried across the broken stone in flashes of sudden movement. Cobwebs hung like sheets of thin, fine linen, clinging in streamers to the company's clothing as they passed.

At the end of the walkway, an entry opened into a huge courtyard littered with debris and filled with the whine of the wind. To either side of an encircling battlement, a broad stairway wound upward toward a balcony that fronted the main tower of the ancient fortress, a monstrous walled citadel that rose hundreds of feet into the night sky, its rugged stone curving back into the shadow of the mountain. Windows marked the rising floors of the tower, overlooking the tangled blackness of the Matted Brakes. At the center of the balcony, a deep alcove sheltered a single wooden door. Below, leading directly from the courtyard into the tower, was a second door. Both stood closed.

Wil glanced about uneasily at the walls and battlements that loomed over him, dark and sinister and crumbling with age. The wind howled in his ears and blew dirt in his eyes, and he tightened the cowl of his cloak about his face for protection. He did not like this place. It frightened him. It was a haven for the ghosts of dead men, a haven in which the living were intruders. He looked at Amberle and saw the same uneasiness reflected in her face.

Crispin had dispatched Dilph to explore the balcony. With Katsin in tow, the Elf Captain moved now to the tower entry before him. He worked the latch unsuccessfully, then put his weight against the door. It held firm. Katsin tried with no better luck. The door was blocked solidly. Wil watched their struggles to free it with growing apprehension. The fortress shut them in like a prison, and he was anxious to be free of it.

Dilph reappeared from the balcony, his words nearly lost in the shriek of the wind. The upper door was open. Crispin nodded. Gathering up several loose sticks of wood that could serve as torches once they had gained access to the tower, he led the company up the balcony stairs and into the shelter of the alcove. The door stood ajar. Stepping just inside, the Elf Captain used tinder to catch fire to one of the brands he carried, lit a second to give to Dilph, then motioned them all inside, pushing the door closed against the wind.

They found themselves in a small anteroom that branched off into a series of darkened hallways. A stairwell cut into the far wall, winding out of the stone-block floor and upward into the gloom. Dust hung heavily in the wind-stirred air, and the rock of the tower was permeated with the smell of musty dampness. Holding out his torch, Crispin paced across the room and back again, tested the heavy iron latch that secured the anteroom door, then turned back to the others. They would rest here until dawn. Katsin and Dilph would stand watch in the courtyard while Wil and Amberle slept. Crispin would go in search of the passageway that would take them through the mountain to the banks of the Mermidon.

Dilph handed his torch to Wil. With Katsin following, he slipped out into the night. Crispin bolted the door behind them, cautioned Wil and Amberle to keep the latch down, and then disappeared into the darkness of one of the hallways. The Valeman and the Elven girl watched until the light from his torch had faded into the gloom. Then Wil moved over to the entry, set his torch into an iron rack fixed in the stone and hunched down with his back against the door. Amberle wrapped herself in her blanket and lay down next to him. Through chinks in the fastenings that held the door, the howl of the wind sounded its eerie call down the tunnel-like halls of the tower.

It was a long time before either of them fell asleep.

Wil was never certain that he did sleep. He seemed to doze more than sleep, a light drifting rest that left him groping uncertainly between wakefulness and slumber. Almost at once, he began to dream, moving through the tangle of half-sleep that hung like a fog across his subconscious. Darkness and mist enfolded him in a forest of imaginings, and he wandered lost. Yet he had been here before, it seemed. It was familiar to him, this darkness and the haze that drifted through it, the mass of jumbled landscapes through which he passed. It was a dream, yet not a dream, that he had had before . . .

Then he felt the terrible presence of the creature as it crouched somewhere in the dark about him and abruptly he remembered. Havenstead—he had dreamed this dream at Havenstead. The creature had come for him and he had fled, but fled in vain, for there had been no escape. He had come awake finally. But could he do so now? Panic surged through him. *It* was out there, the thing, the monster. It was coming for him again. He could not run from it, could not escape it unless he could wake. But he could not find the way out of the dark and this mist.

He heard himself scream as it reached for him.

Instantly, he was awake. In the pocket of his tunic, the Elfstones burned like fire against his body. Lurching up wildly from his blanket, he peered into the smoky haze of the torchlight as it flickered redly from the tower's stone walls. Amberle crouched beside him, sleep clouding her vision, her face pale and frightened. Wil touched the small bulk of the Elfstones uncertainly. Had it been his scream that had wakened them, he wondered? But the Elven girl was not looking at him. She was looking fixedly at the door.

"Out there," she whispered.

Hurriedly, the Valeman rose, drawing the girl up with him. He listened but heard nothing.

"It might have been the wind," he said finally, his voice hushed and filled with doubt. He put his hand on her arm. "I had better have a look. Lock the door after me. Do not open it unless you hear my voice."

He rose, pulled back the heavy bar, and slipped out into the night. Wind whistled sharply through the door as it closed behind him. Amberle pushed the latch securely in place and waited.

Wil crouched for a moment in the shadow of the alcove, staring out into the dark beyond. Moonlight fell across the length of the deserted balcony and across walls and battlements that rose all about. Cautiously, he crossed to the parapet and peered downward into the courtyard. It was empty. There was no sign of Katsin or Dilph. He hesitated, uncertain as to what he should do next. A moment later he started along the length of the balcony. At the top of the stairway, he stopped again to scan the courtyard. Still nothing. He started down.

Tumbleweeds and dust balls blew randomly across the debris-littered court, scattering wildly with each new gust of wind. Wil slipped down the stairs soundlessly. He was almost to the bottom when he saw Katsin. At least he saw what was left of Katsin, his body twisted grotesquely as it slumped against the tower wall beneath the balcony. A few feet beyond lay Dilph, barely visible under what remained of the heavy tower door that earlier had been solidly blocked.

Wil felt himself go cold. The Reaper! It had found them. And it was inside the tower.

In the next instant he was scrambling back up the stairs toward the balcony entry, praying that he was not already too late.

Alone in the tower anteroom, Amberle thought she heard a noise rise out of the gloom of the stairwell behind her, a noise that came from somewhere deep within the structure. Uneasily she glanced about, then listened. She was still listening when a pounding on the tower door startled her so that she jumped away in surprise, crying out.

"Amberle! Open the door!"

It was Wil's voice, so muffled by the wind that it was barely recognizable. Hurriedly she threw back the heavy latch. The Valeman darted inside, shoving the door closed behind him. He was white with fear.

"They're dead—both of them!" He kept his voice low with an effort. "The Reaper got them. It's here, in the tower!"

Amberle started to say something, but Wil quickly put his hand to her mouth, silencing her. A noise—he had heard a noise—there, on the stairwell. It was the Reaper. He knew it with a certainty that defied argument. It was coming for them. Once it found its way up to this room, it would have them. The Valeman felt a moment of utter panic. How could this have happened? How could the Demon have found them so quickly? What was he supposed to do now?

Holding the torch before him like a shield, he moved away from the door, away from the stairwell. Amberle seemed frozen to him, stumbling back mechanically as he did. They could not stay here, he told himself numbly. He glanced at the passageways about him. Which one had Crispin gone into? He was not certain. He chose the one he believed the Elf Captain had gone down, and raced into its darkness, holding tightly to Amberle.

Several hundred feet further on, they stumbled to a halt. The passageway ended, branching into three new corridors. Again the Valeman panicked. Which should he take? He brought the torch close to the tower floor. The passing of a single pair of Elven boots had stirred the dust collected over the years, leaving a clear and easily recognizable trail, one that he could follow to Crispin—one that the Reaper could follow to them. He choked down his fear and rushed quickly on.

Together, Valeman and Elven girl fled down the dark corridors of the fortress, into halls thick with must and cobwebs, through chambers filled with rotting tapestries and crumbling pieces of furniture, and along balconies and parapets that dropped away into pits of blackness. Silence filled the ancient citadel, deep and pervasive within its bowels so that even the sound of the wind faded and there was only the pounding of their boots on the stone flooring as they ran. Twice they lost their way entirely, racing down a wrong corridor before finding that the trail had disappeared and that they had missed a turn in their haste. Several times they found more than one set of prints where Crispin had doubled back on himself in trying to find the right path. Each time precious seconds were used to discover where he had actually gone. Always there was the feeling that at any moment the Reaper would appear from out of the gloom behind them, and their last chance for escape would be gone.

Then a flicker of torchlight cut through the darkness in the corridor ahead of them. They stumbled toward it, watching with relief as Crispin's lean form materialized out of the shadows. The Elf Captain was returning from his search for the passage that led through the mountain. He came up to them at a dead run, sword blade glinting dully in the red firelight.

"What has happened?" he asked, seeing at once the fear in their eyes.

Quickly the Valeman told him. Crispin's face went ashen.

"Dilph and Katsin, too! What will it take to stop this thing?" Staring down at the sword he held, he hesitated, then beckoned for them to follow. "This way. There may yet be a chance for us."

Together they raced back down the passage through which Crispin had come, turning left into another corridor, passing through a massive hall that had once been an armory, hastening down a flight of stairs into an empty rotunda, then into yet another passage. At the end of this final corridor was an iron door, fixed to the rock of the mountain by bolts and crossbars. Crispin drew back the bars and pulled open the heavy door. Wind roared in their faces, bursting through the opening and thrusting them backward violently. Motioning for Wil and Amberle to follow, the Elf Captain discarded his torch, lowered his head resolutely, and pushed through the opening into the darkness beyond.

They found themselves staring out across a deep gorge where the mountain split apart from crest to base. Bridging the two halves was a slender catwalk that led from the small rocky niche in which they stood to a single tower set into the far cliff. Wind howled across the drop of the chasm, shrieking in fury as it buffeted the narrow iron span. Only a thin sliver of moonlight penetrated the deep crevice, its white band falling across a small section of the catwalk near its far end.

Crispin pulled the Valeman and the Elven girl close.

"We have to cross!" he shouted above the roar of the wind. "Hold tight to the railing! Don't look down!"

"I'm not sure I can do this!" Amberle shouted back, looking anxiously out at the catwalk. Wil felt her small hands grip his arm tightly.

"You have to!" Crispin's response left no room for argument. "This is the only way out!"

The wind howled in their ears. Amberle glanced momentarily at the closed door behind her, then looked back again at Crispin. Wordlessly, she nodded.

"Stay close now!" the Elf warned.

In a line, they started onto the catwalk, the Elf Captain leading, Amberle behind him, Wil trailing. They moved slowly, carefully, hands gripping the railing to either side, heads bent low. The wind ripped across their bodies in fierce gusts, tearing at their clothing and shaking the slender iron walk until it seemed certain that it must collapse and fall into the gorge. As they passed from the shelter of the cliff face, the freezing air of the mountain's upper slopes blew down across them. Hands and feet went quickly numb, and the iron of the bridge felt like ice. Step by step, they made their way across, moving at last from the shadow of the cliffs into the slender band of moonlight that marked the final leg of their crossing. Moments later they gained the platform that fronted the solitary tower. The structure rose up before them against the cliff face, its narrow windows recessed and dark, its stone walls trailing moisture frozen to ice. A single door, now closed, marked the entrance into the keep.

Crispin guided Amberle from the walk and placed her against the tower entry. When Wil had scrambled up beside them, the Elf reached into a wooden box built against the tower wall and withdrew a pair of heavy mallets. He handed one to the Valeman and pointed out toward the bridge. His voice was muffled by the wind's shriek.

"There are six pins that hold the supports of the catwalk—three on each side! Knock out those pins and the walk will collapse! It was constructed that way to prevent pursuit by enemies in case the fortress was ever overrun. Take the three on the right!"

Wil hastened onto the platform. Three horizontally fixed pins driven through eyelets secured the struts on each side of the catwalk to the platform on which he stood. Taking the mallet firmly in hand, he began to hammer at the first. Rust and dirt had congealed about it, and it moved very slowly from its seating. When at last it came free, it tumbled soundlessly into the gorge. He went quickly to the next, the wind deafening him to the sound of the blows he struck, the cold numbing his unprotected hands. The second pin edged clear of its seating and fell.

Something heavy shook the bridge. Wil and Crispin looked up together, mallets poised. In the deep shadows at the far end of the walk, something moved.

"Hurry!" the Elf Captain called.

Wil hammered frantically at the final pin, raining blows on its rounded head, desperately trying to knock it free. It was rusted in place. He struck it with both hands, and at last it inched a fraction of the way out.

On the bridge, just beyond the band of moonlight, a shadow darker than the night about it edged into view. Crispin came to his feet with a bound. Two of the pins on his side were free, the third driven halfway through.

But time had run out. The Reaper appeared, stepping forward into the light—huge, cloaked, faceless. Crispin brought up the ash bow and sent his arrows winging at the thing so quickly that Wil could barely follow the archer's movements. All were brushed aside effortlessly. Wil felt his stomach tighten. Desperately he hammered at the pin before him, sending it several inches further through the eyelet. But there it froze.

Then abruptly he remembered the Elfstones. The Elfstones! He must use them now! Determination surged through him. He bounded up, reached into his tunic and pulled free the leather pouch that held them. In seconds, he held the Stones in his hand, gripped so tightly that they cut him. The Reaper was moving toward them, still crouched low upon the catwalk, huge and shadowy. It was not twenty feet away. The Valeman brought up the fist that held the Stones and, with every bit of willpower he could muster, he called up the fire that would destroy this monster.

The Elfstones flared sharply, the blue fire spreading. But then something seemed to lock within Wil. In the next instant the power died.

Terror gripped the Valeman. Desperately, he tried again. Nothing happened. Amberle rushed to his side, calling frantically to him—but her words were lost in the shriek of the wind. Wil staggered back, stunned. He had failed! The power of the Elfstones was no longer his to command!

An instant later, Crispin was on the bridge. He never hesitated. Dropping the bow, he drew his sword and started toward the Demon. The creature seemed to hesitate slightly. It had not expected a direct confrontation. Wind buffeted the catwalk, causing metal supports to creak in protest as the structure swayed unsteadily.

"The pins!" Crispin called back sharply.

In a daze, Wil thrust the Elfstones back into his tunic, retrieved his mallet, and resumed striking futilely at the frozen pin. Still it would not move. From the shadows behind him, Amberle darted forward. Picking up the mallet that Crispin had discarded, she began to hammer wildly at the other pin.

On the catwalk, Crispin closed with the Reaper. Feinting and lunging, the Captain of the Home Guard sought to catch the Demon off balance, hoping that it might slip and tumble from the walk. But the Reaper stayed low upon the slender bridge, warding off the Elf's thrusts with one massive arm, waiting patiently for its chance. Crispin was a skilled swordsman, yet he could not penetrate the creature's defenses. The Reaper edged forward, and the Elf was forced to give ground.

Rage and frustration swept through Wil Ohmsford. Gripping his mallet in both hands, he pounded the rusted pin with every ounce of strength left in him, and at last the pin flew from its seating into the chasm. But as it did, the bridge buckled slightly and Crispin was thrown off balance. As he stumbled back, the Reaper lunged. Claws fastened about the Elf's tunic. As Wil and Amberle watched in horror, the Reaper lifted Crispin clear of the catwalk. The Elf Captain's sword flashed downward toward the Demon's throat, the blade splintering as it struck. The Reaper shrugged off the blow as if it were nothing. Holding Crispin above its shrouded head, it threw the Elf from the catwalk into the void beyond. Crispin fell soundlessly and was gone.

Again, the Reaper started forward.

Then a sudden burst of wind caught the already weakened catwalk with a powerful thrust that snapped the final pin in its seating. Separating from the platform, the narrow span fell away from the cliff face, carrying with it the clinging form of the Reaper. Slowly it dropped, falling with a groan of iron toward the far cliff, metal snapping, breaking, twisting. It swung through the narrow band of moonlight back into the shadows, crashing against the mountainside. Yet it did not break free entirely, but continued to hang from its ruined supports, swinging precariously with the motion of the wind. In the darkness of the cliffs, it was barely visible. The Reaper was nowhere to be seen.

Amberle's voice rose above the pitch of the wind, a thin frightened wail, calling to Wil. Wind howled past the Valeman in frenzied bursts, chilling him to the bone, filling his ears with its whine. He could not understand what the girl was saying. He did not care. His fist still clutched his mallet uselessly. His mind whirled. Crispin and the Elven Hunters were gone. The power of the Elfstones was lost. Amberle and he were alone.

She was crying into his shoulder, pleading with him to come away. He turned to her now and pulled her close against him. For an instant he seemed to hear Allanon's voice telling him that it was he most of all whom the Druid would depend upon. He stood at the edge of the chasm a moment longer, holding the Elven girl, staring helplessly into the blackness below. Then he turned away. With Amberle clutched tightly against him, he disappeared into the shelter of the tower.

XXV

It took them the remainder of the night to find their way out again. With only the single torch that Crispin had left fastened in an iron wall bracket at the tower entry to guide them, they followed a seemingly endless succession of passages and stairways that wound steadily downward through the mountain's rock. Completely exhausted by the ordeal of the past few days, they stumbled mindlessly along the corridors of the ancient keep, eyes fixed on the blackness ahead, hands clasped. They did not speak; they had nothing to say. The shock of all that had happened had left them numb with fright. They wanted only one thing now—to escape this mountain.

Their sense of time slipped quickly away from them until it no longer had meaning. It might have been minutes or hours or even days that they had been shut within the rock; they no longer knew. They had no idea where the passageways were taking them. They were trusting blindly to luck and to instinct, following the tunnels and corridors with a desperate, unvoiced insistence that somehow they would eventually break free. Muscles ached and cramped, and their vision blurred with fatigue. The single torch they carried burned down until it was little more than a stump. Still the passageway burrowed on.

But at last it ended. A massive iron door sealed with double locks and a crossbar stood before them. Wil was reaching for the locks when Amberle seized his arm, her voice weary and strained.

"Wil, what if there are Demons waiting for us out there as well? What if the Reaper wasn't alone?"

The Valeman stared at her wordlessly. He hadn't considered that possibility until now. He hadn't allowed himself to consider it. He thought back to all that had befallen them since Drey Wood. Always, the Demons seemed to find them. There was a sense of inevitability about it. Even if the Reaper were finally gone, there were other Demons. And the spy at Arborlon had heard everything.

"Wil?" Amberle's face was anxious as she waited for him to respond.

He made his decision. "We have to chance it. There is nowhere else for us to go."

Gently he removed her hand from his arm and positioned her behind him. Then cautiously he released the locks, lifted clear the crossbar and swung open the door. Hazy daylight slipped through the opening. Beyond, the murky waters of the Mermidon lapped softly at the walls of a deep grotto that housed the hidden docks of the Elves. Nothing moved. Valeman and Elf girl exchanged quick glances. Wordlessly, Wil dropped the torch to the tunnel floor where it died.

The docks and boats moored to them were rotted and useless. Valeman and Elf girl made their way along a narrow ledge within the grotto until they had emerged onto the forested riverbank that lay at the base of the Pykon. There was no one there. They were alone.

Dawn was just breaking, a chill, frosted morning half-light that had crystallized the dew of nightfall on the trees and brush and left the land white with a covering of false snow. They stared at it wonderingly, seeing their own breath cloud the air before their faces, feeling the chill seep into their damp bodies beneath the covering of their clothes. The river churned noisily between the mountain peaks, flowing eastward through the forestland, its broad surface shrouded in a heavy blanket of fog. The Pykon rose into this fog, massive, dark spires that shadowed the land.

Wil glanced about uncertainly. Within the darkness of the cave, the boats of the Elves lay in ruins. There was nothing here that could help them. Then he caught sight of a small skiff pulled up on the riverbank and partially concealed within the brush just a dozen yards away. Taking hold of

Amberle's hand, he led the way along the heavily overgrown bank until they had reached the skiff. It was a
fishing boat in good condition, secured by lines, obviously
left by someone who from time to time must have enjoyed
the fishing close to the deep grotto waters. The Valeman
released the lines, placed Amberle within the skiff, and
pushed off into the river. Their need for the boat was much
greater than that of the absent fisherman.

They drifted eastward with the river's flow as dawn
lengthened into morning and the day began to warm.
Wrapping herself in her cloak, Amberle was asleep almost
at once. Wil would have slept as well had sleep been
possible. But sleep would not come to him, his weariness
so great that it actually inhibited sleep. His mind filled with
thoughts of what had befallen them. Fitting a small oar that
lay within the skiff into a stern oarlock, he propped himself
at the rear of the little boat and guided it along the river's
channel, watching numbly as the sun rose from behind the
mountains and the haze of early morning burned away. Bit
by bit, the frost melted away in the forest about him. The
peaks of the Pykon disappeared as the river carried them
on, and the damp green of the forestland rose up in their
stead. The sky was free once more from rain clouds and
darkness, turned a brilliant blue and laced with thin white
streamers that floated lazily through the morning sunshine.

Toward noon, the Mermidon began to swing back on
itself, curving slowly south until at last it swung westward
toward the dark line of the Rock Spur. The day had
warmed, and the dampness and chill of dawn had seeped
from their bodies and clothing. Across the span of the
Mermidon flew birds in brilliant bursts of sound and color.
The smell of wildflowers filled the air.

Amberle stretched and came awake, her sleepy eyes
settling quickly on the Valeman.

"Have you slept?" she asked drowsily.

He shook his head. "I couldn't."

She pushed herself into a sitting position. "Then sleep
now. I will steer the boat while you do. You have to get
some rest."

"No, it's okay. I am not tired."

"Wil, you are exhausted." There was concern in her voice. "You have to sleep."

He stared at her wordlessly for a moment, his eyes haunted.

"Do you know what happened to me back there?" he asked finally.

She shook her head slowly. "No. And I don't think you do, either."

"I know, all right. I know exactly what happened. I tried to use the Elfstones and could not. I no longer command their power. I have lost it."

"You don't know that. You had trouble with the Stones before when you tried to use them in the Tirfing. Perhaps this time you tried too hard. Perhaps you did not give yourself enough of a chance."

"I gave myself every chance," he declared softly. "I used everything I had within me to call up the power of the Elfstones. But nothing happened. Nothing. Allanon told me this might happen. It is because of my Elf blood mixing with my human blood. Only the Elf blood commands the Stones, and mine is thin indeed, it seems. There is a block within me, Amberle. I overcame it once, but I can no longer do so."

She moved over to sit close to him, her hand resting lightly on his arm.

"Then we will get by without the Stones."

He smiled faintly at the suggestion. "The Elfstones are the only weapon we have. If the Demons find us again, we are finished. We have nothing with which to protect ourselves."

"Then the Demons must not find us."

"They have found us every time, Amberle, despite every precaution we have taken; they have found us wherever we have gone. They will find us this time as well. You know that."

"I know that you are the one who insisted that we not turn back after our flight from Havenstead," she responded. "I know that you are the one who has never once suggested giving up. I know that you are the one Allanon chose as my protector. Would you desert me?"

Wil flushed. "No. Not ever."

"Nor I you. We began this journey together and we shall end it together. We shall depend on each other, you and I. We shall see each other through. I think maybe that will be enough." She paused, a quick smile crossing her face. "You realize, of course, that you should be giving this talk to me, not I to you. I was the one without faith in my heritage, without belief in the words the Druid spoke. You have always believed."

"If the Stones had not failed me . . ." Wil began glumly.

Amberle's hand came up quickly against his lips, silencing him. "Do not be so certain that they have failed you. Think a moment on what you tried to do with them. You sought to use them as a weapon of destruction. Is this possible for you, Wil? Remember, you are a Healer. It is your code of life to preserve, not destroy. Elven magic is but an extension of the one who wields it. Perhaps you were not meant to use the Elfstones in the way in which you tried to make them act when you faced the Reaper."

The Valeman thought it over. Allanon had told him that the three Stones acted to mesh heart, mind, and body into the power that formed the magic. If any one were lacking . . .

"No." He shook his head emphatically. "The distinction is too finely drawn. My grandfather believed in the preservation of life as strongly as I and yet he used the Elfstones to destroy. And he did so without the difficulty that I have experienced."

"Well then, there is another possibility," she continued. "Allanon warned you of the resistance caused by the mix of human blood with Elven. You have experienced it once already. Perhaps this has caused you to create your own block—a block within your mind that convinces you subconsciously that the power of the Elfstones is lost, when in fact it is not. Perhaps the block you experienced at the catwalk was one of your own making."

Wil stared at her wordlessly. Was that possible? He shook his head. "I don't know. I cannot be sure. It happened so fast."

"Then hear me." She moved close, so that her face was next to his. "Do not be so quick to accept as truth what is only conjecture. You have used the Elfstones once. You have called upon their power and made it your own. I do not think that such a gift is so easily lost. Perhaps it is just misplaced. Take time to look for it before you decide that it is no longer yours."

He looked at her with amazement. "You have more confidence in me than I do. That seems very strange. You thought me worthless on our journey north from Havenstead. You remember that?"

She drew back slightly. "I was wrong to think that. I said things that I should not have said. I was afraid . . ."

For an instant it appeared as if she would say more; but, as on the other occasions when she had seemed ready to explain her fear, she let the matter drop. Wil was wise enough to do likewise.

"Well, you were right about one thing," he offered, trying to keep the tone of his voice light. "I should be giving this talk to you, not you to me."

There was a wistful look in her eyes. "Then remember to do so when you see that I need it. Now will you sleep?"

He nodded. "I think I might—for a little while, at least."

He eased forward, letting the Elf girl slip her arm about the small rudder. Lowering himself into the bottom of the boat, he made a pillow of his cloak and laid his head down wearily. Thoughts of the Elfstones played teasingly within his mind. He closed his eyes, enfolding such thoughts in blackness. Believe in yourself, Allanon had told him. Did he have that belief? Was that belief enough?

The thoughts scattered, drifting. He slept.

He was awake by midafternoon. Cramped and sore, he eased himself up from the hard bottom of the skiff and moved back to take the rudder from Amberle. He was hungry and thirsty, but there was nothing to eat or drink. They had lost everything in their flight through the Pykon.

A short time later, the channel began to narrow, and the limbs of the trees on either bank closed above them like a canopy. Shadows lengthened across the spread of the river; in the west the sun dropped low above the wall of the Rock Spur, its golden light turning red with the coming of dusk. A stretch of rapids bounced the skiff wildly along the channel, but Wil kept their little boat free of the rocks and straight on her course until they were clear. When the river again began to swing south on its long journey back toward the grasslands of Callahorn, the Valeman brought the skiff ashore and they disembarked.

They spent the night at the base of a massive old willow several hundred yards back from the river's edge. Concealing the skiff in the brush beside the riverbank, they gathered fruit and vegetables for an evening meal and set out in search of drinking water. There was none to be found, however, and they were forced to make do with the food. They ate, conversed briefly and fell asleep.

Morning dawned bright and pleasant, and Valeman and Elven girl began the hike westward to the Rock Spur. They walked briskly, enjoying the warmth of the early morning, consuming as they went the remainder of the fruit they had gathered the previous evening. The hours passed quickly, and the stiffness they had experienced on first awakening disappeared as they wound their way steadily ahead. By midmorning, they had discovered a small stream where rapids emptied down into a pond and the water was suitable for drinking. They drank their fill; but, having no containers, they could take nothing with them.

As the day wore on, the mountains of the Rock Spur loomed closer above the wall of the forest in a massive, humped line of peaks that stretched away across the whole of the western horizon. Only to the far south, where lay the vast impenetrable mire of the Shroudslip, were the mountains absent, and there the skyline was filled with thick, gray mist that rose out of the swamp like heavy smoke. For the first time since they had escaped the Pykon, Wil began to worry about where they were going. Their decision to follow the Mermidon down to the forests bordering the mountains had seemed obvious enough. But now that they were there, he found himself wondering how they were ever going to manage a crossing of these monstrous peaks. Neither of them was familiar with this range; neither knew if there were passes that would take them safely through. Without the Elven Hunters to guide them, how were they to keep from becoming hopelessly lost?

By sunset, they were right up against the Rock Spur,

staring upward thousands of feet at a maze of peaks that loomed one above the next and offered no sign of passage nor hint of break. Valeman and Elven girl climbed out of the forest until they had reached the lower slopes of the nearest mountain. Broad, grassy pastures there were covered with brilliant bluebells and red centauries. The sun was almost gone, and they looked for a campsite. They quickly found a stream that emptied down out of the rocks; at a small pool within a grove of pine, they settled in for the night. Another meal of fresh fruit and vegetables was consumed, but Wil found himself hungry for meat and bread and ate what they had without much interest. A new moon and a spectacular display of stars filled the sky. Bidding each other good-night, they rolled themselves into their traveling cloaks and closed their eyes.

Wil was still wondering how they were going to get through the mountains when sleep came to him.

When he awoke, a boy was sitting there, looking at him. It was dawn, and the sun was rising out of the distant forestland in a hazy, golden burst of light that scattered night in fleeting bits of gray. On the broad, open slopes of the mountain which rose above them, the wildflowers were just opening and the dew glistened damply on the grass.

Wil blinked in surprise. At first he thought that his eyes were playing tricks on him, and he waited expectantly for the boy to disappear back into his imagination. But the boy remained where he was, seated on the grass, legs crossed before him, silently contemplating Wil. This was no illusion, the Valeman decided and pushed himself up on one elbow.

"Good morning," he said.

"Good morning," the boy replied solemnly.

Wil brushed the sleep from his eyes and took a moment to study the boy. He was an Elf, rather small, his tousled, sand-colored hair falling down about a rather ordinary face that displayed a light sprinkling of freckles. Leather pants and tunic fitted close on his small frame, and a number of assorted pouches and bags hung about his neck and from his waist. He was very young, certainly much younger than either Wil or Amberle.

"I didn't want to wake you," the boy announced.

Wil nodded. "You were very quiet."

"I know. I can walk through a stretch of dry pine without making a single sound."

"You can?"

"Yes. And I can hunt to a fox lair without starting him. I did that once."

"That's very good."

The boy looked at him curiously. "What are you doing out here?"

Wil grinned in spite of himself. "I was just wondering the same thing about you. Do you live here?"

The boy shook his head. "No. I live to the south, below the Irrybis. In the Wing Hove."

Wil did not have the faintest idea what a Wing Hove might be. Behind him, he heard Amberle stir awake.

"She is very pretty," the boy ventured quietly. "Are you married?"

"Uh, no—just traveling together," the Valeman managed, a bit taken back. "How did you get here?"

"I flew," the boy answered. "I'm a Wing Rider."

Wil stared at him speechlessly. The boy glanced past him to Amberle, who was just sitting up, still wrapped in her cloak.

"Good morning, lady," he greeted.

"Good morning," Amberle replied. Amusement mixed with puzzlement in her green eyes. "What is your name?"

"Perk."

"My name is Amberle." The Elven girl smiled. "This is Wil."

The boy got to his feet and came over to grip Wil's hand in greeting. The Valeman was surprised to find the youngster's palm heavily calloused. The boy seemed conscious of the fact and drew his hand back quickly. He did not offer it to Amberle, but simply nodded.

"Would you like some breakfast?" he asked.

Wil shrugged. "What do you have in mind, Perk?"

"Milk, nuts, cheese, and bread. That is all I have with me."

"That will do nicely." The Valeman grinned, glancing back quickly at Amberle. He had no idea what Perk was doing here, but the food sounded delicious. "We would be very happy to share breakfast with you."

They seated themselves in a circle. From one of the pouches he carried, the young Elf produced the promised nuts, cheese, and bread together with three small cups. The cups he filled with milk he carried in a second pouch. Valeman and Elven girl consumed the small meal ravenously.

"Where did you get the milk?" Amberle asked after a moment.

"Goats," the boy mumbled, his mouth full. "A goatherd keeps a small flock in a meadow several miles north. I milked one earlier this morning."

Amberle glanced questioningly at Wil, who shrugged. "He tells me that he is a Wing Rider. He flies."

"I'm not really a Wing Rider—not yet," the boy interrupted. "I'm too young. But one day I will be."

There was an awkward moment of silence as the three stared wordlessly at one another.

"You didn't say what you were doing out here," Perk said finally. "Are you running away from something?"

"Why do you ask that, Perk?" Amberle wanted to know immediately.

"Because you look like you are running away from something. Your clothes are torn and dirty. You carry no weapons and no food and no blankets. You build no fire. And you look like something has frightened you."

"Perk, you are a bright boy," Wil responded quickly, deciding at once how he was going to handle this. "Will you promise to keep it secret if I tell you something?"

The boy nodded, anticipation showing in his face. "I promise."

"Good." Wil leaned forward confidentially. "This lady—Amberle—is very special. She is a Princess, a granddaughter of Eventine Elessedil, the King of the Elves."

"King of the Land Elves," Perk corrected. When Wil hesitated, confused by the distinction, the boy edged forward anxiously. "Do you go in quest of treasure? Or is the lady enchanted? Is she bewitched?"

"Yes. No." The Valeman stopped. What had he gotten himself into? "We go in search of a . . . a talisman, Perk.

Only the lady can wield it. There is a very great evil that threatens the Elven people. Only the talisman can protect against that evil, and we must find it quickly. Would you be willing to help us?"

Perk's eyes were wide with excitement. "An adventure? A real adventure?"

"Wil, I don't know about this . . ." Amberle interrupted, frowning.

"Trust me, please." Wil held up his hands placatingly. He turned back to Perk. "This is a very dangerous business, Perk. The things that hunt us have already killed a number of Elves. This will not be a game. You must do exactly as I ask, and when I tell you that it is finished, you must leave us at once. Agreed?"

The boy nodded quickly. "What do you want me to do?"

The Valeman pointed toward the Rock Spur. "I want you to show me a way through those mountains. Do you know one?"

"Of course." Perk sounded very indignant. "Where is it that you are going?"

Wil hesitated. He was not certain that he wanted the boy to have that information.

"Does that matter?" he asked finally.

"Certainly it matters," Perk replied at once. "How can I show you how to get to where you want to go if I don't know where it is that you are going?"

"That sounds very sensible," Amberle offered, giving Wil a knowing glance that suggested that he should have foreseen all this. "I think you had better tell him, Wil."

The Valeman nodded. "All right. We are going into the Wilderun."

"The Wilderun?" Perk shook his head solemnly, some of the enthusiasm fading from his eyes. "The Wilderun is forbidden to me. It is very dangerous."

"We know," Amberle agreed. "But we have no choice. We have to go there. Can you help us?"

"I can help you," the boy declared firmly. "But you cannot go through the mountains. That would take days."

"Well, if we don't go through the mountains, then how do we get there?" Wil demanded. "Is there another way?"

Perk grinned. "Sure. We can fly."

Wil looked over at Amberle for help.

"Perk, we cannot . . . really fly," she said gently.

"We can fly," he insisted. "I told you, I'm a Wing Rider—almost a Wing Rider, anyway."

Some imagination, thought Wil. "Look, Perk, you have to have wings to fly and we don't have wings."

"Wings?" The boy looked confused. Then he grinned. "Oh, you thought . . . Oh, I see. No, no, not us. We have Genewen. Here, come with me."

He rose quickly and moved out of the shelter of the pine grove. Mystified, Wil and Amberle trailed after, exchanging confused glances as they went. When they were all beyond the trees and standing on the open slope, Perk reached into a leather pouch tied about his neck and produced a small, silver whistle. Putting the whistle to his lips, the boy blew into it. There was no sound. Wil looked at Amberle a second time and shook his head slowly. This was not working out the way he had intended it. Perk slipped the silver whistle back into its pouch and turned to scan the skyline. Mechanically, the Valeman and the Elven girl looked with him.

Suddenly a great, golden-hued form soared out of the Rock Spur, shimmering brightly in the warm morning sunlight as it dipped downward through the mountains and came toward them. Wil and Amberle started wildly. It was the biggest bird they had ever seen in their lives, a huge creature with a wing span of fully thirty feet, a sleek, crested head the color of fire tinged with flecks of black, a great hooked beak, and powerful talons that extended forward as it approached. For just an instant, both were reminded of the winged black thing that had very nearly caught them in their flight through the Valley of Rhenn, but then they realized that this was not the same creature. It dropped to the meadow not a dozen feet in front of them, wings folding close against its golden, feathered body, crested head arching upward as it came to roost. Its piercing cry split the morning stillness, and it dipped its head sharply toward Perk. The boy gave a quick, odd call in reply, then turned again to his astonished companions.

"This is Genewen," he announced brightly. Then he grinned. "You see? I told you we could fly."

*   *   *

Seeing Genewen made Wil and Amberle more willing to accept the story that Perk then proceeded to tell them.

Before the time of Jerle Shannara and the advent of the Second War of the Races, a small community of Elves migrated south from their traditional homeland—for reasons which had long since been forgotten—to settle below the Irrybis along a rugged, uncharted stretch of mountainous forestland that bordered a vast body of water known to the races as the Blue Divide. These Elves were Perk's ancestors. Over the years, they became hunters and fishermen, their small villages built back upon a string of shoreline cliffs that abutted the Blue Divide west of the Myrian. The Elves quickly discovered that they were sharing the cliffs with a rookery of massive hunting birds that nested within caves opening out over the waters of the Divide. They called the birds Rocs after a legendary bird from the old world. The Rocs and the Elves kept a respectable distance from one another at first, but in time it became apparent to the Elves that the giant birds would be useful to the men if they could be trained to serve as carriers. The Elves were resourceful and determined, and they set out to accomplish this end. After numerous failures, they managed to discover a means of communication with the birds, which in turn led to harnessing several of the young and finally to mastery of the entire rookery. The birds became carriers of the Elves, who were now able to expand their hunting and fishing grounds. The birds became protectors as well, trained to do battle against the enemies of the community. The Elves, in their turn, kept the Rocs safe from creatures that sought to invade their rookery or to encroach upon their feeding grounds. They learned to care for the great birds, to treat them for sickness and injury, to heal them, and to keep them well. With the passage of the years, the bond between the two grew stronger. The community they shared they called the Wing Hove. It was small and isolated in a wilderness only sparsely settled by men and rarely traveled. All contact between the Wing Hove and the larger Elven communities that lay north of the Wilderun had long since ceased. The Elves in the Wing Hove had formed their own government and, although they recognized the sovereignty of the Elven Kings at Arborlon over the majority of the Westland Elves, they considered themselves a separate people. Thus they came to refer to themselves as Sky Elves and to the rest of the Westland Elves as Land Elves.

Perk was the son and grandson of Wing Riders. Wing Riders were the men who trained and rode the giant Rocs, the men who directed the search for food and the defense of the Wing Hove. There were other designations given to the men and women of the Wing Hove, but Wing Rider was the most coveted. Only the Wing Rider was given command over the Roc. Only he was given the power of flight, to ride the skylanes from one corner of the land to the other. The Wing Rider was a man who commanded the honor and trust of his people, who would spend his life in their service, and who would be recognized forever as a symbol of their way of life.

Perk was in the second year of his training to become a Wing Rider. The choice of one who would become a Wing Rider was made at an early age, and the training then continued until the boy reached manhood. Often the choice was virtually predetermined, as in the case of Perk, where both his father and his grandfather were Wing Riders, and it was expected that he should follow in their footsteps. Genewen was his grandfather's mount, but his grandfather was too old to fly in regular service for the Wing Hove; when Perk reached manhood, Genewen would become his. The Rocs lived to be very old, their lives spanning four and sometimes five Elven generations. Thus a Roc would serve several masters during its lifetime. Genewen had seen service first as the carrier of Perk's grandfather, but if her health remained good, she would one day serve Perk's son or grandson as well.

For the moment, however, she served Perk as he trained under the supervision of his grandfather to become a Wing Rider. It was a training exercise that had brought the Elven boy into the Rock Spur and to his meeting with Wil and Amberle. His development as a Wing Rider required that he make longer and longer flights from the Wing Hove. For each flight, he was given certain tasks to accomplish and rules to follow. On this particular outing, he was required to stay away from the Wing Hove for a period of seven days, carrying with him only a small ration of bread and cheese and a container of water. He was to find additional food and drink on his own. He was to explore and be able to describe accurately on his return certain portions of the mountainous country surrounding the Wilderun. The Wilderun itself was forbidden to him, as it was to all who were still in training. He might set down upon the land that bounded the Wilderun, but not within. He was to avoid all contact with its denizens.

The instructions seemed explicit enough, and Perk did not question them. But then on the morning of his second day out, while flying south along the eastern edge of the Rock Spur, he caught sight of Wil and Amberle, two bundled forms asleep in a pine grove below him. After winging downward for a closer look, he found himself faced with an immediate dilemma. Who were these travelers, Elves like himself, a young man and a younger girl, clearly from another part of the land? What were they doing in this rugged country, so poorly equipped? A moment's thought was all that it took, and the decision was made. He had been ordered to avoid any contact with the denizens of the Wilderun, but no directions had been given him regarding his contact with anyone else—an oversight on the part of his grandfather, perhaps, but a fact never-theless. Despite the maturity and caution instilled in Perk by the intense demands of his training, he was still a boy with a boy's spirit of adventure. His grandfather had left the door cracked before him, and it was natural enough that he should want to push it open the rest of the way. After all, although he was an obedient boy, he was also a curious one. Sometimes the former must be permitted to give way to the latter.

Fortunately for Wil and Amberle, this proved to be one such time.

Perk finished his story, then patiently answered questions for a moment or two. But his eagerness to begin his new adventure finally got the better of him. With an unmistakable look of anticipation, he asked his new companions if they were ready yet to depart. Genewen, although not used to carrying more than one rider, could easily do so. She would have them across the mountains of the Rock Spur before they knew it.

Wil and Amberle looked doubtfully at the giant bird. Had there been another way, they would have taken it gladly. Even the thought of flying made their stomachs feel queasy. But there was no alternative, and there the boy stood, hands on hips, waiting for matters to get underway. With a shrug of his shoulders to Amberle, Wil announced that they were ready. After all, if a mere boy could do this, certainly they could also.

With Perk in the lead, they moved over to Genewen. The giant bird was equipped with a leather harness that was bound tightly about her body. Perk showed them foot loops that would allow them to climb the harness to the center of the Roc's feathered back. He held Genewen steady while they did so, then fitted their boots to toe straps, directed their hands to knotted grips, and, as an added precaution, bound them to the harness with safety lines. That way, he informed them, if the wind should blow them loose, they still would not fall. Such assurances gave small comfort to the Valeman and the Elven girl, who were scared enough as it was. Perk then gave each a small section of a brownish root which he told them to chew and swallow. This root, he explained, would ease the discomfort of flying. They ate it hurriedly.

When both were secure, the Elven boy removed a long, leather-bound crop from beneath the harness straps and slapped Genewen smartly. With a piercing cry, the Roc spread her great wings and rose sharply into the morning air. Petrified, Wil and Amberle watched the ground drop away beneath them. The trees of the pine grove shrank as Genewen circled high above the meadowland, catching the wind currents and arcing swiftly west toward the peaks of the mountain range. For the Valeman and the Elven girl, the sensation was indescribable. At first there was a feeling somewhere between sickness and exhilaration, and only the juice of the strange root kept their stomachs from turning over entirely. Then the sickness lessened, and the feeling of exhilaration began to heighten, sweeping through them as they watched the horizons of the land

below broaden and stretch wide, a spectacular panorama
of forestland, swamp, mountains, and rivers. It was an
incredible sight. Before them the black peaks of the Rock
Spur rose up like jagged teeth out of the earth, and the
thin, blue ribbon of the Mermidon wound its way down
out of the rock; to the north was the dark smudge of the
Matted Breaks, set deep within the green of the Westland
forests; to the east, and now far distant, lay the twin towers
of the Pykon; to the south, the haze of the Shroudslip
settled against the threshold of the Irrybis. It was all there,
the whole of the land, spread out below them as if
contained in some hidden valley upon whose crest they
stood, all sharply revealed by a rising morning sun that
burned down out of a cloudless, brilliant blue sky.

Genewen rose to a height of several hundred feet,
winging her way steadily into the Rock Spur, weaving
through its maze of peaks, slipping deftly through breaks
and splits, dipping downward into valleys, then rising
again to clear each new ridge line. Wil and Amberle clung
to the harness with grips of iron, yet the ride was smooth;
the great bird responded to the motions of the small boy
who guided her, his hands and legs nudging and coaxing
with a series of movements familiar to the Roc. The wind
whipped across them in short bursts, yet was light and
warm on this summer's day, blowing softly out of the
south. Perk glanced quickly over his shoulder at his new
companions, a fierce grin splitting his freckled face. The
smiles they returned were less than enthusiastic.

They flew on for nearly an hour, winging deep within the
mountains until the forestland had disappeared from view
entirely. From time to time, they could see the haze of the
Shroudslip appear through breaks in the peaks to the
south, gray and friendless; then even that was gone. The
mountains closed in about them, massive towers of rock
that rose up across the sunlight and left them in shadow.
Wil found himself thinking momentarily of what it would
have been like for Amberle and him, had they attempted to
cross this forbidding range afoot. It was unlikely that they
could have done it, particularly without the aid of the slain
Elven Hunters. He wondered if Demons still tracked them.
Undoubtedly they did, he decided, but he took some small

measure of satisfaction in the knowledge that even the Reaper, had it managed somehow to survive the collapse of the catwalk in the Pykon, would find it impossible to follow their trail this time.

A short while later, Perk guided Genewen down to a high, treeless bluff, covered with long grass and wildflowers, which overlooked a mountain lake. The Roc settled smoothly back upon the earth and her riders disembarked, Perk springing nimbly from the giant bird's back, Wil and Amberle stiff and awkward in their movements, their faces filled with relief.

They rested on the bluff for half an hour, then climbed back upon Genewen and were off once again, winging westward through the massive peaks. Twice more during the morning they landed, resting themselves and Genewen, and then continued on. Each time Perk offered to share food and drink with his companions, and each time they quickly declined. All they would agree to accept was another piece of the strange root. Perk offered it to them without comment. It had been like this for him, too, when he had first flown.

By late morning, they had reached the eastern edge of the Wilderun. From atop Genewen, they could see the whole of the valley clearly, a tangled mass of forest ringed by the mountains of the Rock Spur and Irrybis and the broad, misty sweep of the Shroudslip. It was a forbidding stretch of woodland, heavily overgrown, a jumble of depressions and ridges, spotted with bogs and a scattering of solitary peaks that broke out of the trees like grasping arms. There was no sign of habitation, no villages nor isolated dwellings, no planted fields nor grazing stock. The whole of the valley was wilderness, dark and friendless. Wil and Amberle stared down into it apprehensively.

Moments later, Perk guided Genewen back into the shadow of the mountains and the Wilderun disappeared behind the peaks. They flew on without stopping until shortly after midday, when Perk turned Genewen south again. In a slow, gradual arc, the Roc slipped through a narrow break in the peaks. Ahead of them, the Wilderun again came into view. They flew toward it, dropping along a rugged slide that fell away at its lower end into the bowl of the valley. At the edge of the slide, Genewen banked right, winging downward toward a broad slope that sat back against the base of the peak and overlooked the Wilderun. Scattered clumps of trees dotted the slope, and Perk brought Genewen to rest behind a covering of fir.

Wil and Amberle climbed gingerly from the Roc's back, rubbing muscles that had grown stiff and cramped with the long ride. After a quick command to Genewen, Perk followed them down, his face flushed and excited.

"You see? We did it!" He was grinning from ear to ear.

"We did, indeed." Wil smiled ruefully, massaging his backside.

"What do we do next?" The boy wanted to know immediately.

Wil straightened himself, grimacing. "You don't do anything, Perk. This is as far as you go."

"But I want to help," Perk insisted.

Amberle stepped forward and put her arm about the boy. "You did help, Perk. We would not have gotten this far without you."

"But I want to go . . ."

"No, Perk," Amberle interrupted quickly. "What we must do now is far too dangerous for you to become involved in. Wil and I must go down into the Wilderun. You have said yourself that the Wilderun is forbidden to you. So you must leave us now. Remember, you promised Wil that you would do so when we asked."

The boy nodded glumly. "I am not afraid," he muttered.

"I know." The Elven girl smiled. "I don't think much of anything would frighten you."

Perk brightened a bit with this compliment, a quick smile lighting his face.

"There is one thing more you can do for us." Wil put a hand on his shoulder. "We don't know very much about the Wilderun. Can you tell us anything about what we might find down there?"

"Monsters," the boy answered without hesitation.

"Monsters?"

"All kinds. Witches, too, my grandfather says."

The Valeman could not decide whether to believe that or not. After all, the grandfather was trying to keep the boy out of the Wilderun and that was the kind of warning one would expect him to give.

"Have you ever heard of a place called Safehold?" he asked impulsively.

Perk shook his head no.

"I didn't think so." Wil sighed. "Monsters and witches, huh? Are there any roads?"

The boy nodded. "I will show you."

He led them out of the fir trees to a small rise where they could look down upon the valley.

"See that?" he asked, indicating a mass of fallen trees at the base of the slope. Wil and Amberle peered downward until they saw where he was pointing. "There is a road beyond those trees that leads to the village of Grimpen Ward. All roads in the Wilderun lead to Grimpen Ward. You cannot see anything of it from here, but it's down there, several miles into the forest. My grandfather tells me that it is a bad place, that the people are thieves and cutthroats. Maybe, though, you could find someone there to guide you."

"Maybe we can." Wil smiled his thanks. At least the thieves and cutthroats were preferable to the monsters and witches, he thought to himself. Still, it wouldn't hurt to be careful. Even if all the thieves and cutthroats and witches and monsters were imaginary, there were Demons searching for them, perhaps even waiting for them, who were not.

Perk was deep in thought. After a moment, he looked up. "What will you do when you find this Safehold?" he asked.

Wil hesitated. "Well, Perk, when we find Safehold, we find the talisman I told you about. Then we can return to Arborlon."

The boy's face lighted. "Then there is something more that I can do," he announced eagerly.

He reached into the small pouch that hung about his neck and withdrew the silver whistle, handing it to the Valeman.

"Perk, what . . . ?" Wil began as the whistle was thrust into his palm.

"I have five days more before I must return to the Wing

Hove," the boy interrupted quickly. "Each day I will fly once across the valley at noon. If you need me, signal with that whistle and I will come. The sound cannot be heard by humans—only by the Rocs. If you can find the talisman within the five days that I have left, then Genewen and I will carry you north again to your homeland."

"Perk, I don't think so . . ." Amberle started to object, shaking her head slowly.

"Wait a minute," Wil interjected. "If Genewen could fly us north again, we would save days. We would avoid all of the country we had to travel through to get here. Amberle, we have to get back as quickly as we can—you know that."

He turned quickly to Perk. "Could Genewen make such a trip? Could you?"

The boy nodded confidently.

"But he has said already that the Wilderun is forbidden to him," Amberle pointed out. "How can he land within it, then?"

Perk thought it out. "Well, if I set Genewen down just long enough to pick you up—that would only take a moment."

"I do not like this idea one bit," Amberle declared, frowning at Wil. "It is entirely too dangerous for Perk—and it is a violation of the trust that he has been given."

"I want to help," the boy insisted. "Besides, you told me how important this was."

He sounded so determined that for a moment Amberle could not think of a further argument. Wil took this opportunity to step in again.

"Look, why don't we compromise? I'll make a promise. If there is any danger to Perk, I'll not summon him under any circumstances. Fair enough?"

"But Wil . . ." the boy began.

"And Perk will agree that at the end of five days he will return to the Wing Hove as he has promised his grandfather, whether or not I have summoned him," the Valeman finished, cutting short the objections Perk was about to raise.

Amberle thought it over for a moment, then nodded reluctantly. "All right. But I will hold you to your promise, Wil."

The Valeman's eyes met hers. "Then it is agreed." He turned back to the boy. "We have to be going now, Perk. We owe you a lot."

He took the Elf's rough hand and gripped it firmly in his own.

"Goodbye," Amberle said, bending down to kiss him lightly on the cheek.

Perk flushed, his eyes lowering. "Goodbye, Amberle. Good luck."

With a final wave of farewell, the Valeman and the Elven girl turned and started down the long slope toward the forest wilderness. Perk watched them until they were out of sight.

XXVI

In the late afternoon hours of the second day following the departure of Wil and Amberle with the Elven Hunters who served as their escort from the city of Arborlon, Eventine Elessedil sat alone in the study of his home, maps and charts spread out on the worktable in front of him, his head bent close in concentration. Outside, the rain continued to fall in steady, gray sheets, just as it had fallen for two days past, drenching the whole of the Elven forests. Already dusk was beginning to creep forth, its shadow falling long and dark through the curtained, floor-length windows at the far side of the room.

Manx layed curled at his master's feet, grizzled head resting comfortably on his forepaws, his breathing deep and even.

The old King lifted his head from his work, rubbing his eyes reddened with fatigue. He stared across the room absently, then pushed his chair back from the table. Allanon should have been here by now, he thought anxiously. There was still much to be done, much that could not be done without the aid of the Druid. Eventine had no idea where the big man had gone this time; he had departed early that morning and had not been seen since.

The King stared out into the rain. For three days now he had worked with the Druid and the members of his Council preparing the defense for the Elven homeland—a defense that he knew would be necessary. Time was slipping away from him. The Ellcrys continued to fail, the Forbidding to weaken. With the passage of each day, the King expected to learn that both had crumbled, that the imprisoned Demons had broken free, and that the invasion of the Westland had begun. The Elven army was mobilized and stood ready: pikemen, swordsmen, archers and lancers; foot soldiers and cavalry; Home Guard and Black Watch; regular army and reserve; Elven fighting men from one end of the land to the other. The call had gone out, and all who were able had come to serve, leaving homes and families and pouring into the city to be outfitted with arms and equipment. Yet the King knew that even the iron will of the Elven army would not be enough to withstand an assault of the entire Demon horde, once it had broken free and welded itself into a cohesive unit. He knew this because Allanon had said that it would be so, and Eventine knew better than to question the Druid when he made a pronouncement as dire as this one. The Demons were physically stronger than the Elves; their numbers were greater. They were savage, maddened creatures driven by a hatred that had begun with the day of their banishment from the earth and had focused in whole upon the people responsible for that banishment. For centuries, there had been nothing else. Now that hatred would be given vent. Eventine harbored no illusions. If the Elves did not receive help from some quarter, the Demons would destroy them all.

It was no good depending solely on Amberle and the seed of the Ellcrys. However painful the thought, Eventine knew he must accept the fact that he might never see his granddaughter again. Even before her return to Arborlon, the King had dispatched messengers to the other races, requesting that they stand with the Elves against this evil that threatened his land—an evil that would ultimately consume them all. The messengers had been gone more than a week; as yet, none had returned. It was still too early, of course, to expect an answer from any of the other races, for even Callahorn was several days' ride. Even so, it was doubtful that many would come to stand with them.

Certainly the Dwarves would come, just as they had always come. The Dwarves and the Elves had stood together against every foe the free peoples of the Four Lands had faced since the time of the First Council of the Druids. Yet the Dwarves must come all the way from the deep forests of the Anar. And they must come afoot, for they were not horsemen. Eventine shook his head. They would come as quickly as they could—yet perhaps not quickly enough to save the Elves.

There was Callahorn, of course, but not the Callahorn of old, not the Callahorn of Balinor. Had Balinor still lived, or the Buckhannahs still ruled, the Border Legion would have marched at once. But Balinor was dead, the last of the Buckhannahs, and Callahorn's present ruler, a distant cousin who had ascended the throne more by accident than by acclaim, was an indecisive and overly cautious man who might find it convenient to forget that the Elves had come to the aid of Callahorn when last they called. In any case, the combined councils of Tyrsis and Varfleet and of Kern, rebuilt since its destruction fifty years earlier, wielded more power now than the King. They would be slow to act, even if Eventine's messenger were successful in conveying the urgency of the situation, for they lacked a strong leader to unite them in their thinking. They would debate, and while they debated the Border Legion would sit idle.

Ironically, it was their mistrust of their fellow South-landers—and more particularly, their mistrust of the Feder-ation—that would be likely to delay action on the part of the men of Callahorn. Following the destruction of the Warlock Lord and the defeat of his armies, the major cities of the deep Southland belatedly realized the extent of the threat that the Dark Lord had posed; acting in a haste born of fear, they had formed an alliance with one another, an alliance that began as a loose-knit organization of territories sharing common borders and common fears and quickly grew into the highly structured Federation. The Federation was the first cohesive form of government that the race of Man had known in more than a thousand years. Its professed goal was the final unification of the Southland and the race of Man under a single ruling government. That government, of course, was to be the Federation. To that end, they had begun a concerted effort to unite the remaining cities and provinces. In the four decades since its formation, the Federation had come to dominate almost the whole of the Southland. Of the major Southland cities, only those of Callahorn had resisted the suggested unifica-tion. The decision to do so had resulted in no small amount of friction between the two governments—especially as the

Federation continued its steady advance northward toward Callahorn's borders.

Eventine folded his arms across his chest, frowning. He had dispatched a messenger to the Federation, yet he had little hope that there would be help forthcoming. The Federation had shown scant interest in the affairs of the other races, and it was doubtful that they would see a Demon invasion of the Westland as being of legitimate concern. In fact, it was doubtful that they would even believe that such an invasion was possible. The Men of the deep Southland knew little of the sorcery that had troubled the other lands since the time of the First Council of the Druids; theirs had been a closed, introverted existence, and in their new expansion they had not yet encountered many of the unpleasant realities that lay beyond their own limited experience.

Again the King shook his head. No, the cities of the Federation would not come. Just as had been the case when they were warned of the coming of the Warlock Lord, they would not believe.

No messenger had been sent to the Gnomes. It would have been pointless to do so. The Gnomes were a tribal race. They did not answer to a single ruler or governing council. Their chieftains and their seers were their leaders, and there were different chieftains and seers for each tribe, all constantly feuding with one another. Bitter and disgruntled since their defeat at Tyrsis, the Gnomes had not mixed in the affairs of the other races in the fifty years that had since passed. It was hardly reasonable to expect that they should choose to do so now.

There remained the Trolls. The Trolls, too, were a tribal race, yet since the conclusion of the aborted Third War of the Races, the Trolls had begun unifying within the vast stretches of the Northland, tribes banding together within certain territories under council leadership. The closest and one of the largest of these communities lay within the Kershalt Territory, at the northern borders of the Elven homeland. The Kershalt was occupied principally by Rock Trolls, though some of the lesser tribes inhabited portions of this region as well. Traditionally, Elves and Trolls had been enemies; in the last two Race Wars, they had fought bitterly against one another. But with the fall of the Warlock

Lord, the enmity between the two races had lessened appreciably, and for the past fifty years they had lived in comparatively peaceful coexistence. Relations between Arborlon and the Kershalt had been particularly good. Trade had opened up and plans had been made to exchange delegations. There was a chance then that the Kershalt Trolls might agree to aid them.

The old King checked his thoughts and smiled wanly. A slim chance, he conceded. But he knew he could not afford to pass over any chance. The Elves would have need of whomever they could find to stand with them if they were to survive.

He stood up slowly, stretched, then glanced down again at the array of maps spread out on the worktable. Each depicted a different sector of the Westland, chartings of all the known country that comprised the Elven homeland and the territories surrounding it. Eventine had studied them until he thought it possible to trace their configurations in his sleep. Out of one of those sectors the Demons would come; and there the Elven defenses must be settled. But out of which? Where would the Forbidding crumble first? Where would the invasion begin?

The King let his eyes wander from one map to the next. Allanon had promised that he would discover where the break would come, and it was for that vital piece of information that the Elven army waited. Until then . . .

He sighed and walked to the window-doors that opened onto the manor house grounds. As he stared out through the growing dusk he caught sight of Ander coming up the walkway, head bent against the rain, arms laden with the troop registers and supply listings that he had been instructed to collect. The frown that creased the old King's face softened. Ander had been invaluable these past few days. To his younger son had fallen the tedious, if necessary, task of information gathering—thankless work at best and work that Arion would certainly have disdained. Yet Ander had undertaken the job without a single word of complaint. The King shook his head. Strange, but even though Arion was Crown Prince of the Elves and the closer of his sons, there were times these past few days when he saw more of himself in Ander.

He let his gaze shift then to the leaden evening skies and wondered suddenly if Ander ever felt the same.

Fatigue lined Ander Elessedil's face as he pushed through the manor house doors, shed his rain-soaked cloak, and turned down the darkened hallway that led to his father's study, the troop registers and supply listings cradled protectively in his arms. His day had been a difficult one and it had not been helped any by his brother's continuing refusal to have anything to do with him. It had been like that since he had taken Amberle's part at the High Council. What had always been a rather broad gulf between them had widened into a chasm that he could not begin to bridge. Today's encounter with his brother had illustrated just how wide that chasm had grown. Sent by his father to collect the information he now carried, he had gone to Arion for assistance because Arion had been given responsibility for mobilizing and outfitting the Elven army. Though Arion could have shortened his work by hours, he had refused even to meet with him, sending a junior supply officer in his stead and keeping himself conveniently absent the entire day. It had angered Ander so much that he had very nearly chosen to force a confrontation. But that might have involved his father, and the old King did not need any additional problems to occupy his time. So Ander had kept silent. For as long as the Demon hordes threatened the homeland, personal difficulties must be set aside.

He shook his head. Such reasoning did not make him feel any better, however, about the way things were working out between Arion and him.

He reached the study door, nudged it open with his boot, entered and nudged it closed again. He managed an encouraging smile for his father, who crossed to relieve him of the charts and listings. Then he sank down wearily into an empty chair.

"That's everything," he said. "Inventoried, recorded, and placed in order."

Eventine set the material his son had brought him on the table with the maps and turned back. "You look tired."

Ander rose and stretched. "I am . . ."

In a rush of wind and rain, the window-doors flew open.

Father and son whirled as maps and charts scattered to the floor and oil lamps flickered. Allanon stood framed in the entry, black robes glistening wetly in the dusk, trailing water onto the study floor. The angular features were strained, the thin line of his mouth hard. Both hands held firm a slim wooden staff, its surface the color of silver.

For an instant Ander's eyes met those of the Druid, and the Elven Prince felt his blood turn to ice. There was something terrible in the Druid's expression, glimmerings of fierce determination, power, and death.

The Druid wheeled and shoved closed the window-doors, fastening once again the latch he had somehow managed to loosen from without. When he turned back again, Ander saw clearly the silver staff and his face went deathly pale.

"Allanon, what have you done!" the words slipped out before he could think better of them.

His father saw it as well and cried out in a horrified whisper. "The Ellcrys! Druid, you have cut a branch from the living tree!"

"No, Eventine," the tall man replied softly. "Not cut. Not harmed her who is the life of this land. Never that."

"But the staff . . ." the King began, his hands reaching out as if to touch a thing that would burn.

"Not cut," the other repeated. "Look closely now."

He held forth the staff and turned it slowly so that it could be inspected. Ander and his father bent close. Each end of the staff was smooth and rounded. Nowhere was it splintered or nicked by a blade. Even the boles that roughened its length were healed and free of markings.

Eventine looked bewildered. "Then how . . . ?"

"The staff was given to me, King of the Elves—given by her, given that it might be carried against the enemies who threaten her people and their land." The Druid's voice was so cold that it seemed to freeze the very air of the small room. "Here, then, is magic that will give strength to the Elven army, power to withstand the evil that lives within the Demon hordes. This staff shall be our talisman—the right hand of the Ellcrys, carried forth when the armies meet to do battle."

He stepped forward, the staff still clenched before him, his dark eyes hard within the shadow of his brow.

"Early this morning I went to her, alone, seeking to find a weapon with which we might stand against our enemy. She gave me audience, speaking with the images that are her words, asking why I had come. I told her that the Elves had no magic save my own with which to counter the power of the Demons; I told her that I feared that this alone might not be enough, that I might fail. I told her that I sought something of what she is with which to do battle against the Demons, for she is an anathema to them.

"Then she reached down within herself and stripped away this staff which I hold, this limb of her body. Weakened, knowing that she dies, she yet managed to give to me a part of herself with which to aid the Elven people. I did not touch her, did nothing but stand in awe of her strength of will. Feel this wood, King of the Elves—touch it!"

He thrust the staff into Eventine's hands, and they closed about it. The King's eyes widened in shock. The Druid took the staff from him then and passed it wordlessly to Ander. The Elven Prince started. The wood of the staff was warm, as if the blood of life flowed within.

"It lives!" the Druid breathed reverently. "Apart and separate from her, yet still filled with her life! It is the weapon that I sought. It is the talisman that will protect the Elves against the black sorcery of the Demon hordes. As long as they bear the staff, the power that lives within the Ellcrys shall watch over them and work to keep them safe."

He took the staff from Ander's hands and once more their eyes met. The Elven Prince felt something unspoken pass between them, something he could not quite comprehend—just as it had been that night in the High Council when he had gone to stand with Amberle.

The Druid's eyes shifted to the King. "Now hear me." His voice was low and quick. "The rains will end this night. Does the army stand ready?"

Eventine nodded.

"Then we march at dawn. We must move quickly now."

"But where are we marching to?" the King asked immediately. "Have you discovered where the break will come?"

The Druid's black eyes glistened. "I have. The Ellcrys told me. She senses the Demons massing at a single point within the Forbidding, senses herself weakening where they gather. She knows that it is there that the Forbidding will fail first. The rent has been made once already by the ones who crossed through to slay the Chosen. The breach was closed, but the wound was not healed. There the Forbidding will break. It weakens already, straining with the force that pushes against it. The Demons are summoned to that place by the one who commands them, and who wields the power of sorcery so near my own. He is called the Dagda Mor. With his aid, the breach will be forced once again, and this time it will not be closed.

"But we will be waiting for them." His hand tightened on the staff. "We will be waiting. We will catch them while they stand newly crossed and still disorganized. We will close off their passage to Arborlon for as long as we are able. We will give Amberle the time she needs to find the Bloodfire and return."

Wordlessly he beckoned Ander and his father forward. Then he reached down and pulled from the floor one of the fallen maps, setting it squarely on the work table.

"The break will come here," he said softly.

His finger pointed to the broad expanse of the Hoare Flats.

XXVII

That same afternoon, when the daylight had nearly gone and the rain had turned to fine mist, the Legion Free Corps rode into Arborlon. The people of the city who saw them pass paused in the middle of their endeavors and turned to one another with guarded whispers. From high atop the tree lanes to the forest roadways below, hushed voices spoke as one. There was no mistaking the Free Corps.

Ander Elessedil was still closeted in the manor house study with his father and Allanon—kept there, oddly enough, at the Druid's insistence that he familiarize himself with Westland maps of the Sarandanon and proposed defensive plans—when Gael brought word of their arrival.

"My Lord, a cavalry command of the Border Legion has ridden in from Callahorn," the young aid announced, appearing abruptly at the study door. "Our patrols picked them up an hour east of the city and escorted them in. They should be here in a few minutes."

"The Legion!" A broad smile spread across the old King's weary face. "I hadn't dared to hope. What command, Gael? How many are they?"

"No word, my Lord. A messenger from the patrol brought the news, but there were no details."

"No matter." Eventine was on his feet and moving toward the door. "Any help is welcome, whoever . . ."

"Elven King!" Allanon's deep voice brought Ander's father about sharply. "We have important work to do here, work that should not be interrupted. Perhaps your son might go in your place—if only to give greeting to the Bordermen."

Ander stared at Allanon in surprise and turned eagerly

283

to his father. The King hesitated, then seeing the look in his son's eyes, he nodded.

"Very well, Ander. Extend my compliments to the Legion Commander and advise him that I will meet with him personally later this evening. See that quarters are provided."

Pleased with having been given a responsibility of some importance for a change, Ander hurried from the manor house, an escort of Elven Hunters in tow. The surprise he had experienced at Allanon's unexpected suggestion turned quickly to curiosity. It occurred to him that this was not the first time that Allanon had gone out of his way to include him when the Druid need not have done so. There was that first meeting when he had told Eventine of Amberle and the Bloodfire. There was his admonition to Ander upon leaving for Paranor to assume responsibility for his father's protection. There was that sense of alliance that had brought him to his feet in the High Council to stand with Amberle when no one else would do so. There was this afternoon's meeting when Allanon had given the Ellcrys staff to his father. Arion should have been present for these meetings, not he. Why was Arion never there?

He had just passed through the gates fronting the manor house grounds, still pondering the matter, when the foremost ranks of the Border cavalry crested the roadway leading in and the entire command wound slowly into view. Ander slowed, frowning. He recognized these riders. Long gray cloaks bordered in crimson billowed from their shoulders and wide-brimmed hats with a single crimson feather sat cocked upon their heads. Long bows and broadswords jutted from their saddle harness, and short swords were strapped across their backs. Each rider held a lance from which fluttered a small crimson and gray pennant, and the horses wore light armor of leather with metal fastenings. Escorted by the handful of Elven Hunters who had picked them up while on patrol east of the city, they rode through the rain-soaked streets of Arborlon in their precise, measured lines and glanced neither left nor right at the crowds who gathered to stare after them.

"The Free Corps," Ander murmured to himself. "They have sent us the Free Corps."

There were few who had not heard of the Free Corps,

the most famous and the most controversial command ever attached to the Border Legion of Callahorn. It drew its name from the promise it gave to those who joined its ranks—that its soldiers might leave behind without fear of question or need for explanation all that had come before in their lives. For most, there was much to be left. They came from different lands, different histories, and different lives, but they came for similar reasons. There were thieves among them, killers and cheats, soldiers broken from other armies, men of low blood and high, men with honor and men without, some searching, some fleeing, some drifting—but all seeking to escape what they were, to forget what they had been, and to start anew. The Free Corps gave them that chance. No soldier of the Free Corps was ever asked about his past; his life began with the day he joined. What had come before was finished; only the present mattered and what a man might make of himself for the time that he served.

For most, that time was short. The Free Corps was the Legion's shock unit; as such, it was considered expendable. Its soldiers were the first into battle and the first to die. In every engagement fought since the inception of the Corps some thirty years earlier, its casualty rate had been the highest. While the past had been left behind by the soldiers of the Free Corps, the future was an even more uncertain prospect. Still, it was a fair exchange, most thought. After all, there was a price for everything, and this price was not so unreasonable. If anything, it was a source of pride for the soldiers who paid it; it gave them a sense of importance, an identity that set them apart from any other fighting man in the Four Lands. It was a tradition of the Free Corps that its soldiers should die in battle. It was not important to the men of the Corps that they should die; death was the reality of their existence, and they viewed it as an old acquaintance with whom they had brushed shoulders on more than one occasion. No, it was not important that they should die; it was important only that they should die well.

They had proven it often enough before, Ander knew. Now it appeared they had been sent to Arborlon to prove it once again.

The Legion command drew to a halt before the iron

gates, and a tall, gray-cloaked rider in the forefront dismounted. Catching sight of Ander, he passed the reins of his horse to another and strode forward. On reaching the Elven Prince and his guard, he removed the wide-brimmed hat he wore and inclined his head slightly.

"I am Stee Jans, Commander of the Legion Free Corps."

For an instant Ander did not respond, so startled was he by the other's appearance. Stee Jans was a big man, seeming to tower over Ander. His weathered, yet still-youthful face was crisscrossed with dozens of scars, some of which ran through the light red beard that shaded his jaw, leaving streaks of white. A tangle of rust-colored hair fell to his shoulders, braided and tied. Part of one ear was missing and a single gold ring dangled from the other. Hazel eyes fixed those of the Elven Prince, so hard that they seemed chiseled from stone.

Ander found himself staring and quickly recovered. "I am Ander Elessedil—Eventine is my father." He extended his hand in greeting. Stee Jans' grip was iron hard, the brown hands calloused and knotted. Ander broke the handshake quickly and glanced down the long lines of gray riders, searching in vain for other units of the Legion. "The King has asked me to extend his compliments and to see that you are quartered. How soon can we expect the other commands?"

A faint smile crossed the big man's scarred visage. "There are no other commands, my Lord. Only the soldiers of the Free Corps."

"Only the . . . ?" Ander hesitated in confusion. "How many of you are there, Commander?"

"Six hundred."

"Six hundred!" Ander failed to hide his dismay. "But what of the Border Legion? How soon will it be sent?"

Stee Jans paused. "My Lord, I believe that I should be direct with you. The Legion may not be sent at all. The Council of the Cities has not yet made a decision. Like most councils, it finds it easier to talk about making a decision than to make it. Your ambassador spoke well, I am told, but there are many voices of caution on the Council, some of opposition. The King defers to the Council; the Council looks south. The Federation is a threat that the Council can see; your Demons are little more than a Westland myth."

"A myth!" Ander was appalled.

"You are fortunate to have even the Free Corps," the big man continued calmly. "You would not have that if it were not for the Council's need to sooth its collective conscience. A token force, at least, must be sent to the aid of their Elven allies, they argued. The Free Corps was the logical choice— just as it always is whenever there is an obvious sacrifice to be made."

It was a simple statement of fact, made without rancor or bitterness. The big man's eyes stayed flat and expressionless. Ander flushed.

"I would not have thought that the men of Callahorn would be so stupid!" he snapped, a sense of anger rushing through him.

Stee Jans studied him a moment, as if measuring him. "I understand that when Callahorn was under attack from the armies of the Warlock Lord, the Borderlands sent a request to the Elves for assistance. But Eventine was made prisoner by the Dark Lord, and in his absence the High Council of the Elves found itself unable to act." He paused. "It is much the same with Callahorn now. The Borderlands have no leader; they have had no leader since Balinor."

Ander eyed the other critically, his anger subsiding. "You are an outspoken man, Commander."

"I am an honest man, my Lord. It helps me to see things more clearly."

"What you have told me might not sit so well with some in Callahorn."

The Borderman shrugged. "Perhaps that is why I am here."

Ander smiled slowly. He liked Stee Jans—even without knowing any more about him than he did at this moment. "Commander, I did not mean to seem angry. It has nothing to do with you. Please understand that. And the Free Corps is most welcome. Now let me see to your quarters."

Stee Jans shook his head. "No quarters are necessary; I sleep with my soldiers. My Lord, the Elven army marches in the morning, I am told." Ander nodded. "Then the Free Corps will march as well. We need only rest the night. Please tell this to the King."

"I will tell him," Ander promised.

The Legion Commander saluted, then turned and

walked back to his horse. Remounting, he nodded briefly to the riders of the Elven patrol who escorted his command, and the long gray columns swung left once more down the muddied road.

Ander stared after him with mingled admiration and disbelief. Six hundred men! Thinking of the thousands of Demons that would come against them, he found himself wondering what possible difference six hundred Southlanders would make.

XXVIII

At dawn, the Elves marched forth from Arborlon, to the wail of pipes and the roll of drums, voices raised in song, banners flying in splashes of vivid color against a sky still leaden and clouded. Eventine Elessedil rode at their head, gray hair flowing down chain mail forged of blue iron, his right hand holding firmly the silver-white staff of the Ellcrys. Allanon was at his side, a spectral shadow, tall and black atop a still taller and blacker Artaq, and it was as if Death had ridden from the pits of the earth to stand watch over the Elves. Behind rode the King's sons: Arion, cloaked in white and bearing the Elven standard of battle, a war eagle on a field of crimson; Ander, cloaked in green and carrying the banner of the house of the Elessedils, a crown wreathed in boughs set over a spreading oak. Dardan, Rhoe, and three dozen hardened Elven Hunters came next, the Elessedil guard; then the gray and crimson of the Legion Free Corps, six hundred strong. Pindanon rode alone at the forefront of his command, a gaunt, bent figure atop his warhorse, his battle-scarred armor lashed about his spare frame as if to hold his bones in place. The army followed him, massive and forbidding, six columns wide and thousands strong. They numbered three companies of cavalry, battle lances hoisted out of their midst in a forest of iron-tipped shafts, four companies of foot soldiers with pikes and body shields, and two companies of archers bearing the great Elven long bows— all clad in the traditional manner of the Elven warrior, lightly armored with chain-mail vests and leather guards to assure mobility and quickness.

It was an awesome procession. Trappings and weapons creaked and jingled in the early morning stillness, flashed in dull glimmerings through the new light, and cast the Elves in half-human forms that whispered of death. Booted feet and iron-shod hooves thudded and splashed along the muddied earth as the columns of men and horses wound from the parade grounds north of the city to the bluff of the Carolan and prepared to turn onto the Elfitch, the hooked rampway that led down from the heights of Arborlon to the forestlands beneath. The people of the city had come to watch. Atop the Carolan, on walls and fences, in fields and gardens, lining the way at every step, they bade farewell with cheers of encouragement and hope and with silences born of emotions that had no voice. Before the gates to the Gardens of Life, the Black Watch stood assembled, present to a man, their lances raised in salute. At the bluff's edge were gathered in review the Elven Hunters of the Home Guard and the man who would command them in their King's absence—Emer Chios, First Minister of the High Council, now the designated defender of the city of Arborlon.

Down out of the Carolan the Elven army wound, following the spiral of the stone-block ramp as it dropped along the forested cliffs through seven walled gates that marked its levels of descent. At its lower end, the army swung south toward the narrows. A solitary bridge spanned the Rill Song, the lone passage west from the city, its iron struts nearly awash with the swollen waters of the river. Like a metal-backed snake, the army moved onto the bridge, crossed, and passed into the silent woods beyond. The glitter of weapons and armor twinkled into darkness, banners slipped from view, and the strains of song, the wail of pipes, and the roll of drums faded into echoes quickly lost in the leafy canopy of the trees. By the time the morning sun had broken through the clouds of the departing storm to rise above the crest of the Carolan and light the forestland below, the last remnants of this grand procession had disappeared from view.

For five days the army journeyed west from Arborlon, winding its way through the deep forests of the homeland toward the Sarandanon. The rains had moved east into Callahorn, and the sun shone down out of cloudless blue skies to warm the woodland shadows. Travel was measured, the cavalry forced to slow its place to match that of the soldiers afoot. Evidence of the danger threatening the Elves became steadily more apparent as the army passed westward through the outlying provinces. Tales filtered back from Elven families on their way eastward to the home city with their possessions bundled in carts and on the backs of oxen and horse. Their homes and their villages were abandoned behind them. Terrifying creatures roamed the land west, their frightened voices warned—dark and brutal monsters that killed without reason and disappeared as quickly as they had come. Cottages had been stripped and homes violated, the Elves within left torn and broken. Such incidents were scattered, but that merely served to convince the fleeing villagers that there was no longer any place west of Arborlon that was safe. As the army marched past, the villagers sent up cheers and shouts of encouragement, but their faces remained clouded with doubt.

The march west wore on until, late in the afternoon of the fifth day, the army passed out of the forestland into the valley of the Sarandanon. The valley lay sandwiched between woodlands on the south and east, the Kensrowe Mountains on the north, and the broad expanse of the Innisbore on the west. A flat, fertile stretch of farmland dotted with small clumps of trees and pockets of spring water, the Sarandanon was the breadbasket of the Elven nation. Corn, wheat, and other seed crops were sown and harvested seasonally by the families who lived within the valley, then bartered or sold to the remainder of the homeland. Mild temperatures and a balanced rainfall provided an ideal climate for farming, and for generations the Sarandanon had served as the principal source of food for the Elven people.

The Elven army encamped that night at the eastern end of the valley; at dawn on the following day, it began the journey across. A broad, earthen road wound through the heart of the Sarandanon past fence lines and clusters of small dwellings and sheds, and the army followed it west. In the fields, the families of the valley toiled with quiet determination. Few Elves here had yet gone east. Everything that had meaning in their lives lay rooted in the land they farmed, and they would not be frightened off easily.

By midafternoon, the army had reached the western end

of the valley. In the distance, beyond the Innisbore, the humped ridge of the Breakline rose up against the horizon, curving north above the Kensrowe into the wilderness of the Kershalt Territory. The sun already lay atop the crest of the mountains, brilliant golden light spilling down out of the rock. In the growing darkness of the eastern sky, the moon's whiteness glimmered faintly.

The army swung north. Between the Innisbore and the Kensrowe, Baen Draw opened down out of the rugged hill country below the Breakline into the valley of the Sarandanon. It was there that the army of the Elves made its camp.

At dusk, Allanon came down out of the Kensrowe as silently and unexpectedly as he had gone into them hours before, his tall form moving into the Elven camp like one of night's shadows, dark and solitary as he passed through the maze of cooking fires that dotted the grasslands. He went directly to the tent of the Elven King, oblivious to the soldiers who stared after him, his head lowered within the darkness of his cowl. The Elven Hunters who stood watch before Eventine's quarters stepped aside wordlessly at his approach and let him enter without challenge.

Within, he found the King at a small, makeshift table of planks laid crosswise atop logs, his evening meal spread out before him. Dardan and Rhoe stood silently at the rear of the tent. At a glance from the Druid, Eventine dismissed them. When they were gone, Allanon moved to the table and seated himself.

"Is all in readiness?" he asked quietly.

Eventine nodded.

"And the plan of defense?"

In the light of the oil lamps, the King could see that the Druid's dark face was streaked with sweat. He stared uncertainly at the mystic, then pushed aside his dinner and laid a map of the Elven homeland upon the table.

"At dawn, we march to the Breakline." He traced the route with his finger. "We will secure the passes of Halys Cut and Worl Run and hold them against the Demons for as long as we are able. If the passes are forced, we will fall back to the Sarandanon. Baen Draw will be our second line of defense. Once through the Breakline, the Demons will have three ways to go. If they turn south out of the passes, they must circle below the Innisbore through the forests, then come north again. If they turn north first, they must make their way through the rugged hill country above the Kensrowe and come south. Either route will delay their advance on Arborlon by at least several days. Their only other choice will be to come through the Draw—and through the Elven army."

Allanon's dark gaze fixed on the King. "They will choose the Draw."

"We should be able to hold it for several days," the King continued. "Longer, perhaps, if they do not think to flank us."

"Two days, no more." The Druid's voice was flat, unemotional.

Eventine stiffened. "Very well, two days. But if the Draw is taken, the Sarandanon will be lost. Arborlon will be our last defense."

"So be it." Allanon leaned forward, hands knotting together before him. "We need to speak now of something else, something that I have kept from you." His voice was soft, almost a whisper. "The Demons are no longer with us—those who have crossed already through the Forbidding, the Dagda Mor and his followers. They neither watch us nor follow after us. If they did, I would sense it, and I have sensed nothing from the time that we left Arborlon."

The Elven King stared back at him wordlessly.

"I thought it strange that they should take so little interest in us." The Druid smiled faintly. "This afternoon I went up into the mountains so that I might be alone to discover where it was that they had gone. It is within my power to search out those who are hidden from my eyes. I have that power, but it must be used sparingly, for in using it I reveal to others with powers similar to my own—such as the Dagda Mor—both my own presence and the presence of any whom I seek. I could not risk using it to follow Wil Ohmsford and your granddaughter on their journey south; if I did I might tell the Demons where they could be found. Yet to search out the Dagda Mor himself— that, I felt, was a risk that should be taken.

"I did seek him then, searching the whole of the surrounding land to discover where he had concealed himself. But he was not concealed. I found him beyond the

wall of the Breakline, within the Hoare Flats, he and those
who follow him. Still, I could tell little of what they were
about; their thoughts were closed to me. I could but sense
their presence. The evil that pervades them is so strong
that even brushing against it momentarily caused me great
pain, and I was forced to withdraw at once."

The Druid straightened. "It is certain that the Demons
gather within the Flats in anticipation of the collapse of the
Forbidding. It is certain that they work to hasten that
collapse. They do this openly and without concern for
what the plans of the Elves may be. That suggests to me
that they already know those plans."

Eventine paled. "The spy within my house—the spy
who warned the Demons that you would be at Paranor."

"That would explain why it is the Demons show such an
obvious lack of interest in our movements," Allanon
agreed. "If they already know that we intend to stop them
at the Breakline, they have little need to follow after us to
see what we are about. They have only to await our
coming."

The implication of that statement was not lost on
Eventine. "Then the Breakline may be a trap."

The Druid nodded. "The question is, what kind of trap
do the Demons set? There are not enough of them yet to
withstand an army of this size. They have need of those
still imprisoned within the Forbidding. If we are quick
enough . . ."

He left the sentence unfinished and rose. "One thing
more, Eventine. Be cautious. The spy is still with us. He
may be within this camp, among those you trust. If the
opportunity presents itself, he may seek your death."

He turned and moved back toward the entry, the shadow
of his dark form rising up against the tent wall like some
giant in the flickering light of the oil lamps. The King stared
after him wordlessly for a moment, then lurched sharply to
his feet.

"Allanon!"

The Druid looked back.

"If the Demons know why we march to the Breakline—if
they know that—then they may also know that Amberle
carries the Ellcrys seed into the Wilderun."

There was an unpleasant silence. The two men faced

each other. Then, without replying, the Druid turned and disappeared through the tent flap into the night.

At that same moment, Ander was picking his way through the crowded Elven encampment in search of the Legion Free Corps and Stee Jans. Ostensibly his mission was to inquire into the needs of the Legion soldiers, but underlying this was his personal interest in their Commander. He had not spoken again with Jans since the Free Corps had arrived in Arborlon and he was admittedly curious to know more about the enigmatic Southlander. With nothing else immediate to occupy his time, he had decided to take this opportunity to seek him out and talk further with him.

He found the Free Corps camp at the southern edge of the Kensrowe, their watch already posted, their horses tethered and fed. No one challenged him as he wandered into their midst. When he could not immediately locate the Free Corps Commander's quarters, he stopped a number of soldiers to ask if they knew where Jans could be found and was directed finally to a Legion Captain.

"Him?" The Captain was a burly fellow with a heavy beard and a laugh that rang deep and hollow. "Who knows? He's not in his tent, I can tell you that much. He left almost as soon as we pitched camp. Went out into the hills."

"Scouting?" Ander was incredulous.

The Captain shrugged. "He's like that. Wants to know everything about a place where he might die." He laughed roughly. "Never leaves that kind of checking to another—likes to do it himself."

Ander nodded uncomfortably. "I suppose that's why he's still alive."

"Still alive? Why, that one will never die. You know what they call him? The Iron Man. Iron Man—that's him. That's the Commander."

"He looks hard enough," Ander agreed, his curiosity piqued.

The Captain motioned him closer, and for a moment each forgot whom he was addressing. "You know about Rybeck?" the Borderman asked.

Ander shook his head, and a glint of satisfaction leaped

into the other's hard eyes. "You listen then. Ten years ago a band of Gnome raiders was burning and killing the people at the eastern edge of the borderlands. Vicious little rats, and a bunch of them at that. The Legion tried everything to trap them, but nothing worked. Finally the King sent the Free Corps after them—with orders to track them down and destroy them, even if it took the rest of the year. I remember that hunt; I was with the Corps even then."

He squatted down next to a cooking fire, and Ander hunched down beside him. Others began drifting in to listen.

"Five weeks the hunt went on, and the Corps tracked those Gnomes all the way east into the Upper Anar. Then one day, when we were getting close, a patrol of our men, only twenty-three of them, stumbled into a rear guard of several hundred raiders. The patrol could have fallen back, but it didn't. These were Free Corps soldiers and they chose to fight. One man was sent back for reinforcements and the rest made their stand in this little village called Rybeck—just a bunch of nothing buildings. For three hours those twenty-two soldiers held out against the raiders— threw back every assault they mounted. A lieutenant, three junior officers, and eighteen soldiers. One of those junior officers was just a kid. Just seven months with the Corps—but already a corporal. No one knew much about him. Like most, he didn't say much about his past."

The Captain leaned forward. "After the first two hours, that boy was the only officer still alive. He rallied the half-dozen soldiers left into a small stone cottage. Refused surrender, refused quarter. When the relief force broke through finally, there were dead Gnomes all over the place." The man's hand tightened into a fist before Ander's face. "More than a hundred of them. All of our men were gone, all but two, and one of them died later that day. That left just one. The boy corporal."

He paused and chuckled softly. "That boy was Stee Jans. That's why they call him the Iron Man. And Rybeck?" He shook his head solemnly. "Rybeck shows how a soldier of the Free Corps should fight and die."

The soldiers gathered about him murmured their assent. Ander paused a moment, then rose. The Captain stood up with him, straightening himself as he seemed to remember again who it was that he was conversing with.

"Anyway, my Lord, the Commander's not here right now." He paused. "Can I do something for you?"

Ander shook his head. "I came to ask if there was anything you need."

"A bit to drink," someone cried, but the Captain waved him off with a quick oath.

"We'll be fine, my Lord," he responded. "We have what we need."

Ander nodded slowly. Hard men, these Free Corps soldiers. They had made the long journey to Arborlon and then, with but a single night's rest, a forced march to the Sarandanon. He doubted that there really was much that they needed.

"Then I'll say good-night, Captain," he said.

He turned and walked back toward the Elven camp, mulling over in his mind the tale of the Legion Commander they called the Iron Man.

XXIX

The following morning the army of the Elves and their Legion allies marched north out of the Sarandanon. With the dawn still a faint silver glow above the eastern forestline, the soldiers wound through Baen Draw and turned into the hills that lay beyond. Armor and harness jangled and creaked, boots and hooves thudded in rough cadence, and men and horses huffed clouds of white vapor in the frosty morning air. No one spoke or whistled or sang. A sense of anticipation and wariness pervaded the ranks. On this morning, Elven Hunter and Borderman knew they were marching into battle.

Up into the hills they circled, hills barren and rugged, their slopes sparse with short grass and scrub, rutted and eroded by wind and rain. Ahead, still far distant, the dark mass of the Breakline stood silhouetted against the dying night. Slowly, as the sun brightened the skyline, the mountains etched themselves out of the blackness, a maze of peaks and crags, drops and slides. The day began to warm. The morning hours slipped away and the army swung west, columns of riders and men afoot winding through gullies and over ridges, stretching out across the land. To the south, the waters of the Innisbore sparkled in flashes of blue, and above the choppy surface flew a sprinkling of white-backed gulls, their wings tipped with black, their cries shrill and haunting.

By noon, the army had reached the Breakline, and Eventine signaled a halt. The mountains loomed up against the horizon, a dark and massive wall of rock. Cliffs and spires rose thousands of feet into the sky, massed close as if some giant had gathered them within his hands and squeezed until the stone had broken and split from the pressure. Still and silent, barren and cold, they were filled with emptiness, darkness, and death.

Two passes split the Breakline, slender threads that tied the land of the Elves to the Hoare Flats. South lay Halys Cut. North lay Worl Run. If the Demons were to break through the Forbidding within the Flats as Allanon had foreseen, then, to reach the city of Arborlon, they would be forced to come east through one or both of these passes. It was there that the Elven army would try to stop them.

"We part company here," Eventine announced when he had assembled his officers. Ander edged his mount closer to the small circle of men to hear clearly what was being said. "The army will divide. Half will march north with Prince Arion and Commander Pindanon to secure Worl Run. The other half will march south with me to Halys Cut. Commander Jans?" The bronzed face of the Free Corps Commander pushed into view. "I would like the Free Corps to march south. Pindanon, give the order."

The ring of horsemen broke apart as the word was passed down the line. Ander glanced briefly at Arion, who met his gaze coldly and turned away.

"Ander, I want you to ride with me," his father called over to him.

Kael Pindanon came galloping back to the King. All was in readiness. The two old comrades bade farewell to each other, hands clasping tightly. Ander looked one time more for his brother, but Arion was already moving to the head of his column.

Allanon appeared, dark face impassive. "His anger is misplaced," the Druid said quietly, then nudged Artaq past.

Pindanon's voice rang out. Banners and lances lifted in salute as the army of the Elves split apart. Shouts and cheers broke the morning stillness, echoing through the crags and rifts of the mountain rock. For long moments the air was filled with sound, reckless and fierce. Then Pindanon's command swept north, winding into the hills in a broad cloud of dust until it was lost from view.

The soldiers of the King turned south. For several hours they worked their way along the fringe of the Breakline, following the steady rise and fall of the lowland hills. Overhead, the sun passed west across the ridge of the

mountains, and shadows began to lengthen in dark
swatches. The still, sultry air of midday cooled in a
southerly breeze that swept out of the distant forests.
Gradually the hills broadened into grasslands. At their
edge, straddled by a series of narrow, ragged peaks, the
dark mouth of Halys Cut opened into the rock.

Eventine brought his arm to a halt and held a brief
conference with his officers. Below the eastern entrance to
the pass lay several miles of open plains that ran south to
the forestline. If the Demons were to find a way to cross the
Breakline below Halys Cut, they could slip north through
the forestland and trap the Elven army within the pass. A
rear guard would be necessary to protect against that
possibility. A cavalry unit could best handle the assign-
ment; the cavalry would be of little use in any case within
the narrow confines of the pass.

Ander saw his father's gaze fall briefly on Stee Jans, then
move away. Elven cavalry units would form that guard, the
King announced.

The order was given. The Elven cavalry detached itself
from the main body of the army and began to deploy across
the length of the grasslands. At a signal from Eventine, the
remainder of the army turned into Halys Cut. Through the
broad, shadowed gap the Elves marched, rugged cliffs
towering up about them. The floor of the pass began to
climb almost immediately, and the soldiers trudged upward into the rock. Quickly the air cooled, and the sound
of shod hooves and booted feet striking against stone
echoed eerily. As the trail continued to rise, the footing
grew less sure. Loose rock littered the pathway, and cracks
split its surface. Men and horses stumbled and slid with
each step, and the pace slowed.

Then abruptly it stopped. Before them a huge chasm
opened, a massive fissure that dropped away into black
emptiness, splitting the length of the pass ahead for
hundreds of yards. To the left, the trail sloped down along
the mountainside, broad and even as it ran to a defile at the
far end of the chasm. To the right, a narrow ledge skirted
the fissure, a thin, crumbling pathway that would barely
permit the passage of a single rider. All about, sheer cliff
walls seemed to bend inward as they rose until all that
remained of the sky was a thin, ragged blue line.

The army swung left along the broader path, staying well back of the black mouth of the chasm. When it had gained the defile, it found itself entering a canyon bright with afternoon sunlight and grown green with scrub and saw grass. Clusters of boulders dotted the canyon floor, and a thin stream trickled down out of the cliff walls and pooled in a small, brush-grown hollow. Jackrabbits bounded through the brush at the army's approach, and a scattering of birds drinking at the water's edge took sudden flight.

The Elves crossed to the far end of the canyon. There the pass opened down a broad, winding gorge into the vast emptiness of the Hoare Flats. Eventine's hand came up sharply, signaling a halt. His eyes swept the length of the gorge, past a maze of jumbled rock pockets and drops angling down through hulking cliffs and long, rugged slides. Wordlessly, he nodded. It was here that the army would make its stand.

Dusk crept into the Breakline, shadowed gray light chasing toward a sunset that lit the sky above the Hoare Flats in a blaze of scarlet and gold. Behind the wall of the mountains, the moon's silver disk rose above the forestland and one by one the stars winked into view. Within Halys Cut, the silence began to deepen.

Ander Elessedil stood alone on a small knoll midway down the gorge that ran to the Flats, arms cradling protectively the silver-white staff of the Ellcrys. Wordlessly he surveyed the lines of Elven Hunters and Free Corps soldiers, reconstructing in his mind for the twentieth time in the past half hour the strategy his father had devised for the defense of the pass. A broad rise straddled the pass several hundred yards from its mouth, a flat shelf of rock that overlooked a rugged slide strewn thick with loose stone and scrub. It was here that the army would make its initial stand. Archers would line the front of the rise, shooting into the Demons as they came out of the Flats through the mouth of Halys Cut to scramble up the slide. When the Demons were too close for the longbows to be effective, the archers would be replaced by a phalanx of lancers and pikemen who would bear the brunt of the assault. A second phalanx would be held in reserve to reinforce the first. The defenders would hold the rise for as long as they were able, then fall back several hundred yards to a similar position. If the gorge were lost, they would fall back to the mouth of the canyon. If that, too, were lost, the canyon itself would be defended—and so on, until the army was forced entirely from Halys Cut. It was a good plan. Ander was satisfied on thinking it through that the pass would not be easily taken. The defensive positions had been well chosen; when the attack came, it would find the Elves ready.

He lifted his gaze and stared out toward the Flats. Nothing moved. The land lay silent and empty. There was still no sign of the Demons.

Yet they would come. His hands moved slowly over the smooth wood of the Ellcrys staff, tracing the grain of the skin. His father had left the staff in his care momentarily while he had descended the slide to make his own inspection of the Elven defenses. Ander breathed the night air deeply. Would the staff truly protect the Elves? Would it lend its magic to those who were mortal men now, no longer the creatures of faerie that their forefathers had been? He looked down at it, gripping it tightly within his hands, and tried to find his own strength in its firmness. Allanon had said that the power of the Ellcrys over the Demons was carried within this staff and that it would weaken the evil and make it vulnerable to Elven weapons. Yet doubt clouded Ander's mind. The Demons were an incomprehensible evil, born of a world long since gone, a world that none but they had ever seen nor could begin to imagine.

He caught himself. None but Allanon, he corrected himself. And Allanon was himself perhaps a part of that dark, forgotten world.

His father appeared suddenly from the darkness, slipping from the shadows to stand beside him. Wordlessly, Ander passed back the Ellcrys staff. Fatigue and worry lined the old man's face, reflected in his eyes, and Ander forced himself to look away.

"Is everything all right?" he asked after a moment.

The King nodded distantly. "All of the defensive positions are established."

They were silent again. Ander tried to think of something more that he could say. There was an uneasiness in him that would not settle, one that gave rise to a need to be close to his father. He wanted Eventine to understand this. Yet it was difficult, somehow, to speak with his father of such things. Neither of them had ever been very good at expressing feelings to the other.

His mood darkened. It was that way with Arion as well—particularly with Arion. There was a distance between them that he had never really understood, a distance that might have been shortened had either of them been able to talk about it. But neither had tried. It was worse now, of course. Arion was angered by what had taken place at the High Council, by Ander's refusal to reject Amberle as the rightful bearer of the Ellcrys seed, and by his refusal to demand of her, as Arion thought proper, an accounting of her actions; now he would not talk with his brother at all. There was such bitterness in Arion! Still, it was bitterness that Ander understood. When Amberle had left Arborlon those many months ago, abandoning without explanation her responsibilities as one of the Chosen, both brothers had experienced that bitterness—he as much as Arion because he, too, had loved the child. For too long a time he had let the bitterness blind him to everything that she had once meant to him. Yet seeing her again had allowed him to rediscover something of his old feeling for her. He would have liked to explain that to Arion; he needed to explain it. But somehow he could not seem to find a way to do so.

He started sharply as he realized that Allanon was standing beside him. The Druid had materialized from nowhere, without even the faintest whisper of those black, concealing robes. The cowled face studied him momentarily, then looked past him to his father.

"You do not sleep?"

Eventine seemed distracted. "No. Not yet."

"You must rest, Elven King."

"Soon. Allanon, do you think that Amberle is still alive?"

Ander caught his breath and glanced fleetingly at the Druid. Allanon was quiet a moment before answering.

"She is alive."

When he said nothing more, Eventine looked over. "How can you know that?"

"I cannot know; it is what I think."

"Then why is it that you think she is alive?"

The Druid's head lifted slightly, deep-set eyes studying the sky. "Because Wil Ohmsford has not yet used the Elfstones. If Amberle's life were threatened, the Valeman would use the Stones."

Ander frowned. Elfstones? Wil Ohmsford? What was all this about? Then he remembered the second cloaked figure at the High Council, the one whom Allanon had brought into the chamber with Amberle, and who had never shown himself. That would be Wil Ohmsford.

He turned quickly to Allanon, questions forming on his lips, then caught himself and turned away again. Perhaps this was not something he should be asking about, he thought. After all, nothing had been said before. If Allanon had wanted him to know more, he would have told him. But then why had the Druid said anything at all?

Confused, he stared out across the Flats as the sun slipped beneath the horizon, the colors of the sunset fading slowly into the night.

"There are watch fires laid across the mouth of the pass," his father murmured after a moment. "I must order them lighted."

He walked down into the gorge, and Ander was left alone with Allanon. The two stood wordlessly, motionless statues in the growing dark, looking after the stooped figure of the old King as he wound his way down along the broken rock. The minutes slipped away. Ander thought himself forgotten when the Druid's voice floated up suddenly out of the silence.

"Would you know something more of Wil Ohmsford, Elven Prince?"

Ander stared at the big man in astonishment, then managed a startled nod.

"Then so you shall." Allanon never even glanced at him. "Listen."

Quietly he told Ander of Wil Ohmsford—of his heritage and of his mission to the Elves. Memories came back then to the Elven Prince of his father's stories of the Valemen, Shea and Flick Ohmsford, and of their search for the legendary Sword of Shannara. And now Shea's grandson, heir to the power of a magic that no Elf had wielded since the destruction of the old world, had been made Amberle's protector.

When the Druid finished, Ander was silent for a moment. He stared down into the shadows where his father had disappeared, thinking. Then he glanced once more at the Druid.

"Why have you told me this, Allanon?"

"It is something you should know."

Ander shook his head slowly. "No—I mean, why me?"

Then at last the Druid turned to look at him, hawk face barely visible within the shadows of the cowl. "For many reasons, Ander," he said softly and paused. "Perhaps because when no one else would come forward to stand with Amberle that night in the High Council, you did. Perhaps because of that."

His black eyes remained fixed on Ander for a moment, and then he turned away again. "You should rest now. You should sleep."

Ander nodded, his mind elsewhere. Had the Druid really answered his question? He glanced briefly at Allanon, then looked away again, puzzled. Moments later, when he glanced back once more, the Druid was gone.

XXX

Dawn broke, and a deep, gray mist covered the whole of the Hoare Flats. Thick, still, and impenetrable, it lay stretched across the earth like a death shroud. Night drew away from the mist as the pale, silver light of sunrise crept down out of the Breakline; when the night had gone, the mist came awake. With a sluggish heave, it began to churn against the wall of the mountains like some foul soup stirred within its kettle. Faster and faster it swirled, surging up against the cliffs until it seemed the rock must be swallowed and lost.

High within the shadowed closure of Halys Cut, flanked by his father and Allanon and ringed by the Home Guard, Ander Elessedil stared downward. Below, the army of the Elves prepared to defend against the Demon hordes. Row upon row of archers, lancers, and pikemen bridged the gorge that opened onto the Flats, their weapons held ready, their eyes riveted on the mist as it boiled before the mouth of the pass. Out of this mist must come the Demons, yet nothing could be seen of them. As the minutes slipped by and still the attack did not come, the soldiers began to grow restless. Ander could sense their uneasiness, like his own, turning slowly to fear.

"Stand fast; do not be frightened!" Allanon's voice rang out suddenly, and all eyes turned toward the black-cloaked Druid. "It is but mist, though Demon-wrought! Courage, now! The Forbidding gives way; the Demons are about to cross over!"

Still the mist churned wildly at the entrance to the Cut, as if shut away by some invisible barrier that would not let it advance further. Silence hung across the land, deep and pervasive. Ander's hands were trembling as he gripped the staff from which the banner of the House of the Elessedils hung limply, and he fought silently to still them.

Then abruptly the cries began, distant and haunting, as if drifting out of the bowels of the earth. Within the mist, streaks of red fire lanced upward to the still-darkened morning sky, and the roiling haze seemed to heave. The cries grew louder, turning suddenly to screams that were shrill and savage, filled with madness. They rose steadily, building into a single, unending shriek that emptied out of the Flats into the narrow defile of Halys Cut.

"It comes," Allanon whispered harshly.

The soldiers of the Elven army dropped to their knees, the sound breaking over them like a wave. Arrows were notched quickly in bow strings; spears and pikes were braced against the earth. Across the mouth of the pass, the mist erupted in red fire that turned the whole of the sky and earth crimson with its reflection. The shrieks and screams rose to a deafening pitch, and suddenly the air itself seemed to explode in a thunderous clap that burst out of the wilderness to the wall of the Breakline and shook the rock to its core. Ander cried out in dismay, and the force of the thunder threw them all to the earth. Hurriedly, they scrambled back to their feet, eyes searching. The air had gone silent. The mist hung gray and still once more.

"Allanon?" he questioned softly.

"It is finished—the Forbidding is broken," the Druid breathed.

In the next instant the screams welled up anew from out of the emptiness of the Flats, a maddened roar of exultation, and the Demon hordes, freed at last from their centuries-old prison, spilled through the mouth of Halys Cut. Down the length of the gorge they came, a wave of struggling, dark bodies. The Demons were of all shapes and sizes, bent and twisted by the blackness that had encased them. There were teeth and claws and razor-sharp spines, hair and scales and bristled fur; they slouched and crawled, burrowed and flew, leaped and slithered; all were things of legend and nightmare. Every creature from the oldest tales of horror was there; were-creatures, half-human, half-animal, fleet gray shadows that the eye could barely follow; massive, shambling Ogres with hideously distorted features; Gremlins that flitted about as if blown on the wind; Imps and Goblins, black with muck and slime; serpent forms that hissed their venom and twisted in frenzy; Furies and Demon-wolves; Ghouls and other things that ate of human flesh and drank of human blood; Harpies and bat-things that blackened the sky as they lifted their unwieldy bodies from the mass of their brethren. Surging through the mist, they ripped and tore at one another in their eagerness to break free.

Elven longbows hummed, and a rush of black arrows cut apart the foremost Demons. The rest barely slowed, scrambling quickly over the bodies of those who had fallen. Elven archers shot again and yet again, and still the Demons came at them, screaming their rage and frustration. Less than fifty yards separated the two forces, and now the archers fell back and to either flank as the forward phalanx of lancers and pikemen moved to the crest of the rise, bracing their weapons in readiness. The Demons surged forward, a mass of twisting bodies as they bounded up the broken rock of the gorge to where the Elves waited.

With a muffled crunch, the tide broke against the wall of the phalanx, claws and teeth ripping. The front ranks of the Elven line wavered slightly, but held. Demons hung impaled on spears, their shrieks filling the narrow gorge. With a heave, the Elven Hunters threw them back onto their own, watching in horror as the shattered forms were swallowed in the mass that came after. Again the Demons surged up against the Elves, and this time several knots broke through, only to perish instantly as the rear phalanx moved quickly to plug the gaps in the forward lines. But now the Elves were dying also, buried under the black mass of their attackers, dragged forcibly from their ranks and torn apart. And still the Demons continued to pour out of the mist, thousands strong, spreading out across the floor of the gorge and up its walls. Arrows cut them down in steady numbers; but where one fell, three more appeared to take its place. The Elven flanks were beginning to buckle under the rush of attackers, and the entire line was in danger of being overrun.

Eventine gave the order to fall back. The Elves disengaged hurriedly, retreating to their second line of defense, a broken shelf of rock lying just below the passage that led back into the canyon. Again the longbows sang out, and a hail of arrows flew into the surging mass below. Lancers and pikemen formed their ranks, bracing for the assault. It came almost at once, the wave of struggling dark forms clawing their way over scrub and stone to tear at the hedge of Elven spears. Hundreds died in the rush, pierced through by arrow and lance, trampled beneath the feet of their brethren. Yet still they came, surging forth from the mist into the deep funnel of the gorge, against the lines of Elven defenders. The Elves threw them back—once, twice, a third time. Halys Cut filled with dark bodies, crushed and bleeding, screaming in pain and hatred.

At the mouth of the canyon, Ander watched silently the ebb and flow of the battle. The Elves were losing ground. As Allanon had promised, the Ellcrys staff weakened the Demons who came at the Elves so that they died under the thrust and cut of Elven iron. Yet this was not going to be enough to stop the hordes pouring forth—not even with the gallantry of the soldiers, the defensive positions chosen, or all the careful planning. There were simply too many Demons and not enough of the Elves.

He glanced hurriedly at his father, but the King did not see him. Eventine's hands were fastened on the gnarled length of the Ellcrys staff and the whole of his concentration was fixed on the struggle below. The entire Elven defensive line was beginning to buckle dangerously. Using weapons stripped from Elven dead, rocks and makeshift wooden clubs, teeth and claws and brute strength, the Demons fought to breach the thinning ranks of lancers and pikemen that yet barred their passage forward. The Legion Free Corps, held in reserve until now, threw itself into the center of the Elven line, battle cry ringing out. Still the Demons came on.

"We cannot hold," Eventine muttered and prepared to give the command to withdraw.

"Stay close," Allanon whispered suddenly to Ander.

At that same moment, the Demons broke through the left flank and came streaming up the gorge toward the knot of men who stood before the canyon mouth. The Home Guard stepped in front of the King and Ander protectively, Dardan and Rhoe a pace or two to either side. Short swords slipped from their leather scabbards, the metal glinting. Hurriedly, Ander jammed the Elessedil standard into the rocky earth and drew his own weapon. Sweat ran down his body beneath the chain-mail armor, and his mouth went dry with fear.

Now Allanon moved forward, black robes flying as his arms lifted. Blue fire shattered the half-light, bursting from the Druid's fingers, and the ground about the attackers exploded. Smoke billowed out of the rock, then dispersed across a scattering of lifeless dark bodies. But not all had fallen. For an instant the survivors hesitated. Behind them, the breach had closed again; there could be no turning back. Shrieking in fury, they came on, ripping into the Home Guard. The struggle was desperate. Demons fell dying under the swords of Elven Hunters, yet a handful broke through and hurtled themselves at the King. A lean, black Goblin sprang at Ander, claws ripping for his throat. Frantically the Elven Prince brought up the short sword, warding off the attack. Again the creature lunged at him, but one of the Home Guard came quickly between them, pinning the Demon to the earth with a single thrust.

Ander stumbled back in horror, watching the battle surge closer. The left flank had collapsed anew and again Allanon stepped forward to meet the rush. Blue fire lanced into the attackers, and screams filled the air. A knot of Demons had breached the right flank as well and came charging down off the slope in a desperate effort to aid those of the brethren trapped behind the Elven defensive line. Ander froze. There were not enough Home Guard to stop them all.

Then shockingly, impossibly, Eventine went down, felled by a club thrown from the mass of attackers. The blow caught the old King on the temple, and he toppled instantly to the earth, the Ellcrys staff falling from his hand. A roar rose out of the throats of the Demons, and they pressed forward with renewed fury. Half a dozen from the band that had come down off the slope closed about the fallen King to finish him.

But Ander was already springing to his father's side, his own fear forgotten, his face contorted with fury. With a howl of rage, he charged into the foremost attackers, black Goblins like the one that had nearly finished him moments earlier, and two lay dying before the others realized what had happened. As if gone mad, Ander tore into the rest, thrusting them back from the fallen King.

For an instant, everything was in chaos. On the ridge, the Elven line of defense had been forced backward almost to the mouth of the canyon. Demons surged forward in droves, hacking at the Elves who barred their way, shrieking with glee at the sight of the fallen Eventine. Ander struggled to keep the Demons from his father. In his fury, he tripped over one he had slain and went down. Instantly, they were on him. Claws ripped into him, tearing at his armor, and, for one terrible moment, he believed himself a dead man. But Dardan and Rhoe fought their way to his side, scattered his attackers, and pulled him to safety. Dazed, he stumbled back to where his father lay and knelt down beside the old man, disbelief and shock flooding into his face. His hands groped to find a pulse. It was there, faint and slow. His father was still alive, but fallen, lost to the Elves, lost to Ander—the King, the only one who could save them from what was happening . . .

Then Allanon was beside him. Snatching from the earth the fallen Ellcrys staff, he brought Ander to his feet with a yank and thrust the talisman into his hands.

"Grieve later, Elven Prince." He placed his dark face close to Ander's. "For now, you must command. Quickly—withdraw the Elves into the canyon."

Ander started to object, then stopped. What he saw in the Druid's eyes convinced him that this was neither the time nor the place for argument. Wordlessly he obeyed. He ordered his father carried from the fighting. Then rallying the Home Guard about him at the canyon entrance, he sent runners to the center and both flanks of the Elven defensive line and ordered them to pull back. With Allanon at his shoulder, he placed himself squarely at the head of the gorge where the Elves and the Bordermen might see him and watched the battle sweep toward him.

Back surged the lancers and pikemen of the Elven phalanx and the gray soldiers of the Free Corps, clogging the canyon mouth. Stee Jans appeared, red hair flying, a huge broadsword in his hands. Then Allanon's arms rose high above his head, black robes spreading wide, and the blue fire spurted from his fingers.

"Now!" he commanded Ander. "Back into the canyon!"

Ander lifted the Ellcrys staff and called out. The last of the Elves and Free Corps disengaged from the struggle and

sprinted back through the pass connecting gorge and
canyon. Shrieks of rage broke from the Demons, who
surged forward after them.

Allanon stood alone at the head of the pass. In a rush,
the Demons came for him, scrambling up the gorge, a
wave of black bodies. The Druid seemed to gather himself,
his lean form straightening against the shadow of the rock
walls. Again his hands lifted and the blue fire burst forth.
All across the canyon entrance it burned, rising up like a
wall before the enraged Demons, barring their passage.
Howling and screaming, they backed away.

Within the canyon, Allanon turned to Ander.

"The fire will last only a few moments." The Druid's face
was drawn and streaked with sweat and dirt. "Then they
will be on us again."

"Allanon, how can we stand against such odds . . . ?"
Ander began hopelessly.

"We cannot—not here, not now." The Druid gripped his
arm. "The passes of the Breakline are lost. We must escape
quickly."

Ander was already shouting orders. His command sent
the army of the Elves streaming back across the canyon
floor. Cavalry reserves rode ahead with wounded that
could sit a horse; pikemen, lancers, and archers followed,
carrying those who could not. The Home Guard bore the
unconscious King. Allanon and Ander trailed. They had
gone just beyond the brush-sheltered pool that lay at the
canyon's center when the flame barring the far entrance
flared and went out.

In midflight, the Elves looked back. For an instant the
entrance lay open, but then the Demons poured through,
choking the narrow passage as they fought to gain the
canyon beyond. Howling, they swept after the fleeing
Elves. They were too late. The main body of the army had
already gained the defile that led into the split and had
scrambled through. A rear guard of Free Corps under Stee
Jans set their lines as Allanon, Ander, and the remnants of
the Home Guard crossed the last hundred yards of canyon
floor. At the mouth of the defile, they turned momentarily
to watch the approach of the Demon hordes.

It was an awesome, frightening spectacle. Like a dark
wave, the Demons filled the canyon, spreading out across

its grass-covered floor from wall to wall, their struggling black bodies heaving and tossing like rats driven before the waters of some great flood. The earth grew dark with leaping, twisting, writhing forms, and the air above was dotted with those that flew. Druid and Elves stared back in disbelief. It was as if their numbers were endless.

Then abruptly the wave seemed to part where it broke from the gorge and a monstrous, scaled form lurched into view. Dark green and brutish, it dwarfed its brethren as it reared upward within the canyon pass and shoved its way through, scattering those about it like twigs. The Elves cried out in horror. It was a Dragon, its serpentine body spine-covered and slick with its own secretions. Six ponderous, gnarled legs, clawed and tufted with dark hair, supported its sagging bulk. Its head arched searchingly into the air, horned and crusted, a distorted lump out of which burned a single, lidless green eye. As the scent of Elven blood touched its nostrils, its snout split wide to reveal rows of jagged teeth and its tail thrashed frenziedly behind it, filling the air with shattered bodies. The Demons gave way hurriedly, and the monster shambled forward, shaking the rock with the weight of its passing.

At the far end of the canyon, Allanon watched the Dragon's approach for an instant more before turning to Ander.

"Move back beyond the split. Quickly now."

Ander was pale. "But the Dragon . . ."

". . . is too much for you." The Druid's voice was cold. "Do as I tell you. Leave the Dragon to me."

Ander stepped back to give the command, and the army of the Elves withdrew to the far end of the split. With Stee Jans beside him, Ander turned to watch. Allanon stood alone, staring down into the canyon. The Dragon had passed through the center of the canyon and was lurching up the slope toward the defile. Already it had caught sight of the Druid, that solitary black figure that did not run like the others, and it hungered to reach him so that it might crush out his life. Massive legs churned, tearing apart the rock and earth beneath. Behind and to either side, the Demons followed, shrieking with anticipation, scrambling to stay clear of their monstrous brother.

Allanon held his ground, black robes drawn close about

him, until the Dragon was less then a hundred yards from the defile. Then the robes flew wide and the lean arms lifted, hands extending toward the monster. Blue fire lanced from his fingers, striking the Dragon's head and throat, and the smell of charred flesh filled the air. Yet the creature did not slow, but shrugged aside the attack as if it were little more than bothersome, its huge form surging forward. Again the fire struck, singeing forelegs and chest, leaving trailers of smoke that rose from the Dragon's body. Its hiss of anger was sharp and cold, but it came on.

Allanon slipped back into the defile, moving quickly to the far end. Again he turned. The Dragon reared into view, pushing forward into the narrow passage. Allanon struck, the blue fire searing in sharp, sudden bursts. The Dragon's hiss was venomous as it snapped the air before it, frustrated that it could not yet reach the taunting creature ahead. The walls of the defile hindered its movements as it blundered forward awkwardly. Behind it, the cries of the Demon brethren urged it on.

Slowly Allanon backed away from the mouth of the defile toward the split. The passage was clogged with smoke and dust, and the brutish form of the Dragon was obscured by the haze. Then suddenly it surged into view, its snout gaping hungrily. With both hands locked before him, Allanon sent a bolt of fire into the monster's eye. When the fire struck, the creature's entire head was enveloped. This time the Dragon cried out, a terrible howl that spoke of pain and rage. Its body rose high within the defile, slamming against the stone walls until the cliffs shuddered with the force of the blows. Boulders tumbled down about the monster as it heaved and thrashed with pain.

A moment later the south wall cracked wide and the entire cliff face began to slide slowly into the defile. Sensing the danger it was in, the Dragon lurched forward, desperate to get clear of the pass. Half-blinded by the pain and dust, it broke from the defile as tons of rock crashed down behind it, burying the Demons who tried to follow. Blue fire struck it instantly, but without effect. The Dragon was ready this time, its lumpish head bobbing guardedly to avoid the fire. Before it crouched the dark figure of the Druid. Hissing in fury, the monster shambled toward its enemy, massive jaws snapping. Allanon wheeled and darted back, moving not to the broader trail that lay right, but sprinting onto the narrow ledge that curved left above the split. Maddened beyond reason, heedless of what lay ahead, the Dragon came after him. In a rush it thundered onto the ledge, snout reaching for the human fleeing before it, massive legs driving it forward.

But suddenly the ledge was no longer there. Broken rock gave way beneath the weight of the monstrous creature. With a desperate effort, the Dragon lunged toward the Druid. Allanon sprang back as massive jaws swept barely a foot short of his head. Then with a final, terrible hiss, the Dragon slipped away from the crumbling ledge into the black pit of the chasm, disappearing in an avalanche of earth and stone, screaming its hatred. Down into the emptiness it fell and was gone.

Ander Elessedil stood at the far end of the split and watched as Allanon made his way back along the remains of the ledge. After a moment, his gaze shifted. A quick glance at the defile showed it blocked by tons of rock. A slow, bitter smile creased his bloodied face. The Demons would follow them no further through Halys Cut. The Elves had gained a brief respite, a chance to regroup so that they might make their stand elsewhere.

He turned. Behind him, within the mouth of the pass, the soldiers of the Elven army stared out of the shadows in silence, weariness and uncertainty clouding their faces. The Elven Prince could read what was reflected there. So many Demons had come through the Forbidding—so many more than any of them had believed possible. They had failed utterly to stop them here. How would they stop them at the Sarandanon?

Wordlessly, he looked away again. He did not have the answer. He wondered if anyone did.

XXXI

It was a dispirited army that came down out of Halys Cut, shamed by the defeat that had been inflicted upon it and shocked by the number of its dead and wounded. For the dead, lost in the flight back through the pass, there could be no proper return of the body to the earth which had given it life. For the wounded, there could be no relief from the excruciating pain of injuries inflamed by the poison of Demon claws and teeth; their moans and cries lingered unbearably in the midday stillness. For the rest, those who marched south along the wall of the Breakline, there could be no comfort taken in what had passed that day, nor little in what most certainly lay ahead. As the noon sun beat down upon them, mouths went dry with thirst and thoughts turned black with bitterness.

Ander Elessedil led them, no leader in his own mind, little more than a victim of capricious circumstance, and his thoughts were dark. He wanted this to be ended, his father restored to consciousness, and his brother returned. He held in his hands the gnarled length of the Ellcrys staff and thought himself a fool. None of this was meant to be. Still, he knew he must play the role that had been forced upon him a while longer, at least until the army reached Baen Draw. Mercifully, it would be ended then.

His gaze shifted to Allanon. The Druid rode silently beside him, dark and enigmatic within his concealing robes, his thoughts locked carefully away from Ander. Only once during the march back had he spoken.

"I understand now why they let us come this far," he had said, his voice rather quiet in its suddenness. "They wanted us within these mountains."

"Wanted us?" Ander had questioned.

"Wanted us, Elven Prince." Allanon had replied coldly. "With so many, they knew there was nothing we could do to stop them. They let us trap ourselves."

A rider appeared on the horizon, a solitary horseman, his mount driven almost to exhaustion as it galloped wildly across the grasslands toward the approaching Elves. Lifting the Ellcrys staff, Ander signaled a halt. With Allanon beside him, he rode forward to meet the horseman. Disheveled and dust-streaked, the rider jolted to a stop before them. Ander knew this man, a messenger in his brother's service.

"Flyn," he spoke the Elf's name in greeting.

The messenger hesitated, then glanced quickly past him to the column of soldiers. "I am to report to the King . . ." he began.

"Give your message to the Prince," Allanon snapped.

"My Lord," Flyn saluted, his face white. Suddenly there were tears in his eyes. "My Lord . . ." he began again, but his voice broke and he could not continue.

Ander dismounted and beckoned Flyn down with him. Wordlessly he put an arm about the distraught messenger and led him forward several paces to where they might speak alone. There he faced the Elf squarely.

"Slowly now—give me your message."

Flyn nodded, his face tightening. "My Lord, I am instructed to tell the King that Prince Arion has fallen. My Lord . . . he is dead."

Ander shook his head slowly. "Dead?" It seemed as if someone else were speaking. "How can he be dead? He *can't* be dead!"

"We were attacked at dawn, my lord." Flyn was crying openly. "The Demons . . . there were so many. They forced us from the pass. We were overrun. The battle standard fell . . . and when Prince Arion tried to recover it, the Demons caught him . . ."

Ander quickly put his hand up to check the Elf's words. He did not want to hear the rest. It was a nightmare that could not be happening. His eyes flashed quickly to Allanon, and he found the Druid's dark face turned toward his own. Allanon knew.

"Do we have my brother's body?" Ander forced himself to ask the question.

"Yes, my Lord."

"I want it brought to me."

Flyn nodded silently. "My Lord, there is something more." Ander turned back now, waiting. "My Lord, Worl Run is lost, but Commander Pindanon believes that it can be retaken. He requests additional cavalry to make a sweep back across the grasslands that border the pass so that . . ."

"No!" Ander cut him short, his voice suddenly urgent. With an effort he composed himself. "No, Flyn. Tell Commander Pindanon that he is to withdraw at once. He is to return to the Sarandanon."

The Elf swallowed hard, glancing hurriedly at Allanon. "Forgive me, my Lord, but I was instructed to speak with the King on this. The Commander will ask . . ."

Ander understood. "Tell the Commander that my father has been wounded." Flyn paled further, and Ander took a deep breath. "Tell Kael Pindanon that I command the army of the Elves and that he is to withdraw at once. Take a fresh horse, Flyn, and go quickly. Safe journey, messenger!"

Flyn saluted and hurried off. Ander stood alone, staring out across the empty grasslands, a strange numbness stealing through him as he realized that there no longer remained any chance to bridge that gulf that had always separated Arion and him. Arion was lost to him forever.

His back to Allanon, he let himself cry.

Dusk slipped silently across the valley of the Sarandanon, its shadow lengthening to Baen Draw and the army of the Elves. Within his tent, Eventine Elessedil lay sleeping, unconscious still, his breathing shallow and uneven. Ander sat alone at his bedside, staring down at him wordlessly, wishing that he would come awake again. Until the King woke, it would be impossible to judge how serious his injury might be. He was an old man, and Ander was frightened for him.

Impulsively, he reached for his father's hand and took it gently in his own. The hand was limp. The old man did not stir. Ander held the hand for a moment, then released it again and leaned back wearily.

"Father," he whispered, almost to himself.

He stood up and moved away from the bed, distracted.

How could it have happened—his father fallen, grievously injured; his brother killed; himself become leader of the Elves—how could it have happened? It was a madness that he could not bring himself to accept. Certainly the possibility had always been there that his father and his brother would be gone and that he alone of the Elessedils would be left to rule. But it had been an absurd possibility. No one had believed it would truly happen, least of all he. He was ill prepared for this, he thought gloomily. What had he ever been to his father and his brother but a pair of hands to act in their behalf? It had been their destiny to rule the Elven people, their wish, their expectation—never his. Yet now . . .

He shook his head wearily. Now he must rule, at least for a time. And he must lead this army that his father had led before him. He must defend the Sarandanon and find a way to stop the Demon advance. Halys Cut had shown the Elves how difficult this would be. They knew as well as he that if the rock slide brought about by the battle between Allanon and the Dragon had not blocked Halys Cut, the Demons might have caught and annihilated them all. His first task, then, was to give the Elves reason to believe that this would not happen to them here at Baen Draw, despite the loss of both the King and his firstborn son. In short, he must give them hope.

He sat down again next to his father. Kael Pindanon could help him; he was a veteran of many wars, an experienced soldier. But would he? He knew that Pindanon was angry with him because of his order to the Commander to withdraw from the passes of the Breakline. Pindanon had not returned yet, remaining behind with a rearguard of Elven cavalry to slow the Demon advance on the Sarandanon. But forewarning of his displeasure had already reached Ander's ears through comments voiced by a handful of his officers. When he rode in, he would confront Ander directly. Then things would really come to a head. Ander already knew he would ask that command of the army be given to him. Ander shook his head once more. It would be easy enough to do that, to turn command of the army over to Pindanon and let the old warrior assume responsibility for the defense of the Elven homeland. Perhaps that was what he should do. Yet something inside of him resisted so simplistic a resolution to the dilemma; there was need for caution in shedding too quickly duties that were clearly his.

"What would you do?" he asked softly of his father, knowing there would be no answer, yet needing one.

The minutes slipped past, and the dusk deepened.

Finally Dardan appeared through the tent flap. "Commander Pindanon has returned," he announced. "He asks to speak with you."

Ander nodded and wondered momentarily where Allanon had gone. He had seen nothing of the Druid since their return. Still, this meeting with Pindanon was his problem. He started to his feet, then remembered the Ellcrys staff which lay on the floor next to his father's bed. Lifting it in both hands, he hesitated a moment, staring down at the old man beside him.

"Rest well," he whispered finally, then turned and stepped from the room.

In the adjoining chamber, he found Pindanon waiting. Dust and blood covered the Commander's armor, and his white-bearded face was flushed with anger as he advanced on the Elven Prince.

"Why did you order me to withdraw, Ander?" he snapped.

Ander held his ground. "Lower your voice, Commander. The King lies within."

There was a moment's silence as Pindanon glared at him. Then, more quietly, the Elven Commander asked, "How is he?"

"He sleeps," Ander replied coldly. "Now what is your question?"

Pindanon straightened. "Why was I ordered to withdraw? I could have retaken Worl Run. We could have held the Breakline as your father intended that we should!"

"My father intended that the Breakline be held for as long as it was possible to do so," Ander responded, his eyes locked on Pindanon's. "With my father injured, my brother dead, and Halys Cut lost, it was no longer possible. We were driven from Halys Cut, just as you were driven from Worl Run." Pindanon bristled, but Ander ignored him. "In order to retake Worl Run, I would have had to make a forced march north with an army that had just been routed, knowing that they would immediately be thrown back into battle. If our combined forces were then defeated, they would face an exhausting march back to the Saranda-non with little chance to rest before undertaking a defense of this valley. Worst of all, any battle fought within the passes of the Breakline would be fought without the use of Elven cavalry. If we are to withstand the Demon advance, we will need the whole of our strength to do so. That, Commander, is why you were ordered to withdraw."

Pindanon shook his head slowly. "You are not a trained soldier, my Lord Prince. You had no right to make a decision as crucial as this one without first consulting with the Commander of the Army. Had it not been for my loyalty to your father . . ."

Ander's head came up sharply. "Don't finish that sentence, Commander."

His gaze shifted momentarily as the outer tent flaps parted to admit Allanon and Stee Jans. Allanon's appearance was not unexpected, but Ander was somewhat surprised to find the Free Corps Commander there as well. The Borderman nodded courteously, but said nothing.

Ander turned back to Pindanon. "In any case, the matter is done. We had better concern ourselves with what lies ahead. How much time do we have before the Demons reach us?"

"A day, possibly two," Pindanon offered abruptly. "They must rest, regroup."

Allanon's black eyes lifted. "Dawn tomorrow."

There was instant silence. "You are certain?" Ander asked quietly.

"They are driven beyond the need for sleep. Dawn tomorrow."

Pindanon spat upon the earthen floor.

"Then we must decide now how we will stop them once they are here," Ander declared, hands running lightly over the Ellcrys staff.

"Simple enough," Pindanon snapped impatiently. "Defend Baen Draw. Cordon it off. Stop them at the narrows before they reach the valley."

Ander took a deep breath. "That was tried at Halys Cut. It failed. The Demons forced the Elven phalanx by sheer

strength of numbers. There is no reason to believe that it
would be any different this time."

"There is every reason," Pindanon insisted. "Our
strength is not divided here as it was in the Breakline. Nor
will the Demons be fresh and rested, if they march straight
from the Flats. Cavalry may be used in support where it
could not at the Cut. Oh, much is changed, I promise you.
The result will be different this time."

Ander glanced momentarily at Allanon, but the Druid
said nothing. Pindanon came a step closer.

"Ander, give me command in your father's stead. Let me
set the defense as I know he would set it. The Elves can
hold the Draw against those creatures, whatever their
strength. Your father and I know . . ."

"Commander." The Elven Prince spoke softly, firmly. "I
saw what the Demons are capable of doing at Halys Cut. I
saw what they did to a defensive line that my father felt
certain would hold them. This is a different sort of enemy
we fight. It hates the Elves beyond understanding; it is
driven by that hatred—so much so that dying means
nothing. Can we say the same, we to whom life is so
precious? I think not. We need something more than
standard tactics if we are to survive this encounter."

Out of the corner of his eye, he caught Allanon's brief
nod.

Pindanon bristled. "You lack faith, my Lord Prince. Your
father would not be so quick . . ."

Ander cut him short. "My father is not here. But if he
were, he would speak to you as I have spoken. I seek
suggestions, Commander—not an argument."

Pindanon flushed darkly, then turned suddenly toward
Allanon. "What has this one to say? Has he no thoughts to
offer on how these Demons are to be stopped?"

Allanon's dark face was expressionless. "You cannot stop
them, Commander. You can only slow them."

"Slow them?"

"Slow them so that the bearer of the Ellcrys seed may
gain time enough to find the Bloodfire and return."

"That again!" Pindanon snorted. "Our destiny in the
hands of that girl! Druid, I do not believe in old world
legends. If the Westland is to be saved, it must be saved
through the courage of her men-at-arms—through the skill

and experience of her soldiers. Demons may die as other things of flesh and blood."

"Such as Elves," the Druid replied darkly.

There was a long silence. Pindanon turned away from the others, hands clasping angrily behind his back. After a moment, he wheeled back on them.

"Do we stand at Baen Draw or not, Prince Ander? I hear no suggestions but my own."

Ander hesitated, wishing Allanon would say something. But it was Stee Jans who stepped forward, his rough voice breaking the silence.

"My Lord, may I speak?"

Ander had almost forgotten that the Legion Commander was there. He glanced at the big man and nodded.

"My Lord, the Free Corps has faced similar odds on more than one occasion while in the service of the Borderlands. It is a matter of pride with us that while our enemies have frequently been stronger than we, still we have survived and they have not. We have learned some hard lessons, my Lord. I offer one of them to you now. It is this—never settle a stationary defensive line where superior numbers will overrun you. We have learned to split our defensive front with a series of mobile lines that shift with the flow of battle. These lines attack and retreat in sequence, pulling the enemy first one way, then the other, striking always on the flanks as the enemy turns to repel each new assault, withdrawing beyond the enemy's reach when the strike is done."

Pindanon snorted. "Then you neither gain nor even hold ground, Commander."

Stee Jans turned to him. "When the enemy has been pulled far enough out in his efforts to catch you, when his lines have thinned and split, then you close ranks to either side and collapse on him. Like so."

He placed his hands in a V and brought them together with a clap. There was a startled silence.

"I don't know," Pindanon muttered doubtfully.

"How would you defend Baen Draw?" Ander pressed.

"I would use a variation of what I have just described to you," Stee Jans replied. "Longbows on the slopes of the Kensrowe over the mouth of the Draw to harry the advance. Foot soldiers at its head, as if you meant to hold it as you tried to hold Halys Cut. When the Demons attack, stand for a time, then give way. Let them break through. Give them a rabbit to chase, a cavalry command to draw them on. When their lines are strung out, their flanks exposed, close on them from both sides, quickly, before they can fall back or be reinforced. Use lances to keep them from you. The Demons lack our weapons. If you stay beyond their reach, they cannot harm you. When you have destroyed their front ranks, let the rabbit pull through a second rush. Take them another way; keep them off balance. Concentrate on their flanks."

He finished. The Elves stared at the Borderman. Pindanon frowned.

"Who would be the rabbit in this?"

Stee Jans smiled crookedly. "Who else, Commander?"

Pindanon shrugged. Ander looked over at him questioningly.

"It might work," the old warrior admitted grudgingly. "If the rabbit is any good, that is."

"The rabbit knows a few tricks," Stee Jans replied. "That is why it is still alive after so many chases."

Ander glanced quickly at Allanon. The Druid nodded.

"Then we have our plan for the defense of the Sarandanon," the Elven Prince announced. His hand clasped Pindanon's, then that of the Iron Man. "Let us make certain now that it succeeds."

Later that night, when all was in readiness for the morrow's battle and he was alone, Ander Elessedil paused to reflect on how fortunate it was that Stee Jans had been present at his meeting with Pindanon. It was only then that it occurred to him that it might not have been good fortune at all, but a foresight peculiar to the enigmatic dark wanderer they knew as Allanon.

XXXII

They buried Arion Elessedil at first light of dawn. His brother, Pindanon, and four dozen of the Home Guard interred him in the traditional manner of the Elves, at the birth of the new day, at the time of beginning. They bore him in silence to an oak-shaded bluff below Baen Draw that looked west over the blue expanse of the Innisbore and east across the green valley of the Sarandanon. There the firstborn of Eventine Elessedil was laid to rest, his body returned to the earth that had given it life, his spirit set free once more.

They left no marker to the Crown Prince. Allanon had warned that there were some among the Demons who would search out such testaments and prey upon the dead. There were no songs, no words of praise, no flowers—nothing to show that Arion Elessedil had ever been. There remained nothing of Eventine's firstborn but memories.

Ander saw the tears in the eyes of those who gathered with him and felt that memories might be enough.

Less than an hour later, the Demons attacked the Elves at Baen Draw. Down out of the northern hills they streamed, their screams and howls shattering the stillness of the dawn. They came as they had come at Halys Cut, a mass of twisted dark bodies surging forward like the unleashed waters of a flood.

At the lower end of the Draw, the Elven phalanx waited, rows of lancers and pikemen standing shoulder to shoulder with weapons braced. As the foremost Demons clawed their way toward them, Elven longbows hummed along the slopes of the Kensrowe and the air was filled with feathered arrows. Demons convulsed and fell, buried beneath those who came after. Wave after wave of dark shafts ripped through their ranks, and hundreds died in the rush.

But at last the phalanx was reached and the Demons flung themselves against it, shrieking with pain as the iron-tipped shafts pierced their bodies and held them transfixed. The attack faltered and was thrown back. Again it came, a sudden surge forward of malformed bodies, teeth and claws ripping, and again it was thrown back. The ground before the Elven defensive wall grew littered with dead and dying. Still the horde of Demons pressed ahead, endless in number, and at last the Elven line wavered and broke, its center seeming to fall away. Into the breach surged the Demons, bounding and leaping and scrambling from the draw.

Instantly they were set upon by a body of horsemen, gray-cloaked riders with crimson trim, their leader a tall, scar-faced man on a giant blue roan. The riders swept across the head of the Demon rush, lances scything. Then they were gone, turning back into the valley, gray cloaks flying, lean forms bent low over their mounts as they galloped away. The Demons gave chase in a frenzy. Moments later, the riders came about, charging back into their pursuers, lances lowered, scattering bodies as again they struck and swung quickly away. The Demons howled their frustration and scrambled after them.

Then suddenly the gray-cloaked riders wheeled in a solid line that barred the Demons' path forward, and the arm of the scar-faced man lifted. No longer massed protectively, but strung out along the grasslands for hundreds of yards beyond the mouth of Baen Draw, the Demons who had breached the Elven defensive line stared about wildly, seeing now what had been done to them. To either side, lines of Elven cavalry burst into view, hemming them in like cattle. Behind them, the breach had been closed by a tall, black robed figure, standing atop the lower slopes of the Kensrowe, with fire spurting from his outstretched hands to scatter the Demons who milled uncertainly within the Draw. Desperately, those trapped without sought to break the lines about them. But the Elves converged quickly, sword and lance cutting apart the black forms that reached up for them. In moments, the whole of the Demon advance had been destroyed. Through the length of the Baen Draw, the Elven cry of victory echoed.

It did not end there. For the remainder of the morning and into early afternoon, the battle raged on. Time and again, the Demons massed for a rush on the Elven phalanx that barred passage through Baen Draw. Time and again, they broke through, battling their way past Elven archers and Druid fire, past lancers and pikemen, only to find themselves face to face with the gray riders of the Legion Free Corps. Teased and harassed, they gave chase. Heedless of what lay ahead, they allowed themselves to be drawn on, sometimes toward the shoreline of the Innisbore, sometimes toward the slopes of the Kensrowe, or into the valley of the Sarandanon. Then, when it appeared that they had caught the elusive horsemen, they found themselves encircled by Elven cavalry, their own ranks thinned and unprotected, their thrust having carried them far from those brethren who battled still within the Draw. Raging, they threw themselves at their enemy, but there was no escape. The Elves swept back, and again their lines closed across Baen Draw.

For a time the Demons sought to gain the slopes of the Kensrowe, thinking to put an end to the hated longbows. But, carefully placed, their ranks deep and sheltered within the rocks, the Elven archers cut to pieces those who tried to reach them. In their midst stood the black-robed giant, sorcerous fire lancing from his hands, his awesome power sheltering the Elves who struggled below. All forms of Demons tried to reach him—Demons that burrowed within the earth, Demons that flew, Demons that scaled cliff walls like flies. All failed; all died.

In one attack, the Demons smashed through the Elven phalanx where it bordered the shoreline of the Innisbore, turning it back across the Draw as hundreds of attackers swarmed over the sandswept hills toward the open valley beyond. For a moment it appeared that the Elven defensive line was finally broken. But, with a valiant effort, the cavalry converged east of this new advance and rode into it in a charge that drove the Demons back into the waters of the Innisbore. Again the evil ones could not mass, but were strung out along the beachhead, their backs to the lake. The attack faltered and broke apart, shattered on the lances of the Elves. The breach closed one time more.

Thousands of Demons died that afternoon in senseless, mindless, savage rushes through Baen Draw. They attacked ceaselessly, surging forward on their race to the cliffs with the blind determination of lemmings, oblivious to the destruction that waited. Elves and Bordermen died with them, caught up in their frenzy to break through to the Sarandanon. Yet the rout that had occurred at Halys Cut was not repeated this day; time and again the Demons were thrown back, the forefront of their assault destroyed before it had an opportunity to gain reinforcement from the masses that came after.

Finally, in midafternoon, the Demons launched their final attack. Massing within Baen Draw, they surged against the Elven phalanx, bore it backward by sheer force of numbers, and snapped it apart. Into the seams they poured, and suddenly there was no time for carefully wrought tactics, or for skill and finesse. The Elves and the Legion struck back, their horsemen charging into the midst of the onslaught. Sword and spear cut deep into the tangle of twisted dark forms below. Horses and riders screamed and went down. The lines of fighters surged back and forth desperately. But at last the Demons broke, snarling and clawing as they fled back into the Draw, shrieks of anger rising from their midst. This time they did not turn. They continued on, trampling through their own dead and dying, hobbling and crawling and scrambling into the hills beyond, until Baen Draw stood empty.

The Elves stared after the retreating forms in weary disbelief, watching as the last of them disappeared into the curve of the hills, the sound of their passing fading slowly into silence. Then the Elves looked about them and saw clearly the enormity of the struggle that had taken place. Thousands of tangled dark bodies lay scattered across the grasslands, spreading east out of Baen Draw from Kensrowe to Innisbore, still and lifeless and broken. The Draw itself was massed thick with them. The Elves were appalled. It was as if life had meant nothing to the Demons, as if death were somehow preferable. Eyes began to search out the faces of friends and comrades. Hands stretched out to one another, clasping tightly, and the Elves were filled with relief, grateful that they had somehow survived through such terrible destruction.

At the head of the Draw, Ander Elessedil found Kael Pindanon and impulsively hugged the veteran soldier to him. Cries of elation began to rise from the throats of their countrymen as the realization set in that the day was theirs. Stee Jans rode in at the head of the Free Corps and the Bordermen joined the Elves, lances raising in salute. Down the length of the Sarandanon, the roar of victory swelled and echoed.

Only Allanon stood apart. Alone now on the slopes of the Kensrowe, his dark face turned north toward the hills into which the Demons had so abruptly fled, he found himself wondering why it was that they had been willing to give their lives so cheaply and, perhaps more important still, why it was that through all that slaughter there had been no sign of the one they called the Dagda Mor.

The afternoon faded into dusk and the night slipped silently away. At the mouth of Baen Draw, the army of the Westland waited for the Demons to attack. But the Demons did not come. Nor did they come at dawn, though Elves and Bordermen stood ready once more. The morning hours began to creep past, and a growing uneasiness pervaded the ranks of the defenders.

At midday, Ander went looking for Allanon, hoping that the Druid could give some explanation for what was happening. Alone, he climbed the slopes of the Kensrowe to where Allanon kept a solitary vigil within the shelter of an outcropping of rock, half hidden in shadow as he gazed out across the Sarandanon. The Elven Prince had not spoken with Allanon since yesterday when the Druid had come up into these mountains; no one had. Caught up in the jubilation of the Elven victory over the Demons, he had given little thought to the Druid's going. After all, Allanon came and went all the time, seldom with any explanation. But now, as he approached the Druid, he found himself wondering nevertheless why Allanon had chosen this time to be alone.

He was given his answer the moment the Druid turned to face him. Allanon's face, once so dark, was ashen. Harsh lines creased the skin, giving it a slack and weary cast, and there was a brooding look to the piercing black eyes. Ander drew up short, staring.

The stare brought a faint smile to Allanon's lips. "Does something trouble you, Elven Prince?"

Ander started. "No, I . . . it's just that . . . Allanon, you look . . ."

The Druid shrugged. "There is a price for the ways in which we use ourselves. That is one of nature's laws, though we often choose to disregard it. Even a Druid is subject to its dictates." He paused. "Do you understand what I am saying?"

Ander looked uncertain. "The magic does this to you?"

Allanon nodded. "The magic takes life from the user—it drains strength and being. Something of what is lost can be recovered, but recovery is slow. And there is pain . . ."

The sentence died away, unfinished. Ander felt a sudden chill.

"Allanon, have you lost the magic?"

The cowled head lifted. "The magic is not lost while the user lives. But there are limits that cannot be exceeded, and the limits shorten with the passing of the years. We all grow old, Elven Prince."

"Even you?" Ander asked quietly.

The black eyes were veiled. Allanon changed the subject abruptly. "What brings you to me?"

Ander took a moment to recover his thoughts. "I came to ask why the Demons do not attack."

The Druid looked away. "Because they are not yet ready." He was silent a moment, then his gaze shifted back again. "Do not be misled; they will come. They but delay, and there is a purpose behind that delay. The one who leads them, the one who is called the Dagda Mor, does nothing without reason." He bent forward slightly. "Give thought to this. The Dagda Mor was not among those who attacked us yesterday."

Ander frowned worriedly. "Where was he then?"

Allanon shook his head. "The question we should be asking is where is he now?" He watched Ander for a moment, then drew the black robes close about him. "I have been thinking that it would be wise to send trackers north above the Kensrowe and south below the Innisbore to be certain that the Demons do not intend to flank us."

There was a long silence. "Are there Demons enough to do that?" Ander asked finally, thinking of the thousands that had come against them already at Baen Draw.

Allanon's laugh was brittle. "Demons enough." The Druid turned away. "Leave me alone now, Elven Prince."

Ander went back down out of the Kensrowe, riddled with doubt. On his return, trackers were dispatched, and the waiting resumed. Morning passed into afternoon and afternoon into evening. A heavy bank of clouds rolled across the darkening sky, and shadows lengthened quickly into night.

Still the Demons did not come.

It was nearing midnight when the attack finally came. It was sudden, so sudden that the sentries standing watch had barely enough time to give the alarm before the first of the Demons were upon them. They came through Baen Draw in a massive rush, waves of black, corded bodies surging down out of the darkened northern hills into the light of the watch fires. One by one the fires winked out, smothered by the Demons as they swept through the Draw and onto the slopes of the Kensrowe. With the watch fires gone and the night sky screened by the clouds that had swept east out of the Breakline, the whole of Baen Draw was plunged into blackness. It was a blackness that the Demons knew well, to which they had grown accustomed during the time of their imprisonment within the Forbidding, a darkness that would be made to serve them. For, while the Elves and the Southlanders could now see little, the Demons saw as if it were brightest day. Shrieking in frenzied anticipation, they attacked.

At the head of the Draw, rallying about Ander Elessedil and the gleaming white staff of the Ellcrys, an Elven phalanx met the rush. The impact threw the soldiers backward, yet they held their lines. Hundreds of dark bodies crushed up against them, teeth and claws ripping. The Elves fought back determinedly, lances and pikes thrusting blindly into the mass of Demons that pushed forward, and screams of pain tore through the night. But the Demons kept coming, surging into the Elves, struggling to break apart their defense. For a few desperate minutes, the Elves withstood the savage rush, holding back the masses that hurtled against them. But the darkness confused and hindered them. In the end, they were overwhelmed. The phalanx began to give, falling back raggedly, splitting apart. Seconds later, the Demons broke through.

That would have been the finish if not for Allanon. Gaining the lower slopes of the Kensrowe, where the Elven archers fought a losing battle in the darkness to keep back the onrushing Demons, the Druid seized a handful of glittering dust from a small pouch tied at his waist and tossed the dust high into the air. Instantly the dust spread out across the night sky above the struggling Elves, filling the darkness with a brilliant white glow that lit the land beneath with the brightness of moonlight.

Gone was the blackness and the Demons' concealment. From behind the broken phalanx, a rallying cry went up. Into the main breach, where the largest mass of Demons thrust forward, rode Stee Jans and the men of the Legion Free Corps. Like an iron wedge, they split the forefront of the assault. Less than four hundred now, they hammered into the horde before them and bore it back toward the mouth of Baen Draw. To their aid galloped the Elven cavalry, Kael Pindanon leading, head bare, white hair flying. All along the shattered defensive line, the lances of the horsemen tore into the advancing Demons and drove them back.

On the slopes of the Kensrowe, the Demons had broken through the ranks of archers and were pouring down into the Sarandanon. Allanon stood virtually alone in their path, blue fire lancing from his hands. They came at him from everywhere, howling in frenzy as the fire burned them to ash. The Druid did not give way. When they grew too many for him, he turned the whole of the grasslands about him for hundreds of feet in either direction into an inferno of death, a wall of blue fire that ringed the maddened Demons and destroyed any that tried to breach it.

A hundred yards back from the mouth of Baen Draw, the Elves and the Free Corps fought desperately to keep the main body of Demons from breaking through into the Sarandanon. It was a terrible, frightening battle and the smell of death filled the summer night. At its height, Kael Pindanon went down, his horse stumbling beneath him. The old warrior was shaken and came to his feet unsteadily, fumbling for his broadsword. Instantly, the Demons were upon him, howling. Elven Hunters fought to reach their beleaguered Commander, slashing and cutting their way through the Demons that rose before them. But the Demons were too quick. Clawed hands reached for Pindanon, warding off the blows struck at them, and the old soldier was pulled to his death.

At the same moment, a handful of Demons broke from the crush of fighters about them and hurtled toward Ander Elessedil. Through the ring of Home Guard that battled about him the Demons came, bounding like cats, to lunge for the Elven Prince. In desperation he brought up the Ellcrys staff like a shield and his attackers shrank from it, howling with rage. But Ander was all alone now, surrounded by twisted black forms, and they snapped and tore at him, waiting for a chance to break through the guard of his talisman. Elven Hunters fought desperately to reach the Prince, yet the Demons blocked their way, tearing apart those who came too close, parrying wildly the cut and slash of lance and sword. Their brethren surged to their aid, seeing that they had within their grasp the bearer of the hated talisman. Clawed hands reached out, grasping.

Then through the tangle of fighters hurtled a giant, scar-faced Borderman, gray-cloaked body streaked with dirt and blood. Up against the Demons he went, cutting through corded black bodies with great sweeps of his broadsword until at last he stood next to Ander. Shrieks of rage rose from the Demons, and they threw themselves at him. But Stee Jans held his ground like some immovable rock, keeping Ander's attackers from him as he called to his Bordermen. They came instantly, riding to his aid, gathering about him in a circle of iron. Then he was back atop his roan, sword lifted. The gray riders charged forward, their battle cry ringing out through the night.

For an instant, Ander did not realize what was happening. Then, through the hazy glow of false moonlight, he caught sight of the men of the Free Corps, Stee Jans at their head, red hair flying, one hand gripping the great broadsword, the other the Free Corps standard of battle. Alone, a handful against hundreds, the Free Corps was attacking! At once the Elven Prince seized the reins of a riderless horse, mounted, then spurred the animal ahead, crying out to his countrymen. As the Elves rallied to him from every quarter, he rode into the ranks of the Demons, forward to the side of the Legion Free Corps. In a wave, the Elves and the Bordermen swept down into Baen Draw, driving the Demons before them. Like men gone berserk, they battered their way ahead, horsemen and foot soldiers, with lance and pike and sword, shouting as one the battle cries of their homelands.

For an instant, the Demons stood their ground, shrieking with rage and hate, tearing at the madmen who thrust so recklessly into their midst. But the big man with the broadsword and the Free Corps battle standard had given fresh courage to the Elves, courage that bore them forward to face death without fear, to forget everything but their determination to destroy utterly those twisted black forms that stood before them. The Demons wavered and fell back, slowly at first, then in headlong flight, for the fury generated within the army of the Elves was much greater now than their own. Into the hills north they fled once more, scrambling down from the slopes of the Kensrowe through the rocks and crags of the Draw, flying into the concealing shadows of the night.

In moments, Baen Draw had been cleared, and the Sarandanon was again in the hands of the Elves.

Ander Elessedil sat within his tent, stripped to the waist, as Elven Hunters worked on the wounds the Demons had inflicted upon him during the battle. He sat in silence, his body aching with fatigue and the pain of his injuries. Messengers came and went, reporting on the progress of the army as it prepared to entrench once more across the mouth of Baen Draw. Home Guard ringed the tent, the iron of their weapons glinting in the light of the watch fires.

The Elven Prince had finished with the bandaging and was pulling on his armor when the tent flaps parted suddenly and Stee Jans appeared out of the night, his giant form streaked with dirt and ash and blood. Those within the tent immediately fell silent. With a single word, Ander bade them all leave. The tent emptied, and Ander moved forward to stand before the Borderman. Wordlessly, he clasped the big man's hand in his own.

"You saved all of us tonight, Commander," he said quietly. "There is a debt owed you that will be difficult to repay."

Stee Jans studied him a moment, then shook his head slowly. "My Lord, there is nothing owed to me. I am a soldier. Anything I did this night was no more than I should have done."

Ander smiled wearily. "You will never convince me of that. Still, I respect and admire you far too much to argue the matter. I will simply thank you." He released the big man's hand and stepped back. "Kael Pindanon is dead, and I must find a new field commander. I want you."

The Borderman was quiet a moment. "My Lord, I am not an Elf nor even of this country."

"I have no Elf nor countryman better suited to command this army than you," Ander replied at once. "And it was your plan that enabled us to hold Baen Draw."

Stee Jans did not drop his gaze. "There are some who would question this decision."

"There are some who would question any decision." Ander shook his head. "I am not my father nor my brother nor the leader they thought to have. But be that as it may, the decision is mine to make and I have made it. I want you as field commander. Do you accept?"

The Borderman thought for a long time before he spoke again. "I do."

Ander felt a bit of the weariness slip from him. "Then let us begin . . ."

A sudden movement in the shadows by the entry brought them both about with a start. Allanon stood there, his iron face grim.

"The trackers sent north and south within the valley have returned." The Druid spoke softly, the words almost a hiss as they left his mouth. "Those who went south along the Innisbore found nothing. But those who went north encountered an army of Demons so massive as to dwarf that which battles us within Baen Draw. It comes south along the eastern wall of the Kensrowe. Already it will have entered the Sarandanon."

Ander Elessedil stared silently at the big man, hope fading within his eyes.

"This was their plan from the beginning, Elven Prince—to engage you here at Baen Draw with the lesser force while the greater skirted the Kensrowe north, to come down into the Sarandanon from behind, thereby trapping the army of the Elves between the two. Had you not sent those trackers . . ."

He trailed off meaningfully. Ander started to speak and stopped, choking on the words. Suddenly there were tears in his eyes, tears of rage and frustration.

"All the men who have died here—here and at Halys Cut . . . my brother, Pindanon—all dead that the Sarandanon might be held . . . is there nothing we can do?"

"The army that comes down out of the north contains Demons whose powers far exceed anything you have yet encountered." Allanon's head shook slowly. "Too much power, I am afraid, for you to withstand—too much. If you try to hold the Sarandanon longer, if you attempt to stand here at Baen Draw or even to fall back to some other line of defense within the valley, you shall most certainly be destroyed."

Ander's youthful face was bleak. "Then the Sarandanon is lost."

Allanon nodded slowly. The Elven Prince hesitated, glancing back momentarily toward the rear compartment of the tent where the King still lay unconscious, unknowing, locked in dreamless sleep, far from the pain and the reality that confronted his anguished son. Lost! The Breakline, the Sarandanon, his family, his army—everything! Within, he felt himself breaking apart. Allanon's hand gripped his shoulder. Without turning, he nodded.

"We shall leave at once."

Head bowed, he walked from the tent to give the order.

XXXIII

Wil Ohmsford found the Wilderun as bleak and forbidding as the stories had foretold. Though the afternoon sky had been brilliant with sunlight when he and Amberle had left the Rock Spur, the Wilderun was a tangle of shadows and murky darkness, screened away from the world about it by trees and scrub that was twisted and interwoven until there seemed to be neither beginning nor end to its maze. Trunks thick with mold grew gnarled and bent, the limbs coiling out like spider's legs, choked with vines and brush, heavy with spiny leaves that shimmered in streaks of incandescent silver. Deadwood and scrub littered the valley floor, decaying slowly in the dark ground, giving it an unpleasantly soft, spongy feel. Damp with must and rot, the Wilderun had the look of something misshapen and grotesque. It was as if nature had stunted the land and the life that grew within it, then bent it down within itself, so that it might ever be made to breathe, eat, and drink the stench that rose out of its own slow death.

Down the crooked forest road the Valeman walked, the Elven girl close beside him, peering into the darkness about them with cautious, worried eyes, hearing distantly the sounds of the life that prowled and hunted within. The road was like a tunnel, walled about by forest, lighted only by faint streamers of sunlight that somehow slipped past the tangle overhead to touch faintly the dank earth below. There were no birds within this forest; Wil had noticed that at once. Birds would not live within such blackness, Wil had thought to himself—not while they might fly in sunlight. There were none of the usual small forest animals, nor even such common insects as brightly colored

337

butterflies. What lived here were things best left to blackness, night, and shadow: bats, leathered and reeking of disease; snakes and scaled hunters that nested and fed on vermin that lived within fetid ponds and marsh; cat-things, sleek and quick as they stalked the treeways on silent pads. A time or two their shadows crossed the roadway, and Valeman and Elven girl paused guardedly. Yet as quickly as they had come, they were gone again, lost in the blackness, leaving the humans on the empty path to stare anxiously at the forest and to hurry on.

Once, when they had gone deep into the gloom, the pair heard something massive move, pushing through trees as if it were pushing through fragile twigs, its breath huffing loudly in the stillness that fell across the forest with its passing. Lumbering invisibly through the gloom, it either did not see or did not care to bother with the two small creatures who stood frozen upon the trail. Slowly, deliberately, it moved off. In the silence that followed, Valeman and Elven girl fled quickly away.

They encountered only a handful of travelers as they walked the forest, all but one afoot and that one slouched atop a horse so thin and worn as to appear more an apparition than flesh and blood. Cloaked and hooded, the travelers passed them by singly and in pairs, offering no greeting. Yet within the shadow of their cowls, their heads turned and their eyes blinked with the cold interest of cats, staring after the intruders as if to measure their purpose. Chilled by those looks, the Southlander and the girl found themselves glancing back over their shoulders long after the cloaked forms had disappeared from view.

It was nearing sunset when they passed at last from the gloom of the wilderness forest into the town of Grimpen Ward. A less inviting community would have been hard to imagine. Set down within a hollow, Grimpen Ward was a ramshackle cluster of wooden plank buildings so closely jammed together as to be nearly indistinguishable one from the other. They were a seedy lot, these shops and stalls, inns and taverns. The garish paint that colored them was chipped and faded. Many stood shuttered, bars drawn, locks fastened. Poorly lettered signs hung from swaying posts and over doors, a patchwork maze of promises and prices beneath proprietors' names. Through windows and entryways, lamps of oil and pitch burned, casting their harsh yellow light into the shadows without as dusk closed down about the hollow.

It was in the taverns and inns of Grimpen Ward that her denizens were gathered, at rough-hewn tables and bars formed of boards set atop barrels, about glasses and tankards of ale and wine, their voices loud and rough, their laughter shrill. They drifted from one building to the next, hard-eyed men and women of all races, some dressed gaily, some ragged, bold in the glare of the lamplight, or furtive as they stole through alleyways, many stumbling, lurching, and reeking of drink. Money clinked and changed hands quickly, often in stealth or in violence. Here a lumpish figure slumped down within a doorway, asleep in drunken stupor, his clothes stripped from his body, his purse gone. There a tattered form lay still and twisted within a darkened passage, the lifeblood seeping from the wound at his throat. All about, dogs prowled, ragged and hungry, slinking through the shadows like wraiths.

Thieves and cutthroats, harlots and cheats, traders in life and death and false pleasure. Wil Ohmsford felt the hair on the back of his neck rise. Perk's grandfather had been right about Grimpen Ward.

Holding tight to Amberle's hand, he followed the rutted line of the road as it wound through the tangle of buildings. What were they to do now? Certainly they could not go back into the forest—not at night. He was reluctant to remain in Grimpen Ward, but what other choice did they have? They were both tired and hungry. It had been days since they had slept in a bed or eaten a hot meal. Still, there seemed to be little chance that they would get either here. Neither of them had any money to buy or anything of value to trade for a night's food and lodging. Everything had been lost in their flight out of the Pykon. The Valeman had thought to find someone within the town who might be persuaded to let them work for a meal and a bed, but what he saw about him suggested that no one of that disposition lived in Grimpen Ward.

A drunken Gnome lurched up against him and fumbled for his cloak. Wil shoved the fellow away hurriedly. The Gnome tumbled into the street and lay laughing foolishly at the sky. The Valeman stared down at him a moment, then clasped Amberle's arm and hurried on.

There were other problems facing them as well. Once they left Grimpen Ward, how were they to find their way from there? How were they to keep from becoming quickly lost within the wilderness beyond? They desperately needed someone to guide them, but whom in Grimpen Ward could they trust? If they were forced to continue on without any idea of where they were going, then it would become necessary for Wil to use the Elfstones—or at least attempt to use them—before they had found the tunnels of Safehold and the Bloodfire and long before they were ready to flee. The moment he did that, he would bring the Demons down on them. Yet without the use of the Stones or the aid of a guide, they would have no chance at all of finding Safehold—not if they had all year to do so instead of only days.

Wil paused helplessly, staring at the lighted doors and windows of the buildings of the town, the shadowy figures who milled within, and the backdrop of the wilderness and the night sky. It was an impossible dilemma, and he had no idea at all how he was going to resolve it.

"Wil," Amberle tugged anxiously at his arm. "Let's get off this street."

The Valeman glanced at her quickly and nodded. First things first. They must find a place to sleep for the night; they must have something to eat. The rest would have to wait.

With Amberle's hand in his, he started back up the roadway, studying the inns and taverns at either side. They walked about fifty feet further before the Valeman caught sight of a small, two-story lodging house set back from the other buildings within a grove of scrub pine. Lights burned through the windows of the first floor, while the second story stood dark. The loud voices and raucous laughter were missing here, or at least diminished, and the crowd was small.

Wil moved over to the courtyard fronting the inn and peered through the streaked glass of the windows opening on the main room. Everything appeared quiet. He glanced up. The sign on the gatepost indicated it was the Candle Light Inn. He hesitated a moment longer, then made up his mind. With a reassuring nod to Amberle, who looked more than a little doubtful, he led her through the gate and moved up the walk through the pine. The inn doors stood open to the summer night.

"Put your cowl about your face," he whispered suddenly, and when she stared over at him blankly, quickly did so for her. He gave her a smile which belied his own sense of uncertainty, then took her hand firmly in his and stepped through the entry.

The room within was cramped and thick with smoke from oil lamps and pipes. A short bar stood at the front, and a knot of rough-looking men and women clustered about it, talking among themselves and drinking ale. Various tables ringed by chairs and backless stools filled the back, a few occupied by cloaked figures who hunched over drinks and spoke in low voices. Several doors led from this room to other parts of the building, and a stairway ran up the left wall and disappeared into darkness. The floor was splintered and worn, and cobwebs hung from the corners of the ceiling. Next to the doorway, an aged hound chewed contentedly on a meat bone.

Wil guided Amberle to the back of the room where a small table stood empty save for a fat, low-burning candle, and they seated themselves. A few heads lifted or turned as they passed, then just as quickly looked away again.

"What are we doing here?" Amberle asked anxiously, finding it difficult to keep the tone of her voice low enough that they would not be overheard.

Wil shook his head. "Just be patient."

A few moments later a lumpish, unfriendly-looking woman of uncertain age trudged over to them, a towel thrown loosely across one arm. As she came up to them, Wil noticed that she was limping badly. He thought he recognized that limp, and the germ of an idea began to form.

"Something to drink?" she wanted to know.

Wil smiled pleasantly. "Two glasses of ale."

The woman walked away without comment. Wil watched her go.

"I do not like ale," Amberle protested. "What are you doing?"

"Being sociable. Did you notice the way that woman limped?"

The Elven girl stared at him. "What has that got to do with anything?"

Wil smiled. "Everything. Watch and see."

They sat in silence for a moment, then the woman was back again, carrying with her the glasses of ale. She placed them on the table and stood back, her beefy hand passing through a string of tangled, graying hair.

"That all?"

"Do you have any dinner?" Wil wanted to know, taking a sip of the ale. Amberle ignored her glass entirely.

"Stew, bread, cheese, maybe some cakes—fresh today."

"Mmmm. Hot day for baking."

"Real hot. Waste of effort, too. No one's eating."

Wil shook his head sympathetically. "Shouldn't let that kind of effort go to waste."

"Most would rather drink," the heavy woman offered with a snort. "Me, too, I guess, if I had the time."

Wil grinned. "I suppose. Do you run the inn alone?"

"Me and my boys." She warmed a bit, folding her arms across her chest. "Husband run off. Boys help me when they're not drinking or gambling—which is seldom. I could do it myself if it weren't for this leg. Cramps up all the time. Hurts like there's no quitting."

"Have you tried heat on it?"

"Sure. Helps some."

"Herb mixes?"

She spat. "Worthless."

"Quite a problem. How long has it been that way?"

"Aw, years, I guess. I lost count; doesn't do any good thinking about it."

"Well." Wil looked thoughtful. "The food sounds good. I think we will try it—a plate for each of us."

The proprietress of the Candle Light Inn nodded and moved away again. Amberle leaned forward quickly.

"How do you plan to pay for all this? We don't have any money."

"I know that," the Valeman replied, glancing about. "I don't think we are going to need any."

Amberle looked as if she were going to hit him. "You promised you would not do this again. You promised you would tell me first what it was you were planning to do before you did it—remember? The last time you tried something like this was with the Rovers, and it nearly cost us our lives. These people look a lot more dangerous than the Rovers."

"I know, I know, but I just thought of it. We have to have a meal and a bed, and this looks like our best chance for both."

The Elven girl's face tightened within the shadow of the cowl. "I do not like this place, Wil Ohmsford—this inn, this town, these people, any of it. We could do without the meal and the bed."

Wil shook his head. "We could, but we won't. Shhh, she's coming back."

The woman had returned with their dinner. She set the steaming plates before them and was about to leave when Wil spoke.

"Stay a moment," he asked. The proprietress turned back to them. "I have been thinking about your leg. Maybe I can help."

She stared at him suspiciously. "What do you mean?"

He shrugged. "Well, I think I can stop the pain."

The look of suspicion grew more pronounced. "Why would you want to do that for me?" She scowled.

Wil smiled. "Business. Money."

"I don't have much money."

"Then how about a trade? For the price of the ale, this meal, and a night's lodging, I'll stop the pain. Fair enough?"

"Fair enough." Her lumpish body dropped heavily into the chair next to him. "But can you do it?"

"Bring out a cup of hot tea and a clean cloth and we will see."

The woman came to her feet at once and lumbered off to the kitchen. Wil watched her go, smiling faintly. Amberle shook her head.

"I hope you know what you are doing."

"So do I. Eat your dinner now in case I don't."

They had finished most of their meal by the time she returned with the tea and cloth. Wil glanced past her to the patrons gathered about the bar. A few heads were beginning to turn. Whatever happened next, he thought, he did not want to call further attention to himself. He looked up at the woman and smiled.

"This should be done in private. Do you have somewhere we might go?"

The woman shrugged and led them through one of the closed doors into a small room containing a single table with a candle and six stools. She lit the candle and closed the door. The three seated themselves.

"What happens now?" the woman asked.

The Valeman took a single dried leaf from a pouch about his waist and crumbled it into dust, dropping the dust into the tea. He stirred the mixture about, then handed it back to the woman.

"Drink it down. It will make you a bit sleepy, nothing more."

The woman studied it a moment, then drank it. When the cup was empty, Wil took it from her, dropped in another kind of leaf and poured a small measure of ale from his glass, which he had carried in with him. These he stirred slowly, watching the leaf dissolve away to nothing. Across the table from him, Amberle shook her head.

"Put your leg up on this stool," Wil ordered, shoving a vacant stool in front of the woman, who dutifully placed her leg on it. "Now pull up your skirt."

The proprietress gave him a questioning look, as if wondering what his intentions might be for her, then hiked her skirt up to her thigh. Her leg was corded, veined, and covered with dark splotches. Wil dipped the cloth into the mixture in the cup and began rubbing it into the leg.

"Tingles a bit." The woman giggled.

Wil smiled encouragingly. When the mixture was gone from the cup, he reached into the pouch once more and this time produced a long, silver needle with a rounded head. The woman leaned forward with a start.

"You're not going to stick that in me, are you?"

Wil nodded calmly. "You won't feel it; just a touch." He passed it slowly through the flame of the candle that burned at the center of their table. "Now hold very still," he ordered.

Slowly, carefully, he inserted the needle into the woman's leg, just above the knee joint, until only the rounded head was showing. He left it there a moment, then withdrew it. The woman grimaced slightly, shut her eyes, then opened them again. Wil sat back.

"All done," he announced, hoping that indeed it was. "Stand up and walk about."

The perplexed woman stared at him a moment, then pulled down her skirt indignantly and rose to her feet. Gingerly, she stepped away from the table, testing the feel of the bad leg. Then abruptly she wheeled about, a broad grin creasing her rough face.

"It's gone! The pain's gone! First time in months!" She was laughing excitedly. "I don't believe it. How'd you do that?"

"Magic." Wil grinned with satisfaction, then immediately wished he hadn't said that. Amberle shot him an angry glance.

"Magic, huh?" The woman took a few more steps, shaking her head. "Well, if you say so. It sure feels like magic. No pain at all."

"Well, it wasn't really magic . . ." Wil began anew, but the woman was already moving toward the door.

"I feel so good, I'm going to give everyone a free glass." She opened the door and stepped through. "Can't wait to see their faces when they hear about this!"

"No, wait . . ." Wil called after her, but the door closed and she was gone. "Confound it," he muttered, wishing belatedly that he had made her promise to keep quiet about this.

Amberle folded her hands calmly and looked at him. "How *did* you do that?"

He shrugged. "I'm a Healer, remember? The Stors taught me a few things about aches and pains." He leaned forward conspiratorially. "The trouble is, the treatment doesn't last."

"Doesn't last!" Amberle was horrified.

Wil put a finger to his lips. "The treatment is only temporary. By morning the pain will be back, so we had better be gone."

"Wil, you lied to that woman," the Elven girl cried. "You told her you could cure her."

"No, that was not what I said. I said that I could stop the pain. I did not say for how long. A night's relief for her, a night's sleep and a meal for us. A fair trade."

Amberle stared at him accusingly and did not reply.

Wil sighed. "If it is any comfort to you, the pain will not be as bad as it was before. But her condition is not one that any Healer could cure; it has to do with the life she leads, her age, her weight—a lot of other things over which I have no control. I have done as much as I can for her. Will you please be reasonable?"

"Could you give her something for when the pain returns?"

The Valeman reached over and gripped her hands. "You are a truly gentle person, do you know that? Yes, I could give her something for the pain. But we will leave it for her to find after we are gone, if you don't mind."

A sudden clamor from the other room brought him to his feet, and he moved to the door, slipping it open just a crack. Before, the inn had been all but empty. Now it was nearly filled as people drifted in off the roadway, attracted by the promise of free drinks and the antics of the proprietress, who was gleefully demonstrating her new-found cure.

"Time to be going," Wil muttered and hurriedly led Amberle from the room.

They had not taken a dozen steps when the woman called out shrilly and came rushing over to stop them. Heads shook and fingers pointed at Wil. Too many for the Valeman's comfort.

"A glass of ale, you two?" the heavy woman offered. Her hand clapped Wil on the shoulder and nearly knocked him off his feet. He managed a weak grin.

"I think we should get some sleep. We have a long journey and we are really very tired."

The woman snorted. "Stay up and celebrate. You don't have to pay. Drink all you want."

Wil shook his head. "I think we better get some sleep."

"Sleep? With all this noise?" The woman shrugged. "Take room number ten, top of the stairs and down the hall. Sits at the back of the inn. Might be a little more quiet for you." She paused. "We're even now, right? I don't owe you anything more?"

"Nothing," Wil assured her, anxious to be gone.

The proprietress grinned broadly. "Well, you sold out cheap, you know that? I would have paid you ten times what you asked for what you done. Why, a couple hours without the pain is worth the ale and the meal and the bed! You got to be clever if you expect to get anywhere in this country. Remember that bit of advice, little Elf. It's free."

She laughed roughly and turned back to the bar. The free drinks were over. With a crowd of this size, there was money to be made. The woman scurried along the serving board, snatching the coins up eagerly.

Wil grabbed Amberle's arm and guided her away from the table to the stairway and up the steps. The stares of the patrons followed after them.

"And you were worried about her," the Valeman muttered as they reached the upper hallway and turned down it.

Amberle smiled and said nothing.

XXXIV

They had been asleep several hours when they heard the noises at the door of their room. Wil came awake first, sitting upright in the bed with a start, peering through the deep night blackness. He could hear sounds without—a shuffling of feet, whispered voices, heavy breathing. Not Demons, he told himself quickly, but the chill within him would not subside. The latch on the door jiggled as hands worked quietly to free it.

Amberle was awake as well, sitting next to him, her face white within the shadow of her long chestnut hair. Wil put a finger to his lips.

"Wait here."

Silently he slipped from the bed and moved to the door. The latch continued to rattle, but the Valeman had thrown the bolt above it, so the room was secure. He bent toward the doorway and listened. The voices without were low and muffled.

". . . careful, fool . . . just lift it . . ."

"I am lifting it! Step out of the light!"

". . . waste of time; just break it in . . . there's enough of us."

". . . not if he uses magic."

"The gold is worth the risk . . . break it!"

The voices argued on, whispers laced with the slur of ale, mixed with grunts and ragged breathing. There were at least half a dozen men out there, the Valeman decided—thieves and cutthroats, most probably, undoubtedly led to them by the idle tongue of someone who had heard the tale of their miraculous cure of the proprietress of the inn and who could not resist a few embellishments in a retelling of the story. He backed away hurriedly, groping for the bed. Amberle's hand gripped his arm.

"We have to get out of here," he whispered.

Wordlessly, she moved off the bed into the dark. They had slept in their clothes and it took them only moments to pull on the travel cloaks and boots. Wil hastened to the window at the rear of the room and pushed it open. Immediately below, a veranda roof sloped downward from the wall. From its edge, there was a drop of a dozen feet to the ground. Wil turned back to find Amberle again and brought her to the window.

"Out you go," he whispered and took her arm.

In that same instant, there came a loud oath from the hall, and a heavy body crashed into the door, splintering boards and metal fastenings. The would-be thieves had lost their patience. Wil all but shoved the Elven girl through the open window, glancing back hurriedly to see if the intruders had broken through completely. They had not. The door still held. But then the door was struck again. This time the bolt gave way. Into the room surged a knot of cloaked figures, stumbling over one another, cursing and yelling.

Wil did not wait to see what might happen next. Scrambling through the window, he leaped hurriedly onto the veranda roof.

"Jump!" he yelled to Amberle, who crouched in front of him.

The Elven girl slipped over the edge of the roof and dropped to the earth below. In a moment's time, Wil was beside her. Above them, leaning through the open window, the cloaked figures shouted in anger. Wil pulled Amberle back within the shadows of the building, then looked about hurriedly.

"Which way?" he muttered, suddenly confused.

Wordlessly Amberle took his hand and sprinted to the end of the wall, then broke for the building next to the inn. The shouts of their pursuers rose sharply, followed by the sound of booted feet on the veranda roof. Valeman and Elven girl ran silently through the darkness of the buildings, slipping down passageways, through alleys, and along walls until at last they were back to the edge of the main roadway.

Still the shouts pursued them. Grimpen Ward seemed to come suddenly awake, lights flaring in darkened buildings all about them, voices raising in anger. Amberle started out onto the roadway, but Wil pulled her hastily back. Less than a hundred feet away, in front of the Candle Light Inn, several dark forms fanned out onto the road, searching carefully the shadows about them.

"We have to go back," the Valeman whispered.

They retraced their steps, following the wall of the building until they reached its end. A series of sheds and stalls stood clustered together against the dark backdrop of the forest. Wil hesitated. If they tried to escape into the forest, they would become hopelessly lost. They had to work their way back around the buildings to where the main roadway wound south out of Grimpen Ward. Once beyond the town, they would probably not be pursued further.

Cautiously they moved along the rear of the building. Walls and fences hemmed them in on all sides and barrels of trash cluttered the path forward. But the shouts had quieted now, and the buildings ahead were still dark. A few minutes more and they might be clear of their pursuit.

They turned down a narrow alley that ran through a row of stables behind a feed store. Horses whickered softly at their scent, stamping impatiently within their stalls. A small paddock stretched out before them beyond a line of sheds.

Wil started along the paddock fence with Amberle at his side. They had taken no more than a dozen steps when a sharp cry went up behind them. From out of the shadows of the feed store, a dark form appeared, arms waving, voice raised in alarm. Answering cries sounded from the buildings beyond. Startled by the suddenness of their discovery, Valeman and Elven girl stumbled over one another in their haste to flee, lost their footing, and went down.

Instantly their pursuer was on top of them. Arms flailed and fists pummeled wildly. Wil grappled with the man, a wiry fellow reeking of ale, as Amberle rolled clear. His hands fastened on his attacker's cloak; with a sudden heave, Wil threw the man sideways into the paddock.

There was a sharp whack as the man's head struck the fence boards, and he collapsed in a heap.

Wil scrambled back to his feet. Lights came on in the rooms above the feed store and in the surrounding buildings. In the darkness behind them, torchlight flickered through the night. Cries of pursuit sounded from everywhere. The Valeman seized Amberle's hand and they raced together along the ring of the paddock to the line of sheds. There they turned back toward the main roadway, following a narrow alley that ran between two shuttered buildings. Shadows darkened the passage and the two ran blindly, Wil leading. Ahead, the earthen line of the roadway slipped into view.

"Wil!" Amberle cried out in warning.

Too late. The Valeman's eyes were not as sharp as the Elven girl's, and he stumbled headlong into a pile of loose boards strewn across the alley passage. Down he tumbled, crashing into the side of the building. Pain exploded in his head; for an instant, he lost consciousness completely. Then somehow he was back on his feet, weaving forward dizzily, Amberle's voice a faint buzzing in his ears. His hand reached for his forehead and came away wet with blood.

Abruptly the Elven girl was next to him, her arms wrapping tightly about his waist. He sagged against her weakly, forcing himself to stagger ahead toward the distant light of the street. He felt himself blacking out again and fought against it. He had to keep moving; he had to keep awake. Amberle was talking to him, her voice urgent, but he could not make out the words. He felt like a fool. How could he have let something this stupid happen now?

They staggered clear of the alley and turned into the shadows of a porch. Down its length they stumbled, the Elven girl fighting to keep the Valeman on his feet. Blood ran down into Wil's eyes, blinding him further, and he muttered in anger.

Suddenly he heard Amberle gasp in surprise. Through the haze that blurred his vision, he watched a tangle of shadows appear out of the dark. Voices sounded, low and rough, and there was a hiss of warning. Then Amberle was gone, and he felt himself being lifted. Strong hands bore him quickly through the dark. There was a swirl of color before his clouded eyes, mingled with a rush of torchlight. Then he was being lifted again, this time through a narrow opening of canvas flaps. An oil lamp flickered beside him. Voices sounded, whispers of caution, and he felt a damp cloth wipe his face clean of blood. Hands worked busily to wrap him in blankets and to place a pillow beneath his head.

Slowly he opened his eyes. He lay within a gaily colored wagon, its walls decorated with tapestries, beads, and bright silks. The Valeman started. He knew this wagon.

Then a face bent close, dark and sensuous, framed in ringlets of thick black hair. The smile that greeted him was dazzling.

"I told you we would meet again, Wil Ohmsford."

It was Eretria.

XXXV

For five days the army of the Elves and the Legion Free Corps fought their way back across the Westland to Arborlon. Across the broad valley of the Sarandanon, through woodlands dense and tangled, and down forest roads and rutted trails they fell back slowly, steadily eastward, pursued at every turn by the Demon hordes. They marched in daylight and at night, without rest, often without food, for the creatures that tracked them neither slept nor ate. Unburdened by human needs, free of human limitations, the Demons came after them, purposeful, unrelenting, driven by their own peculiar form of madness. Like dogs at hunt, they harried the withdrawing army, nipping and slashing at its flanks, rushing it now and then in full assault, striving to turn it from its course, to cripple it, to destroy it. The attack was incessant, and the Elves and their allies, already weary from their stand at Baen Draw, grew quickly exhausted. With exhaustion came despair and then fear.

Ander Elessedil fell victim to that fear. It began for the Elven Prince with his own sense of failure. The dead, the defeats of the few days past, and all that the Elves had hoped to accomplish and had not done haunted him. Yet even this was not the worst. For as his battered army struggled eastward and his countrymen continued to die all about him, Ander began to realize that none of them might survive the long march back—that all of them might die. Out of this stark realization was born the fear that became his own private devil—faceless, insidious, lurking just within the shadow of his determination. Leader of the Elves, it asked slyly, what will you do to save them? Are you so helpless, then? So many have been lost—yet what if all those who remain be lost? It teased and tormented him, threatening to turn weary resolve into total despair. Even Allanon's presence did not help, for the black-robed Druid stayed distant and aloof as he rode at Ander's side, veiled in his own world of dark secrets. So Ander fought his fear alone within the silence of his mind, the whole of his strength directed toward its defeat, as slowly, grimly he led his failing soldiers back toward Arborlon.

In the end, it was Stee Jans who saved them all. It was in this darkest time of seeming failure and desperation that the giant Borderman displayed the tenacity, endurance, and courage that had created the legend of the Iron Man. Assembling a rear guard of Elves and Free Corps, he began a defense of the main column of his army as it bore its dead and wounded eastward under cover of night. In a series of lunges and feints, the Legion Commander struck out at his pursuers, drawing them after him, first one way, then another, utilizing the same tactics that he had so successfully employed at Baen Draw. Time and again the Demons came at him, sweeping first through the valley of the Sarandanon, then into the forestland beyond. Time and again they sought to trap the fleet, gray-cloaked Legion riders and the swift Elven horse, always to close an instant too late, finding only an empty grassland, a blind draw, a hollow dark with shadow, or a scrub-choked trail that turned back upon itself. With a deftness that baffled and maddened the Demons, Stee Jans and the riders following him played a deadly cat-and-mouse game that seemed to place them everywhere at once, yet always away from where the main body of the army moved back toward the safety of Arborlon.

Demon anger and frustration mounted; as night became day and day night again, the pursuit grew frenzied. These Demons were different from the lean, black creatures that had swarmed out of the hill country north of Baen Draw to seize the Sarandanon. These were Demons that had gone east above the Kensrowe, more dangerous than their lesser brethren, with powers that no ordinary human could withstand. Some were monstrous in size, corded with muscle and scaled with armor—creatures of mindless destruction. Others were small and fluid and killed with just a touch. Some were slow and ponderous, some quicksilver as they slipped through the forest shadows like wraiths. Some were multilimbed; others had no limbs at all. Some breathed fire as the Dragons of old, and some were eaters of human flesh. Where they passed, the land of the Elves was left blackened and scarred, ravaged so that nothing might live upon it. Yet the Elves themselves remained just beyond their reach.

The chase wore on. Elven Hunters and Free Corps soldier fought side by side in a desperate attempt to slow the Demon advance, watching their numbers dwindle steadily as their pursuers swept after them. Without Stee Jans to lead them, they would have been annihilated. Even with him, hundreds fell wounded and dead along the way, lost in the terrible struggle to prevent the long retreat from turning into a complete rout. Through it all, the Legion Commander's tactics remained the same. The strength of the Demons made it imperative that the Elven army not be forced to stand again this side of Arborlon. So the rear guard continued to strike quickly and slip away, always to swing back for yet another strike and then another—and each time a few more riders were lost.

At last, on the afternoon of the fifth day, the tattered and exhausted army came again to the shores of the Rill Song. With a ragged shout, it crossed back into Arborlon. Then it discovered the price that had been paid. A third of the Elves who had marched west to Sarandanon were dead. Hundreds more lay injured. Of the six hundred soldiers of the Legion Free Corps who had followed after them, less than one in every three remained alive.

And still the Demons advanced.

Dusk fell over the city of Arborlon. The day had gone cool at its end, a bank of heavy stormclouds moving eastward out of the flats to screen away moon and stars and fill the night air with the smell of rain. Lamps began to light within the homes of the city as families and friends gathered together for their evening meal. On the streets and in the treeways, units of the Home Guard began their nightly patrol, slipping through pooled shadows in uneasy silence. Atop the Carolan, on the Elfitch, and along the eastern bank of the Rill Song, the soldiers of the Elven army stood ready, staring past rows of iron stanchions filled with burning pitch to the blackness of the forest beyond. Within the trees, nothing moved.

In the chambers of the Elven High Council, Ander Elessedil came face to face for the first time since his return from the Sarandanon with the King's Ministers, the army commanders, and the few outlanders who had arrived to aid the Elves in their fight against the Demons. He passed through the heavy wooden doors at the end of the council room, carrying the silver Ellcrys staff in his right hand. Dust, sweat, and blood covered the Elven Prince; while he had permitted himself a few brief hours of sleep, he had not yet taken time to wash, preferring to come as quickly as possible before the Council. Beside him walked Allanon, tall and black and forbidding, his shadow rising up against the walls of the chamber as he entered, and Stee Jans, his weapons still strapped about him, his hazel eyes cold with death.

From their high-backed chairs about the council table, the seats of the gallery, and the risers at the edge of the Dais of the Kings, those gathered came at once to their feet. A rush of whispers and mutterings filled the hall, and questions began to rise up in shouts as each man sought to be heard. At the head of the table, Emer Chios brought his open hand down upon the wooden surface with a crash and the room went silent again.

"Be seated," the First Minister directed.

Grumbling, the men assembled did as they were told. Ander waited a moment, then came forward a step. He knew the rules of the High Council. When the King lay disabled, the First Minister presided. Emer Chios was a powerful and respected man, the more so in this situation. Ander had come before the Council with a very specific purpose in mind, and he would need the support of Chios if he were to achieve that purpose. He was tired and he was anxious, but it was necessary that he take time to go about matters in the proper way.

"My Lord First Minister," he addressed the Minister. "I would speak to the Council."

Emer Chios nodded. "Do so then, my Lord Prince."

Slowly, haltingly, for he was not the speaker that his father was or his brother had been, Ander told of all that had befallen the Elven army since its departure to the Sarandanon. He described the injury to the King and the death of Arion. He told them of the battles and defeats at the Breakline, of the withdrawal and gallant stand at Baen Draw, and finally of the retreat back through the Sarandanon and the Westland forests to Arborlon. He told them of the courage of the Legion Free Corps, the leadership of Stee Jans when Pindanon had fallen. Graphically, he described the nature of the enemy they had faced—its size, its shape, its frenzy, and its power. The Demons, he warned them, now approached Arborlon, there to exterminate the last of the Elven people, to lay waste to the city, and to take back again the land they had lost centuries ago. What lay ahead was a battle in which one or the other, Elf or Demon, must surely be destroyed.

As he spoke, he studied the faces of his listeners, seeking in their eyes and expressions something of how they judged his actions since the loss of both their King and his heir-apparent. He accepted now that his father might die, and that he might then be King; he knew that the High Council and the Elven people must come to accept it as well. Acceptance had been difficult for Ander because, before the battle at Halys Cut, the possibility of such a thing happening had always seemed so remote and because he had not wanted to believe that he would lose both his father and his brother. But his father now lay within his bed at the manor house, unchanged since his fall. All the while that the Elves had fought at Baen Draw and on the long march home again, Ander Elessedil had waited for his father to wake, refusing to believe that he would not. But the King had not regained consciousness, and now it seemed that perhaps he would not do so ever. The Elven Prince understood that, accepted it, and thus looked past it to what must then be.

"Elven Lords," he finished, his voice worn and empty. "I am my father's son and I know what is expected of a Prince of the Elves. The Elven army has come out of the Sarandanon and now must stand here. I intend to stand with it. I intend to lead it. I would not have it so if there were any way that this moment could be undone, if all that had happened within these past few weeks might be wiped from the record of our lives. But that cannot be. Were my father here, you would rally to him to a man—I know that. I stand then in my father's place and ask that you rally to me, for I am the last of his blood. These men who stand with me have given me their support. I seek yours as well. Pledge me that support, Elven Lords."

Wordlessly, he waited. He need not have asked for their support, he knew, but merely assumed it. His was the power of the Elessedil rule, and there were few who would dare to challenge that. He could have asked Allanon to speak for him; the Druid's voice alone might have silenced any opposition. Yet Ander wanted no one to intercede for him in this, nor did he wish to take anything for granted. The support of the High Council, and of the outlanders who had come to give them aid, should be won over by what they might see in him—not by fear or any claim of right that did not ground itself squarely on whatever strength of character he had shown in his command of the Elven army since the moment that his father had fallen.

Emer Chios came to his feet. His dark eyes swept briefly over the faces of those assembled. Then he turned to Ander.

"My Lord Prince," his deep voice rumbled. "All who gather in this Council know that I follow no man blindly, even though he be of royal blood and the child of Kings. I have said often and publicly that I trust the judgment of my people better than the judgment of any one man, though he be King of all the known world."

He looked about him slowly. "Yet I am Eventine Elessedil's faithful Minister and his great admirer. He is a King, Elven Lords, as a King was meant to be. I wish that he were here to lead us in this most dangerous time. But he is not. His son offers himself in his place. I know Ander Elessedil—I think I know him as well as any. I have listened to him; I have judged him by his words and by his acts and by what he has shown himself to be. I say now that in the absence of the King there is no man to whom I would more willingly entrust the safety of my homeland and my life than he."

He paused, then carefully placed his right hand over his heart—the Elven pledge of loyalty. There was a moment's silence. Then others rose with him from the table, a few at first, then all, hands placed across their hearts as they faced the Prince. The commanders of the Elven army stepped forward as well—Ehlron Tay, dour-faced and bluff, who, after the death of Pindanon, ranked highest in command; Kobold, the tall, immaculately dressed Captain of the Black Watch; and Kerrin, commanding the Home Guard. In moments, all of the Elves who had assembled within the High Council stood facing their Prince, hands lifted in salute.

At Ander Elessedil's side, a dark figure leaned close. "Now they follow you, Elven Prince," Allanon spoke softly.

Ander nodded. He could almost regret that it was so.

They talked then of the defense of Arborlon.

Preparations for that defense had begun almost immediately following the departure of the Elven army to the Sarandanon two weeks earlier. Emer Chios, as ruler of the home city in the King's absence, had convened the High Council, together with the commanders of the Elven army who had not accompanied the King, for the purpose of deciding what steps should be taken to protect Arborlon in the event the Demons broke out of the Sarandanon. A series of carefully drawn defensive measures had been settled upon. The First Minister reviewed them now with Ander.

There were but two approaches to the city—from the east, along the trails that ran through the Valley of Rhenn and the forests beyond, and from the west, out of the Sarandanon. North and south of Arborlon stood mountains that offered no passage, tall peaks that shut away the lowland woods and ringed the Carolan in a wall of rock. Allanon had warned that the break in the Forbidding would come in the Hoare Flats. That meant the Demons must come east through the Sarandanon, and unless they turned north or south to bypass the mountains sheltering Arborlon—a march that would consume at least several days' additional time—the attack on the Elven home city would come from the west.

Yet it was here that the Elven defenses were strongest. Two natural barriers would immediately confront the Demons. First was the Rill Song, somewhat narrow where it arced eastward below the Carolan, but deep and difficult to navigate in the best weather. Second was the bluff itself, a sheer cliff that rose more than four hundred feet to its summit, its stone face split by a web of deep crevices and choked with scrub and heavy brush. A single bridge spanned the Rill Song below the Carolan at a point where the channel narrowed. There were no shallows for miles in either direction. The Elfitch provided the primary access route to the Carolan, although a series of smaller stairways wound upward through wooded sections of the cliff further south.

The defense of Arborlon depended then upon the river and the bluff. It had been decided that the bridge spanning the Rill Song would be destroyed immediately upon the return of the Elven army. This had been done as planned, Chios pointed out, and the last link between Arborlon and the Sarandanon had been severed. On the east bank, the Elves had anchored hundreds of pitch-burning stanchions to give light in the event a night crossing should be attempted, and they had constructed a stone and earthen redoubt almost at the edge of the Rill Song that ran for several hundred yards along the riverbank at the base of the bluff and arced backward into the cliff face at either side of the Elfitch. The east bank extended back from the river about two hundred feet to the cliffs, and most of this ground was wooded and grown thick with scrub. Here the Elves had set dozens of traps and pitfalls to ensnare any Demons who sought to flank the redoubt.

But it was the Elfitch that provided the major defense to Arborlon. All of the smaller stairways leading to the great tableland of the Carolan had been destroyed. All that remained was the Elfitch—seven stone-block ramps and ironbound gates that ran upward from the base of the bluff to the heights. Battlements ringed each gate to close off passage to the gates and ramps above it. Each ramp and gate was set back slightly from the ones below and, as the Elfitch rose toward the heights, it spiraled upward in a series of evenly measured turns that permitted each successive gate and ramp to offer some measure of protection through the use of longbows and darts to the gates and ramps beneath. In times of peace, the gates to the seven ramps stood open, the battlements were left undefended but for a token watch, and the ancient stone grew thick with flowering vines. But now, with the retreat of the Elven army from the Sarandanon, the ramparts bristled with Elven pikes and lances and the gates stood locked and barred.

No defenses had been constructed atop the Carolan. The plateau ran back to the deep forest in a broad, rolling plain spotted with woods, isolated cottages, and the solitary closure of the Gardens of Life. East, within the fringe of the forest trees, stood Arborlon. If the Demons were successful in reaching the Carolan, the choices left to the defending Elves were few. If enough of them remained, they might stand upon the plain in an attempt to sweep the invaders over the cliff edge. Failing that, they would be forced to fall back to the Valley of Rhenn, there to fight one final battle or face being driven from the Westland altogether.

Chios paused in his report. "Of course if they bypass the mountains and come in from the east . . ." he began.

Allanon cut him short. "They will not. Time becomes important to them now. They will come from the west."

Ander glanced questioningly at Stee Jans, but the Free Corps Commander merely shrugged. Ander turned back to Emer Chios. "What other news, First Minister?"

"Mixed news, I'm afraid, regarding our request to the other lands for aid. Callahorn has sent us another two hundred and fifty horse—Old Guard, the Legion's regular army. There is a vague promise of some additional aid to come, though no indication as to how soon we might expect it. Our messenger reports that the members of the Council of the Cities have not yet been able to resolve their differences over what the extent of Callahorn's involvement in this 'Elven War' should be, and the King has chosen not to intervene. It appears that sending the Old Guard command was basically another compromise solution. The matter is still under debate, but we have heard nothing more."

As Stee Jans had warned, Ander thought darkly.

"The Federation has sent a message as well, my Lord Prince." Chios' smile was bitter. "A message that is brief and to the point, I might add. It is the policy of the Federation that it not become involved in the affairs of other lands and other races. If a threat to others touches upon the sovereignty of its own states, the Federation will act. As matters stand now, that does not appear to be the case. Therefore, until the situation changes, no aid will be forthcoming." He shrugged. "Not altogether unexpected."

"And the Kershalt?" Ander asked quickly. "What of the Trolls?"

Chios shook his head. "Nothing. I took the liberty of dispatching another messenger."

Ander nodded his approval. "And the Dwarves?"

"We're here," a rough voice answered. "Some of us, at least."

A bearded, thickset Dwarf made his way forward through the men gathered about the Council table. Quick blue eyes blinked through a face that was weathered and browned by the sun, and a pair of gnarled hands fastened on the table's edge.

"Druid." The Dwarf nodded briefly to Allanon, then turned to Ander. "My name is Browork, Elder and citizen of Culhaven. I've brought one hundred Sappers to the service of the Elessedils. You can thank the Druid for that. He found us some weeks ago at work on a bridge crossing the Silver River and warned us of the danger. Allanon is known to the Dwarves, so there were no questions asked. We sent word to Culhaven and came on ahead—ten days' march and a hard march at that. But we're here."

He extended his hand and Ander shook it warmly.

"What of the others, Browork?" Allanon asked.

The Dwarf nodded rather impatiently. "On their way by now, I presume. You should have an army of several thousand by week's end." He gave Allanon a disapproving frown. "In the meantime you've got us, Druid, and mighty lucky you are to have us. No one but the Sappers could have rigged that ramp."

"The Elfitch," Chios explained quickly to a puzzled Ander. "Browork and his Sappers have been working with us on our defenses. In the process of studying the Elfitch, he saw that it was possible to rig the fifth ramp to collapse."

"Child's play." Browork dismissed the accomplishment with a wave of his hand. "We undercut the stone block, removed the secondary supports, then split the primary with iron wedges fixed to chains. The chains we concealed in the brush beneath the ramp, ran them to the heights, and lined them to a system of pulleys. If the Demons reach the fifth ramp, just draw in the chains, slip the wedges, and the whole ramp from the fifth gate down falls away. Simple."

"Simple if you have the engineering skill of a Dwarf Sapper, I think." Ander smiled. "Well done, Browork. We have need of you."

"There are others here that you need as well." Allanon put his hand on Ander's shoulder and pointed to the far end of the Council table.

The Elven Prince turned. A lone Elf dressed all in leather stepped forward and placed his hand across his heart in the pledge of loyalty.

"Dayn, my Lord Prince," the Elf said quietly. "I am a Wing Rider."

"A Wing Rider?" Ander stared at the Elf in surprise. He had heard stories from his father of the people who called themselves the Sky Elves—stories almost forgotten by most, for no Wing Rider had come to Arborlon in the last hundred years. "How many of you are there?" he asked finally.

"Five," Dayn replied. "There would be more but for the fear of a Demon attack on the Wing Hove, our own home city. My father has sent those of us who are here. We are all of one family. My father is called Herrol." He paused and glanced at Allanon. "There was a time when the Druid and he were friends."

"We are still friends, Wing Rider," Allanon said quietly.

Dayn acknowledged the Druid's commitment with a nod, then returned his gaze to Ander.

"My father's sense of kinship with the Land Elves is stronger than that of most of his countrymen, my Lord Prince, for most have long since broken all ties with the old ways and the old rule. And my father knows that Allanon stands with the Elessedils—and that has meaning. Thus he sends us. He would be here himself but for the absence of his Roc Genewen, who trains with my brother's son so that he may one day be a Wing Rider as was his father. Still, those of us who are here may be of some use. We can fly the whole of the Westland skies, if need be. We can seek out the Demons who threaten and tell you of their movements. We can spy out strengths and weaknesses. That much, at least, we can offer."

"That much we accept with gratitude, Dayn." Ander returned the Wing Rider's salute. "Be welcome."

Dayn bowed and stepped back. Ander glanced at Chios. "Are there any others come to stand with us, First Minister?"

Chios shook his head slowly. "No, my Lord Prince. These are all."

Ander nodded. "Then these will be enough."

He motioned for all who were gathered to seat themselves with him at the council table, and a general discussion ensued on such matters as soldier placement, weapons distribution, battle tactics, and the taking of additional defensive measures. Reports were heard from Ehlron Tay on the Elven Hunters of the regular army, from Kerrin on the Home Guard, and from Kobold of the Black Watch. Browork gave his assessment of the overall structural efficiency of the Elven defenses, and Stee Jans was consulted on strategies that might be implemented to offset the superior strength of the Demon hordes. Even Dayn spoke briefly on the fighting capabilities of the Rocs and their uses in aerial combat.

Time slipped past rapidly, and the night drifted away. Ander grew light-headed with fatigue, and his thoughts began to wander. It was in the middle of one of these wanderings that a tremendous crash jerked him upright as the doors of the High Council flew open and a disheveled Gael appeared, flanked by the chamber guards. Breathless, the little Elf rushed forward and dropped to his knee before Ander.

"My Lord!" he gasped, his face flushed with excitement. "My Lord, the King is awake!"

Ander stared. "Awake?"

Then he was on his feet and sprinting from the chamber.

* * *

While he slept, it felt to Eventine Elessedil as if he were floating through a blackness layered with gossamer threads that wrapped his body in a seamless blanket. One by one, he felt the threads enfold him, mold about him, join with him. Time and space were nothing; there was only the blackness and the weave of the threads. It was a warm, pleasant sensation at first, much like the feel to an infant of a mother's close embrace, filled with comfort and love. But then the embrace seemed to tighten, and he began to suffocate. Desperately he struggled to break free and found that he could not. He began to sink downward through the blackness, spinning slowly, his blanket a shroud and he no longer a creature of life, but one of death. Terrified, he thrashed within his silken prison, tearing and ripping at its fabric until, with a sudden rending, it flew apart and was gone.

His eyes opened. Light blinded him momentarily, harsh and flickering. He blinked in its glare, disoriented and confused, fighting to gain some sense of where he was and what he was doing. Then the outlines of a room began to gather form, and he recognized the smell of oil lamps and the feel of cotton sheets and woolen blankets wrapped close about his body. All that had happened in the moments before he slept came back again in a rush, images that ran mad and disjointed across his mind: the Breakline; Halys Cut and the Demons attacking from out of the deep mist; lines of Elven archers, lancers, and pikemen spread out below him; cries of pain and death; dark forms hurtling toward him through a wall of blue fire; Allanon, Ander, the glint of weapons, then a sudden blow . . .

He twitched violently beneath the covers, and sweat bathed his body. The room sharpened abruptly before his eyes—it was his sleeping room in the manor house in Arborlon—and there was a figure moving toward him.

"My Lord?" Gael's frightened voice sounded in his ear and the youthful face bent down close to his own. "My Lord, are you awake?"

"What has happened?" he muttered, his own voice thick and barely recognizable.

"You were wounded, my Lord—at Halys Cut. A blow struck here." The Elf pointed to the King's left temple.

"You have been unconscious ever since. My Lord, we were so worried . . ."

"How long . . . have I slept?" he interrupted. His hand reached to touch his head and the pain laced downward through his neck.

"Seven days, my Lord."

"Seven days!"

Gael started to back away. "I will bring your son, my Lord."

His mind whirled. "My son?"

"Prince Ander, my Lord." His aide dashed toward the sleeping room door. "He meets now with the High Council. Lie back—I will bring him at once."

Eventine watched him wrench open the door, heard him talk briefly with someone beyond, then watched the door close again, leaving him in silence. He tried to raise himself, but the effort was too much and he fell back weakly. Ander? Had Gael said that Ander was meeting with the High Council? Where was Arion? Doubt clouded his thoughts, and the questions came in a flurry. What was he doing here in Arborlon? What had befallen the army of the Elves? What had become of their defense of the Sarandanon?

Again he tried to raise himself and again fell back. A wave of nausea swept through him. He felt suddenly old, as if the number of his years was a sickness that had wasted him. His jaw tightened. Oh, that he might have back again five minutes of his youth to give him strength enough to rise from this bed! Anger and determination fired him, and he inched himself upward against his pillows until he lay propped against them, breathing raggedly.

Across the room, Manx raised his grizzled head. The King opened his mouth to call out to the old wolfhound. But suddenly the dog's eyes met his, and the words died in his throat. There was hate in those eyes—hate so cold that it cut through Eventine like a winter frost. He blinked in disbelief, fighting the sense of repulsion that welled up within him. Manx? What was he thinking!

He forced himself to look away, to stare elsewhere in the sleeping room, at walls and their hangings, at furniture, and at the drapes drawn tight across the windows. Desperately, he tried to compose himself and could not. *I am alone,* he thought suddenly, unreasonably, and was filled with fear. *Alone!* He glanced back again at Manx. The wolfhound's eyes fixed him, veiled now, hiding what had been so evident before. Or had he imagined it? He watched as the old dog rose, turned about, and lay down again. *Why does he not come to me,* the King asked himself? *Why does he not come?*

He slipped back against the pillows. *What am I saying?* The words whispered in his mind, and he saw the madness that threatened to slip across him. Seeing hatred in the eyes of an animal that had been faithful to him for years? Seeing in Manx an enemy that might do him harm? What was wrong with him?

Voices sounded in the outer corridor. Then the sleeping room door opened and closed again, and Ander crossed the room to reach down and hold him close. The King hugged his son to him, then broke the clasp, searching Ander's shadowed face as the Prince seated himself on the edge of the bed.

"Tell me what has happened," Eventine ordered softly. Then he saw something flicker in his son's eyes, and he felt a sudden chill pass through him. He forced the question from his lips. "Where is Arion?"

Ander opened his mouth to speak, then stared at the old man wordlessly. Eventine's face froze.

"Is he dead?"

Ander's voice was a whisper. "At Worl Run."

He seemed to search for something more to say, then gave up, shaking his head slowly. Eventine's eyes filled with tears and his hands shook as he grasped his son's arms.

"Arion is dead?" He spoke the words as if they were a lie.

Ander nodded, then looked away. "Kael Pindanon, too."

There was a moment of stunned silence. The King's hands fell away.

"And the Sarandanon?"

"Lost."

They stared at each other wordlessly, father and son, as if some frightening secret had been shared that should never have been told. Then Ander reached down and clasped his father to him. For long moments, they held each other in silence. When at last the King spoke, his voice was flat and distant.

"Tell me about Arion. Everything. Leave nothing out."

Ander told him. Quietly, he related how his brother had died, how they had brought him out of the Breakline to the Sarandanon, and how they had buried him at Baen Draw. Then he spoke of all that had befallen the army of the Elves from that first day of battle at Halys Cut through the long march back to Arborlon. Eventine listened and said nothing. When Ander had finished, he stared blankly at the flicker of the oil lamps for a moment. Then his eyes shifted to his son.

"I want you to return to the High Council, Ander. Do what must be done." He paused, his voice breaking. "Go on. I will be all right."

Ander looked at him uncertainly. "I can ask Gael to come in."

The King shook his head. "No. Not now. I just want to . . ." He stopped, choking back what he was about to say, one hand gripping his son's arm tightly. "I am . . . very proud of you, Ander. I know how difficult . . ."

Ander nodded, his throat tightening. He placed his father's hands within his own. "Gael will be outside in the hall when you need him."

He rose and started toward the door. His hand was on the latch when Eventine called out after him, his voice strangely anxious.

"Take Manx out with you."

Ander stopped, looked at the old wolfhound, whistled him to his side, and led him out. The door closed softly behind him.

Alone again, this time truly alone, the King of the Elves lay back upon the cushion of his pillows and let the enormity of all that had happened wash over him. In a little more than seven days, the finest army in the Four Lands had been driven like a herd of cattle before wolves from its own country—driven from the Breakline, from the Sarandanon, and all the way back to its home city, there to stand or fall. Somewhere deep within him there was a terrible sense of failure. He had let this happen. He was responsible.

"Arion," he whispered suddenly, remembering.

Then the tears welled up in his eyes and he began to cry.

XXXVI

Eretria!" Wil exclaimed softly, surprise and wariness in his voice. Disregarding the pain from his injury, he pushed himself up on one elbow for a closer look. "What are you doing here?"

"Saving you, it would appear." She laughed, her dark eyes mischievous.

Sudden movement caught his eye, and he stared past her into the shadows. Two Rover women busied themselves at a sideboard near the rear of the wagon, rinsing cloths red with his blood in a basin of water. Instinctively, he reached up to his head and found that a bandage had been placed across the wound. He touched it gingerly and winced.

"I wouldn't do that." Eretria brushed his hand aside. "It is the only part of you that is clean."

The Valeman glanced about quickly. "What have you done with Amberle?"

"Your sister?" she mocked. "She is safe enough."

"You will excuse me if I am a bit skeptical about that." He started to rise from the bed.

"Stay, Healer." She forced him down again. Her voice lowered so that the women behind her could not hear. "Do you fear I might seek revenge because of your ill-conceived decision to leave me behind at the Tirfing? Do you think so little of me?" She laughed and tossed her head. "Perhaps now though, if you were given the chance, you would reconsider that decision. Is that possible?"

"Not in the least. Now what about Amberle?"

"Had I intended harm to you, Wil Ohmsford—or to her—I would have left the both of you to the cutthroats

371

who chased you through Grimpen Ward. The Elven girl is
well. I will have her brought after we have talked."

She turned to the women at the sideboard. "Go. Leave
us."

The women stopped what they were doing and disappeared through a flap at the other end of the wagon. When
they had gone, Eretria turned back to the Valeman, her
head cocked to one side.

"Well, what shall I do with you now, Wil Ohmsford?"

He took a deep breath. "How did you find me, Eretria?"

She grinned. "Easily enough. Word of your great healing
power spread the length and breadth of Grimpen Ward
within ten minutes of the time it took you to cure that fat
woman innkeeper. Did you think that such a noisy
performance would go unnoticed? How do you think it
was that you were found by those cutthroats?"

"You knew of that, too, then?"

"Healer, you are a fool." She said it kindly, her hand
reaching up to touch his cheek. "Rovers are the first to
know anything that happens in the places where they
travel. If it were not so, they would not long survive—a
lesson you apparently have yet to learn. Once word spread
of your wondrous act of healing, it was obvious to anyone
with half a brain that there would be some who would
soon decide that one with your talent must surely be a man
of wealth. Greed and drink mix well, Healer. You are lucky
to be alive."

"I suppose so," he acknowledged, chagrined. "I should
have been a bit more careful."

"A bit. Fortunately for you, I realized who you were and
prevailed upon Cephelo to let me find you, once the cry
went up from the inn. Otherwise, you might be food for
the dogs."

"A pleasant thought." Wil grimaced. He glanced at her
quickly. "Cephelo knows that I am here?"

"He knows." She smiled and the mischievousness returned to her eyes. "Does that frighten you?"

"Let's just say that it concerns me," Wil admitted. "Why
should he do anything for me after what happened back in
the Tirfing?"

Eretria leaned close and put her slim, dark arms about
his neck. "Because his daughter is persuasive, Healer—

persuasive enough that at times she may influence even so difficult a man as Cephelo." She shrugged. "Besides, he has had time to rethink what happened at the Tirfing. I have convinced him, I think, that it was none of your doing—that in fact you saved the lives of the Family."

Wil shook his head doubtfully. "I don't trust him."

"Nor should you," she agreed. "But for tonight, at least, he should cause you no concern. He will wait until morning to have you answer to him. By then, at any rate, your pursuers will have worn themselves out chasing shadows and have gone back again to the taverns for fresh ale and a more tangible source of gain."

She rose then, slipped away in a flash of blue silk, and returned a moment later with a damp cloth and a fresh basin of water which she placed on the floor next to the bed.

"We must clean you up, Healer. You reek of sweat and dirt, and your clothes are ruined." She paused. "Take them off and I'll wash you."

Wil shook his head. "I will wash myself. Can you lend me some clothes?"

She nodded, but made no move to go. The Valeman flushed.

"I would like to do this by myself, if you don't mind."

The dazzling smile broke across her face. "Oh, but I do mind."

He shook his head. "You really are incorrigible."

"You are for me, Wil Ohmsford. I told you that before."

The smile faded, replaced by a look so sensuous and compelling as to cause Wil to forget momentarily what it was that he was about. When she started to lean toward him, he forced himself to sit up quickly on the bed. Dizziness washed over him, but he kept himself upright.

"Will you bring me the clothes?"

For an instant her eyes went dark with anger. Then she rose, crossed to a cupboard, removed some clothing, and brought it to him.

"You may have these." She tossed them in his lap.

She started past him, then dipped suddenly and kissed him quickly on the mouth. "Wash and dress yourself then." She sniffed, slipping away.

She opened a door at the end of the wagon and

disappeared into the night, closing the door behind her securely and latching it from without. Wil grinned in spite of himself. Whatever her intentions, she was not about to let him run off. Quickly he stripped away his old clothing, washed, and put on the clothes Eretria had supplied. They fit well, though they were the clothes of a Rover and he felt more than a little strange wearing them.

He had just finished dressing when the door opened again and Eretria appeared with Amberle. The Elven girl was dressed in Rover pants and tunic, with a sash and headband to hold back her waist-length hair. Her face was freshly scrubbed and a bit startled. She glanced at Wil's head and there was immediate concern in her green eyes.

"Are you all right?" she asked quickly.

"I have seen to his needs." Eretria brushed her question aside smoothly. She pointed to the bed opposite Wil's. "You can sleep there. Be certain that you do not try to leave the wagon tonight."

She gave Wil a knowing smile, then turned away and moved to the door. She was halfway through when she glanced back suddenly.

"Good-night, brother Wil. Good-night, sister Amberle. Sleep well."

With a grin, she slipped through the door. The latch fastened behind her with a click.

The Valeman and the Elven girl slept that night within the Rover wagon. It was dawn when they awoke, the new light seeping through cracks in the shuttered windows to light the dusky gloom. Wil lay silent for a time, gathering his thoughts, waiting for the sleep to clear from his eyes. After a moment, he reached within his tunic for the small leather pouch containing the Elfstones, checked to be certain that they were still there, then replaced the pouch. It did not hurt to be careful, he thought. He was halfway out of the bed when Amberle ordered him back in again, scrambling up from the other bed to reach him. Carefully she examined the injury to his head and readjusted the bandage. When she had finished, Wil pushed himself up beside her and surprised her with a quick kiss on one cheek. She flushed slightly and smiled, her child's face beaming.

A short time later the door latch released and Eretria stepped through, carrying a tray of bread, honey, milk, and fruit. Brown limbs slipped from beneath a diaphanous white gown that swirled about the Rover girl like smoke. The dazzling smile flashed at the Valeman.

"Well rested, Wil Ohmsford?" She deposited the tray on his lap and winked. "Cephelo will speak with you now."

She left without saying a word to Amberle. Wil glanced at the Elven girl when Eretria had gone and shrugged helplessly. Amberle's smile was forced.

Minutes later, Cephelo appeared. He entered without knocking, his tall, lean frame stooping slightly as it passed through the entry. Dressed in black and wrapped in the cloak of forest green, he appeared just as he had when they had first observed him on the banks of the Mermidon. The wide-brimmed hat was cocked jauntily on his head, and he removed it with a flourish as he entered, a broad grin splitting his swarthy face.

"Ah, the Elflings, the Healer and his sister. We meet again." He bowed. "Still looking for your horse?"

Wil smiled. "Not this time."

The Rover looked down the length of his hooked nose at them. "No? Have you lost your way then? Arborlon, as I remember, lies north."

"We have been to Arborlon and left again," the Valeman replied, setting aside the tray.

"Come to Grimpen Ward."

"Both of us, it seems."

"Indeed." The tall man seated himself opposite the two. "In my case, business takes me many places that I might not otherwise care to go. But what of yourself, Healer? What brings you to Grimpen Ward? Surely not the prospect of applying your art to the denizens of so shabby a village as this one."

Wil hesitated a moment before responding. He was going to have to be very careful what he told Cephelo. He knew the man well enough by now to appreciate the fact that if the Rover were to discover anything that he might turn to his own advantage, he would be quick to do so.

"We have business of our own," he replied carelessly.

The Rover pursed his lips. "You do not seem to be doing

very well in its pursuit, Healer. Your throat would be cut by now if not for me."

Wil wanted to laugh aloud. The old fox! He was not about to admit that Eretria had anything to do with saving them.

"We seem to be in your debt once again," he offered.

Cephelo shrugged. "I was hasty in my judgment of you at the Tirfing; I let my concern for my people override my common sense. I blamed you for what happened when I should have thanked you for aiding. That has bothered me. Saving you now eases my sense of guilt."

"I am gratified to learn that you feel this way." Wil did not believe one word of it. "This has been a difficult time for my sister and me."

"Difficult?" Cephelo's dark face mirrored sudden concern. "Perhaps there is something more that I can do to aid you—something to be of service. If you would tell me what it is, exactly, that brings you to this most dangerous part of the country . . . ?"

Here it comes, Wil thought. Out of the corner of his eye, he watched Amberle frown in warning.

"I wish that it were within your power to help." Wil did his best to sound sincere. "But I am afraid that it is not. What I need most is the guidance of someone familiar with the history of this valley, its marks, and its legends."

Cephelo clapped his hands lightly. "Well, then, perhaps I can be of assistance after all. I have traveled the Wilderun many times." He lifted a long finger to the side of his head. "I know something of its secrets."

Perhaps, Wil thought. Perhaps not. He wants to know what we are doing here.

The Valeman shrugged. "I do not feel that we should impose further on your hospitality by involving you in our affairs. My sister and I can manage."

The Rover's face was expressionless. "Why not tell me what it is that brings you here—let me judge if the imposition is so great."

Amberle's hand closed tightly on Wil's arm, but he ignored it, keeping his eyes locked on Cephelo's. He knew that he was going to have to tell the Rover something.

"There is a sickness within the house of the Elessedils, rulers of the Elves." He lowered his voice. "The King's granddaughter is very ill. The medicine she needs is an extract from a root that can only be found here, within the Wilderun. I alone know that—I and my sister. We have come here in search of that root, for if we can find it and carry it to the Elven ruler, the reward will be great."

He felt Amberle's grip loosen abruptly. He did not dare to look at her face. Cephelo was silent for a moment before replying.

"Do you know where within the Wilderun this root can be found?"

The Valeman nodded. "There are books, ancient books of healing from the old world, that speak of the root and the name of its location. But it is a name long since forgotten, long since erased from the maps that serve the races now. I doubt that the name would mean anything to you."

The Rover leaned forward. "Tell it to me anyway."

"Safehold," Wil declared, watching the other's dark face. "The name is Safehold."

Cephelo thought a moment, then shook his head. "You were right—the name means nothing. Still . . ." He paused deliberately, rocking back slightly as if deep in thought. "There is one who might know the name, one familiar with the old names of this valley. I could lead you to him, I suppose. Ah, but Healer, the Wilderun is very dangerous country—you know that yourself since you most certainly crossed through some small part of its forests to reach Grimpen Ward. The risk to my people and myself if we were to aid you in such a perilous search would be great." He shrugged apologetically. "Besides, we have other commitments, other places to which we must travel, other business to which we must attend. Time is a precious thing to such as we. Surely you can appreciate that."

"What is it that you are saying?" The Valeman demanded quietly.

"That without me, you will fail in your quest. That you need me; that I in turn wish to offer my help. But such help as you seek cannot be given without, ah . . . adequate recompense."

Wil nodded slowly. "What recompense, Cephelo?"

The Rover's eyes glittered. "The Stones you carry. The ones that hold the power."

The Valeman shook his head. "They would be useless to you."

"Would they? Is their secret so dark?" Cephelo's eyes narrowed. "Do not suppose me a fool. You are no simple Healer. That much was obvious almost from the moment we first met. Still, it matters not to me who you are—only what you have. You have the power of the Stones and I wish it."

"Their magic is Elven." Wil forced himself to remain calm, hoping desperately that he had not lost control of the situation. "Only one of Elven blood can wield their power."

"You lie badly, Healer," the big man's voice was ugly.

"He speaks the truth," Amberle interjected quickly, her face frightened. "If not for the Stones, he would not have even attempted this search. You have no right to ask him to give them up to you."

"I have the right to ask whatever I choose," Cephelo snapped, brushing her words aside with a wave of his hand. "In any case, I believe neither of you."

"Believe what you wish." Wil's voice was steady. "I will not give you the Stones."

The two men stared wordlessly at each other for a moment, the Rover's face hard and threatening. Yet there was fear there as well—fear generated by Cephelo's vivid memory of the power locked within the Elfstones, power that Wil Ohmsford had mastered. With great effort he forced himself to smile.

"What will you give me then, Healer? Am I expected to do this service for nothing? Am I expected to risk lives and property without any form of recompense at all? There must be something of value that you can give me—something that has worth equal to that of the Stones you so stubbornly refuse to yield. What then? What will you give me?"

Wil tried desperately to come up with something, but there was absolutely nothing else he carried that was worth more than a few pennies. Yet just when he had decided that the situation was hopeless, Cephelo snapped his fingers sharply.

"I will make a bargain with you, Healer. You say that the Elven King will reward you if you bring to him the medicine that will cure his granddaughter. Very well. I will do what I can to help you learn something of this place you call Safehold. I will take you to one who might know the name. I will do that and nothing more. In exchange for this, you must give me half of whatever reward you receive from the Elven King. Half. Is it agreed?"

Wil thought it over a moment. A curious bargain, he decided. Rovers seldom, if ever, gave anything away without first getting something in return. What was Cephelo about?

"Are you saying that you will help me learn the location of Safehold . . ."

"If I can."

". . . but you will not come with me to find it?"

Cephelo shrugged. "I have no wish to risk my life unnecessarily. Finding the medicine and conveying it to the Elven King's granddaughter is your problem. My part of the bargain is merely to help you on your way." He paused. "Do not, however, presume that once gone you are therefore free of me. Any attempt to cheat me of what you owe would end very badly for you."

The Valeman frowned. "How will you know whether or not I am successful if you do not come with me?"

Cephelo laughed. "Healer, I am a Rover—I will know! I will know all that happens to you, believe me."

His smile was so wolfish that for an instant Wil was certain that there was another meaning to his words. Something was wrong; he could sense it. Yet they needed help from somewhere in finding their way through the Wilderun—help that would permit him to forgo any use of the Elfstones. If Cephelo were to give them that help, it might mean the difference between success and failure in finding the Bloodfire before the Demons found them.

"Is it agreed?" Cephelo asked again.

Wil shook his head. He would test the Rover. "One half is too much. I will give you a third."

"A third!" Cephelo's face darkened momentarily, then relaxed. "Very well. I am a reasonable man. A third."

That had been entirely too easy, Wil thought. He glanced at Amberle, seeing in her eyes the same mistrust that flickered in his own. But the Elven girl said nothing. She was leaving the decision to him.

"Come, come, Elfling," Cephelo pressed. "Do not be all day about it."

The Valeman nodded. "All right. It is agreed."

"Good." The Rover stood up immediately. "We will leave at once since our business here is ended. But you are to remain within the wagon for a time. It would not do to have you seen again in Grimpen Ward. Once we are into the deep forest, you may come out."

He smiled broadly, dipped the wide-brimmed hat in parting and passed back through the entry. The door closed softly behind him and locked. Wil and Amberle sat staring at each other.

"I don't trust him," Amberle whispered.

Wil nodded. "Not at all."

Moments later, the wagon lurched forward and began to roll and their journey into the Wilderun was under way once more.

XXXVII

The old man hummed softly to himself as he sat in the cane-backed rocker and stared out into the darkening forest. Far to the west beyond the wall of trees that locked tightly about the clearing in which he sat, beyond the valley of the Wilderun and the mountains that ringed it, the sun slipped beneath the earth's horizon and the day's light faded into dusk. It was the old man's favorite time of day, the midday heat cooling into evening shadow, the sunset coloring the far skyline crimson and purple, then deepening into blue night. From atop the ridge line, where the woodland trees broke apart enough to permit glimpses of sky, moon, and stars through a screen of limbs and trunks, the air smelled clean for a time, freed of the damp and mustiness that clung to it through the swelter of the day, and the leaves of the forest whispered in a soft, slow nighttime wind. It was as if, for those few moments, the Wilderun were like any other country, and a man might look upon it as an old and intimate friend.

The old man looked often upon the valley that way, more now than at any other time of the day or night perhaps, but always with that same sense of deep and abiding loyalty. Few others could ever feel as he, but few others knew the valley as he had come to know it. Oh, it was treacherous—hard and filled with dangers to snare and destroy a man. There were creatures within the Wilderun the like of which could be found in no other place this side of a midnight campfire legend, told with hushed whispers and frightened looks. There was death here, death that came with the passing of every hour, harsh, cruel, and certain. It was a land of hunter and hunted, each living creature a bit of both, and the old man had seen the best and worst of each in the sixty years that he had made the valley his home.

He drummed his fingers on the rocker's arms and thought back dreamily. It was sixty years since he had first come to the Wilderun—a long time, yet barely gone. This had been his home for all those years, and it was a home that a man could respect—not simply another place with houses and people all crowded close, safe, secure, and senselessly dull, but a place of solitude and depth, of challenge and heart, a place to which only a few would ever come because only those few would ever belong. A few like himself, he thought, and now only he remained of those who had once come into the valley. All the rest were gone, claimed by the wilderness, buried somewhere deep within her earth. Of course there were those fools that huddled like frightened dogs within the ragged shacks of Grimpen Ward, cheating and robbing each other and any other fool that might venture into their midst. But the valley was not theirs and never would be, for they had no understanding of what the valley was about nor any wish to learn. They might as well be locked within the closet of some castle for all it meant to any claim that they were its lords and ladies.

Crazy, they called him—those fools in Grimpen Ward. Crazy to live in this wilderness, an old man alone. He grinned crookedly at the thought. Madness peculiar to its owner, perhaps; but he would choose his own over theirs.

"Drifter," he called gruffly, and the monstrous black dog that stretched at his feet came awake and rose, a giant animal that had the look of both wolf and bear, its massive body bristling with hair, its muzzle yawning wide.

"Hey, you." The old man grunted, and the dog came over, dropping its great head onto its master's lap, waiting for its ears to be scratched.

The old man obliged. Somewhere in the growing dark, a scream sounded, quick and piercing, to linger in the sudden stillness as a fading echo, then die. Drifter looked up quickly. The old man nodded. Swamp cat. A big one. Something had crossed its path and paid the price.

His gaze wandered idly, picking out familiar shapes and forms in the half-light. Behind him sat the hut in which he lived, a small but solid structure, built of logs and shingles caulked with mortar. A shed and well sat just back of the hut, and a fenced closure that held his mule, and a workbench and lumber. He liked to whittle and carve, liked it well enough that much of his day was spent shaping and honing the wood he took from the great trees about the clearing into odds and ends that it pleased him to look upon. Worthless, he supposed, to everyone but himself, but then he didn't care much about anyone else, so that was all right. He saw little enough of people and little enough was more than enough, and he didn't look to give them reasons to seek him out. Drifter was all the company he needed. And those worthless cats that wandered about looking for new places to sleep and table scraps, as if they were no better than common scavengers. And the mule, a dumb but dependable creature.

He stretched and rose. The sun was down and the night sky was laced with stars and moonlight. It was time to fix something to eat for himself and the dog. He looked momentarily toward the tripod and kettle which sat atop a small cooking fire several yards in front of him. Yesterday's soup, and precious little of that—enough, maybe, for one more meal.

He moved toward the fire, shaking his head. He was a smallish man, old and bent, his stick-thin frame clothed in a ragged shirt and half-pants. White hair ringed his bald head in a thin fringe of snow that ran down the length of a roundish jaw to a beard spotted with soot and bits of sawdust. Brown, wrinkled skin covered his tough old body like leather, and his eyes were barely visible through lids that pouched and drooped. He walked with a sort of hunching motion, as if he had just come awake and, finding his muscles cramped with sleep, was attempting to work out the stiffness.

He halted beside the kettle and stared down into it, trying to decide what he might do to improve the appeal of its contents. It was at that moment that he heard the approach of the horses and wagon, distant still, lost in the dark somewhere up the trail from his hut, winding uncertainly toward him. He turned and stared into the night, waiting. At his side, Drifter growled in an unfriend-

ly manner, and the old man gave him a warning cuff. The
minutes slipped away, and the sounds drew closer. Finally
a line of shadows emerged from the dusk, winding down
over the crest of the rise fronting the clearing—a single
wagon with horses in trace and half a dozen riders in tow.
The old man's mood soured the moment he saw the
wagon. He knew it well enough, knew it to be Rover, knew
it to belong to that rogue Cephelo. He spat to one side with
distaste and thought seriously about loosing Drifter on the
bunch of them.

The riders and wagon halted just inside the fringes of the
clearing. Cephelo's dark form dismounted and came forward. When he reached the old man, the Rover's wide-
brimmed hat swept down in greeting.

"Well met, Hebel. Good evening to you."

The old man snorted. "Cephelo. What do you want?"

Cephelo looked shocked. "Hebel, Hebel, this is no
greeting for two who have done as much for one another as
we. This is no greeting for men who have shared the
hardships and misfortunes of humankind. Hello, now."

The Rover took the old man's hand and shook it firmly.
Hebel neither resisted nor aided the effort.

"Ah, you look well." Cephelo smiled disarmingly. "The
high country is good for the aches and pains of age, I
imagine."

"Aches and pains of age, is it?" Hebel spat and wrinkled
his nose. "What are you selling, Cephelo—some cure-all
for the infirm?"

Cephelo glanced back at those who had come with him
and shrugged apologetically. "You are most unkind, Hebel,
most unkind."

The old man followed his gaze. "What have you done
with the rest of your pack? Have they taken up with some
other thief?"

This time the Rover's face darkened slightly. "I have sent
them on ahead. They follow the main roadway east to
await my coming in the Tirfing. I am here with these few on
a matter of some importance. Might we talk a bit?"

"You're here, aren't you?" Hebel pointed out. "Talk all
you want."

"And share your fire?"

Hebel shrugged. "I don't have the food to feed you all—wouldn't if I did. Maybe you brought something with you, huh?"

Cephelo gave an exaggerated sigh. "We did. Tonight you shall share our dinner."

He called back to the others. The riders dismounted and began caring for the horses. An old woman had been driving the wagon in the company of a young couple. She climbed down now, removed provisions and cookware from the rear of the wagon, and shuffled wordlessly to the cooking fire. The two who sat with her hesitated momentarily, then came forward at Cephelo's invitation. They were joined by a slim, dark-haired girl who had been one of the riders.

Hebel turned away wordlessly and reseated himself in the rocker. There was something peculiar about the two who had come down off the wagon seat, but he could not quite put his finger on what it was. They looked like Rovers and yet at the same time they didn't. He watched them approach with Cephelo and the dark-haired girl. All four seated themselves on the grass about the old man—the dark-haired girl slipping suggestively close to the young man and giving him a bold wink.

"My daughter, Eretria." Cephelo shot the girl an irritated look as he introduced her. "These two are Elves."

"I'm not blind," Hebel snapped, recognizing now why they appeared to be something more than Rovers. "What are they doing with you?"

"We have undertaken a quest," the Rover announced.

Hebel leaned forward. "A quest? With you?" He glanced at the young man, his aged face wrinkling. "You seem like a bright sort. What made you decide to take up with him?"

"He requires a guide through this miserable country," Cephelo answered for him—rather too quickly, Hebel thought. "Why is it, Hebel, that you insist on making this forsaken wilderness your home? One day I'll pass by and find your bones, old man, and all because you were too stubborn to take your worthless hide to safer regions."

"Much you'd care," Hebel grunted. "For a man such as myself, this land is as safe as any other. I know it, know what walks and breathes and hunts it, know how to keep my distance and when to show my teeth. I'll outlive you, Rover—mark my words on that." He pushed back in the rocker, watching Drifter's dark shadow settle in behind him. "What do you want with me?"

Cephelo shrugged. "A bit of talk, just as I've said."

Hebel laughed hoarsely. "A bit of talk? Come now, Cephelo—what do you want? Don't waste my time—there isn't that much of it left."

"For myself, nothing. For these young Elflings, something of the knowledge stored in that balding old pate. It has taken me a great deal of effort to reach you up here, but there are causes that merit special . . ."

Hebel had heard enough. "What are you cooking over there?" He allowed himself to be distracted by the smell of the food simmering in the cooking kettle. "What's in there?"

"How should I know?" Cephelo snapped, irritated by the old man's seeming inattention.

"Beef, I think. Beef and vegetables." Hebel rubbed his weathered hands. "I think we should eat before we talk. Got some of that Rover ale with you, Cephelo?"

So they ate plates of stew, day-old bread, dried fruit, and nuts, with glasses of ale to wash it all down. Not much was said while they ate, though a considerable number of glances were exchanged, and those glances told Hebel a good deal more about the situation than whatever words his visitors might have spoken. The Elves, he decided, were there because they had run out of choices in the matter. They cared nothing more for Cephelo and his band than he did. Cephelo, of course, was there because there was something in all of this for him, but what that might be would undoubtedly be kept carefully concealed. It was the dark-haired girl, the Rover's daughter, who puzzled him most. The way she looked at that Elf lad told him something of what she was about, yet there was more to her than that, more than she was willing to let on. The old man grew increasingly curious as to what it might be.

At last the food was gone and the ale was drunk. Hebel produced a long pipe, struck flint and tinder to its contents, and puffed a broad wreath of smoke into the night air. Cephelo tried again.

"This young Elf and his sister need your help. They have already come a long way, but they won't be able to go any further if you don't give them that help. I told them, of course, that you would."

The old man snorted. He knew this game. "Don't like Elves. They think they're too good for this country, for people like me." He lifted one eyebrow. "Don't like Rovers either, as you well know. Like them even less than Elves."

Eretria smirked. "There seems to be a lot you don't like."

"Shut your mouth!" Cephelo snapped, his face darkening. Eretria went still and Hebel saw the anger in her eyes.

He chuckled softly. "I don't blame you, girl." He looked at Cephelo. "What will you give me if I help the Elflings, Rover? An even trade now, if you want what I know."

Cephelo glowered. "Do not try my patience too severely, Hebel."

"Ha! Will you cut my throat? See what words you find then! Now speak again—what will you give me?"

"Clothes, bedding, leather, silk—I don't care." The Rover brushed aside the question stiffly.

"I got all that." Hebel spat.

Cephelo controlled himself only with a monumental effort. "Well, what is it that you want, then? Speak up, old man!"

From behind the rocker, Drifter growled in warning. Hebel reached back and gave the dog a cuff.

"Knives," he announced. "Half a dozen good blades. An axe head and wedges. Two dozen arrows, ashwood and feathered. And a cutting stone."

The big man nodded, looking less than pleased. "Done, thief. Now give me something back for all that."

Hebel shrugged. "What is it you want to know?"

Cephelo pointed at the young man. "The Elfling is a Healer. He looks for a root that produces a rare medicine. His books of healing say that it can be found here, within the Wilderun, in a place called Safehold."

There was a long moment of silence as the Rover and the old man stared at each other and the others waited.

"Well?" Cephelo demanded finally.

"Well what?" the old man snapped.

"Safehold! Where is it?"

Hebel grinned crookedly. "Right where it's always been, I imagine." He saw the surprise in the other's face. "I know the name, Rover. An old name, forgotten by everyone but me, I'd guess. Tombs of some sort—catacombs beneath a mountain."

"That's it!" The young man came to his feet, his face flushed. Then he saw that everyone was staring at him and he sat down again quickly. "At least that is the way that the books described it," he added lamely.

"Did they now?" Hebel rocked back, puffing. "Did they speak as well of the Hollows?"

The young man shook his head and glanced at the Elf girl, who shook her head as well. It was Cephelo who leaned forward sharply, his eyes narrowing.

"You mean that Safehold lies within the Hollows, old man?"

There was an edge to Cephelo's voice that did not escape Hebel. Cephelo was frightened.

Hebel chuckled. "Within the Hollows. Do you still seek Safehold, Rover?"

The young man hunched forward. "Where can the Hollows be found?"

"South, a day's walk," the old man answered. It was time to put an end to this foolishness. "Deep and dark they are, Elfling—a pit in which anything that drops falls from sight and is lost forever. Death, Elfling. Nothing that goes into the Hollows comes out again. Those who live there choose to keep it so."

The young man shook his head. "I do not understand."

Eretria muttered something under her breath, her eyes darting quickly to the face of the young Elf. She knew, Hebel saw. His voice dropped to a whisper.

"The Witch Sisters, Elfling. Morag and Mallenroh. The Hollows belong to them and to the things they make to serve them—things of Witch power."

"But where within the Hollows lies Safehold?" the other persisted. "You spoke of a mountain . . . ?"

"Spire's Reach—a solitary peak that rises up out of the Hollows like an arm stretched forth from death's grave. There lies Safehold." The old man paused, shrugging. "Or so it was once. I have not been to the Hollows myself in many, many years." He shook his head. "No one goes there anymore."

The young man nodded slowly. "Tell me something of these Witch Sisters."

Hebel's eyes narrowed. "Morag and Mallenroh—the last of their kind. Once, Elfling, there were many such as they—now there are but two. Some say they were the handmaidens of the Warlock Lord. Some say they were here long before even he. Power to match that of the Druids, some say." He spread his hands. "The truth is hidden with them—seek it if you wish. The loss of another Elf, more or less, means nothing to me."

He laughed sharply, choking a bit until he lifted his cup and drank down a swallow or two of ale. His thin frame bent forward as he sought the young man's eyes.

"Sisters, they are, Morag and Mallenroh. Blood sisters. But there is a great hate between them, a hate from some wrong suffered long ago—real or imagined I could not say, nor anyone else I'd guess. But they war within the Hollows, Elfling—Morag holds the east, Mallenroh the west, each trying to destroy the other, each trying to seize for herself her sister's land and power. And at the center of the Hollows, just between the two, stands Spire's Reach—and there, Safehold."

"Have you seen Safehold?"

"I? Not I. The Hollows belong to the Sisters; the valley is room enough for me." Hebel rocked back, remembering. "Once, so many years ago that I no longer care to count, I hunted along the rim of the Hollows. Foolish it was, but I was still of a mind to know the whole of the land that I had chosen for my home, and the stories were but stories. For days I hunted within the shadow of the Hollows, seeing nothing. Then one night as I slept, alone but for the dimming embers of my campfire, she came to me— Mallenroh, tall and like some creature from a dream, gray hair long and woven with nightshade, her face the face of Mistress Death. She came to me, told me she felt the need to speak to one of human blood, one such as I. All the rest of the night she talked and told me of herself and her sister Morag and of the war they fought to own the Hollows."

He was lost in the memory now, his voice distant and

soft. "In the morning she was gone, almost as if she had never been. I never saw her again, of course, not from that moment to this. I might have thought it all imagined, not real at all, except that she took some part of me with her— some bit of life I'd suppose you'd say."

He shook his head slowly. "Most of what she told me scattered like the fragments of some dream. But I remember her words of Safehold, Elfling. Catacombs beneath the arm of Spire's Reach, she said. A place from another age where some strange magic had once been done. So old it was that even the Sisters did not know its meaning. She told me that, did Mallenroh. I remember . . . that much, at least."

He was silent then, thinking back on what had been. Even after all these years, the memory of her was as clear as the faces of those who sat about him. Mallenroh! Strange, he thought, that he should remember her so well.

The young man was speaking quietly, his hand touching the edge of the rocker.

"You remember enough, Hebel."

The old man looked at the Elf in surprise, not understanding. Then he saw in the other's eyes what he intended. He meant to go there, Hebel realized. He meant to go into the Hollows. Impulsively he leaned down.

"Do not go," he whispered, his head shaking slowly. "Do not go."

The young man smiled faintly. "I must, if Cephelo is to have his reward."

The Rover said nothing, his dark face inscrutable. Eretria glanced sharply at him, then turned back to the young man.

"Healer, do not do this," she begged. "Listen to what the old man has said. The Hollows are no place for you. Seek your medicine elsewhere."

The Elf shook his head. "There is nowhere else. Let it alone, Eretria."

For an instant, the Rover girl's entire body seemed to go taut, her dark face flushing with emotions that struggled to break free. Yet she held them carefully in check, rising to her feet and staring down at him coldly.

"You are a fool," she announced, and stalked away into the dark.

Hebel watched the young man, saw his eyes follow after Eretria as she went from them. The Elven girl did not look, her strange green eyes introspective and all but lost in the shadow of her long hair as it fell forward about her child's face.

"Is this root so important?" the old man asked wonderingly, not just to the young man, but to the girl as well. "Can it not be found another place?"

"Let them be." Cephelo spoke up suddenly, his dark eyes slipping from face to face. "The decision is theirs to make and they have made it."

Hebel frowned. "So quick to send them to their deaths, Rover? What then of this reward of which the Elfling speaks?"

Cephelo laughed. "Rewards are given and taken away by the whims of fortune, old man. Where one is lost, another is gained. The Elfling must do what he chooses, he and his sister. We have no right to pass judgment."

"We have to go." The Elven girl spoke softly, for the first time since they had been seated, looking deep into the old man's eyes.

"Well, then." Cephelo rose. "Enough said of the matter. The evening is not yet done and there is good Rover ale to be drunk. Share it with me, friends. We shall talk of the times that have been, rather than guess at what might yet be. Hebel, you shall hear what those fools that people Grimpen Ward have done of late—madness the like of which only men such as you and I can truly appreciate."

He called sharply to the old woman, who scurried to his side with a flask of ale. Several more of the Rovers drifted over to join them, and Cephelo poured freely from the flask into the cups of all. Laughing and joking, he began a series of wild-eyed stories of places he had probably never been and people he had certainly never met. Bold and easy was the Rover, his talk filling the night with the laughter of his people and the clink of their glasses raised in salute. Hebel listened with distrust. Cephelo had been too quick to disparage his warning to the Elflings and to disclaim interest in the supposed reward that would come, it seemed, only if the young Elf found the medicine he sought and returned again. Too quick by far, he thought—for the Rover knew as well as he that no one had ever returned from the Hollows.

He rocked slowly in his cane-backed chair, one hand dropping idly to find Drifter's shaggy head. What more warning could he give this Elf, he wondered? What could he say that he had not already said to discourage his foolishness? Perhaps nothing; the lad seemed determined that he must go.

He wondered then if the Elfling would meet Mallenroh as he had done so many years ago; thinking that he might, he envied him.

It was a short time later when Wil Ohmsford rose from the company of revelers and walked to the well that sat just back of the old man's hut. Amberle already slept, wrapped in blankets close to the fire, exhausted, it seemed, from the day's journey and the events leading up to it. He also was experiencing an unusual drowsiness, though he had drunk little of the Rover ale. The cold water might help, he thought, and a good night's sleep after. He had just taken a long drink from a metal cup hooked to the well-bucket's chain when Eretria stepped from the shadows to stand before him.

"I do not understand you, Healer," she said bluntly.

He replaced the cup within the bucket and seated himself on the stone wall of the well. This was Eretria's first appearance since she had called him a fool in front of the others.

"I went to a considerable amount of trouble to save your life back in Grimpen Ward," she continued. "It was not easy persuading Cephelo that he should allow me to help you—not easy at all. Now it seems that my efforts were wasted. I might as well have let those cutthroats have you, you and this Elven girl you pretend is your sister. Despite the warnings you have been given, you insist on going into the Hollows. I want to know why. Has Cephelo anything to do with this? I don't know what bargain you struck with him, but nothing he promised—even if he were of a mind to deliver, which I doubt he is—would be worth the risk that you take."

"Cephelo has nothing to do with it," Wil replied quietly.

"If he has threatened you in any way, I would stand with you against him," the girl declared firmly. "I would help you."

"I know that. But Cephelo has no part in the decision."

"Then why? Why must you do this?"

The Valeman looked down. "The medicine that is needed for . . ."

"Don't lie to me!" Eretria dropped next to him on the well wall, her dark face angry. "Cephelo may believe that nonsense about roots and medicines, but he reads only the truth of your words, Healer, and not the truth of your eyes. You may disguise the first, but never the second. This girl is not your sister; she is your charge, a responsibility that you clearly hold dear. It is not roots and medicines you seek, but something more. What is it then that lies within the Hollows?"

Wil looked up slowly to meet her gaze and hold it. For a long moment he stared at her without replying. She reached out impulsively, her hands grasping his.

"I would never betray you. Never."

He smiled faintly. "Perhaps that is the one thing about which I am certain, Eretria. I will tell you this. There is a danger that threatens this land—that threatens all the Lands. The thing that will protect against it can be found only in Safehold. Amberle and I have been sent to find it."

The Rover girl's eyes were filled with fire. "Then let me go with you. Take me with you now as you should have taken me before."

Wil sighed. "How can I do that? You have just finished telling me that I am a fool for insisting on going into the Hollows. Now you would have me treat you as a fool as well. No. Your place is with your people—at least for now. Better that you continue east, far from the Westland and what may come."

"Healer, I am to be sold by that devil who masquerades to my father the moment we reach the larger Southland cities!" Her voice was hard, brittle. "Am I to see myself as better off with that fate than any that you might encounter? Take me with you!"

"Eretria . . ."

"Hear me out! I know something of this country, for the Rovers have traveled it since the time of my birth. I may know something that could help you. If not, at least I will be no hindrance to you. I can take care of myself—better than your Elven girl. I ask nothing of you, Healer, that you would not ask of me were our positions reversed. You must let me come!"

"Eretria, even if I were to agree to this, Cephelo would never let you go."

"Cephelo would not know until it was too late to do anything about it." Her voice was quick and excited. "Take me with you, Healer. Say yes to me."

He almost did. She was so wonderfully beautiful that it would have been hard to refuse her anything under normal circumstances. But now, seated next to him, her eyes bright with anticipation, there was a desperation in her words that moved him. She was frightened of Cephelo and what he would do with her. She would not beg, the Valeman knew, but she would come as close to that as possible if it would persuade him to help her get free.

But the Hollows were death, the old man had said. No one went into the Hollows. It would be difficult enough looking after Amberle; and despite what Eretria had said about taking care of herself, Wil knew that, if she were permitted to come with them, he would worry for her just as he worried for the Elven girl.

He shook his head slowly. "I can't, Eretria. I can't."

There was a long moment of silence as she stared at him, disbelief and anger shading her eyes, the excitement and expectation fading. Slowly she rose.

"Though I have saved your life, you will not save mine. Very well." She stepped back from him, tears streaking her face. "Twice you have spurned me, Wil Ohmsford. You will not get the chance to do so again."

She wheeled and started away, only to stop again a dozen paces on.

"There will come a time, Healer, I promise you, when you will wish that you had not been so quick to refuse me aid."

Then she was gone, lost in the night shadows as the

Valeman stared after her. He remained where he was for a time, wishing desperately that things might be different than they were, wishing that there were some sensible way that he might give to her the help she needed.

Then at last he rose, the drowsiness growing, and stumbled off to sleep.

XXXVIII

Dawn broke gray and sullen over the Wilderun, draping the forestland in shadows that spread like bloodstains across the dark earth. Clouds masked the morning sky, hanging still and deep over the valley, and an expectant hush filled the air, warning of the approach of a summer storm. Atop the ridge line, Cephelo and his small band began their descent out of the hills, following the trail that would take them back down to the main roadway and a continuation of their journey toward the Hollows. The Rovers went from Hebel's camp as they had come, like shadows strayed, the horsemen leading the single wagon that bore Wil and Amberle, hands raised in brief farewell to the old man who stood wordlessly before the little hut and watched them depart. Slowly they passed into the gloom of the forest, massive trees wrapping close about them until all but the faintest streamers of light were shut away and there was nothing but the roadway, narrow and rutted and dark, burrowing down into the depths of the valley.

By midmorning they had reached the main road again and turned east. Mist began to gather on the valley floor, sifting through the trees as the day grew hot and the cool of the night turned to steam. Wil and Amberle rode in silence with the old woman, thinking of what lay ahead. There had been no further conversations with Hebel, for they had slept soundly that night and with their awakening, Cephelo had made certain that the old man had kept his distance from them. Now they found themselves wondering what more he might have told them had he been given the chance. As they pondered this, Cephelo rode back to speak with them, yet the smile and the conversation seemed forced and lacking any real purpose. He appeared several times more during the course of the morning and each time it was the same. It was almost as if he were looking for something, yet neither Valeman nor Elven girl had the slightest idea what it was that he might be seeking. Eretria stayed away from them entirely, and while Amberle was mystified as to the Rover girl's sudden change in behavior, Wil understood it all too well.

It was nearing midday when Cephelo signaled a halt at a narrow crossroads somewhere deep within the forest. In the distance, thunder rumbled ominously and the wind blew in sudden gusts that shook the trees and scattered leaves and dust. Cephelo rode back to the wagon and stopped beside Wil.

"This is where we part company, Healer," he announced. He pointed to the crossroads. "Your way lies south, down the smaller road. The path is clear—simply stay on it. You should reach the rim of the Hollows before nightfall."

Wil started to speak, and the Rover quickly held up his hand. "Before you say anything, let me advise you not to ask that I go with you. That was not our bargain, and I have other obligations that I intend to satisfy."

"I was about to ask you if we might have some provisions to take with us," Wil informed him coolly.

The Rover shrugged. "Enough for a day or two, no more."

He nodded to the old woman, who stepped back through the door of the wagon. Wil watched the Rover shift uneasily in his saddle. Something was bothering Cephelo.

"How will I find you to pay you your share of the reward?" he asked suddenly.

"Reward? Oh, yes." Cephelo seemed to have forgotten it momentarily. "Well, as I said before, I will know when you have been paid. I will seek you out, Healer."

The Valeman nodded, rose, and stepped down from the wagon, then turned back to help Amberle. He glanced at her briefly as he lifted her down. She did not feel any easier about the Rover's behavior than he did. He turned back to Cephelo.

"Could you give us a horse? One would . . ."

Cephelo cut him short. "There are no horses to be spared. Now I think you should be going. There is a storm coming."

The old woman reappeared and handed Wil a small sack. The Valeman slung it over one shoulder and thanked her. Then he glanced up at the Rover once more.

"A safe journey, Cephelo."

The big man nodded. "And a quick one to you, Healer. Farewell."

Wil took Amberle's arm and led her through the gathering of horsemen to the crossroads. Eretria sat astride her bay, black hair blowing wildly as the wind swirled past her. When the Valeman reached her side, he stopped momentarily and extended his hand.

"Good-bye, Eretria."

She nodded, her dark face expressionless, cold, and beautiful. Then without a word, she rode back to join Cephelo. The Valeman stared after her a moment, but she did not look at him again. He turned to the pathway leading south. Dirt blew into his eyes, and he shielded them with his hand, squinting into the gloom. With Amberle beside him, he started ahead.

Hebel spent the morning at his workbench behind the little hut, hunched over a carving of a swamp cat. As he worked, his mind drifted back to the events of the previous night, to the Elflings and their strange quest, and the warning he had given them which they had ignored. He could not understand it. Why had they refused to heed him? Certainly he had made it clear enough that it was death to go into the Hollows. And certainly he had made it clear as well that the domain of the Witch Sisters could not be violated. What was it then that could prompt this brother and sister to go there for nothing more than some obscure root medicine?

Then it occurred to him that perhaps there was something more. He thought about that for a moment and the more he thought about it the more plausible it seemed. After all, they would not be so foolish as to entrust a rogue like Cephelo with the truth; no, not that young man—he was too quick for that. Safehold lay within the depths of Spire's Reach; what sort of root would grow deep within a mountain where no sunlight could ever reach to nourish its growth? But magic had once been done within Safehold, the Witch Sister had whispered to him—magic from another age, lost and forgotten. Did the Elflings hope to discover it again?

Overhead, the sky darkened further as the storm rolled out of the far country, the howl of the wind in the trees rising to a higher pitch. The old man paused in his work and looked up momentarily. This would be a big one, he thought idly. Another bad sign for those Elflings who would be caught in the open, for the storm would overtake them before they reached the Hollows. He shook his head. He would go after them if he thought it would do any good, but their minds were obviously made up. Still, it was too bad. Whatever they hoped to find within Safehold, be it root medicine or magic, they would have been better off to have forgotten it entirely. They would never live to use it.

At his feet, Drifter lifted his shaggy head and sniffed the wind. Then abruptly the dog growled, low, deep, and angry. Hebel stared down at him curiously and glanced about. Shadows fell across the clearing from the forest trees, but nothing moved.

Drifter growled again and the hackles on the back of his neck rose. Hebel looked around guardedly. There was something out there, something hidden back in the gloom. He stood up, reaching for the broad axe. Cautiously, he started toward the trees, Drifter crouched beside him, still growling.

But then he stopped. He did not understand why he stopped except that suddenly he felt something cold slip into his body, chilling him so badly that he could barely stand. At his feet, Drifter lay on his belly and cried as if he had been struck, his great body cringing. The old man caught a glimpse of something moving—a shadow, massive and cloaked, there one moment and then gone. A fear passed through him, so terrible that he could not find the will to thrust it from him. It gripped him cruelly and held him fast as he stared helplessly at the dark forest and wished with everything that was left him that he might turn and flee. The axe fell from his hands and tumbled to the earth, useless.

Then the feeling slipped from him, gone as quickly as it

had come. All about him the wind howled, and a spattering of rain struck his leathery face. Drawing a deep breath,
he reached down for the axe and, with Drifter close against
him, backed slowly away until he felt his legs brush up
against the workbench. He paused then, one hand gripping the neck of the big dog to keep himself from shaking.
With frightening certainty he knew that, in sixty years of
struggling to survive the dangers of the valley, never before
had he come so close to dying.

Wil and Amberle had walked for less than an hour when
the storm overtook them. A sprinkling of heavy drops that
slipped teasingly through the dense canopy of trees turned
quickly to a downpour. Sheets of rain swept across the
pathway, driven by a west wind, and thunder boomed and
reverberated through the sodden forest. Ahead, the gloom
of the narrow trail darkened further with the rainfall, and
water-laden tree limbs began to droop about them in damp
trailers. They were soaked in minutes, bereft of the travel
cloaks which they had failed to recover from the Rovers
along with the rest of their clothing. The light garments
they had been fitted with in their stead clung to their
bodies. There was nothing to be done that would ease their
discomfort, however, so they simply put their heads down
and walked on.

For several hours the rain continued to fall at a steady
pace, save for occasional brief lulls that gave false promise
of an end to the storm. Through it all, the Valeman and the
Elven girl trudged on, water dripping from their bodies
and their clothing, mud caking on their boots, their eyes
fixed on the rutted path ahead. When at last the rain did
slow and the storm moved eastward, mist began to seep
out of the forest to mix with the deep gloom. Trees and
brush shone dark and shiny through the haze, and water
dripped noisily in the sudden stillness. Overhead, the sky
stayed clouded and dark; to the east thunder rumbled,
distant and lingering. The mist began to deepen, and the
pace of the travelers slowed.

It was then that the pathway began to slope downward,
a slight dropping off that at first was barely perceptible, but
gradually increased. Valeman and Elven girl slipped and
skidded in the muddied earth as they followed it down,

peering hopefully into the gloom ahead, yet finding nothing more than the dark tunnel of the road and the closure of the trees. The stillness had grown even more pronounced. Even the faint sounds of insects singing at the passing of the storm had faded into silence.

Then suddenly, so suddenly that it was as if someone had removed a veil from before their eyes, the trees of the woods split apart, the slope dropped away, and the great, dark bowl of the Hollows lay spread before them. Valeman and Elven girl stopped where they were in the center of the muddied trail and stared down into the awesome expanse. They knew at once that they had found the Hollows; this massive pit of black forest could be nothing else. It was as if they had come upon some monstrous dead lake, still and lifeless, its dark surface grown thick with vegetation so that what lay beneath its waters could only be guessed at. From its shadowed center rose Spire's Reach, a solitary column of rock thrusting up into the gloom, barren and pitted. The Hollows were bleak like an open grave that whispered of death.

The Valeman and the Elven girl stood silently upon the rim, fighting a sense of revulsion that grew with each passing moment that they gazed down into the soundless gloom. Nothing that either had ever encountered had looked so desolate.

"We have to go down there," Wil ventured finally, hating the idea.

She nodded. "I know."

He cast about hopefully for a way to proceed. Ahead, the trail appeared to stop altogether. Yet when the Valeman walked forward a bit, he saw that it did not end after all, but split to either side to wend downward into the shadows below. He hesitated a moment, studying the two paths, trying to decide which would provide the easier descent, then chose the one that ran left. He held out his arm to Amberle and she gripped it firmly. Leading the way, he started down, feeling his boots slide as the damp earth and rock gave way in clumps. Amberle stayed close, leaning heavily on him for support. Cautiously they moved ahead.

Then abruptly Wil lost his footing and went down. Amberle fell with him, tripping forward across his legs,

tumbling headlong from the muddied path to disappear
with a sharp cry into the wooded darkness. Frantically, Wil
scrambled after her, pushing his way through heavy brush
that ripped his clothing and cut his face. He might not have
found the Elven girl at all but for the bright silk of her
Rover clothing, a splash of red against the dark. She lay
lodged against a clump of scrub, the breath knocked from
her body, her face smeared with mud. Her eyes flickered
uncertainly as he touched her.

"Wil?"

He eased her into a sitting position, cradling her in his
arms. "Are you all right? Are you hurt?"

"No, I don't think so." She smiled. "You're pretty
clumsy, you know that?"

He nodded, grinning with relief. "Let's get you up."

He put his arm about her waist and lifted her clear of the
scrub, her small frame feather-light as he set her back on
her feet. Instantly she cried out and dropped back to the
earth, reaching for her ankle.

"It's twisted!"

Wil felt along the ankle, checking the bones. "Nothing
broken, just a bad sprain." He sat down beside her. "We
can take a few moments to rest, then go on. I can help you
down the slope; I can even carry you if it becomes
necessary."

She shook her head. "Wil, I am so sorry. I should have
been more careful."

"You? I was the one who fell." He grinned, trying to
appear cheerful. "Well, maybe one of the old man's Witch
Sisters will come along to help us out."

"That is not funny." Amberle frowned. She looked about
uneasily. "Maybe we should wait until morning to climb
down any further. My ankle might feel better by then.
Besides, even if we made it down before dark, we would
have to spend the night there, and I don't much care to do
that."

Wil nodded. "Nor I. Nor do I think we should try to find
our way about at night. Daylight will be soon enough."

"Maybe we should go back up to the rim." She looked at
him hopefully.

The Valeman smiled. "Do you really believe the old

man's story? Do you think there are Witches living down there?"

She stared at him darkly. "Don't you?"

He hesitated and then shrugged. "I don't know. Maybe. Yes, I guess so. There is very little I don't believe anymore." He sat forward slowly, arms coming up about his knees. "If there are Witches, I hope they are frightened of Elfstones, because that is just about all the protection we have left. Of course, if I have to use the Stones in order to make them afraid, we may be in a lot of trouble."

"I don't think so," she responded quietly.

"You still think I can use them, don't you—even after what happened on the Pykon?"

"Yes. But you shouldn't."

He looked at her. "You said something like that once before, remember? After the Tirfing, when we camped above the Mermidon. You were worried for me. You said that I should not use the Stones again, even if it meant saving you."

"I remember."

"Then later, when we fled the Pykon, I told you that I could no longer use the Stones, that their power was lost to me, that my Elven blood was not strong enough. You told me that I should not be so quick to judge myself—that you had confidence in me."

"I remember that, too."

"Well, look at what we have been saying. I think I should use the Stones, but don't think I can. You think I can, but don't think I should. Funny, isn't it?" He shook his head. "And we still don't know which of us is right, do we? Here we are, almost to Safehold, and I still haven't found out . . ."

He stopped suddenly, realizing what it was that he was saying.

"Well, it's not important," he finished, looking away. "Better that we never find out. Better that they be given back to my grandfather."

They were silent for a moment. Almost without thinking, Wil reached into the Rover tunic and lifted out the pouch that held the Elfstones. He fingered it idly and was about to return it again when he noticed something odd about its feel. Frowning, he opened the drawstrings and

dumped the contents into his open palm. He found himself
staring at three ordinary pebbles.

"Wil!" Amberle exclaimed in horror.

The Valeman stared at the pebbles in stunned silence, his
mind racing.

"Cephelo," he whispered finally. "Cephelo. Somehow
he switched these for the Stones. Last night, probably,
while we slept. It had to be then; they were in the pouch
that morning in Grimpen Ward—I checked." He rose
slowly, still talking. "But this morning, I forgot. I was so
tired last night—and you fell asleep almost at once. He
must have drugged the ale to be certain I would not awake.
No wonder he was so anxious to be rid of us. No wonder
he made light of Hebel's warning about the Hollows. He
would be happy if we never came back. The reward meant
nothing to him. It was the Elfstones that he wanted all
along."

He started up the trail, his face livid. Then abruptly he
remembered Amberle. Turning quickly back, he lifted the
Elven girl in his arms, held her close against him, and
scrambled back to the rim of the Hollows. For a moment he
looked about, then walked to a clump of high bushes
several yards back. Stepping beneath the shelter of their
boughs, he set the Elven girl down.

"I have to go back for the Elfstones," he declared quietly.
"If I leave you here, will you be all right?"

"Wil, you don't need the Stones."

He shook his head. "If we have to test that theory, I
would prefer that it be done with the Stones in my
possession. You heard what the old man said about the
Hollows. The Stones are all that I have to protect you."

Amberle's face was white. "Cephelo will kill you."

"Maybe. Maybe he has gotten so far up the trail by this
time that I won't even get close to him. But Amberle, I have
to try. If I don't find him by dawn, I'll turn back, I promise.
With or without the Elfstones, I will be with you to go into
the Hollows."

She started to say something more, but then stopped.
Tears ran down her cheeks. Her hands lifted to touch his
face.

"I care for you," she whispered. "I really do."

He looked at her in astonishment. "Amberle!"

"Go on," she urged him, her voice breaking. "Cephelo will have stopped for the night and you may catch him if you hurry. But be careful, Wil Ohmsford—do not give your life foolishly. Come back for me."

She reached up to kiss him. "Go. Quickly."

He stared at her wordlessly for one instant more, then sprang to his feet. Without looking back, he ran from her and in seconds had disappeared into the forest gloom.

XXXIX

At dawn of the same day that found Wil and Amberle faced with the disappearance of the Elfstones, the Demons attacked Arborlon. With a frightening shriek that shattered the morning stillness and reverberated through the lowland forests, they burst from the cover of the trees, a massive wave of humped and twisted bodies that stretched the length of the Carolan. In a frenzy that cast aside reason and thought, the creatures of the dark swept out of the gloom that was still thick within the shadowed woods and threw themselves into the waters of the Rill Song. Like a huge stain spreading over the water, they filled the river, large and small, swift and slow, leaping, crawling, shambling bodies surging and heaving through the swift current. Some swam the river's waters, thrusting and kicking to gain the far bank. Those light and fleet flew above, hopped upon, or skimmed over the river's surface. Others, so huge that they might walk upon the river's bottom, lunged awkwardly ahead, snouts and muzzles stretched high, bobbing and dipping. Many rode crude boats and rafts, poling mindlessly into the river and grasping tightly at whomever or whatever came within reach, thus to be pulled to safety or carried to the bottom with that which had failed to give them aid. Madness gripped the Demon horde, born of frustration with and hatred for the enemy that waited a scant few hundred yards away. This time, certainly, they would see that enemy destroyed.

But the Elves did not panic. Though the number, size, and ferocity of the Demons who came at them might have broken the spirit of a less determined defender, the Elves stood their ground. This was to be their final battle. It was their home city that they defended, the heart of the land that had been theirs for as long as the races had existed. All else had been lost now, from the Rill Song west. But the Elves were determined that they would not lose Arborlon. Better that they fight and die here, the last man, woman and child of them, than that they be driven entirely from their homeland, outcasts in foreign lands, hunted like animals by their pursuers.

Atop the battlements of the Elfitch, Ander Elessedil watched the Demon tide sweep forward. Allanon stood beside him. Neither man spoke. After a moment, Ander's eyes lifted. High overhead a small dot appeared out of the clear blue of the dawn skies, growing in size as it circled downward until it took shape. It was Dayn and his Roc, Dancer. Downward they flew, gliding along the cliffs of the Carolan to settle finally on the open rampway above Ander and the Druid. Dismounting, Dayn came hurriedly to where the Elven Prince waited.

"How many?" Ander asked at once.

Dayn shook his head. "Even the woods and the mist can't hide them all. The ones we see before us are only a handful."

Ander nodded. So many, he thought darkly. But Allanon had said it would be so. He refrained from looking at the Druid. "Do they seek to flank us, Dayn?"

The Wing Rider shook his head. "They come directly against the Carolan—all of them." He glanced down momentarily at the attacking Demons as they struggled and thrashed in the waters of the Rill Song, then turned and started back toward the battlements. "I'll rest Dancer a few minutes more, then fly back for another look. Good luck, my Lord Prince."

Ander barely heard him. "We must hold here," he murmured, almost to himself.

Already the struggle was underway. At the river's edge, row upon row of Elven longbows hummed, and black shafts flew into the mass of heaving bodies that filled the waters of the Rill Song. Arrows bounced like harmless twigs from those armored with scales and leather hides, yet some found their mark, and the screams of their victims rose above the cries of attack. Dark forms twisted and sank into the boiling waters, lost in the wave of bodies that came after. Fire-tipped arrows thudded into the boats, rafts, and logs, but most were quickly extinguished and the craft churned ahead. Again and again the archers shot into the advancing horde as it streamed out of the forest and into the river, but the Demons came on, blackening the whole of the west bank and the river as they struggled to gain the Elven defensive wall.

Then a cry sounded from atop the Carolan, and cheers rang out. In the predawn gloom, Elves turned hurriedly to look, disbelief and joy reflecting in their faces as a tall, gray-haired rider came into view. Down the length of the Elfitch the cry passed on from mouth to mouth. All along the front line of the Rill Song, behind the barricades and walls, it rose into the morning until it became a deafening roar.

"Eventine! Eventine rides to join us!"

In an instant's time the Elves were transformed, filled with new hope, new faith, new life. For here was the King who had ruled them almost sixty years—for many the whole of their lives. Here was the King who had stood against and finally triumphed over the Warlock Lord. Here was the King who had seen them through every crisis the homeland had faced. Wounded at Halys Cut, seemingly lost, he was returned again. With his return surely no evil, however monstrous, could prevail against them.

Eventine!

Yet something was wrong; Ander knew it the instant his father dismounted and turned to face him. This was not the Eventine of old, as his people believed. He saw in the King's eyes a distance separating the Elven ruler from all that was happening about him. It was as if he had withdrawn into himself, not out of fear or uncertainty, for he could master those, but out of deep, abiding sadness that seemed to have broken his spirit. He looked strong enough, the mask of his face reflecting determination and iron will, and he acknowledged those about him with the old, familiar words of encouragement. Yet the eyes betrayed the loss he felt, the despondency that had stripped him of his heart. His son read it there and saw that Allanon read it, too. It was only the shell of the King riding forth that morning to be with his people. Perhaps it was the deaths of Arion and Pindanon that had done this; it might have been the injury he had suffered at Halys Cut, the defeat of his army there, or the terrible devastation of his homeland; but more probably it was all of these and something more—the thought of failing, the knowledge that if the Elves lost this battle they would allow an evil into the Four Lands that no one could stop and which would fall upon all the races and devour them. The responsibility for this must lie with the Elves, yet with no man more than with Eventine, for he was their King.

Ander embraced his father warmly, masking the sadness that he felt. Then he stepped back and held forth the Ellcrys staff.

"This belongs to you, my Lord."

Eventine seemed to hesitate momentarily, then slowly shook his head. "No, Ander. It belongs to you now. You must carry it for me."

Ander stared at his father wordlessly. He saw in the old man's eyes what he had missed before. His father knew. He knew that he was not well, knew that something within him was changed. The pretense he made to others was not to be made to his son.

Ander withdrew the staff. "Then stand with me on the wall, my Lord," he asked softly.

His father nodded, and together they climbed the battlements.

Even as they did so, the foremost of the Demon horde gained the east bank of the Rill Song. Out of the river they surged, heaving up with savage cries to throw themselves against the lances and pikes that bristled from behind the Elven bulwarks. In moments there were Demons emerging from the river's dark waters along the entire length of the defensive line, horned and clawed, a jumble of limbs and jaws ripping and tearing at the defenders that barred their path. At its center, Stee Jans and the last of his Free Corps anchored the defense, the giant red-haired Borderman standing at the forefront of his men, broadsword raised. On the flanks, Ehlron Tay and Kerrin of the Home Guard called out to their soldiers: Hold, Elven Hunters, stand!

But finally they could stand no longer. Outflanked and outnumbered, they saw their line begin to crumble. Huge Demons thrust through the defenders and breached the low walls to open holes to those who followed. The waters of the Rill Song were dark with Demon lifeblood and

twisted bodies; but, for every one that fell, still another
three came on, a savage rush that no lesser force could
hope to stop. Atop the gates of the second level of the
Elfitch, Ander gave the order to fall back. Quickly the Elves
and their allies abandoned the crumbling river wall and
slipped into the forest behind, following carefully memo-
rized paths to the safety of the ramp. Almost before the
Demons realized what was happening, the defenders were
within its walls and the gates were shut behind them.

Instantly the Demons were in pursuit. Pouring through
the forest at the base of the heights, they ran afoul of the
hundreds of snares and pitfalls the Elves had laid for them.
For a few moments, the entire rush stalled. But as their
numbers increased upon the riverbank, they overran those
caught within the traps and came onto the ramp of the
Elfitch. Massing quickly, they attacked. Up the walls of the
first gate they charged, swarming atop one another until
they were pouring over the defenses of the lower level. The
Elves were driven back; almost before the gates to the
second level could be closed, the first had fallen. Without
slowing, the Demons came on, scrambling up the ramp to
the second gate. They swarmed along the walls and even
up the rugged face of the cliff, clinging to the rock like
insects. Bodies clawed, leaped, and bounded up the slope
of the ramp and the bluff face, shrieking with hunger. The
Elves were appalled. The river had not stopped the
Demons. The defenses at the bank had been overrun in
minutes. Now the first level of the Elfitch had been lost and
even the cliff wall did not seem to slow them. It was
beginning to look as if all their defenses would prove
useless.

Demon bodies thudded against the gates of the second
ramp, clawing upward. Spears and pikes thrust down,
impaling the attackers. The gates sagged on their hinges
with the weight of the rush. Yet this time the defenders
held, iron and sinew bracing the gates and repelling the
attack. Cries of pain and death filled the air, and the Demon
force built into a mass of writhing forms, surging mindlessly against the walls of the ramp. Out of their midst came a
handful of Furies, lithe gray forms bounding atop the stone
walls, cat-women's faces twisted with hate. Elven defenders fell back from them, shredded by their claws, crying

out in fear. Then Allanon's blue fire burst amid the Furies, scattering them wildly. The Elves counterattacked, throwing the cat-things from the walls until the last had disappeared into the dark mass below.

The Druid and the Elessedils moved upward to the third gate. From there they watched as the Demon attack gathered force. Still the Elven defenders held, archers from the higher levels lending support to the lancers and pikemen below. Demons clung to the cliff face all about the ramp of the Elfitch, working their way upward toward the heights in a slow, arduous climb. From atop the bluff, the Dwarf Sappers used longbows and boulders to knock the black forms loose. One after another the Demons fell, screaming and twisting to the rocks below.

Then suddenly a monstrous Demon rose out of the attackers that came at the gates of the second ramp, a scaled creature that stood upon its hind legs like a human but had the body and head of a lizard. Hissing in fury, it threw its bulk against the gates, snapping the crossbars and loosening the hinges. In desperation the Elves sought to thrust it back, but the monstrous thing merely shrugged aside the blows, Elven weapons snapping apart on its armored body. A second time it threw itself against the gates and this time they split apart, shattering backward into the Elves. The defenders fell back at once, fleeing up the Elfitch to the third level where the next set of gates stood open to receive them. The lizard thing and its brethren followed after, pouring onto the rampway.

For an instant it did not appear that the Elves would succeed in closing the gates to the third ramp before the Demons breached it. Then Stee Jans appeared at the entrance to the ramp, a huge spear gripped in his hands. Flanked by the veteran soldiers of the Free Corps and by Kerrin and a handful of Home Guard, he stepped in front of the advancing Demons. Dropping forward in a crouch, the lizard Demon reached for him. But the Borderman was too quick. Sidestepping the monster's lunge, he thrust the great spear upward through the back of the gaping jaws. Hissing and choking, the lizard reared back on its hind legs, the shaft driven through its head. Clawed hands ripped at the Legion Commander, but the men of the Free Corps and the Elves rallied about him, warding off the blows. In seconds, they were back within the safety of the battlements, the gates closing behind them. For an instant the lizard Demon stood within the center of the ramphead, trying to pull free the killing shaft. Then its life was gone, and it fell backward into the midst of its brethren, sweeping them from the ramp as it tumbled over the wall and dropped to the forest below.

Snarling, the Demons renewed their attack. But their momentum had been lost. Strung out along the length of the Elfitch, they could not seem to muster a sustained rush. The biggest among them had been slain; lacking another to take his place, they milled uncertainly within the walls of the ramp below. Heartened by the courage of the Free Corps and their own Home Guard, the Elven defenders beat them back. Arrows and spears cut into their midst, and hundreds of black forms collapsed upon the ramp. Still the Demons scrambled forward, but confused now and vulnerable.

Ander recognized his opportunity. He gave the signal to counterattack. At Kerrin's order, the gates to the third ramp were thrown wide and the Elves rushed forth. Into the mass of Demons they charged, driving them back down the Elfitch, back through the shattered gates of the second ramp. Sweeping clear the ramp, the defenders battled downward to the edge of the lower gates before the Demons finally rallied. Back they came, reinforced by the thousands that still poured out of the Rill Song to the base of the cliff. The Elves held a moment only, then retreated to the gates of the second level, bracing them anew with timbers and iron, and there they stood.

So it went for the remainder of the day and into the evening. Back and forth along the rampway the battle raged, from the base of the bluff to the gates of the third level, Elves and Demons hacking and tearing at one another in a struggle where no quarter was asked and none given. Twice the Demons retook the second set of gates and pushed up against the third. Twice they were driven back, once all the way to the base of the bluff. Thousands died, though the dead numbered highest among Demons, for they fought without regard for life, spending themselves willingly on the defenders' carefully drawn formations. Yet Elves were lost as well, injured and dead, and their numbers began to dwindle steadily while the numbers of the Demons never seemed to grow less.

Then abruptly, without warning, the Demons gave up the attack. Back down the length of the Elfitch they went, not in flight nor in haste, but slowly, reluctantly, snarling and rasping as they faded back into the forests. Black forms huddled down in the shadowed gloom of night, crouched motionless and silent as if waiting for something to happen. Behind the gates and walls of the Elfitch and from the rim of the Carolan, the exhausted defenders peered down into the dark. They did not question what had happened, but were merely grateful for it. For one more day, at least, the city of Arborlon was safe.

That same night, scarcely two hours after the Demons had withdrawn into the wooded blackness below the Carolan, a messenger came to Eventine and Ander as they met with the Elven Ministers in the High Council. In an excited voice, he announced that an army of Rock Trolls had arrived from the Kershalt. Hurriedly, the King and his son emerged from the council building, the others trailing after, to find the entire courtyard filled with row upon row of massive, barklike forms, armored with leather and iron. Broadswords and spears glimmered in the smoky light of torches ringing the assemblage, and a sea of deep-set eyes fixed on the Elves' astonished faces.

Their Commander stepped forward, a huge Troll with a great, two-edged axe strapped across his back. With a quick glance at the other Elves, he placed himself before the King.

"I am Amantar, Maturen of this army," he informed them, speaking in the rough Troll dialect. "We are fifteen hundred strong, King Eventine. We come to stand with the Elves."

Eventine was speechless. They had all but given up on the Trolls, believing that the Northlanders had chosen not to become involved in this conflict. Now, to find them suddenly here, just when it appeared that no more help would be coming . . .

Amantar saw the old King's surprise. "King Eventine, you must know that much thought was given to your request for aid," he growled softly. "Always before, Trolls

and Elves have fought against one another; we have been
enemies. That cannot be forgotten all at once. Yet for
everyone, there is a time to begin anew. That time has
come for Elf and Troll. We know of the Demons. There
have been encounters with a scattering of them already.
There have been injuries; there have been deaths. The
Rock Trolls understand the danger that the Demons pose.
The Demons are as great an evil as the Warlock Lord and
the creatures of the Skull mark. Such evil threatens all.
Therefore it is seen that Elf and Troll must put aside their
differences and stand together against this common enemy.
We have come, my countrymen and I, to stand with you."

It was an eloquent statement. Amantar finished and, in a
carefully measured gesture, dropped to one knee, signify-
ing in the manner of the Rock Trolls his pledge of service.
Behind him, his men followed him down, silent as they
knelt before Eventine.

Ander saw the tears that appeared suddenly in the old
man's eyes. For that one moment, Eventine came all the
way back from the place to which he had withdrawn, and
there was hope and fierce pride in his face. Slowly he
placed his right hand on his heart, returning the Trolls'
pledge in the Elven way. Amantar rose, and the two
clasped hands.

Ander found himself wanting to cheer.

Allanon walked the narrow paths of the Gardens of Life
beneath a clouded night sky through which moon and
stars slipped like hunted things. Solitary, noiseless, his tall
form passed through the cooling, fragrant blackness of the
flowered tiers and sculpted hedges, head bent to the walk
before him, arms gathered within the folds of the long,
dark robe. His hard face was lost within the shadow of the
cowl, lean features etched with lines of worry and bitter
resolve. For this night he went to a meeting with death.

He walked to the foot of the rise ringed by the soldiers of
the Black Watch. Impatient, he lifted his hand and slipped
through them with the swiftness of a passing thought, and
they did not see. Slowly he climbed to the top of the rise,
not wishing to look at that which he had come to see, eyes
lowered and fixed upon the grassy slope he trod.

When at last he was atop the rise, his head lifted. Before

him stood the Ellcrys, the once slender and graceful limbs withered and bent like the drying bones of some dead thing. Gone was the fragrance and the color, so that no more than a shadow remained of what had once been so incredibly beautiful. Blood-red leaves lay scattered upon the ground like wads of crumpled parchment. The tree stood bare, nailed against the night sky in a tangle of sticks and peeling bark.

Allanon went cold. Even he had not been prepared for this, not for what he saw, nor for what he felt in seeing. Sorrow welled up within him at the inevitability of what was happening. He was powerless to prevent this, for even the Druids lacked the gift of life eternal. All things must one day pass from the earth, and it was her time.

His hand lifted to touch her withered limbs, then dropped again. He did not want to feel her pain. Yet he knew that he must have the measure of her, and he brought his hand up again, slowly, gently clasping. Just an instant he lingered, willing a sense of comfort and hope to flow from his mind into her own, then withdrew. Another day or two, perhaps three. No more. Then she would be gone.

His tall form straightened, hands falling limply to his sides as his dark eyes fixed upon the dying tree. So little time.

As he turned away he wondered if that little time would be time enough to bring Amberle back again.

XL

Wil Ohmsford raced back through the forest of the Wilderun, following the dark rut of the pathway as it tunneled ahead through mist and gloom. Trailing limbs and vines heavy with dampness brushed and slapped at him as he ran, and water splattered from puddles dotting the rain-soaked trail, leaving him streaked with mud. But the Valeman felt none of it, his mind crowded with emotions that spun and twisted to leave him dazed with despair at the loss of the Elfstones—anger against Cephelo, fear for Amberle, and wonderment at the words she had spoken to him.

I care for you, she had said and meant it. I care for you. So strange to hear her say such a thing to him. Once he would never have believed it possible. She had resented and mistrusted him; she had made that clear enough. And he had not really liked this Elven girl. But the long journey they had begun in the village of Havenstead had taught them much about each other, and the dangers and hardships they had faced and overcome had brought them close. Their lives in that brief span of time had become inextricably bound together. It was not really so unexpected then that out of that binding should come some form of affection. The words throbbed in his head, repeating themselves. I care for you. She did, he knew, and wondered suddenly how much he in turn now cared for her.

He lost his footing and went down, tumbling forward into the muck and the damp. Angrily he scrambled up, brushed the mud and water away as best he could, and ran on. The afternoon was waning far too rapidly; he would be fortunate just to regain the main roadway before nightfall

416

set in. When that happened, he would have to find his way in total blackness, alone in an unfamiliar land, weaponless save for a hunting knife. Stupid! That was the kindest description he could render for what he had done, letting Cephelo fool him into thinking that he could have the Rover's aid for nothing more than a vague promise. Clever Wil Ohmsford, he chided himself, anger burning through him. And Allanon had thought that you were the one to whom he might safely entrust Amberle!

Already his muscles were beginning to cramp with the strain of running. Despair washed through him for a moment as he thought of all that Amberle and he had endured to reach this point, only to face losing everything for want of a bit more caution. Seven Elven Hunters had given their lives so that he and Amberle might reach the Wilderun. Countless more would have already died defending the Westland against the Demons, for surely the Forbidding had given way by now. All for nothing, then? All to no end but this? Shame and then determination rushed through him, carrying away the despair. He would never give up—never! He would retrieve the stolen Elfstones. He would return to Amberle. He would see her safely to Spire's Reach, to the Bloodfire, and back once more to Arborlon. He would do all this because he knew that he must, because to do anything less would be to fail—not just Allanon and the Elves, but himself as well. He was not about to do that.

Even as the thought passed from his mind, a shadow appeared on the trail ahead, materializing out of the gloom like some wraith, tall and silent as it awaited his approach. The Valeman drew up short, frightened so badly that he very nearly bolted from the pathway into the forest. Breathing raggedly, he stared at the shadow, realizing suddenly that what he was looking at was a horse and rider. The horse shifted on the trail and stamped. Wil walked forward cautiously, wariness turning to disbelief and finally to astonishment.

It was Eretria.

"Surprised?" Her voice was cool and measured.

"Very," he admitted.

"I have come to save you one last time, Wil Ohmsford. This time, I think, you will hear better what I have to say."

Wil came up to her and stopped. "Cephelo has the Stones."

"I know that. He drugged your wine, then took them from you last night while you slept."

"And you did nothing to warn me?"

"Warn you?" She shook her head slowly. "I would have warned you, Healer. I would have helped you. But you would not help me—remember? All that I asked of you was that you take me with you when you left. Had you done that, I would have told you of Cephelo's plans for the Elfstones and would have seen to it that you kept them safe. But you spurned me, Healer. You left me. You thought yourself able to manage well enough without me. Very well, I decided, I will see how well the Healer does without me."

She bent down to examine him, her eyes appraising. "It does not appear that you are doing too well."

Wil nodded slowly, his mind racing. This was no time to say something foolish. "Amberle is hurt. She fell and twisted her leg and cannot walk alone. I had to leave her at the rim of the Hollows."

"You seem very good at leaving women in distress," Eretria snapped.

He held his temper. "I guess it must appear that way. But sometimes we cannot always do what we want when it comes to helping others."

"So you have said. I guess that you must believe it. Have you left the Elven girl, then?"

"Only until I get the Stones back again."

"Which you won't without me."

"Which I will, with or without you."

The Rover girl stared down at him for a moment, and her face softened.

"I guess you believe that, too, don't you?"

Wil put his hand on the horse's flank. "Are you here to help me, Eretria?"

She regarded him wordlessly for a moment, then nodded. "If you, in turn, will help me. This time you must, you know." When he did not respond, she continued speaking. "A trade, Wil Ohmsford. I will help you get back the Stones if you will agree to take me with you when you have them back again."

"How will you get the Stones back?" he asked carefully.

She smiled for the first time, that familiar, dazzlingly beautiful smile that took his breath away. "How will I do it? Healer, I am the child of Rovers and the daughter of a thief—bought and paid for. He stole them from you; I will steal them from him. I know the trade better than he. All we need do is find him."

"Won't he be wondering about you by now?"

She shook her head. "When we parted company with you, I told him that I wished to ride ahead to join the caravan. He agreed that I could, for the paths of the Wilderun are well known to the Rovers, and I would be clear of the valley by nightfall. As you know, Healer, he wants to be certain that he keeps me safe. Damaged goods bring a poor price. In any case, I rode but a mile beyond Whistle Ridge, then took a second trail that cuts south and joins this one several hundred yards further back. I thought to catch up to you by nightfall, either at the Hollows or coming back this way, should you discover sooner the loss of the Stones. So you see, Cephelo will not realize what I have done until he reaches the main caravan. The wagon slows him, so he will not do that until sometime tomorrow. Tonight, he will camp on the road leading out of the valley."

"Then we have tonight to get back the Stones," Wil finished.

"Time enough," she replied. "But not if we continue to stand here and talk about it. Besides, you don't want to leave the Elven girl alone at the Hollows for very long, do you?"

The mention of Amberle jarred him. "No. Let's be off."

"One moment." She backed the horse away from him. "First your word. Once I have helped you, then you will help me. You will take me with you when we have the Stones back. You will let me stay with you after that until I am a safe distance from Cephelo—and I will decide when that is the case. Promise me, Healer."

There was very little else that he could do short of taking her horse from her, and he was not at all sure that he could do that.

"Very well. I promise."

She nodded. "Good. To see that you keep that promise, I

will keep the Stones once I have taken them back again until we are both safely out of this valley. Climb up behind me."

Wil mounted the horse without comment. There was no way that he was about to let her keep the Elfstones, once she had retrieved them from Cephelo, but it was pointless to argue about it here. He settled himself behind the girl, and she turned to look at him.

"You do not deserve what I am doing for you—you know that. But I like you; I like your chances in life—especially with me to aid you. Put your hands about my waist."

Wil hesitated, then did as he was told. Eretria leaned back into him.

"Much better," she purred seductively. "I prefer you this way to the way you are when the Elven girl is about. Now hold tight."

With a sudden yell, she put her boots into the flanks of the horse. The startled beast reared up with a scream and shot back along the pathway. Down the wilderness trail they rode, bent low across the horse's neck, limbs whipping against them as they flew through the dark. Eretria seemed to have the eyes of a cat, guiding their mount with a sure and practiced hand past fallen logs and deadwood, over gullies and ruts formed by the sudden rain, down one muddied slope and up the next. Wil hung on desperately, wondering if the girl had lost her mind. At this pace, they were certain to take a fall.

Amazingly, they did not. Scant seconds later, Eretria wheeled their horse from the trail through a narrow gap in the trees that was all but completely grown over. With a surge, the animal sprang into the brush, then broke free along a second trail—one that Wil had missed completely in his trek south to the Hollows—and galloped ahead into the misty gloom. On they rode, Rover girl and Valeman, barely slowing for the obstacles that barred their path forward, racing ahead into the growing dark. What little light there was had begun to fade as dusk approached. The sun, lost somewhere beyond the canopy of the forest, sank downward toward the rim of the mountains. Shadows deepened and the air cooled and still Eretria did not slow. When at last they did stop, they were back once more on the main roadway. Eretria reined the horse in sharply, patted the animal's sweating flanks and glanced back at Wil with an impish grin.

"That was just to let you know that I can hold my own with anyone. I need no looking after from you."

The Valeman felt his stomach begin to settle. "You have made your point, Eretria. Why are we stopping here?"

"Just to check," she replied, and dismounted. Her eyes scanned the trail for a few moments, and then she frowned. "That's odd. There are no wagon tracks."

Wil followed her down. "Are you sure?" He studied the roadway, finding no sign of wheel marks. "Maybe the rain washed them out."

"The wagon was heavy enough that the rain should not have washed away all traces of its passing." She shook her head slowly. "Besides, the rain would have been nearly ended by the time it reached this point. I don't understand it, Healer."

The light was growing steadily dimmer. Wil glanced about apprehensively. "Would Cephelo have stopped to wait out the storm?"

"Maybe." She looked doubtful. "We had better backtrack a bit. Climb on."

They remounted and began riding west, glancing from time to time at the muddied earth for some sign of the Rover wagon. There was nothing. Eretria urged their mount into a slow trot. Ahead, mist curled out of the forest on either side, thin, wispy trailers that slipped like feelers through the gloom. Night sounds came from deep within the trees as the creatures of the valley awoke and began to hunt.

Then a new sound rose from somewhere ahead, faint at first, lingering like an echo in the midst of the sharper, quicker sounds, then stronger and more insistent. It grew into a howl, high-pitched and eerie, as if such pain had been inflicted upon some tortured soul that the limits of endurance had been passed and all that was left before death was that final, terrible cry of anguish.

Wil gripped Eretria's shoulder in alarm. "What is that?"

She glanced back. "Whistle Ridge—just ahead." She grinned nervously. "The wind makes that sound sometimes."

It grew worse, a harsher, more biting cry, and the land began to rise through the forest in a rocky slope that took them above the mist, the trees parting to reveal small patches of blue night sky. The horse had begun to respond to the sounds, huffing nervously, dancing and shifting as Eretria sought to calm it. They moved more slowly now, edging ahead through the dusk until they were atop the ridge line. Beyond, the roadway straightened once more and disappeared into the gloom.

Wil saw something then, a shadow moving toward them, materializing out of the howl of the wind and the night. Eretria saw it as well and reined in sharply. The shadow came closer. It was a horse, a big sorrel, riderless, its reins trailing in the earth. It came slowly up to them and rubbed noses with their own mount. Both Valeman and Rover girl recognized it at once. It was Cephelo's.

Eretria dismounted, handing the reins of her own horse to Wil. Wordlessly, she examined the sorrel, walking quickly about it, patting its flanks and neck to keep it calm. There were no marks on the animal, but it was sweating heavily. When she glanced again at Wil, Eretria's dark face was uncertain.

"Something has happened. His horse would not stray."

The Valeman nodded. He was beginning to get a very bad feeling about this.

Eretria climbed atop Cephelo's horse and took up the reins. "We will go on a bit further," she decided, but there was doubt in her voice.

Side by side, they rode along the ridge line, the wind whistling its eerie cry through the high rock and the trees of the forest. Overhead, the stars winked into view, pale white light shining down into the dark of the Wilderun.

Then something else appeared through the gloom, another shadow, this one black and squarish and motionless upon the trail. Valeman and Rover girl slowed, easing their horses ahead cautiously, uneasiness reflecting in their eyes. Gradually the shadow began to take shape. It was Cephelo's wagon, the garish colors caught in the starlight. They rode closer, and uneasiness then turned to horror. The team of horses that had pulled the wagon was dead, twisted and broken, still locked in their leather and silver-studded traces. Several more of the animals lay close by and, with them, their riders, scattered on the trail like straw men, torn and crumpled, bright clothing stained with blood that seeped through the fabric to mix with the muddied earth.

Quickly Wil looked about, peering into the shadows of the forest, searching for some sign of the thing that had done this. Nothing moved. He glanced at Eretria. She sat rigid on her mount, the color draining from her face as she stared fixedly at the bodies on the trail. Her hands dropped slowly to her lap, and the reins slipped free. Wil dismounted, scooped up the fallen reins, and tried to hand them back to the frightened girl. When Eretria did not move to take them, he gripped her hands, placed the reins of both horses between her fingers, and forced them closed. She glanced down at him wordlessly.

"Wait here," he ordered.

He walked toward the wagon, studying the twisted forms about him as he went. All lay dead, even the old woman who had driven the wagon, bodies broken like deadwood. The Valeman felt his skin crawl. He knew what had done this. One by one, he checked them until at last he found Cephelo. The big man was dead as well, his tall form stretched full length upon the ground, forest-green cloak shredded, angular features frozen with a look of horror. So ruined was his body that it was nearly impossible to recognize.

Wil bent down. Slowly he felt through the dead Rover's clothing, searching for the Elfstones. He found nothing. Fear knotted his stomach. He had to find the Stones. Then he noticed Cephelo's hands. The right hand clutched at the earth in a gesture that spoke of unbearable agony. The left was flung wide and closed into a fist. The Valeman took a deep breath and reached for the left. One by one he pried open the rigid fingers. Blue light winked from between them, and relief flooded through him. Embedded in the flesh of the palm lay the Elfstones. Cephelo had sought to use them as he had seen Wil do in the Tirfing, but the Stones had not responded to the Rover and he had died still clutching them.

The Valeman pulled them free of the dead man's grip, wiped them on his tunic, and dropped them back into their leather pouch. Then he rose, listening to the shriek of the wind whistling through the ridge. Dizziness washed over him as the smell of death filled his nostrils. Only one thing could have done this. He remembered the Elven dead at the camp at Drey Wood and in the fortress of the Pykon. Only one thing. The Reaper. But how had it found them again? How had it trailed them all the way from the Pykon to the Wilderun?

He steadied himself and hastened back to Eretria. She still sat astride Cephelo's horse, dark eyes bright with fear.

"Did you find him?" she asked in a whisper. "Cephelo?"

Wil nodded. "He's dead. They're all dead." He paused. "I took back the Stones."

She did not seem to hear him. "What kind of thing could do this, Healer? Some animal, maybe? Or the Witch Sisters, or . . . ?"

"No." He shook his head quickly. "No, Eretria, I know what did this. The thing that did this tracked Amberle and me all the way south from Arborlon. I thought that we had lost it on the other side of the Rock Spur, but somehow it has found us again."

Her voice shook. "Is it a Devil?"

"A special kind of Devil." He glanced back at the dead upon the trail. "They call it a Reaper." He thought a moment. "It must have believed we were traveling with Cephelo. Perhaps the rain confused it. It followed after him and caught him here . . ."

"Poor Cephelo," she murmured. "He played one game too many." She paused and glanced back at him sharply. "Healer, this thing knows now that you did not come east with Cephelo. Where will it go next?"

Valeman and Rover girl stared wordlessly at each other. Both knew the answer.

At the rim of the Hollows, Amberle crouched within the shelter of the bushes where Wil had hidden her and listened to the sounds of the night. Darkness lay over the Wilderun like a shroud, deep and impenetrable, and the Elven girl sat locked within it, unable to see beyond the covering brush, hearing the creatures that prowled the gloom. Knowing that it would be dawn before Wil could return to her, she tried for a time to sleep. But sleep would not come; her ankle pained her and her mind crowded with thoughts of the Valeman and his quest, of her grandfather, of the dangers all about her. At last she gave it up. With her knees pulled up against her body, she hunched forward, determined that she would become as nearly as she could a part of the forest about her, still, motionless, and unseen.

For a time she succeeded. None of the forest creatures ventured near her, staying back within the deep woods, back from the rim of the Hollows. The Hollows themselves lay wrapped in a silence so profound that the Elven girl could hear it as clearly as she heard the sounds of the night. Once or twice something flew past her shelter, the quick flap of wings breaking the stillness briefly, then fading once more. Time slipped away, and she began to nod sleepily.

Then the chill swept through her suddenly, as if the warmth had been sapped from the air about her. She came awake and rubbed her arms briskly. The chill left and the heat of the summer night slipped back across her. Uncertain now, she glanced about her shelter. Everything was as it had been before; in the darkness nothing moved, nothing sounded. She took a deep breath and closed her eyes again. The chill came back. She waited this time before moving, keeping her eyes tightly shut, trying to trace the source of the chill. She discovered that it came from somewhere within herself. She did not understand. Cold, bitter cold, within her, pushing through her, numbing like the touch of . . . death.

Her eyes snapped wide. Instantly she understood. She was being warned—how she did not know—that something was going to kill her. Had she been anyone but who she was, she might have ignored the feeling as being nothing more than the workings of her imagination. But she was highly sentient; such feelings had come over her before and she knew better than to dismiss them. The warning was real. It was only the source that confused her.

She hunched forward in momentary indecision. Something was coming for her, something monstrous, something that would destroy her. She could not hide from it; she could not stand against it. She could only run.

Ignoring the pain in her ankle, she slipped from beneath the bushes, crouched down beyond them, and stared into

the forest gloom. The thing that stalked her was close; she
could sense its presence clearly now as it moved soundlessly through the night. She thought suddenly of Wil, and she
wished desperately that he were there to help her. But Wil
was not there. She must save herself and she must do so
quickly.

There was only one place for her to go, one place that her
stalker might not follow—the Hollows. She hobbled to
their edge and stared down into the depthless black. Fear
gripped her. The Hollows were as frightening to her as the
thing behind. She steadied herself, green eyes sweeping
across the black to the tower of Spire's Reach. It was there
that she must go. It was there that Wil would look for her.

She found a pathway leading down and started along it,
easing carefully into the shadows. In moments, she was
enveloped by the blackness; the light of the stars and moon
were lost above the trees. Her child's face tightened with
determination, and she felt her way forward. She kept as
still in her movements as she was able, and there was only
the slight scraping of her boots on earth and rock to betray
her passage. Below, there was only silence.

At last she was on the floor of the Hollows. She paused
then, sitting back against a tree trunk, rubbing gingerly the
injured ankle. It was badly swollen by now, aggravated by
her decision to walk upon it. Sweat bathed her face as she
stared upward into the gloom and listened. She heard
nothing. No matter, she told herself. Whatever it was that
sought her, it was up there still, searching. She had to get
deeper into the Hollows. Her eyes had begun to adjust to
the blackness; she could discern vaguely the shapes of
trees and clumps of brush about her. It was time to go on.

She pushed herself up and hobbled ahead into the dark,
trying to keep her weight off her injured ankle. Moving
from one tree to the next, she rested a moment at each,
listening anxiously to the deep silence. The pain was
growing worse, a steady throb that seemed to intensify
with each step forward. The muscles of her good leg had
stiffened and cramped with the constant hobbling; already
she was beginning to tire.

Finally she had to stop. Breathing heavily, she lowered
herself to the ground beside a thicket and leaned back
against the cooling earth. Carefully, she composed herself

and tried to trace anew the source of the warning. For a moment nothing happened. Then the chill swept back across her, penetrating, biting. She caught her breath. The thing that sought her was within the Hollows.

She hauled herself back to her feet and went on, limping blindly through the gloom. At one point it occurred to her that she might be traveling in a circle, but she pushed the thought quickly from her mind. She fell constantly. Several times she went down so hard that she nearly blacked out. Each time she came to her knees gasping for breath, rose, and forced herself to go forward. The minutes slipped by until she lost all track of time. About her, the silence and the dark deepened.

At last she could go no further. She fell to her knees, the sound of her breathing harsh in her ears. Crying with frustration, she began to crawl. Rock and deadwood scraped at her hands and knees as she worked her way through the brush, her ankle throbbing with pain. She would not give up, she swore silently. The thing would not have her. She turned her thoughts to Wil. She saw in her mind the look that had crossed his face when she told him that she cared for him. She should not have said it, she knew. But she had wanted to tell him so badly at that moment; she had needed to tell him. It surprised her how much she had needed to tell him. And the wonder in his eyes . . .

She collapsed on her face, weeping. Wil! She whispered his name like a talisman to ward off the evil that stalked her through the blackness. Then she lifted herself and crawled on. Her mind wandered, and she seemed to sense the presence of other creatures about her, moving with her through the night, quick and all but soundless. Little people, she thought. But the thing, where was the thing? How close to her was it?

She crawled and crawled until her strength was gone entirely; then she lay down upon the forest earth. She was finished, she knew. She had nothing left to draw upon. Her eyes closed and she waited to die. A moment later, she slept.

She was still sleeping when the crooked wooden fingers of a dozen gnarled hands lifted her up and bore her away.

XLI

The Valeman and the Rover girl rode down the rock-strewn trail and off Whistle Ridge, the wind whistling past their ears. Into the blackness of the lower forest they flew, Rover silks whipping about their bodies as they bent low across their horses' necks and peered blindly into the gloom. The trees quickly closed about them and the night sky disappeared. With reckless disregard for their lives, they rode on, trusting to the surefootedness of their mounts and to luck.

There was no discussion of this; they had no time for discussion. The instant that Wil realized that the Reaper would backtrack until it found the trail Amberle and he had taken south to the Hollows after parting company with the Rovers, his mind went blank to every thought but one—Amberle would be at the end of that trail, alone, injured, and unprotected. If he did not reach her before the Reaper did, she would die, and it would be his fault because it had been his decision to leave her. An image of the torn and broken bodies of the Rovers on the trail flashed in his mind. At that moment he forgot everything but his need to get to Amberle. Scrambling back atop his horse, he wheeled the animal about and galloped away.

Eretria gave chase immediately. She might have done otherwise. With Cephelo dead, she had no further need for the Valeman's protection. She no longer belonged to anyone; she was her own person at last. She might have turned her horse about and ridden safely from the valley and the terrible thing that had killed Cephelo and the others. But Eretria did not even stop to consider this. She thought only of Wil, riding off without her, leaving her behind once more. Pride, stubbornness, and the strange attraction she felt for the Valeman flared within her. She could not permit him to do this to her again. Without hesitating, she went after him.

So began their race to save Amberle. Wil Ohmsford, riding as if he were a man possessed, quickly lost all track of where he was. Gloom and mist slipped about him as he came down off the ridge line into the deep forest, and he could barely make out the dark shapes of the trees at either side as he whipped past them. Yet he did not slow; he could not. He heard the sound of another horse following and realized that Eretria had come after him. He muttered a quick oath; did he not have enough to worry about already? But there was no time to concern himself with the Rover girl. He dismissed her from his thoughts and concentrated his efforts on finding the cutoff leading south.

Even so, he rode right past it. If Eretria had not called out to him, he might have kept riding east all the way to the mountains. Wheeling about in surprise, he charged back again. But now Eretria had taken the lead, spurring her mount forward into the darkness. More familiar than he with the trail, she galloped ahead, calling for him to follow. Surprised all over again, he gave chase.

It was a harrowing ride. The darkness was so thorough that even the sharp eyes of the Rover girl could barely pick out the pathway as it twisted through the forest night. Several times the horses almost went down, barely springing clear of gullies and fallen logs that lay across the narrow trail. But these were Rover horses, trained by the finest riders in the Four Lands, and they responded with a quickness and agility that brought a fierce cry from the lips of the Rover girl and left the Valeman breathless.

Then suddenly they were back upon the roadway that Amberle and Wil had followed south to the Hollows, with branches and vines slapping against them and muddied water splashing up from the deep puddles that had collected upon the trail. Without slowing, they turned south. The minutes slipped by.

At last they broke from the forest onto the rim of the Hollows, its black circle spread out before them like some bottomless pit in the earth. Reining in their horses sharply, they sprang to the ground, staring about at the forest gloom. Silence hung across the Hollows, deep and perva-

sive. Wil hesitated only a second, then began searching for
the bushes in which he had hidden Amberle. He found
them almost at once and pushed his way to their center.
There was no one there. For an instant, he panicked. He
groped about for some sign of what might have happened
to the Elven girl, but there was nothing to be found. His
panic increased. Where was she? He rose, backing from the
bushes. Perhaps these were the wrong ones, he thought
suddenly, and began to look about for others. He stopped
almost at once. There were no others like them close
enough to be seen. No, it was here that he had hidden her.

Eretria hurried up to him. "Where is she?"

"I don't know," he whispered, his lean face sweating. "I
can't find her."

He regained control of himself with an effort. Reason it
through, he told himself. Either she fled or the Reaper took
her. If she fled, where would she go? He looked at once to
the Hollows. There, he decided—to Spire's Reach or as
close to it as she could get. What if she had been taken,
what then? But she had not been taken, he realized,
because there was no sign of a struggle. She would have
fought back; she would have left him some sign. If she had
fled, on the other hand, she would have been careful to
leave nothing behind to show her pursuer that she had
been there at all.

He took a deep breath. She must have fled. But then a
new thought struck him. He was assuming in all of this
that Amberle had fled from the Reaper. What if it had not
been the Reaper, but something that had come out of the
Hollows? His jaw locked in frustration. There was no way
to tell. In this blackness, he could not hope to find a trail.
Either he would have to wait until morning, when it might
be too late to help Amberle, or . . .

Or he would have to use the Elfstones.

He was reaching for the pouch when Eretria's hand
gripped his arm sharply, causing him to jump in surprise.

"Healer!" she whispered. "Someone is coming!"

He felt his stomach knot sharply. For an instant he
simply stood there, his gaze following the girl's as it turned
north up the trail they had just traveled. On its shadowed
rut, something moved. Fear welled up within the Valeman.
His hand fumbled within his tunic and lifted free the

Elfstones. At his side, Eretria snatched from her boot a wicked-looking dagger. Together they faced the approaching shadow.

"Just hold on now!" A familiar voice called out to them.

Wil looked at Eretria and she at him. Slowly they lowered Elfstones and dagger. The voice belonged to Hebel. Eretria muttered something under her breath and moved to retrieve the horses, which had strayed back into the forest.

Down the trail trudged Hebel, the shaggy form of Drifter close at his heels. He wore leather woodsman's garb and carried a sack strapped across his back, a longbow and arrows over one shoulder, and a hunting knife at his waist. He moved with a peculiar hunching motion, leaning heavily on a gnarled walking stick. As he came up to them, they could see that he was spattered from head to foot with mud.

"You nearly ran me down, you know!" he snapped. "Look at me! If I'd been foolish enough to stand any further out on the trail than I did when I hailed you back there, I'd be covered with hoof prints as well as mud! What do you think you are doing, riding about the forest like that? It's black as six feet under out there and you ride about like it was broad daylight. Why didn't you stop when I called out to you, for cat's sake?"

"Well . . . because we didn't hear you," Wil answered in bewilderment.

"That's because you weren't listening like you should have been!" Hebel was not about to forgive them. He lurched right up to the Valeman. "Took me all day to get here—all day. Without a horse, I might point out. What took you so confounded long then? The way you were riding a minute ago, you could have been here and gone again half a dozen times!"

He caught sight of Eretria as she reappeared with the horses. "What are you doing here? Where is the Elfling girl? That thing didn't get her, did it?"

Wil started. "You know about the Reaper?"

"Reaper? If that's what it's called, yes, I know about it. It came to my camp earlier today—just after you'd left. Looking for you, it appears now, though at the time I wasn't sure. Never really saw the thing—just caught a glimpse. I think if I'd seen it close up, I'd be dead now."

"I think so, too," the Valeman agreed. "Cephelo and the others are. It caught up with them on Whistle Ridge."

Hebel nodded soberly. "Cephelo was bound to come to that end sooner or later." He glanced at Eretria. "Sorry, girl, but that's the truth of it." Then he turned back to Wil. "Now where's the little Elfling?"

"I don't know," Wil answered him. "I had to go back . . ." He hesitated. "I had to go back for something I left behind with Cephelo. Amberle had injured her ankle, so I hid her in some bushes. I went back a different way than I had come or I would probably be dead as well. I found Eretria, or she found me, I guess; and after we saw what had happened to Cephelo, we came back here as fast as we could. But now Amberle is gone, and I can't be sure what has happened to her. I can't even be sure whether the Reaper has been here yet or is still tracking us."

"It's come and gone," Hebel told him. "Drifter and I have been tracking it while it's been tracking you. Lost the trail at the fork because the Reaper went east to Whistle Ridge while Drifter and I came south after you. But then the trail started up again further south. Thing must have cut through the wilderness. If it could do that, it's dangerous, Elfling."

"Ask Cephelo how dangerous it is," Eretria muttered, glancing about at the forest shadows. "Healer, can we get out of here now?"

"Not until we find out what happened to Amberle," Wil insisted.

Hebel tapped his arm. "Show me where you left the girl."

Wil walked to the clump of bushes, with Eretria, the old man, and the dog trailing after, and pointed to the opening leading in. Hebel bent down, peered inside, and whistled Drifter to him. He spoke quietly to the dog, and the animal came forward, sniffed about, then moved over to the rim of the Hollows as the others watched.

"He has the scent, Drifter has." Hebel grunted with satisfaction. Drifter stopped and growled softly. "She is down in the Hollows, Elfling. The Reaper is down there, too. Probably still tracking her. I'd have guessed as much."

"Then we have to find her right away." Wil started forward.

Hebel caught his arm. "No need to rush, Elfling. That's the Hollows we're talking about, remember? Nothing down there but the Witch Sisters and the things that serve them. Anything else sets one foot in the Hollows gets snatched right up—I know that from what Mallenroh told me sixty years ago." He shook his head. "By now, the girl and the thing tracking her are keeping company with one of the Sisters—that or they're dead."

Wil went white. "Would the Witches kill them, Hebel?"

The old man seemed to think it over. "Oh, not the girl, I'd guess—not right away. The thing they would. And don't think they couldn't, Elfling."

"I don't know what to think anymore," Wil replied slowly. He gazed down into the blackness of the Hollows. "I do know this much—I am going down there and I am going to find Amberle. Right now."

He started to say something to Eretria, but the Rover girl cut him short. "Don't waste your breath, Healer. I'm going with you."

The way she said it left little room for argument. He glanced at Hebel.

"I'm coming, too, Elfling," the old man announced.

"But you said yourself that no one should go into the Hollows," Wil pointed out. "I don't understand why you're even here."

Hebel shrugged. "Because it doesn't matter where I am anymore, Elfling, and hasn't for a long time. I'm an old man; I've done in this life the things I've wanted to do, been where I wanted to go, seen what I've wanted to see. Nothing left for me now—nothing except for maybe this one thing. I want to see what's down there in those Hollows."

He shook his head ruefully. "Thought about it for sixty years, off and on. Always told myself that one day I'd find out—like thinking about a deep pool; you always wonder what's at the bottom." He rubbed his bearded chin. "Well, a sane man wouldn't waste his time with a thing like that, and I was a sane man when I was younger, though I guess some thought different. Now I'm tired of being sane, tired of just thinking about going down there instead of doing it.

You made me decide. When you first told me what you intended, I thought to persuade you otherwise—just as I'd persuaded myself. I was certain that you would lose interest quick enough when you heard what I had to say. I was wrong. I saw that whatever it was that you were looking for was important enough that being afraid didn't matter to you. So why should it matter so much to me, I thought? Then after that Reaper thing passed me by and left me knowing how close I'd come to dying, I realized it didn't. All that really mattered was finding out about those Hollows. So I came after you. I decided that we should go looking together."

Wil understood. "Let's hope that we both find what we are looking for."

"Well, maybe I can be of some help to you." The old man shrugged. "This is Mallenroh's end of the Hollows. She might remember me, Elfling." For an instant his thoughts wandered, then he glanced at Wil. "Drifter can track for as long as it's needed." He whistled. "Take us down, dog. Go, boy."

Drifter disappeared over the rim of the Hollows. Eretria stripped saddles and bridles from the horses and slapped them sharply to send them galloping back through the forest. Then she joined Wil and the old man. In a line, they started down into the Hollows.

"Won't have to rely on Drifter very long," Hebel declared firmly. "Mallenroh—she'll find us quick enough."

If that were so, Wil found himself thinking, then he hoped that she would find Amberle as well.

Amberle came awake in the darkness of the Hollows forest. It was the slight swaying, jostling motion of being carried that awoke her, and for an instant she panicked. Gnarled fingers held her fast, locked tightly about her arms and legs, her body, even her neck and head—fingers so rough they felt as if they were made of wood. Her first reaction was to want to break free, but she resisted it with a desperate effort and forced herself to remain still. Whatever had her did not yet know she was awake. If she were to have any advantage at all, it lay in this. For the moment, at least, she must continue to feign sleep and learn what she could.

She had no idea how long she had slept. It might have been minutes or hours or even longer. She thought, though, that it was still the same night. Logic told her it must be. She thought, too, that whatever it was that had her, it was not the thing that had pursued her into the Hollows. Had that thing found her, it would simply have killed her. This, therefore, must be something else. The old man, Hebel, had told Wil and her that the Hollows were the private domain of the Witch Sisters. Perhaps it was one of them that had her.

She felt somewhat better, having reasoned that much through, and she relaxed a bit, trying to make out something of the terrain through which she was moving. It was difficult to do this; the trees shut away even the smallest trace of stars and moon, leaving everything shrouded in deepest night. Were it not for the familiar woodland smells, she might not have known there was a forest about. The silence was intense. The few sounds were distant and brief, cries that came from the wilderness beyond the Hollows.

Yet there was another sound, she corrected herself, a sort of skittering noise like the chafing of limbs in a breeze—except that there was no breeze, and the sound came from beneath her, not from above. Whatever it was that carried her was making the noise.

The minutes slipped by. She thought briefly of Wil, trying to imagine what he might do in her place. That made her smile in spite of herself. Who could tell what wild stunt Wil might try in such a situation? Then she wondered if she would ever see him again.

Her muscles were beginning to cramp, and she decided to see if she could do something to ease the discomfort without giving herself away. Experimentally she stretched her legs, pretending to stir in her sleep, testing the fingers that held her. They moved with her, but did not release. So much for that.

The sound of running water reached her, growing stronger with each passing second. She could smell it now, fresh and scented with wildflowers—a stream that twisted and churned in the quiet of the forest. Then it was beneath her, and the rustle of the sticks and the night sounds faded in its rush. Footsteps echoed hollowly on wooden planks, and she knew she had been carried over a bridge. The gurgle of the stream faded slightly. Chains clanked and rumbled as if being gathered in, and there was a dull thud. Something had closed behind, a door—a very heavy door. An iron bar and locks snapped into place. She heard them clearly. Night air washed about her as before, but it carried with it the unmistakable smell of stone and mortar. Fear welled up within her once more. She was inside a walled area, a courtyard perhaps, being taken, she now believed, to some sort of confinement, and if she did not break free at once, she would not break free at all. Yet the fingers that constrained her showed not the slightest hint of loosening, and there were many of them. It would take a tremendous effort to wrench free, and she did not believe that she had that kind of strength left in her. Besides, she thought dismally, even if she were to break free, where would she go?

Ahead, another door opened, creaking slightly. Still no light came to her; there was nothing but blackness all about.

"Pretty thing," a voice said suddenly, and the Elven girl started with surprise.

She was carried ahead. Behind her, the door closed and the smells of the forest disappeared. She was inside—but inside of what? Twisting and turning, her captors carried her along passageways that smelled damp and musty; yet there was another odor, a kind of incense, a perfume. The Elven girl breathed it deeply and it left her head in a momentary spin.

Then at last there was a light, suddenly, unexpectedly, glimmering just ahead from within a tall archway. Amberle blinked at the unfamiliar brightness, her eyes still accustomed to the dark. She was carried through the archway and down a winding stair. The light blinked above her, fell behind momentarily, then followed after, weaving and bobbing against the dark.

Her forward motion stopped. She felt herself being lowered onto a thick, woven matting, and the wooden fingers slipped free. She raised herself up on her elbows and squinted toward the light. It hung there before her for just an instant, then retreated slowly behind a wall of iron bars. A door swung shut and the light was gone.

But just before it disappeared, the Elven girl caught a glimpse of her captors, their slender forms outlined clearly in the white glow. They appeared to be made out of sticks.

On the floor of the Hollows, Wil called a halt. It was so black that he could barely see his hand in front of his face; he could not see Hebel or Eretria at all, nor they him. If they attempted to proceed under these conditions, they would soon become separated and hopelessly lost. He waited a few moments for his vision to sharpen. It did, but only slightly. The Hollows remained a dim, barely perceptible mass of shadows.

It was Hebel who came up with a plan to resolve their difficulty. Whistling Drifter to him, he produced a length of rope from the sack he carried, and bound one end to the dog; the rest he fastened about his waist and to the waists of the Valeman and the Rover girl. Thus tied, they could follow after one another without risk of separation. The old man tested the line, then spoke softly to Drifter. The big dog started ahead.

It seemed to Wil as if they walked the Hollows for hours, stumbling through an endless maze of trees and brush, nearly blind in the impenetrable blackness, trusting to the instincts of the dog that led them. They did not talk to one another at all, moving through the forest as silently as they could, all too conscious of the fact that somewhere within that same forest the Reaper prowled. Wil had never felt quite so helpless as he did then. It was bad enough that he could see almost nothing; it was worse knowing that the Reaper was down there with him. He thought constantly of Amberle. If he were frightened, what must it be like for her? His fear made him ashamed. He had no right to be afraid, not when she was the one who was alone and unprotected, and he was the one who had left her that way.

Yet the fear stayed with him. To ward it off, he clutched the pouch with the Elfstones in one hand, grasping it firmly, as if having it there might somehow protect him against whatever hid within the forest night. Yet deep within, the feeling persisted that the Elfstones would not protect him, that their power was lost to him and he could not get it back again. It made no difference what Amberle had told him or what he had told himself. The feeling lacked reason or purpose; it was simply there—haunting, malignant, terrifying. The power of the Elfstones was no longer his.

He was still trying to shake the feeling when the rope before him went suddenly slack. He almost stumbled over Hebel, who had come to a complete stop. Eretria bumped up against him, and the three stood bunched together, peering ahead into the gloom.

"Drifter's found something," the old man whispered to Wil.

Dropping to his knees, he worked his way forward to where Drifter was sniffing the ground, Wil and Eretria following close behind. He patted the dog soothingly and felt along the earth for a time, then rose.

"Mallenroh." He spoke her name softly. "She's got the Elfling girl."

"Are you sure?" Wil whispered back.

The old man nodded. "Has to be. That Reaper thing's somewhere else now. Drifter doesn't smell it anymore."

Wil did not understand how Hebel could be certain of all this, especially when it was so impossibly black, but there was no point in arguing the matter.

"What do we do now?" he asked anxiously.

"Keep going." Hebel grunted. "Drifter—go, boy."

The dog started ahead once more, the three humans trailing after. The minutes slipped away, and gradually the forest began to lighten. At first Wil thought his eyes were playing tricks on him, but finally he realized that night was fading and a new day had begun. Trees and brush began to take shape about him, the dimness sharpening slowly as the sun slipped its faint glow through the forest roof. Ahead, the shaggy black form of Drifter became visible for the first time since they had descended from the Hollows rim, head lowered to the trail as he sniffed his way along the damp earth.

Then abruptly the big head lifted and the dog stopped. The humans stopped with him, startled looks on their faces. Before them stood the strangest creature that any of them had ever seen. It was a man made of sticks—two arms, two legs and a body all of sticks, gnarled roots curling out from the ends of the arms and legs to form fingers and toes. It had no head. It faced them—or at least they thought it faced them since the roots that formed its fingers and toes appeared to point in their direction. Its slender body swayed slightly as if it were a sapling caught in a sudden wind. Then it turned and walked back into the forest.

Hebel glanced quickly at the other two. "I told you. That's Mallenroh's work."

Beckoning hurriedly to them, he started after the creature. Wil and Eretria looked doubtfully at each other, then followed. Wordlessly, the little procession trudged ahead into the gloom, weaving and twisting through the maze of the forest. After a time, other stick men like the first began to appear about them, headless, gnarled things, noiseless but for the slight skittering sound they made as they walked. Almost before the humans knew it, there were dozens of the creatures ringing them, trailing like ghosts through the shadows.

"I told you," Hebel kept whispering back to the Valeman and the Rover girl, his leathered face intense.

Then abruptly the forest thinned. Before them stood a solitary tower, its dark turret rising up into the trees that grew about it. It sat atop a small knoll, a nearly windowless keep, its stone aged, worn, and grown thick with vines and moss. The knoll had become an island, encircled by a stream that flowed from somewhere back in the forest, wending its way down in a series of drops and turns before meandering off into the trees to their left. A low wall ringed the tower, built close to the bank of the stream; where it faced them, a drawbridge stood open and empty, chains hanging limply from small watch houses at either side, a heavy wooden bridgehead spanning the waters beneath. All about the rise and the tower grew massive oaks, ancient trees whose boughs interwove and shut away the morning sky, leaving the isle, like the rest of the Hollows, draped in deepest shadow.

The stick man they had followed stopped. It turned about slightly, as if its headless form would ascertain whether or not they were there. Then it began walking toward the drawbridge. Hebel limped after it without hesitating, Drifter at his side. Wil and Eretria hung back a moment, less certain than the old man that they ought to go further. The tower was a forbidding structure; they knew that they should not set foot within its walls, knew that they had already gone much farther than they should. But the Valeman sensed somehow that it was here he would find Amberle. He looked back at Eretria, and they started forward.

Down to the edge of the stream the little band went, following the silent stick man, its brethren all about them. Except for the sounds of their movements and the flow of the stream, the forest lay wrapped in silence. The stick man stepped onto the bridgehead and walked across, fading from sight in the shadow of the gate. The men, the girl, and the dog passed over the bridge behind it, Wil and Eretria casting apprehensive glances at the massive black tower beyond.

Then they were beneath the gate. The stick man reappeared before them, standing now just beyond the shadowed arch. In a line, they moved forward, watching as it started once more toward the tower. They had barely walked clear of the gateway when they heard the sudden sound of chains creaking and groaning. Behind them, the drawbridge lifted and sealed against the wall.

Now there was no turning back. In a knot, they walked to the tower. The stick man was waiting, standing within a high alcove that sheltered a pair of broad, ironbound wooden doors. One door stood open. The stick man stepped through and was gone. Wil stared upward at the massive stone face of the tower, then reached into his tunic and brought forth the pouch that contained the Elfstones. With the others, he stepped through the doorway into blackness.

For an instant no one moved, standing just within the entry, peering blindly into the gloom. Then the door swung shut behind them, locks snapping into place. Light flared from within a glass-enclosed lamp that hung suspended from above, its glow white and soft, neither from burning oil nor pitch, but something that gave off no flame as it burned. All about stood the stick men, their gnarled shadows cast upon stone walls, swaying gently in the light.

From the gloom behind them, a woman appeared, cloaked all in black and trailing long streamers of crimson nightshade.

"Mallenroh," Hebel whispered, and Wil Ohmsford felt the air about him turn to ice.

XLII

The second day of the battle for Arborlon belonged to Ander Elessedil. It was a day of blood and pain, of death and great courage. All during the night the Demon hordes had continued to ferry their brethren across the waters of the Rill Song, singly and in groups, until, for the first time since their break from the Forbidding, the whole of their army was gathered to strike, massed at the base of the Carolan from cliff face to riverbank, stretched north and south as far as the eye could see, awesome and terrible and endless in number. At dawn, they attacked the city. Up against the walls of the Elfitch they rushed, wave upon wave, maddened and howling with hate. Up against the heights they surged, scrambling onto the sheer rock, clawing their way through a hail of arrows. Onward they came, like a wave that would sweep across the defenders who waited and leave them buried.

It was Ander Elessedil who made the difference. It was as if on that day he became at last the King his father had been, the King who had led the Elves against the armies of the Warlock Lord those fifty years past. Gone was the weariness and the disillusion. Gone was the doubt that had haunted him since Halys Cut. He believed again in himself and in the determination of those who fought with him. It was an historic moment, and the Elven Prince became its focal point. Gathered about him were the armies of four races, battle standards flying in the morning wind. Here were the silver war eagles and spreading oak of the Elves, the gray and crimson slash of the Free Corps, and the black horses of the Old Guard; there flew the forest greens of the Dwarf Sappers split by the twist of the Silver River, and the hammer and twin blue mountains of the Rock Trolls of the

Kershalt. Never before had they flown as one. In the history of the Four Lands the races had never before been united in a common cause, to form a common defense, and to serve a common good. Troll and Dwarf, Elf and Man— the humans of the new world stood together against an evil from ancient times. For that single, wondrous day, Ander Elessedil became the spark that gave them all life.

He was everywhere at once, from the rim of the bluff to the gates of the Elfitch, sometimes on horseback, sometimes afoot, always where the fighting was the heaviest. Chain mail gleaming, Ellcrys staff held high, he stood foremost among the defenders of the city against the Demons who rushed to slay him. Wherever he went, the cry went up and the defenders rallied. Always outnumbered, always pressed, still the Elven Prince and his comrades-at-arms threw back their attackers. Ander Elessedil was something more than human that day, fighting with such ferocity that it seemed as if nothing could stand against him. Time after time, the Demons sought to pull him down, recognizing quickly that this single man was the heart of the Elven defense. Time after time, it seemed as if they would succeed, ringing Ander in a swarm of raging black bodies. But each time he fought his way free. Each time, the Demons were driven back.

It was a day of heroes, for all of the defenders of Arborlon were inspired by the courage of the Elven Prince. Eventine Elessedil stood with his son and fought bravely, his very presence lending heart to the Elves about him. Allanon was there as well, his cloaked form standing head and shoulders above the armored men about him as the blue fire arced from his fingers into the midst of the raging Demons. Twice the Demons broke through the gates of the third ramp, and twice the Rock Trolls under the command of Amantar drove them back again. Stee Jans and the men of the Free Corps broke a third assault, counterattacking with such savagery that they swept the Demons all the way back to the second ramp and for a time threatened to retake its gates. Elven cavalry and Dwarf Sappers repulsed sally after sally along the rim of the Carolan, throwing back scores of Demons who managed to scale the cliff face and threaten to flank the defenders on the Elfitch.

But it was Ander who led them, Ander who gave them

renewed strength when it seemed that they could stand no longer, Ander who rallied them at every point. When the day at last was ended and darkness began to fall, the Demons were forced to withdraw once more, slipping back into the forests below the heights, shrieking with rage and frustration. For yet a second day, the defenders of Arborlon had held. It was Ander Elessedil's finest hour.

Then the fortunes of the defenders of the city took a turn for the worse. With the coming of night, the Demons attacked again, waiting only until the sunlight was gone, then rising up out of the forests to sweep over the Elven defense. One by one, they extinguished the torches that had been lit along the lower Elfitch, battling their way forward to the gates of the third ramp. Desperately, the defenders braced for the assault, massive Rock Trolls blocking the gates while Elves and Legion soldiers fought from atop the walls. But the rush was too strong; the gates buckled and snapped apart. Into the breach surged the Demons, clawing their way forward.

On the heights as well, the Demons began to break through. Dozens of black forms slipped between the lines of cavalry patrolling the bluff and scattered wildly toward the city. Of these, more than a hundred converged on the Gardens of Life, aware that within its gates stood the thing that for so many centuries had held them imprisoned. There they came face to face with the soldiers of the Black Watch who stood ready to fulfill the purpose of their order and to defend to the last man the ancient tree that was their trust. Maddened beyond reason, the Demons attacked. Up against the lowered pikes of the Black Watch they charged and were cut to pieces.

At the southern end of the Carolan, another band of Demons managed to tunnel beneath a line of Dwarf traps set along a dismantled secondary stairway leading up from the Rill Song and thus gain the heights. Skirting the Black Watch and the Gardens of Life, they slipped east away from the Carolan, crawling through the shadows behind the line of torches set against its rim and broke for the city. Half a dozen Elven wounded, en route to their homes from the battle, were caught in the open and killed. More might have perished but for a patrol of Dwarf Sappers, who had agreed to aid the Elves in keeping watch along the perimeter of the city. Realizing that the Demons had broken through the defenders of the bluff, they followed the cries of the dying and fell upon their slayers. When the struggle was ended, only three Dwarves were still standing. All the Demons lay dead.

By dawn, the heights had been cleared and the Demons thrown back once more. But the third ramp of the Elfitch had been lost and the fourth was threatened. At the base of the bluff, the Demons massed anew. Cries rang out through the morning stillness as they charged up the ramp, solidly massed, the foremost among them bearing a massive wooden battering ram. Into the gates they carried the ram, smashing the wooden barrier apart, then pouring through. Trolls and Elves formed quickly into a tight phalanx, a wall of iron spears and lances that cut deep into the writhing black forms. But the Demons came on, surging up against the harried defenders until they had forced them back within the fortress of the fifth ramp.

It was a desperate moment. Four of the seven levels of the Elfitch had been lost. The Demons were halfway to the summit of the bluffs. Ander rallied the defenders, flanked by Amantar and Kerrin and surrounded by Home Guard. The Demons charged, hammering against the gates of the ramp. But just when it seemed that they must break through, Allanon appeared on the walls, arms lifting. Blue flame raced the length of the ramp below, splitting wide the Demon rush, turning the battering ram to ash. Momentarily stunned, the Demons fell back.

All through the morning the Demons sought to breach the Elven defense of the fifth ramp. At midday, they finally succeeded. A pair of monstrous Ogres pushed to the forefront of their brethren and threw themselves against the gates—once, twice. Wood and iron shattered into fragments and the gates broke apart. The Ogres burst through onto the ramp beyond, scattering the defenders. A handful of Rock Trolls tried to stop them, but the Ogres shoved the Trolls aside as if they were made of paper. Again Ander rallied his soldiers, urging them forward. But Demons were pouring through the ruined gates now, sweeping over the defenders.

Then Eventine Elessedil's horse was killed beneath him as he rode back toward the safety of the gates above, and the old King tumbled to the rampway. The Demons saw him fall. With a howl, they surged forward. They would have had him but for Stee Jans. With a scattering of Legion Free Corps, the Borderman sprang into their path, swords cutting. Behind them, Eventine staggered to his knees, dazed and bloodied, but alive. Quickly Kerrin brought the Home Guard to the King's rescue, and they carried him from the battle.

The soldiers of the Free Corps held for a moment longer, then they too were swept aside. The Demons pushed forward, thrusting past the Elves who tried to bar their way. Leading the assault were the Ogres who had forced the gates, crushing all who came within reach. Ander Elessedil leaped to stop them, Ellcrys staff raised high as he called to the defenders of the city to stand with him. But the rush was too strong. Amantar and Stee Jans were fighting for their lives at the walls of the ramp, unable to reach the Elven Prince. For one terrifying moment, he stood virtually alone before the Demon rush.

But only for a moment. Atop the gates of the sixth court, Allanon whistled Dayn down from the edge of the Carolan. Without a word, he snatched Dancer's reins from the surprised Wing Rider and vaulted atop the giant Roc. In the next instant he was winging downward, black robes billowing out like sails. Dancer screamed once, then dropped into the midst of the Demons who threatened Ander, claws and beak tearing. Shrieking, the black forms scattered. Blue fire spurted from the Druid's fingers, and the ramp before him erupted in flame. Then pulling an astonished Ander up beside him, the Druid called out to Dancer and the Roc lifted back into the air; below, the last of the defenders fell back, pouring through the gates of the sixth ramp to safety.

For a few seconds longer, the Druid fire burned, then sputtered and died. Enraged, the Demons charged after the fleeing defenders. But by now the Dwarf Sappers on the heights had been alerted. Winches and pulleys began to turn as the chains wrapped about the supports of the ramp were drawn tight. Browork's carefully concealed trap was about to be sprung. Out from beneath the Elfitch flew the already weakened supports, cracking and snapping as the chains twisted them free. With a shudder, the ramp-

head below the sixth level sank downward and fell apart.
The Demons caught upon it disappeared in a cloud of
rubble. Shrieks and cries filled the air, and the whole of the
lower ramp was lost from view.

When the dust cleared again, the Elfitch was a pile of
crushed stone and shattered wooden beams from the gates
of the sixth ramp downward to the fourth. Demon bodies
lay scattered on the cliff face, lodged within the rubble,
broken and lifeless. Those who had survived fell back
toward the base of the bluff, dodging boulders and debris
that tumbled down about them, disappearing finally into
the woodlands below.

The Demons did not come again that day against the city
of Arborlon.

Suffering from yet another head wound as well as from a
number of smaller cuts and scrapes, Eventine Elessedil was
carried from the battle atop the Elfitch to the seclusion of
his manor house. Faithful Gael was there to care for him, to
wash and dress his wounds, and to help him to his bed.
Then, with Dardan and Rhoe to watch over him, the King
of the Elves was left to sleep.

But Eventine did not sleep. He could not. He lay within
his bed, propped up against the feathered pillows, staring
disconsolately into the darkened corners of the room,
despair washing through him. For all the help that the
Legion, the Dwarves, and the Rock Trolls had given the
Elves, the battle was still being lost. All of their defenses
had failed. Another day, perhaps two, and the sixth and
seventh gates of the Elfitch would fall and the Demons
would be atop the Carolan. That would be the end.
Hopelessly outnumbered, the defenders would be swiftly
overrun and destroyed. The Westland would be lost and
the Elves scattered to the four winds.

The implications behind what he was thinking burned
through him. If the Demons won here, it would mean that
Eventine Elessedil had failed. Not just his own people, but
the peoples of all the Lands—for the Demons would not
stop with the Westland, now that they were free of the
Forbidding. And what of his ancestors who had imprisoned the Demons so many centuries ago, at a time so
remote that he could barely envision its being? He would

ave failed them as well. They had created the Forbidding,
but they had entrusted its care to those who followed after
them, depending on those who came after to keep it
strong. Yet the Forbidding had been forgotten over the
centuries in the upheaval of the old world and the rebirth
of the races, forgotten by them all. Even the Chosen had
come to think of it as little more than a distant part of their
history, a legend that belonged to another age, to the past
or to the future—yet never really to the present.

His throat tightened. If Arborlon fell, if the Westland
were lost, it would be his failure. His! His penetrating blue
eyes turned hard with anger. For eighty-two years he had
lived upon this earth; for more than fifty of them, he had
been the leader of his people. He had accomplished much
in that time—and now it would all be lost. He thought of
Arion, his firstborn, the child who should have lived to
carry on what he had worked so hard to achieve, and of
Kael Pindanon, his old comrade-at-arms, his loyal follower.
He thought of the Elves who had been lost defending the
Sarandanon and Arborlon. All of them dead, and for
nothing.

He eased himself down within the coverings of the bed,
mulling over the choices that were left, the tactics that
might yet be employed, the resources that might be called
upon when the Demons came again. His mind filled with
them, and deep within he felt a sense of hopelessness.
They were not enough; they would never be enough.

Groping for answers to the questions he posed himself,
he suddenly remembered Amberle. It startled him to think
of her, and he sat upright in the bed. In the confusion of the
past few days he had forgotten his granddaughter, she
who was the last of the Chosen, who Allanon had told him
was the only real hope for his people. What, he wondered
sadly, had become of Amberle?

He lay down again and stared through the shadow of the
drapes to the growing darkness beyond. Allanon had said
that Amberle was alive, by now deep within the lower
Westland; but Eventine did not believe that the Druid really
knew. The thought depressed him. If she were dead, he
did not want to know, he decided suddenly. It would be
better that way, not knowing. Yet that was a lie. He needed
to know, desperately. Bitterness welled up within him.

Everything was slipping away from him—his family, his people, his country, everything he loved, everything that had given meaning to his life. There was a basic unfairness to it all that he could not understand. No, it was more than that. The basic unfairness of it all was something he could not accept. If he did, he knew that it would finish him.

He closed his eyes against the light. Where was Amberle? He must know, he insisted stubbornly. He must find a way to reach her, to help her if his help were needed. He must find a way to bring her back to him. He took a deep breath, then another. Still thinking of Amberle, he drifted off to sleep.

It was dark when he awoke. At first he was not certain what it was that brought him awake, his mind still drugged with sleep, his thoughts scattered. A sound, he thought, a cry. He raised himself up against the gathering of pillows and stared into the darkness of the room. Pale, white moonlight seeped through the fabric of the drawn curtains, illuminating faintly the lines of the bolted double windows. Uncertain, he waited.

Then he heard another sound, a muted grunt, quick and surprised, fading almost instantly into silence. It had come from outside his room, from the hall where Dardan and Rhoe stood watch. He sat up slowly, peering into the gloom, straining to hear something more. But there was only the silence, deep and ominous. Eventine slid to the edge of the bed and dropped one leg cautiously to the floor.

The door to his bedchamber swung slowly open, light from the oil lamps of the hallway beyond spilling into the room. The Elven King froze. Through the opening came Manx, heavy body hunched forward in a low crouch, grizzled head swinging to where his master sat upon the bed. The wolfhound's eyes glittered like a cat's, and his dark muzzle was streaked with blood. But it was his forelegs and paws that startled the King most; they seemed in the half-light to have become the corded limbs and claws of a Demon.

Manx passed from the light of the oil lamps into shadow, and Eventine blinked in surprise. In that instant he was certain that what he had seen was something left over from a dream, that he had imagined that Manx was not Manx, but something else. The wolfhound moved toward him slowly, and the King could see that his tail was wagging in a friendly manner. He exhaled in relief. It was just Manx, he told himself.

"Manx, good boy . . ." he started to say and stopped as he caught sight of the reddened tracks that the dog had left on the floor behind him.

Then Manx was springing for his throat, quick and silent, jaws gaping wide, clawed hands reaching. But Eventine was quicker. Snatching the coverings from the bed before him, he caught Manx within their folds. Twisting the coverings about the struggling dog, the King slammed the animal down hard upon the bed and sprang for the open door. In an instant he was through, yanking the door shut behind him, hearing the latch snap into place.

Sweat ran down his body. What was happening? In a daze, he stumbled back from the door, nearly tripping over the lifeless body of Rhoe, who lay sprawled half a dozen feet away, his throat ripped open. Eventine's mind whirled. Manx? Why would Manx . . . ? He caught himself sharply. But it was not Manx. Whatever it was that had come at him within his sleeping chamber was not Manx, just something that looked like Manx. Numb, he started down the hallway, searching for Dardan. He found him near the front entry, a lance driven through his heart.

Then the door to his bedchamber burst open, and the thing that looked like Manx, yet surely was not, bounded into view. Frantic, Eventine sprang for the entry doors, wrenching at the handles. They were jammed, the locks sealed. The old King turned, watching as the beast in the hall stalked slowly toward him, reddened jaws gaping. Fear surged through Eventine, fear so terrible that for an instant it threatened to overwhelm him completely. He was trapped within his own house. There was no one to help him, no one that he might turn to. He was alone.

Down the length of the hall the monster came, the sound of its breathing a slow rasp in the silence. A Demon, Eventine thought in horror, a Demon pretending to be Manx, faithful old Manx. He remembered then awakening after the fall of the Sarandanon to find Manx and thinking suddenly, irrationally, that it was not Manx at all, but something else. An illusion, he had thought—but he had been wrong. Manx was gone, dead he guessed for many days, even weeks . . .

Then the awful truth dawned on him. His meetings with Allanon, the plans they had worked so hard to keep secret, the care they had taken to protect Amberle—Manx had been there. Or the Demon that looked like Manx. There was a spy within the Elven camp, Allanon had warned—a spy that all the while had been as close to them as they had been to each other. The old King thought of the times that he had stroked that grizzled head, and it made his skin crawl.

The Demon was less than a dozen feet from him now, inching along the floor, jaws open, clawed forelegs bent. Eventine knew in that instant that he was a dead man. Then something happened within him, something so sudden that the Elven King was blinded to everything else. Rage swept through him—rage at the deception that had been done him, rage at the deaths that had occurred because of that deception, and most of all, rage at the helplessness he felt now, trapped as he was within his own house.

His body went taut. Next to the fallen Dardan lay the short sword that had been the Elven Hunter's favorite weapon. Keeping his eyes fixed upon those of the Demon, Eventine inched away from the doors. If he could manage to reach that sword . . .

The Demon came at him suddenly, bounding across the space that separated them, launching itself at the Elven King's head. Eventine brought his arms up to protect his face and fell backward, kicking violently. Teeth and claws ripped into his forearms, but his feet caught the underside of the creature and sent it tumbling past him into the darkened recesses of the entry. Quickly he rolled back to his feet, throwing himself over Dardan and grasping the fallen sword. Then he was up again, turning to face his attacker.

Astonishment flooded his face. From the darkened corner where it had tumbled, the Demon slouched, no longer Manx, but something different now. It was changing even as it stalked toward him, changing from Manx into a lean, black thing, corded with muscle, its body sleek and hairless. It came at him on four legs that ended in clawed hands, and its mouth split wide with gleaming teeth. It circled the King, lifting itself from time to time on its hind legs, feinting with its hands like a boxer, hissing with hate. A Changeling, Eventine thought and forced down a new wave of fear. A Demon that could be anything it wanted to be.

The Changeling lunged at him suddenly, claws ripping at his shoulder and side, leaving him torn and bloodied. He swung at the thing with the sword—too late. It was past him and gone before he could reach it. Back the Demon circled, slowly, like a cat watching its cornered prey. I must be quicker this time, the old King told himself. The Demon lunged again, feinted at his chest, and slipped beneath the arc of his sword, tearing at the muscles of his left leg. Pain shot through the leg, and he dropped to his knees, struggling to remain upright. For an instant his vision blurred, then cleared once more as he forced himself to rise.

Before him the Changeling crouched, waiting. When he stayed on his feet, it began to circle once more. Blood streamed down Eventine's body, and he felt himself weakening. He was losing this battle as well, he thought frantically, and it would end in his death if he did not find a way to take the offensive against this monster. Weaving and bobbing, the Demon stalked him. The King tried to corner it, but it stepped nimbly away from him, far too quick for the wounded old man. Eventine stopped his pursuit; it was gaining him nothing. He watched as the Demon continued to circle, hissing.

Then, in a desperate gamble, the Elven King pretended to stumble and fall, staggering heavily to his knees. Pain shot through him as he did so, but the deception worked. Thinking the old man finished, the Changeling lunged. But this time Eventine was waiting. He caught the monster in the chest, the sword biting deep through bone and muscle. Shrieking in pain, the Demon clawed and bit at the Elven King, then twisted free. Blood ran from the slash, a greenish-red ichor that stained the sleek, black body.

They crouched face to face, Elven King and Demon, both wounded, each waiting for the other to drop his guard. Once more, the Demon began to circle, blood trailing after it along the floor. Eventine Elessedil braced, turning to follow the Demon's movement. He was covered with blood, and his strength was ebbing from him. Pain racked his torn body. He knew that he could only last a few minutes more.

Abruptly the Changeling sprang at his throat. It happened so quickly that the King did not have time to do much more than tumble backward, arms raised before his face, sword held high. The Demon landed on top of him, bearing him to the floor, teeth and claws ripping. Eventine screamed in pain as the claws tore into his chest and the jaws closed about his forearm.

Then the doors to the manor house burst apart, locks splintering, hinges ripped from their fastenings. Shouts rang through the darkened entryway as it filled with armed men. In a haze of anguish, Eventine cried out. Someone had heard! Someone had come!

From atop the fallen King, the Changeling rose up, shrieking. In that instant it left its throat exposed. Eventine's sword swept up, glittering. Back flew the Demon, head nearly severed from its body, its voice lost in a sudden gasp. As it fell, the King's rescuers closed in about it, swords thrusting deep into its body.

The Changeling shuddered with the impact of the blows and died.

Eventine Elessedil staggered to his feet, sword still clutched within his hand, blue eyes hard and fixed. A numbing sensation spread through his body as he turned to find Ander reaching out for him. Then the King of the Elves tumbled downward, and the night closed in.

XLIII

Like Mistress Death she came for the humans, taller even than Allanon, gray hair long and woven thick with nightshade, black robes trailing from her slender form, a whisper of silk in the deep silence of the tower. She was beautiful, her face delicate and finely wrought, her skin so pale that she seemed almost ethereal. There was an ageless look to her, a timelessness, as if she were a thing that had always been and would forever be. The stick men fell back from her as she approached, the clicking of their wooden legs a faint rustle in the gloom. She passed them without a glance, her strange violet eyes never leaving the three who stood transfixed in her presence. Her hands stretched forth, small and fragile, their fingers curving as if to draw them close.

"Mallenroh!" Hebel whispered her name a second time, his voice expectant.

She stopped, her perfect features devoid of expression as she looked down upon the old man. Then she turned to Eretria and finally to Wil. The Valeman had gone so cold that he was shaking.

"I am Mallenroh," she said, her voice soft and distant. "Why are you here?"

No one spoke, their eyes riveted on her. She waited a moment, then her pale hand passed before them.

"The Hollows are forbidden. No human is allowed. The Hollows are my home and within them I hold the power of life and death over all living things. To those who please me, I grant life. To those who do not, death. It has always been so. It will always be."

She looked at each of them in turn, carefully this time,

453

violet eyes reaching out to hold their own. Finally her gaze
rested on Hebel.

"Who are you, old man? Why have you come to the
Hollows?"

Hebel swallowed. "I was looking for . . . for you, I
guess." His words stumbled over one another. "I brought
you something, Mallenroh."

Her hand stretched forth. "What have you brought me?"

Hebel removed the sack he carried, lifted its flap and
fumbled through its contents, searching. A moment later
he withdrew a polished wooden figure, a statue carved
from a piece of oak. It was Mallenroh, captured so perfectly
that it seemed as if she had stepped from the carving into
life. She took the wooden figure from the old man and
examined it, her slender fingers running slowly over its
polished surface.

"A pretty thing," she said finally.

"It is you," Hebel told her quickly.

She looked back at him, and Wil did not like what he
saw. The smile she gave the old man was faint and cold.

"I know you," she said, then paused as her eyes studied
anew his leathered face. "Long ago it was, upon the rim of
the Hollows, when you were still young. A night I gave
you . . ."

"I remembered," Hebel whispered, pointing quickly to
the wooden figure. "I remembered . . . what you were
like."

At Hebel's feet, Drifter crouched against the stone floor
of the tower and whined. But the old man never heard
him. He had lost himself completely in the Witch's eyes.
She shook her gray head slowly.

"It was a whim, foolish one," she whispered.

Holding the statue, she stepped past him to where
Eretria stood. The Rover girl's eyes were wide and frightened as the Witch came up to her.

"What have you brought me?" Mallenroh's question
teased through the silence.

Eretria was speechless. Desperately she looked at Wil,
then back again to Mallenroh. The Witch's hand passed
once before her eyes in a gesture that was both soothing
and commanding.

"Pretty thing," Mallenroh smiled. "Have you brought yourself?"

Eretria's slender body shook. "I . . . no, I . . ."

"Do you care for this one?" Mallenroh pointed suddenly to Wil. She turned to face the Valeman. "He cares for someone else, I think. An Elven girl, perhaps? Is this so?"

Wil nodded slowly. Her strange eyes held his own, and her words reached out to him, bold and insistent.

"It is you who holds the magic."

"Magic?" Wil stammered in reply.

Her hands slipped back within the black robes. "Show it to me."

So compelling was her voice that before Wil Ohmsford knew what he had done, he had opened the hand that held the leather pouch. She nodded to him faintly.

"Show it to me," she repeated.

Unable to help himself, the Valeman emptied the Elfstones from the pouch into his outstretched hand. Cupped within his palm, they glittered and flared. Mallenroh drew in her breath sharply, and one hand lifted toward them.

"Elfstones," she said softly. "Blue for the Seeker." Her eyes found Wil's. "Shall they be your gift to me?"

Wil tried to speak, but the cold within him tightened and no words came from his lips. His hand locked before him, and he could not draw it back again. Mallenroh's eyes looked deep into his own; what he saw there terrified him. She wanted him to know what she could do to him.

The Witch stepped back. "Wisp," she called.

From the shadows sidled a small, furry-looking creature, like a Gnome in appearance, with the face of a wizened old man. Scurrying to Mallenroh's side, the creature peered up at the cold face anxiously.

"Yes, Lady. Wisp serves only you."

"There are gifts . . ." She smiled faintly, her voice trailing into silence.

Wordlessly, she handed Wisp the wooden statue of herself, then moved back to stand again before Hebel. Wisp hastened after, crouching down within the folds of her cloak.

"Old man," she addressed Hebel, her pale face bending close to his own. "What would you have me do with you?"

Hebel seemed to have recovered his senses. His eyes

were no longer distant as they glanced quickly at the Witch
and then away again. "Me? I don't know."

Her smile was hard. "Perhaps you should stay here
within the Hollows."

"It doesn't matter," he insisted, as if he sensed somehow
that the Witch would do with him as she pleased anyway.
Then he looked up. "But the Elflings, Mallenroh. Help
them. You could . . ."

"Help them?" she cut him short.

The old man nodded. "If you want me to stay, I will.
There's nothing else for me. But let them go. Give them the
help they need."

She laughed softly. "Perhaps there is something that you
can do to help them, old man."

"But I have done all that I can . . ."

"Perhaps not. If I told you there was something more
that you might do, you would be willing to do it, wouldn't
you?"

Her eyes fixed the old man. Wil saw that the Witch was
toying with him.

Hebel looked uncertain. "I don't know."

"Of course you know," she said softly. "Look at me." His
head lifted. "They are your friends. You want to help them,
don't you?"

The Valeman was frantic. Something was terribly wrong,
but he could neither move nor speak to warn Hebel. He
caught a glimpse of Eretria's frightened face. She, too,
sensed the danger.

Hebel sensed it as well. But he sensed, too, that he could
not escape it. His eyes met those of the Witch. "I want to
help them."

Mallenroh nodded. "Then so you shall, old man."

She reached to touch his face. Hebel saw in the Witch's
eyes what was to become of him. Drifter rose, teeth
suddenly bared, but Hebel's hand caught the back of the
big dog's neck and held him fast. The time for resistance
was over. The Witch's fingers stroked the old man's
bearded cheek gently, and his whole body seemed to go
suddenly rigid. No! Wil tried to scream, but it was already
too late. Mallenroh's cloak enfolded both Hebel and Drifter,
and they were lost from sight. The cloak remained
wrapped about them for a moment, then slipped free.

Mallenroh stood alone. In one hand she held a perfectly sculpted wooden carving of the old man and the dog.

"In this way shall you help them best." She smiled coldly.

She handed the wooden figures to Wisp, who gathered them in. Then she turned to Eretria.

"Now what shall I do with you, pretty one?" she whispered.

Her hand lifted, and a single finger pointed. Eretria was forced to her knees, head bowed. The fingers curled back, and Eretria's hands stretched out to the Witch in a gesture of submission. Tears streaked her face. Mallenroh watched without comment for a moment, then looked abruptly at Wil.

"Would you see her become a wooden statue as well?" Her voice had an edge to it that cut through the Valeman like a knife. Still he could not speak. "Or the Elven girl, perhaps? You know, of course, that I have her."

She did not wait for the response she knew he could not give. She stepped forward, her tall figure bending down until her face was close before his own.

"I wish the Elfstones, and you shall give them to me. You shall give them, Elfling, for I know that if they are taken from you by force, they are useless." Her violet eyes burned into him. "I would have their magic, do you understand? I know their worth far better than you. I am older than this world and its races, older than the Druids who played at Paranor with magics long since mastered by my sister and me. It is so with the Elfstones. Though I am not of Elven blood, yet my blood is the blood of all the races, and so I may command their power. Still, even I cannot break the law that calls their power into being. The Elfstones must be given freely. And so they shall."

Her hand came close before his face, nearly touching it. "I have a sister, Elfling—Morag, she has named herself. For centuries we have lived within these Hollows, called the Witch Sisters, the last of our Coven. Once, long ago, she wronged me greatly, and I have never forgiven. I would have been rid of her except that our powers match so evenly that neither one nor the other of us may prevail. Ah, but the Elfstones are a magic that my sister does not possess, a magic that will enable me to put an end to her.

Morag—odious Morag! Sweet, to see her made to serve me as these men of sticks! Sweet, to still that hateful voice! Oh, I have waited long to be rid of her, Elfling! Long!"

Her voice rose as she spoke until the words rang against the stones of the tower, echoing through the deep stillness. The beautiful, cold face moved back from the Valeman, the slender arms folding within the black robes. Wil Ohmsford could feel the sweat running down his body.

"The Elfstones shall be your gift to me," she whispered. "My gift to you shall be your life and the lives of the women. Accept my gift. Remember the old man. Think of him before you choose."

She stopped as the door to the tower slipped open to admit a handful of the stick men. They came to her in a scuttling of wooden legs, clustering about her. She bent low about them for a moment, then straightened, glancing coldly at Wil.

"You have brought a Demon into the Hollows," she cried. "A Demon—after all these years! It must be found and destroyed. Wisp—his gift!"

The furry creature hastened forward and took from the helpless Valeman the pouch and the Elfstones. The wizened face glanced up at him, then withdrew behind the folds of Mallenroh's cloak. The Witch lifted her hand, and Wil felt himself grow suddenly weak.

"Remember what you have seen, Elfling." Her voice seemed distant now. "I hold the power of life and death. Choose wisely."

She moved past him and disappeared through the open door. His strength began to fail, his vision to blur. At his side, Eretria collapsed on the tower floor.

Then he was also falling. The last thing he remembered was the feel of wooden fingers closing tight about his body.

XLIV

"**W**il."

The sound of his name hung like an echo strayed in the black haze which enveloped him. The voice seemed to come from a great distance, floating downward through the dark to probe him in his sleep. He stirred sluggishly, feeling as if he were weighted and bound. With a great effort, he reached up from within himself, searching.

"Wil, are you all right?"

The voice belonged to Amberle. He blinked, forcing himself awake.

"Wil?"

She was cradling his head in her lap, her face bent close to his own, her long chestnut hair trailing down about him like a veil.

"Amberle?" he asked sleepily, pushing himself upright. Then he reached for her wordlessly and held her close against him.

"I thought I had lost you," he managed.

"And I you." She laughed softly, her arms tight about his neck. "You have been sleeping for hours, ever since they brought you here."

The Valeman nodded into her shoulder, aware suddenly of the pungent smell of incense in the air. He realized it was the incense that was making him feel so groggy. Gently he released the Elven girl and looked about. They were enclosed by a windowless cell, black but for a single light that shone from within a glass container suspended from a ceiling chain, another of the lights that burned neither oil nor pitch and gave off no smoke. One wall of the cell was composed entirely of iron bars fastened vertically into the

460

stone of the floor and ceiling. A single door opened through the bars, fastened in place by hinges on one side and a massive key lock on the other. Within the cell had been placed a pitcher of water, an iron basin, towels, blankets, and three straw-filled sleeping mats. On one of the mats lay Eretria, her breathing deep and even. Beyond the wall of iron bars was a passageway that ran to a set of stairs, then disappeared into blackness.

Amberle followed his gaze to the Rover girl. "I think she is all right—just sleeping. Until now, I have not been able to wake either of you."

"Mallenroh," he whispered, remembering. "Has she harmed you?"

Amberle shook her head. "She has barely spoken to me. In fact, I did not even know who it was that had taken me prisoner at first. The stick men brought me here, and I slept for a time. Then she came to me. She told me that there were others searching for me, that they would be brought to her as I had been brought. Then she left." Sea-green eyes sought his own. "She frightens me, Wil—she is beautiful, but so cold."

"She is a monster. How did she find you in the first place?"

Amberle paled. "Something chased me down into the Hollows. I never saw it, but I could feel it—something evil, searching for me." She paused. "I ran for as long as I was able, then I crawled. Finally I just collapsed. The stick men must have found me and brought me to her. Wil, was it Mallenroh I sensed?"

The Valeman shook his head. "No. It was the Reaper."

She stared at him wordlessly for a moment, then looked away. "And now it is here in the Hollows, isn't it?"

He nodded. "The Witch knows about it, though. She has gone to look for it." He smiled grimly. "Maybe they will destroy each other."

She did not smile back. "How did you manage to find me?"

He told her then everything that had happened since he had left her concealed in the bushes on the rim of the Hollows—the encounter with Eretria, the deaths of Cephelo and the Rovers, the recovery of the Elfstones, the flight back through the Wilderun, the meeting with Hebel and Drifter, the journey down into the Hollows, the discovery of the stick man, and the confrontation with Mallenroh. He finished by telling her what the Witch had done to Hebel.

"That poor old man," she whispered, and there were tears in her eyes. "He meant no harm to her. Why did she do that to him?"

"She doesn't care a whit about any of us," the Valeman replied. "All that interests her are the Elfstones. She means to have them, Amberle. Hebel was just a convenient example for the rest of us—particularly me."

"But you won't give them to her, will you?"

He looked at her uncertainly. "If it means saving our lives, I will. We have to get out of here."

The Elven girl shook her head slowly. "I don't think that she will let us go, Wil—not even if you give her what she wants. Not after what you have told me about Hebel."

He was silent a moment. "I know. But maybe we can bargain with her. She would agree to anything to get the Stones . . ." He stopped abruptly, listening. "Shhh. Someone is coming."

They peered wordlessly through the bars of their cell into the darkness of the corridor beyond. There was a slight shuffling sound upon the stairs. Then a figure appeared within the fringe of their single light. It was Wisp.

"Something to eat," he announced brightly, holding forth a tray with pieces of bread and fruit on it. Shuffling to the cell, he slipped the tray through a narrow slot in the bars at the base of the door.

"Good food," he told them, turning to leave.

"Wisp!" Wil called after him. The furry creature turned, staring at the Valeman quizzically. "Can you stay and talk with us?" Wil asked.

The wizened face broke into a grin. "Wisp will talk with you."

Wil glanced at Amberle. "The ankle—can you walk?"
She nodded. "It's much better," she answered him.

He took her hand and led her to the tray of food. Wordlessly, they seated themselves. Wisp hunched down on the lowest step of the darkened stairway, his head cocking. Wil helped himself to a piece of the bread, chewed, and nodded in appreciation.

"Very good, Wisp."

The little fellow grinned. "Very good."

Wil smiled. "How long have you been here, Wisp?"

"A long time. Wisp serves the Lady."

"Did the Lady make you—as she made those stick men?"

The furry creature laughed. "Stick men—clack, clack. Wisp serves the Lady—but not made of wood." His eyes brightened. "Elf, like you."

Wil was surprised. "But you are so small. And what about the hair?" He pointed to his own arms and legs, then to Wisp. "Did she do that?"

The Elf nodded happily. "Cute, she says. Makes Wisp cute. Roll and jump and play with stick men. Cute." He stopped and glanced past them to where Eretria slept. "Pretty thing." He pointed. "Prettiest of all."

"What do you know about Morag?" the Valeman pressed, ignoring Wisp's obvious interest in the Rover girl.

Wisp's face screwed itself up into a grimace. "Evil Morag. Very bad. A long time she lives within the Hollows, she and the Lady. Sisters. Morag in the east, the Lady in the west. Stick men for both, but just Wisp for the Lady."

"Do they ever go out of the Hollows—Morag and the Lady?"

Wisp shook his head solemnly. "Never."

"Why not?"

"No magic beyond the Hollows." Wisp grinned cunningly.

That told Wil something he had not suspected. The power of the Witch Sisters had its limits; it did not extend beyond the Hollows. That explained why no one had ever encountered them anywhere else within the Westland. He began to see a glimmer of hope. If he could find a way to get clear of the Hollows . . .

"Why does the Lady hate Morag so?" Amberle was asking.

Wisp thought a minute. "Long ago, there was a man. Beautiful, the Lady says. The Lady wanted him. Morag wanted him. Each tried to take the man. The man . . ." He clenched his hands, fingers joining, then wrenched them apart. "No more. Gone." He shook his head. "Morag killed the man. Evil Morag."

Evil Mallenroh, Wil thought. In any case, it was clear enough how the Witch Sisters felt about each other. He decided to find out what else Wisp knew about the Hollows.

"Do you ever go out of the tower, Wisp?" he asked.

The wizened face broke into a proud grin. "Wisp serves the Lady."

Wil took that answer as a yes. "Have you ever gone to Spire's Reach?" he asked.

"Safehold," Wisp replied at once.

There was a hushed silence. Amberle gripped Wil's arm and glanced at him quickly. The Valeman was so stunned by the abruptness of the response that he was left momentarily speechless. Collecting himself, he hunched forward, crooking his finger conspiratorially. Wisp inched a bit closer, head cocked.

"Tunnels and tunnels that wind and twist," Wil said. "Easy to get lost in those tunnels, Wisp."

The furry Elf shook his head. "Not Wisp."

"No?" he challenged. "What of the door made of glass that will not break?"

Wisp thought a moment, then clapped his hands excitedly. "No, no, just pretend glass. Wisp knows pretend glass. Wisp serves the Lady."

Wil was trying to decipher that answer when Wisp pointed past them. "Look. Pretty thing, hello, hello."

The Valeman and the Elven girl turned around. Eretria was sitting up on the straw mat, awake at last, her black tresses falling down about her face as she rubbed the back of her neck. Slowly she looked up at them, started to speak, then caught Wil's warning finger as it passed before his lips. She glanced past him to where Wisp crouched half a dozen feet from the bars of their cell, grinning broadly.

"Pretty thing, hello," Wisp repeated, one hand lifting tentatively.

"Hello," she replied uncertainly. Then, seeing Wil's quick nod of encouragement, she flashed her most dazzling smile. "Hello, Wisp."

"Talk with you, pretty thing." Wisp had forgotten all about Wil and Amberle.

Eretria rose unsteadily, her eyes blinking with sleep, and came over to sit with her companions. She scanned quickly the stairs and the passageway beyond.

"What game are we playing now, Healer?" she whispered out of the corner of her mouth. There was fear in her dark eyes, but she kept her voice even.

The Valeman did not look away from Wisp. "Just trying to learn something that will get us out of here."

She nodded approvingly, then wrinkled her nose. "What is that smell?"

"Incense. I can't be sure, but I think that it acts like a drug when you breathe it in. I think that is what is making us feel so weak."

Eretria turned back to Wisp. "What does the incense do, Wisp?"

The furry Elf reflected, then shrugged. "Nice smell. No worries."

"Indeed," the Rover girl muttered, glancing at Wil. She gave Wisp another broad smile. "Can you open the door, Wisp?" she asked, pointing at the bars.

Wisp smiled back. "Wisp serves the Lady, pretty one. You stay."

Eretria did not change her expression. "Is the Lady here now, in the tower?"

"She looks for the Demon," Wisp answered. "Very bad. Breaks all her stick men apart." His wizened face grimaced. "She will hurt the Demon." He rubbed two fingers together. "Make him go away." Then he brightened. "Wisp could show you wooden statues. Little man and dog. In the box, pretty things like you."

He pointed to Eretria, who went pale and shook her head quickly. "I don't think so, Wisp. Just talk with me."

Wisp nodded agreeably. "Just talk."

Listening to their conversation, Wil had a sudden thought. He sat forward, gripping the bars of their cell.

"Wisp, what did the Lady do with the Elfstones?"

Wisp glanced at him. "In the box, safe in the box."

"What box, Wisp? Where does the Lady keep this box?"

Wisp pointed uninterestedly toward the darkened pas-

sageway behind him, all the while keeping his eyes fixed
on Eretria. "Talk, pretty thing," he pleaded.

Wil glanced at Amberle and shrugged. He was not
having much success coaxing anything more out of Wisp.
The little fellow was only interested in talking with Eretria.

The Rover girl crossed her legs before her and rocked
back. "Would you show me the pretty stones, Wisp? Could
I see them?"

Wisp glanced about furtively. "Wisp serves the Lady.
Faithful Wisp." He paused, considering. "Show you
wooden figures, pretty one."

Eretria shook her head. "Just talk, Wisp. Why do you
have to stay here in the Hollows? Why don't you leave?"

"Wisp serves the Lady." Wisp repeated his favorite
response anxiously, and his face grew troubled. "Never
leaves the Hollows. Cannot leave."

From somewhere high within the tower, a bell rang once
and was still. Wisp rose hurriedly.

"Lady calls," he told them, starting up the stairs.

"Wisp!" Wil called after him. The little fellow stopped.
"Will the Lady let us leave if I give her the Elfstones?"

Wisp did not seem to understand. "Leave?"

"Go out of the Hollows?" Wil pressed.

Wisp shook his head quickly. "Never leave. Never.
Wooden figures." He waved to Eretria. "Pretty thing for
Wisp. Take good care of pretty thing. Talk some more. Talk
later."

He turned and darted up the stairs into the gloom.
Wordlessly, the prisoners watched him go. Above them,
the bell sounded a second time, its echo reverberating into
silence.

Wil spoke first. "Wisp could be wrong. Mallenroh wants
the Elfstones badly. I think she would let us leave the
Hollows if I agreed to give them to her."

They huddled down before the door of their cell, eyes
drifting uneasily to the darkness of the stairway beyond.

"Wisp is not wrong." Amberle shook her head slowly.
"Hebel told us that no one goes into the Hollows. And he
said that no one ever comes out, either."

"The Elven girl is right," Eretria agreed. "The Witch will
never let us go. She will make wooden figures of us all."

"Well, then, we had better come up with another plan."
Vil gripped the bars of the cell, testing their strength.

Eretria rose, peering guardedly into the gloom of the
tairway. "I have another plan, Healer," she said softly.

She reached down into her right boot, separated the
olds of leather along the inner side, and extracted a
1arrow metal rod with a curious hook at one end. Then she
eached into her left boot and pulled forth the dagger she
1ad displayed to Wil when they had been surprised by
Iebel on the rim of the Hollows. She held up the dagger
vith a quick grin, then slipped it back into the boot.

"How did Mallenroh miss that?" Wil asked her in
urprise.

The Rover girl shrugged. "She did not bother to have the
tick men search me. She was too busy making us feel
1elpless."

She moved to the cell door and began examining the
ock.

"What are you doing?" Wil came over to her.

"I am getting us out of here," she declared, peering
arefully into the keyhole. She glanced back at him
1omentarily and indicated the metal rod. "Picklock. No
Rover would be without one. Too many ill-advised citizens
pend their time trying to keep us locked up. I guess they
lon't trust us." She winked at Amberle, who frowned.

"Some of those people probably have good reason not to
rust you," Amberle suggested.

"Probably." Eretria blew dust from the lock. "We all
leceive one another at times—don't we, *sister* Amberle?"

"Wait a minute." Wil dropped down beside her, ignoring
he exchange. "Once you succeed in picking that lock,
:retria, what do we do then?"

The Rover girl looked at him as if he were a fool. "We
un, Healer—just as fast and as far as we can away from
his place."

The Valeman shook his head. "We can't do that. We have
o stay."

"We have to stay?" she repeated in disbelief.

"For a while, at least." Wil glanced momentarily at
\mberle, then made his decision. "Eretria, I think this
night be a good time to put aside a few of those deceptions
ou mentioned. Listen carefully."

He motioned for Amberle to join them, and the three hunched down together in the gloom. Quickly Wil explained to the Rover girl the truth of who Amberle was, who he was, why they had come into the Wilderun, and what it was that they were really seeking. He left nothing out of his narration, for it was necessary now that Eretria appreciate the importance of their search for the Bloodfire. They were in grave danger in this tower, but the danger to them would not lessen, even if they were to get clear of it. If anything were to happen to him, he wanted to be certain that the Rover girl would do what she could to see that Amberle escaped the Hollows.

He finished, and Eretria stared at him wordlessly. She turned to Amberle.

"Is all this true, Elven girl? I trust you better, I think."

Amberle nodded. "It is all true."

"And you are determined to stay until you find this Bloodfire?"

Amberle nodded again.

The Rover girl shook her head doubtfully. "Can I see this seed you carry?"

Amberle withdrew the Ellcrys seed, carefully wrapped in white canvas, from within her tunic. She unwrapped it and held it forth, silver-white and perfectly formed. Eretria stared at it. Then the doubt faded from her eyes, and she turned again to Wil.

"I go where you go, Wil Ohmsford. If you say we must stay, then the matter is settled. Still, we have to get out of this cell."

"All right," Wil agreed. "Then we find Wisp."

"Wisp?"

"We need him. He knows where Mallenroh has hidden the Elfstones and all about Safehold, its tunnels, and its secrets. He knows the Hollows. If we have Wisp to guide us, then we have a chance to do what we came here to do and still escape."

Eretria nodded. "First we have to escape from here. It will take me a while to figure out this lock. Be as quiet as you can. Watch the stairs."

Carefully she inserted the hooked metal rod into the keyhole and began to work it about.

Wil and Amberle moved to the far end of the iron bars,

where they could watch more closely the darkened passageway leading down the flight of stairs from the tower. The minutes slipped away, and still Eretria did not open the cell door. Faint scrapings cut through the deep silence as the hooked rod moved about within the lock, the Rover girl muttering as time and again the latch mechanism slipped free. Amberle crouched close against Wil, and her hand rested loosely on his knee.

"What will you do if she fails?" the Elven girl whispered after a time.

Wil kept his eyes on the passageway. "She won't."

Amberle nodded. "But if she does—what then?"

He shook his head.

"I do not want you to give Mallenroh the Elfstones," Amberle announced quietly.

"We have been over that. I have to get you out of here."

"Once she has the Stones, she will destroy us."

"Not if I handle it right."

"Listen to me!" Her voice was angry. "Mallenroh has no regard for human life. Humans serve no purpose in her eyes beyond the uses she may put them to. Hebel did not understand that when he met her that first time on the rim of the Hollows sixty years ago. All he could see was the beauty and the magic with which she cloaked herself, the dreams she spun with her words, the impressions she left by her passing—all fabrication. He did not see the evil that lay beneath—not until it was too late."

"I am not Hebel."

She took a deep breath. "No. But I worry that your concern for me and what I have come here to do is beginning to color your judgment. You have such determination, Wil. You think that you can overcome any obstacle, however formidable. I envy you your determination—it is something that I sadly lack."

She took his hands in her own. "I just want you to understand that I depend on you. Call it what you wish—I need your strength, your conviction, your determination. But neither that nor what you feel for me must be allowed to distort your judgment. If it does, we are both lost."

"Determination is just about all I have to work with," he responded, eyes shifting momentarily to find hers. "Nor do I agree with you that you lack that same determination."

"But I do, Wil. Allanon knew that when he chose you to be my protector. He knew, I think, how important your own determination would be to our survival. And without it, Wil, we would have been dead long ago." She paused, her voice softening further until she could barely be heard. "But you are wrong when you say that I do not lack that same determination. I do. I always have."

"I do not believe that."

She caught his sudden glance down. "You do not know me as well as you think, Wil."

He studied her face. "What do you mean?"

"I mean that there are things about me . . ." She stopped. "I mean that I am not as strong as I would like to be—not as courageous, not even as dependable as you. Remember, Wil, when we began the journey from Havenstead? You did not think much of me then. I want you to know that I did not think much of me either."

"Amberle, you were frightened. That does not . . ."

"Oh, I was frightened all right," she interrupted quickly. "I am still frightened. My being frightened is the reason for everything that has happened."

By the cell door, Eretria muttered angrily and sat back, eyeing the still tightly locked barrier. She glanced once at the Valeman and went back to work.

"What are you trying to tell me, Amberle?" Wil asked quietly.

Amberle shook her head slowly. "I suppose I am trying to work up enough courage to tell you the one thing that I have been unable to bring myself to tell you since we began this journey." She stared back into the gloomy interior of their little cell. "I suppose I want to tell you now because I do not know if I will have another chance."

"Then tell me," he encouraged.

Her child's face lifted. "The reason that I left Arborlon and did not continue as a Chosen in service to the Ellcrys was that I became so frightened of her that I could no longer bear even to be around her. That sounds foolish, I know, but hear me out, please. I have never told this to anyone. I think that my mother understood, but no one else ever has. I cannot blame them for that. I might have explained myself, but I chose not to. I felt that I could not tell anyone."

She paused. "It was difficult for me once I had been chosen by her. I knew well enough the uniqueness of my selection. I knew that I was the first woman to be chosen in five hundred years, the first woman since the time of the Second War of the Races. I accepted that, though there were many who questioned it and questioned it openly. But I was the granddaughter of Eventine Elessedil; it was not then altogether strange that I should be chosen, I thought. And my family—especially my grandfather—were so proud.

"But the uniqueness of my selection went beyond the fact that I was a woman, I discovered. From the first day of my service, it was different for me from what it was for my companion Chosen. The Ellcrys, it was well known, seldom spoke to anyone. It was virtually unheard of for her to converse with her Chosen after the time of their selection, save in very rare instances. Even then, a conversation with her might take place once during the entire time of a Chosen's service. But from the first day forward, she spoke to me—not once or twice, but every day; not in passing, not in brief, but at length and with purpose. Always, I was alone; the others were never there. She would tell me when to come, and I would do so, of course. I was honored beyond belief; I was special to her, more special than anyone had ever been, and I took great pride in that."

She shook her head at the memory. "It was wonderful at first. She told me things that no one else knew, secrets of the land and the life upon it that had been lost to the races for centuries—lost or forgotten. She told me of the Great Wars, of the Race Wars, of the birth of the Four Lands and their peoples, of all that had been since the beginning of the new world. She told me something of what the old world had been like, though her memory failed her as she went back in time. Some of what she told me, I did not understand. But I understood much. I understood what she told me of growing things, of planting and nurturing. That was her gift to me, the ability to make things grow. It was a beautiful gift. And the talks were magical—just being able to hear about all those wonderful things.

"That was at first. That was when I had just begun my service and the talks were so new and exciting that I accepted what was happening without question. But soon something very unpleasant began to take place. This will sound odd, Wil, but I began to lose myself in her. I began to lose all sense of who I was. I wasn't *me* anymore; I was an extension of her. I still do not know if that was intentional on her part or merely the natural result of our close relationship. At the time, I believed it intentional. I grew frightened of what was happening to me—frightened and then angry. Was I expected as a Chosen to forgo my own personality, my own identity, in order to satisfy her needs? I was being toyed with, I felt; I was being used. It was wrong.

"The rest of the Chosen began to see a change in me. They began to suspect, I think, that there was something different about my relationship with the Ellcrys. I felt them avoiding me; I felt them watching. All the while, I was losing myself in her—a little more of me gone with every day. I was determined to stop it. I began avoiding her as the other Chosen avoided me. I refused to go to her when she asked; I sent another in my stead. When she asked me what was wrong, I would not tell her. I was frightened of her; I was ashamed of myself; I was angry at the whole situation."

Her mouth tightened. "At last I decided that the real problem was that I was never meant to be a Chosen. I did not seem able to cope with the responsibility, to understand what was expected of me. She had done something for me that she had done for no other Chosen—a wondrous, marvelous thing—and I could not accept it. It was wrong that I should feel this way; none of the others would have reacted as I had. My selection as a Chosen had been a mistake.

"So, I left, Wil, barely a month after my choosing. I told my mother and my grandfather that I was leaving, that I could no longer continue to serve. I did not tell them why. I could not bring myself to do that. Failing as a Chosen was bad enough. But to fail because she had made demands on me that anyone else would have been pleased to meet—no. I could admit to myself what had happened between the Ellcrys and me, but I could not admit it to anyone else. My mother seemed to understand. My grandfather did not. There were harsh words exchanged that left us both bitter. I went out of Arborlon disgraced in my own eyes as well as in the eyes of my family and my people, determined that I would not come back again. I swore an Elven vow of outland service; I would make my home in one of the other lands and teach what I knew of the care and preservation of the earth and her life. I traveled until I found Havenstead. That became my home."

There were tears in her eyes. "But I was wrong. I can say that now—I must say it. I walked away from a responsibility that was mine. I walked away from my fears and my frustrations. I disappointed everyone and in the end, I left my companion Chosen to die without me."

"You judge yourself too harshly," Wil admonished her.

"Do I?" Her mouth twisted. "I am afraid that I do not judge myself harshly enough. If I had remained in Arborlon, perhaps the Ellcrys would have spoken sooner of her dying. I was the one to whom she had spoken before—not the others. They did not even realize what had taken place. She might have spoken to me, soon enough that the Bloodfire could have been found and the seed planted before the Forbidding began to crumble and the Demons to break through. Don't you see, Wil? If that is so, then all the Elven dead must be on my conscience."

"It is equally possible," the Valeman pointed out, "that had you not gone out from Arborlon, but remained as you suggest, the warning from the Ellcrys would have come no sooner than it did. Then you would lie dead with the others and be of no use whatsoever to the Elves still living."

"You are asking me to justify my actions through the convenience of hindsight."

He shook his head. "I am asking you not to use hindsight to second-guess what is past. Perhaps it was intended that matters should work out the way they have. You cannot know." His voice hardened. "Now listen to me a minute. Suppose that the Ellcrys had decided to select another of your companion Chosen as the one to whom she would speak. Would that Chosen have reacted any differently from the way you did to the experience? Would another have been immune to the emotions that affected you? I do not think so, Amberle. I know you. Maybe I know you better than anyone, after what we have been through. You have strength of character, you have conviction and, despite what you say, you have determination."

He took her chin in his hand and held it. "I do not know anyone—anyone, Amberle—who would have weathered this journey and all its perils any better than you have. I think that it is time for me to tell you what you are so fond of telling me. Believe in yourself. Stop doubting. Stop second-guessing. Just believe. Put a little trust in yourself. Amberle, you merit that trust."

She was crying openly, silently. "I do care for you."

"And I for you." He kissed her forehead, no longer doubting. "Very much."

She lowered her head against his shoulder, and he held her. When she looked up at him again, the tears were gone.

"I want you to promise me something," she told him.

"All right."

"I want you to promise me that you will make certain that I see this quest through to its conclusion—that I do not falter, that I do not stray, that I do not fail to do what I came to do. Be my strength and my conscience. Promise me."

He smiled gently. "I promise."

"I am still afraid," she confessed softly.

At the door to their cell, Eretria stood up. "Healer!"

Wil scrambled to his feet, Amberle with him, and together they hurried over to join the Rover girl. Her black eyes danced. Wordlessly she slipped the metal rod from the keyhole and returned it to her boot. Then with a wink at the Valeman, she grasped the iron bars to the cell door and pulled. The door swung silently open.

Wil Ohmsford gave her a triumphant grin. Now if they could only find Wisp.

XLV

They found him almost immediately. They had left the cell, moved to the bottom of the stairway, and were peering upward tentatively into the gloom of the passageway when they heard the sound of approaching footfalls. Quickly, Wil motioned Eretria to one side of the passage opening, while drawing Amberle back against the other. Flattened against the stone, they waited expectantly as the footsteps drew closer, a light, familiar scuttling sound that Wil recognized at once.

Seconds later, Wisp's wizened face poked out of the darkness of the passage.

"Pretty one, hello, hello. Talk with Wisp? . . ."

Wil's hand latched firmly onto his neck. Wisp gasped in fright, struggling madly to break free as the Valeman lifted him clear of the floor.

"Keep still!" Wil whispered in warning, yanking the little fellow about so that he could see who had him.

Wisp's eyes went wide. "No, no, cannot leave!"

"Be quiet!" Wil shook him until he was still. "One more word, and I will snap your neck, Wisp."

Wisp nodded frantically, his wiry form squirming in the Valeman's grip. Wil dropped to one knee, lowering his captive to the floor again, still holding tightly to his neck. Wisp's eyes were like saucers.

"Now listen carefully, Wisp," the Valeman said. "I want the Elfstones back again, and you are going to show me what the Witch has done with them. Do you understand?"

Wisp shook his head violently. "Wisp serves the Lady! Cannot leave!"

"In a box, you said." Wil ignored him. "Take me to where she keeps that box."

"Wisp serves the lady! Wisp serves the Lady!" the little fellow repeated in desperation. "You stay! Go back!"

Wil was momentarily at a loss. Then Eretria stepped forward, her dark face just inches from Wisp's. The dagger flashed from her boot and fastened against the little fellow's throat.

"Listen, you little furball!" she said. "If you do not take us to the Elfstones at once, I will cut your throat from one ear to the other. You won't serve anybody then."

Wisp grimaced horribly. "Don't hurt Wisp, pretty one. Like you, pretty one. Care for you. Don't hurt Wisp."

"Where are the Elfstones?" she asked, moving the dagger blade tighter against the Elf's throat.

Abruptly the tower bell sounded—once, twice, three times, then a fourth. Wisp let out a frightened moan and thrashed violently against Wil's grip. The Valeman shook him angrily.

"What's happening, Wisp? What is it?"

Wisp slumped down helplessly. "Morag comes," he whimpered.

"Morag?" Wil felt a sudden sense of desperation. What brought Morag to her sister's keep? He glanced quickly at the others, but the confusion in his eyes was mirrored in theirs.

"Wisp serves the Lady," Wisp muttered and began to cry.

Wil looked about hurriedly. "We need something to bind his hands."

Eretria loosened the long sash about her waist and used it to tie Wisp's hands behind his back. Wil picked up the loose ends and wrapped them about one hand.

"Listen to me, Wisp." He jerked the moaning Elf's chin upright until their eyes met. "Listen to me!" Wisp listened. "I want you to take us to where the Lady keeps the Elfstones. If you try to run or if you try to give any warning, you know what will happen to you, don't you?"

He waited patiently until Wisp nodded. "Then do not be foolish enough to try. Just take us to the Elfstones."

Wisp started to say something, but Eretria brought the dagger up at once. Meekly, the little fellow nodded one time more.

"Good for you, Wisp." Wil released his chin. "Now let's go."

In a line, they started up the stairway, Wisp leading, Wil just a step behind, holding firmly onto the sash that bound Wisp's arms, Eretria and Amberle trailing. Into the blackness they went, eyes peering blindly, hands groping to find the stone walls of the passage. For several moments they were in total blackness. Then a new light glimmered ahead, and the faint outline of the stairs reappeared from the dark. A globe similar to the one that had illuminated their cell came into view, and they passed beneath it. Ahead, others flickered through the gloom.

The climb wore on, the stairway spiraling upward through the tower. From time to time they passed black, empty passageways tunneling through the stone and isolated doors, closed and latched, but Wisp did not slow. The bells had gone still after the first sounding; the entire tower lay wrapped in silence. The musky smell of incense burned more strongly as they climbed, filling the stairwell with its pungent odor. It made the Valeman and the women groggy, and they tried not to breathe it. Wil began to grow suspicious as the minutes slipped away. Perhaps Wisp was smarter than he appeared.

But then they reached a landing and Wisp stopped. He pointed down a dimly lighted corridor that ran a short distance into the tower and ended at a massive, ironbound door. From beyond the door came the sound of voices.

Wil bent down hurriedly. "What is it, Wisp?"

The wizened face was furtive and beaded with sweat. "Morag," Wisp whispered, then shook his head quickly. "Very bad. Very bad."

Wil straightened. "Morag is not our concern. Where are the Elfstones?"

Wisp again pointed to the door. Wil hesitated, staring at him uncertainly. Was Wisp telling him the truth? Then Eretria knelt down next to the little fellow, her voice gentle this time, the dagger no longer in view.

"Wisp, are you certain?"

Wisp nodded. "Not lie, pretty one. Don't hurt Wisp."

"I do not want to hurt you," she assured him, her eyes holding his. "But you serve the Lady, not us. Are we to believe what you say?"

"Wisp serves the Lady," Wisp agreed rather weakly, then shook his head. "Wisp does not lie. Pretty stones there, across great hall, in small room at top of stairs, in box with pretty flowers, red and gold."

Eretria stared at him a moment longer, then glanced at Wil and nodded. She believed him, she was saying. Wil nodded back.

"Is there any other way to get to the box?" Wil pressed the little Elf.

Wisp shook his head. "One door." He pointed down the corridor.

Wil looked at him silently for a moment, then motioned for the others to follow. Quietly, he crept down the short passageway until he stood before the door. Beyond, voices rose, shrill and angry. Whatever was taking place in there, Wil wanted no part of it. He took a deep breath, then slowly, carefully released the latch that held the door before him and pulled. The door slipped open just a crack. The Valeman peered through.

Beyond was the hall where Mallenroh had seized them, massive and shadowed, illuminated faintly by a handful of the strange, smokeless lights that hung like spiders from an invisible ceiling. Immediately past the door, a landing swept downward in a series of half-circle steps to the floor of the hall. There hundreds of the stick men jammed tightly together, encircling two willowy black figures that faced each other at less than a dozen paces and shrieked as if they were cats at bay.

Wil Ohmsford stared. The Witch Sisters, Morag and Mallenroh, last of their Coven, bitter enemies through a centuries-old conflict forgotten by everyone but themselves, were identical twins. Black robes flung back from their tall figures, woven gray hair trailing nightshade, flawless white skin, ghostlike in the dark—they were mirror images. Both were exquisitely formed, both lithe and delicate. But at this moment their beauty was marred by the hatred that contorted their features and hardened their violet eyes. Their words reached out to the Valeman, softer now as the shrieking subsided, yet harsh and biting.

"My power is as strong as your own, Sister, and I fear nothing that you might do. You cannot even keep me from this dreary refuge of yours. We are as rock to stone, and neither one nor the other may prevail." The speaker shook her head mockingly. "But you would change all that, Sister.

You would seek to arm yourself with magic that does not belong to you. In so doing, you would bring an end to our shared dominion over these Hollows. Foolish, Sister. You can have no secrets from me. I know as soon as you what it is that you intend." She paused. "And I know of the Elfstones."

"You know nothing," shrieked the other, whom Wil now saw to be Mallenroh. "Go from my home, Sister. Go while still you may or I will find a way to make you wish that you had."

Morag laughed. "Be still, foolish one. You cannot frighten me. I will leave when I have what I came to get."

"The Elfstones are mine!" Mallenroh snapped. "I have them and will hold onto them. The gift was meant for me."

"Sister, no gift shall be yours if I do not wish it. Such power as the Elfstones offer must belong to her who is best suited to wield it. That one is me. It has always been me."

"You have never been better suited to anything, Sister." Mallenroh spat. "I have permitted you to share this valley with me because you were the last of my sisters, and I felt some pity for one as ugly and purposeless as yourself. Think on it, Sister. I have always had my share of pretty things; but you, you have had nothing but the company of your voiceless stick men." Her voice became a hiss. "Remember the human you tried to take from me, the beautiful one that was mine, the one you wanted so badly? Remember, Sister? Why even that pretty one was lost to you, wasn't he? So careless you were that you let him be destroyed."

Morag stiffened. "It was you who destroyed him, Sister."

"I?" Mallenroh laughed. "One touch from you and he withered with horror."

Morag's face was frozen with rage. "Give me the Elfstones."

"I will give you nothing!"

Crouched motionless behind the massive wooden door, Wil Ohmsford felt a hand on his shoulder and he jumped in surprise. Eretria peered past him through the crack. "What is happening?"

"Stay back," he whispered, and his own eyes returned at once to the confrontation taking place within the hall.

Morag had come forward and now stood directly in front of Mallenroh.

"Give me the Elfstones. You must give them to me."

"Go back to the hole out of which you crawled, lizard." Mallenroh sneered. "Go back to your empty nest."

"Snake! You would feed on your own kind!"

Mallenroh screamed. "Ugly thing! Leave now!"

Morag's hand whipped from beneath her robe and struck Mallenroh a stinging blow across the face. The sound reverberated through the stillness. Mallenroh staggered back in surprise. The wooden limbs of the stick men rattled as they shifted anxiously about the cavernous hall, moving away from the two antagonists.

Then Mallenroh's laughter rose sharply, unexpectedly. "You are pitiful, Sister. You cannot hurt me. Go home. Wait for me to come to you. Wait for me to give you the death you merit. You are not worth having as a slave."

Morag came forward and struck her again, a quick, sudden blow that brought a shriek of rage from Mallenroh. "Give me the Elfstones!" Morag's voice had a desperate edge to it. "I will have them, Sister! I will have them! Give them to me!"

She came at Mallenroh, hands closing about her sister's throat. Mallenroh lurched back again, her beautiful face twisting with rage. Down upon the floor of the tower the Witch Sisters tumbled, scratching and clawing at each other like cats. Then Mallenroh broke free and scrambled back to her feet. One hand stretched forth. Instantly a massive root broke forth from the stone at her feet to wrap tightly about Morag's writhing form. Upward it swept toward the darkness, carrying the struggling Morag with it and growing huge and towering as it reached beyond the glow of the lamps. Morag screamed. Abruptly the darkness blazed with a brilliant flash, and green fire burned the length of the root, turning it to ash. It crumpled lifelessly, smoke billowing out from its remains in thick clouds. Then Morag reappeared, floating downward through the haze like some wraith, to stand again upon the tower floor.

Mallenroh shrieked with frustration, and the green fire swept now from her fingers, engulfing her sister. Morag struck back. For an instant, both were consumed by the fire, their cries filling the hall. Then the fire was gone, and the Sisters stood face to face once more, tall black forms circling slightly away from each other.

"I shall be free of you this time," Mallenroh whispered, her voice filled with cold fury, and she leaped at her sister.

Morag met the rush and threw Mallenroh back. Again the green fire lanced from her fingers. Mallenroh's cry rose high and terrible, and she disappeared in a wall of smoke. An instant later she emerged a dozen feet to the right, fire bursting from her hands. Back and forth the Sisters darted, attacking each other in a frenzied whirl. Sparks from the green fire showered into the hapless stick men; in moments, dozens of them were aflame.

Once more the Sisters closed, grappling wildly, fire lancing from their fingers. Black robes flew wide as they swept together, and the fire burst like a massive pillar out of the stone floor beneath them. A terrible shriek came from both throats as hands locked and their tall forms straightened with the force of their struggle. Flame spattered like water thrown to the far corners of the hall, sparking and burning into the milling stick men. Heat exploded from the pillar of fire with such intensity that it swept through the crack in the door behind which crouched the Valeman and his companions and singed their faces.

Then the tower itself began to shudder, stone and wood shaking free in chips and splinters that cascaded downward through the smoke and gloom. Wil watched the pillar of fire rise from the Witch Sisters to lick hungrily at the great wooden beams that were the tower's support. Everywhere the stick men were burning, spreading the flames across the length and breadth of the hall.

Wil came hurriedly to his feet. If they remained where they were any longer, the flames would trap them. Worse, the entire tower might collapse and bury them. They would have to break out now. It would be dangerous, but less so than staying where they were.

He thrust Wisp before the crack in the door. "Where is the room with the box, Wisp?" Wisp was moaning and sobbing. Wil shook him angrily. "Show me the room!"

Wisp pointed through the door. Far to their right, nearly all the way across the hall, was a narrow, spiraling stairway that ran upward to a landing and a solitary door.

Wil looked quickly at Amberle. Her injured ankle would slow her. "Can you make it?" he asked. She nodded wordlessly. He looked at Eretria, and she nodded as well. He took a deep breath. "Then let's go."

With the struggling Wisp tucked under one arm, he pulled wide the wooden door and darted through. Heat from the flames came at him like a wall, searing his face, burning down his throat. He lowered his head, followed the tower wall to the right, and bounded down the half-circle steps. Stick men milled about him in confusion, but he knocked them aside, clearing the way for his companions. Down to the tower floor they went, skirting the scattered fires, pushing and shoving toward the distant stairs.

Then abruptly the pillar of fire thrust upward in an explosion that threw them all flat. Dazed, they scrambled back to their knees, watching as the struggle between the Witch Sisters intensified. The fire suddenly began to change from mystic green to crackling yellow, a true and natural flame. The Sisters screamed. The fire leaped and streaked along their slender limbs, down the tangle of their long gray hair. It was burning them.

"Sister!" cried one in a wail of recognition and fear.

There was a crackle of burning flesh; with astonishing quickness, the conflagration curled about the Witch Sisters like a shroud and they were consumed. One minute they were standing there, locked in furious battle; the next they were gone. Immune to each other's power, they were unable to survive a joining of the two. All that remained was a shrinking lump of ash and blackened flesh.

Wil heard Amberle gasp in horror. Then the stick men were falling, collapsing like rag dolls, arms and legs separating from bodies, fingers and toes wilting, until nothing was left of them but a vast pile of smoldering deadwood. The magic that had made them and kept them had died with the Witch Sisters. In the burning hall, nothing remained alive but the three outlanders and Wisp.

Their time was growing short. Choking as smoke billowed over him, Wil sprang back to his feet. Holding fast to Wisp, he pushed ahead through the flames and the smoke, kicking aside what remained of the stick men as he went, calling wildly to Amberle and Eretria to follow him. Wisp was crying and muttering, but Wil had little patience with that and ignored him, struggling onto the stairway at the far side of the room and stumbling upward. At the landing, he groped for the latch that held the door closed, praying that it would open. It did. Eyes watering, throat raw and burning, he pushed his way inside.

The roar of the fire followed him, drowning out Wisp's frantic cries. The room was a maze of dark silks and nightshade that trailed along walls and down iron trellis-work. Anxiously the Valeman peered through the dark, finding at last what he sought. On a table at the far side of the chamber, nestled amid clusters of ornaments and jars of incense and perfume, sat a large, intricately carved wooden box, its lid adorned with flowers painted red and gold. The Elfstones! A fierce joy swept through him. Wisp was screaming madly, but Wil did not hear him, dizzied by the heat and the smoke, preoccupied with regaining the Stones. He was vaguely aware of Eretria and Amberle entering the room behind him as he stumbled forward toward the box. He was reaching for the lid when Eretria cried out in warning and knocked him quickly aside.

"How many times must I save you, Healer?" she shouted to make herself heard above the roar of the fire. Snatching an iron latch bar from its hook against one wall, she edged to one side of the box and extended the bar gingerly to flip open the lid. A blur of green shot from within the box, wrapping tightly about the bar. Quickly the Rover girl hammered the bar against the stone floor, leaving the thing still curled about it, a lifeless husk.

Wil stared in horror. It was a viper.

"He was trying to warn you!" Eretria pointed to Wisp. The little fellow had collapsed in tears.

Wil was shaken so badly that for an instant he could neither move nor speak. One bite from that viper . . . Eretria prodded the wooden box with her dagger, pushing it clear of the table. It fell to the chamber floor, and a cluster of precious stones and jewelry tumbled free. In their midst lay the leather pouch. The Rover girl snatched it up, held it a moment as if deciding what should be done with it, then handed it to Wil. He took it wordlessly, loosened the drawstrings, and peered inside.

A faint smile touched his lips. The Elfstones were his once more.

A new shudder swept through the tower; in the hall beyond, one of the massive support timbers gave way, crashing downward in a shower of flames. Wil stuffed the Elfstones into his tunic and started for the door, pulling Wisp and Eretria after him. They had to get out at once.

But a sudden hammering from within a massive wooden wardrobe cabinet brought him about—a hammering that was mixed with muffled cries and the deep snarl of some animal. Wil glanced quickly at Eretria. Something was trapped within that cabinet. The Valeman hesitated only a moment. Whatever it was, it deserved a chance to get clear of the tower. He hastened to the cabinet and flipped clear the restraining latch. The doors flew back and a massive, dark form hurtled into Wil, flinging him back. Shouts rang through the smoke-filled chamber as Wil sought to ward off his attacker. Then the creature was yanked roughly aside and a familiar face came into view.

"Hebel!" Wil exclaimed, in astonishment.

"Back, Drifter!" The old man cuffed the dog sharply, extending a hand down. "What's happening here, anyway? What am I doing in that closet, for cat's sake?"

Wil came to his feet unsteadily. "Hebel! The Witch, Mallenroh—she changed you to wood! Don't you remember?" He grinned in relief. "We thought you were lost! I don't see how you . . ."

Amberle took hold of his arm. "It was the magic, Wil. When Mallenroh died, so did the magic. That was why the stick men collapsed—the magic was gone. It must have happened that way with Hebel and the dog as well."

A fresh wave of smoke poured through the open doorway, and Eretria called out anxiously.

"We have to get out of here." Wil started for the door once more, still cradling the terrified Wisp beneath his arm. "Bring Amberle," he called back to Hebel.

On the landing, they stopped in dismay. The entire hall was in flames. Burning stick men littered the floor. The timbers that spanned the arched ceiling sagged and cracked, the fire burning them through. Even the stone walls had begun to shimmer redly with the heat. At the front of the hall, the entry doors stood closed and barred.

Hesitantly, Wil started down the stairs, searching through the flames and smoke for a path that would take them to those doors.

Then suddenly the doors flew open with a crash, hammered back against the stone by something breaking through from without. At the bottom of the narrow stairway, Wil Ohmsford and the others stopped in surprise, peering through the wall of fire. Daylight streamed through the shattered opening, and Wil thought for just an instant that he saw something shadowy move into the hall. Uncertain, he stared past the flames, trying to decide what it was that he had seen. Had he imagined that shadow . . .

A few steps back, Drifter dropped hurriedly in a crouch, snarling and whining.

And then he knew. The Reaper! He had forgotten about the Reaper.

"Wisp!" he cried frantically, shaking the Elf so hard the wizened face whipped back and forth in front of him. "How do we get out of here? Listen to me! Show me another way out!"

"Wisp . . . out . . . over there." One arm pointed weakly.

Wil saw it—a door, to their left, perhaps twenty yards through the fire. He never hesitated. Calling to his companions to follow, he stumbled through the flames and the smoke for the door. He could almost feel the Reaper breathing over his shoulder. Somewhere back in the hall, it was coming for them.

They reached the door. Choking and gagging, Wil found the handle and twisted. This door, too, was unlocked. Pushing the others before him, he followed them through, slamming the door closed with a heave and throwing the latch bar tight.

Then they ran—down a stairwell that spiraled deep beneath the tower, through gloom lit dimly by the smokeless lights, into musty dampness that cooled their heated bodies, stumbling and lurching, footfalls echoing through the stillness. Only twice did the Valeman turn to speak as he led the others from the ruined tower, once to speak the name of their pursuer, once to warn that the Reaper had found them at last. Then no one spoke again. They simply ran.

At the bottom of the stairs, a passageway opened ahead, tunneling through the light of a scattering of the lamps and twisting from view. Down the corridor they went, Wil carrying the hunched form of Wisp, who moaned and whimpered at every step; Hebel—with Drifter beside him—and Eretria were lending support to Amberle, who still hobbled weakly upon her damaged ankle. The passageway twisted and turned through the earth, angling first one way, then another, filled with insects that skittered and dust that flew as they ran past.

Time and again Wil glanced back through the shadows. Had something moved? Had something sounded? Tears blurred his vision, and he brushed at them angrily. Where was the Reaper? It had tracked them all the way from Arborlon to this tunnel. It was here, close; he could sense it. It was here, hunting.

Ahead, the passageway ended and a second stairwell curled upward, dark and empty. At its foot, the Valeman paused until the others were next to him, then led the way quickly onto the stairs. For long minutes they wound upward through the gloom, watching the curve of the steps slip teasingly ahead, listening for the sounds of the thing that pursued them. But they heard nothing save their own movements. Silence wrapped the passage and those who climbed it.

The stairwell ended at a trapdoor, a latchbolt thrown tight into its stone seating. Wil wrenched the bolt free, placed his shoulder against the door, and heaved upward. With a muffled thud, the trapdoor toppled back; clouded, dull sunlight spilled down into the passage. Quickly the humans and the dog stumbled from the earth.

They stood again within the Hollows, misted, gray, and still. Behind them the island keep of Mallenroh, shrouded in smoke that rose high into the trees and curled down about the moat and wall, crumbled slowly into ruin.

The forest all about lay empty. The Reaper was nowhere to be seen.

XLVI

Wil glanced about uncertainly. Mist and gloom masked everything but the bright flicker of the fires that still burned within the tower of Mallenroh. Nothing else was distinguishable. The Valeman had no idea at all where they should go from there.

"Hebel, where is Spire's Reach?" he asked hurriedly.

The old man shook his head. "Can't be certain, Elfling. Can't see anything."

Wil hesitated, then knelt quickly on the forest earth and brought the cringing form of Wisp out from under his arm. Wisp had buried his face in his hands, and his furry body was curled tightly into a ball. Try as he might, the Valeman could not get the little Elf to unfold. Finally he gave up, holding Wisp by his shoulders and shaking him urgently.

"Wisp, listen to me. Wisp, you have to talk to me. Look at me, Wisp."

The little fellow peeked reluctantly through his fingers. His body shook.

"Wisp, where is Spire's Reach?" Wil asked quickly. "You have to take us to Spire's Reach."

Wisp did not respond, staring out through his parted fingers like a fascinated child for a moment, then locking his hands tight.

"Wisp!" Wil shook him again. "Wisp, answer me!"

"Wisp serves the Lady!" the Elf exclaimed suddenly. "Serves the Lady! Serves the Lady! Serves the . . ."

Wil shook him so hard his teeth rattled. "Stop it! She's dead, Wisp! The Lady is dead! You don't serve her anymore!"

Wisp went still and slowly the hands fell away from his face. He began to cry, great wracking sobs that shook his

487

small frame. "Don't hurt Wisp," he pleaded. "Good Wisp. Don't hurt."

Then he collapsed in a ball, crying and rolling on the ground like a wounded animal. Wil stared down at him helplessly.

"Well done, Healer." Eretria sighed and stepped forward. "You've frightened him half to death. He should be of great use now." She gripped the Valeman's arm and lifted him out of the way. "Let me handle this."

Wil moved over beside Amberle and they watched in silence as the Rover girl knelt beside Wisp and cradled the sobbing Elf in her arms. Whispering softly, she held him close against her and stroked the furry head. Long moments passed and finally Wisp stopped crying. His head lifted slightly.

"Pretty thing?"

"It's all right, Wisp."

"Pretty thing take care of Wisp?"

"I'll take care of you." She gave Wil a stern look. "No one will hurt you."

"Not hurt Wisp?" The wizened face lifted to find her own. "Promise?"

Eretria gave him a reassuring smile. "I promise. But you have to help us, Wisp. Will you do that? Will you help us?"

The little fellow nodded eagerly. "Help you, pretty thing. Good Wisp."

"Good Wisp, indeed," Eretria agreed. Then she bent close to him. "But we have to hurry, Wisp. The Demon—the one that followed us into the Hollows—it still hunts for us. If it finds us, it will hurt us, Wisp."

Wisp shook his head. "Not let it hurt Wisp, pretty one."

"No, it won't hurt you, Wisp—not if we hurry." She stroked his cheek. "But we have to find this mountain—Healer, what is it called?"

"Spire's Reach," Wil offered.

She nodded. "Spire's Reach. Can you show us how to get there, Wisp? Can you take us there?"

Wisp glanced uncertainly at Wil, then past him to the burning tower. His eyes remained fixed on the tower for a moment, then shifted back to Eretria.

"I will take you, pretty one."

Eretria rose and took the little fellow's hand. "Don't worry, now. I'll take care of you, Wisp."

As they moved past Wil, the Rover girl winked. "I told you that you needed me, Healer."

They melted into the gloom of the forest. Wisp led, slipping eel-like through the mist and the tangle of the woods, Eretria's hand gripped firmly in his own. Hebel followed with Drifter, then Wil with Amberle, his arm about her waist to lend support as she limped along gamely beside him. But almost immediately, the others began to widen the distance between them; in trying to catch up, Amberle stumbled and went down. Wil did not hesitate. He simply picked up the Elven girl and went on, cradling her in his arms. To his surprise, Amberle did not protest. He had expected that she would, so fiercely self-reliant had she been throughout their journey. But she was quiet now, her head resting on his shoulder, her arms draped loosely about his neck. Not a single word passed between them.

Wil pondered her behavior momentarily, then his mind was racing on to other matters. Already he was working on a plan for their escape—not just from the Hollows, but from the Reaper as well. For it did them no good to escape from the Hollows, if they did not escape from the Reaper as well. Certainly the Hollows were dangerous, but it was the Reaper that really frightened Wil—a relentless hunter that nothing seemed able to stop, a creature that defied the laws of reason and probability and simply pushed aside the obstacles that hindered its search for the fragile woman-child the Valeman carried. He knew he must not let it find her. Even the Elfstones, could he find a way to unlock their awesome power, might not be enough to stop this creature. They must escape it, and they must escape it quickly.

He thought that he had the means to do so. It was the fifth day of their descent into the Wilderun—the last day that Perk would fly Genewen across the valley before winging home. The Valeman dropped one hand from Amberle momentarily to feel the outline of the small object that nestled in his tunic pocket—the silver whistle that Perk had given him to summon Genewen. It was their sole link to the youthful Wing Rider, and Wil had guarded it carefully. He knew that he had promised Amberle that he would not call upon the boy if their situation were not desperate, but surely it could not be more desperate than this. If they were forced to hike back through the Hollows, back through the Wilderun, and back through the whole of the lower Westland in order to reach the safety of Arborlon, they would never make it. The Reaper would find their trail and catch them. It would be foolish to believe otherwise. They must find another way back, and the only other way he knew was to fly Genewen. The Reaper would still come after them, just as it had come after them before, but by then they would be safely beyond its reach.

Maybe, he cautioned himself. Maybe. They still needed time to escape, and what time remained was slipping rapidly away from them. There had not been much to begin with, and most of that had already been used up. The Reaper hunted them. Even though they had out-maneuvered it in the ruins of the Witch Sister's tower, still it would find them again quickly enough. If they were to escape, they must reach Safehold, locate the Bloodfire, immerse the Ellcrys seed, gain the high slopes of Spire's Reach, signal Perk, who could be anywhere over the Wilderun, board Genewen, if the great Roc could carry them all, and fly to safety—all before the Reaper caught up to them. That was asking a lot, Wil knew.

The forest brushed and tore at him as he followed after Eretria's slim form, branches and vines slapping at his face. He cradled Amberle close, the strain of carrying her already beginning to wear at his arms. All about, the forest lay deep and still.

He wondered momentarily about Arborlon and the Elves. By now, the Demons must have broken through the Forbidding and flooded the Westland, and the Elven people must be engaged in the defense of their homeland. The terrible conflict that Eventine had sought to avoid must have come to pass. And what of the Ellcrys? Had Allanon found a way to protect the dying tree? Had the Druid's power been strong enough to withstand the onslaught of the Demons? Only a rebirth of the Ellcrys could save the Elves, Allanon had said. Yet how much time remained before even that would come too late? Pointless questions, Wil Ohmsford chided himself. Questions that he could not answer, for it was not possible for him to know what was happening beyond the Hollows. Yet he found himself wishing that it were possible for Allanon to reach out to him, tell him something of what was happening in the homeland of the Elves, and let him know that there was still time—if Wil could just find a way to get back again.

Despair washed through him then, sudden, frightening in its certainty—as if he knew that even if he were to succeed here in what he sought to accomplish, still it would be too late for those who awaited his return. And if that were so . . .

Wil Ohmsford did not let the thought finish itself. That way lay madness.

The terrain began to rise, gently at first, then sharply. They were upon the slopes of Spire's Reach. Rock slides and clumps of boulders materialized through the tangle of the woods, and a narrow trail curled upward into the mist. They pushed ahead. Gradually the mist began to fade, and the roof of the forest fell away below them. Large stretches of gray sky appeared through breaks in the trees, and the gloom of the lower forest began to dissipate in small streamers of sunlight. Slowly, carefully, the climbers worked their way up the slopes, catching brief glimpses through the thinning trees of the Hollows spread out beneath them in a sea of tangled limbs.

Then abruptly the trees opened before them and they stood upon a bluff that faced out across the Hollows to the higher walls of the Wilderun. Clusters of scrub and deadwood rose out of deep swatches of saw grass and ran back to the cliff face and a massive cavern that opened down into Spire's Reach like a great dark throat.

Wisp led the little company to the entrance to the cavern, skirting the maze of heavy brush, then stopped just outside and turned quickly to Eretria.

"Safehold, pretty thing—there." He pointed into the cavern. "Tunnels and tunnels that wind and twist. Safehold. Good Wisp."

The Rover girl smiled reassuringly and glanced back to Wil. "Now what?"

Wil came forward and peered unsuccessfully into the darkness. He set Amberle upon her feet momentarily and turned to find Wisp. The little fellow moved at once behind Eretria, hiding his face within the folds of her pants.

"Wisp?" Wil called him gently, but Wisp would have nothing to do with the Valeman. Wil sighed. There was no time for this foolishness.

"Eretria, ask him about a door made of glass that will not break."

The Rover girl bent down so that Wisp was facing her again.

"Wisp, it's all right. I won't let anyone hurt you. Look at me, Wisp." The little fellow raised his head and smiled uncertainly. Eretria stroked his cheek. "Wisp, can you show us a door made of glass that will not break? Do you know of such a door?"

Wisp cocked his head. "Play games, pretty thing? Play games with Wisp?"

Eretria was at a loss. She glanced quickly at Wil, who shrugged and nodded.

"Sure, we can play a game, Wisp." Eretria smiled. "Can you show us this door?"

Wisp's wizened face crinkled with glee. "Wisp can show."

He bounded up, dashed into the mouth of the cavern, then back out again to grab Eretria's hand and pull her after him. Wil shook his head hopelessly. Wisp was more than a little crazed, whether from all that had happened to him during his confinement within the Hollows or from the shock he had suffered at losing his Lady, and they were risking a great deal in believing that he could show them the chamber of the Bloodfire. Still, they had little choice. He glanced again at the blackness of the cavern.

"I'd hate to become lost in there," Hebel muttered next to him.

Eretria seemed to be of the same opinion. "Wisp, we can't see anything." She pulled him to a stop. "We have to make torches."

Wisp froze. "No torches, pretty thing. No fire. Fire burns—destroys. Hurts Wisp. Fire burns the tower of the Lady. The Lady . . . Wisp serves . . ."

He broke down suddenly, tears flooding his eyes, his small arms wrapping tight about the Rover girl's legs. "Not hurt Wisp, pretty thing!"

"No, no, Wisp," she assured him, picking him up and holding him close to her. "No one will hurt you. But we need light, Wisp. We cannot see in this cavern without light."

Wisp raised his tear-streaked face. "Light, pretty thing? Oh, light—there is light. Come. Over here is light."

Mumbling half to himself, he led them to the mouth of the cavern once more. Then, moving to the near wall, he reached into a small niche in the rock and extracted a pair of the strange lamps. As he thrust them into the cavern, the glass-enclosed interiors came alive with the same smokeless light that had burned throughout the Witch Sister's tower.

"Light." Wisp smiled eagerly, handing the lamps to Eretria.

She took them, keeping one for herself and handing the second to Wil. The Valeman turned back to Hebel.

"You don't have to come any further with us if you don't want to," he pointed out.

"Don't be stupid," the old man snorted. "What if you get lost in there? You'll need Drifter and me to get you out again, won't you? Besides, I want a look at this Safehold place."

Wil could see that there was little to be gained by arguing the matter further. He nodded to Eretria. The Rover girl took a firm grip on Wisp's hand; holding the lamp she carried before them both, she started into the cave. Wil lifted Amberle in his arms and followed. Hebel and Drifter brought up the rear.

They moved ahead cautiously. Gradually their eyes began to adjust, and they could see that the cavern ran well back into the core of Spire's Reach, its roof and walls far beyond the glow of the lamps. The floor of the cavern was uneven, but free of obstructions, and they walked deep into the blackness. At last Wisp brought them to the rear wall of the cavern. Before them were a series of openings, little more than narrow clefts in the rock, one very much like another, splitting the cavern wall and disappearing from view.

Wisp had no problem deciding which opening he wanted. Without any hesitation at all, he chose one and led the way through. He took them into a labyrinth of cuts and turns, twisting and winding along a maze of tunnels that sloped steadily downward. The others were soon hopelessly lost. Still Wisp led them on.

Then suddenly they stood before a stairway, and the character of the tunnels underwent an abrupt change. Gone were the naturally formed rock walls, roof, and floor. The stairs and surrounding passageway were formed of stone blocks, rough-hewn and massive, but unquestionably fashioned by hand. Patches of dampness glistened on the walls and roof of the passage, and trailers of water ran upon the steps. There were sounds in the darkness below. Small bodies scattered with a scratching of tiny feet and squeaks of annoyance. Flashes of sudden movement revealed the sleek, dark forms of rats.

Wisp led them down the stairs into the darkness. For hundreds of feet the stairs wore on, bending and turning at odd angles, leveling off once or twice in small rampways, then twisting deep into the mountain. All about them, just beyond the glow of the smokeless lamps, the rats scurried through the dark, their cries faint and unpleasant in the stillness. The air grew pungent with the smell of musty dampness and decay. Still they descended, watching the steps wind away before them.

Finally the steps ended. They stood within a great hall, its high arched ceiling braced with massive columns. Broken stone benches filled the chamber, arranged in widening rows about a low, circular platform. Strange markings were carved in the stone of the columns and walls, and iron stanchions and standards rusted upon the platform. Once this chamber had been a council room or meeting hall, or perhaps even a place of offerings and strange rites, Wil thought. Once another people had gathered here. He stared about momentarily, and then Wisp was leading them through the rows of benches and past the platform to a massive stone door that stood ajar at the far end of the hall. Beyond, another set of stairs led downward.

They descended this new stairway. Wil was growing more than a little concerned. They had come a long way into the mountain, and only Wisp had any idea at all where they were. If the Reaper caught them here . . .

The steps ended. They moved into another passageway. From somewhere ahead, Wil thought he heard the sound of water splashing, as if a brook were tumbling down through the stone. Wisp hurried forward eagerly, pulling at Eretria's hand, casting anxious glances over one shoulder as if to be certain that she still followed him.

Then they were through the passage and standing in a great cavern. Gone were the stone-block walls that formed the tunnels that had led them here. This cavern was nature's work, its walls pocked and split, its roof a mass of jagged stalactites, its floor cratered and littered with broken rock. In the darkness beyond the circle of light cast by their lamps, they could hear water rushing.

Wisp led them across the cavern, stepping nimbly through the rock, muttering as he went. Against the far wall lay stacked a mass of boulders that looked to be the result of a rock slide. Down through their midst, a narrow band of water tumbled and gathered in a pool that spread outward in a series of tiny streams, bubbling and twisting and finally disappearing into the gloom.

"Here," Wisp announced brightly, pointing to the waterfall.

Wil lowered Amberle to her feet and stared at the little fellow blankly.

"Here," Wisp repeated. "Door made of glass that will not break. Funny game for Wisp."

"Wil, he means the waterfall." Amberle spoke up suddenly. "Look closely—where the water spreads out between those rocks above the pool."

Wil did look, seeing now what the Elven girl had seen. Where the water spilled down into the pool, it fell in a thin, even sheet between twin columns of rock, causing it to look very much as if it were a door made of glass. He moved forward several paces, watching the light cast from his lamp reflect back from the water's surface.

"But it is not glass!" Eretria snapped. "It's just water!"

"But would the Ellcrys remember that?" Amberle countered quickly, speaking still to the Valeman. "It has been so long for her. Much of what she once knew has become forgotten in the passing of time. On much she is confused. Perhaps she remembers this waterfall only for what it appeared to be—a door made of glass that will not break."

Eretria looked down at Wisp. "This is the door, Wisp? You're sure?"

Wisp nodded eagerly. "Funny game, pretty thing. Play funny game with Wisp again."

"If this is the door, then there should be a chamber beyond . . ." Wil started forward.

"Wisp can show!" Wisp darted ahead of him, pulling Eretria as he went. "Look, look, pretty thing! Come!"

He drew the Rover girl with him until they stood just to the right of the waterfall beside the pool into which it spilled. The wizened face glanced back briefly, and the little fellow released her hand.

"Look, pretty thing."

An instant later he had stepped into the waterfall and disappeared. The Rover girl stared after him. Almost immediately he was back again, his fur plastered down against his body, his face beaming.

"Look," he beckoned and seized the girl's hand once more, pulling her after him.

In a knot, the little company passed through the waterfall, still holding the smokeless lamps before them, shielding their eyes as they slipped within the rocks. An alcove lay behind the fall, with a narrow passage beyond. Dripping, they followed it back, with Wisp leading them on, until they had walked to its end, where yet another cavern lay, this one much smaller and unexpectedly dry, free of the musty dampness that filled the other, its floor sloping up into the gloom in a series of broad shelves. Wil took a deep breath. If the waterfall were the door made of glass that would not break to which the Ellcrys had directed them, then it was here, in this chamber, that they would find the Bloodfire. He walked wordlessly to the rear of the cavern and back again. There were no other tunnels leading in, no other passages. Rock walls, floor, and cavern roof reflected dully in the glow of his lamp as he held it up and looked carefully about.

The chamber was empty.

At the mouth of the cavern that opened down into Spire's Reach, a shadow passed from the tangle of brush that clogged the bluff and disappeared soundlessly into Safehold. In the wake of its passing, the forest had gone suddenly still.

* * *

A rush of wild imaginings crowded Wil Ohmsford's mind as he stood within that empty cavern and stared helplessly about. There was no Bloodfire. After all they had endured to reach Safehold, there was no Bloodfire. It was lost, perhaps gone from the earth for centuries, gone with the old world. It was a fiction, a vain hope conceived by the Ellcrys in her dying, a magic that had disappeared with the passing of the land of faerie. Or if there was a Bloodfire, it was not here. It lay somewhere else within the Wilderun, somewhere other than these caverns, and they would never find it. It lay beyond their reach. It lay hidden . . .

"Wil!"

Amberle's call broke the stillness, sudden and quick. He turned to find her standing apart from him, one hand groping before her as if she were blind and sought to see.

"Wil, it is here! The Bloodfire is here! I can feel it!"

Her voice trembled with excitement. The others stared at her, watching as she hobbled forward through the cavern gloom, watching the mesmerizing play of her fingers as they stretched forth like feelers into the dark.

Eretria moved quickly over to Wil, still grasping Wisp's hand as the little Elf cowered behind her.

"Healer, what does she . . . ?"

His hand came up to silence her. He shook his head slowly and he did not speak. His eyes remained fixed on the Elven girl. She had moved now to one of the higher levels of the cavern, a small shelf that stood almost in the exact center of the chamber. Painfully, she limped forward, stepping onto the shelf. At its far edge, a large boulder sat. Amberle hobbled to the boulder and stopped, hands reaching down to stroke its surface.

"Here." She breathed the word.

Wil started forward at once, bounding onto the shelf. Instantly the Elven girl turned back to face him.

"No! Come no closer, Wil!"

The Valeman stopped. Something in the tone of her voice forced him to stop. They faced each other wordlessly in the gloom of the cavern for an instant, and in the Elven girl's eyes there was a look of desperation and fear. Her eyes stayed locked on his a moment longer, and then she turned away. Placing her slim body against the boulder, she shoved. As if it were made of paper, the boulder rolled back.

White fire exploded from the earth. Upward toward the roof of the cavern it lifted, the flame glistening like liquid ice. It burned white and brilliant as it rose, yet gave off no heat. Then slowly it began to turn the color of blood.

Wil Ohmsford staggered back in shock, unaware momentarily that in the rush of Fire Amberle had disappeared altogether. Then behind him he heard Wisp scream in horror.

"Burn! Wisp will burn! Hurt Wisp!" His voice became a shriek. His wizened face contorted as the fire flooded the cavern with red light. "The Lady, the Lady, the Lady—burns, she burns! Wisp . . . serves the . . . burns!"

His mind snapped. Wrenching free of Eretria, he ran from the chamber, screaming one long wail of anguish. Hebel grabbed for him and missed.

"Wisp, come back!" Eretria cried. "Wisp!"

But it was too late. They heard him pass through the waterfall and he was gone. In the crimson glare of the Bloodfire, the three who remained faced one another wordlessly.

XLVII

I n the next instant Wil Ohmsford realized that he could no longer see Amberle. He hesitated, thinking that somehow his eyes were deceiving him, that the Fire was hiding her in its mix of shadows and crimson light, that she must still be standing there on that shelf of rock where she had stood a moment earlier. Yet if that were so, why was it that he couldn't see her?

He was starting toward the Bloodfire to find out when the scream sounded—high and terrible as it lingered in the stillness.

"Wisp!" Eretria whispered in horror.

She was already moving toward the passageway when Wil caught up with her and pulled her quickly back toward the Fire. Hebel backed away with them, one hand gripping Drifter's neck as the big dog growled in warning.

Then they heard something pass through the waterfall. Not Wisp, Wil knew; this was something else, something much bigger than Wisp. The sound of its passing told him that much. And if it was not Wisp then . . .

The hackles on the back of Drifter's neck bristled up in fear and the big dog dropped to a crouch, snarling.

"Behind me." Wil motioned Eretria and Hebel back.

Already he was reaching into his tunic, pulling free the pouch that held the Elfstones. Backing to the edge of the rock shelf where the Bloodfire burned, his eyes fixed on the chamber entry, he yanked open the leather drawstrings, his fingers groping frantically.

It was the Reaper.

Its shadow moved in the chamber entry, as soundless as the passing of the moon. The Reaper walked like a man, though it was much larger than any ordinary man, a

massive, dark thing, larger even than Allanon. Robes and a
cowl the color of damp ashes were all that could be seen of
it. As it slipped from the passage, the Fire's crimson light
fell across it like blood.

Eretria's frightened hiss cut through the silence. From a
gathering of great hooked claws dangled the broken form
of Wisp.

Instantly the curved dagger appeared in the Rover girl's
hand. From within the black shadow of its cowl, the
Reaper stared out at her, faceless, implacable. Wil felt
himself go impossibly cold, colder even than when he had
first seen Mallenroh. He felt total evil in the Demon's
presence. He thought suddenly of its victims, of the Elven
watch at Drey Wood, of Crispin, Dilph, and Katsin at the
Pykon, of Cephelo and the Rovers at Whistle Ridge—all of
them destroyed by this monster. And now it had come for
him.

He began to shake, the fear within him so strong that it
was like a living thing. He could not take his eyes from the
Demon, could not bring himself to look away, though
every fiber of his body begged him to do so. At his side,
Eretria's face was gray with terror, her dark eyes darting to
find the Valeman's. Hebel retreated a step further, and
Drifter's snarl became a frightened whine.

When the Reaper stepped clear of the chamber wall, the
motion was smooth and noiseless. Wil Ohmsford braced
himself. The hand that held the Elfstones came up. The
Reaper stopped, its faceless hood lifting slightly. But it was
not the Valeman that caused it to hesitate. It was the
crimson Fire that burned beyond. There was something
about the Fire that disturbed the Reaper. Silently the
Demon studied the blood-red flames as they licked at the
smooth surface of the rock shelf and rose to the chamber
ceiling. The Fire did not appear to threaten. It simply
burned, cool, smokeless, and steady, leaving no mark. The
Reaper waited a moment longer, watching. Then it started
forward.

The dreams came back to Wil Ohmsford in that instant,
the dreams that had plagued his sleep at Havenstead and
again at the fortress in the Pykon, the dreams of the thing
that hunted him through mist and night, the thing from
which he could not escape. The dreams came to him now

as they had come to him in his sleep, and all of the feelings that had swept through him then were reborn, yet stronger and more terrifying. It was the Reaper that had pursued him, its face never seen as it stalked him from one imagined dream world to the next, always just a step away—the Reaper, now come out of nightmare into reality. But this time there was nowhere to flee, nowhere to hide, no waking out of sleep. This time there was no escape.

Allanon! Help me!

He retreated deep within himself and found the Druid's words floating in a sea of unreasoned fear. Believe in yourself. Believe. Have confidence. I depend on you most of all. I depend on you.

He gathered the words to him. Hand steady, he called upon the magic of the Elfstones with everything that he could muster. Down into the Stones he plunged, feeling himself drop through layers of deep blue light. His vision seemed to cloud as he fell, and the scarlet glow of the Bloodfire seemed to fade to gray. He was close now, close. He could feel the fire of the Elfstones' power.

Yet nothing happened.

He panicked then, and for an instant the fear over-whelmed him so completely that he almost broke and ran. It was only the realization that there was nowhere left to run to that made him stand fast. The barrier was still there, still within him—just as it had been within him following the encounter with the Demon in the Tirfing—as it would always be within him because he was not a true master of the Elfstones, not their rightful holder, nothing but a foolish Valeman who had presumed that he could be something more than what he was.

"Healer!" Eretria cried desperately.

Again the Valeman tried and again he failed. The power of the Elfstones would not be called forth. He could not reach it, could not command it. Sweat bathed his face, and he clenched the Elfstones so tightly that the edges cut into his palm. Why would the power not come?

Then Eretria stepped away from him, feinting suddenly with the dagger, calling the Demon after her. The Reaper turned, the faceless cowl following her as she moved slowly down the rock shelf, as if she thought to escape back through the chamber entry. Wil recognized at once what she was doing; she was giving him time—a few precious seconds more to bring the power of the Elfstones to life. He wanted to call out to her, to tell her to come back and to warn her that he could no longer use the magic. But somehow he could not speak. Tears ran from the corners of his eyes as he strained to break the barrier that locked him from the Stones. She was going to die, he thought frantically. The Reaper was going to kill her while he stood there and watched it happen.

Lazily, the Reaper tossed aside what remained of Wisp. From beneath its robes, hooked claws stretched out into the crimson light of the Bloodfire toward the Rover girl.

Eretria!

What happened next was to be etched in his mind as if carved into rock. In a few seconds of frozen time, past and present were gathered into one; as had once happened to his grandfather, Wil Ohmsford came face to face with himself.

He seemed to hear Amberle speaking to him, her voice lifting from out of the red glow cast by the Bloodfire on the chamber rock, steady, calm, and filled with hope. She spoke to him as she had spoken to him that morning after they had fled the Pykon, when the Mermidon was carrying them safely south, far from the horror of the night gone past. She told him, as she had told him then, that despite all that had happened the power of the Elfstones was not lost, that it was still his and that he might use it.

But the power *was* lost. She had seen what had happened on the fortress catwalk. He had wanted desperately to destroy the Demon after what he had seen it do to the gallant Crispin! Yet he had stood there, the Elfstones clutched uselessly in his hand, unable to do anything. If the wind had not caused the catwalk to collapse, the Reaper would have had them. Surely she must see that the power was lost.

Her sigh came back, a whisper in his mind. It was not lost. He was trying too hard. He was trying so hard that he was shutting himself away from the Elfstones, something that would not be happening but for his inability to understand the nature of the power he sought to master.

He must try to understand. He must remember that Elven magic was but an extension of the user . . .

Her voice faded and Allanon's replaced it. Heart and mind and body—one Stone for each. A joining of the three would give life to the Elfstones. But Wil must create that joining. Maybe it would not be as effortless for him as it had been for his grandfather because he was a person different from his grandfather. He was two generations removed from Shea Ohmsford's Elven blood, and what had come to his grandfather with but a thought might not come so easily to him. Much within him resisted the magic.

Yes, yes! Wil cried to himself. The Man blood resisted. It was the Man blood that kept him from the power of the Elfstones. It was the Man blood, the non-Elven part of him that rejected the magic.

Allanon's laugh was low and mocking. If that were so, then how was it that he had been able to use the Elfstones once before . . . ?

The Druid's voice faded as well.

And then Wil Ohmsford saw the deception he had worked upon himself since that moment within the Tirfing when he had called forth the power of the Elfstones and felt the awesome magic flood through him like liquid fire. He had let the lie grow out of doubt that the power of the Elfstones was ever truly his to wield, and he had unwittingly reinforced it with Allanon's startling revelation that only Elven blood gave mastery over the Stones. How quick he had been to conclude that his Man blood was the reason for his failure to use again the very same power that he had used within the Tirfing—even though his mix of Man blood and Elven blood was no different now than it had been then.

He had deceived himself completely! Perhaps not knowingly, perhaps not willingly, but he had deceived himself nevertheless, and in doing so had lost the power of the Elfstones. How had it happened? Amberle had touched upon the truth when twice during their travels she had cautioned that in his use of the Stones within the Tirfing it seemed as if had done something to himself. He had made light of the caution, trying to brush aside her concern—even while admitting to her that she was right. He *had* done something to himself when he had used the Elf-

stones. Yet he could not trace it. He had thought that what
he had done was physical in nature, but he found nothing
wrong. Amberle had suggested that it might be something
more, that Elven magic could affect the spirit as well. But
he hadn't wanted to believe that. When he found nothing
immediately wrong, he had been quick to dismiss the
entire matter, to block it from his mind completely, because
after all he could not afford to spend time worrying about
himself when he had Amberle to look out for. That had
been a very large mistake. He should have seen then, as he
saw now, that Amberle had been right, that his use of the
Elfstones had most certainly done something to his spirit,
something so damaging that, until he came to grips with it,
the power of the Stones would be lost to him.

For what had happened to Wil Ohmsford was that he
had become afraid.

He could admit it now. He must admit it. This was a fear
he had not been able to recognize until now, easily
confused, cleverly concealed. All these weeks it had been
there, and he had not recognized it for what it was. For this
was not a fear of the thing that haunted him in his dreams
or of the Demon that had hunted Amberle and him south
from Arborlon. It was fear of the very thing that he had
relied upon to protect them, of the Elfstones and of the
effect that the use of their awesome, unpredictable power
might have upon him.

Understanding flooded through him. It was not the mix
of his Man blood with his Elven blood that was shutting
him from the power of the Stones. It was his fear of the
magic.

It had been his own doing. So resolved had he been that
he would succeed in the task that Allanon had given him,
and so determined that nothing would prevent him from
carrying it out, that he had buried his fear at the instant of
its birth in a well of determination. He had refused to admit
it might exist, but had hidden it, even from himself. Eventually it had begun to affect his use of the Elfstones. There
could be no joining of himself, of heart and mind and body,
with the power of the Stones while such fear lay unrecog-
nized within him. He had let himself believe that he was
experiencing a rejection of the Elven magic by his Man

blood. With that, he had made the deception complete, and any further use of the Stones had become impossible.

Until now. Now he understood the nature of the barrier that shut him from the power of the Elfstones. It was the fear that had blocked him from the Stones—and he might deal with that.

He reached down within himself, a quick and deliberate act, joining as one heart, mind, and body, willingness and thought and strength, in a single, unbreakable purpose. It did not happen easily. The fear was still there. It rose up before him like a wall, warning him back, eroding his purpose. It was strong, so strong that for an instant Wil thought that he could not go on.

There was danger in his use of the Elfstones, a danger that he could neither see nor touch, define nor understand. It was there, real and tangible, and it could damage body and spirit irreparably. It could destroy him. Worse, it could let him live. There were things more terrible than dying . . .

He fought against it. He thought of his grandfather. When Shea Ohmsford had used the Sword of Shannara, there had been danger that the Valeman had sensed yet not understood. He had told Wil that. But there had been need for the magic of the Sword, and the choice his grandfather had made had been a necessary one. So it was now with Wil. There was need greater than his own. There was a trust that had been given him, and there were lives that only he could preserve.

He thrust himself deep into the blue light of the Elfstones, and the fear shattered before him. Man blood gave way to Elven, and the power of the Stones surged up within him.

Past and present split apart, and the seconds were gone. Eretria!

The Reaper was moving, springing soundlessly through the Bloodfire's crimson glow toward the Rover girl. Wil brought up the Elfstones and their fire exploded from his hands into the Demon, driving the creature back into the cavern wall.

There was no sound as the Reaper struck—only a terrible silence as its robes collapsed against the rock. In the next instant it was on its feet again, lunging for the Valeman.

Wil would not have believed that anything so huge could be that quick. Almost before he could act, the Reaper was before him, claws ripping downward. Again the blue fire burst from the Elfstones, hammering into the Demon, hurtling it backward like a rag doll. Again there was no sound. Wil felt the fire within his body this time, coursing through him as if it were his lifeblood, and the feeling was as it had been in the Tirfing. Something had been done to him—something not altogether pleasant.

But there was no time to think on it. The Reaper's ash-gray form darted like a shadow through the half-light in a soundless rush. Fire burst from the Valeman's outstretched hand, but this time the Reaper was too quick. Dodging the attack, it came on. Again Wil tried to stop it, and again he failed. He stumbled back, frantically trying to bring the Elven magic to bear, but his concentration was broken, and the fire had begun to scatter. The Reaper darted through it, looming up before him. At the last possible moment, Wil managed to gather the fire before him like a shield. Then the Reaper was upon him, knocking him violently back. Down he went, head slamming against the stone of the chamber floor. For an instant he thought he would black out. Claws tore at the blue fire, struggling to reach him. But the Valeman fought the dizziness and the pain, and the Elfstones' magic stayed alive. The Reaper sprang back in frustration and circled silently away.

Dazed, Wil scrambled to his feet. His body ached from the force of the Reaper's attack, and there were spots dancing before his eyes. With an effort, he kept himself erect. Things were not working out as he had expected. He had thought when he had broken through to the Elven magic that the worst was over, that at last he possessed mastery of a weapon against which the Reaper could not stand, that however powerful and dangerous the Demon, it would be no match for the Stones. Now he was no longer certain.

Then he remembered Eretria. Where was Eretria? Within him the Elven fire twisted like an imprisoned creature. For one terrible moment he was afraid that he had lost control of it completely. In that moment, the Reaper attacked him again. It came out of the shadows, silent and swift, bounding into the glare of the Bloodfire and into the

Valeman. Almost of its own volition, the Elven magic flared
up between the combatants in a blinding explosion that
threw both from the narrow shelf. The unprepared Valeman was flung back into the cavern wall, ribs and the
elbow of his free arm cracking like deadwood as he
smashed against the rock. Searing pain lanced through
him, and the arm went quickly numb.

Somehow he struggled up again, bracing himself against
the wall. Fighting the pain and the nausea that washed
through him, he cried out for Eretria. The Rover girl darted
from the shadows, reaching him barely a step ahead of the
Reaper. With a noiseless lunge the monster came for them,
too quickly this time for the dazed Valeman to act. It would
have had them but for Drifter. Forgotten by all, the huge
dog tore free of Hebel's grip and hurtled into the Demon.
The monster tumbled back, a blur of bristling hair and
teeth ripping into the ash-colored robes. For an instant
both disappeared into the shadows at the front of the
cavern. Drifter's snarl was deep and terrible. Then the
Reaper heaved upward, flinging the gallant dog from him,
swatting it as one might swat a fly. Drifter flew through the
air and smashed into the cavern wall, collapsing with a
startled whimper into silence.

Yet even those few seconds gave Wil the time he needed
to recover. His arm rose instantly, and the blue fire thrust
out. It caught the Reaper a glancing blow, but again the
creature twisted free, circling swiftly away through the
cavern half-light until the pillar of the Bloodfire screened it
from view.

The Valeman waited, eyes sweeping the chamber. There
was no sign of the Demon. Frantically he searched the
shadows, knowing that it would come again. He could not
find it. Eretria crouched sobbing beside him, one hand still
clutching the dagger, her face streaked with dirt and sweat.
Hebel bent close to Drifter, whispering urgently. The
seconds slipped away. Still nothing moved.

Then Wil glanced up. The Reaper was on the cavern
roof.

He saw it just as it dropped toward him, gray robes
flying wide. Frantically he shoved Eretria aside and
brought up the Elfstones. Like a cat, the Demon landed
before them, massive and soundless. Eretria screamed and

stumbled back in horror. Slowly, slowly, the black hole of
the cowl widened, freezing Wil Ohmsford with its empty
stare. The Valeman could not move. The blackness held
him, faceless and deep.

Then the Reaper lunged, and for just an instant Wil felt
himself swallowed by the thing. He would have died then
but for the power of the Elfstones. Seeking stones, Allanon
had called them, and the warning cried out in his mind—
seek the Reaper's face! Quicker than thought, the magic
acted, blinding him to the terrible monster, to his fear and
pain, and to everything but a primitive instinct for survival.
He heard himself scream, and the blue fire exploded from
him. It tore through the Reaper's faceless cowl, gripped the
Demon like a vice about its invisible head and held it fast.
Twisting desperately, the monster sought to break free. Wil
Ohmsford's hands locked before him, and the Elven magic
swept from his shattered body into the Reaper, lifting it,
thrusting it back against the cavern wall. There the Reaper
hung, impaled upon the blue fire, writhing in fury as it
burned. An instant later the fire swept downward through
the Demon's robes and exploded in a flare of blinding light.

When the fire died, all that remained of the Reaper was a
charred outline of its twisted robes burned deep into the
cavern rock.

XLVIII

The Bloodfire enfolded Amberle Elessedil with the gentle touch of a mother's hands. All about her the flames rose, a crimson wall that shut away the whole of the world beyond, yet did no harm to the wondering girl. How strange, she thought, that the Fire did not burn. Yet when she had pushed away the rock and the Fire had burst forth about her, somehow she had known that it would be so. The Fire had consumed her, but there had been no pain; there had been no heat or smoke or even smell. There had been only the color, deep hazy scarlet, and a sense of being wrapped in something familiar and comforting.

A drowsiness crept through her and the pain and fear of the past few days seemed to drain slowly away. Her eyes wandered curiously through the flames, trying to catch a glimpse of the cavern that housed the Fire and the companions who had come with her. But there was nothing; there was only the Fire. She thought to step through it momentarily; to reach beyond its haze, yet something within her dissuaded her from doing so. She should remain here, she sensed. She should do what she had come here to do.

What she had come here to do—she repeated the words and sighed. Such a long journey it had been; such a terrible ordeal. But now it was ended. She had found the Bloodfire. Curious how that had happened, she thought suddenly. She had been standing there within that darkened, empty cavern, as dispirited as her companions that there was no Bloodfire to be found beyond the door made of glass that would not break, that all of their efforts had been for nothing, when suddenly . . . suddenly she had sensed the Fire's presence. She hesitated in describing it so, but there was no better way. The sensing was similar to what she had experienced upon the rim of the Hollows when she had hidden within that clump of bushes to await Wil's return, similar to what had warned her of the Reaper's approach. It was a feeling that came from deep inside, telling her that the Bloodfire was there within that cavern and that she must find it. She had groped her way forward then, trusting to her instincts, not understanding what it was that made her do so. Even when she had found the Fire beneath that cavern shelf and warned Wil back from her, even when she had pushed aside the rock to free the Fire, she had not understood what it was that was guiding her.

The thought disturbed her. She still did not understand. Something had touched her. She needed to know what it was. She closed her eyes and sought it out.

Understanding came slowly.

At first she thought it must be the Bloodfire, for it was the Fire to which she had been drawn. Yet the Fire was not a sentient thing; it was an impersonal force, old and vital and life-giving, yet without thought. It was not the Fire. Then she thought that if it was not the Fire, it must be the seed she carried, that tiny bit of life given her by the Ellcrys. The Ellcrys was sentient; her seed could be sentient as well. The seed could have warned her of the Reaper and the Fire. . . . But that, too, was wrong. The Ellcrys seed would possess no life until bathed in the flames of the Bloodfire. It lay dormant now; the Fire was needed to awaken it. It was not the seed.

But if it was not the Bloodfire and it was not the seed, what was left?

Then she saw it. It was she. Something within her had warned of the Reaper. Something within her had warned of the Bloodfire. The warnings had come from within her because they belonged to her. It was the only answer that made any sense. Her eyes opened in surprise, then quickly closed again. Why were the warnings hers? Memories flooded through her of the strange influence the Ellcrys had exercised over her, of the way the tree had begun to make her over until she had felt no longer so much herself as an extension of the tree. Had the tree done this to her? Had she been affected even more than she believed?

She was frightened momentarily by the possibility, just as she was always frightened when she thought of the way the Ellcrys had stolen her away from herself. With an effort, she forced down her fear. There was no reason to be frightened now. That was all behind her. The journey to find the Bloodfire was done. Her promises were kept. All that remained was to give life back to the Ellcrys.

Her hand slipped down within her tunic and closed about the seed that was the source of that life. It felt warm and alive, as if anticipating an end to its dormancy. She was about to withdraw her hand when the fears came back again, sudden and intense. She hesitated, feeling her strength of will begin to ebb. Was there more to this ritual than she imagined? Where was Wil? He had promised to see her through this. He had promised to make certain that she did not falter. Where was he? She needed the Valeman; she needed him to come to her.

But Wil Ohmsford would not come. He was beyond the Fire's wall, and she knew that he could not reach her. She must do this by herself. It was the task she had been given; it was the responsibility she had accepted. She took a deep breath. A moment's time to place the Ellcrys seed in the flames of the Bloodfire and the task would be finished. It was what she had come all this way to do; now she should do it. Yet the fear persisted. It filled her like a sickness and she hated it, because she did not understand it. Why was it that she was so frightened?

In her hand, the seed began to pulsate softly.

She glanced down. Even this seed frightened her, even so small a part of the tree as this. Memories came and fled again. In the beginning they had been close, the Ellcrys and she. There had been no fear, only love. There had been joy and sharing. What had changed that? Why had she begun to feel that she was losing herself in the tree? Such a frightening thing that had been! Even now it haunted her. What right had the Ellcrys to do that to her? What right had the Ellcrys to use her so? What right . . . ?

Shame filled her. Such questions served no purpose. The Ellcrys was dying and she needed help, not recrimination. The Elven people needed help. The Elven girl opened her

eyes and blinked into the Bloodfire's crimson glow. Ther
was no time to indulge her bitterness or to explore her fea
There was only time to do what she had come to do—
bathe the seed she held in the Fire.

She started. The Fire! Why had the seed not already bee
affected by the fire? Could the flames not reach it within h
tunic? Had they not already touched it? What differenc
whether she took the seed out?

More questions. Pointless questions. Again she starte
to withdraw the seed and again the fear held her back
Tears filled her eyes. Oh, that there might be someone el
to do this thing! She was not a Chosen! She was not suite
She was not . . . she was not . . .

With a cry, she wrenched the seed from her tunic an
held it forth into the Bloodfire's scarlet flame. It flare
within her hand, alive with the Fire's touch. From dee
within the Elven girl the feeling came again, the feelir
that had warned her of the Reaper's coming, the feelir
that had called her to the Bloodfire, flooding through h
now in a dazzling sweep of images that wracked her wit
such intense emotions that she dropped weakly to h
knees.

Slowly she brought the Ellcrys seed to her breast, feelir
the life within it stir. Tears ran down her cheeks.

It was she. It was she.

Now at last, she understood. She held the seed clos
against her and drew the Bloodfire in.

XLIX

huddled against the cavern wall, Wil Ohmsford and Eretria watched the Fire's crimson glow wink into darkness. It happened suddenly—a final spurt of flame and then the Bloodfire was gone. All that remained to light the chamber gloom were the discarded lamps they had carried in, their soft white glimmer faint and small.

Valeman and Rover girl blinked in the sudden night, peering blindly through the shadows. Slowly their vision sharpened, and they saw movement from atop the shelf where the Bloodfire had burned. Guardedly Wil brought up the hand that held the Elfstones, and the Elven magic rose in a flicker of blue fire.

"Wil . . ."

It was Amberle! She emerged from the gloom like a lost child, her voice a thin, desperate whisper. Ignoring the pain that racked his body, the Valeman started toward her, Eretria a step behind. They reached her as she stumbled from the shelf, caught her in their arms, and held her.

"Wil," she murmured softly, sobbing.

Her head lifted and the long chestnut hair fell back from her face. Her eyes burned crimson with the Bloodfire.

"Shades!" Eretria gasped and stepped back from the Elven girl.

Wil caught Amberle up in his arms; despite the pain that lanced through his injured arm, he cradled her against him. She was feather-light, as if the bones had withered within her and all that remained was a shell of flesh. She was crying still, her head buried in his shoulder.

"Oh, Wil, I was wrong, I was wrong. It was never her. It was me. It was always me."

The words came in a rush, as if she could not speak them fast enough. The Valeman stroked her pale cheek.

"It's all right, Amberle," he whispered back to her. "It' over."

She looked up at him again, the blood-red eyes fixed and terrible.

"I didn't understand. She knew . . . all along. She knew, and she tried . . . and she tried to tell me, to let me see . . . but I didn't understand, I was frightened . . ."

"Don't talk." The Valeman gripped her tightly, a sudden unreasoning fear slipping through him. They had to get free of this blackness. They had to get back to the light. He turned quickly to Eretria. "Pick up the lamps."

The Rover girl didn't argue. She retrieved the smokeless lights and hurried back to him. "I have them, Healer."

"Then let us hurry from this . . ." he began and caught himself. The Ellcrys. The seed. Had the Elven girl . . . "Amberle," he whispered gently. "Has the seed been placed within the Fire? Amberle?"

"It . . . is done," she said so softly he barely caught her words.

How much had this cost her, he wondered bitterly? What had happened to her within the Fire . . . ? But no, there was no time for this. They must hurry. They must climb from these catacombs back to the slopes of Spire's Reach and then return to Arborlon. There Amberle could be made well again. There she would be all right.

"Hebel!" he called out.

"Here, Elfling." The old man's voice was thin and harsh. He appeared out of the shadows, cradling Drifter in his arms. "Leg's broke. Maybe something more." There were tears in Hebel's eyes. "I can't leave him."

"Healer!" Eretria's dark face was suddenly close before his own. "How are we to find our way back without the dog?"

He stared at her as if he had forgotten she existed, and she flushed with shame, thinking him angry for her reaction to the Elven girl.

"The Elfstones," he muttered finally and did not stop to question whether he could use them. "The Elfstones will show us the way."

He shifted Amberle slightly in his arms, grimacing as the pain from his shattered body rose up in waves.

Eretria caught his arm. "You cannot carry the Elven girl and use the Stones as well. Give the girl to me."

He shook his head. "I can manage," he insisted. He wanted Amberle to stay close to him.

"Don't be so stubborn," she pleaded softly. Her jaw tightened, and it was with difficulty that she spoke. "I know how you feel about her, Healer. I know. But this is too much for you. Please, let me help. Give her to me to carry."

Their eyes met momentarily in the half-light, and Wil saw the tears that glistened on her cheeks. That admission had hurt her. Slowly he nodded.

"You are right. I cannot do this alone."

He gave Amberle to the Rover girl, who cradled her as if she were a baby. Amberle's head slipped down against Eretria's shoulder and she slept.

"Stay close," Wil admonished, taking one of the smoke-less lamps and turning away.

They went back through the waterfall and through the cavern that housed it, picking their way carefully across the rock-strewn floor. Blood and sweat mingled freely on Wil Ohmsford's body, and the pain grew worse. By the time they had reached the passageway leading up into the maze, the Valeman could barely walk. Yet there was no time to rest. They had to reach Perk quickly, for it was his final day. They had to get free of Safehold, back to the surface of the Hollows, to the slopes of Spire's Reach, before the sun set, or the little Wing Rider would be gone. That would be the finish for them. Without Perk and Genewen to carry them to Arborlon, they would never get clear of the Wilderun.

Staggering to a halt before the passage entry, Wil fumbled through the compartments of the pouch he carried at his waist. Within were the herbs and roots that aided him in his healing. After a moment's search, he brought forth a dark purple root, its six-inch length coiled tight. He held it before him, hesitating. If he ate it, its juice would kill the pain. He would be able to go on until they reached the slopes of the mountain above. But the root had other effects. It would make him drowsy and eventually render him unconscious. Worse, it would cause him to become increasingly less coherent. If it took effect too quickly, before they succeeded in finding their way clear of the catacombs . . .

Eretria was watching him wordlessly. He glanced up at her and the frail body she carried. Then he bit into the root and began to chew. It was a chance he had to take.

They stumbled ahead in the dark. When the maze began to open up before them, the Valeman brought up the hand that held the Elfstones and called forth the magic within. It came quickly this time, flooding through him like a sudden rush of heat, whirling through his limbs and exploding outward into the dark. Like a beacon, it curled before them through the catacombs, leading them on. They followed, shadows in the passage gloom. Onward they trudged, the crippled Valeman willing forth the blue fire to give them direction, the Rover girl close beside him, holding the sleeping Elf girl gently, and the old man cradling the giant dog. The minutes slipped slowly away.

Pain from the wounds suffered in the battle with the Reaper faded into numbness, and Wil Ohmsford felt himself drift through the darkness like a thing filled with air. Slowly the juice of the root worked through him, sapping his strength until his body felt as if it were made of damp clay, sapping his reason until it was all that he could do to remember that he must go on. All the while the Elven magic stirred his blood, and, as it did so, he felt himself changing in that same unexplainable way. He was no longer the same, he knew. He would never be the same. The magic burned him through and left an invisible, permanent scar upon his body and his consciousness. Helpless to prevent it, he let it happen, wondering as he did what effect it would have upon his life.

Yet it did not matter, he told himself. Nothing mattered but seeing that Amberle was made safe.

The little company pushed ahead in the wake of the brilliant blue fire, and the tunnels and corridors and stairways disappeared into the blackness behind them.

When they finally staggered from the cavern mouth of Safehold, into the air and light of the valley, they had spent themselves. The Rover girl had carried Amberle the entire way, and her strength was gone. The Valeman was barely conscious, numbed through by the painkilling root, drifting in and out of coherence as if wandering directionless through a deep mist. Even Hebel was exhausted. Together they stood upon the open bluff high on the slopes of Spire's Reach and blinked in the mix of fading sunlight and lengthening shadow, their eyes following its sweep across the expanse of the Hollows westward to where the sun set slowly into the forest, a brilliant blaze of golden fire.

Wil felt his hopes fall away from him.

"The sun . . . Eretria!"

She came to him and together they laid Amberle upon the ground, dropping wearily to their knees as they finished. The Elven girl slept still, her soft breathing the only sign of life she had shown during the whole of their journey up from the catacombs. She stirred slightly now, as if she might wake, yet her eyes remained closed.

"Eretria . . . here," Wil called to her, his hand fumbling within his tunic. His eyes were lidded and his words slurred. His tongue felt thick and useless. Struggling to hold himself upright, he produced the tiny silver whistle and passed it to the girl. "Here . . . use it . . . quickly."

"Healer, what am I . . . ?" she began, but he seized her hand angrily.

"Use it!" he gasped, and fell back weakly. Too late, he was thinking. Too late. The day is finished. Perk is gone.

He was losing consciousness rapidly now—just a few minutes more and he would be asleep. His hand still clutched the Elfstones, and he felt their edges bite against the palm. A few minutes more. Then what would protect them?

He watched Eretria rise and place the whistle to her lips. Then she turned to him, her dark eyes questioning.

"There is no sound!"

He nodded. "Blow . . . again."

She did, then turned a second time.

"Watch . . ." he pointed toward the sky.

She turned away. Hebel had laid Drifter upon a bed of saw grass, and the big dog was licking his hand. Wil took a deep breath and glanced down at Amberle. So pale, as if the life had been drained from her. A sense of desperation gripped him. He had to do something to help her; he couldn't leave her like this. He needed Perk badly! If only they had been a little quicker, a little swifter in their flight! If only he had not been hindered by his injuries! Now the day was gone!

Shadows fell about them, and the pinnacle of the mountain was cloaked in dusk's gray light. The sun had slipped into the west, a small crest of gold glimmering against the distant treeline as it died.

Perk, don't be gone, he cried soundlessly. Help us.

"Wil."

His head jerked sharply about. Amberle was staring up at him through blood-red eyes. Her hand found his.

"It's all right . . . Amberle," he managed, swallowing against the dryness that coated his throat. "We're . . . out."

"Wil, listen to me," she whispered. Her words were clear now, no longer vague or hurried, only faint. He tried to answer her, but her fingers came up to seal his lips, and her head shook slowly. "No, listen to me. Don't speak. Just listen."

He nodded, bending down as she moved her body close.

"I was wrong about her, Wil—about the Ellcrys. She was not trying to use me; there were no games being played. The fear . . . that was unintentional, caused by my failure to understand what it was that she was doing. Wil, she was trying to make me see, to let me know why it was that I was there, why it was that I was so special. You see, she knew that I was to be the one. She knew. Her time was gone, and she saw . . ."

She stopped then, biting her lip against the emotions welling up within her. Tears began rolling down her cheeks.

"Amberle . . ." he started to say, but she shook her head.

"Listen to me. I made a choice back there. It is my choice and there is no one but me to answer for it. Do you understand? No one. I made it because I had to. I made it for a lot of reasons, for reasons that I cannot . . ." She faltered, her head shaking. "For the Chosen, Wil. For Crispin and Dilph and the other Elven Hunters. For the soldiers at Drey Wood. For poor little Wisp. All of them are dead, Wil, and I can't let it be for nothing. You see, you and I have to . . . forget what we . . ."

The words would not come for her, and she began to sob.

"Wil, I need you, I need you so much . . ."

Fear rushed through him. He was losing her. He could feel it, deep down within him. He struggled to free himself from the numbness that weighted him.

Then Eretria called out to them, her voice sharp with excitement. They turned, eyes lifting to follow the line of her outstretched arm as it pointed skyward. Far to the west, through a haze of dying sunlight, a great golden bird soared downward toward the bluff face.

"Perk!" Wil cried softly. "Perk!"

Amberle's arm went about him and held him close.

Then he was being carried and through a fog of half-sleep he heard Perk's voice speaking to him.

"It was the smoke from that burning tower, Wil. Genewen and I circled all day. I knew you were down here. I knew it. Even when the day was almost gone and it was time to return to the Wing Hove, I couldn't leave. I knew the lady would need me. Wil, she looks so pale."

The Valeman felt himself being hoisted onto Genewen's back, and Eretria's slim brown arms began fastening the harness straps tightly about him.

"Amberle," he whispered.

"She's here, Healer," the Rover girl responded quietly. "We are all safe now."

Wil let himself sag back against her, drifting slowly toward unconsciousness as the night about him deepened.

"Elfling," a voice called gently, and his eyes opened to find Hebel's weathered face looking up. "Goodbye, Elfling. I'll go no further with you now. The wilderness is my home. I've taken my search as far as I care to. And Drifter, he's going to be fine. The Rover girl helped me splint the leg, and he's going to be just fine. He's a tough one, that dog."

The old man bent close. "You and the Elfling girl—I wish you luck."

Wil swallowed hard. "We . . . owe you, Hebel."

"Me?" The old man laughed gently. "Not me, Elfling. Not a thing. Luck, now."

He stepped away and was gone. Then Amberle appeared, her slim form hunching down in front of him, and Perk was back, quickly checking harness straps and lines. A moment later the boy's strange call sounded; with a sudden lurch, Genewen lifted slowly into the sky, her great wings spanning outward across the dark bowl of the Hollows. Upward rose the giant Roc, the forests of the Wilderun falling away below. In the distance, the wall of the Rock Spur came into view.

Wil Ohmsford's arms tightened around Amberle. A moment later, he was asleep.

L

Night lay over Arborlon. In the solitude of the Gardens of Life, Allanon walked alone to the top of the small rise where the Ellcrys stood, his black robes wrapped close to ward off the evening chill, the silver staff she had entrusted to his care cradled within his arms. He had come to be with her, to comfort her in whatever way he might, to give to her what companionship he could. These were to be her final hours; the burden that had been given her so many years ago was about to be lifted.

He paused momentarily, staring up at her. It would have seemed curious had someone come upon them, he thought —the Druid and the Ellcrys, stark black silhouettes framed against a moonlit summer sky, the man standing wordlessly before the withered, barren tree as if lost in some private reverie, his dark face an impassive mask that told nothing of what feelings might lie beneath. But no one would come. He had decreed that the tree and he should spend this night alone and that no one should be witness to her dying but he.

He stepped forward then, her name whispered in his mind. Her limbs reached for him at once, frightened and urgent, and his thoughts went quickly to comfort her. Do not despair, he soothed. This very afternoon, while the battle to save Arborlon was at its most furious, while the Elves fought so gallantly to stem the Demon advance, something unexpected happened, something that should give us hope. Far, far to the south in the dark of the wilderness forests where the Chosen has gone, her protector brought to life the magic of the Elfstones. The moment that he did so, I knew. I reached out to him then and I touched his thoughts with my own—quickly, for but a moment's time, because the Dagda Mor could sense what I did. Still, that moment was enough. Gentle Lady, the Bloodfire has been found! The rebirth can still come to pass!

Tinged with expectancy, the thoughts rushed from him. Yet nothing came back. Weakened almost to the point of senselessness, the Ellcrys had not heard or understood. She was conscious only of his presence, he realized then, conscious only of the fact that in her final moments she was not alone. What he might say to her now would have no meaning; she was blind to everything but her desperate, hopeless struggle to fulfill her trust—to live, and by living to protect the Elven people.

A sadness filled him. He had come to her too late.

He went quiet then, for there was nothing more that he could do, except to stay with her. Time slipped away, agonizingly slow in its passing. Now and again her random thoughts reached him, filtered down like scattered bits of color in his mind, some lost in the history of what had been, some cloaked in wishes and dreams of what might yet be, all hopelessly tangled and fragmented by her dying. Patiently he caught those thoughts as they slipped from her, and he let her know that he was there, that he had heard, that he was listening. Patiently he shared with her the trappings of the death that sought to cloak her. He felt the chill of those trappings, for they spoke all too eloquently of his own mortality. All must pass the way that she was passing, they whispered. Even a Druid.

It caused him to ponder momentarily the inevitability of his own death. Even though he slept to prolong his life, to lengthen it far beyond the lives of ordinary men, still one day he, too, must die. And like the tree, he was the last of his kind. There were no Druids to follow him. When he was gone, who then would preserve the secrets handed down since the time of the First Council at Paranor? Who then would wield the magic that only he had mastered? Who then would be guardian of the races?

His dark face lifted. Was there yet time, he wondered suddenly, to find that guardian?

Night sped away with soundless steps, and dawn's pale light broke across the darkness of the eastern sky. Within the vast Westland forests, life began to stir. Allanon felt something change in the Ellcrys' touch. He was losing her. He stared fixedly at the tree, hands gripping tightly the silver staff as if by clasping it so he might hold fast to the life that drained from her. The morning sky brightened; as it did, the images came less frequently. The pain that washed into him lessened, and a curious detachment replaced it. Bit by bit, the detachment widened the distance between them. In the east, a crest of sunlight edged above the horizon, and the night stars faded away.

Then the images ceased altogether. Allanon stiffened. In his hands, the silver staff had gone cold. It was over.

Gently he laid the staff beneath the tree. Then he turned and walked from the Gardens and did not look back.

Ander Elessedil stood silently by his father's bed and stared down at the old man. Torn and battered, the King's frail body lay wrapped in bandages and blankets, and only the shallow rise and fall of his chest gave evidence of life. He slept now, a fitful, restless sleep, hovering in the gray zone between life and death.

A rush of feelings swept through the Elven Prince, scattering like leaves in a strong wind. It was Gael who had wakened him, fightened and unsure. The young aide had come back to the manor house, restless, unable to sleep, thinking to do some work in preparation for the coming day. But the doors were jammed, he told Ander—the sentries gone. Did the King sleep unguarded? Should something be done? Instantly Ander had come to his feet, dashing from his cottage and calling out to the gate watch. In a rush they had broken through the front entry, frantic, hearing the old King's cries from within. There they had witnessed the finish of the death struggle between his father and that monster—the Demon that had masqueraded as Manx. His father had regained consciousness for just a short time as they carried him, bleeding and broken, to his bedchamber, to whisper in horror of the battle that had been fought and the betrayal he had suffered. The consciousness had left him, and he had slept.

How could his father have survived? Where had he found the strength? Ander shook his head. Only the few who had found him could begin to appreciate what it must have taken. The others, the Ministers and the commanders, the guards and the retainers, had come later. They had not seen the old King sprawled in that blood-smeared entry, torn and shredded. They had not seen what had been done to him.

There was speculation, of course—speculation that bred rumors. The King was dead, they whispered. The city was lost. Ander's jaw tightened. He had silenced them quickly enough. It would take more than a single Demon to kill Eventine Elessedil!

He knelt suddenly beside his father and touched the limp hand. He would have cried had there been tears left to cry. How terribly fate had treated the old King. His firstborn and his closest friend were dead. His beloved granddaughter was lost. His country was overrun by an enemy he could not defeat. He himself had been betrayed in the end by an animal that he had trusted. Everything had been stripped from him. What was it that kept him alive after all that he had suffered? Surely death would come as a welcome relief.

He clasped the hand gently. Eventine Elessedil, King of the Elves—there would never be another such King. He was the last. And what would be left to remember him by, other than a land destroyed and a people driven into exile? Ander was not bitter for himself, he knew. He was bitter for his father, who had spent his entire life working for that land and those people. There was nothing owed to Ander Elessedil perhaps. But what of that old man whose heart was wedded to this land that would be ravaged and this people that would be destroyed? Was not something owed him? He loved the Westland and the Elves more than the life he was about to give up, and that he should be forced to see it all taken away . . . it was so terribly unjust!

Ander bent down impulsively and kissed his father's cheek. Then he straightened and turned away. Through the curtained windows, he could see the sky brightening with the new day. He had to find Allanon, he thought suddenly. The Druid did not yet know. Then he must return to the Carolan, to stand with his people where his father would have stood had he been able. No matter the bitterness. No matter the regrets. What was needed now was the same courage and strength that his father had shown in his last battle, a courage and strength that would sustain the Elves in theirs. Whatever was to happen this day, he must be his father's son.

Tightening his armor as he went, Ander Elessedil walked quickly from the darkened room.

On the threshold of the entry to the manor house he paused momentarily and peered toward the brightening eastern sky. Dark circles shadowed his eyes, and his face was haggard and drawn. The dawn air chilled him, and he drew his heavy cloak close. Behind him the manor house windows blazed with light, and grim-faced Elven Hunters prowled the hallways like hunting dogs.

"Useless now . . ." he murmured to himself.

He set off toward the front gates, moving alone down the gravel walk, his mind clouded by his need for sleep. How long had he slumbered before Gael had come to him? One hour? Two? He could no longer remember. When he tried, it was the face of his father that appeared, blood-spattered and terrible, piercing blue eyes fixed upon his own.

Betrayed, those eyes cried out. Betrayed!

He passed through the wrought-iron gates into the street beyond, failing to notice the giant figure that emerged from the shadows where the war horses were tethered.

"Prince Ander?"

He started at the sound of his name, stopped, and turned. The dark figure approached silently, the new light glinting from chain-mail armor. It was the Free Corps Commander, Stee Jans.

"Commander." He nodded wearily.

The big man nodded in reply, the scarred face impassive. "A bad night, I am told."

"Then you have heard?"

Stee Jans glanced toward the manor house. "A Demon found its way into the King's house. His guard was slain, and he himself struck down when he slew the creature. You can scarcely expect to keep such news a secret, my Lord."

"No—nor have we tried." Ander sighed. "The Demon was a Changeling. It made itself appear as my father's wolfhound, an animal he had had with him for many years. None of us know how long it has been there, playing this game, but tonight it decided the game was finished. It killed the guards, bolted the doors leading out, and attacked the King. A monster, Commander—I saw what was left of it. I don't know how my father managed . . ."

He trailed off hopelessly and shook his head. The Borderman's eyes shifted back to him.

"So the King still lives."

Ander nodded slowly. "But I don't know what it is that keeps him alive."

They were silent then, their eyes glancing back toward the lighted manor house and the armed figures that patrolled its shadowed grounds.

"Perhaps he waits for the rest of us, my Lord," Stee Jans said quietly.

Their eyes met. "What do you mean?" Ander asked him.

"I mean that time draws short for all of us."

Ander took a deep breath. "How much longer do we have?"

"Today."

The hard face remained expressionless, as if the Borderman spoke of nothing more significant than what the weather might be that day.

Ander straightened. "You seem resigned to this, Commander."

"I am an honest man, my Lord. I told you that when we met. Would you wish to hear something other than the truth?"

"No." Ander shook his head firmly. "Is there no chance that we can hold longer?"

Stee Jans shrugged. "There is always a chance. Measure it as you would measure the King's chances of surviving beyond this day. That is the chance we all have."

The Elven Prince nodded slowly. "I accept that, Commander." He extended his hand. "The Elves have been fortunate to have you and the Free Corps soldiers to stand with them. I wish that we could find a better way to thank you."

The Iron Man gripped the other's hand. "I wish that we could offer you the opportunity. Good fortune, Prince Ander."

He saluted and was gone. Ander stared after him for a moment, then turned and started back up the street.

* * *

Moments later Allanon found him as he was preparing to ride to the Carolan. The Druid rode out of the predawn gloom aboard Artaq, black shadows slipping from the forest mist. Ander stood wordlessly as the big man reined Artaq to a halt and stared down at him.

"I know what has happened," the deep voice rumbled softly. "I am sorry, Ander Elessedil."

Ander nodded. "Allanon, where is the staff?"

"Gone." The Druid stared past him toward the manor house. "The Ellcrys is dead."

Ander felt the strength drain from him. "Then that's the end, isn't it? Without the magic of the Ellcrys to aid us, we are finished."

Allanon's eyes were hard. "Perhaps not."

Ander stared at him in disbelief, but the Druid was already turning Artaq back up the roadway.

"I will wait for you at the gates to the Gardens of Life, Elven Prince," he called back. "Follow quickly, now. There is still hope for us."

Then he put his heels into the black and they disappeared from view.

LI

Daybreak was an hour gone when the Demons attacked. They swarmed up the face of the Carolan, scrambling over the rubble of the shattered Elfitch to converge on the walls and gates of the sixth ramp. No longer weakened by the power of the Ellcrys or held back by the anathema of the Forbidding, the Demons shrugged aside the arrows and spears that showered down on them and came on. Wave upon wave of black bodies surged upward from the forests. In moments the cliffs were thick with them. Crude grappling hooks forged of captured weapons and trailing heavy vines were flung atop the walls and gates to catch upon the massive stone blocks. Hand over hand, the Demons began to climb.

The defenders stood ready—Kerrin and the Home Guard atop the gates, Stee Jans and the Free Corps upon the left wall, Amantar and the Rock Trolls upon the right. As their attackers climbed toward them, the defenders hacked and cut the scaling ropes. Back the Demons fell, screaming. Elven longbows hummed, and a hail of black arrows cut into the attackers. But still the Demons came, throwing up new hooks, new vines. Heavy wooden beams, hewn from whole trees and notched with steps, were flung against the gates, and the Demons scrambled up. Clubs and rocks flew out of the black mass below, cutting into the defenders as they tried to withstand the assault. Again and again the Demons were beaten back. But in the end they gained the walls, and the Elves and their allies found themselves locked in fierce hand-to-hand combat.

To either side of the Elfitch, the Demons spread wide along the cliff face, clawing their way determinedly toward the rim of the Carolan. There waited the Elven horse, Legion Old Guard, Dwarf Sappers, and scattered units of the other companies of defenders. Ehlron Tay was in command. Leading one charge after another into the swarms of attackers that appeared above the bluff rim, he thrust them back, sweeping them from the Carolan. But the defenders' lines were thin and the bluff was long and dotted with bits of sheltering forest which hid the Demons' approach. Isolated groups began to break through, and the Elven flanks began to buckle.

On the Elfitch, the Demons breached the gates of the sixth ramp. Breaking through the defenders' ranks, they shattered the bolts and crossbars that secured the gates and flung them wide. Into the gap they poured, clawing their way upward through the bodies of their dead. Amantar still held the right wall, but Stee Jans and his decimated Bordermen were being forced steadily back. At the center of the Elven defense, Kerrin rallied the Home Guard and counterattacked the Demon rush, desperately trying to throw it back. Into the howling mass the Elven Hunters charged, hammering the Demons aside, slowing the assault. For an instant it appeared that the Home Guard would recapture the gates. But then a handful of Furies launched themselves from the walls onto the attacking Elves, claws and teeth ripping. Kerrin went down, dying. The counterattack stalled, then fell back, broken.

Slowly the defenders retreated up the Elfitch through the open gates of the seventh and last ramp, keeping their lines tightly formed as the enemy tried to break through. With Amantar and Stee Jans holding the center, the defenders slipped back within the walls, and the gates slammed shut. Below, the Demons massed once more.

Three hundred yards east of the ramphead, Ander Elessedil stared out over the battlefield and felt his hopes begin to fade. At his back, the soldiers of the Black Watch ringed the Gardens of Life. He glanced quickly to Kobold, who stood at their head, then to Allanon. The Druid was at his side, seated on Artaq, dark face impassive as he watched the tide of battle shift back and forth.

"Allanon, we must do something," he whispered finally. The Druid did not turn. "Not yet. Wait."

All along the rim of the Carolan, the Demons continued

to scramble to the top of the cliffs, battling to turn the Elven flanks. To the south, they had gained a toehold on the bluff and were swelling their ranks, turning back the assaults of Elven horse that sought to dislodge them. To the north, the Dwarf Sappers still held their ground against repeated attacks, the resourceful Browork rallying horse and foot soldiers in a succession of strikes that time and time again threw the Demons from the heights. Ehlron Tay rode south, leading a reserve company of horse to regain the lower bluff. They charged into the Demons, lances lowered. There was a frightful clash of bodies, screams and cries rising up, and the battle raged so heatedly that, from a distance, it was impossible to tell friend from foe. But when at last the struggle broke off, it was the Elves who were in retreat. The left flank of the defense curled up quickly now, and the Demons surged forward, howling with glee.

Then the gates of the seventh ramp splintered and broke, and the Demons poured through. The defenders were flung back, and it appeared that they would be overrun completely. But the Trolls led a sudden, savage counterattack that swept the Demons back through the broken gates, and for an instant the walls were regained. Then the Demons rallied, the largest, most brutal moving to the fore, and the hordes broke through again. This time even the Rock Trolls could not stem the advance. Dragging their wounded with them, the defenders abandoned the gates and moved back up the ramp toward the bluff rim.

By now the Demons had gained the north end of the Carolan as well as the south, thrusting back the determined Dwarves, and the flanks folded in toward the center point. Slowly, surely, the Gardens of Life became an island on the battlefield as the Demons surged toward it. Ehlron Tay went down, ripped from his horse. Torn and battered, he was pulled to safety by his soldiers and carried from the bluff. Browork had suffered half a dozen wounds, and the Demons were all about him. The Old Guard had lost a third of its strength. Two of the Wing Riders were down and the three who remained, including Dayn, had flown back to the Gardens of Life to stand with Allanon Everywhere, the Elves and their allies were in retreat.

The defenders on the Elfitch had been forced back to the ramphead by their attackers. Stee Jans held the center position in the defense, surrounded by his Free Corps soldiers. Elves and Trolls held the flanks. It was clear to all that they could not hold long. The scar-faced Borderman recognized the danger of their position at a glance. Below, the Demons massed for another assault. To either side along the bluff rim, the defenders' lines had collapsed and were pinching in upon the ramphead. In moments, all would be caught in a vice from which none would escape. They had to fall back at once, to reform their lines at the perimeter of the Gardens of Life where they might consolidate their strength and gain the support of the Black Watch. But they needed time to do that, and someone must give them that time.

Red hair flying, the Free Corps Commander snatched the crimson and gray battle standard of his company and jammed it between the ramp stones. Here the Free Corps would make its stand. Rallying his Bordermen to him, he formed a narrow phalanx at the center of the ramphead. Then he ordered the Elves and Trolls to fall back. No one questioned the order; Stee Jans had been given command of the army. Quickly they abandoned the Elfitch, moving back toward the ranks of Black Watch that ringed the Gardens of Life. In moments, the remnants of the Free Corps stood alone.

"What is he doing!" Ander screamed to Allanon, horrified. But the Druid did not answer.

The Demons attacked. Up the ramp they charged, howling with rage. Incredibly, the Free Corps withstood the assault and thrust it back. All the while the Elven defenders continued to slip free of the noose that had threatened to snare them. Again the Demons came up the Elfitch, and again the Free Corps thrust them back. No more than two dozen Bordermen remained alive. At their head stood the tall figure of Stee Jans. Regrouping before the Gardens of Life, the defenders who had fled the Elfitch looked back, watching the tiny knot of men who still held against the Demon rush. A silence settled over their ranks. They knew how this must end.

Now the whole of the Carolan lay open. Stee Jans wrenched free the battle standard, lifted the gray and crimson pennant high above his head, and the Free Corps battle cry rang out. Then slowly, deliberately, the little band

began to move back across the Carolan, back toward the
Elven defenders who ringed the Gardens of Life. Not a
single Borderman broke formation. Not a single Borderman ran.

Ander's breath escaped from his lips with a sharp hiss. It
was a hopeless retreat. At his elbow, Browork's battered
face shoved into view.

"It's too far, Bordermen!" he muttered, almost to himself.

A wave of Demons edged over the lip of the ramphead,
snarling. North and south along the Carolan, they began to
mass.

"Run!" Ander whispered. "Run, Stee Jans!"

But there was no time left to run. Shrieks filled the
morning air, shattering the momentary stillness, and the
whole of the Demon army swept forward.

Then Allanon was moving. A quick word to Dayn and
Dancer's reins were in his hands. A moment later he had
swung astride the giant Roc and was lifting skyward.
Ander Elessedil and those who stood with him stared after
the Druid in astonishment. High above the Gardens
Allanon flew, black robes billowing out, lean arms raised.
On the Carolan, the converging Demons slowed abruptly
and stared skyward. Then a monstrous clap of thunder
burst across the grasslands as if the earth had split apart in
anger, and blue fire spurted from the Druid's fingers. In an
arc that reached from one end of the Demon advance to the
other, the fire swept the foremost ranks of the attackers and
burned them to ash. Howls and shrieks rose from the
Demons as a wall of flame lifted before them, forcing them
back from the encircled Free Corps.

A roar of excitement went up from the Elves. A narrow
corridor had opened through the ring of fire to the Gardens
and the embattled army of the Elves. Back through this
corridor came the Bordermen—quickly now, for their trap
might close again at any moment. All about them the
Demons raged, but the fire held them at bay. Run! Ander
cried silently. There is still a chance! Back raced the
Bordermen, and the distance between them narrowed. A
handful of Furies gave chase, maddened beyond reason,
hurtling through the flames. But Allanon saw them. One
dark hand raised, clenching. Druid fire lanced into the cat-

hings and they disappeared in a brilliant explosion, a pillar
f fire rising skyward to mark their end. High overhead,
Dancer screamed his battle cry.

And then Stee Jans and his Free Corps soldiers broke
lear of the fire and were back once more within the safety
f the Elven lines. Shouts and cheers welcomed them, and
he battle standards of the Four Lands lifted in the morning
uir.

On the Carolan, the Druid fire burned lower now, but
till the Demons did not try to cross. With the Furies so
easily destroyed, none cared to face Allanon alone. Milling
behind the wall of flames, they snarled and raged at the
one black flyer. And they waited.

The Druid glided past, eyes searching. He knew what
must happen now. A challenge had been issued, and one
among the Demons must answer it. Only the Dagda Mor
was strong enough to do so—and answer he would,
Allanon believed, because he had no other choice. The
Dagda Mor could sense the magic of the Elfstones as well
as Allanon. He, too, would know that Wil Ohmsford had
used the Stones, that the quest for the Bloodfire had been
successful, and that the thing he feared most might yet
come to pass—a rebirth of the hated Ellcrys and a restoration of the Forbidding. It was a dangerous moment for the
Demon Lord. His Changeling was dead. His Reaper had
failed. His army had stalled. If he were stopped now, even
though all that remained of the Westland was his, he had
lost. The Ellcrys was the key to the Demons' survival. The
mother tree must be destroyed and the earth in which she
rooted razed so that nothing could ever again grow there.
Then the seed could be hunted at leisure and the last
Chosen found. Then the Demons could be assured that
they would not again be banished from the land. Yet none
of this would come to pass if Allanon were not first
destroyed. The Dagda Mor knew that, and now he would
have to act . . .

A frightful shriek rose from the Demons. From beneath
the rim of the Carolan, a massive black shadow lifted into
the clear morning sky. Allanon turned. It was the winged
creature that had nearly caught Wil Ohmsford and Amberle in the Valley of Rhenn on their flight north from
Havenstead. The Druid saw the thing clearly now, a

monstrous bat, sleek and leathery, its blunt snout split wide to reveal gleaming fangs, its legs crooked and taloned. He had heard rumors of such bats living deep in the mountains of the far Northland, but even he had never seen one until now. It hovered above the Demon hordes, its cry a high, grating squeal that froze the black mass beneath it into sudden stillness.

Allanon tensed. Seated astride the creature's hooked neck was the Dagda Mor. The challenge had been accepted.

The Druid swung Dancer about sharply. Downward flew the bat, the Demon's humped form bent close. In one hand, the Staff of Power began to gleam redly. Allanon waited, holding Dancer steady beneath him. The bat squealed in anticipation. Out from the Demon's Staff of Power the red fire lanced, but just an instant too late. Dancer banked sharply, guided by the Druid's touch, then swung abruptly left. As the winged monster swooped down, taloned feet reaching and missing, Demon fire exploding into the Carolan, Allanon wheeled Dancer about. The bat was ponderous and slow in its flight; as it rose, the Druid flew beneath it and struck back. Blue fire burned the monster's wings and body, searing its leathered skin, and it cried out shrilly.

But it flew back, and again the Dagda Mor brought down the Staff of Power. Demon fire knifed across the morning sky, sweeping in front of the Druid and his mount. A wall of flame hung in the air before them, and this time there was no chance to turn. Dancer never hesitated. With a scream, the giant Roc looped upward, carrying Allanon clear of the fire, then straightened and swept downward across the Carolan. From the Gardens of Life, cheers rose from the throats of the Elves and their allies.

Again the Demon attacked, his massive carrier dropping swiftly. Again Dancer was too quick. Back across the bluff the giant Roc flew. Demon fire burst from the Staff of Power, lancing past the Roc, burning the grasslands to ash. Dancer swung right, then left, changing directions so quickly that the Dagda Mor could not bring the fire to bear. All the while Allanon fought back, Druid fire ripping into the monstrous bat, burning it over and over again until smoke trailed from its ruined body in small swirls as it flew.

The battle wore on, a terrifying duel that carried Druid and Demon back and forth above the scarred surface of the Carolan, twisting and turning, each trying to outmaneuver the other. For a time they fought evenly, and neither could gain an advantage over the other. The bat was ponderous and easily struck, but it was also strong and seemed unaffected by its injuries. Dancer was simply too quick; the fire never touched him. But as the minutes slipped by and still the struggle did not end, the Roc began to tire. For three days he had flown in battle, and his strength was ebbing fast. Each time he swept back above the bluff, the Demon fire burned closer. Silence fell over the ranks of the defenders. Through each mind the same thought passed. Sooner or later, the Roc would falter or the Druid would guess wrong. Then the Demon Lord would have them.

Moments later, their fears were realized. Fire lanced across Dancer's path of flight as the Roc banked suddenly left, shattering the great bird's wing. Instantly Dancer faltered and began to spiral downward toward the Carolan. A cry of horror went up from the Elves. Again the Staff of Power flared, and again the fire burned into the broken Roc. Down swept the bat, taloned feet flexed. Desperately Allanon turned as the monstrous thing dropped toward him, and his arms stretched skyward, hands clenched. The bat was almost on top of him when blue fire burst from the Druid's fingers. The bat's entire head seemed to explode and disappear. But its momentum carried it into the stricken Dancer. Thirty feet above the Carolan, the bat and the Roc collided, slamming into each other with terrifying force. Locked together, they dropped earthward, carrying their riders with them. Downward they plummeted and struck the ground with crushing force. Dancer shuddered once and lay still. The bat never moved.

In that instant it appeared to all as if the battle were lost. Dancer and the bat were dead. Allanon lay stretched upon the ground, still and burned. Only the Dagda Mor was in motion. One leg was smashed, but the Demon pulled himself free of the stricken bat and started toward the Druid. Allanon stirred, head lifting weakly. Slowly the Dagda Mor dragged himself forward until he stood not ten feet from the fallen Druid. Face twisting with hate, the

Demon braced. In his hands, the Staff of Power began to glow.

"Allanon!" Ander Elessedil heard himself cry out, and the echo reverberated in the sudden stillness.

Perhaps the Druid heard. Somehow he was on his feet, sidestepping the bolt of fire that lanced past him, moving so swiftly that he was on top of the Dagda Mor before the Staff of Power could be brought to bear a second time. The Demon tried to swing the Staff about, and then Allanon's hands were locked on its gnarled length. Demon fire flared within the Staff, and pain swept through the Druid. But his own magic rose in defense, and blue fire mingled with the red. Back and forth the Druid and the Demon wrestled, bodies straining, each trying to wrench the Staff free from the other's hands.

Then Allanon reached deep within some final well of strength, some last inner reserve, and the blue fire exploded from him. It burst from his hands and swept the length of the Staff of Power, smothering the Demon fire, coursing into the body of the Dagda Mor. The Demon's eyes went wide with horror, and he screamed once, high and terrible. Allanon heaved upward, throwing back the humped form, forcing the Demon slowly to his knees. Again the Demon screamed, the hatred spilling out of him. Desperately he fought against the fire that engulfed his body, struggling to break the Druid's hold. But Allanon's hands closed over his own like iron locks, fastening them tightly to the failing Staff. The Dagda Mor shuddered wildly and sagged, his cry dying into a whisper, and the terrible eyes went blank.

The Druid fire swept through him unhindered then, cloaking him in a shroud of blue light until his body exploded into ash and was gone.

A silence fell over the Carolan. Allanon stood alone, the Staff of Power still clutched within his hands. He stared down wordlessly at the ruined bit of wood, charred and smoking. Then he snapped it apart and threw the pieces to the ground.

Turning back toward the Gardens of Life, he whistled Artaq to him. Alone, the black trotted out from the Elven lines. Allanon knew he had only moments left. His

strength was gone, and he was still on his feet only through sheer force of will. Before him the wall of fire that had held back the Demons was dying. Already they massed along its perimeter, eyes fixed hungrily upon him, waiting to see what would happen next. The destruction of the Dagda Mor meant nothing to them. Their hatred of the Elves was what mattered. The Druid returned their stares, his smile slow and mocking. All that held them back now was their fear of him. The moment they lost that, they would attack.

Artaq nudged his shoulder and whickered softly. His eyes never leaving the Demons, Allanon edged carefully back until he could grip the horse's mane and harness. Then painfully he pulled himself into the saddle, nearly blacking out with the effort. Grasping the reins, he turned Artaq about. Seemingly unhurried, he started back toward the Elven defensive lines.

It was an agonizingly slow escape. He kept Artaq at a deliberate walk; a faster gait would have been too much for him. Foot by foot, the Gardens of Life drew closer. Out of the corner of his eye he could see movement in the lines of the encircling Demons. A few among them were already darting challengingly past the dying flames, shrieking at his back. Others quickly began to follow their lead. He gripped the saddle harness with both hands and did not turn. Soon now, he thought, soon.

Then suddenly the entire mass broke, howling and screaming. From all sides the Demons came after him. He knew at once that he was still too far from the Gardens of Life to escape them at this pace. He had no choice. He put his boots into Artaq's flanks, and the black leaped forward. Across the Carolan the big horse raced, powerful body leveled out and straining. Dizziness washed over the Druid, and he felt his grip loosening. He was going to fall.

Yet somehow he did not. Somehow he managed to hold on until finally the Elven lines were before him. With a lunge, Artaq was through, carrying him past the outstretched hands of Elf and Troll and Dwarf to the Gardens' iron gates, there at last to thunder to a halt.

Even then Allanon did not fall. Iron determination kept him astride the black. His face streaked with sweat, he turned to look back across the bluff as the Demon hordes converged upon the Gardens. At its walls, the defenders braced.

At least they have a chance now, he thought. At least I have given them that.

Then a flurry of shouts rose all about him and hands pointed skyward. Dayn was beside him, disbelief reflecting in his cry.

"Genewen! It's Genewen!"

The Druid's eyes lifted. Far to the south, nearly lost in the glare of the noonday sun, a great golden bird was winging its way downward toward Arborlon.

LII

Wil Ohmsford stared downward in horror. The sun was a dazzling burst of white light that made him squint. Within him, the fever still burned. He felt weak and lightheaded, and sweat bathed his body, drying in the rush of the wind. Genewen bore him high above the green, wooded landscape of the Westland, her wings stretched wide as she glided smoothly in the currents of the wind. Leather straps bound Wil to the Roc, and his shattered arm was splinted and wrapped. In front of him sat Perk, the small body swaying easily with Genewen's movements, his hands and voice guiding her flight. Huddled close against the little Wing Rider, nearly lost within a covering of heavy robes, was Amberle. The arms about his waist belonged to Eretria. He turned, and the Rover girl's dark eyes met his. The look she gave him was stricken.

Below lay the Elven city of Arborlon. Bodies littered the Carolan, fires burned across its bluff, and the Elfitch lay in ruins. Horsemen and lancers, pikemen and bowmen, ringed the Gardens of Life like an iron wall. All about them a wave of twisted black bodies swarmed, thousands strong, and it seemed as if at any moment the defenders might all be swept away.

The Demons, he whispered soundlessly. The Demons!

He was conscious suddenly of movement from Amberle. The Elven girl had straightened slightly, still bent close to Perk, and she was speaking to the boy. One small hand gripped the Wing Rider's shoulder. He nodded. Then Genewen began to descend, dropping swiftly toward the Carolan and the Gardens of Life. The Gardens stood like an island, sculpted hedgerows and flower beds carefully ordered and serene, awash in a sea of scarred grasslands and shrieking black Demons. Wil watched the glitter of weapons in the sunlight as the defenders fought back against the hordes that came against them. Already the black creatures were breaking through. A scattered few were within the walls.

On the small rise at the Gardens' center, the lifeless husk that had once been the Ellcrys stood forgotten.

Genewen cried out suddenly, a piercing shriek that cut through the din of the battle taking place below. For an instant all eyes were turned upon the giant Roc. Downward she plunged, like a falling piece of sunlight. Scattered cries of recognition rose from among the Elves. A Wing Rider, they cried, and searched futilely for others.

Then Genewen was within the Gardens, dropping slowly to the foot of the small rise. Great wings folded in and the scarlet head dipped sharply. Perk scrambled down, working swiftly to release the harness straps that secured the others. He freed Amberle first, and she slid limply from Genewen's back, crumpling to her knees as her feet touched the ground. Wil struggled to reach her, but the fever had weakened him and the straps would not loosen.

Beyond the hedgerows and flowered tiers, the sounds of battle drew closer.

"Amberle!" he called.

She was on her feet again, standing not a dozen paces from him, her child's face lifting. For an instant the terrible blood-red eyes fixed upon his, and it seemed as if she would speak. Then, wordlessly, she turned and started up the rise.

"Amberle!" Wil screamed and thrashed against the straps that bound him. Genewen lurched sharply, crying out, and Perk fought to steady her.

"Be still, Healer!" Eretria tried to caution him, but he was beyond being cautioned. All he could see was Amberle moving away from him. He was losing her. He could sense it.

Genewen started to rise then, frightened by the Valeman's struggles. Perk grasped her harness and pulled himself up, vainly trying to bring her under control. Then Eretria's knife was out, severing the straps that secured both Wil and her. An instant later they were falling, tumbling headlong into a line of bushes. Pain shot through the Valeman's injured body as he struggled back to his feet. Eretria called out to him, but he ignored her, stumbling after the retreating figure of the Elven girl. Already she was halfway up the rise, moving slowly toward the tree.

Howls rose from close at hand. Abruptly half a dozen Demons broke from the hedgerows. Perk had Genewen grounded again and had just dismounted and gone after Wil. Instantly the Demons came at him. But the Valeman had seen them. His fist swung about, the Elfstones gripped within it. Blue fire exploded into the Demons and they disappeared.

"Get away!" he called back to Perk. "Fly, Wing Rider!"

Eretria stumbled to his side, Other Demons began to emerge from the sheltering hedgerows, shrieking as they came. A scattering of Black Watch burst through to intercept them, pikes lowered. But the Demons fought their way past the Elves and came at Wil. The Valeman turned to face them, and again the Elfstones flared. Perk was back atop Genewen, but instead of flying to safety, the little Wing Rider had turned the giant Roc toward the closest attackers, driving them back. Yet there were dozens more, converging from everywhere, and even the fire of the Elfstones was not enough to stop them all.

Then a single piercing cry rose above those of the Demons and seemed to hang in the heat of the summer noon. Wil turned. Atop the rise stood Amberle, arms stretched forth to clasp the trunk of the Ellcrys. At her touch the tree appeared to shimmer like the waters of a stream caught in a blaze of sunlight, then disintegrate in a shower of silver dust that fell about the Elven girl like snow. She stood alone then, arms lifting, frail body straightening.

And she began to change.

"Amberle!" Wil screamed one final time, falling stricken to his knees.

The Elven girl's body began to lose its shape, the human form melting, clothing shredding and falling from her; her legs fused and tendrils from her feet slipped downward into the earth; slowly, her upraised arms lengthened and split.

"Oh, Wil!" Eretria whispered as she sank down beside him.

Amberle was gone. In her place stood the Ellcrys, perfectly formed, silver bark and crimson leaves gleaming in the sunlight, born anew into the world of the Elves.

A wail of anguish rose from the Demons. The Forbidding was restored. All across the Carolan they cried out as it began to draw them back again. Frantically they stumbled away, fighting to escape the blackness that closed inexorably about them. But there was no escape. One by one they faded from the light, hundreds and then thousands, large and small, black forms writhing, until finally the last had vanished.

Silence fell over the defenders of Arborlon as they stared wordlessly about. It was as if the Demons had never been.

In the Gardens of Life, Wil Ohmsford wept.

LIII

The Elves found him there moments later. At Ander Elessedil's command, they carried him to Arborlon Too stunned by the loss of Amberle to argue, his body racked with fever, he let them take him. He was carried to the manor house of the Elessedils, down its hallways and corridors, silent and shadowed, to a room where he was bedded. Elven Healers washed and dressed his wounds and bound his shattered arm. They gave him a bitter liquid to drink that made him drowsy, and they wrapped him carefully in linen and blankets. Then they left him, closing the door quietly as they went. In seconds, he was asleep.

As he slept, he dreamed that he wandered through a deep, impenetrable darkness, hopelessly lost. Somewhere within the same darkness was Amberle, but he could no find her; when he called, her response was faint and distant. Gradually he became aware of another presence cold and evil and strangely familiar—a thing that he had encountered before. Terrified, he began to run, faster and faster, fighting his way through webs of black silence. But the thing pursued him; though it made no sound, he could sense it nevertheless, always just a step behind. At last its fingers touched him, and he cried out in fear. Then abruptly the darkness disappeared. There were gardens all about him, beautiful and rich with color, and the thing was gone. Relief flooded through him; he was safe again. But in the next instant the ground beneath his feet buckled and he was lifted into the air. Suddenly he could see that a black wave beyond the gardens was sweeping slowly inward closing about him, rising like an ocean in which he would surely drown. Desperately he turned to find Amberle, and

544

he saw her now, darting like some voiceless wraith through the garden's center—just a glimpse and then she was gone. Over and over he called for her, but there was no answer. Then the black wave washed over him, and he began to sink . . .

Amberle!

He awoke with a start, his body damp with sweat. On a small table set against the far wall, a single candle burned. Shadows wrapped the room, and nightfall lay over the city.

"Wil Ohmsford."

He turned at the sound of his name, searching. A tall, cowled figure sat at his bedside, black and faceless against the faint glow of the candle's flame.

The Valeman blinked slowly in recognition.

Allanon.

Then everything came back to him in a rush. Bitterness stirred within him, bitterness so tangible that he could taste it. When at last he was able to speak, his voice was a low hiss.

"You knew, Allanon. You knew all the time."

There was no reply. Tears stung the Valeman's eyes. He thought back to that first night in Storlock, when he had met the Druid. He had known then that he could not afford to trust Allanon, that he must not trust him. Flick had warned him; Allanon was a man of secrets, and he hid those secrets well.

But this—how could he have hidden this!

"Why didn't you tell me?" The words were a whisper. "You could have told me."

There was a movement within the shadows of the cowl. "It would not have helped you to know, Valeman."

"It would not have helped *you*—isn't that what you mean? You used me! You let me think that if I could protect Amberle from the Demons, if she could be brought safely back to Arborlon, then everything would be all right. You knew that was what I believed and you knew it wasn't so!"

The Druid was silent. Wil shook his head in disbelief. "Couldn't you at least have told her?"

"No, Valeman. She would not have believed me. She would not have let herself. It would have been too much to ask of her. Think back to what happened when I spoke with her at Havenstead. She did not even want to believe that she was still a Chosen. Her selection as a Chosen had been a mistake, she insisted. No, she would not have believed me. Not then. She needed time to learn the truth about herself and to understand that truth. It was not something that I could have explained to her; it was something that she had to discover for herself."

The Valeman's voice shook. "Words, Allanon—you are so practiced in their use. You can persuade so easily. You persuaded me once, didn't you? But I will not be persuaded this time; I know what you did."

"Then you must know also what I did not do," Allanon replied quietly. He bent forward. "The final decision was hers, Valeman—not mine. I was never there to make that decision, only to see to it that she was given the opportunity to make it herself. I did that and nothing more."

"Nothing more? You made certain that she made the decision the way you wanted it made. I wouldn't call that nothing."

"I made certain she understood what the consequences of the decision would be, whichever way she chose to make it. That is somewhat different . . ."

"Consequences!" Wil's head jerked up from the pillow and his sudden laugh was laced with irony. "What do you know about consequences, Allanon?" His voice broke. "Do you know what she meant to me? Do you know?"

Tears streamed down his face. Slowly he lay back again, feeling strangely ashamed. All of the bitterness drained out of him, and he ached with the emptiness that was left. He looked away from Allanon self-consciously, and they both stayed silent. In the darkness of the sleeping room, the lone candle's glow touched them softly.

It was a long time before the Valeman looked back again. "Well, it's finished now. She's gone." He swallowed hard. "Would you at least explain why?"

The Druid said nothing for a moment, hunched down within the concealing shadows of his robe. When he finally spoke, his voice was almost a whisper.

"Listen then, Valeman. She is a marvelous creature—this tree, this Ellcrys—a living bit of magic formed by the bonding of human life with earth-fire. Before the Great Wars, she was made. The Elven wizards conceived her when the Demons were finally brought to bay and there was a need to prevent them from again threatening the land of faerie. The Elves, you remember, were not a violent people. Preservation of life was their purpose and their work. Even with creatures as destructive and evil as the Demons, they would not consider deliberate annihilation of a species. Banishment from the land appeared the most acceptable alternative, but they knew it would have to be a banishment of such power that the Demons thousands of years hence would still be subject to its laws. And the banishment would have to be to a place where no harm would come to others. So the Elven wizards used their most powerful magics, the ones that called for the greatest sacrifice of all, the willing gift of life. It was this gift that enabled the Ellcrys to come into being and the Forbidding to be created."

He was quiet a moment. "You must understand the Elven way of life, the nature of the code that governs that way of life, to appreciate what the Ellcrys truly represents and why, therefore, Amberle chose to become her. The Elves believe that they owe a debt to the land, for the land is the creator of and the provider for all life. The Elves believe that when one takes from the land, one must give something back in return. This belief is traditional; it is ritual. Their lives are given them; therefore they must give life back again. They accomplish this, Valeman, through a life marked by service to the land, endeavoring each in his own way to see to it that the land is preserved. The Ellcrys is but an expansion of that dedication. She is the embodiment of the belief that the land and the Elves are mutually dependent. The Ellcrys is a joining of the land with Elven life, a joining conceived to protect against an evil that would see both destroyed. Amberle understood that in the end. She saw that the only way in which the Westland and her people could be saved was through her sacrifice, her willingness to become the Ellcrys. She saw that the seed she bore could be given life only through a giving up of her own."

He paused and bent forward slowly, his dark figure casting its shadow over the listening Valeman. "You realize that the first Ellcrys was a woman also; it is not by chance that we refer to the tree as a lady. The Ellcrys must always be a woman, for only a woman can reproduce others of her kind. The wizards foresaw this need for procreation, though they were not able to foresee how often it might be necessary. They chose a woman, a young girl who, I would imagine, was very much like Amberle, and they transformed her. Then they established the order of the Chosen so that she might be cared for and when the time came might have the means to select her successor. But it was men, not women, that she selected as her Chosen down through the years, all but a handful. The histories do not record why—even she no longer knew. The selections had been made from habit for a very long time; she chose women only when the need was there. Perhaps it had something to do with her creation in the time of the Elven wizards. Perhaps they promised her young men to serve her—perhaps she requested it. Perhaps the choice of young men to serve was more acceptable to the Elves. I don't know.

"In any case, when she chose Amberle, the Ellcrys suspected that she might be dying. She could not be certain, of course, because she was the first of her kind, and no one had ever known when her death might come or what signs might foretell it. Indeed, many believed that she could not die. And the physical characteristics of that part of her that had been human had long since evolved into something far different, so there was no help there. There had been other times in her life when she had thought she might be dying, when she had thought she was in such danger that she must choose the one who would succeed her. Each time she selected a woman—a handful of times only. The last was five hundred years ago. I don't know what prompted it, so don't ask. It isn't really important.

"When Amberle was made a Chosen, the first woman in five hundred years, there was no small amount of surprise among the Elves. But the selection of Amberle had far greater significance than anyone realized because the Ellcrys in making her choice was looking upon the girl as a possible successor. And more than that really. She was looking upon Amberle as a mother would her unborn child. An odd characterization you might argue, but consider the circumstances. If the tree were to die, she would then produce a seed, and that seed and Amberle would become one, a new Ellcrys born in part at least from the old. The selection of Amberle was made with that foreknowledge, and it necessarily entailed much of the feeling that a mother would bear for an unborn child. Physically the woman that had been the Ellcrys had changed, but emotionally she retained much of what she had been. Something of this the tree sensed in the Elven girl. That was why they were so close in the beginning."

He reflected a moment. "Unfortunately it was this closeness that eventually caused problems. When I first came to Arborlon, awakened by the erosion of the Forbidding and the threatened crossover of the Demons, I went to the Gardens of Life to speak with the Ellcrys. She told me that after her selection of Amberle as a Chosen, she attempted to strengthen the ties that bound the Elven girl to her. She did this because she felt the sickness within her growing. Her life, she realized, was coming to an end; the seed that was beginning even then to form within her was to be passed to Amberle. In her dying, she responded to the girl with that same mothering instinct. She wanted to prepare her for what was to come, to see something of the beauty and grace and peace that she had enjoyed in her life. She wanted Amberle to be able to appreciate what it meant to become one with the land, to see its evolution through the years, to experience its changes—in short, I suppose, to understand a little of the growing up that a mother knows and a child does not."

Wil nodded slowly. He was thinking of the dream that Amberle and he had shared after the King of the Silver River had rescued them from the Demons. In that dream they had searched for each other—he within a beautiful garden, so breathtaking that it had made him want to cry; she in darkness, calling out as he stood there but would not answer. Neither had understood that the dream was a prophecy. Neither had understood that the King of the Silver River had given them a glimpse of what was destined to be.

The Druid continued. "The Ellcrys was well intentioned, but overzealous. She frightened Amberle with her visions and her constant motherings and her stealing away of Amberle's identity. The Elven girl was not yet ready for the transition that the Ellcrys was so anxious for her to make.

She became frightened and angry, and she left Arborlon. The Ellcrys did not understand; she kept waiting for Amberle to come back. When the sickness grew irreversible and the seed was completely formed, she called the Chosen to her."

"But not Amberle?" Wil was listening closely now.

"No, not Amberle. She thought Amberle would come on her own, you see. She did not want to send for her because, when she had done that before, it had only driven the girl further away. She was certain that once Amberle knew that she was dying, the girl would come. Unfortunately there was less time remaining to her than she thought. The Forbidding began to erode, and she could not maintain it. A handful of the Demons broke through and the Chosen were slain—all but Amberle. When I appeared, the Ellcrys was desperate. She told me that Amberle must be found, so I went to seek her out."

A hint of renewed bitterness darkened the Valeman's face.

"Then you knew at Havenstead that the Ellcrys still considered Amberle a Chosen."

"I knew."

"And you knew that she would give Amberle the seed to bear."

"I will save you the trouble of asking further questions. I knew everything. The Druid histories at Paranor revealed to me the truth of how the Ellcrys had come into being—the truth of how she must come into being again."

There was a brief hesitation. "Understand something, Valeman. I cared for this girl also. I had no desire to deceive her, if you wish to characterize my omissions as deceptions. But it was necessary that Amberle discover the truth about herself another way than through me. I gave her a path to follow; I did not give her a map that would explain its twists and turns. Such choices as might be necessary I thought were hers. Neither you, I, nor anyone else had the right to make those choices for her. Only she had that right."

Wil Ohmsford's eyes lowered. "Perhaps so. And perhaps it would have been better if she had known from the beginning where that path you set her upon would end." He shook his head slowly. "Odd. I thought that hearing the truth about everything that has happened would help somehow. But it doesn't. It doesn't help at all."

There was a long silence. Then Wil looked up again. "In any case, I do not have the right to blame you for what has happened. You did what you had to do—I know that. I know that the choices were really Amberle's. I know. But to lose her like this—it's so hard . . ." He trailed off.

The Druid nodded. "I am sorry, Valeman."

He started to rise, and Wil asked suddenly. "Why did you wake me now, Allanon? To tell me this?"

The big man straightened, black and faceless. "To tell you this, and to tell you goodbye, Wil Ohmsford."

Wil stared up at him. "Goodbye?"

"Until another day, Valeman."

"But . . . where are you going?"

There was no response. Wil felt himself grow sleepy again; the Druid was letting him drift back into the slumber from which he had been awakened. Stubbornly he fought against it. There were things yet to be said, and he meant to say them. Allanon could not leave him like this, disappearing into the night as unexpectedly as he had come, cloaked and hooded like some thief who feared that even the slightest glimpse of his face might give him away . . .

A sudden suspicion crossed his mind in that instant. Weakly he stretched forth his hand and caught the front of the Druid's robe.

"Allanon."

Silence filled the little sleeping room.

"Allanon—let me see your face."

For a moment he thought the Druid had not heard him. Allanon stood motionlessly at his bedside, staring down from the shadows of his robe. The Valeman waited. Then slowly the Druid's big hands reached up and pulled back the hood.

"Allanon!" Wil Ohmsford whispered.

The Druid's hair and beard, once coal black, were shot through with streaks of gray. Allanon had aged!

"The price one pays for use of the magic." Allanon's smile was slow and mocking. "This time I fear that I used too much; it drained more from me than I wished to give."

He shrugged. "There is only so much life allotted to each of us, Valeman—only so much and no more."

"Allanon," Wil cried softly. "Allanon, I'm sorry. Don't go yet."

Allanon replaced the hood, and his hand stretched down to grasp Wil's. "It is time for me to go. We both need to rest. Sleep well, Wil Ohmsford. Try not to think ill of me; I believe that Amberle would not. Be comforted in this: You are a Healer, and a Healer must preserve life. You have done so here—for the Elves, for the Westland. And though Amberle may seem lost to you, remember that she may be found always within the land. Touch it, and she will be with you."

He stepped away into the dark and pinched out the candle's flame.

"Don't go," Wil called out sleepily.

"Goodbye, Wil." The deep voice drifted out of a fog. "Tell Flick that he was right about me. He will like that."

"Allanon," the Valeman mumbled softly and then he was asleep.

Through the dimly lit corridors of the Elessedil home the Druid stole, as silent as the shadows of the night. Home Guard patrolled these corridors, Elven Hunters who had fought and survived in the battle of the Elfitch, hard men and not easily moved. Yet they stepped aside for Allanon; something in the Druid's glance suggested that they should.

Moments later he stood within the bedchamber of the Elven King, the door closing softly behind him. Candlelight illuminated the room with a dim, hazy glow that seeped through the gloom into shadowed corners and hidden nooks with a blind man's touch. Windows stood closed and drapes drawn, masking the room in silence. On a wide double bed at the far end of the chamber lay Eventine, swathed in bandages and linen sheets. At his side Ander dozed fitfully in a high-backed wicker chair.

Wordlessly Allanon came forward and stopped at the foot of the bed. The old King slept, his breathing ragged and slow, his skin the color of new parchment. The end of his life was near. It was the passing of an age, the Druid thought. They would all be gone now, all those who had stood against the Warlock Lord, all those who had aided in the quest for the elusive Sword of Shannara—all but the Ohmsfords, Shea and Flick.

A grim, ironic smile passed slowly across his lips. And himself, of course. He was still there. He was always there.

Beneath the linen coverings, Eventine stirred. It will happen now, Allanon told himself. For the first time that night, a touch of bitterness showed in his hard face.

Silently he moved back within the concealing shadows at the rear of the room and waited.

Ander Elessedil came awake with a start. Eyes blurred with sleep, he peered guardedly about the empty bed-chamber, searching for ghosts that were not there. A frightening sense of aloneness swept through him. So many of those who should have been there were not— Arion, Pindanon, Crispin, Ehlron Tay, Kerrin. All dead.

He slumped back in the wicker chair, weariness numbing him until he could feel nothing but the ache of joints and muscles. How long had he slept, he wondered? He didn't know. Gael would be back soon, bringing food and drink, and together they would keep this vigil, watching over the stricken King. Waiting.

Memories haunted him, memories of his father and what had been, spectral images of the past, of times and places and events that would never be again. They were bitter-sweet, a reminder both of the happiness shared and its transience. On balance, he would have preferred that the memories leave him in peace this night.

He thought suddenly of his father and Amberle, of the special affection they had felt for each other, the closeness that had been lost and found again—gone now, all of it. It was difficult even now to comprehend the transformation that Amberle had undergone. He had to keep reminding himself that it was real, that it was not imagined. He could still see the little Wing Rider, Perk, telling him what he had witnessed, his child's face awestruck and frightened all at once, so determined and so concerned that he should not be doubted.

His head tilted back and his eyes closed. Few knew the truth yet. He was still undecided as to whether or not it should remain that way.

"Ander."

He jerked upright, and his father's penetrating blue eyes met his own. He was so surprised that, for an instant, he simply stared down at the old man.

"Ander—what has happened?"

The Elven King's voice was a thin, harsh whisper in the stillness. Quickly Ander knelt down beside him.

"It is over," he replied softly. "We have won. The Demons are locked once more within the Forbidding. The Ellcrys . . ."

He could not finish. He did not have the words. His father's hand slipped from beneath the coverings to find his own.

"Amberle?"

Ander took a deep breath, and there were tears in his eyes. He forced himself to meet his father's gaze.

"Safe," he whispered. "Resting now."

There was a long pause. A trace of a smile slipped across his father's face.

Then his eyes closed. A moment later he was dead.

Allanon stood within the shadows several minutes more before stepping forward.

"Ander," he called softly.

The Elven Prince rose, releasing his father's hand. "He's gone, Allanon."

"And you are King. Be the King he would have wanted you to be."

Ander turned, his eyes searching. "Did you know, Allanon? I have wondered often since Baen Draw. Did you know that all this would happen, that I would be King?"

The Druid's features seemed to close in about him momentarily, and his dark face lost all expression. "I could not have prevented from happening that which happened, Elven Prince," he replied slowly. "I could only try to prepare you for what was to be."

"Then you knew?"

Allanon nodded. "I knew. I am a Druid."

Ander took a deep breath. "I will do the best that I can, Allanon."

"Then you will do well, Ander Elessedil."

He watched the Elven Prince move back to the dead

King, saw him cover his father as he would a sleeping child, then kneel once more at the bedside.

Allanon turned and slipped noiselessly from the room, from the manor house, from the city, and from the land. No one saw him go.

It was dawn when Wil Ohmsford was shaken gently awake, silver-gray light seeping through curtained windows to chase the fading dark. His eyes blinked slowly open and he found himself staring up at Perk.

"Wil?" The little Wing Rider's face was a mask of seriousness.

"Hello, Perk."

"How are you feeling?"

"A little better, I think."

"That's good." Perk tried a quick smile. "I was really worried."

Wil smiled back. "Me, too."

Perk sat down on the edge of the bed. "I'm sorry to wake you, but I didn't want to leave without saying goodbye."

"You're leaving?"

The youth nodded. "I should have left last night, but I had to rest Genewen. She was pretty tired after that long flight. But I have to leave now. I should have been back at the Wing Hove two days ago. They will probably be searching for me." He paused. "But they'll understand when I explain what happened. They won't be mad."

"I hope not. I wouldn't want that."

"My Uncle Dayn said he would explain it to them, too. Did you know that my Uncle Dayn was here, Wil? My grandfather sent him. Uncle Dayn said I acted like a true Wing Rider. He said what Genewen and I did was very important."

Wil pushed himself up slightly against his pillows. "So it was, Perk. Very important."

"I couldn't just leave you. I knew you might need me."

"We needed you very much."

"And I didn't think my grandfather would mind if I disobeyed just this once."

"I don't think he will mind."

Perk looked down at his hands. "Wil, I'm sorry about the Lady Amberle. I really am."

Wil nodded slowly. "I know, Perk."

"She really was enchanted, wasn't she? She was enchanted and the enchantment turned her into the tree." He looked up quickly. "That was what she wanted, wasn't it? To turn into the tree so the Demons would disappear? That was the way it was supposed to be?"

The Valeman swallowed hard. "Yes."

"I was really scared, you know," Perk said quietly. "I wasn't sure whether that was supposed to happen or not. It was so sudden. She never said anything about it to me before it happened, so when it did happen it scared me."

"I don't think she wanted to scare you."

"No, I don't think so either."

"She just didn't have time enough to explain."

Perk shrugged. "Oh, I know that. It was just so sudden."

They were quiet a moment, and then the little Wing Rider rose. "I just wanted to say goodbye, Wil. Would you come visit me sometime? Or I could come to see you—but that wouldn't be until I'm older. My family won't let me fly out of the Westland."

"I will come visit you," Wil promised. "Soon."

Perk gave a sort of half-wave and walked to the door. His hand was on the latch when he paused and glanced back at the Valeman.

"I really liked her, Wil—a whole lot."

"I liked her, too, Perk."

The little Wing Rider smiled briefly and disappeared through the door.

LIV

They went home then, all those who had come to Arborlon to stand with the Elves, all but two.

The Wing Riders went first, at the dawn of the day that began the reign of Ander Elessedil as the new King of the Land Elves—three who remained of the five who had flown north together and the boy called Perk. They left quietly, with barely a word to anyone but the young King, and were gone before the sun fully crested the eastern forests, their golden-hued Rocs chasing after the disappearing night like the first rays of the morning sun.

At midday the Rock Trolls departed, Amantar at their head, as fierce and proud as when they had come, weapons raised in salute as the Elven people gathered along the streets and in the tree-lanes to cheer their passing. For the first time in more than a thousand years, Troll and Elf parted not as enemies, but as friends.

The Dwarves stayed several days longer, lending to the Elves the benefit of their vast engineering expertise by assisting in the drafting of plans for the rebuilding of the shattered Elfitch. A most difficult task lay ahead in that rebuilding, for not only was it necessary to replace the demolished fifth rampway, but most of the remainder of the structure was in need of shoring up as well. It was the kind of challenge that the redoubtable Browork relished; with the aid of those Sappers yet able to work, he traced for the Elves the steps by which the task might best be accomplished. When finally he did take leave of Ander and the Elven people, he did so with the promise that another company of Dwarf Sappers—one in better condition to serve than his own—would be sent at once to give whatever aid was necessary.

"We know that we can depend upon the Dwarves."
Ander gripped Browork's rough hand in parting.

"Always," the crusty Dwarf agreed with a nod. "See that
you remember that when we have need of you."

Finally it was the turn of the men of Callahorn to
depart—the handful of Legion Free Corps and Old Guard
who had survived the ferocious struggle to hold the Elfitch.
Not a dozen of the former remained and of those not six
would fight again. The command had virtually ceased to
exist, the bodies of its soldiers scattered between the passes
of the Breakline and Arborlon. Yet once more the tall, scar-
faced Borderman called Stee Jans had survived where so
many others had not.

He came to Ander Elessedil early on the morning of the
sixth day following their victory over the Demon hordes,
riding out on his great blue roan to where the Elven King
stood at the edge of the Carolan and reviewed with his
engineers the plans drafted by the Dwarf Sappers. Excusing himself hurriedly, Ander walked quickly to where the
Free Corps Commander had dismounted and stood waiting. Ignoring the nod of respect the big man gave him,
Ander seized the other's hand and gripped it firmly.

"You are well again, Commander?" he greeted him,
smiling.

"Well enough, my Lord," Stee Jans smiled back. "I came
to thank you and to say goodbye. The Legion rides again
for Callahorn."

Ander shook his head slowly. "It is not for you to thank
me. It is for me—and for the Elven people—to thank you.
No one gave more to us and to this land than the men of
the Free Corps. And you, Stee Jans—what would we have
done without you?"

The Borderman was quiet for a moment before speaking.
"My Lord, I think we found in the people and the land a
cause worth fighting for. All that we gave, we gave freely.
And you did not lose this fight—that is what matters."

"How could we lose with you to aid us?" Ander gripped
his hand anew. He paused. "What will you do now?"

Stee Jans shrugged. "The Free Corps is gone. Perhaps
they'll rebuild. Perhaps not. If not, perhaps there will be a
new Legion command. I will ask for one, in any case."

Ander nodded slowly. "Ask me, Stee Jans—ask me and

the command is yours. I would be honored to have you. And the Elven people would be honored. You are one of us. Will you consider it?"

The Borderman smiled, turned, and swung back into the saddle. "I am already considering it, King Ander Elessedil." He saluted smartly. "Until we meet again, my Lord—strength to you and to the Elves."

He reined the big roan about, gray cloak flying, and rode east across the Carolan. Ander watched him go, waving after him. Until we meet again, Borderman, he replied without speaking.

Thus they went home, all those who had come to Arborlon to stand with the Elves, all the brave ones, all but two.

One was the Valeman, Wil Ohmsford.

Sunshine lay across the Carolan in a blanket of warmth and hazy brightness as the noonday neared and Wil Ohmsford approached the gates leading into the Gardens of Life. Down the gravel pathway the Valeman walked, his stride measured and even, and there was no sign of hesitation in his coming. Yet when he stood at last before the gates, he was not sure that he could go further.

It had taken him a week to come this far. The first three days following his collapse in these same Gardens had been spent in his chambers in the Elessedil manor house, asleep most of the time. Two more had been spent in the seclusion of the grounds surrounding the ancient home, wrestling with the jumble of emotions that seethed within him as memories of Amberle came and went. The last two days he had spent studiously avoiding the very thing he had now come to do.

He stood for a long time at the Gardens' entrance, staring upward at the arch of silver scroll and inlaid ivory, at the ivy-grown walls, and the pines and hedgerows leading in. Heads turned toward him questioningly as the people of the city came and went, passing into and out of the gates before which he stood. They were there for the same reason that had brought him and were wondering as they saw him if he were perhaps even more awed and self-conscious than they. Sentries of the Black Watch stood rigid and aloof to either side, eyes shifting momentarily to watch the motionless figure of the Valeman, then looking quickly away again. Still Wil Ohmsford did not go forward.

Yet he knew he must. He had thought it through quite carefully. He must see her one time more. One final time There could be no peace within him until it was done.

Almost before he realized it, he was through the gates, following the curve of the pathway that would take him to the tree.

He felt oddly relieved as he went, as if in making the decision to go to her he was doing something not only necessary, but right. A bit of the determination that had seen him through so much these past few weeks returned to him now—determination that had been drained from him when he had lost the Elven girl, so complete was his belief that he had failed her. He thought he understood that feeling better now. It was not so much a sense of failure that he had experienced as a sense of his own limitations. You cannot do everything you might wish that you could do, Uncle Flick had told him once. And so, while he had been able to save Amberle from the Demons, he had not been able to save her from becoming the Ellcrys Yet saving her from that, he knew, was not something that had ever been within his power. It had only been within hers. Her choice, as she had told him—as Allanon, too had told him. No amount of anger, bitterness, or self remorse would change that or bring him the peace he needed. He must reconcile what had happened another way. He thought he knew that way now. This visit to her was the first step.

Then he passed through an opening in a tall row of evergreens and she was before him. The Ellcrys rose up against the clear blue of the noonday sky, tall silver trunk and scarlet leaves rippling in the golden sunlight, a thing of such exquisite beauty that in the instant he saw her tears came to his eyes.

"Amberle . . ." he whispered.

Gathered at the foot of the small rise upon which she stood were Elven families from the city, their eyes fixed upon the tree, their voices lowered and hushed. Wil Ohmsford hesitated, then moved forward to join them.

"You see, the sickness is gone," a mother was saying to a little girl. "She is well again."

And her land and her people are safe, the Valeman added silently. Because of Amberle—because she had sacrificed herself for both. He took a deep breath, gazing upward at the tree. It was something she had wanted to do, something she had had to do—not just because it was needed but because in the end she had come to believe it to be the purpose for her existence. The Elven ethic, the creed that had governed her life—something of the self must be given back to the land. Even when she had banished herself from Arborlon, she had not forgotten the creed. It had been reflected in her work with the children of Havenstead. It had been a part of the reason that she had returned with him to discover the truth of her destiny.

Something of the self must be given back to the land.

In the end, she had given back everything.

He smiled sadly. But she had not lost everything. In becoming the Ellcrys, she had gained an entire world.

"Will she keep the Demons from us, Mommy?" the little girl was asking.

"Far, far away from us." Her mother smiled.

"And protect us always?"

"Yes—and protect us always."

The little girl's eyes flitted from her mother's face to the tree. "She is so pretty." Her small voice was filled with wonderment.

Amberle.

Wil gazed upon her for an instant longer, then turned and walked slowly from the Gardens.

He had just passed back through the gates leading in when he spied Eretria. She stood a little to one side on the pathway leading up from the city, her dark eyes shifting quickly to meet his own. The bright Rover silks were gone, replaced by ordinary Elven garb. Yet there could never be anything ordinary about Eretria. She was as stunningly beautiful now as she had been the first time Wil had laid eyes on her. Her long black hair shimmered in the sunlight as it curled down about her shoulders, and that dazzling smile broke over her dusky face as she caught sight of him.

Wordlessly, he walked over to greet her, permitting himself a small grin in reply.

"You look like a whole man again," she said lightly.

He nodded. "You can take whatever credit is due fo
that. You're the one who got me back on my feet."

Her smile broadened at the compliment. Every day fo
the past week she had come to him—feeding him, dressin
his wounds, giving him company when she had sensed h
needed it, giving him peace when she had seen that h
needed to be alone. His recovery, both physical anc
emotional, was due in no small part to her efforts.

"I was told that you had gone out." She glanced briefly
toward the Gardens. "It didn't require much imaginatio
to know where you had gone. So I thought I would follov
and wait for you." She looked back at him, the smil
winsome. "Are all the ghosts laid to rest at last, Healer?

Wil saw the concern in her eyes. She understood bette
than any what the loss of Amberle had done to him. The
had talked about it constantly in the time they had sper
together during his recovery. Ghosts, she had calle
them—all those purposeless feelings of guilt that had
haunted him.

"I think maybe they're resting now," he answered
"Coming here helped, and in a little more time, may
be . . ."

He trailed off, shrugged and smiled. "Amberle believec
that something was owed to the land for the life it gave her
She told me once that her belief was a part of her Elver
heritage. My heritage, too, I think she was suggesting. Yo
see, she always thought of me more as a Healer than as
protector. And a Healer is what I should be. A Healer give
something to the land through the care he provides to th
people who look after her. That will be my gift, Eretria.'

She nodded solemnly. "So you will go back now t
Storlock?"

"Home first, to Shady Vale—then to Storlock."

"Soon?"

"I think so. I think I should go now." He cleared hi
throat uneasily. "Did you know that Allanon left me th
black—the stallion Artaq? A gift. I suppose he felt it migh
help make up for losing Amberle."

Her dark face glanced away. "I suppose. Can we wal
back now?"

Without waiting for his answer, she began to retrace he
steps along the pathway. He hesitated in confusion

noment, then hurried after her. Together, they walked in ilence.

"Have you decided to keep the Elfstones?" she asked fter several minutes had passed.

He had told her once, when his depression had been leepest, that he intended to give them up. The Elven nagic had done something to him, he knew. Just as surely s magic had aged Allanon, it had affected him as well— hough as yet he could not tell how. Such power frightened im still. Yet the responsibility for that power remained his; e could not simply pass it carelessly to another.

"I'll keep them," he answered her. "But I'll never use hem again. Never."

"No," she said quietly. "A Healer would have no use for he Stones."

They walked past the Gardens' walls and turned down he pathway toward Arborlon. Neither spoke. Wil could ense the distance separating them, a widening gulf caused y her certainty that he would be leaving her once again. he wanted to go with him, of course. She had always vanted to go with him. But she would not ask—not this me, not again. Her pride would not let her. He mulled the natter over in his mind.

"Where will you go now?" he asked her a moment later.

She shrugged casually. "Oh, I don't know. Callahorn, naybe. This Rover girl can go where she chooses, be what he wants." She paused. "Maybe I'll come to see you. You eem to require a great deal of looking after."

There it was. She said it lightly, jokingly almost, but here was no mistaking the intent. I am for you, Wil)hmsford, she had told him that night in the Tirfing. She vas saying it again. He glanced over at her dark face, hinking fleetingly of all that she had done for him, all that he had risked for him. If he left her now, she would have o one. She had no home, no family, no people. Before, vhen she had wanted to go with him, there had been a eason to refuse her. What was his reason now?

"It was just a thought," she added, brushing the matter ff quickly.

"A nice thought," he said quietly. "But I was thinking hat maybe you'd like to come back with me now."

The words were spoken almost before he realized what

he had decided. There was a long, long silence, and they kept walking along the pathway, neither one looking at the other, almost as if nothing at all had been said.

"Maybe I would," she replied finally. "If you mean it."

"I mean it."

Then he saw her smile—that wondrous, dazzling smile. She stopped and turned toward him.

"It is reassuring to see, Wil Ohmsford, that you have come to your senses at last."

Her hand reached for his and clasped it tightly.

Riding back along the Carolan toward the city, his mind still occupied by thoughts of the rebuilding of the Elfitch, Ander Elessedil caught sight of the Valeman and the Rover girl as they walked back from the Gardens of Life. Reining in his horse for a moment, he watched the two who had not yet gone home, saw them stop, then saw the girl take the Valeman's hand in her own.

A slow smile creased his face as he swung his horse wide of where they stood. It looked very much as if Wil Ohmsford, too, would be going home now. But not alone.